Flowers in the Attic
___
Petals on the Wind

V.C. Andrews® Books

The Dollanganger Family Series
Flowers in the Attic
Petals on the Wind
If There Be Thorns
Seeds of Yesterday
Garden of Shadows

The Casteel Family Series
Heaven
Dark Angel
Fallen Hearts
Gates of Paradise
Web of Dreams

The Cutler Family Series
Dawn
Secrets of the Morning
Twilight's Child
Midnight Whispers
Darkest Hour

The Landry Family Series
Ruby
Pearl in the Mist
All That Glitters
Hidden Jewel
Tarnished Gold

The Logan Family Series
Melody
Heart Song
Unfinished Symphony
Music in the Night
Olivia

My Sweet Audrina
(does not belong to a series)

The Orphans Miniseries
Butterfly
Crystal
Brooke
Raven
Runaways (full-length novel)

The Wildflowers Miniseries
Misty
Star
Jade
Cat
Into the Garden (full-length novel)

The Hudson Family Series
Rain
Lightning Strikes
Eye of the Storm
The End of the Rainbow

The Shooting Stars Series
Cinnamon
Ice
Rose
Honey
Falling Stars

The De Beers Family Series
Willow
Wicked Forest
Twisted Roots
Into the Woods
Hidden Leaves

The Broken Wings Series
Broken Wings
Midnight Flight

The Gemini Series
Celeste
Black Cat
Child of Darkness

Flowers in the Attic

Petals on the Wind

By V.C. Andrews

SIMON PULSE

New York   London   Toronto   Sydney

SIMON PULSE
An imprint of Simon & Schuster Children's Publishing Division
1230 Avenue of the Americas, New York, NY 10020
This Simon Pulse paperback edition November 2009
Flowers in the Attic Copyright © 1979 by the Vanda General Partnership
Petals on the Wind Copyright © 1980 by the Vanda General Partnership
These titles were originally published individually by Pocket Books.
All rights reserved, including the right of reproduction in whole or in part in any form.
SIMON PULSE and colophon are registered trademarks of Simon & Schuster, Inc.
V.C. Andrews® and Virginia Andrews® are registered trademarks
of the Vanda General Partnership.
For information about special discounts for bulk purchases, please contact
Simon & Schuster Special Sales at 1-866-506-1949 or
business@simonandschuster.com.
Manufactured in the United States of America
12 14 16 18 20 19 17 15 13 11
Library of Congress Control Number 2009933048
ISBN 978-1-4424-0301-7
These books were originally published individually by Pocket Books.

Flowers in the Attic

This book is dedicated to my mother.

PART ONE

Shall the clay say to him that fashioneth it, What makest thou?

Isaiah 45:9

Prologue

It is so appropriate to color hope yellow, like that sun we seldom saw. And as I begin to copy from the old memorandum journals that I kept for so long, a title comes as if inspired. *Open the Window and Stand in the Sunshine.* Yet, I hesitate to name our story that. For I think of us more as flowers in the attic. Paper flowers. Born so brightly colored, and fading duller through all those long, grim, dreary, nightmarish days when we were held prisoners of hope, and kept captives by greed. But, we were never to color even one of our paper blossoms yellow.

Charles Dickens would often start his novels with the birth of the protagonist and, being a favorite author of both mine and Chris's, I would duplicate his style—if I could. But he was a genius born to write without difficulty while I find every word I put down, I put down with tears, with bitter blood, with sour gall, well mixed and blended with shame and guilt. I thought I would never feel ashamed or guilty, that these were burdens for others to bear. Years have passed and I am older and wiser now, accepting, too. The tempest of rage that once stormed within me has simmered down so I can write, I hope, with truth and with less hatred and prejudice than would have been the case a few years ago.

So, like Charles Dickens, in this work of "fiction" I will hide myself away behind a false name, and live in fake places, and I will pray to God that those who should will hurt when they read what I have to say. Certainly God in his infinite mercy will see that some understanding publisher will put my words in a book, and help grind the knife that I hope to wield.

Good-bye, Daddy

Truly, when I was very young, way back in the Fifties, I believed all of life would be like one long and perfect summer day. After all, it did start out that way. There's not much I can say about our earliest childhood except that it was very good, and for that, I should be everlastingly grateful. We weren't rich, we weren't poor. If we lacked some necessity, I couldn't name it; if we had luxuries, I couldn't name those, either, without comparing what we had to what others had, and nobody had more or less in our middleclass neighborhood. In other words, short and simple, we were just ordinary, run-of-the-mill children.

Our daddy was a P.R. man for a large computer manufacturing firm located in Gladstone, Pennsylvania: population, 12,602. He was a huge success, our father, for often his boss dined with us, and bragged about the job Daddy seemed to perform so well. "It's that all-American, wholesome, devastatingly good-looking face and charming manner that does them in. Great God in heaven, Chris, what sensible person could resist a fella like you?"

Heartily, I agreed with that. Our father was perfect. He stood six feet two, weighed 180 pounds, and his hair was thick and flaxen blond, and waved just enough to be perfect; his eyes were cerulean blue and they sparkled with laughter, with his great zest for living and having fun. His nose was straight and neither too long nor too narrow, nor too thick. He played tennis and golf like a pro and swam so much he kept a suntan all through the year. He was always dashing off on airplanes to California, to Florida, to Arizona, or to Hawaii, or even abroad on business, while we were left at home in the care of our mother.

When he came through the front door late on Friday afternoons—every Friday afternoon (he said he couldn't bear to be separated from us for longer than five days)—even if it were raining or snowing, the sun shone when he beamed his broad, happy smile on us.

His booming greeting rang out as soon as he put down his suitcase and briefcase: "Come greet me with kisses if you love me!"

Somewhere near the front door, my brother and I would be hiding, and after he'd called out his greeting, we'd dash out from behind a chair or the sofa to crash into his wide open arms, which seized us up at once and held us close, and he warmed our lips with his kisses. Fridays—they were the best days of all, for they brought Daddy home to us again. In his suit pockets he carried small gifts for us; in his suitcases he stored the larger ones to dole out after he greeted our mother, who would hang back and wait patiently until he had done with us.

And after we had our little gifts from his pockets, Christopher and I would back off to watch Momma drift slowly forward, her lips curved in a welcoming smile that lit up our father's eyes, and he'd take her in his arms, and stare down into her face as if he hadn't seen her for at least a year.

On Fridays, Momma spent half the day in the beauty parlor having her hair shampooed and set and her fingernails polished, and then she'd come home to take a long bath in perfumed-oiled water. I'd perch in her dressing room, and wait to watch her emerge in a filmy negligee. She'd sit at her dressing table to meticulously apply makeup. And I, so eager to learn, drank in everything she did to turn herself from just a pretty woman into a creature so ravishingly beautiful she didn't look real. The most amazing part of this was our father thought she *didn't* wear makeup! He believed she was naturally a striking beauty.

Love was a word lavished about in our home. "Do you love me?—For I most certainly love you; did you miss me?—Are you glad I'm home?—Did you think about me when I was gone? Every night? Did you toss and turn and wish I were beside you, holding you close? For if you didn't, Corrine, I might want to die."

Momma knew exactly how to answer questions like these—with her eyes, with soft whispers and with kisses.

One day Christopher and I came speeding home from school with the wintery wind blowing us through the front door. "Take off your boots in the foyer," Momma called out from the living room, where I could see her sitting before the fireplace knitting a little white sweater fit for a doll to wear. I thought it was a Christmas gift for me, for one of my dolls.

"And kick off your shoes before you come in here," she added.

We shed our boots and heavy coats and hoods in the foyer, then raced in stockinged feet into the living room, with its plush white carpet. That pastel room, decorated to flatter our mother's fair beauty, was off limits for us most of the time. This was our company room, our mother's room, and never could we feel really comfortable on the apricot brocade sofa or the cut-velvet chairs. We preferred Daddy's room, with its dark paneled walls and tough plaid sofa, where we could wallow and fight and never fear we were damaging anything.

"It's freezing outside, Momma!" I said breathlessly as I fell at her feet, thrusting my legs toward the fire. "But the ride home on our bikes was just beautiful. All the trees are sparkled with diamond icicles, and crystal prisms on the shrubs. It's a fairyland out there, Momma. I wouldn't live down south where it never snows, for anything!"

Christopher did not talk about the weather and its freezing beauty. He was two years and five months my senior and he was far wiser than I; I know that now. He warmed his icy feet as I did, but he stared up at Momma's face, a worried frown drawing his dark brows together.

I glanced up at her, too, wondering what he saw that made him show such concern. She was knitting at a fast and skilled pace, glancing from time to time at instructions.

"Momma, are you feeling all right?" he asked.

"Yes, of course," she answered, giving him a soft, sweet smile.

"You look tired to me."

She laid aside the tiny sweater. "I visited my doctor today," she said, leaning forward to caress Christopher's rosy cold cheek.

"Momma!" he cried, taking alarm. "Are you sick?"

She chuckled softly, then ran her long, slim fingers through his tousled blond curls. "Christopher Dollanganger, you know better than that. I've seen you looking at me with suspicious thoughts in your head." She caught his hand, and one of mine, and placed them both on her bulging middle.

"Do you feel anything?" she asked, that secret, pleased look on her face again.

Quickly, Christopher snatched his hand away as his face turned blood-red. But I left my hand where it was, wondering, waiting.

"What do *you* feel, Cathy?"

Beneath my hand, under her clothes, something weird was going on. Little faint movements quivered her flesh. I lifted my head and stared up in her face, and to this day, I can still recall how lovely she looked, like a Raphael madonna.

"Momma, your lunch is moving around, or else you have

gas." Laughter made her blue eyes sparkle, and she told me to guess again.

Her voice was sweet and concerned as she told us her news. "Darlings, I'm going to have a baby in early May. In fact when I visited my doctor today, he said he heard *two* heartbeats. So that means I am going to have twins . . . or, God forbid, triplets. Not even your father knows this yet, so don't tell him until I have a chance."

Stunned, I threw Christopher a look to see how he was taking this. He seemed bemused, and still embarrassed. I looked again at her lovely firelit face. Then I jumped up, and raced for my room!

I hurled myself face down on my bed, and bawled, really let go! Babies—two or more! *I* was the baby! I didn't want any little whining, crying babies coming along to take my place! I sobbed and beat at the pillows, wanting to hurt something, if not someone. Then I sat up and thought about running away.

Someone rapped softly on my closed and locked door. "Cathy," said my mother, "may I come in and talk this over with you?"

"Go away!" I yelled. "I already hate your babies!"

Yes, I knew what was in store for me, the middle child, the one parents didn't care about. I'd be forgotten; there'd be no more Friday gifts. Daddy would think only of Momma, of Christopher, and those hateful babies that would displace me.

My father came to me that evening, soon after he arrived home. I'd unlocked the door, just in case he wanted to see me. I stole a peek to see his face, for I loved him very much. He looked sad, and he carried a large box wrapped in silver foil, topped by a huge bow of pink satin.

"How's my Cathy been?" he asked softly, as I peeked from beneath my arm. "You didn't run to greet me when I came home. You haven't said hello; you haven't even looked at me. Cathy, it hurts when you don't run into my arms and give me kisses."

I didn't say anything, but rolled over on my back to glare at him fiercely. Didn't he know I was supposed to be his favorite all his life through? Why did he and Momma have to go and send for more children? Weren't two enough?

He sighed, then came to sit on the edge of my bed. "You know something? This is the first time in your life you have ever glared at me like that. This is the first Friday you haven't run to leap up into my arms. You may not believe this, but I don't really come alive until I come home on weekends."

Pouting, I refused to be won over. He didn't need me now. He had his son, and now heaps of wailing babies on the way. I'd be forgotten in the multitude.

"You know something else," he began, closely watching me, "I used to believe, perhaps foolishly, that if I came home on Fridays, and didn't bring one single gift for you, or your brother . . . I still believed the two of you would have run for me like crazy, and welcomed me home, anyway. I believed you loved *me* and not my gifts. I mistakenly believed that I'd been a good father, and somehow I'd managed to win your love, and that you'd know you would always have a big place in my heart, even if your mother and I have a dozen children." He paused, sighed, and his blue eyes darkened. "I thought my Cathy knew she would still be my very special girl, because she was my first."

I threw him an angry, hurt look. Then I choked, "But if Momma has another girl, you'll say the same thing to her!"

"Will I?"

"Yes," I sobbed, aching so badly I could scream from jealousy already. "You might even love her *more* than you do me, 'cause she'll be little and cuter."

"I may love her as much, but I won't love her more." He held out his arms and I could resist no longer. I flung myself into his arms, and clung to him for dear life. "Ssh," he soothed as I cried. "Don't cry, don't feel jealous. You won't be loved any the less. And Cathy, real babies are much more fun than dolls. Your mother will have more than she can handle, so she's going to depend on you to help her. When I'm away from home, I'll feel better knowing your mother has a loving daughter who will do what she can to make life easier and better for all of us." His warm lips pressed against my teary cheek. "Come now, open your box, and tell me what you think of what's inside."

First I had to smother his face with a dozen kisses and give him bear hugs to make up for the anxiety I'd put in his eyes. In the beautiful box was a silver music box made in England. The music played and a ballerina dressed in pink turned slowly around and around before a mirror. "It's a jewel box, as well," explained Daddy, slipping on my finger a tiny gold ring with a red stone he called a garnet. "The moment I saw that box, I knew you had to have it. And with this ring, I do vow to forever love my Cathy just a little bit more than any other daughter—as long as she never says that to anyone but herself."

There came a sunny Tuesday in May, when Daddy was home. For two weeks Daddy had been hanging around home, waiting for those babies to show up. Momma seemed irritable, uncomfortable, and Mrs. Bertha Simpson was in our kitchen, preparing our meals, and looking at Christopher and me with a smirky face. She was our most dependable baby-sitter. She lived next door, and was always saying Momma and Daddy looked more like brother and sister than husband and wife. She was a grim, grouchy sort of person who seldom had anything nice to say about anybody. And she was cooking cabbage. I hated cabbage.

Around dinnertime, Daddy came rushing into the dining room to tell my brother and me that he was driving Momma to the hospital. "Now don't be worried. Everything will work out fine. Mind Mrs. Simpson, and do your homework, and maybe in a few hours you'll know if you have brothers or sisters . . . or one of each."

He didn't return until the next morning. He was unshaven, tired looking, his suit rumpled, but he grinned at us happily. "Take a guess! Boys or girls?"

"Boys!" chimed up Christopher, who wanted two brothers he could teach to play ball. I wanted boys, too . . . no little girl to steal Daddy's affection from his first daughter.

"A boy *and* a girl," Daddy said proudly. "The prettiest little things you ever saw. Come, put your clothes on, and I'll drive you to see them yourselves."

Sulkily, I went, still reluctant to look even when Daddy picked me up and held me high so I could peer through the nursery room glass at two little babies a nurse held in her arms. They were so tiny! Their heads were no bigger than small apples, and small red fists waved in the air. One was screaming like pins were sticking it.

"Ah," sighed Daddy, kissing my cheek and hugging me close, "God has been good to me, sending me another son and daughter as perfect as my first pair."

I thought I would hate them both, especially the loud-mouthed one named Carrie, who wailed and bellowed ten times louder than the quiet one named Cory. It was nearly impossible to get a full night's rest with the two of them across the hall from my room. And yet, as they began to grow and smile, and their eyes lit up when I came in and lifted them, something warm and motherly replaced the green in my eyes. The first thing you knew, I was racing home to see *them;* to play with *them;* to change diapers and hold nursing bottles, and burp them on my shoulder. They *were* more fun than dolls.

I soon learned that parents have room in their hearts for more than two children, and I had room in my heart to love them, too—even Carrie, who was just as pretty as me, and maybe more so. They grew so quickly, like weeds, said Daddy, though Momma would often look at them with anxiety, for she said they were not growing as rapidly as Christopher and I had grown. This was laid before her doctor, who quickly assured her that often twins were smaller than single births.

"See," said Christopher, "doctors *do* know everything."

Daddy looked up from the newspaper he was reading and

smiled. "That's my son the doctor talking—but nobody knows everything, Chris."

Daddy was the only one who called my older brother Chris.

We had a funny surname, the very devil to learn to spell. Dollanganger. Just because we were all blond, flaxon haired, with fair complexions (except Daddy, with his perpetual tan), Jim Johnston, Daddy's best friend, pinned on us a nickname, "The Dresden dolls." He said we looked like those fancy porcelain people who grace whatnot shelves and fireplace mantels. Soon everyone in our neighborhood was calling us the Dresden dolls; certainly it was easier to say than Dollanganger.

When the twins were four, and Christopher was fourteen, and I had just turned twelve, there came a very special Friday. It was Daddy's thirty-sixth birthday and we were having a surprise party for him. Momma looked like a fairy-tale princess with her freshly washed and set hair. Her nails gleamed with pearly polish, her long formal gown was of softest aqua color, and her knotted string of pearls swayed as she glided from here to there, setting the table in the dining room so it would look perfect for Daddy's birthday party. His many gifts were piled high on the buffet. It was going to be a small, intimate party, just for our family and our closest friends.

"Cathy," said Momma, throwing me a quick look, "would you mind bathing the twins again for me? I gave them both baths before their naps, but as soon as they were up, they took off for the sandbox, and now they need another bath."

I didn't mind. She looked far too fancy to give two dirty four-year-olds splashy baths that would ruin her hair, her nails, and her lovely dress.

"And when you finish with them, both you and Christopher jump in the tub and bathe, too, and put on that pretty new pink dress, Cathy, and curl your hair. And, Christopher, no blue jeans, please. I want you to put on a dress shirt and a tie, and wear that light blue sports jacket with your cream-colored trousers."

"Aw, heck, Momma, I hate dressing up," he complained, scuffing his sneakers and scowling.

"Do as I say, Christopher, for your father. You know he does a lot for you; the least you can do is make him proud of his family."

He grouched off, leaving me to run out to the back garden and fetch the twins, who immediately began to wail. "One bath a day is enough!" screamed Carrie. "We're already clean! Stop! We don't like soap! We don't like hair washings! Don't you do that to us again, Cathy, or we'll tell Momma!"

"Hah!" I said. "Who do you think sent me out here to clean up two filthy little monsters? Good golly, how can the two of you get so dirty so quickly?"

As soon as their naked skins hit the warm water, and the little yellow rubber ducks and rubber boats began to float, and they could splash all over me, they were content enough to be bathed, shampooed, and dressed in their very best clothes. For, after all, they were going to a party—and, after all, this was Friday, and Daddy was coming home.

First I dressed Cory in a pretty little white suit with short pants. Strangely enough, he was more apt to keep himself clean than his twin. Try as I would, I couldn't tame down that stubborn cowlick of his. It curled over to the right, like a cute pig's tail, and—would you believe it?—Carrie wanted her hair to do the same thing!

When I had them both dressed, and looking like dolls come alive, I turned the twins over to Christopher with stern warnings to keep an ever observant eye on them. Now it was my turn to dress up.

The twins wailed and complained while I hurriedly took a bath, washed my hair, and rolled it up on fat curlers. I peeked around the bathroom door to see Christopher trying his best to entertain them by reading to them from *Mother Goose*.

"Hey," said Christopher when I came out wearing my pink dress with the fluted ruffles, "you don't look half-bad."

"Half-bad? Is that the best you can manage?"

"Best I can for a sister." He glanced at his watch, slammed the picture book closed, seized the twins by their dimpled hands and cried out, "Daddy will be here any minute—hurry, Cathy!"

Five o'clock came and went, and though we waited and waited, we didn't see our father's green Cadillac turn into our curving drive. The invited guests sat around and tried to keep up a cheerful conversation, as Momma got up and began to pace around nervously. Usually Daddy flung open the door at four, and sometimes even sooner.

Seven o'clock, and still we were waiting.

The wonderful meal Momma had spent so much time preparing was drying out from being too long in the warming oven. Seven was the time we usually put the twins to bed, and they were growing hungry, sleepy and cross, demanding every second, "When is Daddy coming?"

Their white clothes didn't look so virgin now. Carrie's smoothly waved hair began to curl up and look windblown. Cory's nose began to run, and repeatedly he wiped it on the back of his hand until I hurried over with a Kleenex to clean off his upper lip.

"Well, Corinne," joked Jim Johnston, "I guess Chris has found himself another super-broad."

His wife threw him an angry look for saying something so tasteless.

My stomach was growling, and I was beginning to feel as worried as Momma looked. She kept pacing back and forth, going to the wide picture window and staring out.

"Oh!" I cried, having caught sight of a car turning into our tree lined driveway, "maybe that's Daddy coming now!"

But the car that drew to a stop before our front door was white, not green. And on the top was one of those spinning red lights. An emblem on the side of that white car read STATE POLICE.

Momma smothered a cry when two policemen dressed in

blue uniforms approached our front door and rang our doorbell.

Momma seemed frozen. Her hand hovered near her throat; her heart came up and darkened her eyes. Something wild and frightening burgeoned in my heart just from watching her reactions.

It was Jim Johnston who answered the door, and allowed the two state troopers to enter, glancing about uneasily, seeing, I'm sure, that this was an assembly gathered together for a birthday party. All they had to do was glance into the dining room and see the festive table, the balloons suspended from the chandelier, and the gifts on the buffet.

"Mrs. Christopher Garland Dollanganger?" inquired the older of the two officers as he looked from woman to woman.

Our mother nodded slightly, stiffly. I drew nearer, as did Christopher. The twins were on the floor, playing with tiny cars, and they showed little interest in the unexpected arrival of police officers.

The kindly looking uniformed man with the deep red face stepped closer to Momma. "Mrs. Dollanganger," he began in a flat voice that sent immediate panic into my heart, "we're terribly sorry, but there's been an accident on Greenfield Highway."

"Oh . . ." breathed Momma, reaching to draw both Christopher and me against her sides. I could feel her quivering all over, just as I was. My eyes were magnetized by those brass buttons; I couldn't see anything else.

"Your husband was involved, Mrs. Dollanganger."

A long sigh escaped from Momma's choked throat. She swayed and would have fallen if Chris and I hadn't been there to support her.

"We've already questioned motorists who witnessed the accident, and it wasn't your husband's fault, Mrs. Dollanganger," that voice continued on, without emotion. "According to the accounts, which we've recorded, there was a motorist driving a blue Ford weaving in and out of the lefthand lane, apparently drunk, and he crashed head-on into your husband's car. But it seems your husband must have seen the accident coming, for he swerved to avoid a head-on collision, but a piece of machinery had fallen from another car, or truck, and this kept him from completing his correct defensive driving maneuver, which would have saved his life. But as it was, your husband's much heavier car turned over several times, and still he might have survived, but an oncoming truck, unable to stop, crashed into his car, and again the Cadillac spun over . . . and then . . . it caught on fire."

Never had a room full of people stilled so quickly. Even the young twins looked up from their innocent play, and stared at the two troopers.

"My husband?" whispered Momma, her voice so weak it was hardly audible. "He isn't . . . he isn't . . . dead . . . ?"

"Ma'am," said the red-faced officer very solemnly, "it pains me dreadfully to bring you bad news on what seems a special occasion." He faltered and glanced around with embarrassment. "I'm terribly sorry, ma'am—everybody did what they could to get him out . . . but, well ma'am . . . he was, well, killed instantly, from what the doc says."

Someone sitting on the sofa screamed.

Momma didn't scream. Her eyes went bleak, dark, haunted. Despair washed the radiant color from her beautiful face; it resembled a death mask. I stared up at her, trying to tell her with my eyes that none of this could be true. Not Daddy! Not my daddy! He couldn't be dead . . . he couldn't be! Death was for old people, sick people . . . not for somebody as loved and needed, and young.

Yet there was my mother with her gray face, her stark eyes, her hands wringing out the invisible wet cloths, and each second I watched, her eyes sank deeper into her skull.

I began to cry.

"Ma'am, we've got a few things of his that were thrown out on the first impact. We saved what we could."

"Go away!" I screamed at the officer. "Get out of here! It's not my daddy! I know it's not! He's stopped by a store to buy ice cream. He'll be coming in the door any minute! Get out of here!" I ran forward and beat on the officer's chest. He tried to hold me off, and Christopher came up and pulled me away.

"Please," said the trooper, "won't someone please help this child?"

My mother's arms encircled my shoulders and drew me close to her side. People were murmuring in shocked voices, and whispering, and the food in the warming oven was beginning to smell burned.

I waited for someone to come up and take my hand and say that God didn't ever take the life of a man like my father, yet no one came near me. Only Christopher came to put his arm about my waist, so we three were in a huddle,—Momma, Christopher, and me.

It was Christopher who finally found a voice to speak and such a strange, husky voice: "Are you positive it was our father? If the green Cadillac caught on fire, then the man inside must have been badly burned, so it could have been someone else, not Daddy."

Deep, rasping sobs tore from Momma's throat, though not a tear fell from her eyes. She believed! She believed those two men were speaking the truth!

The guests who had come so prettily dressed to attend a birthday party swarmed about us now and said those consoling things people say when there just aren't any right words.

"We're so sorry, Corinne, really shocked . . . it's terrible. . . ."

"What an awful thing to happen to Chris."

"Our days are numbered . . . that's the way it is, from the day we're born, our days are numbered."

It went on and on, and slowly, like water into concrete, it sank in. Daddy was really dead. We were never going to see him alive again. We'd only see him in a coffin, laid out in a box that would end up in the ground, with a marble headstone that bore his name and his day of birth and his day of death. Numbered the same, but for the year.

I looked around, to see what was happening to the twins, who shouldn't have been feeling what I was. Someone kind had taken them into the kitchen and was preparing them a light meal before they were tucked into bed. My eyes met Christopher's. He seemed as caught in this nightmare as I was, his young face pale and shocked; a hollow look of grief shadowed his eyes and made them dark.

One of the state troopers had gone out to his car, and now he came back with a bundle of things which he carefully spread out on the coffee table. I stood frozen, watching the display of all the things Daddy kept in his pockets: a lizard-skinned wallet Momma had given him as a Christmas gift; his leather notepad and date book; his wristwatch; his wedding band. Everything was blackened and charred by smoke and fire.

Last came the soft pastel animals meant for Cory and Carrie, all found, so the red-faced trooper said, scattered on the high-way. A plushy blue elephant with pink velvet ears, and a purple pony with a red saddle and golden reins—oh, that just had to be for Carrie. Then the saddest articles of all—Daddy's clothes, which had burst the confines of his suitcases when the trunk lock sprang.

I knew those suits, those shirts, ties, socks. There was the same tie I had given him on his last birthday.

"Someone will have to identify the body," said the trooper.

Now I knew positively. It was real, our father would never come home without presents for all of us—even on his own birthday.

I ran from that room! Ran from all the things spread out that tore my heart and made me ache worse than any pain I had yet experienced. I ran out of the house and into the back garden, and there I beat my fists upon an old maple tree. I beat my fists until they ached and blood began to come from the many small cuts; then I flung myself down on the grass and cried—cried ten oceans of tears, for Daddy who should be alive. I cried for us, who would have to go on living without him. And the twins, they hadn't even had the chance to know how wonderful he was—or had been. And when my tears were over, and my eyes swollen and red, and hurt from the rubbing, I heard soft footsteps coming to me—my mother.

She sat down on the grass beside me and took my hand in hers. A quarter-horned moon was out, and millions of stars, and the breezes were sweet with the newborn fragrances of spring. "Cathy," she said eventually when the silence between us stretched so long it might never come to an end, "your father is up in heaven looking down on you, and you know he would want you to be brave."

"He's not dead, Momma!" I denied vehemently.

"You've been out in this yard a long time; perhaps you don't realize it's ten o'clock. Someone had to identify your father's body, and though Jim Johnston offered to do this, and spare me the pain, I had to see for myself. For, you see, I found it hard to believe too. Your father is dead, Cathy. Christopher is on his bed crying, and the twins are asleep; they don't fully realize what 'dead' means."

She put her arms around me, and cradled my head down on her shoulder.

"Come," she said, standing and pulling me up with her, keeping her arm about my waist, "You've been out here much too long. I thought you were in the house with the others, and the others thought you were in your room, or with me. It's not good to be alone when you feel bereft. It's better to be with people and share your grief, and not keep it locked up inside."

She said this dry-eyed, with not a tear, but somewhere deep inside her she was crying, screaming. I could tell by her tone, by the very bleakness that had sunk deeper into her eyes.

With our father's death, a nightmare began to shadow our days. I gazed reproachfully at Momma and thought she should have prepared us in advance for something like this, for we'd never been allowed to own pets that suddenly pass away and teach us a little about losing through death. Someone, some adult, should have warned us that the young, the handsome, and the needed can die, too.

How do you say things like this to a mother who looked like fate was pulling her through a knothole and stretching her out thin and flat? Could you speak honestly to someone who didn't want to talk, or eat, or brush her hair, or put on the pretty clothes that filled her closet? Nor did she want to attend to our needs. It was a good thing the kindly neighborhood women came in and took us over, bringing with them food prepared in their own kitchens. Our house filled to overflowing with flowers, with homemade casseroles, hams, hot rolls, cakes, and pies.

They came in droves, all the people who loved, admired, and respected our father, and I was surprised he was so well known. Yet I hated it every time someone asked how he died, and what a pity someone so young should die, when so many who were useless and unfit, lived on and on, and were a burden to society.

From all that I heard, and overheard, fate was a grim reaper, never kind, with little respect for who was loved and needed.

Spring days passed on toward summer. And grief, no matter how you try to cater to its wail, has a way of fading away, and the person so real, so beloved, becomes a dim, slightly out-of-focus shadow.

One day Momma sat so sad-faced that she seemed to have forgotten how to smile. "Momma," I said brightly, in an effort to cheer her, "I'm going to pretend Daddy is still alive, and away on another of his business trips, and soon he'll come, and stride in the door, and he'll call out, just as he used to, 'Come and greet me with kisses if you love me.' And—don't you see?—we'll feel better, all of us, like he *is* alive somewhere, living where we can't see him, but where we can expect him at any moment."

"No, Cathy," Momma flared, "you must accept the truth. You are not to find solace in pretending. Do you hear that! Your father is dead, and his soul has gone on to heaven, and you should understand at your age that no one ever has come back from heaven. As for us, we'll make do the best we can without him— and that doesn't mean escaping reality by not facing up to it."

I watched her rise from her chair and begin to take things from the refrigerator to start breakfast.

"Momma . . ." I began again, feeling my way along cautiously lest she turn hard and angry again. "Will we be able to go on, without him?"

"I will do the best I can to see that we survive," she said dully, flatly.

"Will you have to go to work now, like Mrs. Johnston?"

"Maybe, maybe not. Life holds all sorts of surprises, Cathy, and some of them are unpleasant, as you are finding out. But remember always you were blessed to have for almost twelve years a father who thought you were something very special."

"Because I look like you," I said, still feeling some of that envy I always had, because I came in second after her.

She threw me a glance as she rambled through the contents of the jam-packed fridge. "I'm going to tell you something now, Cathy, that I've never told you before. You look very much as I did at your age, but you are not like me in your personality. You are much more aggressive, and much more determined. Your father used to say that you were like his mother, and he loved his mother."

"Doesn't everybody love their mother?"

"No," she said with a queer expression, "there are some mothers you just can't love, for they don't want you to love them."

She took bacon and eggs from the refrigerator, then turned to take me in her arms. "Dear Cathy, you and your father had a very special close relationship, and I guess you must miss him more because of that, more than Christopher does, or the twins."

I sobbed against her shoulder. "I hate God for taking him! He should have lived to be an old man! He won't be there when I dance and when Christopher is a doctor. Nothing seems to matter now that he's gone."

"Sometimes," she began in a tight voice, "death is not as terrible as you think. Your father will never grow old, or infirm. He'll always stay young; you'll remember him that way—young, handsome, strong. Don't cry anymore, Cathy, for as your father used to say, there is a reason for everything and a solution for every problem, and I'm trying, trying hard to do what I think best."

We were four children stumbling around in the broken pieces of our grief and loss. We would play in the back garden, trying to find solace in the sunshine, quite unaware that our lives were soon to change so drastically, so dramatically, that the words "backyard" and "garden" were to become for us synonyms for heaven—and just as remote.

It was an afternoon shortly after Daddy's funeral, and Christopher and I were with the twins in the backyard. They sat in the sandbox with small shovels and sand pails. Over and over again they transferred sand from one pail to another, gibbering back and forth in the strange language only they could understand. Cory and Carrie were fraternal rather than identical twins, yet they were like one unit, very much satisfied with each other. They built a wall about themselves so they were the castle-keeps, and full guardians of their larder of secrets. They had each other and that was enough.

The time for dinner came and went. We were afraid that now even meals might be cancelled, so even without our mother's voice to call us in, we caught hold of the dimpled, fat hands of the twins and dragged them along toward the house. We found our mother seated behind Daddy's big desk; she was writing what appeared to be a very difficult letter, if the evidence of many discarded beginnings meant anything. She frowned as she wrote in longhand, pausing every so often to lift her head and stare off into space.

"Momma," I said, "it's almost six o'clock. The twins are growing hungry."

"In a minute, in a minute," she said in an off-hand way. "I'm writing to your grandparents who live in Virginia. The neighbors have brought us food enough for a week—you could put one of the casseroles in the oven, Cathy."

It was the first meal I almost prepared myself. I had the table set, and the casserole heating, and the milk poured, when Momma came in to help.

It seemed to me that every day after our father had gone, our mother had letters to write, and places to go, leaving us in the care of the neighbor next door. At night Momma would sit at Daddy's desk, a green ledger book opened in front of her, checking over stacks of bills. Nothing felt good anymore, nothing. Often now my brother and I bathed the twins, put on their pajamas, and tucked them into bed. Then Christopher would hurry off to his room to study, while I would hurry back to my mother to seek a way to bring happiness to her eyes again.

A few weeks later a letter came in response to the many our mother had written home to her parents. Immediately Momma began to cry—even before she had opened the thick, creamy envelope, she cried. Clumsily, she used a letter opener, and with trembling hands she held three sheets, reading over the letter three times. All the while she read, tears trickled slowly down her cheeks, smearing her makeup with long, pale, shiny streaks.

She had called us in from the backyard as soon as she had collected the mail from the box near the front door, and now we four were seated on the living room sofa. As I watched I saw her soft fair Dresden face turn into something cold, hard, resolute. A cold chill shivered down my spine. Maybe it was because she stared at us for so long—too long. Then she looked down at the sheets held in her trembling hands, then to the windows, as if there she could find some answer to the question of the letter.

Momma was acting so strangely. It made us all uneasy and

unusually quiet, for we were already intimidated enough in a fatherless home without a creamy letter of three sheets to glue our mother's tongue and harden her eyes. Why did she look at us so oddly?

Finally, she cleared her throat and began to speak, but in a cold voice, totally unlike her customary soft, warm cadence. "Your grandmother has at last replied to my letters," she said in that icy voice. "All those letters I wrote to her . . . well . . . she has agreed. She is willing to let us come and live with her."

Good news! Just what we had been waiting to hear—and we should have been happy. But Momma fell into that moody silence again, and she just sat there staring at us. What was the matter with her? Didn't she know we were hers, and not some stranger's four perched in a row like birds on a clothesline?

"Christopher, Cathy, at fourteen and twelve, you two should be old enough to understand, and old enough to cooperate, and help your mother out of a desperate situation." She paused, fluttered one hand up to nervously finger the beads at her throat and sighed heavily. She seemed on the verge of tears. And I felt sorry, so sorry for poor Momma, without a husband.

"Momma," I said, "is everything all right?"

"Of course, darling, of course." She tried to smile. "Your father, God rest his soul, expected to live to a ripe old age and acquire in the meantime a sizable fortune. He came from people who know how to make money, so I don't have any doubts he would have done just what he planned, if given the time. But thirty-six is so young to die. People have a way of believing nothing terrible will ever happen to them, only to others. We don't anticipate accidents, nor do we expect to die young. Why, your father and I thought we would grow old together, and we hoped to see our grandchildren before we both died on the same day. Then neither of us would be left alone to grieve for the one who went first."

Again she sighed. "I have to confess we lived way beyond our present means, and we charged against the future. We spent money before we had it. Don't blame him; it was my fault. He knew all about poverty. I knew nothing about it. You know how he used to scold me. Why, when we bought this house, he said we needed only three bedrooms, but I wanted four. Even four didn't seem enough. Look around, there's a thirty year mortgage on this house. Nothing here is really ours: not this furniture, not the cars, not the appliances in the kitchen or laundry room—not one single thing is fully paid for."

Did we look frightened? Scared? She paused as her face flushed deeply red, and her eyes moved around the lovely room that set off her beauty so well. Her delicate brows screwed into an anxious frown. "Though your father would chastise me a little, still he wanted them, too. He indulged me, because he loved me, and I believe I convinced him finally that luxuries were absolute necessities, and he gave in, for we had a way, the two of us, of indulging our desires too much. It was just another of the things we had in common."

Her expression collapsed into one of forlorn reminiscence before she continued on in her stranger's voice. "Now all our beautiful things will be taken away. The legal term is repossession. That's what they do when you don't have enough money to finish paying for what you've bought. Take that sofa, for example. Three years ago it cost eight hundred dollars. And we've paid all but one hundred, but still they're going to take it. We'll lose all that we've paid on everything, and that's still legal. Not only will we lose this furniture and the house, but also the cars—in fact, everything but our clothes and your toys. They're going to allow me to keep my wedding band, and I've hidden away my engagement diamond—so please don't mention I ever had an engagement ring to anyone who might come to check."

Who "they" were, not one of us asked. It didn't occur to me to ask. Not then. And later it just didn't seem to matter.

Christopher's eyes met mine. I floundered in the desire to understand, and struggled not to drown in the understanding. Already I was sinking, drowning in the adult world of death and debts. My brother reached out and took my hand, then squeezed my fingers in a gesture of unusual brotherly reassurance.

Was I a windowpane, so easy to read, that even he, my archtormentor, would seek to comfort me? I tried to smile, to prove to him how adult I was, and in this way gloss over that trembling and weak thing I was cringing into because "they" were going to take everything. I didn't want any other little girl living in my pretty peppermint pink room, sleeping in my bed, playing with the things I cherished—my miniature dolls in their shadowbox frames, and my sterling-silver music box with the pink ballerina—would they take those, too?

Momma watched the exchange between my brother and me very closely. She spoke again with a bit of her former sweet self showing. "Don't look so heartbroken. It's not really as bad as I've made it seem. You must forgive me if I was thoughtless and forgot how young you still are. I've told you the bad news first, and saved the best for the last. Now hold your breath! You are not going to believe what I have to tell you—for my parents are rich! Not middle-class rich, or upper-class rich, but very, very rich! Filthy, unbelievably, sinfully rich! They live in a fine big house in Virginia—such a house as you've never seen before. I know, I was born there, and grew up there, and when you see that house, this one will seem like a shack in comparison. And didn't I say we are going to live with them—my mother, and my father?"

She offered this straw of cheer with a weak and nervously fluttering smile that did not succeed in releasing me from doubts which her demeanor and her information had pitched me into. I didn't like the way her eyes skipped guiltily away when I tried to catch them. I thought she was hiding something.

But she was my mother.

And Daddy was gone.

I picked up Carrie and sat her on my lap, pressing her small, warm body close against mine. I smoothed back the damp golden curls that fell over her rounded forehead. Her eyelids drooped, and her full rosebud lips pouted. I glanced at Cory, crouching against Christopher. "The twins are tired, Momma. They need their dinner."

"Time enough for dinner later," she snapped impatiently. "We have plans to make, and clothes to pack, for tonight we have to catch a train. The twins can eat while we pack. Everything you four wear must be crowded into only two suitcases. I want you to take only your favorite clothes and the small toys you cannot bear to leave. Only one game. I'll buy you many games after you are there. Cathy, you select what clothes and toys you think the twins like best—but only a few. We can't take along more than four suitcases, and I need two for my own things."

Oh, golly-lolly! This was real! We had to leave, abandon everything! I had to crowd everything into two suitcases my brothers and sister would share as well. My Raggedy Ann doll alone would half fill *one* suitcase! Yet how could I leave her, my most beloved doll, the one Daddy gave me when I was only three? I sobbed.

So, we sat with our shocked faces staring at Momma. We made her terribly uneasy, for she jumped up and began to pace the room.

"As I said before, my parents are extremely wealthy." She shot Christopher and me an appraising glance, then quickly turned to hide her face.

"Momma," said Christopher, "is something wrong?"

I marveled that he could ask such a thing, when it was only too obvious, *everything* was wrong.

She paced, her long shapely legs appearing through the front opening of her filmy black negligee. Even in her grief, wearing black, she was beautiful—shadowed, troubled eyes and all. She was so lovely, and I loved her,—oh, how I loved her then!

How we all loved her then.

Directly in front of the sofa, our mother spun around and the black chiffon of her negligee flared like a dancer's skirt, revealing her beautiful legs from feet to hips.

"Darlings," she began, "what could possibly be wrong about living in such a fine home as my parents own? I was born there; I grew up there, except for those years when I was sent away to school. It's a huge, beautiful house, and they keep adding new rooms to it, though Lord knows they have enough rooms already."

She smiled, but something about her smile seemed false. "There is, however, one small thing I have to tell you before you meet my father—your grandfather." Here again she faltered, and again smiled that queer, shadowy smile. "Years ago, when I was eighteen, I did something serious, of which your grandfather disapproved, and my mother wasn't approving, either, but she wouldn't leave me anything, anyway, so she doesn't count. But, because of what I did, my father had me written out of his will, and so now I am disinherited. Your father used to gallantly call this 'fallen from grace.' Your father always made the best of everything, and he said it didn't matter."

Fallen from grace? Whatever did that mean? I couldn't imagine my mother doing anything so bad that her own father would turn against her and take away what she should have.

"Yes, Momma, I know exactly what you mean," Christopher piped up. "You did something of which your father disapproved, and so, even though you were included in his will, he had his lawyer write you out instead of thinking twice, and now you won't inherit any of his worldly goods when he passes on to the great beyond." He grinned, pleased with himself for knowing more than me. He always had the answers to everything. He had his nose in a book whenever he was in the house. Outside, under the sky, he was just as wild, just as mean as any other kid on the block. But indoors, away from the television, my older brother was a bookworm!

Naturally, he was right.

"Yes, Christopher. None of your grandfather's wealth will come to me when he dies, or through me, to you. That's why I had to keep writing so many letters home when my mother didn't respond." Again she smiled, this time with bitter irony.

"But, since I am the sole heir left, I am hopeful of winning back his approval. You see, once I had two older brothers, but both have died in accidents, and now I am the only one left to inherit." Her restless pacing stopped. Her hand rose to cover her mouth; she shook her head, then said in a new parrot-like voice, "I guess I'd better tell you something else. Your real surname is not Dollanganger; it is Foxworth. And Foxworth is a very important name in Virginia."

"Momma!" I exclaimed in shock. "Is it legal to change your name, and put that fake name on our birth certificates?"

Her voice became impatient. "For heaven's sake, Cathy, names can be changed legally. And the name Dollanganger does belong to us, more or less. Your father borrowed that name from way back in his ancestry. He thought it an amusing name, a joke, and it served its purpose well enough."

"What purpose?" I asked. "Why would Daddy legally change his name from something like Foxworth, so easy to spell, to something long and difficult like Dollanganger?"

"Cathy, I'm tired," said Momma, falling into the nearest chair. "There's so much for me to do, so many legal details. Soon enough you'll know everything; I'll explain. I swear to be totally honest; but please, now, let me catch my breath."

Oh, what a day this was. First we hear the mysterious "they" were coming to take away all our things, even our house. And then we learn even our own last name wasn't really ours.

The twins, curled up on our laps, were already half-asleep, and they were too young to understand, anyway. Even I, now twelve years old, and almost a woman, could not comprehend why Momma didn't really look happy to be going home again to parents she hadn't seen in fifteen years. Secret grandparents we'd thought were dead until after our father's funeral. Only this day had we heard of two uncles who'd died in accidents. It dawned on me strongly then, that our parents had lived full lives even before they had children, that we were not so important after all.

"Momma," Christopher began slowly, "your fine, grand home in Virginia sounds nice, but we like it here. Our friends are here, everybody knows us, likes us, and I know I don't want to move. Can't you see Daddy's attorney and ask him to help find a way so we can stay on, and keep our house and our furnishings?"

"Yes, Momma, please, let us stay here," I added.

Quickly Momma was out of her chair and striding across the room. She dropped down on her knees before us, her eyes on the level with ours. "Now listen to me," she ordered, catching my brother's hand and mine and pressing them both against her breasts. "I have thought, and I have thought of how we can manage to stay on here, but there is no way—no way at all, because we have no money to meet the monthly bills, and I don't have the skills to earn an adequate salary to support four children and myself as well. Look at me," she said, throwing wide her arms, appearing vulnerable, beautiful, helpless. "Do you know what I am? I am a pretty, useless ornament who always believed she'd have a man to take care of her. I don't know how to do anything. I can't even type. I'm not very good with arithmetic. I *can* embroider beautiful needlepoint and crewelwork stitches, but that kind of thing doesn't earn any money. You can't live without money. It's not love that makes the world go 'round—it's money. And my father has more money than he knows what to do with. He has only one living heir—me! Once he cared more for me than he did for either of his sons, so it shouldn't be difficult to win back his affection. Then he will have his attorney draw me into a new will, and I will inherit everything! He is sixty-six years old, and he is dying of heart disease. From what my mother wrote on a separate sheet of paper which my father didn't read, your grandfather cannot possibly live more than two or three months longer at the most. That will give me plenty of time to charm him into loving me like he used to—and when he dies, his entire fortune will be mine! Mine! *Ours!* We will be free forever of all financial worries. Free to go anywhere we want. Free to do anything we want. Free to travel, to buy what our hearts desire—anything our hearts desire! I'm not speaking of only a million or two, but many, many millions—maybe even billions! People with that kind of money don't even know their own net value, for it's invested here and there, and they own this and that, including banks, airlines, hotels, department stores, shipping lines. Oh, you just don't realize the kind of empire your grandfather controls, even now, while he's on his last legs. He has a genius for making money. Everything he touches turns to gold."

Her blue eyes gleamed. The sun shone through the front windows, casting diamond strands of light on her hair. Already she seemed rich beyond value. Momma, Momma, how had all of this come about only after our father died?

"Christopher, Cathy, are you listening, using your imaginations? Do you realize what a tremendous amount of money can do? The world, and everything in it is yours! You have power, influence, respect. Trust me. Soon enough I will win back my father's heart. He'll take one look at me, and realize instantly how all those fifteen years we've been separated have been such a waste. He's old, sick, he always stays on the first floor, in a small room beyond the library, and he has nurses to take care of him night and day, and servants to wait on him hand and foot. But only your own flesh and blood means anything, and I'm all he has left, only me. Even the nurses don't find it necessary to climb the stairs, for they have their own bath. *One* night, I will prepare him to meet his four grandchildren, and then I will bring you down the stairs, and into his room, and he will be charmed, enchanted by what he sees: four beautiful children who are perfect in every way—he is bound to love you, each and every one of you. Believe me, it will work out, just the way I say. I promise that whatever my father requires of me, I will do. On my life, on all I hold sacred and dear—and that is the children my love for your father made—you can believe I will soon be the heiress to a fortune beyond belief, and through me, every dream you've ever had will come true."

My mouth gaped open. I was overwhelmed by her passion. I glanced at Christopher to see him staring at Momma with incredulity. Both the twins were on the soft fringes of sleep. They had heard none of this.

We were going to live in a house as big and rich as a palace.

In that palace so grand, where servants waited on you hand and foot, we would be introduced to King Midas, who would soon die, and then *we* would have all the money, to put the world at our feet. We were stepping into riches beyond belief! I would be just like a princess!

Yet, why didn't I feel really happy?

"Cathy," said Christopher, beaming on me a broad, happy smile, "you can still be a ballerina. I don't think money can buy talent, nor can it make a good doctor out of a playboy. But, until the time comes when we have to be dedicated and serious, my, aren't we gonna have a ball?"

I couldn't take the sterling-silver music box with the pink ballerina inside. The music box was expensive and had been listed as something of value for "them" to claim.

I couldn't take down the shadowboxes from the walls, or hide away the miniature dolls. There was hardly anything I could take that Daddy had given me except the small ring on my finger, with a semiprecious gem stone shaped like a heart.

And, just like Christopher said, after we were rich, our lives would be one big ball, one long, long party. That's the way rich people lived—happily ever after as they counted their money and made their fun plans.

Fun, games, parties, riches beyond belief, a house as big as a palace, with servants who lived over a huge garage that stored away at least nine or ten expensive automobiles. Who would ever have guessed my mother came from a family like that? Why had Daddy argued with her so many times about spending money lavishly, when she could have written letters home before, and done a bit of humiliating begging?

Slowly I walked down the hall to my room, to stand before the silver music box where the pink ballerina stood in arabesque position when the lid was opened, and she could see herself in the reflecting mirror. And I heard the tinkling music play, "Whirl, ballerina, whirl. . . ."

I could steal it, if I had a place to hide it.

Good-bye, pink-and-white room with the peppermint walls. Good-bye, little white bed with the dotted-Swiss canopy that had seen me sick with measles, mumps, chicken pox.

Good-bye again to you, Daddy, for when I'm gone, I can't picture you sitting on the side of my bed, and holding my hand, and I won't see you coming from the bathroom with a glass of water. *I really don't want to go too much, Daddy. I'd rather stay and keep your memory close and near.*

"Cathy"—Momma was at the door—"don't just stand there and cry. A room is just a room. You'll live in many rooms before you die, so hurry up, pack your things and the twins' things, while I do my own packing."

Before I died, I was going to live in a thousand rooms or more, a little voice whispered this in my ear . . . and I believed.

The Road to Riches

While Momma packed, Christopher and I threw our clothes into two suitcases, along with a few toys and one game. In the early twilight of evening, a taxi drove us to the train station. We had slipped away furtively, without saying good-bye to even one friend, and this hurt. I didn't know why it had to be that way, but Momma insisted. Our bicycles were left in the garage along with everything else too large to take.

The train lumbered through a dark and starry night, heading toward a distant mountain estate in Virginia. We passed many a sleepy town and village, and scattered farmhouses where golden rectangles of light were the only evidence to show they were there at all. My brother and I didn't want to fall asleep and miss out on anything, and oh, did we have a lot to talk about! Mostly we speculated on that grand rich house where we would live in splendor, and eat from golden plates, and be served by a butler wearing livery. And I supposed I'd have my own maid to lay out my clothes, draw my bath, brush my hair, and jump when I commanded. But I wouldn't be too stern with her. I would be sweet, understanding, the kind of mistress every servant desired—

unless she broke something I really cherished! Then there'd be hell to pay—I'd throw a temper tantrum, and hurl a few things I didn't like, anyway.

Looking backward to that night ride on the train, I realize that was the very night I began to grow up, and philosophize. With everything you gained, you had to lose something—so I might as well get used to it, and make the best of it.

While my brother and I speculated on how we would spend the money when it came to us, the portly, balding conductor entered our small compartment and gazed admiringly at our mother from head to toes before he softly spoke: "Mrs. Patterson, in fifteen minutes we'll reach your depot."

Now why was he calling her "Mrs. Patterson"? I wondered. I shot a questioning look at Christopher, who also seemed perplexed by this.

Jolted awake, appearing startled and disoriented, Momma's eyes flew wide open. Her gaze jumped from the conductor, who hovered so close above her, over to Christopher and me, and then she looked down in despair at the sleeping twins. Next came ready tears and she was reaching in her purse and pulled out tissues, dabbing at her eyes daintily. Then came a sigh so heavy, so full of woe, my heart began to beat in a nervous tempo. "Yes, thank you," she said to the conductor, who was still watching her with great approval and admiration. "Don't fear, we'll be ready to leave."

"Ma'am," he said, most concerned when he glanced at his pocket watch, "it's three o'clock in the morning. Will someone be there to meet you?" He flicked his worried gaze to Christopher and me, then to the sleeping twins.

"It's all right," assured our mother.

"Ma'am, it's very dark out there."

"I could find my way home asleep."

The grandfatherly conductor wasn't satisfied with this. "Lady," he said, "it's an hour's ride to Charlottesville. We are letting you and your children off in the middle of nowhere. There's not a house in sight."

To forbid any further questioning, Momma answered in her most arrogant manner, "Someone *is* meeting us." Funny how she could put on that kind of haughty manner like a hat, and just as easily discard it.

We arrived at the depot in the middle of nowhere, and we were let off. No one was there to meet us.

It was totally dark when we stepped from the train, and as the conductor had warned, there was not a house in sight. Alone in the night, far from any sign of civilization, we stood and waved good-bye to the conductor on the train steps, holding on by one hand, waving with the other. His expression revealed that he wasn't too happy about leaving "Mrs. Patterson" and her brood of four sleepy children waiting for someone coming in a car. I looked around and saw nothing but a rusty, tin roof supported by four wooden posts, and a rickety green bench. This was our train depot. We didn't sit on that bench, just stood and watched until the train disappeared in the darkness, hearing one single, mournful whistle calling back, as if wishing us good luck and Godspeed.

We were surrounded by fields and meadows. From the deep woods in back of the "depot", something made a weird noise. I jumped and spun about to see what it was, making Christopher laugh. "That was only an owl! Did you think it was a ghost?"

"Now there is to be none of that!" said Momma sharply. "And you don't have to whisper. No one is about. This is farm country, dairy cows mostly. Look around. See the fields of wheat and oats, some barley, too. The nearby farmers supply all the fresh produce for the wealthy people who live on the hill."

There were hills aplenty, looking like lumpy patchwork quilts, with trees parading up and down to separate them into distinct sections. Sentinels of the night, I called them, but Momma told us the many trees in straight rows acted as windbreaks, and held back the heavy drifts of snow. Just the right words to make Christopher very excited. He loved all kinds of winter sports, and he hadn't thought a southern state like Virginia would have heavy snow.

"Oh, yes, it snows here," said Momma. "You bet it snows. We are in the foothills of the Blue Ridge Mountains, and it gets very, very cold here, just as cold as it did in Gladstone. But the summers will be warmer during the day. The nights are always cool enough for at least one blanket. Now if the sun were out, you'd be feasting your eyes on very beautiful countryside, as pretty as there is anywhere in the world. We have to hurry, though. It's a long, long walk to my home, and we have to reach there before dawn, when the servants get up."

How strange. "Why?" I asked. "And why did that conductor call you Mrs. Patterson?"

"Cathy, I don't have time to explain to you now. We've got to walk fast." She bent to pick up the two heaviest suitcases, and said in a firm voice that we were to follow where she led. Christopher and I were forced to carry the twins, who were too sleepy to walk, or make even an attempt.

"Momma!" I cried out, when we had moved on a few steps, "the conductor forgot to give us *your* two suitcases!"

"It's all right, Cathy," she said breathlessly, as if the two suitcases she was carrying were enough to tax her strength. "I asked the conductor to take my two bags on to Charlottesville and put them in a locker for me to pick up tomorrow morning."

"Why would you do that?" asked Christopher in a tight voice.

"Well, for one thing, I certainly couldn't handle *four* suitcases, could I? And, for another thing, I want the chance to talk to my father first before he learns about my children. And it just wouldn't seem right if I arrived home in the middle of the night after being gone for fifteen years, now would it?"

It sounded reasonable, I guess, for we did have all we could handle since the twins refused to walk. We set off, tagging along behind our mother, over uneven ground, following faint paths between rocks and trees and shrubbery that clawed at our clothes. We trekked a long, long, long way. Christopher and I became tired, irritable, as the twins grew heavier and heavier, and our arms began to ache. It was an adventure already beginning to pall. We complained, we nagged, we dragged our feet, wanting to sit down and rest. We wanted to be back in Gladstone, in our own beds, with our own things—better than here—better than that big old house with servants and grandparents we didn't even know.

"Wake up the twins!" snapped Momma, grown impatient with our complaining. "Stand them on their feet, and force them to walk, whether or not they want to." Then she mumbled something faint into the fur collar of her jacket that just barely reached my keen ears: "Lord knows, they'd better walk outside while they can."

A ripple of apprehension shot down my spine. I glanced at my older brother to see if he'd heard, just as he turned his head to look at me. He smiled. I smiled in return.

Tomorrow, when Momma arrived at a proper time, in a taxi, she would go to the sick grandfather and she'd smile, and she'd speak, and he'd be charmed, won over. Just one look at her lovely face, and just one word from her soft beautiful voice, and he'd hold out his arms, and forgive her for whatever she'd done to make her "fall from grace."

From what she'd already told us, her father was a cantankerous *old* man, for sixty-six did seem like incredibly old age to me. And a man on the verge of death couldn't afford to hold grudges against his sole remaining child, a daughter he'd once loved very much. He'd have to forgive her, so he could go peacefully, blissfully into his grave, and know he'd done the right thing. Then, once she had him under her spell, she'd bring us down from the bedroom, and we'd be looking our best, and acting our sweetest selves, and he'd soon see we weren't ugly, or really bad, and nobody, absolutely nobody with a heart could resist loving the twins. Why, people in shopping centers stopped to pat the twins, and compliment our mother on having such beautiful babies. And just wait until Grandfather learned how smart Christopher was! A straight-A student! And what was even more remarkable, he didn't have to study and study the way I did. Everything came so easily for him. His eyes could scan a page just once or twice, and all the information would be written indelibly on his brain, never to be forgotten. Oh, how I did envy him that gift.

I had a gift too; not the bright and shining coin that was Christopher's. It was my way to turn over all that glittered and look for the tarnish. We had gleaned but a bit of information about that unknown grandfather, but putting the pieces together, I already had the idea he was not the kind to easily forgive—not when he could deny a once-beloved daughter for fifteen years. Yet, could he be so hard he could resist all Momma's wheedling charms, which were considerable? I doubted it. I had seen and heard her wheedle with our father about money matters, and always Daddy was the one to give in and be won over to her way. Just a kiss, a hug, a soft stroking caress and Daddy would brighten up and smile, and agree, yes, somehow or other they could manage to pay for everything expensive she bought.

"Cathy," said Christopher, "take that worried look off your face. If God didn't plan for people to grow old, and sick, and to eventually die, he wouldn't keep on letting people have babies."

I felt Christopher staring at me, as if reading my thoughts, and I flushed. He grinned cheerfully. He was the perpetual cock-eyed optimist, never gloomy, doubtful, or moody, as I often was.

We followed Momma's advice and woke up the twins. We stood them on their feet and told them they would have to make an effort to walk, tired or not. We pulled them along while they whined and complained with sniffling sobs of rebellion. "Don't wanna go where we're going," sobbed a teary Carrie.

Cory only wailed.

"Don't like walkin' in woods when it's dark!" screamed Carrie, trying to pull her tiny hand free from mine. "I'm going home! Let me go, Cathy, let me go!"

Cory howled louder.

I wanted to pick Carrie up again, and carry her on, but my arms were just too aching to make another effort. Then

Christopher released Cory's hand and ran ahead to assist
Momma with her two heavy suitcases, so I had two unwilling,
resisting twins to lug along in the darkness.

   The air was cool and sharply pungent. Though Momma called
this hill country, those shadowy, high forms in the distance
looked like mountains to me. I stared up at the sky. It seemed to
me like an inverted deep bowl of navy-blue velvet, sparkled all
over with crystallized snowflakes instead of stars—or were they
tears of ice that I was going to cry in the future? Why did they
seem to be looking down at me with pity, making me feel ant-
sized, overwhelmed, completely insignificant? It was too big,
that close sky, too beautiful, and it filled me with a strange sense
of foreboding. Still I knew that under other circumstances, I
could love a countryside like this.

   We came at last upon a cluster of large and very fine homes,
nestled on a steep hillside. Stealthily, we approached the largest
and, by far, the grandest of all the sleeping mountain homes.
Momma said in a hushed voice that her ancestral home was
named Foxworth Hall, and was more than two hundred years
old!

   "Is there a lake nearby for ice-skating, and swimming?"
asked Christopher. He gave serious attention to the hillside. "It's
not good ski country—too many trees and rocks."

   "Yes," said Momma, "there's a small lake about a quarter of a
mile away." And she pointed in the direction where a lake could
be found.

   We circled that enormous house, almost on tiptoes. Once at
the back door, an old lady let us in. She must have been waiting,
and seen us coming, for she opened that door so readily we
didn't even have to knock. Just like thieves in the night, we stole
silently inside. Not a word did she speak to welcome us. Could
this be one of the servants? I wondered.

   Immediately we were inside the dark house, and she hustled
us up a steep and narrow back staircase, not allowing us one second to pause and take a look around the grand rooms we only

glimpsed in our swift and mute passage. She led us down many halls, past many closed doors, and finally we came to an end room, where she swung open a door and gestured us inside. It was a relief to have our long night journey over, and be in a large bedroom where a single lamp was lit. Heavy, tapestried draperies covered two tall windows. The old woman in her gray dress turned to look us over as she closed the heavy door to the hall and leaned against it.

She spoke, and I was jolted. "Just as you said, Corrine. Your children are beautiful."

There she was, paying us a compliment that should warm our hearts—but it chilled mine. Her voice was cold and uncaring, as if we were without ears to hear, and without minds to comprehend her displeasure, despite her flattery. And I was right to judge her so. Her next words proved that.

"But are you sure they are intelligent? Do they have some invisible afflictions not apparent to the eyes?"

"None!" cried our mother, taking offense, as did I. "My children are perfect, as you can plainly see, physically and mentally!" She glared at that old woman in gray before she squatted down on her heels and began to undress Carrie, who was nodding on her feet. I knelt before Cory and unbuttoned his small blue jacket, as Christopher lifted one of the suitcases up on one of the big beds. He opened it and took out two pairs of small yellow pajamas with feet.

Furtively, as I helped Cory off with his clothes and into his yellow pajamas, I studied that tall, big woman, who was, I presumed, our grandmother. As I looked her over, seeking wrinkles and heavy jowls, I found out she was not as old as I had at first presumed. Her hair was a strong, steel-blue color, drawn back from her face in a severe style which made her eyes appear somewhat long and cat-like. Why, you could even see how each strand of hair pulled her skin up in little resentful hills—and even as I watched, I saw one hair spring free from its moorings! Her nose was an eagle's beak, her shoulders were wide, and her mouth was like a thin, crooked knife slash. Her dress, of gray taffeta, had a diamond brooch at the throat of a high, severe neckline. Nothing about her appeared soft or yielding; even her bosom looked like twin hills of concrete. There would be no funning with her, as we had played with our mother and father.

I didn't like her. I wanted to go home. My lips quivered. I wanted Daddy alive again. How could such a woman as this make someone as lovely and sweet as our mother? From whom had our mother inherited her beauty, her gaiety? I shivered, and tried to forbid those tears that welled in my eyes. Momma had prepared us in advance for an unloving, uncaring, unrelenting grandfather—but the grandmother who had arranged for our coming—she came as a harsh, astonishing surprise. I blinked back my tears, fearful Christopher would see them and mock me later. But to reassure me, there was our mother smiling warmly as she lifted a pajamaed Cory into one of the big beds, and then she put Carrie in beside him. Oh, how they did look sweet, lying there, like big, rosy-cheeked dolls. Momma leaned over the twins and pressed kisses on their flushed cheeks, and her hand tenderly brushed back the curls on their foreheads, and then she tucked the covers high under their chins. "Good night, my darlings," she whispered in the loving voice we knew so well.

The twins didn't hear. Already they were deeply asleep.

However, standing firmly as a rooted tree, the grandmother was obviously displeased as she gazed upon the twins in one bed, then over to where Christopher and I were huddled close together. We were tired, and half-supporting each other. Strong disapproval glinted in her gray-stone eyes. She wore a fixed, piercing scowl that Momma seemed to understand, although I did not. Momma's face flushed as the grandmother said, "Your two older children cannot sleep in one bed!"

"They're only children," Momma flared back with unusual fire. "Mother, you haven't changed one bit, have you? You still have a nasty, suspicious mind! Christopher and Cathy are innocent!"

"Innocent?" she snapped back, her mean look so sharp it

could cut and draw blood. "That is exactly what your father and I always presumed about you and your half-uncle!"

I looked from one to the other, my eyes wide. I glanced at my brother. Years seemed to melt from him, and he stood there vulnerable, helpless, as a child of six or seven, no more comprehending than I.

A tempest of hot anger made our mother's ruddy color depart. "If you think like that, then give them separate rooms, and separate beds! Lord knows this house has enough of them!"

"That is impossible," the grandmother said in her fire ice voice. "This is the only bedroom with its own adjoining bath, and where my husband won't hear them walking overhead, or flushing the toilet. If they are separated, and scattered about all over upstairs, he will hear their voices, or their noise, or the servants will. Now, I have given this arrangement a great deal of thought. This is the only safe room."

Safe room? We were going to sleep, all of us, in only one room? In a grand, rich house with twenty, thirty, forty rooms, we were going to stay in one room? Even so, now that I gave it more thought, I didn't want to be in a room alone in this mammoth house.

"Put the two girls in one bed, and the two boys in the other," the grandmother ordered.

Momma lifted Cory and put him in the remaining double bed, thus, casually establishing the way it was to be from then on. The boys in the bed nearest the bathroom door, and Carrie and I in the bed nearest the windows.

The old woman turned her hard gaze on me, then on Christopher. "Now hear this," she began like a drill sergeant, "it will be up to you two older children to keep the younger ones quiet, and you two will be responsible if they break even one of the rules I lay down. Keep this always in your minds: if your grandfather learns too soon you are up here, then he will throw all of you out without one red penny—*after* he has severely punished you for being alive! And you will keep this room clean, neat, tidy, and the bathroom, too, just as if no one lived here. And you will be quiet; you will not yell, or cry, or run about to pound on the ceilings below. When your mother and I leave this room tonight, I will close and lock the door behind me. For I will not have you roaming from room to room, and into the other sections of this house. Until the day your grandfather dies, you are here, but you don't really exist."

Oh, God! My eyes flashed to Momma. This couldn't be true! She was lying, wasn't she? Saying mean things just to scare us. I drew closer to Christopher, pressing against his side, gone cold and shaky. The grandmother scowled, and quickly I stepped away. I tried to look at Momma, but she had turned her back, and her head was lowered, but her shoulders sagged and quivered as if she were crying.

Panic filled me, and I would have screamed out something if Momma hadn't turned then and sat down on a bed, and stretched out her arms to Christopher and me. We ran to her, grateful for her arms that drew us close, and her hands that stroked our hair and backs, and smoothed down our wind-rumpled hair. "It's all right," she whispered. "Trust me. One night only will you be in here, and my father will welcome you into his home, to use it as you would your own—all of it, every room, and the gardens, too."

Then she glared up at her mother so tall, so stern, so forbidding. "Mother, have some pity and compassion for my children. They are of your flesh and blood too; keep that in *your* mind. They are very good children, but they are also normal children, and they need room to play and run and make noise. Do you expect them to speak in whispers? You don't have to lock the door to this room; you can lock the door at the end of the hall. Now why can't they have all the rooms of this north wing to use as their very own? I know you never cared for this older section very much."

The grandmother shook her head vigorously. "Corrine, I make the decisions here—not you! Do you think I can just close and lock the door to this wing and the servants won't wonder why? Everything must stay just as it was. They understand why I keep this particular room locked, for the stairway to the attic is in here, and I don't like for them to snoop around where they don't belong. Very early in the mornings, I will bring the children food and milk—before the cook and the maids enter the kitchen. This north wing is never entered except on the last Friday of each month, when it is thoroughly cleaned. On those days, the children will hide in the attic until the maids finish. And before the maids enter, I myself will check everything over to see they leave behind no evidence of their occupancy."

Momma voiced more objections. "That is impossible! They are bound to give themselves away, leave a clue. Mother, lock the door at the end of the hall!"

The grandmother gnashed her teeth. "Corrine, give me time; with time I can figure out some reason why the servants cannot enter this wing at all, even to clean. But I have to tread carefully, and not raise their suspicions. They don't like me; they would run to your father with tales, hoping he would reward them. Can't you see? The closure of this wing cannot coincide with your return, Corrine."

Our mother nodded, giving in. She and the grandmother plotted on and on, while Christopher and I grew sleepier and sleepier. It seemed an endless day. I wanted so much to crawl into the bed beside Carrie, and nestle down so I could fall into sweet oblivion, where problems didn't live.

Eventually, just when I thought she never would, Momma took notice of how tired Christopher and I were, and we were allowed to undress in the bathroom, and then to climb into bed—at long last.

Momma came to me, looking tired and concerned, with dark shadows in her eyes, and she pressed her warm lips on my forehead. I saw tears glistening in the corners of her eyes, and her mascara pooled the tears into black streaks. Why was she crying again?

"Go to sleep," she said hoarsely. "Don't worry. Pay no attention to what you just heard. As soon as my father forgives me, and forgets what I did to displease him, he'll open up his arms and welcome his grandchildren—the only grandchildren he's likely to live long enough to see."

"Momma"—I frowned, full of anguish, "why do you keep crying so much?"

With jerky movements she brushed away her tears and tried to smile. "Cathy, I'm afraid it may take more than just one day to win back my father's affection and approval. It may take two days, or more."

"More?"

"Maybe, maybe even a week, but not longer, possibly much less time. I just don't know exactly . . . but it won't be long. You can count on that." Her soft hand smoothed back my hair. "Dear sweet Cathy, your father loved you so very much, and so do I." She drifted over to Christopher, to kiss his forehead and stroke his hair, but what she whispered to him, I couldn't hear.

At the door she turned to say, "Have a good night's rest, and I'll see you tomorrow as soon as I can. You know my plans. I have to walk back to the train depot, and catch another train to Charlottesville where my two suitcases will be waiting, and tomorrow morning, early, I'll taxi back here, and I'll sneak up to visit with you when I can."

The grandmother ruthlessly shoved our mother through the open doorway, but Momma twisted around to peer back at us over her shoulder, her bleak eyes silently pleading with us even before her voice sounded again: "Please be good. Behave yourselves. Don't make any noise. Obey your grandmother and her rules, and never give her any reason to punish you. Please, please do this; and make the twins obey, and keep them from crying and missing me too much. Make this seem a game, lots of fun. Do what you can to entertain them until I'm back with toys and games for you all to play. I'll be back tomorrow, and every second I'm gone, I'll be thinking of you, and praying for you, and loving you."

We promised we'd be as good as gold, and quiet as mice, and like angels we'd obey and keep to whatever rules were laid down. We'd do the best we could for the twins and I'd do anything, say anything, to take the anxiety from her eyes.

"Good night, Momma," said both Christopher and I as she stood falteringly in the hall with the grandmother's large cruel hands on her shoulders. "Don't worry about us. We'll all be fine. We know what to do for the twins, and how to entertain ourselves. We're not little children anymore." All of this came from my brother.

"You'll see me early tomorrow morning," the grandmother said before she pushed Momma into the hall, then closed and locked the door.

Scary to be locked in, children alone. What if a fire started? Fire. Always I was to think of fire and how to escape. If we were going to be here locked in, no one would hear us if we cried out for help. Who *could* hear us in this remote, forbidden room on the second floor, where no one came but once a month, on the last Friday?

Thank God this was just a temporary arrangement—one night. And then, tomorrow Momma would win over the dying grandfather.

And we were alone. Locked in. All the lights were turned off. Around us, below us, this huge house seemed a monster, holding us in its sharp-toothed mouth. If we moved, whispered, breathed heavily, we'd be swallowed and digested.

It was sleep I wanted as I lay there, not the long, long silence that stretched interminably. For the first time in my life I didn't fall into dreams the moment my head touched the pillow. Christopher broke the silence, and we began, in whispers, to discuss our situation.

"It won't be so bad," he said softly, his eyes liquid and gleaming in the dimness. "That grandmother—she can't possibly be as mean as she seems."

"You mean to tell me you didn't think she was a sweet old lady?"

He sort of chuckled. "Yeah, you bet, sweet—sweet as a boa constrictor."

"She's awful big. How tall do you think she is?"

"Gosh, that's hard to guess. Maybe six feet, and two hundred pounds."

"Seven feet! Five hundred pounds!"

"Cathy, one thing you've got to learn—stop exaggerating! Stop making so much out of small things. Now, take a real look at our situation, and realize this is only a room in a big house, nothing at all frightening. We have one night to spend here before Momma comes back."

"Christopher, did you hear what the grandmother said about a half-uncle? Did you understand what she meant?"

"No, but I suppose Momma will explain everything. Now go to sleep, and say a prayer. Isn't that about all we can do?"

I got right out of the bed, fell down on my knees, and folded my hands beneath my chin. I closed my eyes tightly and prayed, prayed for God to help Momma be her most charming, disarming, and winning self. "And God, please don't let the grandfather be as hateful and mean as his wife."

Then, fatigued and drowning in many emotions, I hopped back into bed, hugged Carrie close against my chest, and fell, as I wanted, into dreams.

The Grandmother's House

The day dawned dim behind the heavy, drawn draperies that we had been forbidden to open. Christopher sat up first, yawning, stretching, grinning over at me. "Hi, tousle-head," he greeted. His hair was as tousled as mine, much more so. I don't know why God chose to give him and Cory such curly hair, when he gave Carrie and me only waves. And all boy that he was, he tried with mighty effort to brush out those curls, as I sat and hoped they would jump from his head over to mine.

I sat up and looked around this room that was, perhaps, sixteen-by-sixteen. Large, but with two double beds, a massive highboy, a large dresser, two overstuffed chairs, a dressing table between the two front windows, with its own small chair, plus a mahogany table with four chairs, it seemed a small room. Cluttered. Between the two big beds was another table with a lamp. Altogether there were four lamps in the room. Beneath all the ponderous dark furniture was a faded Oriental red rug with gold fringe. At one time it must have been a beautiful thing, but now it was old and worn. The walls were papered in cream with white flocking. The bedspreads were gold-colored and made of some heavy fabric like quilted satin. There were three paintings on the walls. Golly-lolly, they did steal your breath away! Grotesque demons chased naked people in underground caverns colored mostly red. Unearthly monsters devoured other pitiful souls. Even as their legs still kicked, they dangled from slobbering mouths filled with long, shiny, sharp teeth.

"You are now gazing on hell, as some might see it," my know-it-all brother informed me. "Ten to one, our angel grandmother hung those reproductions herself just to let us know what we're in for if we dare to disobey. Look like Goya's work to me," he said.

My brother did know everything. Next to being a doctor, he wanted to be an artist. He was exceptionally good at drawing, using watercolors, oil paints, and so on. He was good at most everything except picking up after himself, and waiting on himself.

Just as I made a move to get up and go into the bath, Christopher jumped from his bed and beat me to it. Why did Carrie and I have to be so far from the bath? Impatiently I sat on the edge of the bed, swinging my legs, and waited for him to come out.

With many little restless movements, Carrie and Cory fluttered awake simultaneously. They sat up and yawned, as if mirrored reflections, rubbed at their eyes, and looked sleepily around. Then Carrie pronounced in definite tones, "I don't like it here!"

That was not at all surprising. Carrie was born opinionated. Even before she could talk, and she talked at nine months, she knew what she liked and what she hated. There was never a middle road for Carrie—it was down low, or up sky-high. She had the cutest little voice when she was pleased, sounding very much like a sweet little bird chirping happily in the mornings. Trouble was, she chirped all day long, unless she was asleep. Carrie talked to dolls, teacups, Teddy bears and other stuffed animals. Anything that sat and didn't answer back was worthy of her conversation. After a while, I got so I didn't even hear her incessant chatter; I just turned it off and let her rattle on and on.

Cory was entirely different. While Carrie chattered on and on, he'd sit and listen attentively. I recall Mrs. Simpson saying Cory was "a still water that ran deep." I still don't know what she meant by that, except quiet people did exude some illusion of mystery that kept you wondering just what they really were beneath the surface.

"Cathy," twittered my baby-faced small sister, "did you hear me say I don't like it here?"

Hearing this, Cory scrambled from his bed and ran to jump into ours, and there he reached for his twin and held her tight, his eyes wide and scared. In his solemn way, he asked, "How did we get here?"

"Last night, on a train. Don't you remember?"

"No, I don't remember."

"And we walked through the woods in the moonlight. It was very pretty."

"Where is the sun? Is it still night?"

Behind the draperies the sun hid. But if I dared to tell Cory that, then he was for sure going to want to open those draperies and look outside. And once he saw outside, he was going to want to go outside. I didn't know what to say.

Someone in the hall fumbled with the door lock, saving me from giving any answer at all. Our grandmother carried into the room a large tray laden with food, covered with a large white towel. In a very brisk, businesslike way she explained that she couldn't be running up and down the stairs all day carrying heavy trays. Once a day only. If she came too often, the servants might notice.

"I think from now on I'll use a picnic basket," she said as she set the tray down on the little table. She turned to look at me, as if I were in charge of the meals. "You are to make this food last throughout the day. Divide it into three meals. The bacon, eggs, toast and cereal are for breakfast. The sandwiches and the hot soup in the small thermos are for your lunch. The fried chicken, potato salad and string beans are for your dinner. You can eat the fruit for dessert. And if at the end of the day, you are silent and good, I may bring you ice cream and cookies, or cake. No candy, ever. We can't have you getting tooth cavities. There won't be any trips to a dentist until your grandfather dies."

Christopher had come from the bathroom, fully dressed, and he, too, stood and stared at the grandmother who could so easily talk of the death of her husband, showing no distress. It was as if she were speaking of some goldfish in China that would soon die in a fishbowl. "And clean your teeth after every meal," she went on, "and keep your hair brushed neatly, and your bodies clean and fully clothed. I do despise children with dirty faces and hands and runny noses."

Even as she said this, Cory's nose was running. Surrep—titiously, I used a tissue to wipe it for him. Poor Cory, he had hay fever most of the time, and she hated children with runny noses.

"And be modest in the bathroom," she said, looking particularly hard at me and then Christopher who was now lounging insolently against the doorframe of the bath. "Girls and boys are never to use the bathroom together."

I felt a hot blush stain my cheeks! What kind of kids did she think we were?

Next we heard something for the first time, which we were to hear over and over again like a needle stuck in a scratched record: "And remember, children, God sees everything! God will see what evil you do behind my back! And God will be the one to punish when I don't!"

From her dress pocket, she pulled a sheet of paper. "Now, on this paper, I have listed the rules you are to follow while you are in my home." She laid the list down on the table and told us we should read and memorize them. Then she spun around to leave . . . but no, she headed toward the closet that we hadn't yet investigated. "Children, beyond this door, and in the far end of the closet, is a small door concealing the steps to the attic. Up in the attic there is ample space for you to run and play and make a rea—sonable amount of noise. But you are never to go up there until after ten o'clock. Before ten, the maids will be on the second floor doing their morning chores, and they could hear you running about. Therefore, always be conscious you can be heard below if you are too noisy. After ten, the servants are forbidden to use the second floor. One of them has started stealing. Until that thief is caught red-handed, I'm always present when they straighten up the bedrooms. In this house, we make our own rules, and execute the deserved punishment. As I said last night, on the last Friday of each month, you will go into the attic very early, and sit quietly without talking, or scuffling your feet—do you understand me?" She stared at each of us in turn, impounding her words with mean, hard eyes. Christopher and I nodded. The twins only gazed at her in a strange kind of fascination, close to awe. Further explanations informed us that she would check our room and bath to see we left no hint of ourselves on that Friday.

Everything said, she left. Once more she locked us in.

Now we could breathe.

Grimly, with determination, I set out to make a game of this. "Christopher Doll, I appoint you the father."

He laughed, then said with sarcasm, "What else? As the man, and the head of this family, let it be known hitherto that I am to be waited on hand and foot—the same as a king. Wife, as my inferior, and my slave, set the table, dish out the food, make ready for your lord and master."

"Repeat again what you said, *brother.*"

"From now on, I am not your brother, but your lord and master; you are to do my bidding, whatever I say."

"And if I don't do as you say—what will you do next, lord and master?"

"I don't like the tone of your voice. Speak respectfully when you speak to me."

"La-dee-da, and ho-ho-ho! The day I speak respectfully to you, Christopher, will be the day you *earn* my respect—and that will be the day you stand twelve feet high, and the moon is at noon, and a blizzard blows in a unicorn ridden by a gallant knight wearing pure white shining armor, with a green dragon's head perched on the point of his lance!" And so said, and so satisfied with his disgruntled expression, I caught hold of Carrie's small hand and led her haughtily into the bathroom where we could take our time to wash, dress and brush, and ignore poor Cory, who kept calling out that he had to go.

"Please, Cathy. Let me come in! I won't look!"

Eventually a bathroom grows boring, and we came out, and, believe it or not, Christopher had Cory fully dressed! And what was even more shocking—now Cory didn't need to use the bathroom!

"Why?" I asked. "Now don't you dare tell me you got back into bed and did it there!"

Silently, Cory pointed to a large blue vase without flowers.

Christopher lounged against the highboy, his arms folded across his chest, pleased with himself. "That should teach you to ignore a male in need. We men are not like you sit-down females. Any little thing will do in an emergency."

Before I would allow anyone to begin breakfast, I had to empty the blue vase, and rinse it out well. Really, it wouldn't be such a bad idea to keep the vase near Cory's side of the bed, just in case.

Near the windows we sat down to the little table meant for card-playing. The twins sat on doubled-over pillows so they could see what they were eating. All four lamps were turned on. Still it was depressing, having to eat breakfast in what looked like twilight.

"Cheer up, sober face," said my unpredictable older brother. "I was only kidding. You don't have to be my slave. I just love the gems you spurt forth when provoked. I admit, in verbosity you females are blessed, just as we males are gifted with the perfect instrument for picnic bathrooming." And to prove he wasn't going to be an overbearing brute, he helped me pour the milk, finding out, as I had, that hefting a gallon-sized thermos and pouring without spilling was no mean feat.

Carrie gave those fried eggs and bacon just one glance and

she was wailing. *"We-ee* don't like bacon and eggs! *Cold* CEREAL is what we-ee like! We-ee don't want no hot, lumpy, bumpy food that's greasy. *Cold* CEREAL IS WHAT WE LIKE!" she shrieked. *"Cold* CEREAL WITH RAISINS!"

"Now you listen to me," said their new, smaller-edition father, "you will eat what is put before you, and you will make no complaints, and you will not yell, or cry, or scream! Hear that? And it is not hot food, it is cold food. You can scrape off the grease. It is solid, anyway."

In a wink Christopher gobbled down his cold, greasy food, plus his cold toast without butter. Those twins, for some odd reason I'll never understand, ate their breakfast without another word of complaint. I had the uneasy queasy feeling our luck with the twins just couldn't hold out. They might be impressed now by a forceful older brother, but watch out later!

The meal finished, I neatly stacked the dishes back on the tray. And only then did I remember we'd forgotten to say grace. Hastily we gathered together at the table and sat down to bow our heads, and clasp our palms together.

"Lord, forgive us for eating without asking your permission. Please don't let the grandmother know. We vow to do it right next time. Amen." Finished, I handed Christopher the list of do's and don'ts that were carefully typed in capital letters as if we were so stupid we couldn't understand longhand.

And just so the twins, who'd been too sleepy last night to understand our situation, fully realized what they were in for, my brother began at the top of the list of rules not to be broken—or else!

First he pursed his mouth up in a good imitation of the grandmother's hateful lips, and you'd never believe such a finely shaped mouth as his could be made to look so grim, but somehow he managed to mimic her austerity.

"One:"—he read in a cold, flat voice—"you are *always* to be fully dressed." And, boy, did he make *"always"* sound impossible.

"Two: you will never take the Lord's name in vain, and will

always say grace before each meal. And if I am not in the room to see that you do this, you may be sure that He above will be listening, and watching.

"Three: you are *never* to open the draperies, not even to peek out.

"Four: you will *never* speak to me unless I speak to you first.

"Five: you will keep this room neat and orderly, *always* with the beds made.

"Six: you are *never* to be idle. You will devote five hours each day to studying, and use the remainder of your time to develop your abilities in some meaningful way. *If* you have any skills, abilities or talents, you will seek to improve upon them, and if you have no abilities, or talents, or skills, you will read the Bible; and if you cannot read, then you will sit and stare at the Bible, and try to absorb through the purity of your thoughts the meaning of the Lord and his ways.

"Seven: you will clean your teeth after breakfast each day, and before retiring each night.

"Eight: if I ever catch boys and girls using the bathroom at the same time, I will quite relentlessly, and without mercy, peel the skins from your backs."

My heart seemed to flip over. Good-golly day, what kind of grandmother did we have?

"Nine: you will, all four, be modest and discreet at *all* times—in deportment, in speech, and in thought.

"Ten: you *will not* handle or play with the private parts of your bodies; nor will you look at them in the mirrors; nor will you think about them, even when you are cleansing those parts of your bodies."

Unabashed, with a funny little gleam in his eyes, Christopher read on, mimicking the grandmother with some skill.

"Eleven: you *will not* allow wicked, sinful, or lusting thoughts to dwell in your minds. You will keep your thoughts clean, pure, and away from wicked subjects that will corrupt you morally.

"Twelve: you will refrain from looking at members of the opposite sex unless it is absolutely necessary.

"Thirteen: those of you who can read, and I hope at least two of you can, will each, alternately, take turns reading aloud from the Bible at least one page per day, so the two younger children will benefit from the Lord's teachings.

"Fourteen: you will each bathe daily, and clean the ring from the tub, and keep the bathroom as spotless as it was when you found it.

"Fifteen: you will each learn, including the twins, at least one quote from the Bible per day. And if I so request, you will repeat to me such quotes as I demand, as I keep track of what passages you have read.

"Sixteen: you will eat all of the food I bring to you, and not waste one single bit, or throw it away, or hide it away. It is sinful to waste good food when so many in this world are starving.

"Seventeen: you will not stride about in the bedroom wearing only your nightclothes, even if you are only going from bed to bath, or bath to bed. You will, at *all* times wear a robe of some kind over your nightclothes, and over your undergarments if at some time you feel the need to suddenly leave the bathroom without fully dressing yourself, so that another child may enter in an emergency. I demand that everyone who lives under this roof be modest and discreet—in all things, and in all ways.

"Eighteen: you will stand at attention when I enter your room, with your arms straight down at your sides; you will not clench your hands into fists to show silent defiance; nor will you allow your eyes to meet with mine; nor will you seek to show signs of affection toward me, nor hope to gain my friendship, nor my pity, nor my love, nor my compassion. All of that is impossible. Neither your grandfather nor myself can allow ourselves to feel anything for what is not wholesome."

Ohhh! Those were words to really sting! Even Christopher paused, and a flicker of despair fleeted over his face, quickly put away by a grin as his eyes met with mine. He reached out and tickled Carrie to make her giggle, and then he tweaked Cory's nose, so he, too, giggled.

"Christopher," I cried, alarm in my voice. "From the way she puts it, our mother can never hope to win over her father again! Much less will he want his eyes to rest upon us! Why? What have we done? We weren't here the day our mother fell from grace by doing something so terrible her father disinherited her! We weren't even born then! Why do they hate us?"

"Keep your cool," said Chris, his eyes scanning down the long list. "Don't take any of this seriously. She's a nut, a loony-bird. Nobody as smart as our grandfather can have the idiot ideas his wife does—or else how could he make millions of dollars?"

"Maybe he didn't make the money, but inherited it."

"Yes, Momma told us he inherited some, but he has increased that a hundred times over, so he must have a *little* brains in his head. But he somehow picked the Queen Bee nut from the balmy tree for his wife." He grinned and then went on with the rule reading.

"Nineteen: when I come into this room to bring you food and milk, you will not look at me, or speak to me, or think of me with disrespect, or of your grandfather with disrespect, for God is above and is able to read your minds. My husband is a very determined man, and seldom has any one bested him in any way. He has an army of doctors and nurses and technicians to tend to his every need, and machines to function for his organs in case they fail, so don't think something as weakly motivated as his heart can fail a man made of steel."

Wow! A man of steel to make the opposite bookend to his wife. His eyes must be gray, too. Flint, hard, steel-gray eyes— for, as our very own mother and father had proved, likes do attract.

"Twenty:"—read Christopher—"you will not jump, yell, shout, or speak in loud voices so the servants below can hear you. And you will wear sneakers and never hard-soled shoes.

"Twenty-One: you will not waste toilet tissue, or the soap, and you will clean up the mess if you clog up the toilet bowl so it overflows. And if you put it out of order, then it will stay that way until the day you leave, and you will use the chamberpots that you will find in the attic, and your mother can empty them for you.

"Twenty-Two: the boys will wash their own clothes in the bathtub, as will the girls. Your mother will take care of the bed linens and the towels you use. The quilted mattress covers will be changed once a week, and if a child soils the covers, then I will order your mother to bring you rubber sheets to use, and thrash severely the child who cannot be toilet-trained."

I sighed and put my arm about Cory who whimpered and clung to me on hearing this. "Ssssh! Don't be afraid. She'll never know what you do. We'll protect you. We'll find a way to cover up your mistakes, if you make any."

Chris read: "Conclusion, and this is not a do or a don't, just a warning. She's written: 'You may rightly assume that I will add to this list from time to time as I see the need arise, for I am a very observant woman who misses nothing. Do not think you can deceive me, mock me, or play jokes at my expense, for if you do, your punishment will be so severe that your skins, and your egos, will bear lifetime scars, and your pride will go down in permanent defeat. And let it be known from now on, that never in my presence will you mention your father's name, or refer to him in the slightest way, and I, myself, will refrain from looking at the child who resembles him most.' "

It was over. I flashed Christopher a questioning look. Was he inferring, as I was, what that last paragraph implied—that for some reason our father was the cause of our mother being disinherited, and now hated by her parents?

And did he infer, too, that we were going to be locked up here for a long, long time?

Oh, God, oh God, oh God! I couldn't stand even a week!

We weren't devils, but most certainly we weren't angels, either! And we needed each other, to touch, to look at.

"Cathy," said my brother calmly, a wry smile cocking his lips while the twins looked from one to the other of us, ready to mimic our panic, our joy, or our screams, "are we so ugly and without charm that an old woman who very obviously hates our mother, and also our father, for some reason I don't know, can forever resist us? She's a fake, a fraud. She doesn't mean any of this." He gestured toward the list, which he folded and flung away toward the dresser. It made a poor airplane.

"Are we to believe an old woman like that, who must be demented, and should be locked up—or should we believe the woman who loves us, the woman we know and trust? Our mother will take care of us. She knows what she's doing, on that you can depend."

Yes, of course, he was right. Momma was the one to believe in and trust, not that stern old crazy woman with her idiot ideas, and her gunshot eyes, and her crooked, knife-slashed mouth.

In no time at all the grandfather downstairs would succumb to our mother's beauty and charm, and down the stairs we'd trip, dressed in our best, wearing happy smiles. And he'd see us, and know we weren't ugly, or stupid, but normal enough to like a little, if not a lot. And perhaps, who knows, maybe someday he might even find a *little* love to give to his grandchildren.

The Attic

The morning hour of ten came and went.

What remained of our daily ration of food, we stored in the coolest spot we could find in the room, under the highboy. The servants who made the beds, and tidied up in the upstairs rooms of other wings, must surely have departed for lower sections, and they would not see this floor again for another twenty-four hours.

We were, of course, already tired of that room, and very eager to explore the outer confines of our limited domain. Christopher and I each caught hold of a twin's hand, and we headed silently toward the closet that held our two suitcases with all the clothes still inside. We'd wait to unpack. When we had more roomy, pleasant quarters, the servants could unpack for us, as they did in movies, and we could take off outdoors. Indeed, we wouldn't be in this room when the servants came in on the last Friday of the month to clean. We'd be set free by then.

With my older brother in the lead, holding onto the small hand of my younger brother so he wouldn't trip or fall, and with me close at Cory's heels, as Carrie clung to my hand, we headed up the dark, narrow, steep steps. The walls of that passageway were so narrow your shoulders almost brushed them.

And there it was!

Attics we'd seen before, who hasn't? But never such an attic as this one!

We stood as if rooted, and gazed around with incredulity. Huge, dim, dirty, dusty, this attic stretched for miles! The farthest walls were so distant they seemed hazy, out of focus. The air was not clear, but murky; it had an odor, an unpleasant odor of decay, of old rotting things, of dead things left unburied, and because it was cloudy with dust, everything seemed to move, to shimmer, especially in the darker, gloomier corners.

Four sets of deep dormer windows stretched across the front, four sets across the back. The sides, what we could see of them, were without windows—but there were wings where we couldn't see unless we dared to move forward and brave the stifling heat of the place.

Step by step we moved as one away from the stairwell.

The floor was of wide wooden planks, soft and rotting. As we inched along cautiously, feeling fearful, small creatures on the floor went scuttling off in all directions. There was enough furniture stored in the attic to furnish several houses. Dark, massive furniture, and chamber pots, and pitchers set in larger bowls, perhaps twenty or thirty sets of them. And there was a round wooden thing that looked like a tub banded with iron. Imagine keeping a bathtub like that!

Everything that seemed of value was draped over by sheets where dust had accumulated to turn the white cloth dingy gray. And what was covered by sheets for protection shivered my spine, for I saw these things as weird, eerie, furniture ghosts, whispering, whispering. And I didn't want to hear what they had to say.

Dozens of old leather-bound trunks with heavy brass locks and corners lined one entire wall, each trunk stuck all over with travel labels. Why, they must have been around the world several or more times. Big trunks, fit for coffins.

Giant armoires stood in a silent row against the farthest wall, and when we checked, we found each one full of ancient clothes. We saw both Union and Confederate uniforms, giving Christopher and me much to speculate upon as the twins cringed close against us and looked around with big, scared eyes.

"Do you think our ancestors were so undecided during the Civil War they didn't know which side they were on, Christopher?"

"The War Between the States sounds better," he answered.

"Spies, you think?"

"How would I know?"

Secrets, secrets, everywhere! Brother against brother I saw it—oh, what fun to find out! If only we could find diaries!

"Look here," said Christopher, pulling out a man's suit of pale cream-colored wool, with brown velvet lapels, and piped smartly with darker brown satin. He waved the suit. Disgusting winged creatures took off in all directions, despite the stench of mothballs.

I yelped, as did Carrie.

"Don't be such babies," he said, not in the least disturbed by those things. "What you saw were moths, harmless moths. It's the larvae that do the chewing and make the holes."

I didn't care! Bugs were bugs—infants or adults. I don't know why that darned suit interested him so much, anyway. Why did we have to examine the fly to see if men in those days used buttons or zippers? "Gosh," he said, finally disturbed, "what a pain to unfasten buttons every time."

That was his opinion.

In my opinion, olden-day people really knew how to dress! How I would love to flounce around in a frilly chemise over pantaloons, with dozens of fancy petticoats over the wire hoops, all bedecked in ruffles, lace, embroidery, with flowing ribbons of velvet or satin, and my shoes would be of satin and over all this bedazzling finery would be a lacy parasol to shade my golden curls, and keep the sun from my fair, unwrinkled complexion. And I'd carry a fan to elegantly cool myself, and my eyelids would flutter and bewitch. Oh, what a beauty I'd be!

Subdued by the immense attic until now, Carrie let out a howl that took me swiftly from sweet speculations and right back to the here and now, which was where I didn't want to be.

"It's hot up here, Cathy!"

"Yes, it is."

"I hate it up here, Cathy!"

I glanced at Cory, his small face awed as he looked around and clung to my side, and catching his hand, and Carrie's, I left behind the fascination of the old clothes, and all of us wandered off to pry into everything this attic had to offer. And that was considerable. Thousands of old books in stacks, dark ledgers, office desks, two upright pianos, radios, phonographs, cartons filled with the unwanted accoutrements of generations long gone. Dress forms, all sizes and shapes, bird cages and stands to hold them, rakes, shovels, framed photographs of peculiar pale and sickly looking people who were, I presumed, dead relatives of ours. Some had light hair, some dark; all had eyes sharp, cruel, hard, bitter, sad, wistful, yearning, hopeless, empty, but never, I swear, never did I see any happy eyes. Some smiled. Most didn't. I was drawn in particular to a pretty girl of perhaps eighteen; she wore a faint, enigmatic smile which reminded me of Mona Lisa, only she was more beautiful. Her bosom swelled out beneath a ruffled bodice most impressively, making Christopher point to one of the dress forms and declare emphatically, "Hers!"

I looked. "Now," he continued with admiring eyes, "that is what you call an hourglass figure. See the wasp waist, the ballooning hips, the swelling bosom? Inherit a shape like that, Cathy, and you will make a fortune."

"Really," I said in disgust, "you don't know very much. That is not a woman's natural form. She's wearing a corset, cinched in at the waist so much her flesh is squeezed out at the top and the bottom. And that is exactly why women used to faint so much and then call for smelling salts."

"How can one faint and still manage to call for smelling salts?" he asked sarcastically. "Besides, you can't squeeze out at the top what isn't there." He took another look at the shapely young woman. "You know, she kind of looks like Momma. If she wore her hair differently and her clothes were modern— she'd be Momma."

Hah! Our mother would have more sense than to wear a laced-up cage and suffer. "But this girl is only pretty," Christopher concluded. "Our mother is beautiful."

The silence of that huge space was so deep you could hear your heartbeat. Yet it would be fun to explore every trunk; to examine the contents of every box; to try on all those rotting, smelly, fancy clothes, and pretend, pretend, pretend. But it was so hot! So stifling! So stuffy! Already my lungs seemed clogged with dirt and dust and stale air. Not only that, spider webs laced the corners and draped down from the rafters, and crawling or slithering things rambled about on the floor or up the walls. Though I didn't see any, I thought of rats and mice. We'd seen a movie once on TV where a man went crazy and hung himself from an attic rafter. And in another movie, a man shoved his wife in an old trunk with brass corners and locks, just like these, and then he slammed down the lid and left her there to die. I took another look at those trunks, wondering what secrets they held that the servants shouldn't know.

Disconcerting, the curious way my brother was watching me and my reactions. I whirled to hide what I was feeling—but he saw. He stepped closer and caught my hand, and said so much like Daddy, "Cathy, it is going to be all right. There must be very simple explanations for everything that seems to us very complex and mysterious."

Slowly I turned to him, surprised he'd come to comfort and not to tease. "Why do you suppose the grandmother hates us, too? Why should the grandfather hate us? What have *we* done?"

He shrugged, as baffled as I was, and with his hand still holding mine, we both pivoted to look the attic over again. Even our untrained eyes could tell where new sections had been added to the older house. Thick, square, upright beams divided the attic into distinct sections. I thought if we wandered here, and wandered there, we would come upon a place for comfortable, fresh breathing.

The twins began to cough and sneeze. They fixed resentful blue eyes on us for keeping them where they didn't want to be.

"Now look," said Christopher when the twins started to really complain, "we can open up the windows an inch or so, enough to let in a little fresh air, and no one will notice such a little opening from the ground." Then he released my hand and ran on ahead, leaping over boxes, trunks, furniture, showing off, while I stood frozen, holding to the hands of both my little ones, who were terrified of where they were.

"Come see what I've found!" called Christopher, who was out of sight. Excitement was in his voice. "You just wait and see my discovery!"

We ran, eager to see something exciting, wonderful, fun—and all he had to show us was a room, a real room with plaster walls. It had never been painted, but it did have a regular ceiling, not just beams. This seemed to be a schoolroom with five desks, facing a larger desk up front. Blackboards lined three walls over low bookcases filled with faded and dusty old volumes that my perpetual seeker of all knowledge had to immediately inspect by crawling around and reading the book titles aloud. Books were enough to send him off on a high tangent, knowing he had a way to escape to other worlds.

I was drawn to the small desks, where names and dates were etched, such as Jonathan, age 11, 1864! And Adelaide, age 9, 1879! Oh, how very old this house was! They were dust in their graves by now, but they had left their names behind to let us know that once, they, too, had been sent up here. But why would parents send their children into an attic to study? They had been wanted children, surely—unlike us, whom the grandparents despised. Maybe for *them* the windows had been opened wide. And for them, servants had carried up coal or wood to burn in the two stoves we saw in the corners.

An old rocking horse with a missing amber eye wobbled unsteadily, and his matted yellow tail was a woebegone thing. But this white-and-black-spotted pony was enough to bring a delighted cry from Cory. Instantly he clambered up on the peeling red saddle, crying out, "Getty-up, horsy!" And the pony, not ridden for ever so long, galloped along, squealing, rattling, protesting with every rusty joint.

"I want to ride, too!" bellowed Carrie. "Where is *my* horsy?"

Quickly I ran to lift Carrie up behind Cory, so she could cling to his waist, and laugh, and kick her heels to make the dilapidated horse go faster and faster. I marveled that the poor thing stayed hinged together.

Now I had the chance to look over the old books that had charmed Christopher. Heedlessly, I reached in and took out a book, not caring what the title read. I flipped through the pages and sent legions of flat bugs with centipede legs madly scampering everywhere! I dropped that book,—then stared down at the loose pages that had scattered. I hated bugs, spiders most of all, worms next. And what swarmed from those pages seemed a combination of both.

Such a girlish performance was enough to send Christopher into hysterics, and when he calmed down, he called my squeamishness overdone. The twins reined in their bucking bronco and stared at me in astonishment. Quickly I had to reach for my poise. Even pretend mothers didn't squeal at the sight of a few bugs.

"Cathy, you're twelve, and it's time you grew up. Nobody screams to see a few bookworms. Bugs are a part of life. We humans are the masters, the supreme rulers over all. This isn't such a bad room at all. Lots of space, full of big windows, plenty of books, and even a few toys for the twins."

Yeah. There was a rusty red wagon with a broken handle, and

a missing wheel—great. A broken green scooter, too. Terrific. Yet there stood Christopher looking around and expressing his pleasure in finding a room where people hid away their children so they couldn't see them, or hear them, or maybe not even think about them, and he saw it as a room with possibilities.

Sure, somebody could clean all the dark secret places where creeping horrors lived, and they could spray all over with insect repellent so nothing sinister was left that was small enough to step on. But how to step on the grandmother, the grandfather? How to turn an attic room into a paradise where flowers bloomed, and not just another prison like the one below?

I ran to the dormer windows and climbed upon a box to reach the high window ledge. Desperate to see the ground, to see how far we were above it, and if we jumped how many bones we'd break. Desperate to see the trees, the grass, where the flowers grew, where sunlight was, where birds flew, where real life lived. But all I saw was a slate black roof expanding wide beneath the windows, blocking out the view of the ground. Beyond the roofs were treetops; beyond the treetops, enclosing mountains hovered over by blue mists.

Christopher climbed up beside me and looked, too. His shoulder brushing mine quivered, as did his voice when he said softly, "We can still see the sky, the sun, and at night we'll see the moon and stars, and birds and planes will fly over. We can watch them for amusement until the day we don't come up here again."

He paused, seeming to think back to the night we came—was it only last night? "I'll bet if we leave a window open wide, an owl might fly in. I've always wanted an owl for a pet."

"For heaven's sake, why in the world would you want one of those things?"

"Owls can turn their heads all the way around. Can you do that?"

"I don't want to do that."

"But if you wanted to, you still couldn't."

"Well, neither can you!" I flared, wanting to make him face up to reality, like he insisted I do. No bird as wise as an owl would want to live locked up with us for even an hour.

"I want a kitty," spoke up Carrie, holding her arms up so she could be lifted to where she could see, too.

"I want a puppy," said Cory before he glanced out of the window. Then he quickly forgot about pets, for he began to chant, "Outside, outside, Cory wants outside. Cory wants to play in the garden. Cory wants to swing!"

Quickly Carrie followed suit. She too wanted outside, the garden, and the swings. And with her bull-moose voice, she was far more persistent with her wants than Cory.

Now they were both near driving Christopher and me up the wall with their demands to go outside, outside, outside!

"Why can't we go outside?" screamed Carrie, doubling up her fists and beating them against my chest. "We-ee don't like it here! Where is Momma? Where is the sunshine? Where did the flowers go? Why is it so hot?"

"Look," said Christopher, catching her small battering fists and saving me from a bruising, "think of this place as outside. There's no reason you can't swing up here, like in a garden. Cathy, let's search around and see if we can't find some rope."

We did search. And we did find rope in an old trunk that held all sorts of junk. It was very apparent the Foxworths didn't throw anything away—they stored their trash in the attic. Maybe they were afraid of one day being poor, and suddenly needing what was put away so miserly.

With great diligence my older brother worked to make swings for both Cory and Carrie, for when you have twins, you must never, ever give them only one of a kind—of anything. For seats he used boards ripped from a lid of a trunk. He found sandpaper and smoothed away the splinters. While he did this, I hunted around until I found an old ladder with a few missing rungs that didn't hinder Christopher in the least from quickly reaching the rafters high above. I watched him climbing nimbly around up there, crawling out on a wide beam—and every move he made endangered his life! He stood up to show off his balancing skill. He swayed suddenly off balance! Quickly he adjusted himself by putting out his arms, but my heart had jumped up, terrified to see him taking such chances, risking his life, just to show off! There was no adult to call him down. If I tried to order him down, he'd laugh, and do even more foolish things. So I kept my mouth shut and closed my eyes, and I tried to shut out the visions I had of him falling, splattering down, breaking his arms, legs or, even worse, his back or neck! And he didn't have to put on any act. I knew he was brave. He had the knots securely tied, so why couldn't he come down and give my heart a chance to beat normally again?

It had taken Christopher hours to make those swings, and then he risked his life to hang them. And when he was down, and the twins were seated on the swings, fanning back and forth and stirring up the dusty air, they were satisfied for, perhaps, three minutes.

Then it began. Carrie started off. "Take us out of here! Don't like these swings! Don't like in here! This is a baa-ad place!"

No sooner did her wails cease than Cory's began. "Outside, outside, we want outside! Take us outside! Outside!" And Carrie added her chants to his. Patience—I had to have patience, deep self-control, act adult, not scream just because I wanted outside just as much as they did.

"Now stop that racket!" snapped Christopher to the twins. "We're playing a game, and all games have rules. The main rule of this game is to stay inside and be as quiet as possible. Screaming and yelling is forbidden." His tone turned softer as he gazed down at their tear-streaked, grimy faces. "Pretend this is the garden under a bright blue sky, and tree leaves are overhead, and the sun is shining bright. And when we go downstairs, that room will be our home with many rooms."

He gave us all a whimsical, disarming smile. "When we're rich as Rockefellers, we'll never need to see this attic again, or that bedroom below. We'll live like princesses and princes."

"Do you think the Foxworths have as much money as the

Rockefellers?" I asked disbelievingly. Golly-day, wow! We'd be
able to have everything! Yet, yet, I was terribly troubled . . . that
grandmother, something about her, the way she treated us, as if
we didn't have a right to be alive. Such horrible words she'd
said: "You are here, but you don't really exist."

We rambled about the attic, half-heartedly exploring this and
that, until someone's stomach rumbled. I glanced at my wristwatch. Two. My older brother stared at me, as I glanced at the
twins. It must have been one of their stomachs, for they ate so
little, but, nevertheless, their digestive systems were automatically set on seven for breakfast, twelve for lunch, and five for
dinner, and seven for bedtime, and a snack before.

"Lunch time," I announced cheerfully.

Down the stairs we tripped single file, back into that hateful
dim room. If only we could open the draperies wide to let in
some light and cheer. If only . . .

My thoughts could have been spoken aloud, for Christopher was
perceptive enough to say that even if the draperies were opened
wide, this room faced north and the sunlight would never enter.

And my, just look at the chimney sweeps in the mirrors! Just
like those from *Mary Poppins*, a spoken comparison to put
smiles on the dirty faces of the twins. They dearly loved being
compared with those charming people who lived in their kind of
picture books.

Since we'd been taught from our earliest years never to sit
down to eat when we were less than spotlessly clean, and since
God had His keenest eye riveted on us, we would obey all the
rules and please Him. Now, it didn't really offend God's eyes if
we put Cory and Carrie in the same bathtub, when they'd come
from the same womb, did it? Christopher took over Cory, as I
shampooed Carrie, then bathed her, dressed her, and brushed her
silky hair until it shone, and then I curled her hair around my
fingers till it spiraled down in pretty coils. Next I tied on a green
satin ribbon.

And it wouldn't really hurt anyone if Chistopher talked to me while I bathed. We weren't adults—yet. It wasn't the same thing as "using" the bathroom together. Momma and Daddy had seen nothing wrong about bare skin, but as I washed my face, the memory of the grandmother's stern, uncompromising expression flashed before my eyes. *She* would think it was wrong.

"We can't do this again," I said to Christopher. "That grandmother—she might catch us, and then she would think it evil." He nodded as if it didn't really matter. He must have seen something on my face that made him move forward to the tub so he could put his arms about me. How did he know I needed a shoulder to cry on? Which was exactly what I did.

"Cathy," he soothed while my head was tucked down on his shoulder and my sobs came, "keep thinking about the future, and all that will be ours when we're rich. I've always wanted to be filthy rich so I can be a playboy for a while, only a little while, for Daddy said everybody should contribute something useful and meaningful to mankind, and I'd like to do that. But until I'm in college, and med school, I could sneak in a little fooling around until I settle down seriously."

"Oh, I see you mean do everything a poor guy can't afford to do. Well, if that's what you want, go to it. But what I want is a horse. All my life I've wanted a pony, and we've never lived in a place that would allow a pony, and now I'm too big for a pony. So it will have to be a horse. And, of course, all the while I'll be working my way to fame and fortune as the world's leading prima ballerina. And you know how dancers have to eat and eat or else they'd be just skin and bones, so I'm going to eat a whole gallon of ice cream each day, and one day I'm going to eat nothing but cheese—every kind of cheese there is, put on cheese crackers. Then, I want lots and lots of new clothes: a different outfit for each day of the year. I'll give them away after one wearing, then sit down to eat cheese on crackers, and top it off with ice cream. And I'll work off the fat by dancing."

He was stroking my wet back, and when I turned to see his profile, he looked dreamy, wistful.

"You see, Cathy, it's not going to be so bad, this short time while we're shut up here. We won't have time to feel depressed, for we'll be too busy thinking of ways to spend all of our money. Let's ask Momma to bring us a chess game. I've always wanted to learn to play chess. And we can read; reading is almost as good as doing. Momma won't let us get bored; she'll bring us new games and things to do. This week will pass in a flash." He smiled at me brilliantly. "And please stop calling me Christopher! I can't be confused with Daddy anymore, so from now on, I am only Chris, okay?"

"Okay, Chris," I said. "But the grandmother—what do you think she'd do if she caught us in the bathroom together?"

"Give us hell—and God knows what else."

Still, when I was out of the tub, drying off, I started to tell him not to look. However, he wasn't looking. Already we knew each other's bodies well, having been looking at them naked since I could remember. And in my opinion, mine was the best. Neater.

All of us wearing clean clothes, and smelling good, we sat down to eat our ham sandwiches, and lukewarm vegetable soup from the small thermos, and more milk to drink. Lunch without cookies was an abysmal thing.

Furtively, Chris kept glancing at his watch. It might be a long, long time before our mother showed up. The twins prowled around restlessly after lunch was over. They were cranky, and they expressed their displeasure with everything by kicking at it, and from time to time as they prowled the room, they shot both me and Chris scowling looks. Chris headed for the closet, and the attic, to the schoolroom for books to read, and I started to follow.

"No!" screamed Carrie. "Don't go up in the attic! Don't like it up there! Don't like it down here! Don't like nothin'! Don't want you being my momma, Cathy! Where is my real momma? Where'd she go? You tell her to come back and let us go out to the sandbox!" She took off for the door to the hall and turned the

knob, then screamed like an animal in terror when the door
wouldn't open. Wildly she beat her small fists against the hard
oak and all the while she screamed for Momma to come and
take her out of this dark room!

I ran to catch her up in my arms while she kicked and kept
right on yelling. It was like holding a wildcat. Chris seized Cory,
who ran to protect his twin. All we could do was put them down
on one of the big beds, haul out their storybooks, and suggest
naps. Teary and resentful, both twins glared up at us.

"Is it night already?" whimpered Carrie, gone hoarse from so
many fruitless screams for freedom, and a mother who wouldn't
come. "I want my momma so bad. Why don't she come?"

"Peter Rabbit," I said, picking up Cory's favorite storybook
with colorful illustrations on every page, and this alone made
Peter Rabbit a very good book. Bad books had no pictures.
Carrie had a fondness for *The Three Little Pigs,* but Chris would
have to read like Daddy used to, and huff and puff, and make his
voice deep like the wolf's. And I wasn't sure he would.

"Please let Chris go up in the attic and find himself a book to
read, and while he does that, I'll read to you from *Peter Rabbit.*
And let's see if Peter will steal into the farmer's garden tonight
and eat his fill of carrots and cabbages. And if you fall asleep
while I'm still reading, the story will end in your dreams."

Maybe five minutes passed before both the twins were asleep.
Cory clutched his storybook against his small chest to make the
transportation of *Peter Rabbit* into his dreams as easy as possible. A soft, warm feeling swept over me, making my heart ache
for little ones who really needed a grown-up mother, not one
only twelve. I didn't feel much different than I had at ten. If
womanhood was just around the corner, it hadn't reared its head
to make me feel mature and capable. Thank God we weren't
going to be shut up here long, for what would I do if they got
sick? What would happen if there was an accident, a fall, a broken bone? If I banged hard on the locked door, would the despicable grandmother come running in response? There was no

telephone in this room. If I cried out for help, who would hear me from this remote, forbidden wing?

While I stewed and fretted, Chris was up in the attic school-room, collecting an assortment of dusty, buggy books to bring down to the bedroom for us to read. We had brought along a checker board, and that's what I wanted to do—not stick my nose in an old book.

"Here," he said, thrusting an old book into my hands. He said he'd shaken it free of all bugs that might send me off into hysteria again. "Let's save the checkers until later when the twins are awake. You know how you cut up when you lose."

He settled down in a comfortable chair, flinging his leg across the fat, rounded chair arm, and opened up *Tom Sawyer.* I flung myself down on the only empty bed and began to read about King Arthur and the Knights of the Round Table. And, believe it or not, that day a door opened I hadn't known existed before: a beautiful world when knighthood was in flower, and there was romantic love, and fair ladies were put on pedestals and wor-shipped from afar. A love affair with the medieval age began that day for me, one I was never to lose, for, after all, weren't most ballets based on fairy tales? And weren't all fairy tales written from folklore of medieval times?

I was the kind of child who'd always looked for fairies danc-ing on the grass. I wanted to believe in witches, wizards, ogres, giants, and enchanted spells. I didn't want all of the magic taken out of the world by scientific explanation. I didn't know at that time that I had come to live in what was virtually a strong and dark castle, ruled over by a witch and an ogre. I didn't guess that some modern-day wizards could weave money to create a spell. . . .

As daylight drew away behind the heavy drawn draperies, we sat down at our small table to eat our meal of fried chicken (cold) and potato salad (warm) and string beans (cold and greasy). At least Chris and I ate most of our meal, cold and unappetizing or not. But the twins just picked at their food, complaining all the time that it didn't taste good. I felt that if Carrie had said less, then Cory would have eaten more.

"Oranges are not funny looking," said Chris, handing me an orange to peel, "or supposed to be hot. Actually, oranges are liquid sunshine." Boy, he did say the right thing that time. Now the twins had something they could eat with pleasure—liquid sunshine.

Now it was night, and really not much different than the day had been. We turned on all four lamps, and one tiny little rose nightlamp our mother had brought along to comfort the twins who didn't like the dark.

After their naps, we had dressed the twins again in their clean clothes, and brushed their hair, and washed their faces, so they looked sweet and appealing as they settled down on the floor to put large pieces of puzzles together. Those puzzles were old ones and they knew exactly which piece fitted into the other, and it was not so much of a problem, but a race to see who could fit in the most pieces first. Soon the race to put puzzles together bored the twins, so we piled all on one of the beds and Chris and I told stories we made up. That too grew boring for the twins, though my brother and I could have gone on longer, competing to see who had the most imagination. Next we hauled the small cars and trucks from the suitcases so the twins could crawl around and push cars from New York to San Francisco, by route of wriggling under the beds and between the table legs—and soon they were dirty again. When we tired of that, Chris suggested we play checkers, and the twins could transport orange peels in their trucks and dump them down in Florida, which was the trash can in the corner.

"You can have the red pieces," announced Chris patronizingly. "I don't believe as you do, that black is a losing color."

I scowled, sulked away. It seemed an eternity had passed between dawn and dusk, enough to change me so I'd never be the same again. "I don't want to play checkers!" I said nastily.

So I fell on a bed and gave up the struggle to keep my thoughts from roaming up and down endless alleys of dark suspicious fears, and tormenting nagging doubts, wondering always if Momma had told us all of the truth. And while we all four waited, and waited, and waited for Momma to show up, there wasn't a calamity my thoughts didn't touch upon. Mostly fire. Ghosts, monsters, and other specters lived in the attic. But in this locked room fire was the uppermost threat.

And time passed so slowly. Chris in his chair, with his book, kept sneaking glances at his watch. The twins crawled to Florida, dumped their orange peels, and now they didn't know where to go. There were no oceans to cross, for they had no boats. Why hadn't we brought a boat?

I whipped a glance at the paintings depicting hell and all its torments, and marveled at how clever and cruel the grandmother was. Why did she have to think of everything? It just wasn't fair for God to keep an ever watchful eye on four children, when outside in the world so many others were doing worse. In God's place, from His all-seeing perspective, I wouldn't waste my time looking at four fatherless children locked up in a bedroom. I'd be staring at something far more entertaining. Besides, Daddy was up there—he'd make God take good care of us, and overlook a few mistakes.

Disregarding my sulky ways and objections, Chris put down his book and carried over the gaming box, which held equipment enough to play forty different games.

"What's the matter with you?" he asked, as he began to place the red and black rounds on the board. "Why are you sitting so quiet, so scared looking? Afraid I'll win again?"

Games, I wasn't thinking of games. I told him my thoughts of fire, and my idea of ripping up sheets and knotting them together to form a ladder to reach the ground, just like they did in many an old movie. Then if a fire started, maybe tonight, we'd have a way to reach the ground after we broke a window, and each of us could tie a twin to our back.

I'd never seen his blue eyes show so much respect as they lit up with admiration. "Wow, what a fantastic idea, Cathy! Terrific! Exactly what we'll do if a fire starts—which it won't. And boy, it sure is good to know you're not going to be a cry-baby after all. When you think ahead and plan for unexpected contingencies it shows you're growing up, and I like that."

Golly-day, in twelve years of hard striving, I had at last won his respect and approval, and reached a goal I thought impossible. It was sweet knowing we could get along when shut up so close. Our exchanged smiles promised that together we were going to manage to survive until the end of the week. Our new-found camaraderie constructed some security, a bit of happiness to grab hold of, like hands clasping.

Then, what we'd found was shattered. Into our room came our mother, walking so funny, wearing the strangest expression. We'd waited so long for her return, and somehow it didn't give us the anticipated joy to be with her again. Maybe it was only the grandmother, who followed so close at her heels, with her flint hard, mean gray eyes that quickly quelled our enthusiasm.

My hand rose to my mouth. Something dreadful had happened. I knew it! I just knew it!

Chris and I were sitting on a bed, playing a checker game and from time to time looking at each other while we rumpled the bedspread.

One rule broken . . . no, two . . . looking was forbidden as well as rumpling.

And the twins had puzzle pieces here and there, and their cars and marbles were scattered about, so the room wasn't exactly tidy.

Three rules broken.

And boys and girls had been in the bathroom together.

And maybe we'd even broken another rule, for we were always to feel, no matter what we did, that God and the grandmother had some secret communication between them.

The Wrath of God

Momma came into our room this first night, tight-limbed and stiff-jointed, as if every movement she made hurt. Her lovely face was pale and bloated; her swollen eyes red-rimmed. At the age of thirty-three, someone had humiliated her so much she couldn't squarely meet a pair of our eyes. Looking defeated, forlorn, humbled, she stood in the center of the room like a child brutally chastised. Thoughtlessly, the twins ran to greet her. They threw enthusiastic arms about her legs, laughing and crying out in happy voices, "Momma, Momma! Where have you been?"

Chris and I ambled over to tentatively hug her. One might have thought she had been gone a decade of Sundays, and not just one Wednesday, but she represented our hope, our reality, our line to the world outside.

Did we kiss her too much? Did our eager, hungry, clinging embraces make her wince from pain, or from the obligations? While fat and slow tears slid silently down her pale cheeks, I thought she cried only for the pity she felt for us. When we sat, all wanting to be as close to her as possible, it was on one of the big beds. She lifted both twins to her lap so Chris and I could cuddle close on either side. She looked us over, and complimented our glowing cleanliness, and smiled because I had tied a green ribbon in Carrie's hair to match the green stripes on her dress. She spoke, her voice hoarse, as if she had a cold, or that fabled frog had lodged in her throat. "Now, tell me honestly, how did it go for you today?"

Resentfully, Cory's plump face pouted, mutely saying his day had *not* gone well at all. Carrie put her unspoken umbrage into words. "Cathy and Chris are mean!" she screamed, and it was no sweet bird twitter. "They made us stay inside all day! We don't like inside! We don't like that big dirty place they told us was nice! Momma, it's not nice!"

Troubled and pained looking, Momma tried to soothe Carrie, telling the twins that circumstances had changed, and now they had to mind their older brother and sister, and think of them as parents to obey.

"No! No!" shrilled an even more irate bundle of red-faced fury. "We hate it here! We want the garden; it's dark here. We don't want Chris and Cathy, Momma, we want *you!* Take us home! Take us out of here!"

Carrie hit at Momma, at me, at Chris, yelling how much she wanted her home, as Momma sat there not defending herself, apparently unhearing, and not knowing how to handle a situation in which a five-year-old ruled. The more unhearing Momma became, the louder Carrie screamed. I covered my ears.

"Corrine!" commanded the grandmother. "You stop that child from screaming this very second!" I knew, just looking at her stone cold face, that she would know exactly how to shut Carrie up, and at once. However, sitting on Momma's other knee was a little boy whose eyes grew wide as he stared up at the tall grandmother—someone who threatened his twin sister, who had jumped down from Momma's lap and was now standing in front of the grandmother. Planting her small feet wide apart, Carrie threw back her head, opened up her rosebud mouth and she really let go! Like an opera star who'd saved her best for the grand aria finale, her former cries seemed like weak mewings from a small kitten. Now we had a tigress—enraged!

Oh, boy, was I impressed, awed, terrified of what would happen next.

The grandmother seized hold of Carrie by the hair, lifting her up enough to make Cory jump from Momma's lap. Quick as a cat he pounced on the grandmother! Faster than I could wink, he ran to bite her leg! I cringed inside, knowing now we were all in for it. She gazed down at him, then shook him off as one does a small, annoying lap-dog. But the bite did make her release Carrie's hair. Down she dropped to the floor, to quickly scamper to her feet, and take a quick swipe, just missing the grandmother's leg with her foot.

Not to be outdone by his twin sister, Cory raised his small white shoe, took careful aim, then kicked the grandmother's leg as hard as he could manage.

In the meanwhile, Carrie had scuttled over to the corner where she crouched down and wailed like an Irish banshee set on fire!

Oh, indeed, it was a scene worthy of remembering, and recording.

So far Cory hadn't said a word, or uttered one cry, as was his silent and resolute way. But no one was going to hurt or threaten his twin sister—even if that "no one" stood close to six feet, and weighed in at close to 200 pounds! And Cory was very small for his age.

If Cory didn't like what was happening to Carrie, or the potential threat to himself, the grandmother didn't like what was happening to her either! She glared down at his small, defiant, angry face, which was tilted up to hers. She waited for him to cower, to take the scowl from his face, and the defiance from his blue eyes, but he stood determinedly before her, daring, challenging her to do her worst. Her thin and colorless lips tightened into a fine, crooked pencil line.

Up came her hand—a huge, heavy hand, flashing with diamond rings. Cory didn't flinch, his only reaction to this very
obvious threat was a deeper, more fierce scowl as his small
hands knotted into fists raised in professional boxer technique.

Good-golly day! Did he think he could fight her—and win?

I heard Momma call Cory's name, her voice so choked it was
only a whisper.

Decided on her course of action now, the grandmother delivered against his round, defiant baby face a stinging slap so hard
it sent him reeling! He stumbled backward, then fell to the floor,
but was up in a flash, spinning around to consider a fresh assault
against that huge mountain of hateful flesh. His indecision then
was a pitiful thing. He faltered, reconsidered, and common
sense won out over anger. He scampered over to where Carrie
crouched, half-crawling, half-running, and then flinging his
arms about her, they knelt, holding one to the other, cheek
pressed to cheek, and he added his siren howls to hers!

Beside me, Chris mumbled something that sounded like a
prayer.

"Corrine, they are your children—shut them up! This
instant!"

However, the buttercup twins, once started, were practically
impossible to quiet. Reasoning never reached their ears. They
heard only their own terror, and like mechanical toys, they had
to run down from pure exhaustion.

When Daddy was alive and knew how to handle situations like
this, he would pick them up as sacks of corn, one under each
arm, and off he'd carry them to their room and order them sternly
to shut up, or else they'd stay alone until they could, without TV,
toys, without anything. Without an audience to witness their defiance, or hear their impressive wails, their screams seldom lasted
more than a few minutes after the door closed on them. Then
they would sulk out, quiet, meek and they would snuggle down
on Daddy's lap and say in small voices, "We're sorry."

But Daddy was dead. There wasn't a distant bedroom where

they could wind down. This one room was our mansion, and in here the twins held their captive audience painfully enthralled. They screamed until their faces went from pink to red, from red to magenta, and then on to purple. Their blue eyes went glassy and unfocused from their combined efforts. Oh, it was a grand show all right—and a foolhardy one!

Apparently, until now our grandmother had been held mesmerized by such a display. Then, whatever had held her motionless released its spell. She came alive. Purposefully, she strode over to the corner where the twins huddled. Down she reached to seize up ruthlessly, by their scruffs, two yelling children. Holding them stiff-armed away from her, as they kicked, hollered, and flailed their arms, trying ineffectively to inflict some injury on their tormentor, the twins were hauled up before our mother. Then down on the floor they were dropped like so much unwanted trash. In a loud, firm voice that punctuated through their yelling, she stated flatly, "I will whip you both until the blood runs from your skin if you don't stop that yelling this very instant!"

That inhuman quality, plus the cold force of this appalling threat, convinced the twins, as it did me, that she meant exactly what she said. In astonished and horrified belief, the twins stared up at her—and with open mouths they choked off their cries. They knew what blood was, and pain came with it. It hurt to see them handled so brutally, as if she didn't care if frail bones broke, or tender flesh was bruised. She towered above them, above all of us. Then, she pivoted about and fired at our mother: "Corrine, I will not have a scene so disgusting as this happen again! Obviously your children have been spoiled and indulged, and are in desperate need of lessons in discipline and obedience. No child who lives in this house will disobey, or scream, or show defiance. Hear that! They will speak when spoken to. They will jump to obey my voice. Now take off your blouse, daughter, and show those who disobey just how punishment is dealt out in this house!"

During this our mother had risen. She seemed to shrink smaller into her high-heeled shoes as she turned waxen white. "No!" she breathed, "that is not necessary now. See, the twins have stopped crying . . . they are obeying now."

The old woman's face grew very grim. "Corrine, are you heedless enough to disobey? When I tell you to do something, you will do it without question! And immediately! Look at what you have raised. Weak, spoiled, unruly children, all four! They think they can scream and get what they want. Screams will not avail them here. They might as well know there is no mercy for those who disobey and break my rules. You should know that, Corrine. Did I ever show you mercy? Even before you betrayed us, did I ever let your pretty face and beguiling ways stay my ready hand? Oh, I remember when your father loved you well, and he would turn against me in defense of you. But those days are over. You proved to him you are just what I always said you were—a deceitful, lying bit of trash!"

She turned those hard, flintstone eyes on Chris and me. "Yes, you and your half-uncle did make exceedingly beautiful children, I readily admit that, though they should never have been born. But they also appear soft, useless nothings!" Her mean eyes raked over our mother scornfully, as if we had caught all these demeaning faults from her. But she had not yet finished.

"Corrine, definitely your children need an object lesson. When they observe what has happened to their mother, then they will have no doubt as to what can happen to them."

I saw my mother straighten and stiffen her spine, facing up bravely to the large, raw-boned woman who topped her by at least four inches, and was many, many pounds heavier.

"If you are cruel to my children," began Momma in a voice that quavered, "I will take them out of this house tonight, and you will never see them, or me, again!" This she stated defiantly, lifting her beautiful face and staring with some determined fierceness at that hulking woman who was *her* mother!

A small smile, tight and cold, met Momma's challenge. No, it was not a smile, it was a sneer. "Take them away tonight—now! Take yourself away, Corrine! If I never see your children again, or hear from you again, do you think I care?"

Our mother's Dresden blues clashed with those steely tones while we children watched. Inside I was screaming with joy. Momma was going to take us out of here. We were leaving! *Good-bye, room! Good-bye, attic! Good-bye, all those millions I don't want anyway!*

But, as I watched, as I waited for Momma to spin on her heel and head for the closet, for our suitcases, I saw instead something that was noble and fine in our mother crumble. Her eyes lowered in defeat and slowly her head bowed to hide her expression.

Shaken and trembling myself, I watched the grandmother's sneer become a large, cruel smile of victory. Momma! Momma! Momma! My soul was screaming. Don't let her do this to you!

"Now, Corrine, *take off that blouse.*"

Slowly, reluctantly, her face as white as death, Momma pivoted around, presenting her back just as a violent shudder shivered down her spine. Stiffly her arms lifted. With great difficulty each button of her white blouse was unfastened. Carefully, she eased down the blouse to expose her back.

Under the blouse she didn't wear a slip, or a bra, and it was easy enough to see why. I heard Chris pull in his breath. And Carrie and Cory must have looked, for their whimpers reached my ears. Now I knew why Momma, usually so graceful, had walked stiffly into our room, with eyes red from weeping.

Her back was striped with long, angry red welts from her neck on down to the waistband of her blue skirt. Some of the puffier welts were crusted over with dried blood. There was barely an inch of uncut, unmarred skin between the hideous whip marks.

Unfeeling, uncaring, disregarding our sensitivities, or those of our mother, new instructions issued from our grandmother: "Take a good long look, children. Know that those whip marks go *all* the way down to your mother's feet. Thirty-three lashes, one for each year of her life. And fifteen extra lashes for each year she lived in sin with your father. Your grandfather ordered this punishment, but I was the one who applied the whip. Your mother's crimes are against God, and the moral principles society lives by. Hers was an unholy marriage, a sacrilege! A marriage that was an abomination in the eyes of the Lord. And, as if that wasn't enough, they had to have children—four of them! Children spawned from the Devil! Evil from the moment of conception!"

My eyes bulged at the sight of those pitiful welts on the creamy tender flesh that our father had handled with so much love and gentleness. I floundered in a maelstrom of uncertainty, aching inside, not knowing who or what I was, if I had the right to be living on an earth the Lord reserved for those born with his blessings and permission. We had lost our father, our home, our friends and our possessions. That night I no longer believed that God was the perfect judge. So, in a way, I lost God too.

I wanted a whip in my hands to strike back at that old woman who had ruthlessly ripped so much from us. I stared at the ladder of bloody welts on Momma's back, and never had I felt such hate before, or such anger. I hated not only for what she had done to our mother, but for the ugly words that gushed forth from that mean mouth.

She looked at me then, that detestable old woman, as if sensing all that I felt. I glared back defiantly, hoping that she *could* see how I denied her blood relationship from that moment on— not only her, but that old man downstairs as well. Never again would I pity him.

Perhaps my eyes were only glass to reveal all the spinning wheels of revenge I harbored, and vowed to let loose one day. Maybe she did see something vengeful on those white worms of brains, for she directed her next words solely at me, though she used the noun "children."

"So you see, children, this house can be hard and relentless in dealing with those who disobey and break our rules. We will dole out food, drink, and shelter, but never kindness, sympathy or love. It's impossible to feel anything but revulsion for what is not wholesome. Keep to my rules, and you won't feel the bite of my whip, nor will you be deprived of necessities. Dare to disobey me, and you will soon learn all I can do to you, and all I can keep from you." She stared in turn at each of us.

Yes, she wanted to make us undone that night, when we were young, innocent, trusting, having known only the sweetest part of living. She wanted to wither our souls and shrivel us small and dry, perhaps never to feel pride again.

But she didn't know us.

Nobody was ever going to make me hate my father or my mother! Nobody was going to have the power of life and death over me—not while I was alive and could still fight back!

I shot Chris a quick glance. He was staring at her, too. His eyes swept up and down her height, considering what damage he could inflict if he attacked. But he was only fourteen. He would have to grow into a man before he could overcome the likes of her. Still, his hands clenched into fists, which he forced to keep tight at his sides. The restraint pressed his lips into a line as thin and hard as the lips of the grandmother. Only his eyes were cold, hard as blue ice.

Of us all, he loved our mother best. He had her high on a pedestal of perfection, considering her the dearest, sweetest, most understanding woman alive. He'd already told me when he grew up, he'd marry a woman who was like our mother. Yet he could only glare fiercely. He was too young to do anything.

Our grandmother bestowed on us one last, long, contemptuous look. Then she shoved the door key into Momma's hand and left the room.

One question loomed sky-high, above all others.

Why? *Why* had we been brought to *this* house?

This was no safe harbor, no refuge, no sanctuary. Certainly Momma must have known how it would be, and yet, she'd led us here in the dead of night. Why?

Momma's Story

After the grandmother's departure, we did not know what to do, or what to say, or how to feel, except unhappy and miserable. My heart was fluttering madly as I watched Momma slip up her blouse, button it, and tuck it into the waistband of her skirt before she turned to give us all a tremulous smile that sought to reassure. Pitiful that I could find a straw to grasp in such a smile as that one. Chris lowered his eyes to the floor; his restless torment was expressed by his shoe diligently following the intricate scrollwork of the Oriental rug.

"Now look," said Momma with forced cheerfulness, "it was just a willow switching, and it didn't hurt too much. My pride suffered more than my flesh. It's humiliating to be whipped like a slave, or an animal, and by your own parents. But don't worry that such a whipping will occur again, for it never will. Only this one time. I would suffer a hundred times over what whip weals I bear to live again those fifteen years of happiness I had with your father, and with you. Though it cringes my soul, she made me show what they did. . . ." She sat on a bed and held out her arms so we could cluster close about and be comforted, though I was careful not to embrace her again and cause more pain. She lifted the twins to her lap and patted the bed to indicate we should crowd up against her. Then she began to talk. What she said was obviously hard to say, and equally difficult for us to hear.

"I want you to listen very carefully, and remember all your lives every word I say tonight." She paused, hesitating as she scanned the room and stared at the cream-flocked walls as if they were transparent, and through them she could see into all the rooms of this gigantic house. "This is a strange house, and the people who reside here are even stranger—not the servants, but my parents. I should have warned you that your grandparents are fanatically religious. To believe in God is a good thing, a right thing. But when you reinforce your belief with words you take from the Old Testament that you seek out, and interpret in the ways that suit your needs best, that is hypocrisy, and that is exactly what my parents do.

"My father is dying, yes, but every Sunday he is carried into church either in his wheelchair, if he is feeling that well, or lying on a stretcher if he is feeling worse, and he gives his tithe—a tenth share of his yearly income, which is considerable. So naturally, he is very welcomed. He paid to have the church built, he bought all the stained-glass windows, he controls the minister and his sermons, for he is paving his way to heaven with gold, and if St. Peter can be bribed, my father will surely gain entrance. In that church he is treated like a god himself, or a living saint. And then he comes home, feeling completely justified in doing anything he wants, because he has done his duty, and paid his way, and therefore he is safe from hell.

"When I was growing up, with my two older brothers, we were literally forced to go to church. Even if we were sick enough to stay in bed, we still had to go. Religion was rammed down our throats. Be good, be good, be good—that's all we ever heard. Everyday, normal pleasures that were right for other people were made sinful for us. My brothers and I were not allowed to go swimming, for that meant wearing bathing suits and exposing most of our bodies. We were forbidden card games, or any sort of game that implied gambling. We weren't allowed to go to dances, for that meant your body might be pressed close to that of the other sex. We were ordered to control our thoughts, to keep them off lusting, sinful subjects for they said the thought was as evil as the deed. Oh, I could go on and on about all we were forbidden to do—it seemed everything that was fun and exciting was sinful to them. And there is something in the young that rebels when life is made too strict, making us want to do most of all the very things denied to us. Our parents, in seeking to make their three children into living angels or saints, only succeeded in making us worse than we would have been otherwise."

My eyes widened. I sat spellbound, all of us did, even the twins.

"Then one day," Momma went on, "into all this, a beautiful young man came to live. His father had been my grandfather, a man who died when this young man was only three. His mother was named Alicia, and she was only sixteen when she married my grandfather who was fifty-five years old. So, when she gave birth to a boy, she should have lived to see him a man. Unfortunately, Alicia died very young. My grandfather's name was Garland Christopher Foxworth, and when he died, half of his estate should have gone to his youngest son, who was three. But Malcolm, my father, gained control of his father's estate by having himself appointed administrator, for, of course, a three-year-old boy had no voice in the matter, nor was Alicia given a vote. Once my father had everything under his thumb, he kicked out Alicia and her young son. They fled back to Richmond, to Alicia's parents, and there she lived until she married a second time. She had a few years of happiness with a young man she'd loved since her childhood, and then he, too, died. Twice married, twice widowed, left with a young son, and now her parents were dead as well. And then one day she found a lump in her breast, and a few years later she died of cancer. That was when her son, Garland Christopher Foxworth the Fourth, came to live here. We never called him anything but Chris." She hesitated, tightened her arms about Chris and me. "Do you know who I'm talking about? Have you guessed who this young man was?"

I shivered. The mysterious half-uncle. And I whispered, "Daddy . . . you're talking about Daddy."

"Yes," she said, then sighed heavily.

I leaned forward to glance at my older brother. He sat so still, with the queerest expression on his face, and his eyes were glassy.

Momma continued: "Your father was my half-uncle, but he was only three years older than I. I remember the first time I saw him. I knew he was coming, this young half-uncle I'd never seen or heard much about, and I wanted to make a good impression, so all day I prepared myself, curling my hair, bathing and I put on what I thought were my prettiest and most becoming clothes. I was fourteen years old—and that is an age when a girl just begins to feel her power over men. And I knew I was what most boys and men considered beautiful, and I guess, in a way, I was ripe for falling in love.

"Your father was seventeen. It was late spring, and he was standing in the middle of the hall with two suitcases near his shabby shoes—his clothes were very worn looking, and he'd outgrown them. My mother and father were with him, but he was turning around, staring at everything, dazzled by the display of wealth. I myself had never paid much attention to what was around me. It was there, I accepted it as part of my heritage, and until I was married, and began to live a life without wealth, I hardly realized that I'd been raised in an exceptional home.

"You see, my father is a 'collector.' He buys everything that is considered a unique work of art—not because he appreciates art, but he likes to own things. He would like to own *everything,* if possible, especially beautiful things. I used to think I was part of his collection of *objets d'art* . . . and he meant to keep me for himself, not to enjoy, but to keep others from enjoying what was his."

My mother continued, her face flushed, her eyes staring off into space, apparently looking backward to that exceptional day

when a young half-uncle came into her life to make such a difference.

"Your father came to us so innocent, so trusting, so sweet, and
vulnerable, having known only honest affection, and genuine
love, and a great deal of poverty. He came from a four-room cottage into this huge, grand house that widened his eyes and dazzled his hopes, and he thought that he had stumbled onto good
luck, into heaven on earth. He was looking at my mother and
father with all of that gratefulness plain in his eyes. Hah! The
pity of him coming here and being grateful still hurts. For half of
what he was looking at, by all rights, should have been his. My
parents did all they could to make him feel like a poor relation.

"I saw him there, standing in the sunlight, beaming down
through the windows, and paused halfway down the staircase.
His golden hair was haloed by an aura of silver light. He was so
beautiful, not just handsome, but beautiful—there's a difference, you know. Real beauty radiates from the inside out, and
he had that.

"I made some slight noise that made him lift his head, and his
blue eyes lit up—and oh, I can remember how they lit up—and
then when we were introduced, the light went out. I was his half-
niece, and forbidden, and he was disappointed, just as I was. For
on that very day, with me on the staircase and him down there on
the floor, a spark was lit between us, a little red glow that was to
grow larger and larger until we could deny it no longer.

"I won't embarrass you with the telling of our romance," she
said uneasily when I shifted, and Chris moved to hide his face.
"Let it suffice to say that it was love at first sight with us, for it
happens that way sometimes. Perhaps he was ready to fall in
love, as was I, or perhaps it was because we were both needing
someone to give us warmth and affection. My older brothers
were both dead by this time, killed by accidents; I had only a
few friends, for no one was 'good enough' for the daughter of
Malcolm Foxworth. I was his prize, his joy; if ever a man took
me from him, it would be for a dear, dear price. So, your father

and I would meet furtively in the gardens and just sit and talk for hours and hours, and sometimes he'd push me in a swing, or I'd push him, and sometimes we'd stand on the swing and work it with our legs, and just look at each other as we flew higher and higher. He told me all his secrets and I told him all of mine. And soon enough it had to come out, we had to confess that we were deeply in love, and right or wrong, we had to marry. And we had to escape this house, and the rule of my parents, before they had a chance to make us into duplicates of themselves—for that was their purpose, you know, to take your father and change him, make him pay for the evil his mother had done in marrying a man so much older. They gave him everything, I will admit that. They treated him as their own son, for he was to replace the two sons they had lost. They sent him to Yale, and he was brilliant. You get your intelligence from him, Christopher. He graduated in three years—but he could never use the master's degree he earned, for it had his rightful name on it, and we had to hide who we were from the world. It was hard for us in the first years of our marriage because he had to deny his college education."

She paused. She glanced reflectively at Chris, then at me. She hugged the twins and kissed the top of their fair heads, and a troubled frown came to worry her face and pucker her brow. "Cathy, Christopher, you are the ones I am expecting to understand. The twins are too young. You are trying to understand how it was with us?"

Yes, yes, both Chris and I nodded.

She was talking my language, the language of music and ballet, romance, and love, beautiful faces in lovely places. Fairy tales can come true!

Love at first sight. Oh, that was going to happen to me, I just knew it would and he'd be as beautiful as Daddy had been, radiating beauty, touching my heart. You had to have love or you withered away and died.

"Listen attentively, now," she said in a low voice, and this gave her words greater impact. "I am here to do what I can to make my father like me again, and forgive me for marrying his half-brother. You see, as soon as I reached my eighteenth birthday, your father and I eloped, and two weeks later we came back and told my parents. My father nearly threw a fit. He raged, he stormed, he ordered us both out of his house, and told us never to come back, never! And that is why I was disinherited, and your father too—for I think my father did plan to leave him a little, not much, but some. The main portion was to be mine, for my mother has money in her own right. Why, to hear tell it, the money she inherited from her parents is the main reason why my father married her, though in her youth she was what is called a *handsome* woman, not a great beauty, but she had a regal, powerful kind of noble good looks."

No, I thought bitterly to myself . . . that old woman was born ugly!

"I am here to do what I can to make my father like me again, and forgive me for marrying my half-uncle. And in order to do this, I am going to have to play the role of the dutiful, humbled, thoroughly chastised daughter. And sometimes, when you begin to play a role you assume that character, so I want to say now, while I am still fully myself, all you have to hear. That's why I'm telling you all of this, and being as honest as I can. I confess, I am not strong-willed, nor am I a self-starter. I was strong only when I had your father to back me up, and now I don't have him. And downstairs, on the first floor, in a small room beyond a giant library, is a man the likes of whom you have never encountered. You have met my mother, and know a little of what she is like, but you have not met my father. And I don't want you to meet him until he forgives me and accepts the fact that I have four children fathered by his much younger half-brother. This is going to be very difficult for him to take. But I don't think it is going to be *too* difficult for him to forgive me, since your father *is* dead, and it is difficult to hold grudges against the dead and buried."

I don't know why I felt so scared.

"In order to have my father write me into his will again, I am going to be forced to do anything he wants."

"What could he want from you but obedience and a show of respect?" asked Chris in the most somber, adult way, as if he understood what this was all about.

Momma gave him the longest look, full of sweet compassion as her hand lifted to caress his boyish cheek. He was a younger smaller edition of the husband she'd so recently buried. No wonder tears came into her eyes.

"I don't know what he'll want, darling, but whatever I have to do, I will do. Somehow he must include me in his will. But let's forget all of that now. I saw your faces when I was talking. I don't want you to feel what my mother said is true. What your father and I did was *not* immoral. We were properly married in church, just as any other young couple in love. There was nothing 'unholy' about it. And you are not the Devil's spawn, or evil—your father would call that hogwash. My mother would have you think yourselves unworthy as another way to punish me, and you. People make the rules of society, not God. In some parts of the world closer relatives marry and produce children, and it is considered perfectly all right, though I'm not going to try and justify what we did, for we do have to abide by the laws of our own society. That society believes closely related men and women should not marry, for if they do, they can produce children who are mentally or physically less than perfect. But who is perfect?"

Then she was laughing, half-crying, and hugging us all close. "Your grandfather predicted our children would be born with horns, humped backs, forked tails, hooves for feet—he was like a crazy man, trying to curse us, and make our children deformed, because he wanted us cursed! Did any of his dire predictions come true?" she cried, seemingly half-wild herself. "No!" She answered her own question. "Your father and I did worry some when I was pregnant the first time. He paced the hospital corridors all night, until nearly dawn, when a nurse came up and told him he had a son, perfect in every way. Then he had to run to the nursery to see for himself. You should have been there to see the joy on his face when he entered my room, bearing in his arms two dozen red roses, and tears were in his eyes when he kissed me. He was so proud of you, Christopher, so proud. He gave away six boxes of cigars, and went right out and bought you a plastic baseball bat, and a catcher's mitt, and a football, too. When you were teething, you'd chew on the bat, and beat on the crib and the wall to let us know you wanted out.

"Next came Cathy, and you, darling, were just as beautiful, and just as perfect as your brother. And you know how your father loved you, his beautiful dancing Cathy, who would make the world sit up and take notice when she came on stage. Recall your first ballet performance, when you were four? You wore your first pink tutu, and made a few mistakes, and everybody in the audience laughed, and you clapped your hands like you were proud, even so. And your father sent you a dozen roses—remember? He never saw any mistakes you made. In his eyes you were perfect. And seven years after you came to bless us, our twins were born. Now we had two boys, and two girls, and had tempted fate four times—and had won! Four perfect children. So if God had wanted to punish us, he had four chances to give us deformed or mentally retarded children. Instead, he gave us the very best. So never let your grandmother or anyone else convince you that you are less than competent, less than worthy, or less than wholly pleasing in God's eyes. If there was a sin committed, it was the sin of your parents, not yours. You are the same four children all our friends in Gladstone envied and called the Dresden dolls. Keep remembering what you had in Gladstone—hold on to that. Keep believing in yourselves, and in me, and in your father. Even if he is dead, keep on loving and respecting him. He deserves that. He tried so hard to be a good parent. I don't think there are many men who care as much as he did." She smiled brightly through glistening tears. "Now, tell me who you are."

"The Dresden dolls!" Chris and I cried out.

"Now, will you ever believe what your grandmother says about being the Devil's spawn?"

No! *Never, never!*

Yet, yet, half of what I'd heard from both women I would have to ponder over later, and ponder deeply too. I wanted to believe God was pleased with us, and in who and what we were. I had to believe, needed to believe. Nod, I told myself, say yes, just as Chris did. Don't be like the twins who only stared at Momma, not comprehending anything. Don't be so suspicious—don't!

Chris chimed up in the firmest of convincing voices, "Yes, Momma, I do believe what you say, for if God had disapproved of your marriage to our father, then he *would* have punished you and Daddy through your children. I believe God is not narrow-minded and bigoted—not as our grandparents are. How can that old woman speak so ugly, when she does have eyes, and she can see we are not ugly, and not deformed, and certainly we are not retarded?"

Relief, like a river dammed and released, caused tears to stream down Momma's beautiful face. She drew Chris close against her breast, kissing the top of his head. Then she cupped his face between her palms, stared deep into his eyes, ignoring the rest of us. "Thank you, my son, for understanding," she said in a husky whisper. "Thank you again for not condemning your parents for what they did."

"I love you, Momma. No matter what you did, or do, I'll always understand."

"Yes," she murmured, "you will, I know *You* will." Uneasily she glanced at me who stood back, taking all of this in, weighing it, and her. "Love doesn't always come when you want it to. Sometimes it just happens, despite your will." She bowed her head, reaching for my brother's hands, and clinging to them. "My father adored me when I was young. He wanted to keep me always for himself. He never wanted me to marry anyone. I recall when I was only twelve, he said he'd leave me his entire estate if I stayed with him until he died of old age."

Suddenly, she jerked up her head and looked at me. Did she see something doubting, something questioning? Her eyes shadowed, grew deep, dark. "Join hands," she ordered forcefully, bracing her shoulders, releasing one of Chris's hands. "I want you to repeat after me: We are perfect children. Mentally, physically, emotionally, we are wholesome, and godly in every way possible. We have as much right to live, love, and enjoy life as any other children on this earth."

She smiled at me, and reached for my hand to hold in her free one, and asked that Carrie and Cory join the family chain. "Up here, you are going to need small rituals to get you through the days, little stepping stones. Let me lay down a few for you to use when I'm gone. Cathy, when I look at you, I see myself at your age. Love me, Cathy, trust me, please."

Haltingly, we did as she directed, and repeated the litany that was ours to say whenever we felt in doubt. And when we had finished, she smiled at us with approval and reassurance.

"There!" she said with a happier look. "Now don't think I have lived through this day without the four of you constantly on my mind. I have thought and I have thought of our future, and I've decided we cannot continue to live here, where all of us are ruled over by my mother and father. My mother is a cruel, heartless woman who just happened to give birth to me, but who's never given me an ounce of love—she gave all of that to her sons. It was my foolish belief, when her letter came, that she would treat you differently from the way she treated me. I thought by now she would have mellowed with age, and once she saw you, and knew you, she would be like all grandmothers and welcome you with open arms, and be charmed and delighted to have children to love again. I so hoped once she got a look at your faces . . ." She choked up, near tears again, as if no one with good sense could help but love her children. "I can understand her dislike for Christopher"—and here she hugged him tightly, and kissed his cheek—"for he looks so much like his father. And I know she can look at you, Cathy, and see me, and she never liked me—I don't know why, except, perhaps, my father liked me too much, and that made her jealous. But never did it cross my mind that she could be cruel to any of you, or my little twins. I made myself believe people change with age, and they realize their mistakes, but now I know how wrong I was." She wiped away her tears.

"So, that is why tomorrow morning, early, I am driving away from here, and in the nearest big city, I will enroll in a business school that will teach me how to be a secretary. I'll learn to type, take shorthand, do bookkeeping and how to file—and everything a good secretary has to know, I'll learn. When I know how to do all of these things, I'll be able to find a good job that will pay an adequate salary. And then I'll have enough money to take you all out of this room. We'll find an apartment somewhere nearby, so I can still visit my father. Soon, we'll all be living under the same roof, our roof, and we'll be a real family again."

"Oh, Momma!" Chris cried happily, "I knew you would find a way! I knew you wouldn't keep us locked up in this room." He leaned forward to give me a look of smug satisfaction, as if he'd known all along *his* beloved mother would solve all problems, no matter how complicated.

"Trust me," said Momma, smiling and confident now. Again she had kisses for Chris.

I wished somehow I could be like my brother Chris, and take everything she said as a sacred vow. But my treacherous thoughts were dwelling overlong on her words of not being strong-willed or a self-starter, without Daddy nearby to give her support. Dejectedly, I put in my question. "Just how long does it take to learn how to be a good secretary?"

Quickly—I thought too quickly—she answered. "Only a little while, Cathy. Perhaps a month. But if it takes a bit longer, you have to be patient and realize I'm not too smart about things like that. It's not really my fault," she went on hastily, as if she could see I was blaming her for being inadequate.

"When you're born rich, and you're educated in boarding schools only for the daughters of the extremely rich and powerful, and then you're sent to a girls' finishing school, you are taught polite rules of social etiquette, academic subjects, but most of all, you're made ready for the whirl of romance, debutante parties, and how to entertain and be the perfect hostess. I wasn't taught anything practical. I didn't think I'd ever need any business skills. I thought I'd always have a husband to take care of me, and if not a husband, then my father would—and besides, all the time I was in love with your father. I knew the day I turned eighteen we'd be married."

She was at that very minute teaching me well. Never would I become so dependent on a man I couldn't make my way in the world, no matter what cruel blow life delivered! But most of all I felt mean, mad, ashamed, guilty—feeling she was to blame for everything, and how could she have know what lay ahead?

"I'm going now," she said as she stood to leave. The twins burst into tears.

"Momma, don't go! Don't leave us!" They both wrapped their small arms around her legs.

"I'll be back early tomorrow morning, before I leave for that school. Really, Cathy," she said, looking straight at me, "I promise to do the best I can. I want you out of this place just as much as you want to be out."

At the door she said it was a good thing we'd seen her back, for now we knew how heartless her mother could be. "For God's sake, keep to her rules. Be modest in the bathroom. Realize she can be inhuman not only to me, but to those who are mine." She held out her arms to all of us, and we ran into them, forgetting her whip-lashed back. "I love all of you so much," she sobbed. "Hold on to that. I'll apply myself as never before, I swear. I feel as much a prisoner as you do, just as trapped by circumstances as you are, in a way. Go to bed tonight with happy thoughts, know that no matter how bad it may seem, seldom is anything *that* bad. I am likable, you know that, and my father did love me extremely well once. So that will make it easy for him to love me again, won't it?"

Yes, yes, it would. To love anything once extremely well made you vulnerable to another loving attack. I knew; I'd already been in love six times.

"And while you're in your beds, and in the dimness of this room, remember that tomorrow after I enroll in that school, I'll go shopping for new toys and games to keep your hours up here busy and happy. And it's not going to be a long time until I have my father loving me again, and forgiving me for everything."

"Momma," I said, "do you have enough money to buy us things?"

"Yes, yes," she said hurriedly, "I have enough, and my mother and father are proud people. They would not have me seen by their friends and neighbors looking shabby, or ill-groomed. They will provide for me and they'll provide for you, as well. You'll see. And every spare minute I have, and every spare dollar I don't use, I'll put away, and I'll plan for the day when we can all be free to live in our own home, as we used to, and be a family again."

Those were her parting words before she blew us kisses, and then she closed and locked the door.

Our second night behind a locked door.

Now we knew so much more . . . maybe too much.

After Momma had left, both Chris and I settled into bed. He grinned over at me as he curled his body against Cory's back, and already his eyes were sleepy, too. He closed his eyes and murmured, "Good night, Cathy. Don't let the bedbugs bite."

As Christopher had done, I curled around Carrie's small warm body, and she was cupped spoon-like in my arms, and my face lowered into her sweet, soft hair.

I was restless, and soon enough I was supine, staring upward, and sensing the great silence of this huge house as it settled down, and went to sleep. I heard not a whisper of movement in the huge house; not the faint shrills of a telephone ringing; not a kitchen appliance could be heard switching on and off; not even a dog barked outside; nor did a car pass to throw light that might, hopefully, penetrate through the heavy draperies.

Snide thoughts came and told me we were unwanted, locked up . . . Devil's spawn. Those thoughts wanted to lounge around in my head and make me miserable. I had to find a way to drive them out. Momma, she loved us, she wanted us, she'd try hard to be a good secretary to some lucky man. She would. I knew she would. She would resist the ways the grandparents sought to turn her away from us. She would, she would.

God, I prayed, please help Momma learn quickly!

It was horribly hot and stuffy in that room. Outside, I could hear the wind rustling the leaves, but not enough of it came in to cool us off, only enough to hint that it was cool out there, and would be in here if only we could open the windows wide. Wistfully, I sighed, longing for fresh air. Hadn't Momma told us mountain nights, even in the summertime, were always cool? And this was summertime and it wasn't cool with the windows down.

In the rosy darkness, Chris whispered my name. "What are you thinking?"

"About the wind. It sounds like a wolf."

"I knew you'd be thinking something cheery like that. Gosh, if you aren't the one to take the cake for depressing thoughts."

"I've got another goodie—whispering winds like dead souls trying to tell us something."

He groaned. "Now you listen to me, Catherine Doll (the stage name I planned to use one day), I order you *not* to lie there and think your kind of scary thoughts. We will take each hour as it comes, and never pause to think ahead to the next one, and by using this method, it will be much easier than thinking in terms of days and weeks. Think about music, about dancing, singing. Haven't I heard you say you never feel sad when music is dancing in your head?"

"What will you think about?"

"If I were less sleepy, I would pour out ten volumes of thoughts, but as it is, I'm too tired to answer. And you know my goal, anyway. As for now, I'll just think of the games we'll have time to play." He yawned, stretched, and smiled over at me. "What did you think of all that talk about half-uncles marrying half-nieces, and creating children with hooves, tails, and horns?"

"As a seeker of all knowledge, and a future doctor, is it medically, scientifically possible?"

"Nope!" he answered, as if well-educated on the subject. "If so, the world would abound in freaks resembling devils and to tell you the truth, I would like to see a devil, just once."

"I see them all the time, in my dreams."

"Hah!" he scoffed. "You and your crazy dreams. Weren't the twins something, though? I was really rather proud of them when they faced up to that giant grandmother so defiantly. Gosh, they got spunk. But then I was afraid she'd really do something awful."

"What she did wasn't awful? She picked Carrie up by her hair. That must have hurt. And she slapped Cory and sent him reeling, and that must have hurt. What more did you want?"

"She could have done worse."

"I think she's crazy herself."

"You may be right," he mumbled sleepily.

"The twins are only babies. Cory was only protecting Carrie—you know how he is about her, and she is about him." I hesitated. "Chris, did our mother and father do right by falling in love? Couldn't they have done something to stop it?"

"I don't know. Let's not talk about that; it makes me feel uneasy."

"Me, too. But I guess that explains why we all have blue eyes and blond hair."

"Yeah," he yawned, "the Dresden dolls; that's us."

"You're right. I've always wanted to play games all day long. And just think, when our mother does bring us that new deluxe Monopoly game, we will at last have time to finish a game." For we had never finished a game. "And Chris, the silver ballerina slippers are to be mine."

"Right," he murmured, "and I'll take the top hat, or the racing car."

"The top hat, please."

"Right. Sorry, I forgot. And we can teach the twins to be bankers and count out the money."

"First we'll have to teach them to count."

"That will be no trick at all, for Foxworths know all about money."

"We are *not Foxworths!*"

"Then what are we?"

"Dollangangers! That's who!"

"Okay, have it your way." And again he said good night.

Once more I knelt by the side of the bed and put my hands in prayer position under my chin. Silently I began: *Now I lay me down to sleep, I pray the Lord my soul to keep* . . . But somehow I just couldn't say those words about taking my soul if I should die before I wake. Again I had to skip that part, and again I asked blessings for Momma, for Chris, and the twins, and for Daddy, too, wherever he was in heaven.

Then, when I was back in bed again, I had to go and think of the cake or cookies, and the ice cream the grandmother had half-promised last night—if we were good.

And we had been good.

At least until Carrie started cutting up—and still the grandmother hadn't come into the room with desserts.

How could she have known that later on we would be so undeserving?

"What are you thinking now?" asked Chris in a sleepy monotone. I thought he was already asleep, and certainly not watching me.

"Nuthin' much. Just little thoughts of the ice cream, and cake or cookies the grandmother said she'd bring if we were good."

"Tomorrow's another day, so don't give up on treats. And maybe tomorrow the twins will forget about outdoors. They don't have very long memories."

No, they didn't. Already they'd forgotten Daddy, and he'd been killed only last April. How easily Cory and Carrie let go of a father who had loved them very much. And I couldn't let him go; I was never going to let him go, even if I couldn't see him so clearly now . . . I could feel him.

Minutes Like Hours

All the days dragged by. Monotonously.

What did you do with time when you had it in super-abundance? Where did you put your eyes when you had already seen everything? What direction should your thoughts take, when daydreams could lead you into so much trouble? I could imagine how it would be to run outside, wild and free in the woods, with dry leaves crackling under my feet. I could picture swimming in the nearby lake, or wading in a cool mountain stream. But daydreams were merely cobwebs, easily torn into shreds, and I'd quickly be dropped back into reality. And where was happiness? In the yesterdays? In the tomorrows? Not in this hour, this minute, this second. We had one thing, and one thing only, to give us a spark of joy. Hope.

Chris said it was a deadly crime to waste time. Time was valuable. No one ever had time enough, or lived long enough to learn enough. All about us the world was on the way to the fire, crying, "Hurry, hurry, hurry!" And look at us: we had time to spare, hours to fill, a million books to read, time to let our imaginations take wing. The creative genius begins in the idle moment, dreaming up the impossible, and later making it come true.

Momma came to see us, as she promised, bearing new games and toys to occupy our time. Chris and I adored Monopoly, Scrabble, Chinese checkers, plain checkers, and when Momma brought us a double deck of bridge cards, and a book on how to play card games, boy, did we become the card sharks!

It was harder with the twins, who weren't old enough to play games with rules. Nothing held their interest for long, not the many tiny cars Momma bought, nor the dump trucks, nor the electric tram that Chris hooked together so the tracks ran under our beds, under the dressing table, over to the dresser, and under the highboy. No matter where we turned something was underfoot. One thing for sure, they did hate the attic— everything about it seemed scary to them.

Every day we got up early. We didn't have an alarm clock, only our wristwatches. But some automatic timing-system in my body took over and wouldn't let me sleep late, even when I wanted to.

As soon as we were out of bed, on alternate days, the boys would use the bathroom first, and then Carrie and I would go in. We had to be fully dressed before the grandmother entered—or else.

Into our grim, dim room the grandmother would stalk, while we stood at attention, waiting for her to put down the picnic basket and depart. Seldom did she speak to us, and when she did, it was only to ask if we had said grace before every meal, said prayers before retiring and had read a page from the Bible yesterday.

"No," said Chris one morning, "we don't read a page—we read chapters. If you consider reading the Bible a form of punishment, then forget it. We find it fascinating reading. It's bloodier and lustier than any movie we ever saw, and talks more about sin than any book we ever read."

"Shut up, boy!" she barked at him. "I was asking your sister, *not you!*"

Next she was asking me to repeat some quote I'd learned, and in this way we often had our little jokes, at her expense, for when you looked hard and long enough, you found words in the Bible to suit any occasion. I answered on this particular morning, "Wherefore have you rewarded evil for good? Genesis 44:4."

She scowled and pivoted about and left us. It was another few days before she snapped at Chris, without looking his way, and keeping her back turned, "Repeat to me a quote from the Book of Job. And do not try to fool me into believing you read the Bible when you do not!"

Chris seemed well prepared and confidant "Job, 28:12.—But where shall wisdom be found? And where is the place of understanding? Job 28:28,—Behold, the fear of the Lord, that is wisdom; and to depart from evil is understanding. Job, 31:35—My desire is that the Almighty would answer me, and that mine adversity had written a book. Job, 32:9—Great men are not always wise." And he would have gone on and on endlessly, but anger colored the grandmother's face. Never again did she ask Chris to quote from the Bible. She eventually stopped asking me also, for I, too, could always come up with some stinging quote.

Around six o'clock each evening Momma would show up, breathless, always in a great hurry. She came loaded down with gifts, new things for us to do, new books to read, more games to play. Then she'd dash off to bathe and dress in her suite of rooms for a formal dinner downstairs, where a butler and a maid waited on the table, and it seemed, from what she breathlessly explained, that often guests dined with them. "A great deal of business is done over lunch and dinner tables," we were informed.

The best times were when she sneaked up fancy little canapés, and tasty hors d'oeuvres, but she never brought us candy to rot our teeth.

Only on Saturdays and Sundays could she spend more than a few moments with us, and sit down at our small table to eat lunch. Once she patted her stomach. "Look how fat I'm becoming, eating lunch with my father, then saying I want to nap, so I can come up and eat again with my children."

Meals with Momma were wonderful, because it reminded me of the old days when we were living with Daddy.

One Sunday Momma came in, smelling fresh from outside, bringing a quart of vanilla ice cream and a chocolate cake from a bakery. The ice cream had melted almost to soup, but still we ate it. We begged her to stay all night, to sleep between Carrie and me, so we could wake up in the morning and we could see her there. But she took a long look around the cluttered bedroom, and shook her head. "I'm sorry, I can't, I really can't. You see, the maids would wonder why my bed wasn't used. And three in a bed would be too crowded."

"Momma," I asked, "how much longer? We've been here two weeks—it seems like two years. Hasn't the grandfather forgiven you yet for marrying Daddy? Have you told him about us yet?"

"My father has given me one of his cars to drive," she said with what I considered evasiveness. "And I believe he is going to forgive me, or else he wouldn't be letting me use his car, or sleep under his roof, or eat his food. But no, I haven't had the nerve to tell him yet that I have four children hidden away. I have to time this very carefully, and you have to have patience."

"What would he do if he knew about us?" I asked, ignoring Chris, who kept frowning at me. Already he'd told me if I kept asking so many questions, Momma would stop coming to see us everyday. Then what would we do?

"God knows what he'd do," she whispered fearfully. "Cathy, promise me you will not try to make the servants hear! He is a cruel, heartless man, and one who wields a great deal of power. Let me time carefully the moment I believe he's *ready* to hear."

She went away about seven, and soon after we retired. We went to bed early, because we got up early. And the longer you could stay asleep, the shorter were the days. We would drag our twins into the attic as soon as the hour of ten passed. Exploring the giant attic was one of the best ways to occupy our time. There were two pianos up there, uprights. Cory climbed on a round seat that twirled higher or lower, and round and round he spun. He banged on the yellow piano keys, cocked his head and listened attentively. It was out of tune, and the noise he made was so discordant it made your head ache. "Don't sound right," he said. "Why don't it sound right?"

"It needs tuning," said Chris, who tried to tune it, but when he did, the wires broke. That was the end of trying to make music on two old pianos. There were five Victrolas, each with a small, white dog that cocked its head charmingly, as if enchanted to hear the music—but only one of these machines worked well. We'd wind up this one, put on a warped old record, and listen to the weirdest music we'd ever heard!

There were stacks and stacks of Enrico Caruso records, but, unfortunately, they were not well cared for, just stacked on the floor, not even put in cardboard cartons. We sat in a semicircle to listen to him sing. Christopher and I knew he was the greatest of all male singers, and now was our chance to hear him. His voice was so high-pitched it sounded false, and we wondered what had been so great about him. But for some crazy reason, Cory loved it.

Then, slowly, slowly, the machine would wind down, and would spin Caruso's voice into only a whine, and that's when one of us would race like mad to crank the handle so tight he'd sing fast and funny so he sounded like Donald Duck talking jibberty-junk—and the twins would break up in laughter. Naturally. It was their kind of talk, their secret language.

Cory would spend all of his days in the attic, playing the records. But Carrie was a restless prowler, ever discontented, an incessant seeker of something better to do.

"I don't like this *big bad place!*" she wailed for the zillionth time. "Take me out of this *baa-aad place! Take me out now! This minute! You take me out or I'm gonna kick down the walls! I will! I can! I can, too!*"

She ran to the walls to attack with small feet and flailing little fists that she managed to bruise severely before she gave up.

I felt sorry for her, and for Cory. All of us would have liked to kick down the walls and escape. With Carrie, though, it was more likely the walls would tumble down just from the crescendo trumpet of her powerful voice, like the walls of Jericho tumbling down.

Indeed, it was a relief when Carrie braved the dangers of the attic and found her own way to the stairway, and to the bedroom below, where she could play with her dolls, and her tea-cups, and her tiny stove, and her little ironing board with the iron that didn't heat up.

For the first time, Cory and Carrie could spend a few hours separated from each other, and Chris said that was a good thing. Up in the attic was the music which charmed Cory, while Carrie would chatter on to her "things."

Taking many baths was another way to use up excess time, and shampooing hair made it last longer—oh, we were the cleanest children alive. We napped after lunch, which lasted as long as we could stretch it. Chris and I made a contest of peeling apples so the skin came off in one long, long spiraling cord. We peeled oranges and took off every bit of white string that the twins detested. We had little boxes of cheese crackers that we counted out to divide equally into four portions.

Our most dangerous and amusing game was to mimic the grandmother—ever fearful she'd walk in and catch us draped with some filthy gray sheet from the attic, to represent her gray taffeta uniforms. Chris and I were the best at this. The twins were too afraid of her to even lift their eyes when she was in the room.

"Children!" snapped Chris while he stood by the door, holding an invisible picnic basket. "Have you been decent, honorable, proper? This room looks a terrible mess! Girl—you over there—smooth out that rumpled pillow before I crush your head in with the mere glare of my eyes!"

"Mercy, Grandmother!" I cried, falling down on my knees

and crawling to her with my hands folded under my chin. "I was dead tired from scrubbing down all the walls in the attic. I had to rest."

"Rest!" snapped the grandmother at the door, her dress about to fall off. "There is no *rest* for the evil, the corrupt, the unholy and the unworthy—there is only work until you are dead, and hung forever over hell's eternal roasting fires!" Then he lifted his arms beneath the sheet in some horrible gestures that made the twins shriek from fright, and in a witch's way, the grandmother disappeared, and only Chris was left, grinning at us.

The first weeks were like seconds turned into hours despite all we did to entertain ourselves, and we managed to do quite a lot. It was the doubts and the fears, the hopes and expectations that kept us so in suspense, waiting, waiting—and we were no closer to being let out and taken downstairs.

Now the twins ran to me with their small cuts and bruises, and the splinters garnered from the rotten wood in the attic. I carefully plucked them out with tweezers, Chris would apply the antiseptic, and the adhesive plaster they both loved. An injured small finger was enough reason to demand cuddly-baby things, and lullabies sung as I tucked them into bed, and kissed their faces, and tickled where laughter had to be freed. Their thin little arms wrapped tightly about my neck. I was loved, very loved . . . and needed.

Our twins were more like three-year-olds than children of five. Not in the way they talked, but in the way they rubbed their eyes with small fists, and pouted when they were denied anything, and the way they had of holding their breath until they turned magenta and forced you to give them what they wanted. I was much more susceptible to this kind of ploy than Chris, who reasoned it was impossible for anyone to suffocate themselves in such a way. Still, to see them purple was a terrifying sight.

"Next time they behave like that," he told me in private, "I want you to ignore them, even if you have to go into the bathroom and lock the door. And, believe me, they won't die."

That was exactly what they forced me to do—and they didn't die. That was the last time they pulled that stunt as a way to keep from eating food they didn't like—and they didn't like anything, or hardly anything.

Carrie had the swayback posture of all little girls, protruding in front in a strong arc, and she adored skipping around the room, holding out her skirts so her ruffled panties showed. (Lace ruffled panties were the only kind she would wear.) And if they had little roses made of ribbons, or embroidered somewhere in front, you had to see them at least a dozen times a day, and comment on how charming she looked in her panties.

Of course, Cory wore briefs like Chris, and he was very proud of this. Somewhere, lurking in his memory, were the diapers not too long ago discarded. If he had a temperamental bladder. Carrie was the one who got diarrhea if she ate one teensy bit of any fruit but citrus. I actually hated the days when peaches and grapes were brought up to us—for dear Carrie adored green grapes without seeds, and peaches, and apples . . . and all three had the same effect. Believe me, when fruit came in the door, I blanched, knowing who would have to wash the ruffled, lacy panties unless I moved fast as lightening, running with Carrie under my arm, and plopping her down in the nick of time. Chris's laughter would ring out when I didn't make it—or Carrie *did* make it. He kept that blue vase handy, for when Cory had to go, he had to let loose immediately, and woe if a girl was in the bathroom with the door locked. More than once he had wet his short pants, and then he'd bury his face in my lap, so ashamed. (Carrie was never ashamed—my fault for being slow.)

"Cathy, when do we get to go outside?" he whispered after one accident.

"As soon as Momma says we can."

"Why doesn't Momma say we can?"

"There is an old man downstairs who doesn't know we're up here. And we have to wait until he likes Momma again, enough to accept us too."

"Who is the old man?"

"Our grandfather."

"Is he like the grandmother?"

"Yeah, I'm afraid he is."

"Why don't he like us?"

"He doesn't like us because . . . because, well, because he hasn't got good sense. I think he's sick in the head, as well as in the heart."

"Does Momma still like us?"

Now, that was a question to keep me awake at night.

More than weeks had passed when a Sunday came where Momma didn't show up during the day. It hurt not having her with us, when we knew she had the day off from school, and we knew she was somewhere in this very house.

I lay flat on my stomach on the floor where it was cooler, reading *Jude the Obscure*. Chris was up in the attic searching for new reading material, and the twins were crawling around pushing tiny cars and trucks.

The day dragged on into evening before finally the door opened and Momma came gliding into our room, wearing tennis shoes, white shorts and a white top with a sailor collar trimmed in red and blue braid, and an anchor design. Her face was rosy tan from being outdoors. She looked so vibrantly healthy, so unbelievably happy, while we wilted and felt half-sick from the oppressive heat of this room.

Sailing clothes—oh I knew them—that's what she'd been doing. I stared at her resentfully, longing for my skin to be tanned by the sun, with my legs as healthily colored as hers. Her hair was windblown, and it flattered her well, making her seem almost ten times more beautiful, earthy, sexy. And she was almost old, almost forty.

Very obviously, this afternoon had given her more pleasure than any day since our father died. And it was almost five o'clock. Dinner was served at seven downstairs. That meant she would have very little time to spend with us before she had to leave for her own rooms, where she could bathe, then change into something more suitable for the meal.

I laid aside my book and turned over to sit up. I was hurting, and I wanted to hurt her, too: "Where have you been?" I demanded in an ugly tone. What right did she have to be enjoying herself when we were locked away, and kept from doing the youthful things that were our right? I would never have a summer when I was twelve again, nor would Chris enjoy this fourteenth summer, or the twins their fifth.

The ugly, accusing tone of my voice paled her radiance. She blanched and her lips quivered, and perhaps she regretted bringing us a big wall calendar so we could know when it was Saturday or Sunday. The calendar was filled with our big red X's to mark off our imprisoned days, our hot, lonely, suspenseful, hurting days.

She fell into a chair and crossed her lovely legs, picking up a magazine to fan herself. "I'm sorry to have kept you waiting," she said, with a loving smile in my direction. "I wanted to stop by and visit this morning, but my father demanded all of my attention, and I'd made plans for this afternoon, though I did cut them short so I could spend some time with my children before dinner." Though she didn't look sweaty, she raised a sleeveless arm and fanned her armpit as though this room was more than she could bear. "I've been sailing, Cathy," she said. "My brothers taught me how to sail when I was nine, and then when your father came here to live, I taught him how. We used to spend a lot of time on the lake. Sailing is almost like flying . . . wonderful fun," she ended lamely, realizing her fun had stolen *our* fun.

"Sailing?" I just about screamed. "Why weren't you downstairs telling the grandfather about us? How long do you intend to keep us locked up here? Forever?"

Her blue eyes skipped nervously about the room; she appeared on the verge of getting up from the chair we seldom used, for we saved it especially for her—her throne. Maybe she would have gone then and there if Chris hadn't come down from the attic with his arms loaded down with encyclopedias so old they didn't include television or jet planes.

"Cathy, don't shout at our mother," he scolded. "Hi, Mom. Boy, do you look great! I love that sailing outfit you've got on." He put down his load of books on the dressing table he used for a desk, then strolled over to put his arms around her. I felt betrayed, not only by Momma, but by my brother. The summer was almost over, and we hadn't done anything, been on a picnic or had a swim, or walked in the woods, even seen a boat or put on a bathing suit to wade in a backyard pool.

"Momma!" I cried out, jumping to my feet, and ready to do battle for our freedom. "I think it's time you told your father about us! I'm sick of living in this one room, and playing in the attic! I want our twins out in the fresh air and sunshine, and I want out, too! *I* want to go sailing! If the grandfather has forgiven you for marrying Daddy, then why can't he accept us? Are we so ugly, so terrible, so stupid he'd be ashamed to claim us as his blood kin?"

She shoved Chris away from her, then sank weakly down into the chair she'd just abandoned, leaned forward, and bowed her face down into her hands. Intuitively, I guessed she was going to reveal some truth she'd previously held back. I called to Cory and Carrie and told them to sit close at my sides so I could put my arm about each. And Chris, though I thought he would stay close by Momma's side, came over to sit on the bed next to Cory. We were again, as we'd been before, small fledgling birds sitting on a clothesline waiting for a strong gust of wind to blow us asunder.

"Cathy, Christopher," she began, her head still bowed, though her hands were in her lap nervously working, "I haven't been completely honest with you."

As if I hadn't guessed that already.

"Will you be staying for dinner with us tonight?" I asked, for some reason wanting to put off the full truth.

"Thank you for asking me. I'd like to stay, but I've made other plans for this evening."

And this was our day, our time to be with her until dark. And yesterday she'd spent only half an hour with us.

"The letter," she murmured, and her head lifted and shadows darkened the blue of her eyes into green, "the letter my mother wrote when we were still in Gladstone. That letter invited us to live here. I didn't tell you that my father wrote a short note on the bottom."

"Yes, Momma, go on," I urged. "Whatever you have to tell us, we can take it."

Our mother was a poised woman, cool and self-possessed. But there was one thing she could never control, and that was her hands. Always they betrayed her emotions. One willful, capricious hand rose to flutter near her throat, fingering there, seeking some string of pearls to twist and untwist, and since she wore no jewelry, her fingers just endlessly sought. The fingers on the hand she kept in her lap restlessly rasped together, as if to cleanse themselves.

"Your grandmother, she wrote the letter, signed it, but at the end, my father added his note." She hesitated, closing her eyes, waited a second or two, and then opened them to glance at us again. "Your grandfather wrote he was glad your father was dead. He wrote the evil and corrupt always get what they deserve. He wrote the only good thing about my marriage was it hadn't created any Devil's issue."

Once I would have asked: What was that? Now I knew. Devil's issue was the same as Devil's spawn—something evil, rotten, born to be bad.

I sat on the bed with my arms about the twins, and I looked at Chris, who must be much like Daddy had been at his age, and a vision flashed of my father in his white tennis clothes, standing tall, proud, golden-haired, and bronze-skinned. Evil was dark, crooked, crouched and small—it didn't stand straight and smile at you with clear sky-blue eyes that never lied.

"My mother made the plans for your concealment on a page of the letter my father didn't read," she concluded lamely, her face flushed.

"Was our father considered evil and corrupt only because he married his half-niece?" asked Chris, in the same controlled, cool voice our mother had used. "Is that the only thing he ever did wrong?"

"Yes!" she cried, happy that he, her beloved, understood. "Your father in all his life committed one single, unforgivable sin—and that was to fall in love with me. The law forbids marriage between an uncle and niece, even those who are only half-related. Please don't condemn us. I explained how it was with us. Of us all, your father was the best . . ." She faltered, on the verge of tears, and pleaded with her eyes, and I knew, I knew what was coming next.

"What is evil, and what is corrupt, is in the eyes of the beholder," she rushed on, eager to make us see it her way. "Your grandfather could find these faults in an angel. He is the kind of man who expects perfection from everyone in his family, and he is far from perfect. But just try and tell him that, and he would smack you down." She swallowed nervously then, appearing near sick with what she had to say. "Christopher, I thought once we were here, and I could tell him about you, how you were the most brilliant boy in your class, and always have been a straight-A student, and I thought when he saw Cathy, and knew of her great talent for dancing—I thought surely those two things alone would win him over without him even seeing the twins, how beautiful they are and how sweet—and who knows what talent they have waiting to be developed? I thought, foolishly, hopefully, that he would easily yield and say he'd made a mistake in believing our marriage was so wrong."

"Momma," I said weakly, almost crying myself, "you make it sound as if you're never going to tell him. He's never going to like us, no matter how pretty the twins are, or how smart Chris is, or how good I can dance. None of it's gonna make any difference to him. He'll still hate us, and think of us as Devil's issue, won't he?"

She got up and came to us, and she fell down on her knees again and tried to wrap us all in her embrace. "Haven't I told you before he hasn't got long to live? He gasps for breath every time he exerts himself in the least way? And if he doesn't die soon, I'll find a way to tell him about you. I swear I will. Just have patience. Be understanding. What fun you lose now, I'll make up for later on, a thousandfold!"

Her teary eyes were beseeching. "Please, please, for me, because you love me, and I love you, keep on having patience. It won't be long, it can't be long, and I'll do what I can to make your lives as enjoyable as possible. And think of the riches we'll have one day soon!"

"It's all right, Momma," said Chris, drawing her into his embrace just as our father would. "What you ask isn't too much, not when we have so much to gain."

"Yes," Momma said eagerly, "just a short while more to sacrifice, and a little more patience, and all that is sweet and good in life will be yours."

What was there left for me to say? How could I protest? Already we'd sacrificed over three weeks—what was a few more days, or weeks, or even another month?

At the end of the rainbow waited the pot of gold. But rainbows were made of faint and fragile gossamer—and gold weighed a ton—and since the world began, gold was the reason to do most anything.

To Make a Garden Grow

Now we knew the full truth.

We would be in this room until the day our grandfather died. And it came to me in the night, when I was low and dreary, that perhaps she had known from the very beginning that her father was not the kind to forgive anyone anything.

"But," said my cheerful optimist Christopher, "any day could see him gone. That is the way of heart disease. A clot could break free and find its way to his heart or lung and snuff him out like a candle."

Chris and I said cruel and irreverent things between ourselves, but in our hearts we ached, knowing it was wrong, and we were disrespectful as a way to salve the pain of our bleeding self-esteem.

"Now look," he said, "since we are going to be up here a while longer, we should set about with more determination to placate the twins, and ourselves, with more entertaining things to do. And when we really apply ourselves, gosh knows, we might just dream up some pretty wild and fantastic things."

When you have an attic full of junk, and great armoires full of rotting, stinking, but nevertheless very fancy costumes, you are inspired to put on plays, naturally. And since one day I was going to be on stage, I would be the producer, the director, the choreographer, as well as the female star. Chris, of course, would have to play all the male lead roles, and the twins could participate and play minor parts.

But they didn't want to participate! They wanted to be the audience, and sit and watch and applaud.

It wasn't such a bad idea, for what was a play without an audience! It was a great pity they didn't have any money to buy tickets.

"We'll call this dress rehearsal," said Chris, "and since you seem to be everything else, and know everything about theatrical productions, you write the script."

Hah! As if I needed to write the script. This was my chance to play Scarlett O'Hara. We had the hoops to wear under the flouncy ruffled skirts, and the stays to squeeze you tight, and just the clothes for Chris to wear, and fancy parasols with a few holes. The trunks and the armoires offered a great deal to select from, and I had to have the best costume, hauled from one of the armoires, and the underwear and petticoats came from one of the trunks. I'd curled my hair in rags so it hung in long, spiraling curls, and on my head I wore a floppy old Leghorn hat of straw, bedecked with faded silk flowers and banded by green satin ribbon, that was browning about the edges. My ruffled gown worn over wire hoops was of some flimsy stuff that felt like voile. Once, I think, it might have been pink, now it was hard to say just what color it was.

Rhett Butler wore the fancy costume of cream-colored trousers, and a brown velvet jacket with pearl buttons, and a satin vest underneath with fault red roses scattered on it. "Come, Scarlett," he said to me, "We've got to escape Atlanta before Sherman reaches here and sets the town on fire."

Chris had strung ropes on which we draped blankets to act as stage curtains, and our audience of two were stomping their feet impatiently, eager to see Atlanta burn. I followed Rhett onto the "stage" and was ready to taunt and tease, flirt and bewitch, and put *him* on fire before I rushed off to some pale-haired Ashley Wilkes, when one of my bedraggled ruffles caught beneath my too large, funny-looking old shoe, and down I sprawled in an undignified heap that showed my dirty pantaloons with lace hanging in ragged strings. The audience gave me a standing ovation, thinking this was a pratfall and part of the act. "Play's over!" I announced, and began to rip off the smelly old clothes.

"Let's eat!" cried Carrie, who'd say anything to take us down from this despised attic.

Cory pouted his lower lip and looked around. "I wish we had the garden again," he said so wistfully it hurt. "I don't like to swing when the flowers don't sway in the wind." His flaxen hair had grown long enough to touch his shirt collar, and it curled in ringlets, while Carrie's hair hung halfway down her back and rippled like cascading waves. They were wearing blue today, for Monday. We had colors for each day. Yellow was our Sunday color. Red was for Saturday.

The wish spoken by Cory put thoughts into Chris's head, for he turned in a slow circle, giving the huge attic an appraising survey. "Admittedly this attic is a grim and dreary place," he mused, "but why can't we, as a constructive way to use our creative talents, bring about a metamorphosis and turn this ugly caterpillar into a brilliant soaring butterfly?" He smiled at me, at the twins, in such a charming, convincing way that I was immediately won over. It *would* be fun to attempt to pretty up this dismal place, and give the twins a colorful fake garden where they could swing and enjoy looking at beauty. Of course, we'd never finish decorating all of the attic, it was so tremendous—and any day the grandfather could die, and then we'd leave, never to return again.

We couldn't wait for Momma to come that evening, and when she did, Chris and I enthusiastically told her our plans of decorating the attic, and turning it into a cheerful garden the twins wouldn't be afraid of. The strangest expression flickered momentarily in her eyes.

"Well, now," she said brightly, "if you're going to make the attic pretty, first you must make it clean. And I'll do what I can to help."

Momma sneaked up mops, pails, brooms, scrub brushes, and boxes of soap powder. She went down on her knees beside us to scrub in the attic corners, and around the edges, and under the large pieces of furniture. I marveled that our mother knew how to scrub and clean. When we lived in Gladstone, we had a twice weekly maid who came in to do all the hard, dreary things that would redden Momma's hands and break her fingernails. And here she was, on her hands and knees, wearing faded old blue jeans, an old shirt, her hair pinned up in a bun. I really admired her. It was hard, hot, demeaning work—and she never once complained, only laughed and chatted and acted as if this was great fun.

In a week of hard work, we had most of the attic as clean as possible. Then she brought us insect repellent to kill what bugs had hidden from us while we cleaned. We swept up dead spiders and other crawlers by the bucketfuls. We threw them out of a back window, where they rolled to a lower section of the roof. Later the rain came to wash them down into the gutters. Then the birds found them and had a grisly feast while we four sat on a window ledge and watched. We never saw a rat or a mouse—but we saw droppings. We presumed they were waiting for all the hustle and bustle to calm down before they ventured out of their dark and secret places.

Now that the attic was clean, Momma brought us green plants, plus a spiky amaryllis that was supposed to bloom at Christmastime. I frowned when she said this—for we wouldn't be here then. "We'll take it with us," said Momma, reaching out to stroke my cheek. "We'll take all of our plants when we go, so don't frown and look unhappy. We wouldn't want to leave anything living, and loving of sunshine, in this attic."

We put our plants in the attic schoolroom for that room had windows facing east. Happy and gay, we all tripped down the narrow stairs, and Momma washed up in our bathroom, then fell exhausted into her special chair. The twins climbed up on her lap as I set the table for lunch. That was a good day, for she stayed until dinnertime, then sighed and said she'd have to go. Her father made such demands on her, wanting to know where she went every Saturday, and why she stayed so long.

"Can you sneak back to see us before bedtime?" Chris asked.

"I'm going to the movies tonight," she said evenly, "but before I leave, I'll slip in to see you again. I've got some of those little boxes of raisins that you can snack on between meals. I forgot to bring them with me."

The twins were crazy about raisins, and I was happy for them. "Are you going to the movies alone?" I asked.

"No. There's a girl I grew up with—she used to be my best friend, and she's married now. I'm going to the movies with them. She lives only a few houses from here." She got up and went to the windows, and when Chris had the lights turned out, she parted the draperies and pointed in the direction of the house where her best friend lived. "Elena has two unmarried brothers, one is studying to be a lawyer. He goes to Harvard Law School, and the other is a tennis pro."

"Momma!" I cried. "Are you dating one of those brothers?"

She laughed and let the draperies fall. "Turn on the lights, Chris. No, Cathy, I am not dating anyone. To tell you the truth, I'd rather go right to bed, I'm that tired. I really don't care for musicals, anyway. I'd rather stay with my children, but Elena keeps insisting I get out, and when I keep refusing, she keeps asking why. I don't want people to wonder why I stay home every weekend; that's why occasionally I do have to go sailing, or to the movies."

To make the attic even pretty seemed highly improbable—to make it a beautiful garden soared over the rainbow! It was going to take an enormous amount of hard work and creative ability, but that darned brother of mine was convinced we could do it *in no time at all*. He soon had our mother so sold on the idea that

every day she went to secretarial school, she came back to us
bearing coloring books from which we could cut out pre-drawn
flowers. She brought us watercolor sets, many brushes, boxes of
crayons, huge amounts of colored craft paper, fat pots of white
paste, and four pairs of blunt-nosed scissors.

"Teach the twins to color and cut out flowers," she instructed,
"and let them participate in all you undertake. I nominate you
their kindergarten teachers."

She came from that city an hour's train ride away, glowing with
radiant good health, her skin fresh and rosy from outside air, her
clothes so beautiful they took my breath away. She had shoes of
every color, and bit by bit she was accumulating new pieces
of jewelry which she called "junk" jewelry, but somehow those
rhinestones looked more like diamonds to me from the way they
sparkled. She fell into "her" chair, exhausted, but happy, and told
her of her day. "Oh, how I wish those typewriters had letters on
the keys. I can't seem to remember but one row. I have to look up
at the wall chart everytime and that slows me down, and I'm not
very good at remembering the bottom row, either. But I do know
where all the vowels are. You use those keys more than any others, you know. So far my typing speed is twenty words per
minute, and that's not too good. Plus I make about four mistakes
in those twenty words. And those shorthand squiggles . . ." She
sighed, as if they, too, had her baffled. "Well, I guess I'll learn
eventually; after all, other women do, and if they can, then I can."

"Do you like your teachers, Momma?" asked Chris.

She giggled girlishly before she answered. "First, let me tell
you about my typing teacher. Her name is Mrs. Helena Brady.
She's shaped very much like your grandmother—huge. Only
her bosom is much larger! Really, hers is the most remarkable
bosom I've ever seen! And her bra straps keep slipping off her
shoulders, and if it isn't her bra straps, then it's her slip straps,
and she's always reaching into the neckline of her dress to haul
them back into place, and the men in the class always snicker."

"Do men take typing classes?" asked I, very surprised.

"Yes, there are a few young men there. Some are journalists, writers, or have some good reason for wanting to know how to type. And Mrs. Brady is divorced, and has a keen eye for one of those young men. She flirts with him, while he tries to ignore her. She's about ten years older than he is, at least, and he keeps looking at me. Now don't get any ideas, Cathy. He's much too short for me. I couldn't marry a man who couldn't pick me up and carry me over the threshold. I could pick *him* up—he's only five feet two."

We all had a good laugh, for Daddy had been a full foot taller, and he had easily picked our mother up. We'd seen him do that many times—especially on those Friday nights when he came home, and they'd look at each other so funny.

"Momma, you're not thinking of getting married again, are you?" Chris asked in the tightest of voices. Swiftly her arms went around him. "No darling, of course not. I loved your father dearly. It would take a very special man to fill his shoes, and so far I haven't met one who measures up to even his outgrown socks."

To play kindergarten teachers was great fun, or could have been, if our student body had been the least bit willing. But as soon as we had breakfast finished, our dishes washed and put away, our food stashed in the coldest place, and the hour of ten had come and gone with servants from the second floor, Chris and I each dragged a wailing twin up into the attic schoolroom. There we could sit at the student desks and make a grand mess cutting flower forms from the colored craft paper, using the crayons to glorify the colors with stripes and polka-dots. Chris and I made the best flowers—what the twins made looked like colored blobs.

"Modern art," Chris named the flowers they made.

On the dull and gray slat walls we pasted up our goliath flowers. Chris ascended the old ladder with the missing rungs again so he could dangle down long strings tied to the attic rafters, and to these strings we fastened colorful blossoms that constantly moved in the attic drafts.

Our mother came up to view our efforts, and she gave us all a pleased smile. "Yes, you're doing marvelously well. You *are* making it pretty up here." And thoughtfully she moved closer to the daisies, as if considering something else she could bring us. The next day she came with a huge flat box containing colored glass beads and sequins, so we could add sparkle and glamor to our garden. Oh, we did slave over making those flowers, for whatever occupation we pursued, we pursued it with diligent, fervid zeal. The twins caught some of our enthusiasm, and they stopped howling and fighting and biting when we mentioned the word attic. For after all, the attic was slowly, but surely, turning into a cheerful garden. And the more it changed, the more determined we became to cover over every last wall in that endless attic!

Each day, of course, when Momma was home from that secretarial school, she had to view the day's accomplishments. "Momma," gushed Carrie in her breathless bird twitter, "that's all we do all day, make flowers, and sometimes Cathy, she don't want us to go downstairs and eat lunch!"

"Cathy, you mustn't become so preoccupied with decorating the attic that you forget to eat your meals."

"But, Momma, we're doing it for them, so they won't be so scared up there."

She laughed and hugged me. "My, you are the persistent one, you and your older brother both. You must have inherited that from your father, certainly not from me. I give up so easily."

"Momma!" I cried, made uneasy. "Are you still going to school? You are getting better at typing, aren't you?"

"Yes, of course I am." She smiled again, and then settled back in her chair, holding up her hand and seeming to admire the bracelet she wore. I started to ask why she needed so much jewelry to attend secretarial school, but she spoke instead. "What you need to make now is animals for your garden."

"But, Momma, if roses are impossible to make, how can we even *draw* animals?"

She gave me a wry little smile as she traced a cool finger over my nose "Oh, Cathy, what a doubting Thomas you are. You question everything, doubt everything, when you should know by now, you can do anything you want to, if you want to badly enough. And I'm going to tell you a secret I've known about for some time—in this world, where everything is complicated, there is also a book to teach you how simple everything can be."

That I was to find out.

Momma brought us art instruction books by the dozens. The first of these books taught us to reduce all complicated designs into basic spheres, cylinders, cones, rectangles and cubes. A chair was just a cube—I hadn't known that before. A Christmas tree was just an inverted ice-cream cone—I hadn't known that before, either. People were just combinations of all those basic forms: spheres for heads; arms, necks, legs, torso, upper and lower, were only rectangular cubes or cylinders, and triangles made for feet. And believe it or not, using this basic method, with just a few simple additions, we soon had rabbits, squirrels, birds, and other small friendly creatures—all made by our very own hands.

True, they were peculiar looking. I thought their oddities made them all the sweeter. Chris colored all his animals realistically. I decorated mine with polka-dots, gingham checks, plaids, and put lace-edged pockets on the laying hens. Because our mother had shopped in a sewing notions store, we had lace, cords of all colors, buttons, sequins, felt, pebbles and other decorative materials. The possibilities were endless. When she put that box into my hands, I know my eyes must have shown all the love I felt for her then. For this did prove she thought of us when she was out in the world. She wasn't just thinking of new clothes for herself, and new jewelry and cosmetics. She *was* trying to make our confined lives as pleasant as possible.

One rainy afternoon Cory came running to me with an orange paper snail he'd laboriously worked on the entire morning, and half of the afternoon. He'd eaten but a little of his favorite lunch, peanut-butter-and-jelly sandwiches, he was that anxious to get back to his "work" and put on the "things that stick out of the head."

Proudly, he stood back, small legs spread wide, as he watched each flicker of expression on my face. What he'd made resembled nothing more than a lopsided beachball with trembling feelers.

"Do you think it's a good snail?" he asked, frowning up and looking worried when I couldn't find words to say.

"Yes," I said quickly, "it's a wonderful, beautiful snail."

"You don't think it looks like an orange?"

"No, of course not—oranges don't have swirls, like this snail does—or crooked feelers."

Chris stepped closer to view the pitiful creature I held in my hands. "You don't call those things feelers," he corrected. "A snail is a member of the mollusc family, which have soft bodies without any backbones—and those little things are called antennae, which are connected to its brain; it has tubular intestines that end with its mouth, and it moves by a gear-edged foot."

"Christopher," I said coolly, "when Cory and I want to know about a snail's tubular intestines, we'll send you a telegram, and please go sit on a tack and wait for it."

"Do you want to be ignorant all your life?"

"Yes!" I flared back, "When it comes to snails, I prefer knowing nothing!"

Cory tagged behind me as we went to watch Carrie pasting pieces of purple paper together. Her working method was slapdash, unlike Cory's careful plodding. Carrie used her pair of scissors to ruthlessly stab a hole into her purple . . . thing. Behind the hole she pasted a bit of red paper. When she had this . . . thing . . . put together, she named it a worm. It undulated like a giant boa constrictor, flashing a single mean red eye with black spider-leg lashes. "Its name is Charlie," she said, handing over her four feet of "worm" to me. (When things came to us without a name of their own, we made their names begin with a C to make them one of us.)

On the attic walls, in our beautiful garden of paper flowers, we pasted up the epileptic snail beside the fierce and menacing worm. Oh, they did make a pair. Chris sat down and lettered a big sign in red: ALL ANIMALS BEWARE OF EARTH-WORM!!!

I lettered my own sign, feeling Cory's small snail was the one in jeopardy, IS THERE A DOCTOR IN THE HOUSE? (Cory named this snail Cindy Lou.)

Momma viewed this day's accomplishments with laughter, all smiles, because we were having fun. "Yes, of course there is a doctor in the house," she said, and leaned to kiss Chris's cheek. "This son of mine has always known what to do for a sick animal. And Cory, I adore your snail—she looks . . . so . . . so sensitive."

"Do you like my Charlie?" asked Carrie anxiously. "I made him good. I used all the purple to make him big. Now we don't have no more purple."

"It's a beautiful worm, really a gorgeous worm," said Momma, taking the twins onto her lap and giving them the hugs and kisses she sometimes forgot. "I especially like the black lashes you put around that red eye—very effective."

It was a cozy, homey scene, the three of them in her chair, with Chris perched on the arm, his face close to his mother's. Then I had to go and spoil it all, as was my hateful way.

"How many words can you type per minute now, Momma?"

"I'm getting better."

"How much better?"

"I'm doing the best I can, really, Cathy—I told you the keyboard doesn't have any letters."

"What about shorthand—how fast can you take dictation?"

"I'm trying. You've got to have patience. You don't learn things like that overnight."

Patience. I colored patience gray, hung over with black clouds. I colored hope yellow, just like that sun we could see for a few short morning hours. Too soon the sun rose high in the sky and disappeared from view, leaving us bereft, and staring at blue.

When you grow up, and have a million adult things to do, you forget how long a day can be for a child. It seemed we lived through four years in the course of seven weeks. Then came another dreaded Friday when we had to get up at dawn and scurry around like mad to rid the bedroom, and the bathroom, of all evidence that we existed. I stripped off the sheets from the bed and rolled them into a ball along with the pillowcases and blankets, and I put the bedspreads directly over the mattress covers—the way the grandmother had ordered me to do. The night before, Chris had taken apart the train tracks. Like crazy we worked to make the room neat, spotless, plus the bathroom, and then the grandmother came in with the picnic basket and ordered us to take it into the attic, and we could eat breakfast there. I had most carefully wiped away all our fingerprints, and the mahogany furniture shone. She scowled heavily when she saw this, and darn if she didn't use dust from a vacuum cleaner bag to make all the furniture tops dull again.

At seven we were in the attic schoolroom, eating our cold cereal with raisins and milk. Down below we could faintly hear the maids moving around in our room. On tippy-toes we moved to the stairwell, and huddled there on the top step listening to what went on below, though we were scared every minute of being discovered.

Hearing the maids move about, laughing and chatting, while the grandmother hovered near the closet door directing them to clean the mirrors, use the lemon wax, air the mattresses—it all gave me the queerest feeling. Why didn't those maids notice something different? Didn't we leave any odor behind to let them know Cory often wet his bed? It was as if we really *didn't* exist, and weren't alive, and the only scents we had were imaginary. We wrapped our arms about each other and held onto each other tightly, tightly.

The maids didn't enter the closet; they didn't open the tall, narrow door. They didn't see us, or hear us, nor did they seem to think it odd the grandmother never left the room for a second while they were in there scrubbing the tub, cleaning the toilet bowl, scrubbing the tile floor.

That Friday did something strange to all of us. I believe we shriveled in our own estimations of ourselves, for afterwards we couldn't find words to say. We didn't enjoy our games, or our books, and so silently we cut out tulips and daisies and waited for Momma to come and bring hope with her again.

Still, we were young, and hope has strong roots in the young, right down to their toes, and when we entered the attic and saw our growing garden, we could laugh, and pretend. After all, we were making our mark in the world. We were making something beautiful out of what had been drab and ugly.

Now the twins took off like butterflies, fluttering through the mobile flowers. We pushed them high on the swings and created windstorms to shake the flowers madly. We hid behind cardboard trees no taller than Chris, and sat on mushrooms made of papier-mâché, with colorful foam cushions on top, which were, honestly, better than the real thing—unless you had an appetite for eating mushrooms.

"It's pretty!" cried Carrie, spinning around and around, holding to her short pleated skirt so we just had to see the new lace ruffled panties Momma had given her yesterday. All new clothes and shoes had to spend their first night with Carrie and Cory in their beds. (It's terrible to wake up at night with your cheek resting on the sole of a sneaker.) "I'm going to be a ballerina, too," she said happily, spinning and spinning until she eventually fell, and Cory went rushing to see if she had hurt herself. She screamed to see the blood ooze from a cut on her knee. "Oh—I don't want to be a ballerina if it hurts!"

I didn't dare let her know it hurt—oh, boy, did it hurt!

Yesterdays ago, I'd ambled through real gardens, real forests—and always I felt their mystical aura—as if something magic and marvelous was waiting just around the bend. To make our attic garden enchanted, too, Chris and I crawled around and drew white-chalk daisies on the floor, joining them in a ring. Inside that fairy ring of white flowers, all that was evil was banished. There we could sit cross-legged on the floor, and by the light of a single candle burning, Chris and I would spin long, involved tales of good fairies who took care of small children, and wicked witches who always went down in defeat.

Then Cory spoke up. As always, he was the one to ask the most difficult questions to answer. "Where has all the grass gone?"

"God took the grass to heaven." And thusly, Carrie saved me from answering.

"Why?"

"For Daddy. Daddy likes to mow the lawn."

Chris's eyes met with mine—and we'd thought they'd forgotten Daddy.

Cory puckered up his faint brows, staring at the little cardboard trees Chris had made. "Where are all the big trees?"

"Same place," said Carrie. "Daddy likes big trees." This time my eyes took wild flight. How I hated lying to them—telling them this was only a game, an endless game they seemed to endure with more patience than Chris or me. And they never once asked why we had to play such a game.

Never once did the grandmother come up to the attic to ask what we were doing, though very often she opened the bedroom door as silently as possible, hoping we wouldn't notice the noise of the key turning in the lock. She'd peer in the crack, trying to catch us doing something "unholy" or "wicked."

In the attic we were free to do anything we wanted without fear of retaliation, unless God wielded a whip. Not one time did the grandmother leave our room without reminding us that God was up above to see, even when she was not. Because she never went even into the closet to open the door of the attic stairwell, my curiosity was aroused. I reminded myself to ask of Momma as soon as she came in, so I wouldn't forget again. "Why doesn't the grandmother go into the attic herself and check to see what we do? Why does she just ask, and think we'll tell the truth?"

Tired and dejected looking, Momma wilted in her special chair. Her new green wool suit looked very expensive. She had been to a hairdresser, and the style was changed. She answered my question in an offhand manner, as if her thoughts were dwelling on something more appealing, "Oh, haven't I told you before? Your grandmother suffers from claustrophobia. That's an emotional affliction that makes it difficult for her to breathe in any small, confined area. You see, when she was a child, her parents used to lock her in a closet for punishment."

Wow! How difficult to think that large old woman had once been young, and small enough to punish. I could almost feel sorry for the child she'd been, but I knew she was happy to see *us* locked up. Every time she glanced our way, it showed in her eyes—her smug satisfaction to have us so neatly captured. Still, it was a peculiar thing that fate would give her such a fear, and thus give Chris and me reason enough to kiss the dear, sweet, close walls of that narrow passageway. Often Chris and I speculated on how all the massive furniture had been taken up into the attic. Certainly it couldn't have been maneuvered up through the small closet and then up the stairway, which was barely more than a foot wide. And though we searched diligently to find another larger doorway into the attic, we never found one. Maybe one was hidden behind one of the giant armoires too heavy for us to move. Chris thought the largest furniture could have been hauled up to the roof, then passed through one of the big windows.

Every day the witch-grandmother came into our room, to stab with her flintstone eyes, to snarl with her thin, crooked lips. Every day she asked the same old questions: "What have you been up to? What do you do in the attic? Did you say grace before today's meals? Did you go down on your knees last night and ask God to forgive your parents for the sin they committed? Are you teaching the youngest two the words of the Lord? Do you use the bathroom together, boys and girls?" Boy, did her eyes flash mean then! "Are you modest, always? Do you keep the private parts of your bodies from the eyes of others? Do you touch your bodies when it's not necessary for cleanliness?"

God! How dirty she made skin seem. Chris laughed when she was gone. "I think she must glue on her underwear," he joked.

"No! She nails it on!" I topped.

"Have you noticed how much she likes the color gray?"

Noticed? Who wouldn't notice? Always gray. Sometimes the gray had fine pinstripes of red or blue, or a dainty plaid design, very faint, or jacquard—but always the fabric was taffeta with the diamond brooch at the throat of a high and severe neckline, softened a bit by hand-crocheted collars. Momma had already told us a widow-lady in the nearest village custom made these uniforms that looked like armor. "This lady is a dear friend of my mother's. And she wears gray because it is cheaper to buy material by the bolt than by the yard—and your grandfather owns a mill that makes fine fabrics down in Georgia somewhere."

Good golly, even the rich had to be stingy.

One September afternoon I raced down the attic stairs in a terrible hurry to reach the bathroom—and I collided smack into the grandmother! She seized hold of my shoulders, and glared down into my face. "Watch where you're going, girl!" she snapped. "Why are you in such a hurry?"

Her fingers felt like steel through the thin fabric of my blue blouse. She had spoken first, so I could answer. "Chris is painting the most beautiful landscape," I breathlessly explained, "and I've got to get right back with fresh water before his large wash dries. It's important to keep the colors clean."

"Why doesn't he come for his own water? Why do you wait on him?"

"He's painting, and he asked if I'd mind fetching him fresh water, and I wasn't doing anything but watching, and the twins would spill the water."

"Fool! Never wait on a man! Make him wait on himself. Now, spill out the truth—what are you *really* doing up there?"

"Honest, I'm telling the truth. We're working hard to make the attic pretty so the twins won't be afraid up there, and Chris is a wonderful artist."

She sneered and asked with contempt, "How would *you* know?"

"He is gifted artistically, Grandmother—all his teachers said so."

"Has he asked you to pose for him—without clothes?"

I was shocked. "No. Of course not!"

"Then why are you trembling?"

"I'm . . . I'm scared of . . . of you," I stammered. "Every day you come in and ask what sinful, unholy thing we're doing, and truly, I don't know what it is you think we're doing. If you don't tell us exactly, how can we avoid doing something bad, not knowing it *is* bad?"

She looked me over, down to my bare feet, and smiled sarcastically. "Ask your older brother—he'll know what I mean. The male of the species is born knowing everything evil."

Boy, did I blink! Chris wasn't evil, or bad. There were times when he was tormenting, but not unholy. I tried to tell her this, but she didn't want to hear.

Later on in the day she came into our room bearing a clay pot of yellow chrysanthemums. Striding directly to me, she put that pot in my hands. "Here are real flowers for your fake garden," she said without warmth. It was such an unwitch-like thing for her to do, it took my breath away. Was she going to change, see us differently? Could she learn to like us? I thanked her effusively for the flowers, perhaps too much, for she spun around and stalked out, as if embarrassed.

Carrie came running to put her small face into the mass of yellow petals. "Pretty," she said. "Cathy, can I have them?" Of course she could have them. With reverence that pot of flowers was placed on the eastern windowsills in the attic to receive the morning sunshine. There was nothing to see but hills and far off mountains and the trees in between, and above everything hovered a blue mist. The real flowers spent the nights with us, so the twins could wake up in the morning and see something beautiful and alive growing near them.

Whenever I think of being young, I see again those blue-misted mountains and hills, and the trees that paraded stiffly up and down the slopes. And I smell again the dry and dusty air that was ours to breathe daily. I see again the shadows in the attic that blended so well with the shadows in my mind, and I hear again the unspoken, unanswered questions of Why? When? How much longer?

Love . . . I put so much faith in it.

Truth . . . I kept believing it falls always from the lips of the one you love and trust the most.

Faith . . . it's all bound up to love and trust. Where does one end and the other start, and how do you tell when love is the blindest of all?

More than two months had passed, and still the grandfather lived on.

We stood, we sat, we lay on the wide ledges of the attic dormer windows. We wistfully watched as the treetops of summer's old dark green turned overnight into the brilliant scarlets, golds, oranges, and browns of autumn. It moved me; I think it moved all of us, even the twins, to see the summer go away, and see the fall begin. And we could only watch, but never participate.

My thoughts took frantic flight, wanting to escape this prison, and seek out the wind so it could fan my hair and sting my skin, and make me feel alive again. I yearned for all those children out there who were running wild and free on the browning grass, and scuffling their feet in the dry, crackling leaves, just as I used to do.

Why was it I never realized when I was able to run wild and free that I was experiencing happiness? Why did I think back then, that happiness was always just ahead in the future, when I would be an adult, able to make my own decisions, go my own way, be my own person? Why had it seemed that being a child was never enough? Why had I thought that happiness reserved itself for those grown to full size?

"You're looking sad," said Chris, who was crowded close beside me, with Cory on the other side of him, and Carrie on the other side of me. Nowadays Carrie was my little shadow to follow where I led, and mimic what I did, and imitate the way she thought I felt—just as Chris had his small mimicking shadow too, in Cory. If there were ever four siblings closer than we were, they would have had to have been Siamese quadruplets.

"Aren't you going to answer me?" asked Chris. "Why are you looking so sad? The trees look beautiful, don't they? When it's summer, I like summer best; yet when fall comes, I like fall best, and when winter comes, then that's my favorite season, and then comes spring, and I think spring is best."

Yes, that was my Christopher Doll. He could make do with the here and now, and always think it best, no matter what the circumstances.

"I was thinking back to old Mrs. Bertram and her boring talk of the Boston Tea Party. She made history seem so dull, and the people so unreal. Yet, I'd like to be bored like that again."

"Yeah," he agreed, "I know what you mean. I thought school a bore, too, and history a dull subject, particularly American history—all but the Indians, and the old West. But at least when we were in school, we were doing what other kids our ages did. Now we're just wasting time, doing nothing. Cathy, let's not waste one minute! Let's prepare ourselves for the day we get out. If you don't set your goals firmly in mind, and strive always to reach them, then you never do. I'll convince myself if I can't be a doctor, then I won't want to be anything else, or want anything more that money can buy!"

He said that so intensely. I wanted to be a prima ballerina, though I would settle for something else. Chris scowled as if reading my mind. He turned his summer-blue eyes on me and scolded because I hadn't practiced my ballet exercises once since I'd come upstairs to exist. "Cathy, tomorrow I'm attaching a barre in the portion of the attic we've finished decorating—and five or six hours each day, you are going to practice, just like in ballet class!"

"I am not! Nobody is going to tell me I have to do anything! Besides, you can't do ballet positions unless you are properly dressed for it!"

"What a stupid thing to say!"

"That's because I *am* stupid! *You,* Christopher, have *all* the brains!" With that I burst into tears and fled from the attic, racing past all the paper flora and fauna. Run, run, run for the stairs. Fly, fly, fly down the steep and narrow wooden steps, daring fate to make you fall. Break a leg, a neck, put you in a coffin dead. Make everybody sorry then; make them cry for the dancer I should have been.

I threw myself down on my bed and sobbed into the pillow. There was nothing here but dreams, hopes—nothing real. I'd grow old, ugly, never see lots of people again. That old man downstairs could live to be a hundred and ten! All those doctors would keep him living forever—and I would miss out on Halloween—no tricking, no treating, no parties, no candy. Oh, I felt sorry for myself, and I vowed somebody was going to pay, pay, pay for all of this, somebody was, somebody was!

Wearing their dirty white sneakers, they came to me, my two brothers, my small sister, and each sought to give me comfort with small gifts of cherished possessions: Carrie's red and purple crayons, Cory's *Peter Rabbit* story book; but Chris, he just sat and looked at me. I never felt so small.

One evening quite late, Momma came in with a large box that she put in my hands to open. There amidst sheets of white tissue were ballet costumes, one a bright pink, the other azure-blue, with leotards and toe shoes to match the tulle tutus. "From

Christopher," was written on the enclosed small card. And there were records of ballet music. I started to cry as I flung my arms around my mother, then around my brother. This time they weren't tears of frustration, or despair. Now I had something to work toward.

"I wanted most of all to buy you a white costume," said Momma, still hugging me. "They had a beauty in a size too large to fit you, and with it comes a tight cap of white feathers that curl over your ears—for *Swan Lake*—and I ordered it for you, Cathy. Three costumes should be enough to give you inspiration, shouldn't they?"

Oh, yes! When Chris had the barre nailed securely to an attic wall, I practiced for hours on end while the music played. There wasn't a large mirror behind the barre, like there had been in the classes I had attended, but there was a huge mirror in my mind, and I saw myself as Pavlova, performing before ten thousand enraptured people, and encore after encore I took, bowing and accepting dozens of bouquets, every one red roses. In time, Momma brought me every one of Tchaikovsky's ballets to play on the record player, which had been hooked up to a dozen extension cords, which went down the stairs and plugged into a socket in our bedroom.

Dancing to beautiful music took me out of myself, and made me forget momentarily that life was passing us by. What did it matter when I was dancing? Better to pirouette and pretend I had a partner to support me when I did the most difficult positions. I'd fall, get up, then dance on again until I was out of breath and ached in every muscle, and my leotards were glued to me with sweat, and my hair was wet. I'd fall down flat on the floor to rest, and pant, then up again at the barre to do pliés. Sometimes I would be the Princess Aurora in *The Sleeping Beauty* and sometimes I'd dance the part of the prince, as well, and leap high into the air and beat my feet together.

Once I looked up from my concluding dying swan spasms,

and I saw Chris standing in the attic shadows, watching with the oddest expression on his face. Soon he'd be having a birthday, his fifteenth. How had it come about that already he seemed a man and not a boy? Was it only that vague look in his eyes that said he was moving quickly from childhood?

On full pointe I performed a sequence of those very small, even steps which are supposed to give the impression the dancer is gliding across the stage and creating what is poetically called "a string of pearls." In such a way I flitter-glided over to Chris and held out my arms. "Come, Chris, be my *danseur;* let me teach you the way."

He smiled, seeming bemused, but he shook his head and said that was impossible. "Ballet dancing is not for me. But I'd like to learn to waltz—if the music is Strauss."

He made me laugh. At that time the only waltz music we had (except ballet) were old Strauss records. I hurried over to the record player to take off the *Swan Lake* records, and I put on *The Blue Danube.*

Chris was clumsy. He held me awkwardly, as if embarrassed. He stepped on my pink pointe shoes. But it was touching how hard he tried to get simple steps right, and I couldn't tell him all his talents must reside in his brain, and in the skill of his artistic hands, for certainly none of it drifted down to his legs and feet. And yet, and yet, there was something sweet and endearing about a Strauss waltz, easy to do, and romantic, and so unlike those athletic ballet waltzes that put you in a sweat, and left you panting for breath.

When Momma finally came through the door with that smashing white outfit for dancing *Swan Lake,* a beautifully feathered brief bodice, tight cap, white slippers, and white leotards so sheer the pink of my skin showed through, I gasped!

Oh, it seemed that love, hope, and happiness *could be* brought upstairs in one single giant-sized slippery-satin white box with a violet ribbon and given to me by someone who really cared when another who really cared, put this idea in her head.

"Dance, Ballerina, dance, and do your pirouette
In rhythm with your aching heart,
Dance, Ballerina, dance, you mustn't once forget
A dancer has to dance the part,
Once you said his love must wait its turn,
You wanted fame instead, I guess that's your concern,
We live and learn . . . and love is gone, Ballerina, gone . . ."

Eventually, Chris could do the waltz and the foxtrot. When I tried to teach him the Charleston, he refused: "I don't need to learn every kind of dance, like you do. I'm not going to be on stage; all I want to learn is how to get out on the dance floor with a girl in my arms, and not make a jackass of myself."

I'd always been dancing. There wasn't any kind of dance I couldn't do, and didn't want to do.

"Chris, there's one thing you've got to know: you cannot waltz your whole life through, or do the foxtrot. Every year brings about changes, like in clothes. You've got to keep up with the times, and adapt. Come on, let's jazz it up a bit, so you can limber up your creaky joints that must be going stiff from so much sitting and reading."

I stopped waltzing and ran to put on another record: "You ain't nothin' but a hound dog."

I raised my arms, and began to gyrate my hips.

"Rock 'n' roll, Chris, you've got to learn how. Listen to the beat, let go, and learn to swivel your hips like Elvis. Come on, half-close your eyes, look sleepy, sexy, and pout your lips, for if you don't, no girl is ever going to love you."

"Then no girl is ever gonna love me."

That's the way he said it, dead flat, and dead serious. He would never let anyone force him to do anything that didn't fit his image of himself, and in a way I liked him for being what he was, strong, resolute, determined to be his own person, even if his kind of person had long ago gone out of style. My Sir Christopher, the knight gallant.

*   *   *

God-like, we changed the seasons in the attic. We took down the flowers and hung up autumn leaves of brown, russet, scarlet and gold. If we were still here when winter's snowflakes fell, we'd then substitute lacy white designs that we were all four cutting out in preparation, just in case. We made wild ducks and geese from white, gray, and black craft paper, and aimed our mobile birds in wide-arrowed skeins, heading them south. Birds were easy to make: just elongated ovals with spheres for heads, teardrops with wings.

When Chris wasn't sitting with his head stuck in a book, he was painting watercolor scenes of snow-covered hills with lakes where ice skaters skimmed. He put small houses of yellow and pink deeply buried in snow, and smoke curled from the chimneys, and in the distance rose a misty church steeple. And when he was done, he painted all around this a dark window-frame. When this was hung on the wall, we had a room with a view!

Once Chris had been a tease I could never please. An older brother. . . . But, we changed up there, he and I, just as much as we altered our attic world. We lay side by side on an old mattress, stained and smelly, for hours on end, and talked and talked, making plans for the kind of lives we'd live once we were free and rich as Midas. We'd travel around the world. He would meet and fall in love with the most beautiful, sexy woman who was brilliant, understanding, charming, witty and enormous fun to be with; she'd be the perfect housekeeper, the most faithful of devoted wives, the best of mothers, and she'd never nag, or complain, or cry, or doubt his judgment, or be disappointed or discouraged if he made stupid mistakes on the stock market and lost all of their money. She'd understand he'd done his best, and soon he'd make a fortune again with his wits and clever brains.

Boy, did he leave me feeling low. How in the world was I ever going to fill the needs of a man like Chris? Somehow or other, I knew he was setting the standard from which I'd judge all my future suitors.

"Chris, this intelligent, charming, witty, gorgeous woman, can't she have even one little flaw?"

"Why should she have flaws?"

"Take our mother, for instance, you think she is all of those things, except, perhaps, brilliant."

"Momma's not stupid!" he defended vehemently. "She's just grown up in the wrong kind of environment! She was put down as a child, and made to feel inferior because she was a girl."

As for me, after I'd been a prima ballerina for a number of years and was ready to marry and settle down, I didn't know what kind of man I wanted if he didn't measure up to Chris, or my father. I wanted him handsome, I knew that, for I wanted beautiful children. And I wanted him brilliant, or I might not respect him. Before I accepted his diamond engagement ring, I'd sit him down to play games, and if I won time and again, I'd smile, shake my head, and tell him to take his ring back to the store.

And as we made our plans for the future, our pots of philo-dendron drooped limp; our ivy leaves turned yellow before they died. We bustled about, giving our plants tender loving care, talking to them, pleading with them, asking them to please stop looking sick, and perk up and straighten up their necks. After all, they were getting the healthiest of all sunlight—that eastern morning light.

In a few more weeks Cory and Carrie stopped pleading to go outside. No longer did Carrie beat her small fists against the oak door, and Cory stopped trying to kick it down with his ineffec-tual small feet, wearing only soft sneakers that didn't keep his small toes from bruising.

They now docilely accepted what before they'd denied—the attic "garden" was the only "outside" available to them. And in time, pitiful as it was, they soon forgot there was a world other than the one we were locked up in.

Chris and I had dragged several old mattresses close to the

eastern windows, so we could open the windows wide and sun-bathe in the beneficial rays that didn't have to pass through dirty window glass first. Children needed sunlight in order to grow. All we had to do was look at our dying plants, and register what the attic air was doing to our greenery.

Unabashedly, we stripped off all our clothes and sun-bathed in the short time the sun visited our windows. We saw each other's differences, and thought little about them, and frankly told Momma what we did, so we, too, wouldn't die from lack of sunlight. She glanced from Chris to me and weakly smiled. "It's all right, but don't let your grandmother know. She wouldn't approve, as you well know."

I know now that she looked at Chris, and then at me for signs to indicate our innocence, or our awakening sexuality. And what she saw must have given her some assurance we were still only children, though she should have known better.

The twins loved to be naked and play as babies. They laughed and giggled when they used terms such as "do-do" and "twiddle-dee" and, enjoyed looking at the places where do-do came from, and wondered why Cory's twiddle-dee maker was so different from Carrie's.

"Why, Chris?" asked Carrie, pointing at what he had, and Cory had, and she and I didn't have.

I went right on reading *Wuthering Heights* and tried to ignore such silly talk.

But Chris tried to give an answer that was correct as well as truthful: "All male creatures have their sexual organs on the out-side, and females have theirs tucked away inside."

"Neatly inside," I said.

"Yes, Cathy, I know you approve of your *neat* body and I approve of my *un-neat* body, so let all of us rejoice that we have what we do. Our parents accepted our bare skins just as they did our eyes and hair, and so shall we. And I forgot, male birds have their organs 'neatly' tucked away inside, too, like females."

Intrigued, I asked, "How do you know?"

"I just know."

"You read it in a book?"

"What else—do you think I caught a bird and examined it?"

"I wouldn't put it past you."

"At least I read to improve my brain, not just to entertain it."

"You are going to make a very dull man, I'm warning—and if a male bird has tucked away sexual organs, doesn't that make him a her?"

"No!"

"But, Christopher, I don't understand: Why are birds different?"

"They have to be streamlined in order to fly."

It was another of those puzzlements, and he had the answers. I just knew the brain of brains had the answers.

"All right, but why are male birds made the way they are? And leave out the streamlined part."

He floundered, his face turned deeply red, and he sought a way to say something delicately. "Male birds can be aroused, and that makes what is in, come out."

"How are they aroused?"

"Shut up and read your book—and let me read mine!"

Some days were too chilly for sunbathing. Then it grew frigid, so even wearing our heaviest and warmest clothes, we still shivered unless we ran. Too soon the morning sun stole away from the east, leaving us desolate and wishing there were windows on the southern side. But the windows were shuttered over and locked.

"It doesn't matter," said Momma, "the morning sun is the healthiest."

Words that didn't cheer us, since our plants were dying one by one while living in the healthiest sunlight of all.

As November began, the attic began to turn Arctic cold. Our teeth chattered, our noses ran, we sneezed often and complained to Momma that we needed a stove with a chimney, since the two stoves in the schoolroom had been disconnected. Momma spoke of bringing up an electric or gas heater. But she feared an electric stove might start a fire if connected to many extension cords. And a chimney was also needed for a gas heater.

She brought us long heavy underwear, and thick ski jackets with attached hoods, and bright ski pants with wool fleece lining. Wearing these clothes, we went daily into the attic where we could run free and escape the grandmother's ever observant eyes.

In our cluttered bedroom we barely had room to walk without colliding into something to bruise our shins. In the attic we went frantic, screaming as we chased one another: hiding, finding, putting on small plays with frenzied activity. We fought sometimes, argued, cried, then went back to fierce play. We had a passion for hide and seek. Chris and I enjoyed making this game terribly threatening but only mildly so for the twins, who were already terrified enough of the many "bad things" that lingered in the dark attic shadows. Carrie earnestly said she saw monsters hiding behind the shrouded furniture.

One day, we were up in the attic polar zone, and searching to find Cory. "I'm going downstairs," said Carrie, her small face resentful, her lips pouted. No good to try and make her stay and exercise—she was too stubborn. She sashayed off in her little red ski outfit, leaving me and Chris to hunt around to find Cory. Customarily, he was just too easy to find. His way was to choose the last place Chris had hidden. So it was our belief we could go straight to the third massive armoire and there would be Cory, crouched down on the floor, hiding under the old clothes, and grinning up at us. We indulged him, avoiding this particular wardrobe for a specific length of time. Then we decided to "find" him. And lo, when we looked—he wasn't there!

"Well, I'll be damned!" exclaimed Chris. "He's finally going to be innovative and find an original place to hide."

That's what came of reading so many books. Big words stuck

to his brains. I swiped at my leaky nose, and then took another look around. If truly innovative, there were a million good hiding places in this multi-winged attic. Why, it might take us hours and hours to find Cory. And I was cold, tired and irritable, sick of playing this game Chris insisted on daily to keep us active.

"Cory!" I yelled. "Come out from wherever you are! It's time to eat lunch!" Now, that should bring him. Meals were a cozy and homey thing to do, and they broke up our long days into separate portions.

Still, he didn't answer. I flashed angry eyes at Chris. "Peanut-butter-and-grape-jelly sandwiches," I added. Cory's favorite meal, which should bring him running. Still, not a sound, not a cry, nothing.

Suddenly I was scared. I couldn't believe Cory had overcome his fear of the immense, shadowy attic, and was at last taking the game seriously—but just suppose he was trying to imitate Chris or me? Oh, God! "Chris!" I cried. "We've got to find Cory, and fast!"

He caught my panic, and whirled about to run, crying out Cory's name, ordering him to come out, stop hiding! Both of us ran and hunted, calling Cory repeatedly. Hide-and-seek-time was over—lunchtime now! No answer, and I was nearly freezing, despite all my clothes. Even my hands looked blue.

"Oh, my God," murmured Chris, pulling up short, "just suppose he hid in one of the trunks, and the lid came down and accidently latched?"

Cory would suffocate. He'd die!

Like crazy we ran and looked, throwing open the lids of every old trunk. We tossed out pantaloons, shifts, camisoles, petticoats, stays, suits, all with insane, distressed terror. And while I ran and searched, I prayed over and over again for God not to let Cory die.

"Cathy, I've found him!" shouted Chris. I spun around to see Chris lifting Cory's small, inert form from a trunk that had latched and kept him inside. Weak with relief, I stumbled over and kissed

Cory's small, pale face, turned a funny color from lack of oxygen. His slitted eyes were unfocused. He was very nearly unconscious. "Momma," he whispered, "I want my momma."

But Momma was miles away, learning how to type and take shorthand. There was only a pitiless grandmother we didn't know how to reach in an emergency.

"Run quick and fill the bathtub with hot water," said Chris, "but not too hot. We don't want to scald him." Then he was racing with Cory in his arms toward the stairwell.

I reached the bedroom first, then sped on toward the bath. I glanced backward to see Chris lay Cory down on his bed. Then he bent above, held Cory's nostrils, and then Chris lowered his head until his mouth covered Cory's blue lips, which were spread apart. My heart jumped! Was he dead? Had he stopped breathing?

Carrie took one glance at what was going on—her small twin blue and not moving—and she began to scream.

In the bathroom I turned on both faucets as far as they would go; full blast they gushed. Cory was going to die! Always I was dreaming of death and dying . . . and most of the times my dreams came true! And as always, just when I thought God had turned his back on us and didn't care, I whirled to grab hold of my faith, and prayed, demanding Him not to let Cory die . . . *please God, please God, please, please, please . . ."*

Maybe my desperate prayers did as much to help Cory back to life as the artificial resuscitation Chris performed.

"He's breathing again," said Chris, pale-faced and trembling as he carried Cory to the tub. "Now all we have to do is warm him up."

In no time at all we had Cory undressed and in the tub of warm water.

"Momma," whispered Cory as he came to, "I want Momma." Over and over again he kept saying it, and I could have pounded my fists through the walls it was so damned unfair! He should have his mother, and not just a pretend mother who didn't know what to do. I wanted out of this, even if I had to beg in the streets!

But I said in a calm way that made Chris lift his head and smile at me with approval, "Why can't you pretend *I'm* Momma? I'll do everything for you that she would. I'll hold you on my lap, and rock you to sleep while I sing you a lullaby, just as soon as you eat a little lunch, and drink some milk."

Both Chris and I were kneeling as I said this. He was massaging Cory's small feet, while I rubbed his cold hands and made them warm again. When his flesh was colored normally again, we dried Cory off, put on his warmest pajamas, wrapped him in a blanket, and, in the old rocker Chris had brought down from the attic, I sat down and cuddled my small brother on my lap. I covered his wan face with kisses, and whispered sweet nothings in his ear that made him giggle.

If he could laugh, he could eat, and I fed him tiny bits of sandwich, and gave him sips of lukewarm soup, and long drinks of milk. And as I did this, I grew older. Ten years I aged in ten minutes. I glanced over at Chris as he sat down to eat his lunch, and saw that he, too, had changed. Now we knew there was real danger in the attic beyond that of slow withering from lack of sunlight and fresh air. We all faced threats much worse than the mice and spiders that insisted on living, despite all we did to kill every last one.

All alone Chris stalked up the narrow, steep stairs to the attic, his face grim as he entered the closet. I rocked on and on, holding both Carrie and Cory on my lap, and singing "Rock-a-bye, Baby." Suddenly there was a fierce hammering coming from above, a terrible clamor the servants might hear.

"Cathy," said Cory in a small whisper while Carrie nodded off into sleep, "I don't like not having a momma anymore."

"You do have a momma—you have me."

"Are you as good as a real momma?"

"Yes, I think I am. I love you very much, Cory, and that's what makes a real mother."

Cory stared up at me with wide blue eyes, to see if I was sincere, or if I were only mocking his need. Then his small arms crept up around my neck, and he cuddled his head on my shoulder. "I'm so sleepy, Momma, but don't stop singing."

I was still rocking, still singing softly, when Chris came back wearing a satisfied expression. "Never again will a trunk lock inadvertently," he said, "for I smashed every last lock and the wardrobes, now they won't lock, either!"

I nodded.

He sat on the nearest bed and watched the slow rhythm of the rocking chair, listening to the childish tune I kept right on singing. A slow flush heated his face so he seemed embarrassed. "I feel so left out, Cathy. Would it be all right if I sat in the rocker first, and then the three of you piled on?"

Daddy used to do that. He'd hold all of us on his lap, even Momma. His arms had been long enough, and strong enough, to embrace us all, and give us the nicest, warmest feeling of security and love. I wondered if Chris could do the same.

As we sat in the rocker with Chris underneath, I caught a glimpse of us in the dresser mirror across the way. An eerie feeling stole over me, making all of this seem so unreal. He and I looked like doll parents, younger editions of Momma and Daddy.

"The Bible says there is a time for everything," whispered Chris so as not to awaken the twins, "a time to be born, a time to plant, a time to harvest, a time to die, and so on, and this is our time to sacrifice. Later on will come our time to live and enjoy."

I turned my head and nestled it down on his boyish shoulder, grateful he was always so optimistic, always so cheerful. It felt good to have his strong young arms about me—almost as protective and good as Daddy's arms had been.

Chris was right, too. Our happy time would come the day we left this room and went downstairs to attend a funeral.

Holidays

On the tall stalk of the amaryllis a single bud appeared—a living calendar to remind us that Thanksgiving and Christmas were drawing nigh. It was our only plant alive now, and it was, by far, our most cherished possession. We carried it down from the attic to spend warm nights with us in the bedroom. Up first every morning, Cory rushed to see the bud, wanting to know if it had survived the night. Then Carrie would shortly follow him, to stand close at his side and admire a hardy plant, valiant, victorious, where others had failed. They checked the wall calendar to see if a day was encircled with green, indicating the plant needed to be fertilized. They felt the dirt to see if it needed water. They never trusted their own judgment, but would come to me and ask, "Should we give Amaryllis water? Do you think she's thirsty?"

We never owned anything, inanimate or alive, that we didn't name, and Amaryllis was determined to live. Neither Cory nor Carrie would trust their frail strength to carry the heavy pot up to the attic windows, where the sunshine lingered but shortly. I was allowed to carry Amaryllis up, but Chris had to bring her

down at night. And each night we took turns marking off a day
with a big red X. We now had crossed off one hundred days.

The cold rains came, the fierce winds blew—sometimes heavy
fog shut out the morning sunlight The dry branches of the trees
scraped the house at night and woke me up, making me suck in
my breath, waiting, waiting, waiting for some horror to come
in and eat me up.

On a day when it was pouring rain that might later turn into
snow, Momma came breathless into our bedroom, bringing with
her a box of pretty party decorations to put on our Thanksgiving
Day table and make it festive. She had included a bright yellow
tablecloth and orange linen napkins with fringe.

"We're having guests tomorrow for a midday dinner," she
explained, dumping her box on the bed nearest the door, and
already turning to leave. "And two turkeys are being roasted:
one for us, one for the servants. But they won't be ready early
enough for your grandmother to put in the picnic basket. Now
don't worry, I'm not allowing my children to live through a
Thanksgiving Day without the feast to fit the occasion.
Somehow I'll find a way to slip up some hot food, a little bit of
everything we have. I think I'll make a big to-do about wanting
to serve my father myself, and while I'm preparing his tray, I
can put food on another tray to bring up to you. Expect to see
me about one tomorrow."

Like the wind through the door, she blew in, blew out, leaving
us with happy anticipations of a huge, hot, Thanksgiving Day
meal.

Carrie asked, "What's Thanksgiving?"

Cory answered, "Same as saying grace before meals."

In a way he was right, I think. And since he'd said something
voluntarily, darned if I was going to squelch him by any criticism.

While Chris cuddled the twins on his lap, sitting in one of the
big lounge chairs, and told them of the first Thanksgiving Day

so long ago, I bustled about like any hausfrau, very happy to set a festive holiday table. Our place cards were four small turkeys with tails that fanned out to make orange and yellow honeycombed paper plumage. We had two big pumpkin candles to burn, two Pilgrim men, two Pilgrim women, and two Indian candles, but darned if I could light such pretty candles and see them melt down into puddles. I put plain candles on the table to light, and saved the costly candles for other Thanksgiving Day meals when we were out of this place. On our little turkeys, I carefully lettered our names then fanned them open and placed one of them before each plate. Our dining table had a small shelf underneath, and that's where we kept our dishes and silverware. After each meal I washed them in the bathroom in a pink plastic basin. Chris dried, then stacked the dishes in a rubber rack under the table to await the next meal.

I laid out the silverware most carefully, forks to the left, the knives to the right, blades facing the plates, and next to the knives, the spoons. Our china was Lenox with a wide blue rim, and edged in twenty-four-karat gold—all that was written on the back. Momma had already told me this was old dinnerware that the servants wouldn't miss. Our crystal today was footed, and I couldn't help but stand back to admire my own artistry. The only thing missing was flowers. Momma should have remembered to bring flowers.

One o'clock came and went. Carrie complained loudly. "Let's eat our lunch now, Cathy!"

"Be patient. Momma is bringing us special hot food, turkey and all the fixings—and this will be dinner, not lunch." My housewifely chores done for a while, I curled up happily on the bed to read more of *Lorna Doone*.

"Cathy, my stomach don't have patience," said Cory now, bringing me back from the mid-seventeenth century. Chris was deep into some Sherlock Holmes mystery that would be solved fast on the last page. Wouldn't it be wonderful if the twins could calm their stomachs, capacity about two ounces, by reading as Chris and I did?

"Eat a couple of raisins, Cory."

"Don't have no more."

"The correct way to say that is: I don't have anymore, or there aren't anymore."

"Don't have no more, honest."

"Eat a peanut."

"Peanuts are all gone—did I say that right?"

"Yes," I sighed. "Eat a cracker."

"Carrie ate the last cracker."

"Carrie, why didn't you share those crackers with your brother?"

"He didn't want none then."

Two o'clock. Now all of us were starving. We had trained our stomachs to eat at twelve o'clock sharp. Whatever was keeping Momma? Was she going to eat first herself, and then bring us our food? She hadn't told it that way.

A little after three o'clock, Momma rushed in, bearing a huge silver tray laden with covered dishes. She wore a dress of periwinkle-blue wool jersey, and her hair was waved back from her face and caught low at the nape of her neck with a silver barrette. Boy, did she look pretty!

"I know you're starving," she immediately began to apologize, "but my father changed his mind and decided at the last minute to use his wheelchair and eat with the rest of us." She threw us a harried smile. "Your table-setting is lovely, Cathy. You did everything just right. I'm sorry I forgot the flowers. I shouldn't have forgotten. We have nine guests, all busy talking to me, and asking a thousand questions about where I was for so long, and you just don't know the trouble I had slipping into the butler's pantry when John wasn't looking—that man has eyes in back of his head. And you never saw anyone hop up and down as much as I did; the guests must have thought I was very impolite, or just plain foolish—but I did manage to fill your dishes, and hide them away, then back to the dining table I'd dash, and smile, and eat a bite before I had to get up again to blow my nose in another room. I answered three telephone calls that I made to myself from the private line in my bedroom. I had to disguise my voice so no one would guess, and I really did want to bring you slices of pumpkin pie, but John had it sliced and already put on the dessert plates, so what could I do? He'd have noticed four missing pieces."

She blew us a kiss, bestowed a dazzling, but hurried smile, and disappeared out the door.

Good-golly day! We sure did complicate her life, all right!

We rushed to the table to eat.

Chris bowed his head to say a hasty grace that couldn't have impressed God very much on this day, of all days, when His ears must ring with more eloquent phrasing: "Thank you, Lord, for this belated Thanksgiving Day meal. Amen."

Inwardly I smiled, for it was so like Chris to get directly to the point, and that was to play host, and dish up the food onto the plates we handed him one by one. He gave "Finicky" and "Picky" one slice of white turkey meat apiece, and tiny portions of the vegetables, and to each a salad that had been shaped in a pretty mold. The medium-sized portions were mine, and, of course, he served himself last—huge amounts for the one who needed it most, the brain.

Chris appeared ravenous. He forked into his mouth huge gobs of mashed potatoes that were almost cold. Everything was on the verge of being cold, the gelatin salad was beginning to soften, and the lettuce beneath it was wilted.

"We-ee don't like cold food!" Carrie wailed as she stared down at her pretty plate with such dainty portions placed neatly in a circle. One thing you could say for Chris, he was precise.

You would have thought Miss Picky was looking at snakes and worms from the way she scowled at that plate, and Mr. Finicky duplicated his twin's sour expression of distaste.

Honestly, I felt kind of sorry for Momma, who had tried so

hard to bring us up a really good hot meal, and messed up her own meal in the process, making herself look silly in front of the guests, too. And now those two weren't going to eat anything! After three hours of complaining, and telling us how hungry they were! Kids!

The egghead across the way closed his eyes to savor the delight of having something different: deliciously prepared food, and not the hasty picnic junk thrown together in a hurry before six o'clock in the morning. Although to be fair to the grandmother, she didn't ever forget us. She must have had to get up in the dark to beat the chef and the maids into the kitchen.

Chris then did something that really shocked me. He knew better than to stab into a huge slice of white turkey meat and shove the whole slice into his mouth! What was the matter with him?

"Don't eat like that, Chris. It sets a bad example for you-know-who."

"They aren't watching me," he said with a mouthful, "and I'm starving. I've never been so hungry before in my whole life, and everything tastes so good."

Daintily, I cut my turkey into small bits, and put some in my mouth to show the hog across the way how it was properly done. I swallowed first, then said, "I pity the wife you'll have. She'll divorce you within a year."

He went on eating, deaf and dumb to everything but enjoyment.

"Cathy," said Carrie, "don't be mean to Chris, 'cause we don't like cold food, anyway, so we don't want to eat."

"My wife will adore me so much, she'll be charmed to pick up my dirty socks. And Carrie, you and Cory like cold cereal with raisins, so *eat!*"

"We don't like cold turkey . . . and that brown stuff on the potatoes looks funny."

"That brown stuff is called gravy, and it tastes delicious. And Eskimos *love* cold food."

"Cathy, do Eskimos like cold food?"

"I don't know, Carrie. I suppose they'd better like it, or starve to death." For the life of me, I couldn't understand what Eskimos had to do with Thanksgiving. "Chris, couldn't you have said something better? Why bring up Eskimos?"

"Eskimos are Indians. Indians are part of the Thanksgiving Day tradition."

"Oh."

"You know, of course, the North American continent used to be connected with Asia," he said between mouthfuls. "Indians trekked over from Asia, and some liked ice and snow so much, they just stayed on, while others had better sense, and moved on down."

"Cathy, what's this lumpy and bumpy stuff that looks like Jell-O?"

"It's cranberry salad. The lumps are whole cranberries; the bumps are pecan nuts; and the white stuff is sour cream." And, boy, was it good! It had bits of pineapple, too.

"We don't like lumpy-bumpy stuff."

"Carrie," said Chris, "I get tired of what you like and don't like—*eat!*"

"Your brother is right, Carrie. Cranberries are delicious, and so are nuts. Birds love to eat berries, and you like birds, don't you?"

"Birds don't eat berries. They eat dead spiders and other bugs. We saw them, we did. They picked them out of the gutters, and ate them without chewing! We can't eat what birds eat."

"Shut up and eat," said Chris, with a mouthful.

Here we were with the best food (even if it was almost cold) since we'd come upstairs to live in this hateful house, and all the twins could do was stare down at their plates, and so far hadn't eaten a single bite!

And Chris—he was demolishing everything in sight like the prize-winning hog at the county fair!

The twins tasted the mashed potatoes with the mushroom

gravy. The potatoes were "grainy" and the gravy was "funny." They tasted the absolutely divine stuffing, and declared that "lumpy, grainy, and funny."

"Eat the sweet potatoes, then!" I almost yelled. "Look at how pretty they are. They're smooth because they've been whipped, and marshmallows have been added, and you love marshmallows, and it's flavored with orange and lemon juice." And pray to God they didn't notice the "lumpy" pecans.

I guess between the two of them, sitting across from one another, fussily stirring the food into mishmash, they managed to put away three or four ounces of food.

While Chris was longing for dessert, pumpkin pie, or mincemeat pie, I began to clear away the table. Then, for some reason extraordinaire, Chris began to help! I couldn't believe it. He smiled at me disarmingly, and even kissed my cheeks. And, boy, if good food could do that for a man, I was all for learning gourmet cooking. He even picked up his socks before he came to help me wash and dry the dishes, glasses, and silverware.

Ten minutes after Chris and I had everything neatly stored away under the table and covered over with the clean towel, the twins simultaneously announced, "We're hungry! Our stomachs hurt!"

Chris read on at his desk. I got up from the bed after laying aside *Lorna Doone,* and without saying one word, I gave to each of the twins a peanut-butter-and-jelly sandwich from the picnic basket.

As they ate, taking tiny bites, I threw myself down on the bed and watched them with real puzzlement. Why did they enjoy that junk? Being a parent wasn't as easy as I used to presume, nor was it such a delight.

"Don't sit on the floor, Cory. It's colder down there than in a chair."

"Don't like chairs," said Cory. Then he sneezed.

*   *   *

The very next day, Cory came down with a severe cold. His small face was red and hot. He complained that he ached all over and his bones hurt. "Cathy, where is my momma, my real momma?" Oh, how he wanted his mother. Finally, she did show up.

Immediately she became anxious as she viewed Cory's flushed face, and she rushed away to fetch a thermometer. Unhappily, she returned, trailed by the detested grandmother.

With the slim stem of glass in his mouth, Cory stared up at his mother as if at a golden angel come to save him in his time of distress. And I, his pretend mother, was forgotten.

"Sweetheart, darling baby," she crooned. And she picked him up from the bed and carried him to the rocker, where she sat down to put kisses on his brow. "I'm here, darling. I love you. I'll take care of you and make the pains go away. Just eat your meals, and drink your orange juice like a good little boy, and soon you'll be well."

She put him to bed again, and hovered over him before she popped an aspirin into his mouth and gave him water to swallow it down. Her blue eyes were misted over with troubled tears, and her slim white hands worked nervously.

I narrowed my eyes as I watched her eyes close, and her lips move as if in silent prayer.

Two days later Carrie was in the bed beside Cory, sneezing and coughing, too, and her temperature raged upward with terrifying swiftness, enough to panic me. Chris looked scared, too. Listless and pale, the two of them lay side by side in the big bed, with little fingers clutching the covers high under their rounded chins.

They seemed made of porcelain, they were so waxy white, and their blue eyes grew larger and larger as they sank deeper and deeper into their skulls. Dark shadows came under their eyes, to make them seem haunted children. When our mother wasn't there, those two sets of eyes pleaded mutely with Chris and me to do something, anything, to make the misery go away.

Momma took a week off from the secretarial school so she could be with her twins as much as possible. I hated it that the grandmother felt it so necessary to trail after her every time she showed up. Always putting her nose in where it didn't belong, and her advice, when we didn't want her advice. Already she'd told us we didn't exist, and had no right to be alive on God's earth, save for those saintly and pure—like herself. Did she come merely to distress us more, and take from us the comfort of having our mother to ourselves?

The whisper of her menacing gray dresses, the sound of her voice, the tread of her heavy feet, the sight of her huge pale hands, soft and puffy, flashing with diamond rings, and spotted brown with dying pigment . . . oh, yes, just to see her was to loathe her.

Then there was our mother, rushing to us often, doing what she could to help the twins back to health. Shadows were under her eyes, too, as she gave the twins aspirins and water, and later on orange juice, and hot chicken soup.

One morning Momma rushed in carrying a big thermos of orange juice she had just squeezed. "It's better than the frozen or canned kind," she explained, "full of vitamins C and A, and that's good for colds." Next she listed what she wanted Chris and me to do, saying that Chris and I were to give orange juice often. We stored the thermos on the attic steps—as good as any refrigerator in the wintertime.

One glance at the thermometer from Carrie's lips, and a frenzied panic blew away all of Momma's cool. "Oh, God!" she cried out in distress. "One hundred three-point-six. I have to take them to a doctor, a hospital!"

I was before the heavy dresser holding to it lightly with one hand and exercising my legs, as I did each day, now that the attic was too cold to limber up in. I threw my grandmother a quick glance, trying to read her reactions to this.

The grandmother had no patience for those who lost control and made waves. "Don't be ridiculous, Corrine. All children run high fevers when they are sick. Doesn't mean a thing. You should know that by now. A cold is just a cold."

Chris jerked his head up from the book he was pursuing. He believed the twins had the flu, though how they had caught the virus he couldn't guess.

The grandmother continued: "Doctors, what do they know about curing a cold? We know just as much. There are only three things to do: stay in bed, drink lots of liquids, and take aspirins—what else? And aren't we doing all of those things?" She flashed me a mean look. "Stop swinging your legs, girl. You make me nervous." Again she directed her eyes, and her words, at our mother. "Now, *my* mother had a saying, colds take three days coming, three days staying, and three days leaving."

"What if they have the flu?" asked Chris. The grandmother turned her back and ignored his question. She didn't like his face; he resembled our father too much. "I hate it when people who should know better question those who are older and far wiser. Everyone knows the rule for colds: six days to start and stay, and three days to leave. That's the way it is—they'll recover."

As the grandmother predicted, the twins recovered. Not in nine days . . . in nineteen days. Only bed rest, aspirins, and fluids did the trick—no perscriptions from a doctor to help them back to health more quickly. By day the twins stayed in the same bed; by night Carrie slept with me, and Cory with his brother. I don't know why Chris and I didn't come down with the same thing.

All night long we jumped up and down, to run for water, for orange juice kept cold on the attic stairs. They cried for cookies, for Momma, for something to unstop their nostrils. They tossed and fretted, weak and uneasy, worried by bothersome things they couldn't express except by large fearful eyes that tore at my heart. They asked questions while they were sick that they didn't ask while they were well . . . and wasn't that odd?

"Why do we stay upstairs all the time?"

"Has downstairs gone away?"

"Did it go where the sun hides?"

"Don't Momma like us no more?"

"Anymore," I corrected.

"Why are the walls fuzzy?"

"Are they fuzzy?" I asked in return.

"Chris, he looks fuzzy, too."

"Chris is tired."

"Are you tired, Chris?"

"Kinda. I'd like for you both to go to sleep and stop asking so many questions. And Cathy is tired, too. We'd both like to go to sleep, and know the two of you are sleeping soundly, too."

"We don't *sound* when we sleep."

Chris sighed, picked up Cory, and carried him over to the rocker, and soon Carrie and I were seated on his lap. There we rocked back and forth, back and forth, telling stories at three o'clock in the morning. We read stories on other nights till four in the morning. If they cried and wanted Momma, as they incessantly did, Chris and I acted as mother and father and did what we could to soothe them with soft lullabies. We rocked so much the floorboards started to creak, and surely below someone could have heard.

And all the while we heard the wind blowing through the hills. It scraped the skeleton tree branches, and squeaked the house, and whispered of death and dying, and in the cracks and crevices it howled, moaned, sobbed, and sought in all ways to make us aware we weren't safe.

We read so much aloud, sang so much, both Chris and I grew hoarse and half-sick ourselves from fatigue. We prayed every night, down on our knees, asking God to make our twins well again. "Please, God, give them back to us the way they were."

A day came when the coughing eased, and sleepless eyelids drooped, and eventually closed in peaceful sleep. The cold, bony hands of death had reached for our little ones, and was reluctant to let go, for so tortuously, slowly, the twins drifted back to health. When they were "well" they were not the same robust, lively pair. Cory, who had said little before, now said even less. Carrie, who had adored the sound of her own constant chatter, now became almost as truculent as Cory. And now that I had the quiet I so often longed for, I wanted back the bird-like chitchat that rattled on incessantly to dolls, trucks, trains, boats, pillows, plants, shoes, dresses, underpants, toys, puzzles, and games.

I checked her tongue, and it seemed pale, and white. Fearfully, I straightened to gaze down on two small faces side by side on one pillow. Why had I wanted them to grow up and act their proper ages? This long illness had brought about instant age. It put dark circles under their large blue eyes, and stole their healthy color. The high temperatures and the coughing had left them with a wise look, a sometimes sly look of the old, the tired, the ones who just lay and didn't care if the sun came up, or if it went down, and stayed down. They scared me; their haunted faces took me into dreams of death.

And all the while the wind kept blowing.

Eventually they left their beds and walked about slowly. Legs once so plump and rosy and able to hop, jump, and skip were now as weak as thin straws. Now they were inclined to only creep instead of fly, and smile instead of laugh.

Wearily, I fell face down on my bed and thought and thought and thought—what could Chris and I do to restore their babyish charm?

There was nothing either he or I could do, though we would have given our health to restore theirs.

"Vitamins!" proclaimed Momma when Chris and I took pains to point out the unhealthy differences in our twins. "Vitamins are exactly what they need, and what you two need, as well—from now on, each one of you must take a daily vitamin capsule." Even as she said this, her slim and elegant hand rose to fluff the glory of her beautifully coiffed, shining hair.

"Does fresh air and sunshine come in capsules?" I asked, perching on a nearby bed, and glaring hard at a mother who refused to see what was wrong. "When each of us has swallowed a vitamin capsule a day, will that give to us the radiant good health we had when we lived normal lives, and spent most of our days outside?"

Momma was wearing pink—she did look lovely in pink. It put roses in her cheeks, and her hair glowed with rosy warmth.

"Cathy," she said, tossing me a patronizing glance while she moved to hide her hands, "why do you incessantly persist in making everything so hard for me? I do the best I can. Really I do. And, yes, if you want the truth, in vitamins you *can* swallow the good health the outdoors bestows—that is exactly the reason so many vitamins are made."

Her indifference put more pain in my heart. My eyes flashed over to Chris, who had bowed his head low, taking all this in, but saying nothing. "How long is our imprisonment going to last, Momma?"

"A short while, Cathy, only a short while longer—believe that."

"Another month?"

"Possibly."

"Could you manage, somehow, to sneak up here and take the twins outside, say, for a ride in your car? You could plan it so the servants wouldn't see. I think it would make an immense amount of difference. Chris and I don't have to go."

She spun around and glanced at my older brother to see if he were in this plot with me, but surprise was a dead giveaway on his face. "No! Of course not! I can't take a risk tike that! Eight servants work in this house, and though their quarters are quite cut off from the main house, there is always someone looking out a window, and they would hear me start up the car. Being curious, they'd look to see which direction I took."

My voice turned cold. "Then would you please see if you can manage to bring up fresh fruit, especially bananas. You know how the twins love bananas, and they haven't had one since we came."

"Tomorrow I'll bring bananas. Your grandfather doesn't like them."

"What has *he* got to do with it?"

"It's the reason bananas are not purchased."

"You drive back and forth to secretarial school every week-day—stop yourself and buy the bananas—and more peanuts, and raisins. And why can't they have a box of popcorn once in a while? Certainly that won't rot their teeth!"

Pleasantly she nodded, and verbally agreed. "And what would you like for yourself?" she asked.

"Freedom! I want to be let out. I'm tired of being in a locked room. I want the twins out; I want Chris out. I want you to rent a house, buy a house, steal a house—but get us out of *this* house!"

"Cathy," she began to plead, "I'm doing the best I can. Don't I bring you gifts every time I come through the door? What is it you lack besides bananas? Name it!"

"You promised we'd stay up here but a short while—and it's been months."

She spread her hands in a supplicating gesture. "Do you expect me to kill my father?"

Numbly I shook my head.

"You leave her alone!" Chris exploded the moment the door closed behind his goddess. "She does try to do the best she can by us! Stop picking on her! It's a wonder she comes to see us at all, what with you riding her back, with your everlasting questions, like you don't trust her. How do you know how much she suffers? Do you believe she's happy knowing her four children are locked in one room, and left to play in an attic?"

It was hard to tell about someone like our mother, just what she was thinking, and what she was feeling. Her expression was always calm, unruffled, though she often appeared tired. If her clothes were new, and expensive, and we seldom saw her wear the same thing twice, she brought us many new and expensive clothes, too. Not that it mattered what we wore. Nobody saw us but the the grandmother, and we could have worn rags, which, indeed, might have put a smile of pleasure on her face.

We didn't go up to the attic when it rained, or when it snowed. Even on clear days, there was that wind to snarl fiercely as it blew, screaming and tearing through the cracks of the old house.

One night Cory woke up and called to me, "Make the wind go away, Cathy."

I left my bed and Carrie, who was fast asleep on her side, crawled under the covers beside Cory, and tightly I held him in my arms. Poor little thin body, wanting to be loved so much by his real mother . . . and he had only me. He felt too small, so fragile, as if that rampaging wind could blow him away. I lowered my face into his clean, sweet-smelling curly blond hair and kissed him there, as I had when he was a baby, and I had replaced my dolls with living babies. "I can't make the wind go away, Cory. Only God can do that."

"Then tell God I don't like the wind," he said sleepily. "Tell God the wind wants to come in and get me."

I gathered him closer, held him tighter . . . *never going to let the wind take Cory away, never!* But I knew what he meant

"Tell me a story, Cathy, so I can forget the wind."

There was a favorite story I had concocted to please Cory, all about a fantasy world where little children lived in a small cozy home, with a mother and father who were much, much bigger, and powerful enough to scare away frightening things. A family of six, with a garden out in back, where giant trees held swings, and where real flowers grew—the kind that knew how to die in the fall, and how to come up again in the spring. There was a pet dog named Clover, and a cat named Calico, and a yellow bird sang in a golden cage, all day long, and everybody loved everybody, and nobody was ever whipped, spanked, yelled at, nor were any of the doors locked, nor the draperies closed.

"Sing me a song, Cathy. I like it when you sing me to sleep."

I held him snugly in my arms and began to sing lyrics I had written myself to music I had heard Cory hum over and over again . . . his own mind-music. It was a song meant to take away from his fear of the wind, and perhaps take from me my fears too. It was my very first attempt to rhyme.

> I hear the wind when it sweeps down from the hill,
> It speaks to me, when the night is still,
> It whispers in my ear,
> The words I never hear,
> Even when he's near.
>
> I feel the breeze when it blows in from the sea,
> It lifts my hair, it caresses me,
> It never takes my hand,
> To show it understands,
> It never touches me, ten-der-ly.
>
> Someday I know I'm gonna climb this hill,
> I'll find another day,
> Some other voice to say the words I've gotta hear,
> If I'm to live, another year. . . .

And my little one was asleep in my arms, breathing evenly, feeling safe. Beyond his head Chris lay with his eyes wide open, fixed upward on the ceiling. When my song was over, he turned his head and met my eyes. His fifteenth birthday had come and gone, with a bakery cake, and ice cream to mark the occasion as special. Gifts—they came every day, almost. Now he had a polaroid camera, a new and better watch. Great. Wonderful. How could he be so easily pleased?

Didn't he see our mother wasn't the same anymore? Didn't he notice she no longer came every day? Was he so gullible he believed everything she said, every excuse she made?

Christmas Eve. We had been five months at Foxworth Hall. Not once had we been down into the lower sections of this enormous house, much less to the outside. We kept to the rules: we said grace before every meal; we knelt and said prayers beside our beds every night; we were modest in the bathroom; we kept our thoughts clean, pure, innocent . . . and yet, it seemed to me, day by day our meals grew poorer and poorer in quality.

I convinced myself it didn't really matter if we missed out on one Christmas shopping spree. There would be other Christmases when we were rich, rich, rich, when we could go into a store and buy anything we wanted. How beautiful we'd be in our magnificent clothes, with our stylish manners, and soft, eloquent voices that told the world we were somebodies . . . somebodies who were special . . . loved, wanted, needed somebodies.

Of course Chris and I knew there wasn't a real Santa Claus. But we very much wanted the twins to believe in Santa Claus, and not miss out on all that glorious enchantment of a fat jolly man who whizzed about the world to deliver to all children exactly what they wanted—even when they didn't know what they wanted until they had it.

What would childhood be like without believing in Santa Claus? Not the kind of childhood I wanted for our twins!

Even for those locked away, Christmas was a busy time, even for one beginning to despair, and doubt, and distrust. Secretly, Chris and I had been making gifts for Momma (who really didn't need anything), and gifts for the twins—plushy stuffed animals that we tediously backstitched by hand, and then filled with cotton. I did all the embroidery work on the faces when they were still flat. I was, in private in the bathroom, knitting Chris a cap of scarlet wool—it grew and it grew and it grew; I think Momma must have forgotten to tell me something about gauge.

Then Chris came up with an absolutely idiotic and horrific suggestion. "Let's make the grandmother a gift, too. It's really not right to leave her out. She does bring up our food and milk, and who knows, a token like this may be just the thing needed to win over her affection. And think how much more enjoyable our lives would be if she could tolerate us."

I was dopey enough to think it might work, and for hours and hours we slaved on a gift for an old witch who hated us. In all this time she had never even once said our names.

We bonded tan linen to a stretcher frame, glued on different colored stones, then carefully applied gold and brown cording. If we made a mistake, ever so painstakingly we'd do it over and make it right so *she* wouldn't notice. She was bound to be a perfectionist who'd see the slightest flaw and frown. And never, truly, would we give *her* anything less than our best efforts could produce.

"You see," said Chris again, "I really do believe we have a chance in winning her over to our side. After all, she is our grandmother, and people *do* change. No one is static. While Momma works to charm her father, we must work to charm her mother. And even if she refuses to look at me, she does look at you."

She didn't look at me, not really, she only saw my hair—for some reason she was fascinated by my hair.

"Remember, Cathy, she did give us yellow chrysanthemums." He was right—that alone was a strong straw to grasp.

In the late afternoon, toward dusk, Momma came to our room bearing a live Christmas tree in a small wooden tub. A balsam tree—what could smell more like Christmas? Momma's wool dress was of bright red jersey; it clung and showed off all the curves I hoped to have one day. She was laughing and gay, making us happy, too, as she stayed to help us trim the tree with the miniature ornaments and lights she'd brought along. She gave us four stockings to drape on the bedposts for Santa to find and fill.

"Next year this time we'll be living in our own house," she said brightly, and I believed.

"Yes," said Momma, smiling, filling all of us with cheer, "next year this time life will be so wonderful for all of us. We'll have plenty of money to buy a grand home of our own, and everything you want will be yours. In no time at all, you'll forget this room, the attic. And all the days you have all endured so bravely will be forgotten, just like it never happened."

She kissed us, and said she loved us. We watched her leave and didn't feel bereft, as before. She filled all our eyes, all our hopes and dreams.

Momma came in the night while we slept. In the morning I woke up to see the stockings filled to the brim. And gifts galore were stacked under the small table where the tree was, and in every empty, available space in that room were all the toys for the twins that were too large and awkward to wrap.

My eyes met with Chris's. He winked, grinned, then bounded from his bed. He grabbed for the silver bells attached to red plastic reins, and he shook them vigorously above his head. "Merry Christmas!" he boomed. "Wake up, everybody! Cory, Carrie, you sleepyheads—open your eyes, get up, and behold! Look and see what Santa Claus brought!"

They came so slowly out of dreams, rubbing at sticky eyes, staring in disbelief at the many toys, at the beautifully wrapped packages with name tags, at the striped stockings stuffed with cookies, nuts, candy, fruit, chewing gum, peppermint sticks, chocolate Santas.

Real candy—at last! Hard candy, that colorful kind that churches and schools gave out at their parties, the best kind of candy for making black holes in your teeth. Oh, but it looked and tasted so Christmasy!

Cory sat on his bed, bedazzled, and again his small fists lifted to rub at his eyes, and he appeared too bewildered for speech.

But Carrie could always find words. "How did Santa Claus find us?"

"Oh, Santa has magic eyes," explained Chris, who lifted Carrie up and swung her to his shoulder, and then he reached to do this to Cory, too. He was doing as Daddy would have done, and tears came to my eyes.

"Santa would never overlook children deliberately," he said, "and besides, he knew you were here. I made sure he knew, for I sat down and wrote him one very long letter, and gave him our address, and I made out a list of things we wanted that was three feet long."

How funny, I thought. For the list of what all four of us wanted was so short and simple. We wanted outside. We wanted our freedom.

I sat up in bed and looked around, and felt a sour-sweet lump in my throat. Momma had tried, oh, yes. She'd tried, done her best from the way it looked. She did love us, she did care. Why, it must have taken her months to buy all of this.

I was ashamed and full of contrition for everything mean and ugly I'd thought. That's what came from wanting everything, and at once, and having no patience, and no faith.

Chris turned to look at me questioningly. "Aren't you ever gonna get up? Gonna sit there the whole day through—you don't like gifts anymore?"

While Cory and Carrie tore off gift wrappings, Chris came over to me and stretched out his hand. "Come, Cathy, enjoy the only Christmas you'll have in your twelfth year. Make this a unique Christmas, different from any we will experience in the future." His blue eyes pleaded.

He was wearing rumpled red pajamas piped in white, and his gold hair fluffed out wildly. I was wearing a red nightgown made of fleece, and my long hair was far more disheveled than his. Into his warm hand I put my own, and I laughed. Christmas was Christmas, no matter where you were, and whatever the circumstances, it was still a day to enjoy. We opened everything wrapped, and we tried on our new clothes while stuffing candy into our mouths before breakfast. And "Santa" had left a note telling us to hide the candy from a certain "you-know-who." After all, candy still caused cavities. Even on Christmas Day.

I sat on the floor wearing a stunning new robe of green velvet. Chris had a new robe of red flannel to match his pajamas. I dressed the twins in their new robes of bright blue. I don't think there could have been four happier children than we were early that morning. Chocolate bars were devilishly divine and made even sweeter because they were forbidden. It was pure heaven to hold that chocolate in my mouth and slowly, slowly let it melt while I squeezed my eyelids tight to better savor the taste. And when I looked, Chris had his eyes closed too. Funny how the twins ate their chocolate, with wide open eyes, so full of surprise. Had they forgotten about candy? It seemed so, for they appeared to be holding paradise in their mouths. When we heard the doorknob rattle, we quickly hid the candy under the nearest bed.

It was the grandmother. She came in quietly, with the picnic basket. She put the basket on the gaming table. She didn't greet us with "Merry Christmas," nor did she say good morning, nor even smile, or show in any way that this was a special day. And we were not to speak to her unless she spoke to us first.

It was with reluctance and fear, and also with great hope, that I picked up the long package wrapped in red foil that had come from one of Momma's gifts to us. Beneath that beautiful paper was our collage painting on which all four of us had worked to create a child's version of the perfect garden. The old trunks in the attic had provided us with fine materials, such as the gossamer silk to make the pastel butterflies that hovered over bright yarn flowers. How Carrie had wanted to make purple butterflies with red spots—she loved purple combined with red! If ever a more glorious butterfly existed—it wouldn't be a live one—it would be Cory's made of yellow, with green and black splotches, and tiny little red stone eyes. Our trees were made of brown cording, combined with tiny tan pebbles to look like bark, and the branches gracefully entwined so brightly colored birds could perch or fly between the leaves. Chris and I had taken chicken feathers from old pillows and dipped them in watercolors, and dried them, and used an old toothbrush to comb the matted hairs, and make them lovely again.

It may be conceited to say that our picture showed signs of true artistry, and a great deal of creative ingenuity. Our composi-

tion was balanced, yet it had rhythm, style . . . and a charm that
had brought tears to our mother's eyes when we showed it to
her. She had to turn her back so we, too, wouldn't cry. Oh, yes,
by far this collage was the very best piece of artwork we had as
yet turned out.

Trembling, apprehensive, I waited to time my approach so
her hands would be empty. Since the grandmother never looked
at Chris, and the twins were so terrified of her they shriveled in
her presence, it was up to me to give her the gift . . . and darned
if I could make my feet move. Sharply, Chris nudged me with
his elbow. "Go on," he whispered, "she'll go out the door in a
minute."

My feet seemed nailed to the floor. I held the long red package across both my arms. From the very positioning it seemed a
sacrificial offering, for it wasn't easy to give her anything, when
she had given us nothing but hostility, and was waiting her
chance to give us pain.

That Christmas morning, she succeeded very well in giving
us pain, even without a whip or a word.

I wanted to greet her in the proper way and say, "Merry
Christmas Day, Grandmother. We wanted to give you a little
something. Really, don't thank us; it was no trouble at all. Just a
little something to show how much we appreciate the food you
bring to us each day, and the shelter you have given us." No, no,
she would think me sarcastic if I put it that way. Much better to
say something like this: "Merry Christmas, we hope you like
this gift. We all worked on it, even Cory and Carrie, and you can
keep it so when we're gone, you'll know we did try, we did."

Just to see me near with the gift held before me took her by
surprise.

Slowly, with my eyes lifting to bravely meet hers, I held out
our Christmas offering. I didn't want to plead with my eyes. I
wanted her to take it, and like it, and say thank you, even if she
said it coldly. I wanted her to go to bed this night and think about
us, that maybe we weren't so bad, after all. I wanted her to digest

and savor all the work we'd put into her gift, and I wanted her to question the right and wrong of how she treated us.

In the most withering way, her cold and scornful eyes lowered to the long box we'd wrapped in red. On the top was a sprig of artificial holly and a huge silver bow. A card was tied to the bow, and read: "To Grandmother, from Chris, Cathy, Cory, and Carrie."

Her gray-stone eyes lingered on the card long enough to read it. Then she lifted her gaze to stare directly into my hopeful eyes, pleading, begging, wanting so much to be assured we weren't—as I sometimes feared—evil. Back to the box her eyes skipped, then deliberately she turned her back. Without a word she stalked out of the door, slammed it hard, then locked it from the other side. I was left in the middle of the room, holding the end product of many long hours of striving for perfection and beauty.

Fools!—that's what we'd been! Damned fools!

We'd never win her over! She'd always consider us Devil's spawn! As far as she was concerned, we really *didn't* exist.

And it hurt, oh, you bet, it did hurt. Right down to my bare feet I ached, and my heart became a hollow ball shooting pains through my chest. Behind me, I could hear Chris raspily breathing in and out, and the twins began to whimper.

This was my time to be adult, and keep the poise that Momma used so well and so effectively. I patterned my movements, and my expressions, after those of my mother. I used my hands the way she used hers. I smiled as she did, slow and beguiling.

And what did I do to demonstrate my maturity?

I hurled the package to the floor! I swore, using words I'd never said aloud before! I raised my foot and stomped down on it, and heard the cardboard box crunch. I screamed! Wild with fury, I jumped with both feet onto the gift, and I wildly stomped and jumped until I heard the cracking of the beautiful old frame we'd found in the attic, and reglued, and refinished and made it look almost like new again. I hated Chris for persuading me that we could win over a woman made of stone! I hated Momma for putting us in this position! She should have known her mother better; she should have sold shoes in a department store; certainly there was something she could have done but what she did.

Beneath the assault of someone wild and frenzied, the dry frame shattered into splinters; all our labor was gone, gone.

"Stop!" cried Chris. "We can keep it for ourselves!"

Though he ran fast to prevent total destruction, the fragile painting was ruined. Forever gone. I was in tears.

Then I was bending down, crying, and picking up the silk butterflies Cory and Carrie had made so painstakingly, with so much effort wasted to color the wings gloriously. Pastel butterflies I was to keep all my life long.

Chris held me fast in his arms while I sobbed as he tried to comfort me with fatherly words: "It's all right. It doesn't matter what she does. We were right, and she was wrong. We tried. She never tries."

We sat on the floor silent now amidst our gifts. The twins were quiet, their big eyes full of doubts, wanting to play with their toys, and undecided because they were our mirrors, and they would reflect our emotions—whatever they were. Oh, the pity of seeing them so made me ache again. I was twelve. I should learn at some time in my life how to act my age, and hold onto my poise, and not be a stick of dynamite always ready to explode.

Into our room Momma came, smiling and calling out her Christmas greetings. She came bearing more gifts, including a huge dollhouse that once had been hers . . . and her hateful mother's. "This gift is *not* from Santa Claus," she said, putting down the house on the floor with great care, and now, I swear, there wasn't one inch of uncluttered space left. "This is my present to Cory and Carrie." She hugged them both, and kissed their cheeks, and told them now they could "pretend house" and "pretend parents" and "pretend host and hostess," just as she used to do when she was a child of five.

If she noticed none of us was really excited by that grand dollhouse, she didn't comment. With laughter, and gay charm, she knelt on the floor and sat back on her heels, and told us of how very much she used to love this dollhouse.

"It is very valuable, too," she gushed. "On the right market, a dollhouse like this would bring a fabulous fortune. Just the miniature porcelain dolls with the moveable joints alone are priceless, their faces all hand-painted. The dolls are made in scale to the house, as is the furniture, the paintings—everything, in fact. The house was handcrafted by an artist who lived in England. Each chair, table, bed, lamp, chandelier—all are genuine reproductions of antiques. I understand it took the craftsman twelve years to complete this.

"Look at how the little doors open and close, perfectly hung—which is more than you can say for the house you're living in," she went on. "And all the drawers slide in and out. There's a tiny little key to lock the desk, and look how some of the doors slide into the walls—pocket doors, they are called. I wish this house had doors like that; I don't know why they went out of fashion. And see the hand-carved moldings near the ceiling, and the wainscoting in the dining room and library—and the teensy books on the shelves. Believe it or not, if you have a microscope, you can read the text!"

She demonstrated with knowing, careful fingers all the fascinations of a dollhouse only children of the extremely wealthy could ever hope to own.

Chris, of course, had to pull out a tiny book and hold it close to his squinting eyes, to see for himself print so small you needed a microscope. (There was a very special type of microscope he hoped to own someday . . . and I hoped to be the one to give it to him.)

I couldn't help but admire the skill and patience it would take to make such small furniture. There was a grand piano in the front parlor of the Elizabethan house. The piano was covered with a silken paisly shawl, with fringes of gold. Little-bitty silk flowers were centered on the dining room table. Bitsy fruit made of wax was in a silver bowl on the buffet. Two crystal chandeliers hung down, and real candles were fitted into sockets. Servants were in the kitchen, wearing aprons while they prepared dinner. A butler wore livery white while he stood near the front door to greet the arriving guests, while in the front parlor the beautifully gowned ladies stood stiffly near poker-faced men.

Upstairs in the nursery were three children, and a baby was in the crib, arms outstretched and ready to be lifted up. A side building was attached, somewhat to the rear, and in there was such a coach! And two horses were in the stables! Golly day! Who would ever dream people could make things so small! My eyes jumped to the windows, drinking in the dainty white curtains and heavy drapes, and dishes were on the dining table, and silverware, and pots and pans were in the kitchen cupboards—all so tiny they were no bigger than large green peas.

"Cathy," said Momma, putting her arm around me, "look at this little rug. It is a genuine Persian, made of pure silk. The rug in the dining room is an Oriental." And on and on she extolled the virtues of this remarkable plaything.

"How can it look so new, yet be so old?" I asked.

A dark cloud passed over Momma and shadowed her face. "When it belonged to my mother, it was kept in a huge glass box. She was allowed to look at it, but she could never touch it. When it was given to me, my father took a hammer and broke the glass box, and he allowed me to play with everything—on the condition that I would swear, with my hand on the Bible, not to break anything."

"Did you swear and did you break anything?" questioned Chris.

"Yes, I swore, and yes, I did break something." Her head bowed low so we couldn't watch her eyes. "There was another doll, a very handsome young man, and his arm came off when I tried to take off his coat. I was whipped, not only for breaking the doll, but for wanting to see what was underneath the clothes."

Chris and I sat silent, but Carrie perked up and showed great interest in the funny little dolls in their fancy, colorful costumes. She particularly favored the baby in the crib. Because she was so interested, Cory moved so he, too, could investigate the many treasures of the dollhouse.

That was when Momma turned her attention on me. "Cathy, why were you looking so solemn when I came in? Didn't you like your gifts?"

Because I couldn't answer, Chris answered for me. "She's unhappy because the grandmother refused the gift we made for her." Momma patted my shoulder but she avoided my eyes. Chris continued, "And thank you for everything—there's nothing you didn't remind Santa Claus to bring. Thank you most of all for the dollhouse. I think our twins are going to have more fun with that than anything else."

I fixed my gaze on the two tricycles for the twins to ride in the attic and strengthen their thin, weak legs while they pedaled. There were roller skates for Chris and me to use in the attic schoolroom only. That room was insulated with plastered walls, and hardwood flooring, making it more soundproof than the rest of the attic.

Momma got up from her knees, smiling mysteriously before she left. Just outside the door she said she'd be back in a second or two, and that is when she really gave us the best gift of all—a small, portable TV set! "My father gave this to me to use in my bedroom. And immediately I knew just who would enjoy it the most. Now you have a real window through which you can view the world."

Just the right words to send my hopes flying high into the sky! "Momma!" I cried out. "Your father gave you an expensive gift? Does that mean he likes you now? Has he forgiven you for marrying Daddy? Can we go downstairs now?"

Her blue eyes went dark and troubled again, and there was no joy when she told us that yes, her father was friendlier—he had forgiven her for committing a sin against God, and society. Then she said something that jumped my heart right up against my throat.

"Next week, my father is having his lawyer write me into his will. He is going to leave me everything; even this house will be mine after my mother dies. He isn't planning on leaving her money, because she has wealth she inherited from *her* father and mother."

Money—I didn't care anything about it. All I wanted was out! And suddenly I was very happy—so happy I flung my arms around Momma, kissed her cheek, and hugged her tight. Golly-lolly, this was the best day since we'd come to this house . . . and then I remembered, Momma hadn't said we could go downstairs yet. *But,* we were one step on our way to freedom.

Our mother sat on the bed and smiled with her lips, though not her eyes. She laughed at some silly things Chris and I said, and it was laughter brittle and hard, not at all her kind of laugh. "Yes, Cathy, I have become the dutiful, obedient daughter your grandfather always wanted. He speaks, I obey. He orders, I jump. I have at last managed to please him." She stopped abruptly and looked toward the double windows and the pale light beyond. "As a matter of fact, I have pleased him so well he is giving me a party tonight to reintroduce me to my old friends, and the local society. It is to be a grand affair, for my parents do everything in a big way when they entertain. They don't imbibe themselves, but they don't mind serving liquor to those who don't fear hell. So, of course, it will be catered, and there will also be a small orchestra for dancing." A party! A Christmas party! With an orchestra for dancing! And catered! And Momma was being written into the new will. Was there ever such a happy wonderful day?

"Can we watch?" Chris and I cried out almost simultaneously.

"We'll be very quiet."

"We'll hide so no one can see us."

"Please, Momma, please, it's been so long since we saw other people, and we've never been to a Christmas Day party."

We pleaded and pleaded until at last she could resist no longer. She drew Chris and me aside, to a far corner where the twins couldn't overhear, and she whispered, "There is one place where the two of you can hide and still be able to watch, but I cannot risk the twins. They're too young to be trusted and you know they can't sit still for longer than two seconds, and Carrie would probably scream out in delight, and rivet everyone's attention. So, swear on your word of honor you will not tell them."

We promised. No, of course we wouldn't tell them, even without a vow to keep our silence. We loved our little twins, and we wouldn't hurt their feelings by letting them know they were missing out.

We sang Christmas carols after Momma had gone, and the day passed cheerfully enough, though there was nothing special in the picnic basket for us to eat: ham sandwiches, which the twins didn't like, and cold slices of turkey that were still icy, as if they had been taken from the freezer. Leftovers from Thanksgiving Day.

As evening came on so early, I sat for the longest time gazing over at the dollhouse, where Carrie and Cory played happily with the tiny porcelain people and the priceless miniatures.

Funny how much you can learn from inanimate objects that a little girl had once owned, and been allowed to look at, but never touch. And then another little girl came along, and the dollhouse was given to her, and the glass box smashed just so she *could* touch the objects inside so she could be punished—when she broke something.

A shivering thought came: I wondered just what Carrie or Cory would break, and what their punishment would be.

I shoved a bit of chocolate into my mouth, and sweetened the sourness of my roving, wicked thoughts.

The Christmas Party

True to her word, not long after the twins were sound asleep, Momma slipped into our room. She looked so beautiful my heart swelled with pride and admiration, and with some envy too. Her long formal gown had a skirt of flowing green chiffon; the bodice was of a deeper green velvet, cut low to show off a lot of cleavage. Underneath the streaming panels of lighter green chiffon were shoestring straps that glittered. Diamond-and-emerald earrings dangled long and sparkling. Her scent reminded me of a musky, perfumed garden on a moonlit night somewhere in the Orient. No wonder Chris stared at her as if dazzled. Wistfully I sighed. *Oh God, please let me look like that one day . . . let me have all those swelling curves that men so admire.*

And when she moved, the panels of chiffon floated as wings, leading us out of our sequestered dim place for the first time. Down all the dark and wide halls of the northern wing we followed close at Momma's silver heels. She whispered, "There's a place where I used to hide when I was a child, to watch the adult parties without my parents knowing. It's going to be cramped for the two of you, but it's the only place where you can hide and still see. Now promise again to be quiet, and if you get sleepy, slip unseen back to your room—remember how to get there." She told us not to watch longer than an hour, for the twins would be frightened to wake up and find themselves alone. Then, possibly, they'd wander out into the hall, looking for us—and God alone knew what could happen if they did.

We were secreted inside a massive oblong dark table, with cabinet doors underneath. It was uncomfortable, and very stuffy, but we could see well enough through the fine, mesh-like screen on the back side.

Silently, Momma stole away.

Far below us was a mammoth room brilliantly lit with candles fitted in the five tiers of three gigantic crystal and gold chandeliers suspended from a ceiling so high above, we couldn't see it. I never saw so many candles burning all at once! The scent of them, the way flickering lights glowed and caught in the sparkling prisms, to scatter and refract beams of iridescence from all the jewelry the women wore, made it a scene from a dream—no, better, more like a movie, sharp, clear, a ballroom where Cinderella and Prince Charming might dance!

Hundreds of richly dressed people milled about, laughing, talking. And over in the corner towered a Christmas tree that was beyond belief! It must have been more than twenty feet high, and it sparkled all over with thousands of golden lights to shine on the colorful ornaments and bedazzle your eyes!

Dozens of servants in black-and-red uniforms flowed in and out of the ballroom, bearing silver trays laden with dainty party food, and they set them on long tables where a giant crystal fountain sprayed pale amber fluid into a silver receiving bowl. Many men and women came to hold stemmed goblets and catch the sparkling liquid. There were two other punchbowls of silver, with small matching cups—both bowls large enough for a child to bathe in. It was beautiful, glamorous, exciting, exhilarating, . . . and so good to know that happy living was still going on outside our locked door.

"Cathy," whispered Chris into my ear, "I'd sell my soul to the Devil to have just one single sip from that crystal-and-silver fountain!"

My very same thought!

Never had I felt so hungry, so thirsty, so deprived. Yet we both were charmed, enchanted, and bedazzled by all the splendor of what great wealth could buy and display. The floor where couples danced was laid out in mosaic patterns, and was waxed so it gleamed like reflecting glass. Huge gold-framed mirrors were on the walls, reflecting back the dancers so you could hardly tell the images from the reality. The frames of the many chairs and sofas lining the walls were gold-colored, and the padded seats and backs were of red velvet, or white brocade. French chairs, of course—they just had to be Louis XIV or XV. Fancy, good-golly day!

Chris and I stared at the couples, who were the most beautiful and young. We commented on their clothing, their hairstyles, and speculated on what relationships they had going for them. But most of all we watched our mother, who was the center of attention. Most often she danced with a tall, handsome man with dark hair and a big moustache. He was the one who brought her stemmed goblets, and a plate of food, and they sat on a velvet couch to eat canapes and hors d'oeuvres. I thought they sat too close. Quickly I took my eyes from them, to take a look at the three chefs behind the long tables, still cooking what looked like pancakes to me, and little sausages to be stuffed with fillings. The aroma of all that drifted up to us, making our salivary glands overwork.

Our meals were monotonous, boring things: sandwiches, soups, and that everlasting fried chicken and eternal potato salad. Down there was a gourmet feast of everything delicious. Food was hot down there. Ours was seldom even warm. We kept our milk on the attic stairs so it wouldn't sour—and sometimes we found ice on the top. If we kept our picnic basket of food on the attic stairs, the mice stole down to nibble on everything.

From time to time, Momma disappeared with that man. Where did they go, and what did they do? Did they kiss? Was she falling in love? Even from my high and remote place in the cabinet, I could tell that man was fascinated by Momma. He couldn't take his eyes from her face, or keep his hands from touching her. And when they danced to music that was slow, he held her so his cheek pressed to hers. When they stopped dancing, he kept his arm around her shoulders, or her waist—and once he dared to even touch her breast!

I thought that now she would slap his good-looking face—for I would! But she only turned and laughed, and pushed him away, saying something that must have been a warning not to do that in public. And he smiled and took her hand and raised it to his lips while their eyes locked long and meaningfully—or so I thought.

"Chris, do you see Momma with that man?"

"Sure I see them. He's just as tall as Daddy was."

"Did you see what he just did?"

"They're eating and drinking, and laughing and talking, and dancing, just like everybody else. Cathy, just think, when Momma inherits all that money, we can have parties like this on Christmas, and on our birthdays. Why, in the future, we might even have some of the very same guests we see now. Let's send invitations to our friends back in Gladstone. Boy, won't they be surprised to see what we inherit!"

Just then, Momma and that man got up from the couch and left. So we fastened our charmed eyes on the second most attractive woman in the group below and watched her, and pitied her, for how could she compete with our mother?

Then into the ballroom strode our grandmother looking neither left nor right, nor smiling at anyone. Her dress wasn't gray—and that alone was enough to astonish us. Her long formal gown was of ruby-red velvet, tight in the front and flowing in the back, and her hair was piled high on her head, and curled elaborately, and ruby and diamond jewelry sparkled on her neck, ears, arms and fingers. Who would ever think that impressive, regal-looking woman down there was the menacing grandmother who visited us each day?

Reluctantly, we had to admit in whispers back and forth: "She does look magnificent."

"Yes, very impressive. Like an Amazon, too big."

"A mean Amazon."

"Yeah, a warrior Amazon, ready to do battle with the glare of her eyes alone. She doesn't really need any other weapon."

That's when we saw him! Our unknown grandfather!

It stole my breath away to look down and see a man so very much like our father, if he had lived long enough to become old and feeble. He sat in a shiny wheelchair, dressed in a tuxedo, and his formal shirt was white with black trim. His thinning blond hair was almost white, and it shone silver under the lights. His skin was unlined, at least viewed from our far and high and hidden place. Appalled, as well as fascinated, neither Chris nor I could move our eyes anywhere else once we spied him.

He was fragile looking, but still unnaturally handsome for a man of his great age of sixty-seven, and a man who was near dead. Suddenly, frighteningly, he raised his head and he gazed upward, directly at our hiding place! For one awful, terrifying moment, it seemed he knew we were there, hidden behind the wire screen! A small smile played on his lips. Oh, dear God, what did that smile mean?

Still, he didn't look nearly as heartless as the grandmother. Could he truly be the cruel and arbitrary tyrant we presumed him to be? From the gentle, kindly smiles he bestowed on all those who came up to greet him, and shake his hand, and pat his shoulder, he seemed benign enough. Just an old man in a wheel chair, who really didn't look very sick. Yet, he was the one who had ordered our mother to be stripped and whipped from her neck down to her heels, and he had watched. So, how could we ever forgive him for that?

"I didn't know he would look like Daddy," I whispered to Chris.

"Why not? Daddy was his much younger half-brother. Grandfather was a grown man before our father was born, and married, too, with two sons of his own, before he had a half-brother."

That was Malcolm Neal Foxworth down there, the one who had kicked out his younger step-mother and her little son.

Poor Momma. How could we blame her for falling in love with a half-uncle when he was as young, and as handsome and charming as our father had been? With such parents as she'd described, she *did* have to have someone to love, and she *did* need to be loved in return—she did . . . he did.

Love, it came unbidden.

You couldn't help whom you fell in love with—cupid's arrows were ill aimed. Such ran the whispered comments between Chris and me.

Then, we were suddenly hushed by the footfalls and voices of two people approaching our hiding place.

"Corrine hasn't changed at all," said a man unseen by us, "only to grow more beautiful, and even more mysterious. She's a very intriguing woman."

"Hah! That's because you always did have a yen for her, Al," responded his female companion. "Too bad she didn't have eyes for you instead of Christopher Foxworth. Now there was a man who was really something else. But I marvel that those two narrow-minded bigots down there would allow themselves to forgive Corrine for marrying her half-uncle."

"They have to forgive her. When you have only one child left out of three, you are forced to take that one back into the fold."

"Isn't it peculiar how things work out?" asked the woman, her voice thick and guttural from too much liquor. "Three children . . . and only the despised, regretted one is left to inherit all of this."

The half-drunken man chortled. "Corrine wasn't always so

despised. Remember how the old man adored her? She could do no wrong in his eyes until she eloped with Christopher. But that harridan mother of hers never had any patience with her daughter. Jealous, maybe. But what a luscious, rich plum to fall into the hands of Bartholomew Winslow. Wish it were mine!" said the unseen Al, wistfully.

"I'll bet you do!" sarcastically scoffed the woman, who set something down on our table that sounded like a glass with ice inside. "A beautiful, young, and rich woman is indeed a plum for any man. Much too heady for a slob like you, Albert Donne. Corrine Foxworth would never look at you, not now, not even when you were young. Besides, you're stuck with me."

The bickering pair drifted out of earshot. Other voices came and went as the long hours passed. My brother and I were tired now of watching, and we were both very much needing the bathroom. Plus we were worried about the twins, left alone in the bedroom. What if one of the guests wandered into the forbidden room and saw the sleeping twins? Then all the world—and our grandfather—would know that our mother had four children.

A crowd gathered around our hiding place to laugh, talk, and drink. It took them forever to move away and give us the opportunity to open the cabinet door with extreme caution. Seeing no one, we scampered out, then dashed pell-mell in the direction from which we'd come. Breathless and panting, our bladders full enough to pop, we reached our quiet, cloistered place unseen, unheard.

And just as we'd left them, our twins lay deeply asleep in separate beds. They seemed identical, weak-looking pale dolls . . . like children used to look a long time ago in the pictures in history books. They weren't today's kind of children at all—but once they'd been. And they would be again, I vowed!

Next thing, Chris and I were arguing over who got to use the bathroom first—and this was easily settled. He just pushed me down on a bed and took took off, slamming the bathroom door behind him and locking it. I fumed that it seemed to take him forever to empty his bladder. Good golly, how could he hold so much?

Nature's calls eased, bickering over, we huddled together to discuss what we'd just witnessed and overheard.

"Do you think Momma plans to marry Bartholomew Winslow?" I asked, twisting my ever-present anxieties into a knot

"How do I know?" answered Chris in an offhand manner. "Though it certainly seems everybody else thinks she will, and, of course, they know more about that side of her than we do."

What an odd thing to say. Didn't we, her children, know our mother better than anyone else?

"Chris, why did you say that?"

"What?"

"What you did—about others knowing her better than we do."

"People are multi-faceted, Cathy. To us, our mother is only our mother. To others, she is a beautiful, sexy young widow who is likely to inherit a fortune. No wonder the moths all come swarming to encircle the kind of bright flame she is."

Wow! And he was taking all of this so casually, just as if it didn't matter to him one whit—when I knew it did. I thought I knew my brother very well. He must be suffering inside, just as I was, for I knew he didn't want our mother to marry again. I turned my most intuitive eyes upon him . . . ah, he wasn't nearly as detached as he seemed, and that pleased me.

I sighed, though, for I would so much like to be the eternal optimist, like him. Deep down I thought life was sure to always put me between Scylla and Charybdis, and give to me always Hobson's Choice. I had to make myself over, make myself better, and become like Chris—eternally cheerful. When I suffered, I had to learn to hide it, as he did. I had to learn to smile and never frown, and not be the genuine clairvoyant I was.

Already we had discussed between us the possibility that our mother might marry again, and neither one of us wanted that to happen. We thought of her as still belonging to our father; we wanted her to be faithful to his memory, ever constant to his first love. And if she remarried, just where would the four of us fit in? Would that Winslow man, with his handsome face and big moustache want four children who weren't his?

"Cathy," mused Chris aloud. "Do you realize this is the perfect time to explore this house? Our door is unlocked, the grandparents are downstairs. Momma is occupied—the perfect chance to find out all we can about this house."

"No!" I cried, frightened. "Suppose the grandmother found out? She'd whip the skin off all of us!"

"Then you stay with the twins," he said with surprising firmness. "If I'm caught, which I won't be, I'll suffer the whipping and take all the blame. Think of it this way, someday we may need to know how to escape this house." An amused smile curved his lips before he went on. "I'm going to disguise myself, anyway, just in case I'm seen."

Disguise? How?

But I'd forgotten the treasure trove of old clothes in the attic. He was up there only a few minutes before he came down, wearing an old-fashioned dark suit that wasn't much too large. Chris was big for his age. Over his blond head he'd fitted a ratty, dark wig he'd found in a trunk. Just possibly he *might* be mistaken for a small man if the lights were dim enough—a ridiculously funny-looking man!

Jauntily, he paraded back and forth in front of me. Then he leaned forward and stalked around Groucho Marx–style, holding an invisible cigar. He stopped directly in front of me, grinning self-consciously as he bowed deeply and doffed an invisble top hat in a wide and gentlemanly gesture of respect. I had to laugh, and he laughed too, and not just with his eyes, then he straightened up to say, "Now, tell me truthfully, who could recognize this dark and sinister small man as belonging to the giant Foxworth clan?"

No one! For who had ever seen a Foxworth such as he? An awkward, lean and gangling one, with clear-cut features, and dark birdnest hair, plus a smudgy pencil moustache? Not a photograph in the attic resembled what swaggered about, showing off.

"Okay, Chris, cut the act. Go on, find out what you can, but don't stay away too long, either. I don't like it here without you."

He came closer to whisper in a sly and conspiratorial stage whisper, "I'll be back soon, my fair beauty, and when I'm back, I shall bring with me all the dark and mysterious secrets of this huge, huge, old, old house." And suddenly, he caught me by surprise, and swooped to plant a kiss on my cheek.

Secrets? And he said *I* was given to exaggerations! What was the matter with him? Didn't he know that *we* were the secrets?

I was already bathed and shampooed and dressed for bed, and, of course, on Christmas night, I couldn't go to bed in a nightgown I'd worn before—not when I had several new ones "Santa" had brought. It was a lovely gown I wore, white, with full long sleeves that ruffled at the wrists, and was beaded through with blue satin ribbon, and everything was lace-edged, with smocking across the front and back of the bodice, and dainty pink roses with a tracery of delicately embroidered green leaves. It was one lovely nightgown, exquisitely made, and it made me feel beautiful and exquisite just to have it on.

Chris swept his eyes from my hair down to my bare toes that just barely peeked from beneath my long gown, and his eyes told me something they'd never said quite as eloquently before. He stared at my face, at my hair that cascaded down past my waist, and I knew it gleamed from all the brushing I gave it every day. He seemed impressed and dazzled, just as he had when he'd gazed so long at Momma's swelling bosom above the green velvet bodice.

And no wonder he had kissed me voluntarily—I was so princess-like.

He stood in the doorway, hesitating, still looking at me in my new nightgown, and I guess he was very happy to be playing the knight gallant, protective of his lady fair, of small children, and everyone who relied upon his audacity.

"Take care until you see me again," he whispered.

"Christopher," I whispered back, "all you need is a white horse and a shield."

"No," he whispered again, "a unicorn, and a lance with a green dragon's head upon its point, and back I'll gallop in my shining white armor while the blizzard blows in the month of August and the sun is mid-sky, and when I dismount you'll be looking up at someone who stands twelve feet high, so speak respectfully when you speak to me, my lady Cath-er-ine."

"Yes, my lord. Go forth and slay yonder dragon—but take not overlong, for I could be undone by all that menaces me and mine in this stone-cold castle, where all the drawbridges are up, and the portcullises are down."

"Farewell," he whispered. "Have no fear. Soon I'll be back to care for thee and thine."

I giggled as I climbed into bed to lie down beside Carrie. Sleep was an elusive stranger that night as I thought about my mother and that man, about Chris, about all boys, about men, about romance—and love. As I slipped softly into dreams, with music playing down below, my hand lifted to touch the small ring with the garnet heart-stone that my father had put on my finger when I was only seven years old. A ring I'd outgrown so long ago. My touchstone. My talisman, worn now on a very fine gold chain.

Merry Christmas, Daddy.

Christopher's Exploration
and Its Repercussions

Suddenly rough hands seized me by the shoulders and shook me awake! Jolted, startled, I stared with frightened eyes at a woman I hardly recognized as my mother. She glared at me and demanded in an angry voice, "Where is your brother?"

Taken aback that she could speak and look as she did, so out of control, I cringed from her attack, then rolled my head to look at the bed three feet from the one I was in. Empty. Oh, he had stayed too long.

Should I lie? Protect him, and say he was in the attic? No, this was our mother who loved us; she'd understand. "Chris went to look over the rooms on this floor."

Honesty was the best policy, wasn't it? And we never lied to our mother, or to each other. Only to the grandmother, and then only when necessary.

"Damn, damn, damn!" she swore, reddened by a new flood of temper that was now directed at me. Most certainly her precious older son, whom she favored above all, would never betray her without my devilish influence. She shook me until I felt like a rag doll, and my eyes were loose and rolling.

"Just for this, I will never, for any reason, or any special occasion, allow you and Christopher out of this room again! You both gave me your word—and you broke it! How can I trust either one of you now? And I thought I could. I thought you loved me, that you would never betray me!"

My eyes widened more. Had we betrayed her? I was shocked too that she could act the way she was—it seemed to me she was betraying *us*.

"Momma, we haven't done anything bad. We were very quiet in the chest. People came and went all around us, but nobody knew we were there. We *were* quiet. No one knows we're here. And you can't say you won't let us out again. You've got to let us out of here! You can't keep us locked up and hidden away forever."

She stared at me in an odd, harassed way, without answering. I thought she might slap me, but no, she released her hold on my shoulders and spun around to leave. The flaring chiffon panels of her couturier gown seemed like wild fluttering wings, wafting sweet, flowery perfume that went ill with her fierce demeanor.

Just as she was about to leave the room, apparently going to hunt up Chris herself, the door opened, and my brother stole quietly inside. He eased to the door, then turned and looked in my direction. His lips parted to speak. That's when he saw our mother and the strangest expression came over his face.

For some reason, his eyes didn't light up as they customarily did when he saw our mother.

Moving swiftly and with strong purpose, Momma reached his side. Her hand lifted and she delivered a hard, stinging slap against his cheek! Then, before he could recover from the shock of that, her left hand lifted, and the opposite cheek felt the strength of her anger!

Now Chris's pale and stunned face wore two large red splotches.

"If you ever do anything like this again, Christopher Foxworth, I will myself whip not only you, but Cathy, as well."

What color Chris had left in his unnaturally pale face drained away, leaving those red slap marks on his wan cheeks like smeary handprints of blood.

I felt my own blood drain down into my feet; a stinging sensation began behind my ears as my strength grew small, and I stared at that woman who seemed a stranger now, like some woman we didn't know, and one I didn't care to know. Was that our mother who usually spoke to us only with kindness and love? Was that the mother who was so understanding of our misery from such a long, long confinement? Was the house already doing "things" to her—making her different? It came then in a rush . . . yes, all the little things totaled up . . . she *was* changing. She didn't come as often as she used to, not every day, most certainly not twice a day as she had in the beginning. And, oh, I was scared, like everything trusted and dependable was torn from beneath our feet—and only toys, games, and other gifts were left.

She must have seen something in Chris's stunned expression, something that made her hot anger disappear. She drew him into her open arms and covered his wan, splotched, moustached face with quick little kisses that sought to take away the harm she'd done. Kiss, kiss, kiss, finger his hair, stroke his cheek, draw his head against her soft, swelling breasts, and let him drown in the sensuality of being cuddled close to that creamy flesh that must excite even a youth of his tender years.

"I'm sorry, darling," she whispered, tears in her eyes and in her voice, "forgive me, please forgive me. Don't look so frightened. How can you be afraid of me? I didn't mean it about the whippings. I love you. You know that. I would never whip you or Cathy. Have I ever? I'm not myself, because I have everything going my way now—our way. You just can't do anything to spoil it for all of us. And that's the only reason I slapped you."

She cupped his face between her palms and kissed him full on lips that were puckered from the tight squeeze of her hands. And those diamonds, those emeralds kept flashing, flashing . . . signal lights, meaning something. And I sat and watched, and wondered, and felt . . . felt, oh, I didn't know how I felt, except confused and bewildered, and very, very young. And the world all about us was wise, and old, so old.

Of course he forgave her, just as I did. And of course we had to know what was going her way, and our way.

"Please, Momma, tell us what it is—please."

"Another time," she said, in a terrible hurry to get back to the party before she was missed. More kisses for the both of us. And it came to me then, I had never felt my cheek against the softness of her breast.

"Another time, perhaps tomorrow, and I'll tell you everything," she said, hurriedly giving us more kisses, and saying more soothing words to take away our anxieties. She leaned over me to kiss Carrie, and then went over to Cory to kiss his cheek too.

"You have forgiven me, Christopher?"

"Yes, Momma. I understand, Momma. We should have stayed in this room. I should never have gone exploring."

She smiled and said "Merry Christmas, and I'll be seeing you soon." And then out the door she went, closing and locking it behind her.

Our first Christmas Day upstairs was over. The clock down the hall had struck one. We had a room full of gifts, a TV set, the chess game we'd asked for, one red and one blue tricycle, new clothes that were heavy and warm, plus many sweet things to eat, and Chris and I had been to a magnificent party—in a way. Yet, something new had come into our lives, a facet of our mother's character we had never experienced before. For just a brief moment or two, Momma seemed exactly like our grandmother!

In the dark, on one bed, with Carrie on one side of me, and Chris on the other, he and I lay holding each other. He smelled different than I did. My head was on his boyish chest and he was losing weight. I could hear his heart throbbing along with the faint music still drifting to our ears. He had his hand in my hair, curling a tendril over and over around his fingers.

"Chris, being grown up is awfully complicated, isn't it?"

"Guess so."

"I always thought when you were an adult you knew how to handle any situation. You were never in doubt as to what is wrong, and what is right. I never guessed adults floundered around, too, just like us."

"If you're thinking of Momma, she didn't mean what she said and did. I believe, though I'm not sure, once you are an adult, and come back to the home of your parents to live, for some odd reason, you're reduced to being a child again, and dependent. Her parents tug her one way—and we pull her another way—and now she's got that man with the moustache. He must be tugging her his way, too."

"I hope she never marries again! We need her more than that man does!"

Chris didn't say anything.

"And that TV set she brought us—she waited for her father to give her one, when she could have bought us one herself months ago, instead of buying herself so many clothes. And the jewelry! She's always wearing new rings, and new bracelets, earrings and necklaces."

Very slowly he expressed a careful explanation of our mother's motives. "Look at it this way, Cathy. If she had given us a TV the first day we came, we would have sat down in front of it and stared all day long. Then we wouldn't have created a garden in the attic where the twins can play happily. We wouldn't have done anything but sit and watch. And look how much we've learned during our long, long days, like how to make flowers and animals. I paint better now than when I came, and look at the books we've read to improve our minds. And you, Cathy, you've changed too."

"How? How have I changed? Name it."

He rolled his head from side to side on the pillow, expressing a sort of embarrassed helplessness.

"All right. You don't have to say anything nice to me. But

before you leave this bed and get into your own, tell me all you found out—everything. Don't leave out a thing, not even your thoughts. I want you to make me feel I was there with you, at your side, seeing and feeling what you did."

He turned his head so our eyes locked and he said in the weirdest voice, "You *were* there beside me. I felt you there, holding onto my hand, whispering in my ear, and I looked all the harder, just so you could see what I did."

This giant house, ruled by the sick ogre beneath, had intimidated him; I could tell that by his voice. "It's an awfully big house, Cathy, like a hotel. There are rooms and rooms, all furnished with beautiful expensive things, but you can tell they are never used. I counted fourteen rooms on this floor alone, and I think I missed a few small ones."

"Chris!" I cried out, disappointed. "Don't tell it to me that way! Make me feel I was there beside you. Start over, and tell me how it went from the second you were out of my sight."

"Well," he said, sighing, like he'd rather not, "I stole along the dark corridor of this wing, and I ran to where this hall joins that large center rotunda where we hid in the chest near the balcony. I didn't bother looking in any of the northern-wing rooms. As soon as I was where people might see me, I had to be careful. The party was nearing its peak. The revelry down there was even louder, everybody sounded drunk. In fact, one man was singing in a foolish way something about wanting his missing two front teeth. It was so funny sounding, I stole over to the balustrade and looked down on all the people. They looked odd, foreshortened, and I thought, I'll have to remember that, so when I draw people from an above the eye-level viewpoint, they'll look natural. Perspective makes all the difference in a painting."

It made all the difference in everything, if you asked me.

"Of course it was Momma I searched for," he continued after I urged him on, "and the only people I recognized down there were our grandparents. Our grandfather was beginning to look tired, and even as I watched, a nurse came and pushed him out of sight. And I watched, for it gave me the general direction to his room in back of the library."

"Was she wearing a white uniform?"

"Of course. How else would I know she was a nurse?"

"Okay, go on. Don't leave out a thing."

"Well, no sooner did the grandfather leave than the grand-mother left, too, and then I heard voices coming up one of the stairways! You never saw anyone move quicker than I did! I couldn't hide in the chest without revealing myself, so I ducked into a corner where a suit of armor stood on a pedestal. You know that armor must have been worn by a fully grown man, and yet I'll bet you a hundred it wouldn't fit me, though I would have liked to try it on. And as for who was coming up the stairs, it was Momma, and with her she had the same dark-haired man with the moustache."

"What did they do? Why were they upstairs?"

"They didn't see me hiding in the shadows, I guess, because they were so preoccupied with each other. That man wanted to see some bed Momma has in her room."

"Her bed—he wanted to see her bed? Why?"

"It's a special kind of bed, Cathy. He said to her, 'C'mon, you've held out long enough.' His voice sounded teasing. Then he added, 'It's time you showed me that fabulous swan bed I've heard so much about.' Apparently Momma was worried that we might still be hidden in the chest. She glanced that way, looking uneasy. But she agreed and said, 'All right, Bart—however, we can linger but a moment, for you know what everyone will sus-pect if we stay away too long.' And he chuckled and teased back, 'No, I can't guess what everyone would think. Tell me what they will suspect.' To me, this sounded like a challenge to let every-one think what they would. It made me angry, him saying that." And at this point Chris paused, and his breathing got heavier and faster.

"You're holding something back," I said, knowing him like a book I'd read a hundred times over. "You're protecting her! You saw something you don't want to tell me! Now that's not fair! You know we agreed the first day we came here to always be honest and fully truthful with each other—now you tell me what you saw!"

"Good gosh," he said, squirming and turning his head and refusing to look me straight in the eyes, "what difference does a few kisses make?"

"*A FEW kisses?*" I stormed. "You saw him kiss Momma more than once? What kind of kisses? Hand kisses—or real mouth-to-mouth kisses?"

A blush heated up his chest, on which my cheek was resting. It burned right through his pajamas. "They were passionate kisses, weren't they?" I threw out, convinced even without his say-so. "He kissed her, and she let him, and maybe he even touched her breasts, and stroked her buttocks, like I once saw Daddy do when he didn't know I was in the room and watching! Is that what you saw, Christopher?"

"What difference does it make?" he answered, a choke in his voice. "Whatever he did, she didn't seem to mind, though it made me feel sick."

It made me feel sick, too. Momma was only a widow of eight months then. But, sometimes eight months can feel more like eight years, and, after all, of what value was the past when the present was so thrilling, and pleasing . . . for, you bet, I could guess a lot went on that Chris wasn't ever going to tell me.

"Now, Cathy, I don't know what you're thinking, but Momma did command him to stop, and if he didn't, she wouldn't show him her bedroom."

"Oh boy, I bet he was doing something gross!"

"Kisses," said Chris, staring over at the Christmas tree, "only kisses, and a few caresses, but they did make her eyes glow, and then that Bart, he was asking her if the swan bed had once belonged to a French courtesan."

"For heaven's sake, what is a French courtesan?"

Chris cleared his throat. "It's a noun I looked up in the dictionary, and it means a woman who saves her favors for men of the aristocracy, or royalty."

"Favors—what kind of favors?"

"The kind rich men pay for," he said quickly, and went on, putting his hand over my mouth to shut me up. "And, of course, Momma denied such a bed would be in this house. She said a bed with a sinful reputation, no matter how beautiful, would be burned at night, while prayers were said for its redemption, and the swan bed was her grandmother's bed, and when she was a girl, she wanted her grandmother's bedroom suite more than she wanted anything else. But her parents wouldn't let her have those rooms, fearful she'd be contaminated by the ghost of her grandmother who wasn't exactly a saint, and not exactly a courtesan either. And then Momma laughed, kind of hard and bitterly, and told Bart her parents believed she was now so corrupted that nothing could, or would make her worse than she already was. And you know, that made me feel so bad. Momma isn't corrupted— Daddy loved her . . . they were married . . . and what married people do in private is no one else's business."

My breath caught and held. Chris always knew everything— absolutely everything!

"Well, Momma said, 'One quick look, Bart, and then back to the party.' They disappeared down a wing softly lit and inviting, and of course that gave me the general directions of her room. I cautiously peered in all directions first, before I came from out of hiding, and dashed away from the suit of armor, and into the first closed door that I saw. I rushed in, thinking that since it was dark, and the door was closed, it would be unoccupied. I closed the door behind me very softly, and then stood perfectly still, just to absorb the scent and feel of the place, the way you say you do. I had my flashlight, and I could have beamed that around right away, but I wanted to learn how you can be so intuitive, and so wary and suspicious, when everything seems perfectly normal to me. And darned if you aren't right. If the lights had been on, and I'd used the flashlight, maybe I wouldn't have noticed the strangest unnatural odor that filled the room. An odor that made me feel uneasy and kind of scared. Then, by golly, I nearly dropped my skin!"

"What—what?" I said, pushing his hand that tried to hush me. "What did you see—a monster?"

"Monster? Oh, you bet I saw *monsters! Dozens* of monsters! At least I saw their heads mounted and hung on the walls. All about me eyes were glistening—amber, green, topaz, and lemon eyes. Boy, was it scary! The light coming through the windows was colored bluish because of the snow, and it caught on the shiny teeth, and on the fangs of the lion which had its mouth wide open and was silently roaring. It had a tawny ruff of mane that made its head seem huge—it had a mute expression of anguish, or anger. And for some reason, I felt sorry for it, decapitated, mounted, stuffed—made just a thing to decorate when it should have lived out its life stalking free on the veld."

Oh, yes, I knew what he meant. My anguish was always like a mountain of rage.

"It was a trophy room, Cathy, a huge room with many animal heads. There was a tiger, and an elephant with its trunk uplifted. All the animals from Asia and Africa were displayed on one side of the huge room, and the big game from America was on the opposite wall: a grizzly bear, a brown-and-black bear, an antelope, a mountain lion, and so on. Not a fish or bird was represented, as if they didn't present enough of a challenge to the hunter who had killed to decorate that room. It was a creepy room, and yet I wanted so much for you to see it. You've just got to see it!"

Oh, heck—what did I care about the trophy room? I wanted to know about people—their secrets—that's what I wanted.

"There was a stone fireplace at least twenty feet long on the wall with the windows on either side, and above it hung a life-size oil portrait of a young man who was so much like our father it made me want to cry out. But it wasn't Daddy's portrait. As I neared, I saw a man much like our father, except in the eyes. He wore a khaki hunting outfit, with a blue shirt. The hunter rested on his rifle and he had one leg up on a log that lay on the ground. I know a little about art, enough to know that painting is a masterpiece. The artist really captured the soul of the hunter. You never saw such hard, cold, cruel and pitiless blue eyes. That alone told me it couldn't be our father even before I read the small metal plate fastened to the bottom of the goldleaf frame. It was a painting of Malcolm Neal Foxworth, our grandfather. The date showed Daddy had been five years old when that portrait was painted. And as you know, when Daddy was three, he and his mother, Alicia, had been driven away from Foxworth Hall, and he and his mother were living in Richmond then."

"Go on."

"Well, I was very fortunate nobody saw me stealing around, for I really did poke into every room. And finally I found Momma's suite of rooms. It has double doors over two steps up, and, boy, when I took a look inside, I thought I was looking into a palace! The other rooms made me anticipate something splendid, but her rooms are just beyond belief! And they had to be our mother's rooms, for Daddy's photograph was on her nightstand, and the rooms smelled of her perfume. In the center of the room, on a dais, was the fabulous swan bed! Oh! What a bed! You've never seen anything like it! It has a sleek ivory head, turned in profile, and appears ready to plunge its head under the ruffled underside of a lifted wing. It has one sleepy red eye. The wings curve gently to cup the head of an almost oval bed—I don't know how they fit sheets on it, unless they are custom-made. The designers arranged for the wingtip feathers to act as fingers, and they hold back the delicate, transparent draperies that are in all shades of pink and rose, and violet, and purple. It is really some bed . . . and those bed curtains . . . why, she must feel like a princess sleeping there. The pale mauve carpet is so thick you sink up to your ankles, and there's a large rug of white fur near the bed. There are lamps four feet high of cut-crystal, decorated with gold and silver, and two of them have black shades. There's

an ivory chaise lounge upholstered in rose-colored velvet—
something like you'd see in a Roman orgy. And at the foot of
that big swan bed—and hold your breath, for you're not going
to believe this—there was an infant swan bed! Imagine that!
Placed at the foot, and crossways. I just had to stand and wonder
why anyone would need a big wide bed, and then a little narrow
bed across the bottom. There must be a good reason, beside that
of taking a nap and not mussing the larger bed. Cathy, you've
just got to see that bed to believe it!"

I knew he'd seen a whole lot more that he didn't mention.
More that I was to see later for myself. So much I did see that I
knew why he came back and made so much of the bed without
telling me everything.

"Is this house prettier than our house in Gladstone?" I asked,
for, to me, our ranch house—eight rooms and two and a half
baths—had been the best possible.

He hesitated. It took him some time to find the right words to
say, for he was not one to speak hastily. He weighed his words
carefully that night, and that alone told much. "This is not a
pretty house. It's grand, it's big, it's beautiful, but I wouldn't call
it pretty."

I thought I knew what he meant. Prettiness was more akin to
coziness than grand, rich, and beautiful, plus huge.

And now there was nothing left to say but good night—and
don't let the bedbugs bite. I put a kiss on his cheek and pushed
him off the bed. This time he didn't complain that kisses were
only for babies and sissies—and girls. Soon he was snuggled
down beside Cory, only three feet away.

In the dark, the little live Christmas tree, two feet tall,
sparkled with tiny colored lights, like the tears I saw glistening
in my brother's eyes.

The Long Winter, and Spring, and Summer

Never had our mother spoken truer words when she said now we had a real window to look into the lives of others. That winter, the TV set took over our lives. Like others—invalids, sick people, old people—we ate, bathed, and dressed, so we could sit down to watch other people living fake lives.

During January, February, and most of March the attic was much too cold to enter. A frigid vapor hung in the air up there, eerily misting everything over, and it was scary, you bet. And miserable; even Chris had to admit that.

All of this made us very content to stay in the warmer bedroom, cuddled close together as we stared and stared and stared. The twins adored the TV so they never wanted to turn it off; even at night while we slept they wanted it on, knowing it would then wake them up in the mornings. Even the scramble of dots after the late-late shows was better to them than nothing at all. Cory, in particular, liked to wake up and see the little people behind the desks giving the news, talking about the weather; for certainly their voices welcomed him more cheerfully into another day than did the covered, dim windows.

The TV shaped us, molded us, taught us how to spell and pro-nounce difficult words. We learned how important it was to be clean, odorless, and never let wax accumulate on your kitchen floor; never let the wind muss your hair, and God forbid if you had dandruff! Then the entire world would hold you in scorn. In April I'd be thirteen, approaching the age of acne! Each day I examined my skin to see what horrors might pop up any moment. Really, we took commercials literally, believing in their value as a book of rules to see us safely through the dangers life held.

Each day that passed brought about changes in Chris and in me. Peculiar things were happening to our bodies. We grew hair where we hadn't had hair before—funny looking, crispy, amber-colored hair, darker than what was on our heads. I didn't like them, and I took the tweezers and plucked them out whenever they appeared, but they were like weeds: the more you plucked, the more came back. Chris found me one day with my arm upraised, seeking diligently to grasp one single, crinkly amber hair and ruthlessly yank it out.

"What the heck are you doing?" he shot out.

"I don't want to have to shave under my arms and I don't want to use that depilatory cream that Momma uses—it stinks!"

"You mean you've been pulling hairs from your body wher-ever they appear?"

"Sure I do. I like my body nice and neat—even if you don't."

"You're fighting a losing battle," he said with a wicked grin. "That hair is supposed to grow where it does—so leave it alone and stop thinking about looking childishly neat, and begin to think of that hair as sexy."

Sexy? Big bosoms were sexy, not crinkly, wiry hair. But I didn't say this, for little hard apples were beginning to poke out my chest, and I just hoped Chris hadn't noticed. I was very pleased I was beginning to swell out in front—when I was alone, in a private place—but I didn't want anyone else to notice. I had to abandon that forlorn hope, for I saw Chris glance quite often at my chest, and no matter how loosely my sweaters or blouses fitted, I believe those little hills betrayed my modesty.

I was coming alive, feeling things I hadn't felt before. Strange achings, longings. Wanting something, and not knowing what it was that woke me up at night, pulsating, throbbing, excited, and knowing a man was there with me, doing something I wanted him to complete, and he never did . . . he never did . . . always I woke up too soon, before I reached those climactic heights I knew he would take me to—if only I wouldn't wake up and spoil it all.

Then there was another puzzling thing. It was me who made up the beds every morning, as soon as we were up and dressed, and before the witch came in with the picnic basket. I kept seeing stains on the sheets, and they weren't large enough to be another of Cory's dreams of going to the bathroom. They were on Chris's side of the bed. "For heaven's sakes, Chris. I sure hope *you* don't take to dreaming of being in the bathroom while you're still asleep in bed." I just couldn't believe his fantastic tale of something he called "nocturnal emissions!"

"Chris, I think you should tell Momma, so she can take you to a doctor. Whatever you have might be contagious, something Cory could catch, and he's messy enough already in the bed without adding more."

He threw me a look of contempt while red color heated his face. "I don't need to see a doctor," he said in the stiffest way. "I've heard older boys talk in the school restrooms, and what is happening to me is perfectly normal."

"It cannot be normal—it is much too messy to be normal."

"Hah!" he scoffed, flashing his eyes with hidden laughter sparkling them. "Your time to mess up your sheets is coming."

"What do you mean?"

"Ask Momma. It's about time she told you. I've already noticed you're beginning to develop—and that's a sure sign."

I hated that he always knew more about everything than I did! Where did he learn so much—from nasty, idle talk in the boy's room? I'd heard some nasty, idle talk in the girls' room too, but darned if I was gonna believe one word of it. It was all just too gross!

The twins seldom used a chair, and they couldn't loll about on the beds, for that would make them rumpled, and the grandmother insisted that we keep everything "shipshape." And though they liked the soaps, they still kept on playing as they occasionally glanced up to see the most spellbinding scenes. Carrie had that dollhouse, with all its little people and its many small fascinations, to keep her constantly chattering in a singsong, lilting way that could grate on your nerves. Many an annoyed glance I'd throw her way, hoping she'd shut up for two seconds, and let me hear and enjoy without all the chitchat—but I never said anything to her, for that would bring about howls worse than the low murmur of her back-and-forth conversations.

While Carrie moved the dolls about, and conversed for male and female, Cory would fiddle with his many boxes of Tinkertoys. He refused to use the directions that Chris tried to teach him how to follow. Cory would design whatever suited his needs most, and what he constructed was always something he could beat upon to make musical notes. With the television to make noise and give a constantly changing variety of scenes, the dollhouse with its many charms to please Carrie, and the Tinkertoys which happied away the hours for Cory, the twins managed to make the best of their confined lives. The young are very adaptable; I know that from watching them. Sure, they complained some,about two things the most. Why didn't momma come as often as she used to? That hurt, really hurt, for what could I tell them? And then there was the food; they never liked the food. They wanted icecream cones that they saw on TV, and the hot dogs TV children were always eating. In fact, they wanted everything that was aimed at a child's appetite for sweet things, or toy things. The toys they got. The sweets they didn't.

And while the twins crawled about on the floor, or sat cross-legged making their particular kind of annoying racket, Chris and I tried to keep our minds concentrated on the complicated situations that unfolded daily before our eyes. We watched unfaithful husbands deceive loving wives, or nagging wives or wives too concerned with their children to give the husbands the attentions they deemed so necessary. It was vice-versa, too. Wives could be just as unfaithful to husbands good, or husbands bad. We learned love was just like a soap bubble, so shining and bright one day, and the next day it popped. Then came the tears, the woebegone expressions, the anguish over endless cups of coffee while seated at the kitchen table with a best friend who had her own troubles, or his own troubles. But, no sooner was one love over and done with, then along came another love to start that shining soap bubble soaring again. Oh, how very hard those beautiful people sought to find the perfect love and lock it away, keep it safe; and they never could.

One afternoon in late March Momma came into the room with a large box tucked under her arm. We were accustomed to seeing her enter our room with many gifts, not just one, and the strangest thing was she nodded at Chris, who seemed to understand for he got up from where he sat to study, caught hold of the small hands of our twins, and he took them up into the attic. I didn't understand in the least. It was still cold up there. Was this some secret? Was she bringing a gift just for me?

We sat side by side on the bed Carrie and I shared and before I could have a look at the "gift" meant especially for me, Momma said we had to have a "woman-to-woman" talk.

Now, I'd heard about man-to-man talks from watching old Andy Hardy movies, and I knew these particular kinds of discussions had something to do with growing up and sex, so I grew thoughtful and tried not to show too much interest, which would be unladylike—though I was dying to know at last.

And did she tell me what I'd waited to hear for many a year? No! While I sat solemnly and awaited the disclosing of all the evil, unholy things boys knew from the moment they were born, according to one particular witch-grandmother, I sat stunned and disbelieving while she did the explaining of how likely any day I would start to bleed!

Not from a wound, an injury, but from God's plan of how a woman's body should function. And, to add to my amazement, not only was I going to bleed once every month from now on until I was an old woman of fifty, this bloody thing was going to last five days!

"Until I'm fifty?" I asked in a voice weak and small, afraid, oh so afraid she wasn't joking.

She gave me a sweet and tender smile. "Sometimes it stops before you're fifty, and sometimes it goes on for a few years more—there's no set rule. But somewhere around that age bracket you can expect to go into 'the change of life.' And that is called menopause."

"Is it going to hurt?" was the most important thing I needed to know at that moment.

"Your monthly periods? There may be a little crampy pain, but it's not so bad, and I can tell you this from my own experience, and that from other women I know, the more you dread it, the more it pains."

I knew it! Never did I see blood that I didn't feel pain—unless it was the blood of someone else. And all this mess, this pain, these cramps, just so my uterus could ready itself to receive a "fertilized egg" that would grow into a baby. Then she gave me the box which contained everything I would need for "that time of month."

"Hold up, Momma!" I cried, having found a way to avoid all of this. "You've forgotten I plan to be a ballerina, and dancers are never supposed to have babies. Miss Danielle was always telling us it was better never to have a child. And I don't want any, not ever. So you can take all this stuff back to the store, and get back your money, for I'm calling off this monthly period mess!"

She chuckled, then hugged me closer and put on my cheek a

kiss. "I guess I must have overlooked telling you something—for there isn't anything you can do to prevent menstruation. You have to accept all of nature's ways of changing your body from that of a child, into that of a woman. Certainly you don't want to remain a child all your life, do you?"

I floundered, wanting very much to be a grown woman, with all the curves she had, and yet I wasn't prepared for the shock of such messiness—and once each month!

"And, Cathy, please don't be ashamed, or embarrassed, or dread a little discomfort, and the trouble—having babies is very rewarding. Someday you'll fall in love and marry, and you'll want to give your husband children—if you love him enough."

"Momma, there's something you're not telling me. If girls go through this sort of thing to become a woman, what must Chris endure to become a man?"

She giggled girlishly and pressed her cheek to mine. "They have changes, too, though none that make them bleed. Chris will soon have to be shaving—and every day too. And there are certain other things he will have to learn to accomplish, and control, that you don't have to worry about."

"What?" asked I, eager to have the male gender share some of the miseries of maturing. When she didn't answer, I asked, "Chris, he sent you to me with instructions to tell me, didn't he?" She nodded and said yes, though she had meant to tell me long ago, but downstairs there was a hassle every day to keep her from doing what she should.

"Chris—what does he have to endure that's painful?"

She laughed, seemingly amused. "Another day, Cathy. Now put your things away, and use them when you have the need. Don't panic if it starts in the night, or while you're dancing. I was twelve the day mine started, and out riding a bicycle, and you know I rode home at least six times and changed my panties before my mother finally noticed, and took the time to explain to me what it was all about. I was furious because she hadn't warned me in advance. She never told me anything. Believe it or

not, you'll soon get used to it, and it won't make one bit of difference in your lifestyle."

Despite the boxes of hateful things I wished I would never
need—for I wasn't going to have a baby, that was a very good
warm talk that my mother and I shared.

And yet, when she called Chris and the twins down from the
attic, and she kissed Chris and ruffled his blond curls, and played
with him in teasing ways, and almost ignored the twins, the closeness shared but a moment ago began to fade. Carrie and Cory
seemed ill at ease in her presence now. They came running to me
and climbed up on my lap, and with my arms hugging them close,
they watched as Chris was fondled, kissed, and fawned over. It
bothered me so much the way she treated the twins, as if she
didn't like to look at them. As Chris and I moved on into puberty,
and toward adulthood, the twins stagnated, went nowhere.

The long cold winter passed into spring. Gradually the attic
grew warmer. We went, all four, up there to take down the paper
snowflakes, and we made it bloom again with our brilliant
spring flowers.

My birthday came in April, and Momma didn't fail to come
with presents, and the treats of ice cream and bakery cake. She
sat down to spend the Sunday afternoon, and taught me how to
do crewel embroidery, and a few needlepoint stitches. Thus,
with the kits she gave me, I had another way to fill my time.

My birthday was followed by the twins' day—their sixth
birthday. Again, Momma bought the cake, the ice cream, and the
many gifts, including musical instruments that made Cory's
blue eyes light up. He took one long, charmed look at that toy
accordion, gave it a squeeze or two while punching the keys,
cocking his head to listen attentively to the sounds he made. And
darned, if he wasn't soon playing a tune on that thing! None of
us could believe it. Then again we were dumbfounded, for he
turned to Carrie's toy piano and did the same thing. "Happy
birthday to you, happy birthday dear Carrie, happy birthday to
you and me."

"Cory has an ear for music," said Momma, looking sad and yearning as she at last turned her gaze upon her youngest son. "Both my brothers were musicians. The pity of it was my father had no patience for the arts, or the type of men who were artists—not only those who were musicians, but painters, poets, and so forth. He thought them weak and effeminate. He forced this older brother to work in a bank he owned, not caring if his son detested the job that didn't suit him at all. He was named after my father, but we called him Mal. He was a very goodlooking young man, and on weekends, Mal would escape the life he hated by riding up into the mountains on his motorcycle. In his own private retreat, a log cabin he had built himself, he composed music. One day he took a curve too fast in the rain. He careened off the road and crashed down hundreds of feet into a chasm. He was twenty-two years old and dead.

"My younger brother was named Joel, and he ran away the day of his brother's funeral. He and Mal had been very close, and I guess he just couldn't bear the thought that now he would have to take Mal's place, and be the heir to his father's business dynasty. We received one single postcard from Paris, in which Joel told us he had a job with an orchestra touring Europe. Next thing we heard, perhaps three weeks later, Joel had been killed in a skiing accident in Switzerland. He was nineteen when he died. He had fallen into some deep ravine filled with snow, and to this day, they never found his body."

Oh, golly! I was greatly disturbed, kind of numb-feeling inside. So many accidents. Two brothers dead, and Daddy, too, all from accidents. My bleak look met with Chris's. He wasn't smiling. As soon as our mother was gone, we escaped to the attic and our books.

"We've read every damned thing!" said Chris in deep disgust, flashing me an annoyed look. Wasn't my fault he could read a book in a few hours!

"We could read through those Shakespeare books again," I suggested.

"I don't like to read plays!"

Gosh-golly, I loved reading Shakespeare and Eugene O'Neill, and anything that was dramatic, fanciful, and fraught with tempestuous emotions.

"Let's teach the twins to read and write," I suggested, I was that frantic to do something different. And in this way we could give *them* another way to entertain themselves. "And Chris, we'll save their brains from turning into mush from looking at that tube so much, and keep them from going blind, too."

Down the stairs we determinedly stalked, and right up to the twins who had their eyes glued to Bugs Bunny, who was signing off.

"We are going to teach the two of you to read and write," said Chris.

With loud wails they protested. *"No!"* howled Carrie. *"We don't want to learn to read and write! We don't write letters! We want to watch* 'I Love Lucy'!"

Chris grabbed her, and I seized hold of Cory, and quite literally we had to drag them both into the attic. It was like trying to handle slippery snakes. One of them could bellow like a mad bull charging!

Cory didn't speak, nor did he scream, nor did he beat at me with small fists to inflict some damage; he just clung fiercely to whatever came within reach of his hands, and he used his legs to wrap around things, too.

Never did two amateur teachers have a more unwilling student body. But finally, through tricks and threats and fairy tales, we began to interest them. Maybe it was pity for *us* that soon had them carefully toiling over books, and tediously memorizing and reciting letters. We gave them a McGuffey's first grade primer to copy words from.

Not acquainted with other children the same age as our twins, Chris and I thought our six-year-olds did remarkably well. And though Momma didn't come every day now as she had in the beginning, or every other day, she did show up once or twice a week. How anxiously we waited to give her the short note Cory and Carrie had printed, making sure each had the same amount of words to print.

They printed in letters at least two inches high, and very crooked:

Dear Momma,

We love you,
And candy, too.

Good-bye,
Carrie and Cory

Such sweating diligence they used to concoct their own message, not coached by either Chris or me—a message which they hoped our mother would get. Which she didn't.

Tooth cavities, of course.

Then summer was upon us. And again it was hot and sweltering, so horribly stuffy, though, strangely, not as unbearable as it had been the previous summer. Chris reasoned our blood was thinner now, so we could tolerate the heat better.

Our summer was filled with books. Apparently Momma just reached in and took books from the shelves downstairs without bothering to read the titles, or wondering if they would be of interest to us, or suitable reading for young minds so easily impressed. It didn't really matter. Chris and I would read anything.

One of our favorite books that summer was a historical novel that made history better than that taught in school. We were surprised to read that in the old days women didn't go to the hospitals to have babies. They had them at home on a small, narrow cot, so the doctor could reach them more easily than on a large, wide bed. And sometimes only "midwives" were in attendance.

"A baby swan bed, to give birth to an infant child," mused Chris aloud, lifting his head to stare off into space.

I rolled over on my back and smiled at him wickedly. We were in the attic, both lying on the old stained mattress near the open windows that let in soft warm breezes. "And kings and queens who held court in their bedroom—or bedchambers, as they called them—and having the nerve to sit up in bed entirely naked. Do you think everything that's written in books can be entirely true?"

"Of course not! But much of it is. After all, people didn't used to wear nightgowns, or pajamas to bed. They only wore nightcaps to keep their skulls warm, and the heck with the rest."

We laughed, both of us, picturing kings and queens who weren't embarrassed to be naked in front of their nobles and foreign dignitaries.

"Naked skin wasn't sinful then, was it? Way back in medieval days?"

"Guess not," he answered.

"It's what you do when you're naked that's sinful, isn't it?"

"Guess so."

For the second time now, I was coping with that curse nature sent to make me a woman, and it did hurt so much the first time that I stayed in bed all day, and made a big to-do about feeling crampy.

"You don't think it's disgusting, what is happening to me—do you?" I asked Chris.

His face lowered into my hair. "Cathy, I don't think anything about the human body and the way it functions is disgusting or revolting. I guess this is the doctor in me coming out. I think like this about your particular situation . . . if it takes a few days a month to make you into a woman like our mother, then I'm all for it. And if it pains, and you don't like it, then think about dancing, for that hurts, too, you've told me so. And yet, you think the price you pay is worth the rewards." My arms closed tighter about him when he paused. "And I pay a price too in becoming a man. I don't have a man to talk to, as you have Momma. I'm all alone in a sticky situation, full of frustrations, and sometimes I don't know which way to turn, and how to get away from temptations, and I'm so damned scared I'll never get to be a doctor."

"Chris," I began, then stumbled on quicksand, I knew, "don't you ever have any doubts about her?"

I saw his frown, and spoke again before he could fire back some angry retort, "Doesn't it strike you as . . . as *odd,* that she keeps us locked up for so long? She's got lots of money, Chris, I know she has. Those rings and bracelets, they're not fake like she tells us. I know they're not!"

He had drawn away when first I brought up "her." He adored his goddess of all female perfection, but then he was embracing me again, and his cheek was on my hair, his voice tight with thick emotion, "Sometimes I am not the eternal cockeyed optimist you call me. Sometimes I am just as doubting of what she does as you are. But I think back to the time before we came here, and I feel I have to trust her, and believe in her, and be like Daddy was. Remember how he used to say, 'For everything that seems strange, there is a good reason? And everything always works out for the best.' That's what I make myself believe—she has good reasons for keeping us here, and not sneaking us out to some boarding school. She knows what she's doing, and Cathy, I love her so much. I just can't help it. No matter what she does, I feel I will go right on loving her."

He loved her more than me, I thought bitterly.

Our mother now came and went with no regularity. Once, a whole week passed with no visit. When she finally arrived she told us her father was very ill. I was overjoyed to hear the news.

"Is he getting worse?" I asked, feeling a little pang of guilt. I knew it was wrong to wish him dead, but his death meant our salvation.

"Yes," she said solemnly, "much worse. Any day now, Cathy, any day. You wouldn't believe his pallor, his pain; soon as he goes, you'll be free."

Oh, good-golly, to think I was so evil as to want that old man to die this very second! God forgive me. But it wasn't right for us to be shut up all the time; we needed to be outside, in the warm sunlight, and we did get so lonesome, seeing no new people.

"It could be any hour," said Momma, and got up to leave.

"Swing low, sweet chariot, comin' for t' carry me home . . ." was the tune I hummed as I made the beds, and waited for the news to come that our grandfather was on his way to heaven if his gold counted, and to hell if the Devil couldn't be bribed.

"If you get there before I do . . ."

And Momma was at the door, tired looking as she poked only her face in. "He's passed the crisis . . . he's going to recover— this time." The door closed, and we were alone, with dashed hopes.

I tucked the twins into bed that night for seldom did Momma show up to do this. I was the one who kissed their cheeks and heard their prayers. And Chris did his share, too. They loved us, it was easy to read in their big, shadowed blue eyes. After they fell asleep, we went to the calendar to make an "X" through another day. August had come again. We had now lived in this prison a full year.

PART TWO

Until the day break,
and the shadows flee away.

The Song of Solomon 2:17

Growing Up,
Growing Wiser

Another year passed, much as the first did. Mother came less and less frequently, but always with the promises that kept us hoping, kept us believing our deliverance was only a few weeks away. The last thing we did each night was to mark off that day with a big red X.

We now had three calendars with big red X's. The first one was only half-bloodied with red, the second one X'd all the way through, and now a third over half filled with X's. And the dying grandfather, now sixty-eight, always about to breathe his last breath, lived on, and on, and on while we waited in limbo. It seemed he'd live to be sixty-nine.

On Thursdays, the servants of Foxworth Hall went into town, and that was when Chris and I stole out onto the black roof, to lie on a steep slope, soaking up the sunlight, and airing under the moon and stars. Though it was high and dangerous, it was the real outdoors, where we could feel fresh air on our thirsting skins.

In a place where two wings met and formed a corner, we

could brace our feet against a sturdy chimney and feel quite safe. Our positioning on the roof hid us from anyone who might be on the ground.

Because the grandmother's wrath had not yet materialized, Chris and I had grown careless. We were not always modest in the bedroom, nor were we always fully dressed. It was difficult to live, day in, day out, and always keep the intimate places of our bodies secret from the other sex.

And to be perfectly honest, none of us cared very much who saw what.

We should have cared.

We should have been careful.

We should have kept the memory of Momma's bloody welted back sharply before us, and never, never have forgotten. But the day she'd been whipped seemed so long, long ago. An eternity ago.

Here I was a teen-ager, and I'd never seen myself naked all over, for the mirror on the medicine cabinet door was placed too high for good viewing. I'd never seen a naked woman, or even a picture of one, and paintings and marble statues didn't show details. So I awaited a time when I had the bedroom to myself, and before the dresser mirror I stripped off everything, and then I stared, preened, and admired. Incredible the changes hormones brought about! Certainly I was much prettier than when I came here, even my face, my hair, my legs—much less that curvy body. From side to side I twisted, keeping my eyes glued to my reflection as I performed ballet positions.

A rippling sensation on the back of my neck gave me the awareness that someone was near, and watching. I whirled about suddenly to catch Chris standing in the deep shadows of the closet. Silently he'd come from the attic. How long had he been there? Had he seen all the silly, immodest things I'd done? Oh, God, I hoped not!

He stood as one frozen. A queer look glazed his blue eyes, as if he'd never seen me before without my clothes on—and he had, many a time. Perhaps when the twins were there, sunbathing with us, he kept his thoughts brotherly and pure, and didn't really stare.

His eyes lowered from my flushed face down to my breasts, then lower, and lower, and down to my feet before they traveled upward ever so slowly.

I stood trembling, uncertain, wondering what to do that wouldn't make me seem a foolish prude in the judgment of a brother who knew well how to mock me when he chose. He seemed a stranger, older, like someone I had never met before. He also seemed weak, dazed, perplexed, and if I moved to cover myself, I'd steal from him something he'd been starving to see.

Time seemed to stand still as he lingered in the closet, and I hesitated before the dresser which revealed to him the rear view, too, for I saw his eyes flick to the mirror to take in what that reflected.

"Chris, please go away."

He didn't seem to hear.

He only stared.

I blushed all over and felt perspiration under my arms, and a funny pounding began in my pulse. I felt like a child caught with her hand in the cookie jar, guilty of some petty crime, and terribly afraid of being severely punished for almost nothing. But his look, his eyes, made me come alive, and my heart began a fierce, mad throbbing, full of fright. Why should I be afraid? It was only Chris.

For the first time I felt embarrassed, ashamed of what I had now, and quickly I reached to pick up the dress I'd just taken off. Behind that I would shield myself, and I'd tell him to go away.

"Don't," he said when I had the dress in my hands.

"You shouldn't . . ." I stammered, trembling more.

"I know I shouldn't be, but you look so beautiful. It's like I never saw you before. How did you grow so lovely, when I was here all the time?"

How to answer a question like that? Except to look at him, and plead with my eyes.

Just then, behind me, a key turned in the door lock. Swiftly I tried to put the dress over my head and pull it down before she came in. Oh, God! I couldn't find the sleeves. My head was all covered by the dress, while the rest of me was bare, and *she* was there—the grandmother! I couldn't see her, but I *felt* her!

Finally I found the armholes, and quickly I yanked the dress down. But she had seen me in my naked glory, it was in those glittering gray stone eyes. She turned those eyes away from me and nailed Chris with a stabbing glare. He was still in the daze that put him nowhere.

"So!" she spat. "I have at last caught you! I knew I would sooner or later!"

She had spoken to us first. This was just like one of my nightmares . . . without clothes in front of the grandmother and God.

Chris snapped out of the fog and stepped forward to fire back, "You have caught us? What have you caught? Nothing!"

Nothing . . .

Nothing . . .

Nothing . . .

One word that reverberated. In her eyes, she had caught us doing everything!

"Sinners!" she hissed as she once again turned those cruel eyes on me. They held no mercy. "You think you look pretty? You think those new young curves are attractive? You like that long, golden hair that you brush and brush and curl?" She smiled then—the most frightening smile I ever saw.

My knees were clicking nervously together; my hands were working too. How vulnerable I felt without underwear and with a wide open zipper in back. I darted a glance to Chris. He advanced slowly, his eyes flicking around to search out some weapon.

"How many times have you allowed your brother to use your body?" shot out the grandmother. I just stood there, unable to speak, not comprehending what she meant.

"Use? What do you mean?"

Her eyes narrowed to mere slits that sharply turned to catch an embarrassed blush on Chris's face, clearly revealing even to me that he knew what she meant, even if I didn't.

"What I mean is," he said, turning redder, "we haven't really done anything bad." He had a man's voice now, deep and strong. "Go on, look at me with your hateful, suspicious eyes. Believe what you will, but Cathy and I have never done one single, wicked, sinful or unholy thing!"

"Your sister was naked—she has allowed you to look on her body—so, you have done wrong." She whipped her eyes to me and flared them with hate before she pivoted around and stalked from the room. She left me quivering. Chris was furious with me.

"Cathy, why the hell did you have to undress in this room! You know she spies on us, just hoping to catch us doing something!" A wild, distraught look came upon him, making him seem older and terribly violent. "She's going to punish us. Just because she left without doing anything, doesn't mean she won't come back."

I knew that . . . I knew it. She was coming back—with the whip!

Sleepy and irritable, the twins drifted down from the attic. Carrie settled in front of the dollhouse. Cory squatted down on his heels to watch TV. He picked up his expensive, professional guitar and began to play. Chris sat on his bed and faced the door. I hedged, ready to run when she came back. I'd run into the bath, lock the door . . . I'd . . .

The key turned in the door. The doorknob twisted.

I jumped to my feet, as did Chris. He said, "Get in the bathroom, Cathy, and stay there."

Our grandmother walked into the room, towering like a tree; and she bore not a whip, but a huge pair of scissors, the kind women use when cutting fabric to make clothes. They were chrome-colored, shiny, long, and looked very sharp.

"Sit down, girl!" she snapped. "I am going to cut off your hair to the scalp—and then maybe you won't feel pride when you look in the mirror."

Scornfully, cruelly, she smiled when she saw my surprise—the first time I'd seen her smile.

My worst fear! I'd rather be whipped! My skin would heal, but it would take years and years to grow back the beautiful, long hair I'd cherished since Daddy first said it was pretty, and he liked long hair on little girls. Oh, dear God, how could she know that almost every night I dreamed she stole into this room while I slept and sheared me as one does a sheep? And sometimes I dreamed not only did I wake up in the mornings bald and ugly, but she cut off my breasts, too!

Whenever she looked at me, it was at some particular place. She didn't see me as a whole person, but in sections that seemed to arouse her anger . . . and she would destroy whatever made her angry!

I tried to dash into the bathroom, and lock the door behind me. But for some reason my dancer's legs, trained so well, refused to move. I was paralyzed by the very threat of those long, shiny scissors and above them—the grandmother's chrome-colored eyes were sparked with hate, scorn, contempt.

That's when Chris spoke up in a stong man's voice. "You are not going to cut off one strand of Cathy's hair, Grandmother! Take just one step in her direction, and I will pound you over the head with this chair!"

He held one of the chairs we used for dining, ready to carry out his threat. His blue eyes snapped fire as hers shot hate.

She flicked him a scathing glance, as if what he threatened were of no consequence, as if his puny strength could never overcome the mountain of steel she appeared. "All right. Have it your way. I will give you your choice, girl—the loss of your hair, or no food or milk for an entire week."

"The twins have done nothing wrong," I implored. "Chris has done nothing. He didn't know I was unclothed when he came down from the attic—it was all my fault. I can go without food and milk for a week. I won't starve, and besides, Momma won't let you do this to me. She'll bring us food."

I didn't say that with any confidence, though. Momma had been gone so long. She didn't come very often; I'd grow very hungry.

"Your hair—or no food for a week," she repeated, untouched and unflinching.

"You are wrong to do this, old woman," said Chris, coming closer with his lifted chair. "I caught Cathy by surprise. We did nothing sinful. We never have. You judge us by circumstantial evidence."

"Your hair, or *none* of you will eat for a week," she said to me, ignoring Chris, as she always did. "And if you lock yourself in the bathroom, or hide yourself in the attic, then not one of you will eat for two weeks! Or when you come down with a bald head!" Next, she riveted her cold and calculating eyes on Chris for a long, excruciating moment. "I think *you* will be the one to shear off your sister's long, cherished hair," she said with a secret smile. On the dresser top she laid the shiny scissors. "When I come back, and see your sister without hair, then the four of you will eat."

She left us, locked us in, left us in a quandary, with Chris staring at me, and me staring back at him.

Chris smiled. "Come now, Cathy, she's all bluff! Momma will come any hour. We'll tell her . . . no problem. I'll never cut off your hair." He came to put his arm around me. "Isn't it fortunate we've hidden a box of crackers and a pound of cheddar cheese in the attic? And we still have today's food—the old witch forgot that."

We seldom ate very much. We ate even less that day, just in case Momma didn't show up. We saved half our milk, and the oranges. The day ended without a visit from Momma. All night I tossed and turned, fretting in and out of sleep. When I slept I had horrible nightmares. I dreamed Chris and I were in a deep dark woods, running lost, looking for Carrie and Cory. We called their names in the silent voices of dreams. The twins never answered. We panicked and ran in utter blackness.

Then suddenly, out of the dark loomed up a cottage made of gingerbread! Made of cheese, too, with a roof of Oreo cookies, and hard Christmas candy made a colorful winding path to the Hershey bar door. The picket fence was of peppermint sticks, the shrubbery of ice-cream cones, seven flavors. I flashed a thought over to Chris. *No!* This is a trick! We can't go in!

He messaged back: We have to go in! We have to save the twins!

Quietly we stole inside and saw the hot-roll cushions, dripping with golden butter, and the sofa was of freshly baked bread, buttered, too.

In the kitchen was the witch to end all witches! Beak-nosed, jutting jaw, sunken, toothless mouth, and her head was a mop of strings colored gray and pointing wildly in all directions.

She held up our twins by their long golden hair. They were about to be thrust into her hot oven! Already they were frosted pink and blue, and their flesh, without cooking, was beginning to turn into gingerbread, and their blue eyes into black raisins!

I screamed! Over and over again I screamed!

The witch whirled to glare at me with her gray flintstone eyes, and her sunken mouth, thin as a red knife slash, opened wide to laugh! Hysterically, she laughed on and on as Chris and I cringed in shock. She threw back her head, her wide open mouth exposing fang-like tonsils—and startlingly, frighteningly, she began to change from the grandmother. From a caterpillar into a butterfly she emerged as we stood frozen, and could only watch . . . and there from the horror came our mother!

Momma! Her blond hair flowed as silken, streaming ribbons, writhing forward on the floor to snare us both like snakes! Slithering coils of her hair twined up and around our legs, to creep nearer our throats . . . trying to strangle us into silence . . . no threat to her inheritance then!

I love you, I love you, I love you, she whispered without words.

I woke up, but Chris slept on and on, just as the twins did.

I grew desperate as sleep wanted to come and take me again. I tried to fight it off, the terrible drowsiness of drowning, drowning, and then again I was sunken deep in dreams, in nightmarish dreams. I ran wild into the dark, and into a pool of blood I fell. Blood sticky as tar, smelling of tar, and diamond-spangled fish with swan heads and red eyes came and nibbled on my arms and legs so they went numb and unfeeling, and the fish with the swan heads laughed, laughed, laughed, glad to see me done in, and made bloody all over. See! See! They shouted in whiny voices that echoed and re-echoed. *You can't get away!*

The morning came pale behind the heavy drawn draperies that shut out the yellow light of hope.

Carrie turned over in her sleep and cuddled up closer to me, "Momma," she murmured, "I don't like this house." Her silky hair on my arm felt like goose-down, as slowly, slowly, feeling began to return to my hands and arms, feet and legs.

I lay still on the bed as Carrie squirmed restlessly, wanting my arms about her, and I felt so drugged I couldn't move my arms. What was wrong with me? My head so heavy, as if it were stuffed full of rocks so my skull was pressured from the inside and the pain was so great my skull was likely to split wide open! My toes and fingers still tingled. My body was leaden. The walls advanced, then retreated, and nothing had straight vertical lines.

I tried to see my reflection in the shimmering mirror across the way, yet when I tried to turn my swollen head, it refused to budge. And always before I went to sleep, I spread my hair on my pillow so I could turn my head, and nestle my cheek in the sweet-smelling silkiness of very pampered, well-cared-for, healthy, strong hair. It was one of the sensual things I enjoyed, the feel of my hair against my cheek to take me into sweet dreams of love.

And yet, today, there was no hair on my pillow. Where was my hair?

The scissors, they still lay on the dresser top. I could vaguely

see them. Swallowing repeatedly to clear the way, I forced out a
small cry, uttering Chris's name, not Momma's. I prayed to God
to make Him let my brother hear. "Chris," I finally managed to
whisper in the strangest, gritty voice, "something is the matter
with me."

My whispered, weak words roused Chris, though I don't
know how he heard. He sat up and sleepily rubbed his eyes.
"What yuh want, Cathy?" he asked.

I mumbled something that took him from his bed, and in his
rumpled blue pajamas, his hair a golden mop, he ambled over to
my bed. He jerked up short. He drew in his breath and made
small gasping sounds of horror and shock.

"Cathy, oh my God!"

His cry sent shivers of fear down my spine.

"Cathy . . . oh, Cathy," he moaned.

As he stared, and as I wondered what he was seeing that
made his eyes bulge, I tried to lift my leaden arms and feel my
swollen, heavy head. Somehow I managed to get my hands up
there—and that's when I found a loud voice to scream! Really
scream! Over and over again I howled like someone demented
until Chris ran to gather me in his arms.

"Stop, please stop," he sobbed. " 'Remember the twins . . .
don't scare them more . . . please don't scream again, Cathy.
They've been through so much, and I know you don't want to
scar them permanently, and you will, if you don't calm down.
It's all right, I'll get rid of it. I swear on my life, that today,
somehow, I'll get the tar from your hair."

He found a small red prick on my arm where the grandmother
had plunged in a hypodermic needle to keep me asleep with
some drug. And while I slept, she had poured hot tar on my hair.
She must have gathered it all into a neat bunch before she used
the tar, for not a strand was left free of the gook.

Chris tried to keep me from looking into the mirror, but I
shoved him away, and had to stare with my mouth agape at the
horrible black blob that was my head now. Like a huge wad of

black bubble gum, chewed and left in an unsightly mess, it even ran down my face and streaked my cheeks with black tears!

I looked, and I knew that he'd never get the tar out. Never!

Cory woke up first, ready to run to the windows and draw aside the closed draperies and peek outside to see the sun that kept hiding from him. He was out of bed and ready to dash to the windows when he saw me.

His eyes widened. His lips parted. His small fluttering hands reached upward to rub at his eyes with fists, and then he was staring at me again with so much disbelief. "Cathy," he managed finally, "is that you?"

"I guess it is."

"Why is your hair black?"

Before I could reply to that question, Carrie was awake. *"Oooh!"* she howled. "Cathy—your head looks funny!" Big tears came to glisten her eyes and slide down her cheeks. "I don't like your head now!" she wailed, then began to sob as if the tar were on *her hair.*

"Calm down, Carrie," said Chris, in the most ordinary, everyday tone of voice. "It's only tar on Cathy's hair—and when she takes a bath, and shampoos her hair, it will be the same as yesterday. While she does that, I want the two of you to eat the oranges for breakfast, and look at TV. Later on we'll all eat a real breakfast, when Cathy's hair is clean." He didn't mention our grandmother for fear of instilling in them even more terror of our situation. So they sat on the floor close as bookends, supporting only each other, and peeled and ate orange sections, losing themselves in the sweet nothingness of cartoons and other Saturday morning violence and foolishness.

Chris ordered me into a tub full of hot water. In that almost scalding water I dunked my head over and over again while Chris used shampoo to soften the tar. The tar did soften, but it didn't come out and leave my hair clean. His fingers moved in a sodden mass of sticky goo. I heard myself making small whimpering sounds. He did try, oh, he did try to take out the tar without taking out all my hair. And all I could think of was the scissors—the shiny scissors the grandmother had laid on the dresser top.

On his knees by the tub, Chris finally managed to work his fingers through the mass, but when he withdrew them, they were clogged with sticky black hair. "You'll have to use the scissors!" I cried out, tired of the whole thing after two hours. But no, the scissors were the last resort. He reasoned there must be some chemical solution that would dissolve the tar, without dissolving my hair. He had a very professional chemistry set Momma had given him. On the lid was a stern warning: "This is not a toy. This box contains dangerous chemicals and is for professional use only."

"Cathy," he said, sitting back on his bare heels, "I'm going up to the attic schoolroom and mix some compound to take the tar from your hair." He grinned at me shyly then. The light from the ceiling caught on the soft downy fuzz that covered his upper lip, and I knew he had stronger, darker hair on the lower part of his body, the same as I did. "I've got to use the John, Cathy. I've never done that in front of you, and I'm kind of embarrassed. You can turn your back, and put your fingers in your ears, and maybe if you go in the water too, the ammonia might unglue your hair."

I couldn't help but stare at him in amazement. The day had taken on nightmarish proportions. To sit in boiling water and use it for a toilet and then wash my hair in that? Could it be real that I would do this as Chris streamed urine into the commode behind my back? I said to myself, no, this wasn't real, just a dream. Carrie and Cory wouldn't use the bathroom, too, while I was in the tub, dunking my hair in foul water.

It was real enough. Hand in hand, Cory and Carrie came to the tub and stared at me, wanting to know why I was taking so long.

"Cathy, what is that stuff on your head?"

"Tar."

"Why did you put tar in your hair?"

"I must have done it in my sleep."

"Where did you find the tar?"

"In the attic."

"Why did you want to put tar in your hair?"

I hated lying! I wanted to tell her who put the tar in my hair, but I couldn't let her know. Already she and Cory were scared enough of that old woman. "Go back and look at TV, Carrie," I ordered, testy and irritable from all the questions she asked, and hating to look at her thin, hollowed-out cheeks, her sunken eyes.

"Cathy, don't you like me no more?"

"Anymore . . ."

"Don't you?"

"Of course I like you, Cory. I love you both, but I put the tar on my hair by mistake, and now I'm mad at myself."

Carrie wandered off to sit once more near Cory. They whispered back and forth in that strange language that only they could understand. Sometimes, I think they were far wiser than Chris and I suspected.

For hours I was in the tub, while Chris concocted a dozen different compounds to test on a bit of my hair. He tried everything, making me change the water often, always making it hotter. I shriveled into a puckered prune as bit by bit he cleared the gooey mess from my hair. The tar came out, eventually, along with a great loss of hair. But I had a lot, and could afford to lose much without making a noticeable difference. And when it was over, the day was gone, and neither Chris nor I had eaten a bite. He had given cheese and crackers to the twins, but he himself hadn't wasted time to eat. Wrapped in a towel, I sat on the bed and dried my much thinned hair. What was left was fragile. It broke easily, and the color was almost platinum.

"You might as well have saved yourself the effort," I said to Chris, who was hungrily eating two crackers with cheese. "She hasn't brought up any food—and she won't bring any up until you cut it all off."

He came to me, bearing a plate with cheese and crackers, and holding a glass of water. "Eat and drink. We will outsmart her. If by tomorrow she doesn't bring up some food, or if Momma doesn't show up, I'll cut off just your front hair, over your forehead. Then you can wrap your head with a scarf, like you're ashamed to be seen bald-headed, and soon enough that hair will grow back in."

Sparingly, I ate the cheese and crackers, not answering. I washed down my one meal of the day with water from the bathroom tap. Then Chris brushed that pale, pale weak hair that had endured so much. Peculiar how fate works things out: my hair had never gleamed more, or felt so much like gossamer silk, and I was grateful to have any left at all. I lay back on the bed, worn out, enervated by emotion torn asunder, and watched Chris sitting on the bed just looking at me. When I fell asleep, he was still there, watching me, and in his hand he held a long coil of my spiderweb, silken hair.

That night I fretted in and out of sleep, restless, tormented. I felt helpless, angry, frustrated.

And then I saw Chris.

He was still in the clothes he'd worn all day. He'd moved the heaviest chair in the room so that it was against the door, and in that chair he sat and dozed, while in his hand he held the pair of long and sharp scissors. He had barred the way, so the grandmother couldn't sneak in again and use the scissors. He was, even in his sleep, guarding me from her.

As I stared over at him, his eyes opened, jolted, as if he hadn't meant to doze off and leave me unprotected. In the dimness of that locked room, always rosy at night, he caught my gaze, and our eyes locked, and ever so slowly he smiled. "Hi."

"Chris," I sobbed, "go to bed. You can't keep her out forever."

"I can while you sleep."

"Then let me be the sentry. We'll take turns."

"Who's the man here, you or me? Besides, I eat more than you do."

"What's that got to do with it?"

"You're too thin now, and staying awake all night would make you thinner, whereas I can afford to lose weight."

He was underweight, too. We all were, and his slight weight wouldn't keep that grandmother out if she really wanted to shove the door open. I got up and went to sit with him in the chair, though he gallantly protested.

"Ssh," I whispered. "The two of us together can keep her out better, and we can both sleep." Embraced in each other's arms, we fell asleep.

And the morning came . . . without the grandmother . . . without food.

The hungry days passed by endlessly, miserably.

Only too soon the cheese and crackers were gone, though we ate most sparingly of what we had. And that was when we really began to suffer. Chris and I drank only water, and saved what milk there was for the twins.

Chris came to me with the shears in his hand, and reluctantly, with tears, he cut off the front top hair close to my scalp. I wouldn't look in a mirror when it was done. The long part that was left, I wrapped about my head, and over that I formed a scarf into a turban.

Then came the irony, the bitter irony of the grandmother not coming to check!

She didn't bring us food, or milk, or clean linens, or towels, or even the soap and toothpaste we had run out of. Not even toilet paper. Now I regretted throwing out all the tissue our expensive clothes came in. There was nothing left to do but tear pages from the oldest books in the attic and use that.

Then the toilet bowl stopped up, and overflowed, and Cory began to scream as filth flooded over and filled the bathroom. We didn't have a plunger. Frantically, Chris and I wondered what to do. As he ran for a coat hanger made of wire to straighten out and push down whatever clogged the drain, I ran to the attic to fetch old clothes to mop up the flooding mess.

Somehow Chris managed to use the wire coat hanger, and the commode worked normally again. Then, without a word, he got down on his knees beside me, and we both mopped up the floor with the old clothes from the attic trunks.

Now we had filthy, smelly rags to fill up a trunk, and add to the secrets of the attic.

We escaped the full horror of our situation by not talking about it much. We just got up in the mornings, splashed water on our faces, cleaned our teeth with plain water, drank a little water, moved about a little, then lay down to watch TV, or to read, and the devil to pay if she came in and caught us rumpling a bedspread. What did we care now?

To hear the twins cry for food put scars on my soul that I would bear for the rest of my life. And I hated, oh, how I hated that old woman—and Momma—for doing this to us!

And when mealtimes rolled by with no food, we slept. For hours on end we slept. Asleep you don't feel pain or hunger, or loneliness, or bitterness. In sleep you can drown in false euphoria, and when you awaken, you just don't care about anything.

There was one hazy, unreal day when we lay listless, all four of us, with the only life going on confined to the small box over in the corner. Dazed and tired, I turned my head for no reason at all just to look at Chris and Cory, and I lay without much feeling at all as I watched Chris take his pocket knife and slash his wrist. He put his bleeding arm to Cory's mouth, and made him drink his blood, though Cory protested. Then it was Carrie's turn. The two of them, who wouldn't eat anything lumpy, bumpy, grainy, too tough, too stringy, or just plain "funny looking," drank of their older brother's blood and stared up at him with dull, wide, accepting eyes.

I turned my head away, sickened by what he had to do, and full of admiration that he *could* do it. He could always solve a difficult problem.

Chris came to my side of the bed and perched on the edge, and looked at me for the longest moment, then his eyes lowered to the cut on his wrist that wasn't bleeding as freely now. He lifted his pocket-knife and prepared to make a second slash so I too could be nourished by his blood. I stopped him, and seized hold of his jack-knife and hurled it away. He ran fast to get it, and again he cleaned it with alcohol, despite my vow never to taste his blood, and drain from him more of his strength.

"What will we do, Chris, if she never comes back?" I asked dully. "She will let us starve to death." Meaning the grandmother, of course, whom we hadn't seen in two weeks. And Chris had exaggerated when he said we had a full pound of cheddar cheese stashed away. We baited our mousetraps with cheese, and had been forced to take back the bits of cheese to eat ourselves, when everything else was gone. Now we'd been without one bit of food in our stomachs for three whole days and four days with only a little cheese and crackers. And the milk we saved for the twins to drink—gone ten days ago, too.

"She won't let us starve to death," said Chris as he lay down beside me and took me into his weak embrace. "We'd be idiots, and spineless, to allow her to do that to us. Tomorrow, if she doesn't show up with food, and our mother doesn't show up, we'll use our sheet-ladder to reach the ground."

My head was on his chest and I could hear his heart thumping. "How do you know what she'd do? She hates us. She wants us dead—hasn't she told us that time and time again we should never have been born?"

"Cathy, the old witch is not dumb. She'll bring food soon, before Momma comes back from wherever she's been."

I moved to bandage his slashed wrist. Two weeks ago Chris and I should have tried to escape, when both of us had the strength to make the perilous descent. Now, if we tried to make it, surely we'd fall to our deaths, what with the twins tied to our backs to make it even more difficult.

But when morning came, and there was still no food brought up to us, Chris forced us into the attic. He and I carried the twins who were too weak to walk. It was a torrid zone up there.

Sleepily, the twins sagged in the corner of the schoolroom where we put them down. Chris set about fashioning slings so we could attach the twins securely to our backs. Neither of us mentioned the possibility that we could be committing suicide, and murder, too, if we fell.

"We'll do it another way," said Chris, reconsidering. "I'll go first. When I reach the ground, you'll put Cory into a sling, tie him in fast so he can't kick free, and then you'll lower him down to me. Next, you can do that for Carrie. And you can come down last. And for God's sake, put forth your very best efforts! Call upon God to give you the strength—don't be apathetic! Feel anger, wrath, think of revenge! I've heard great anger gives you super-human strength in an emergency!"

"Let me go first. You're stronger." I said weakly.

"No! I want to be down there to catch in case anyone comes down too fast, and your arms don't have the strength mine do. I'll brace the rope about a chimney so all the weight won't be on you—and Cathy, this is really an emergency!"

God, I couldn't believe what he expected me to do next!

With horror I stared at the four dead mice in our traps. "We've got to eat these mice to gain some strength," he said to me grimly, "and what we have to do, we *can* do!"

Raw meat? Raw mice? "No," I whispered, revolted by the sight of those tiny stiff and dead things.

He grew forceful, angry, telling me I could do anything that was necessary to keep the twins alive, and myself alive. "Look, Cathy, I'll eat my two first, after I've run downstairs for salt and pepper. And I need that coat hanger to tighten up the knots— leverage, you know. My hands, they're not working too good now."

Of course they weren't. We were all so weak we could barely move.

He shot me a quick appraising glance. "Really, with salt and pepper, I think the mice might be tasty."

Tasty.

He sliced off the heads, then skinned and gutted them next. I watched him slice open the small bellies and withdraw long, slimy intestines, little bitty hearts, and other miniature "innards."

I could have vomited if there had been anything in my stomach.

And he didn't run for the salt and pepper, or the coat hanger. He only walked, and slowly at that—telling me in this way he wasn't too eager to partake of raw mice, either.

While he was gone, my eyes stayed glued to the skinned mice that were to be our next meal. I closed my eyes and tried to will myself into taking the first bite. I was hungry but not hungry enough to enjoy the prospects.

I thought then of the twins, who sagged in the corner with their eyes closed, holding each other, their foreheads pressed together, and I thought they must have embraced like that when they were inside Momma's womb, waiting to be born, so they could be put away behind a locked door, and starved. Our poor little buttercups who once had known a father and mother who loved them well.

Yet, there was the hope the mice would give Chris and me enough strength and we could take them safely to the ground, and some kind neighbor who was at home would give them food, give all of us food—if we lived through the next hour.

I heard the slow returning steps of Chris. He hesitated in the doorframe, half-smiling, his blue eyes meeting with mine . . . and shining. In both of his hands he carried the huge picnic basket we knew so well. It was so filled with food the wooden lids that folded backwards couldn't lie flat.

He lifted out two thermos jugs: one with vegetable soup, the other with cold milk, and I felt so numb, confused, hopeful. Had Momma come back and sent this up to us? Then why hadn't she called for us to come down? Or why didn't she come looking for us?

Chris took Carrie and I took Cory on our laps, and we spooned soup into their mouths. They accepted the soup as they had accepted his blood—as just another event in their extraordinary lives. We fed them bits of sandwich. We ate most sparingly, as Chris cautioned, lest we throw it all up.

I wanted to stuff the food into Cory's mouth, so I could get around to ramming food into my own ravenous stomach. He ate so darned slow! A thousand questions ran through my brain: Why today? Why bring food today and not yesterday, or the day before? What was her reasoning? When finally I could eat, I was too apathetic to be overjoyed, and too suspicious to be relieved.

Chris, after slowly eating some soup, and half a sandwich, unwrapped a foil package. Four powdered-sugar doughnuts were disclosed. We, who were never given sweets, were given a dessert—from the grandmother—for the first time. Was this her way of asking our forgiveness? We took it that way, whatever her purpose.

During our week of near starvation, something peculiar had happened between Chris and me. Perhaps it became enhanced that day when I sat in the hot tub of concealing bubble bath, and he toiled so valiantly to rid my hair of the tar. Before that horrible day, we'd been only brother and sister, play-acting the roles of parents to the twins. Now our relationship had changed. We weren't play-acting anymore. We were the genuine parents of Carrie and Cory. They were our responsibility, our obligation, and we committed ourselves to them totally, and to each other.

It was obviously drawn now. Our mother didn't care anymore what happened to us.

Chris didn't need to speak and say how he felt to recognize her indifference. His bleak eyes told me. His listless movements said more. He'd kept her picture near his bed, and now he put that away. He'd always believed in her more than I, so naturally he was hurt the most. And if he ached more than I was aching, then he was in agony.

Tenderly he took my hand, indicating that now we could go back to the bedroom. Down the stairs we drifted as pale sleepy ghosts, in subnormal states of shock, all of us feeling sick and weak, especially the twins. I doubted they weighed thirty pounds each. I could see how they looked, and how Chris looked, but I couldn't see myself. I glanced toward the tall, wide mirror over the dresser, expecting to see a circus freak, short-cropped hair on top, long, lank pale hair in back. And lo, when I looked, there was no mirror there!

Quickly I ran to the bathroom to find the medicine cabinet mirror smashed! Back I raced to the bedroom, to lift the lid of the dressing table that Chris often used as a desk . . . and that mirror, too, was broken!

We could gaze in shattered glass and see distorted reflections of ourselves. Yes, we could view our faces in faceted broken pieces as a fly would, one side of the nose riding up higher than the other. It wasn't pleasant viewing. Turning away from the dressing table, I put the basket of food down on the floor where it was coldest, then went to lie down. I didn't question the reason for the broken mirrors, and the one taken away. I knew why she'd done what she did. Pride was sinful. And in her eyes Chris and I were sinners of the worst kind. To punish us, the twins would suffer, as well, but why she brought us food again, I couldn't guess.

Other mornings came, with baskets of food carried up to us. The grandmother refused to look our way. She kept her eyes averted and swiftly retreated out the door. I wore a turban made of a pink towel around my head which revealed the front portion over my brow, but if she noticed, she didn't comment. We watched her come and go, not asking where Momma was, or when she was coming back. Those so easily punished learn their lesson well, and don't speak unless spoken to first. Both Chris and I stared at her, filling our eyes with hostility, with anger and hate, hoping she'd turn and see how we felt. But she didn't meet a pair of our eyes. And then I would cry out and make her see, and make her look at the twins, and see for herself how thin they were, how shadowed their large eyes were. But she wouldn't see.

Lying on the bed beside Carrie, I looked deep into myself and realized how I was making all of this worse than it ought to be. Now Chris, once the cheerful optimist, was turning into a gloomy imitation of me. I wanted him back the way he used to be—smiling and bright, making the best out of the worst.

He sat at the dressing table with the lid down, with open medical books before him, his shoulders sagging. He wasn't reading, just sitting there.

"Chris," I said, sitting up to brush my hair, "in your opinion, what percentage of teen-aged girls in the world have gone to bed with clean, shining hair and awakened a tar baby?"

Swiveling around, he shot me a glance full of surprise that I would mention that horrible day. "Well," he drawled, "in my opinion, I suspect you might well be the one and only . . . unique."

"Oh, I don't know about that. Remember when they were putting down asphalt on our street? Mary Lou Baker and I turned over a huge tub of that stuff, and we made little tar babies, and put black beds in black houses, and the man in charge of the street-repair gang came along and bawled us out."

"Yeah," he said, "I remember you came home looking filthy-dirty, and you had a wad of tar in your mouth, chewing to make your teeth whiter. Gosh, Cathy, all you did was pull out a filling."

"One good thing about this room, we don't have to visit dentists twice a year." He gave me a funny look. "And another nice thing is to have so much time! We'll complete our Monopoly tournament. The champion player has to wash everyone's underwear in the bathtub."

Boy, he was all for that. He hated bending over the tub, kneeling on the hard tile, doing his wash and Cory's.

We set up the game, and counted out the money, and looked around for the twins. Both had disappeared! Where was there to go but up in the attic? They'd never go there without us, and the bathroom was empty. Then we heard some small twittering noises behind the TV set.

There they were, crouched in the corner in back of the set, sitting and waiting for the tiny people inside to come out. "We thought maybe Momma was in there," explained Carrie.

"I think I'll go up in the attic and dance," I said, getting up from the bed and moving toward the closet.

"Cathy! What about our tournament Monopoly game?"

Pausing, I half-turned. "Oh, you'd only win. Forget the tournament."

"Coward!" he taunted now, the same as he used to. "Come on, let's play." He looked long and hard at the twins, who always acted as our bankers. "And no cheating this time," he warned sternly, "if I catch one of you slipping Cathy money when you think I'm not looking—then I'll eat every one of those four doughnuts myself!"

I'll be darned if he would! The doughnuts were the best part of our meals, and saved for nighttime dessert. I threw myself down on the floor, crossed my legs, and busied my brain with clever ways in which I could get to buy the best property first, and the railroads, and the utilities, and I'd get my red houses up first, then the hotels. He'd see who was good at doing something better than him.

For hours and hours we played, stopping only to eat meals or go to the bathroom. When the twins grew tired of playing bankers, we counted out the money ourselves, closely watching each other to see if any cheating was going on. And Chris kept landing up in jail, and had to miss out on passing Go and collecting two hundred dollars, and the Community Chest made him give, and he had to pay inheritance tax . . . and *still* he won!

Late in August Chris came to me one night and whispered in my ear, "The twins are sound asleep. And it's so hot in here. Wouldn't it be just great if we could go for a swim?"

"Go away—leave me alone—you know we can't go swimming." I was, of course, still sulky from always losing at Monopoly.

Swimming, what an idiotic idea. Even if we could, I didn't want to do anything in which he excelled, like swimming. "And just where are we going to swim? In the bathtub?"

"In the lake Momma told us about. It's not far from here," he whispered. "We ought to practice reaching the ground with that rope we made, anyway, just in case there's a fire. We're stronger now. We can reach the ground easily, and we won't be gone long." On and on he pleaded, as if his very existence depended on escaping this house just once—just to prove that we could.

"The twins might wake up and find us gone."

"We'll leave a note on the bathroom door, telling them we're up in the attic. And besides, they never wake up until morning, not even to go to the bathroom."

He argued, and pleaded until I was won over. Up into the attic we went, and out onto the roof where he fastened the sheet-ladder securely to the chimney closest to the back side of the house. There were eight chimneys on the roof.

Testing the knots one by one, Chris gave me instructions: "Use the large knots as a ladder rung. Keep your hands just above the higher knot. Go down slowly, feeling with your feet for the next knot—and be sure to keep the rope twisted between your legs, so you can't slip and fall."

Smiling with confidence, he held to the rope and inched his way to the very edge of the roof. We were going down to the ground for the first time in more than two years.

A Taste of Heaven

Slowly, carefully, hand under hand, and foot under foot, Chris descended to the ground while I lay flat on my stomach near the roof's edge watching his descent. The moon was out and shining brightly as he lifted his hand and waved: his signal to send me on my way. I had watched the way he handled himself, so I could duplicate his method. I told myself it was no different from swinging on the ropes tied to the attic rafters. The knots were big and strong, and we had judiciously made them about four and a half feet apart. He had told me not to look down once I left the roof, just to concentrate on notching one foot securely on a lower knot before I reached with my other foot to find an even lower knot. In less than ten minutes, I was standing on the ground next to Chris.

"Wow!" he whispered, hugging me close. "You did that better than me!"

We were in the back gardens of Foxworth Hall, where all the rooms were dark, though in the servants' quarters over the huge garage every window was brightly yellow. "Lead on, MacDuff, to the swimming hole," I said in a low voice, "if you know the way."

Sure, he knew the way. Momma had told us how she and her brothers used to steal away and go swimming with their friends.

He caught my hand as we tiptoed away from the huge house. It felt so strange to be outside, on the ground, on a warm summer night. Leaving our small brother and sister alone in a locked room. When we crossed over a small footbridge, and knew we were now outside the realm of Foxworth property, we felt happy, almost free. Still we had to be cautious and not let anyone see us. We ran toward the woods, and the lake Momma had told us about.

It was ten o'clock when we went out on the roof; it was ten-thirty when we found the small body of water surrounded by trees. We were fearful others would be there to spoil it for us, and send us back unsatisfied, but the lake water was smooth, unruffled by winds, or bathers, or sailboats.

In the moonlight, under a bright and starry sky, I looked on that lake and thought I'd never beheld such beautiful water, or felt a night that filled me with such rapture.

"Are we going to skinny-dip?" asked Chris, looking at me in a peculiar way.

"No. We are going to swim in our underwear."

The trouble was, I didn't own a single bra. But now that we were here, silly prudery wasn't going to stop me from enjoying that moonlit water. "Last one in is a rotten egg!" I called. And I took off, on the run toward a short dock. But when I reached the end of the dock, I somehow sensed the water might be icy cold, and most gingerly I cautiously stuck a toe in first—and it was ice cold! I glanced back at Chris, who had taken off his watch and flung it aside, and now he was coming at me fast. So darned fast, before I could brave myself to dive into the water, he was behind me, and shoved me! Splash—flat down in the water I was, soaked from head to toe, and not inch by inch, as I would have had it!

I shivered as I came to the surface and paddled around, looking for Chris. Then I spied him crawling up a pile of rocks, and

for a moment he was silhouetted. He lifted his arms and gracefully made a swan dive into the middle of the lake. I gasped!
What if the water wasn't deep enough? What if he hit the bottom
and broke his neck or back?

And then, and then . . . he didn't surface! Oh God, . . . he was
dead . . . drowned!

"Chris," I called, sobbing, and began to swim toward the spot
where he had disappeared beneath the cold water.

Suddenly I was seized by the legs! I screamed and went
under, pulled down by Chris, who kicked his legs strongly and
took us both up to the surface, where we laughed, and I splashed
water into his face for playing such a dirty trick.

"Isn't this better than being shut up in that damned hot
room?" he asked, frolicking around like someone demented,
delirious, wild, and crazy! It was as if this bit of freedom had
gone to his head like strong wine, and he was drunk! He swam
in circles around me, and tried again to catch my legs and drag
me under. But I was wise to him now. He kicked to the surface
and backstroked, he also did the breaststroke, the crawl, side-
stroked, and named what he did as he performed. "This is the
back crawl," he said as he demonstrated, showing off techniques
I'd never seen before.

He surfaced from a dive under, and treaded water as he began
to sing, "Dance, ballerina, dance,"—and in my face he threw
water, as I splashed it back at him—"and do your pirouette in
rhythm with your aching heart. . . ." And then he had me in his
embrace, and laughing and screaming, we fought, gone crazy
just to be children again. Oh, he was wonderful in the water, like
a dancer. Suddenly I was tired, extremely tired, so tired I felt
weak as a wet dishcloth. Chris put his arm about me and assisted
me up onto shore.

Both of us fell on a grassy bank to lie back and talk.

"One more swim, and then back to the twins," he said, lying
supine on the gentle slope beside me. Both of us stared up at a
sky full of glittering, twinkling stars, and there was a quarter-

moon out, colored silvery-gold, and it ducked and hid, and played hide and seek with the strung-out long, dark clouds.

"Suppose we can't make it back up to the roof?"

"We'll make it, because we have to make it."

That was my Christopher Doll, the eternal optimist, sprawled beside me, all wet and glistening, with his fair hair pasted to his forehead. His nose was the same as Daddy's as it aimed at the heavens, his full lips so beautifully shaped he didn't need to pout to make them sensual, his chin square, strong, clefted, and his chest was beginning to broaden . . . and there was that hillock of his growing maleness before his strong thighs, beginning to swell. There was something about a man's strong, well-shaped thighs that excited me. I turned away my head, unable to feast my eyes on his beauty without feeling guilty and ashamed.

Birds were nested overhead in the tree branches. They made sleepy little twittery noises that for some reason made me think of the twins, and that made me sad and put tears in my eyes.

Fireflies bobbed up every so often and flashed their lemon-colored tail-lights off and on, signaling male to female, or vice-versa. "Chris, is it the male firefly that lights up, or the female?"

"I'm really not sure," he said as if he didn't care. "I think they both light up, but the female stays on the ground signaling, while the male flies around looking for her."

"You mean you aren't positive about everything—you, the all-knowing?"

"Cathy, let's not quibble. I don't know everything—a long way from it." He turned his head and met my eyes; our gazes locked and neither of us seemed capable of looking elsewhere.

Soft southern breezes came and played in my hair and dried the wisps about my face. I felt them tickling like small kisses, and again I wanted to cry, for no reason at all, except the night was so sweet, so lovely, and I was at the age for high romantic yearning. And the breeze whispered loving words in my ears . . . words I was so afraid no one was ever going to say. Still, the night was so lovely under the trees, near the shimmering moonlit water, and I sighed. I felt that I'd been here before, on this grass near the lake. Oh, the strange thoughts I had as the night-fliers hummed and whirred, and the mosquitoes buzzed and somewhere far off an owl hooted, taking me quickly back to the night when first we came to live as fugitives, hidden from a world that didn't want us.

"Chris, you're almost seventeen, the same age Daddy was when he first met Momma."

"And you're fourteen, the same age she was," he said in a hoarse voice.

"Do you believe in love at first sight?"

He hesitated, mulling that over . . . his way, not mine. "I'm not an authority on that subject. I know when I was in school, I'd see a pretty girl and right away feel in love with her. Then when we'd talk, and she was kind of stupid, then I didn't feel anything at all about her. But if her beauty had been matched by other assets, I think I could fall in love at first sight, though I've read that kind of love is only physical attraction."

"Do you think I'm stupid?"

He grinned and reached out to touch my hair. "Gosh, no. And I hope you don't think you are, because you're not. Your trouble is, Cathy, you have too many talents; you want to be everything, and that's not possible."

"How do you know I'd like to be a singer and an actress, too?"

He laughed soft and low. "Silly girl, you're acting ninety percent of the time, and singing to yourself when you feel contented; unfortunately, that's not very often."

"Are *you* contented often?"

"No."

So we lay, silent, from time to time staring at something that drew our attention, like the fireflies that met on the grass and mated, and the whispering leaves, and the floating clouds, and the play of the moonlight on the water. The night seemed enchanted and set me to thinking again of nature, and all its strange ways. Though I didn't understand fully many of its ways, why I dreamed as I did at night now, why I woke up throbbing and yearning for some fulfillment that I could never reach.

I was glad Chris had persuaded me into coming. It was wonderful to be lying on grass again, feeling cool and refreshed, and most of all, feeling fully alive again.

"Chris," I began tentatively, afraid to spoil the soft beauty of this star-filled moonlit night, "where do you think our mother is?"

He kept right on staring at Polaris, the north star.

"I have no idea where she is," he answered finally.

"Don't you have any suspicions?"

"Sure. Of course I do."

"What are they?"

"She could be sick."

"She's not sick; Momma's never sick."

"She could be away on a business trip for her father."

"Then why didn't she come and tell us she was going, and when to expect her back?"

"I don't know!" he said irritably, like I was spoiling the evening for him, and of course he couldn't know, any more than I could.

"Chris, do you love and trust her as much as you used to?"

"Don't ask me questions like that! She's my mother. She's all we've got, and if you expect me to lie here and say mean things about her, I'm not going to do it! Wherever she is tonight, she's thinking of us, and she's coming back. She'll have a perfectly good reason for going away and staying so long, you can count on that."

I couldn't say to him what I was really thinking, that she could have found time to come in and tell us of her plans—for he knew that as well as I did.

There was a husky tone to his voice that came about only when he was feeling pain—and not the physical kind. I wanted to take away the hurt I'd inflicted with my questions. "Chris, on

TV, girls my age, and boys your age—they start to date. Would you know how to act on a date?"

"Sure, I've watched a lot on TV."

"But watching isn't the same as doing."

"Still it gives you the general idea of what to do, and what to say. And besides, you're still too young to date guys."

"Now let me tell you something, Mr. Big Brain, a girl of my age is actually one year older than a boy of your age."

"You're crazy!"

"Crazy? I read that fact in a magazine article, written by an authority on the subject—a doctor of psychology," I said, thinking he was sure to be impressed. "He said girls mature emotionally much quicker than boys do."

"The author of that article was judging all mankind by *his own* immaturity."

"Chris, you think you know everything—and nobody knows everything!"

He turned his head and met my eyes and scowled, like he used to do so often. "You're right," he agreed pleasantly. "I know only what I read, and what I'm feeling inside has me as mystified as any first-grader. I'm mad as hell at Momma because of what she's done, and I'm feeling so many different things, and I don't have a man to talk them over with." He rose on an elbow to stare down in my face. "I wish it wasn't taking your hair so long to grow back. I wish now I hadn't used the scissors . . . didn't do any good, anyway."

It was better when he didn't say anything to make me think of Foxworth Hall. I just wanted to look up at the sky and feel the fresh night air on my wet skin. My pajamas were of thin white batiste, scattered all over with rosebuds, and edged with lace. They clung to me like a second skin, just as Chris's white jockey shorts clung to him.

"Let's go now, Chris."

Reluctantly, he got up and stretched out a hand. "Another swim?"

"No. Let's go back."

Silently, we headed away from the lake, walking slowly through the woods, drinking in the sensation of being outside, on the ground.

We headed back to our responsibilities. For the longest time we stood by the rope we'd made, fastened to a chimney far above. I wasn't thinking of how we'd make the ascent, only wondering what we'd gained by this brief little escape from a prison we had to enter again.

"Chris, do you feel different?"

"Yes. We didn't do very much but walk and run on the ground, and swim for a short while, but I feel more alive and more hopeful."

"We could get away if we wanted to—tonight—and not wait for Momma to come back. We could go up, make slings to carry the twins, and while they sleep we could carry them down. We could run away! We'd be *free!*"

He didn't answer, but began the ascent to the roof, hand over hand, with the sheet-ladder caught fast between his legs as he worked his way up. As soon as he was on the roof, I began, for we didn't trust the rope to hold the weight of two people. It was much harder going up than coming down. My legs seemed so much stronger than my arms. I reached above for the next knot, and lifted my right leg. Suddenly my left foot slipped from where I'd notched it and I was swinging free—held only by weak hands!

A short scream tore from my lips! I was more than twenty feet from the ground!

"Hold on!" called Chris from above. "The rope is directly between both your legs. All you have to do is squeeze them together quick!"

I couldn't see what I was doing. All I could do was follow his directions. I grasped the rope between my thighs, quivering all over. Fear made me weaker. The longer I stayed in one place, the more fearful I became. I began to gasp, to tremble. And then came the tears . . . stupid girlish tears!

"You are almost within reach of my hands," called Chris. "Just a few more feet up, and I can reach you. Cathy, don't panic. Think of how much the twins need you! Try . . . try hard!"

I had to talk myself into letting go with one hand, to reach higher for another knot. I said over and over again to myself, I *can* do it. I can. My feet were slippery from the grass—but then, Chris's feet had been slippery, too, and he had managed. And if he could do it, then I could too.

Bit by terrifying bit I climbed up that rope to where Chris could reach down and grasp my wrists. Once his strong hands had me, a surge of relief tingled my blood down to my fingertips and to my toes. In a few seconds he hauled me up, and I was seized in a tight embrace while we both laughed and then almost cried. Then we crawled up the steep slope, keeping fast hold of the rope until we reached the chimney. That's when we fell down in our accustomed place and shivered all over.

Oh, the irony of it—that we would be glad to be back!

Chris lay on his bed and stared over at me. "Cathy, for just a second or two, when we were lying on the bank of the lake, it seemed a bit like heaven. Then when you faltered on the rope, I thought I might die too, if you did. We can't do that again. You don't have the strength in your arms that I do. I'm sorry I forgot about that."

The night lamp was burning with a rosy glow over in the corner. Our eyes met in the dimness. "I'm not sorry we went. I'm glad. It's been so long since I felt real."

"Did you feel like that?" he asked. "So did I . . . just like we had left a bad dream that was lasting too long."

I dared again, had to. "Chris, where *do* you think Momma is? She's drifting away from us gradually, and she never really looks at the twins, like they scare her now. But she's never stayed away this long before. She's been gone over a month."

I heard his heavy, sad sigh. "Honestly, Cathy, I just don't

know. She hasn't told me anymore than she's told you—but you can bet she's got a good reason."

"But what kind of reason could she have to leave without an explanation? Isn't that the least she could do?"

"I don't know what to say."

"If I had children, I would never leave them the way she does. I'd never stick my four children away in a locked room and then forget them."

"You're not going to have any children, remember?"

"Chris, someday I'm going to dance in the arms of a husband who loves me, and if he really wants a baby, then I might agree to have one."

"Sure, I knew all along you'd change your mind once you grew up."

"You really think I'm pretty enough for a man to love?"

"You're *more* than pretty enough." He sounded embarrassed.

"Chris, remember when Momma told us that it was money that made the world go around and not love? Well, I think she's wrong."

"Yeah? Give that a bit more thought. Why can't you have both?"

I gave it thought. Plenty of thought. I lay and stared up at the ceiling that was my dancing floor, and I mulled life and love over and over. And from every book I'd ever read, I took one wise bead of philosophy and strung them all into a rosary to believe in for the rest of my life.

Love, when it came and knocked on my door, was going to be enough.

And that unknown author who'd written that if you had fame, it was not enough, and if you had wealth as well, it was still not enough, and if you had fame, wealth, and also love . . . still it was not enough—boy, did I feel sorry for him.

One Rainy Afternoon

Chris was at the windows, both hands holding open the heavy tapestry draperies. The sky was leaden, the rain came down in a solid sheet. Every lamp in our room was lit, and the TV was on, as usual. Chris was waiting to see the train that would pass by around four. You could hear its mournful whistle before dawn, around four, and then later if you were awake. You could just barely catch a glimpse of the train that appeared to be a toy, it was so far away.

He was in his world, I was in mine. Sitting cross-legged on the bed Carrie and I shared, I cut pictures from decorating magazines Momma had brought up for my entertainment before she went away to stay so long. I cut each photograph out carefully and pasted them into a large scrapbook. I was planning my dream house, where I would live happily ever after, with a tall, strong, dark-haired husband who loved only me and not a thousand others on the side.

I had my life mapped out: my career first, a husband and children when I was ready to retire and give someone else a chance. And when I had my dream home, I'd have an emerald-glass tub

situated on a dais where I could soak in beauty oil all day long if
I wanted to—and nobody would be outside the door, banging
and telling me to hurry up! (I never had the chance to sit in the
tub long enough.) From that emerald tub I'd step, smelling
sweet of flowered perfume, and my skin soft as satin, and my
pores would be forever cleansed of the rotten stench of dry old
wood and attic dust permeated with all the miseries of
antiquity . . . so that we, who were young, smelled as old as this
house.

"Chris," I said, turning to stare at his back, "why should we
stay on and on, and wait for Momma to come back, much less
wait for that old man to die? Now that we are strong, why don't
we find a way to escape?"

He didn't say a word. But I saw his hands clutch the fabric of
the draperies harder.

"Chris . . ."

"I don't want to talk about it!" he flared.

"Why are you standing there waiting for the train to pass, if
you aren't thinking about getting away?"

"I'm not waiting for the train! I'm just looking out, that's
all!"

His forehead was pressed against the glass, daring a close
neighbor to look out and see him.

"Chris, come away from the window. Someone might see
you."

"I don't give a damn who sees me!"

My first impulse was to run to him, to put my arms around
him, and lavish a million kisses on his face to make up for those
he was missing from Momma. I'd draw his head down against
my breast and cuddle it there as she used to do, and he'd go back
to being the cheerful, sunny optimist who never had a sullen
angry day like I used to. Even if I did all that Momma did once,
I was wise enough to know it wouldn't be the same. It was *her*
he wanted. He had all his hopes, dreams, and faith wrapped up
in one single woman—Momma.

She'd been gone more than two months! Didn't she realize one day up here was longer than a month of normal living? Didn't she worry about us, and wonder how we were faring? Did she believe that Chris would always be her staunchest supporter when she left us without an excuse, a reason, an explanation? Did she really believe that love, once gained, couldn't be torn asunder by doubts and fears, and could never, never be put back together again?

"Cathy," said Chris suddenly, "Where would you go if you had your choice of anywhere?"

"South," I said, "down to some warm, sunny beach, where the waves wash in gentle and low . . . don't want high surf with white caps . . . don't want the gray sea chafing against big rocks . . . I want to go where the wind never blows, I just want soft warm breezes to whisper in my hair and on my cheeks, while I lie on pure white sand, and drink up the sunlight."

"Yeah," he agreed, sounding wistful, "sounds nice the way you say it. Only I wouldn't mind a strong surf; I'd like to ride the crest of a wave on one of those surfboards. It would sort of be like skiing."

I put my scissors down, my magazines, my pot of rubber cement, and laid aside the magazines and scrapbook to fully concentrate on Chris. He was missing out on so many sports he loved, shut up here in one room, made old and sad beyond his years. Oh, how I wanted to comfort him, and I didn't know how.

"Come away from the windows, Chris, please."

"Leave me alone! I get so damned sick and tired of this place! Don't do this, don't do that! Don't speak until spoken to—eat those damned meals every day, none of it hot enough, or seasoned right—I think *she* does it deliberately, just so we'll never have anything to enjoy, even food. Then I think about all that money— half of it should be Momma's, and ours. And I tell myself, no matter what, it is worth it! That old man can't live forever!"

"All the money in the world isn't worth the days of living we've lost!" I flared back.

He spun around, his face red. "The hell it isn't! Maybe you can get by with your talent, but I've got years and years of education ahead of me! You know Daddy expected me to be a doctor, so come hell or high water, I'm getting my M.D.! And if we run away, I'll never be a doctor—you know that! Name what I can do to earn a living for us—quick, list the jobs I can get other than a dishwasher, a fruit-picker, a short-order cook—will any of those put me through college, and then through med school? And I'll have you and the twins to support, as well as myself—a ready-made family at age sixteen!"

Fiery anger filled me. He didn't give me credit for being able to contribute anything! "I can work, too!" I snapped back. "Between us we can manage. Chris, when we were starving, you brought me four dead mice, and you said God gives people extra strength and abilities in the time of great stress. Well, I believe He does. When we leave here and are on our own, somehow or other we will make our way, and you will be a doctor! I'll do anything to see that you get that damned M.D. behind your name!"

"What can *you* do?" he asked in a hateful, sneering way. Before I could reply, the door behind us opened and the grandmother was there! She paused without stepping into the room and fixed her glare on Chris. And he, stubborn and unwilling to cooperate as before, refused to be intimidated. He didn't move from the window, but he turned to stare out at the rain again.

"Boy!" she lashed out. *"Move away from that window—this instant!"*

"My name is not *'boy.'* My name is Christopher. You can address me by my given name, or don't address me at all—but never call me *'boy'* again!"

She spat at his back: "I hate that particular name! It was your father's; out of the kindness of my heart, I pleaded his cause when his mother died, and he didn't have a home. My husband didn't want him here, but I felt pity for a young boy without parents, or means, and robbed of so much. So I kept nagging my husband to let his younger half-brother live under our roof. So your father came . . . brilliant, handsome, and he took advantage of our generosity. Deceived us! We sent him to the best of schools, bought him the best of everything, and he stole our daughter, his own half-niece! She was all we had left then . . . the only one left . . . and they eloped in the night, and came back two weeks later, smiling, happy, asking us to forgive them for falling in love. That night, my husband had his first heart attack. Has your mother told you that—that she and that man were the cause of her father's heart disease? He ordered her out—told her never to come back—and then he fell down on the floor."

She stopped, gasping for breath, putting a large, strong hand flashing with diamonds to her throat. Chris turned away from the window and stared at her, as did I. This was more than she had said to us since we came up the stairs to live, an eternity ago.

"We are not to blame for what our parents did," Chris said flatly.

"You are to blame for what you and your sister have done!"

"What have we done so sinful?" he asked. "Do you think we can live in one room, year after year, and not see each other? You helped put us here. You have locked this wing so the servants cannot enter. You *want* to catch us doing something you consider evil. You want Cathy and me to prove your judgment of our mother's marriage is right! Look at you, standing there in your iron-gray dress, feeling pious and self-righteous while you starve small children!"

"Stop!" I cried, terrified by what I saw on the grandmother's face. "Chris, don't say anything else!"

But he had already said too much. She slammed out of the room as my heart came up in my throat. "We'll go up in the attic," said Chris calmly. "The coward is afraid of the stairwell. We'll be safe enough, and if she starves us, we'll use the sheet-ladder and reach the ground."

Again the door opened. The grandmother came in, striding

forward with a green willow switch in her hand, and grim determination in her eyes. She must have stashed the switch somewhere nearby, to have fetched it so quickly. "Run into the attic and hide," she lashed out, reaching to seize Chris by his upper arm, "and none of you will eat for another week! And not only will I whip you, but your sister, as well, if you resist, and the twins."

It was October. In November, Chris would be seventeen. He was still only a boy compared to her huge size. He was considering resistance, but glanced at me, then at the twins, who whimpered and clung to each other, and he allowed that old woman to drag him into the bathroom. She closed and locked the door. She ordered him to strip, and to lean over the bathtub.

The twins came running to me, burying their faces in my lap. "Make her stop!" pleaded Carrie. "Don't let her whip Chris!"

He didn't make a sound as that whip slashed down on his bare skin. I heard the sickening thuds of green willow biting into flesh. And I felt every painful blow! Chris and I had become as one in the past year; he was like the other side of me, the way I'd like to be, strong and forceful, and able to stand that whip without crying out. I hated her. I sat on that bed, and gathered the twins in my arms, and felt hate so large looming up inside of me that I didn't know how to release it except by screaming. He felt the whip, and I let loose his cries of pain. I hoped God heard! I hoped the servants heard! I hoped that dying grandfather heard!

Out of the bathroom she came, with her whip in her hand. Behind her, Chris trailed, a towel swathed around his hips. He was dead-white. I couldn't stop screaming.

"Shut up!" she ordered, snapping the whip before my eyes. "Silence this second, unless you want more of the same!"

I couldn't stop screaming, not even when she dragged me off to the bed and threw the twins aside when they tried to protect me. Cory went for her leg with his teeth. She sent him reeling with one blow. I went then, my hysteria quelled, into the bathroom, where I, too, was ordered to strip. I stood there looking at her diamond brooch, the one she always wore, counting the stones, seventeen tiny ones. Her gray taffeta was patterned with fine red lines, and the white collar was hand-crocheted. She fixed her eyes on the short stubble of hair the scarf about my head revealed with an expression of gloating satisfaction.

"Undress, or I will rip off your clothes."

I began to undress, slowly working on the buttons of my blouse. I didn't wear a bra then, though I needed one. I saw her eyeing my breasts, my flat stomach, before she turned her eyes away, apparently offended. "I'm going to get even one day, old woman," I said. "There's going to come a day when you are going to be the helpless one, and I'm going to hold the whip in my hands. And there's going to be food in the kitchen that you are never going to eat, for, as you incessantly say, God sees everything, and he has his way of working justice, an eye for an eye is his way, Grandmother!"

"Never speak to me again!" she snapped. She smiled then, confident there would never come that day when I was in control of her fate. Foolishly, I had spoken, using the worst possible timing, and she let me have it. While the whip bit down on my tender flesh, in the bedroom the twins screamed, "Chris, make her stop! Don't let Cathy be hurt!"

I fell down on my knees near the tub, crouching in a tight ball to protect my face, my breasts, my most vulnerable areas. Like a wild woman out of control, she lashed at me until the willow switch broke. The pain was like fire. When the switch broke, I thought it was over, but she picked up a long-handled brush and with that she beat me about the head and shoulders. Try as I would to keep from screaming, like the brave silence Chris had kept, I had to let it out. I yelled, "You're not a woman! You're a monster! Something unhuman and inhumane!" My reward for this was a belting whack against the right side of my skull. Everything went black.

I drifted into reality, hurting all over, my head splitting with pain. Up in the attic a record was playing the "Rose Adiago"

from the ballet *The Sleeping Beauty*. If I live to be a hundred I
will never forget that music, and the way I felt when I opened
my eyes to see Chris bending over me, applying antiseptic, taping on adhesive plasters, tears in his eyes dropping down on me.
He'd ordered the twins up into the attic to play, to study, to
color, to do anything to keep their minds off of what was going
on down here. When he had done for me all that he could with
his inadequate medical supplies, I took care of his welted,
bloody back. Neither of us wore clothes. Clothes would adhere
to our oozing cuts. I had the most bruises from the brush she'd
wielded so cruelly. On my head was a dark lump that Chris
feared might be a concussion.

Doctoring over, we turned on our sides, facing one another
under the sheet. Our eyes locked and melded as one set. He
touched my cheek, the softest, most loving caress. "Don't we
have fun, my brother . . . don't we have fun?" I sang in a parody
of that song about Bill Bailey. "We'll hurt the livelong da-ay . . .
you'll do the doctoring and I'll pay the rent . . ."

"Stop!" he cried out, looking hurt and defenseless. "I know it
was my fault! I stood at the window. She didn't have to hurt you,
too!"

"It doesn't matter, sooner or later she would do it. From the
very first day, she planned to punish us for some trifling reason.
I just marvel that she held back for so long in using that whip."

"When she was lashing me, I heard you screaming—and I
didn't have to. You did it for me, Cathy, and it helped; I didn't
feel any pain but yours."

We held each other carefully. Our bare bodies pressed
together; my breasts flattened out against his chest. Then he was
murmuring my name, and tugging off the wrapping from my
head, letting loose my spill of long hair before he cupped my
head in his hands to gently ease it closer to his lips. It felt odd
to be kissed while lying naked in his arms . . . and not right.
"Stop," I whispered fearfully, feeling that male part of him grow
hard against me. "This is just what she thought we did."

Bitterly, he laughed before he drew away, telling me I didn't know anything. There was more to making love than just kissing, and we hadn't done more than kiss, ever.

"And never will," I said, but weakly.

That night I went to sleep after thinking of his kiss, and not the whipping or the blows from the brush. Swelling up in both of us was a turmoil of whirling emotions. Something sleeping deep inside of me had awakened, quickened, just as Aurora slept until the Prince came to put on her quiet lips a long lover's kiss.

That was the way of all fairy tales—ending with the kiss, and the happy ever after. There had to be some other prince for me to bring about a happy ending.

To Find a Friend

Somebody was screaming on the attic stairs! I bolted awake and looked around to see who was missing. Cory!

Oh, God—what had happened now?

I bounded from bed and raced toward the closet, and I heard Carrie wake up and add her yowls to Cory's, not even knowing what he was yelling about. Chris cried out, "What the hell is going on now?"

I sped through the closet, raced up six steps, and then stopped dead and just stared. There was Cory in his white pajamas, yelling his head off—and darned if I could see why.

"Do something! Do something!" he screamed at me, and finally he pointed to the object of his distress.

Ohhh . . . on the step was a mousetrap, the same place we left one every night, set with cheese. But this time the mouse wasn't dead. It had tried to be clever, and steal the cheese with a forepaw instead of his teeth, and it was a tiny foot caught beneath the strong wire spring. Savagely, that little gray mouse was chewing on that trapped foot to free itself, despite the pain it must have felt.

"Cathy, do something quick!" cried Cory, throwing himself into my arms. "Save his life! Don't let him bite off his foot! I want him alive! I want a friend! I've never had a pet; you know I always wanted a pet. Why do you and Chris always have to kill all the mice?"

Carrie came up behind me to beat on my back with her tiny fists. "You're *mean*, Cathy! *Mean! Mean! You won't let Cory have nothin'!*"

As far as I knew, Cory had just about everything money could buy except a pet, his freedom and the great outdoors. And truly, Carrie might have slaughtered me on the stairs if Chris hadn't rushed to my defense and unhinged the jaws clenched on my leg, which was fortunately well covered over with a very full nightgown that reached my ankles.

"Stop all this racket!" he ordered firmly. And he bent over to use the wash cloth he must have gone for just to pick up a savage mouse, and save his hand from being bitten.

"Make him well, Chris," pleaded Cory. "Please don't let him die!"

"Since you seem to want this mouse so badly, Cory, I'll do what I can to save his foot and leg, though it's pretty mangled."

Oh, what a hustle and bustle to save the life of one mouse, when we had killed hundreds. First Chris had to carefully lift the wire spring, and when he did, that uncomprehending wild thing almost hissed as Cory turned his back and sobbed, and Carrie screamed. Then the mouse seemed to half-faint, from relief, I suppose.

We raced down to the bathroom, where Chris and I scrubbed up and Cory held his near-dead mouse well wrapped in the pale blue washcloth, as Chris warned not to squeeze too tight.

On the countertop I spread all the medication we had on a clean towel.

"He's dead!" yelled Carrie, and she struck Chris. "You killed Cory's only pet!"

"This mouse is not dead," said Chris calmly. "Now please, all of you, be quiet, and don't move. Cathy, hold him still. I've got to do what I can to repair the torn flesh, and then I'll have to splint up that leg."

First he used antiseptic to clean the wound, while the mouse lay as if dead, only its eyes were open and staring up at me in a pitiful way. Next he used gauze that had to be split lengthwise to fit such a tiny foot and leg, and then over that he wrapped cotton and for a splint he used a toothpick, broke it in half and taped that in place with adhesive.

"I'm going to call him Mickey," said Cory—a thousand candles behind his eyes because one small mouse would live to become his pet.

"It may be a girl," said Chris, who flicked his eyes to check.

"No! Don't want no girl mouse—want a Mickey mouse!"

"It's a boy all right," said Chris. "Mickey will live and survive to eat all of our cheese," said the doctor, having completed his first surgery, and made his first cast, and looking, I must admit, rather proud of himself.

He washed the blood from his hands, and Cory and Carrie were lit up like something marvelous had finally come into their lives.

"Let me hold Mickey now!" cried Cory.

"No, Cory, let Cathy hold him for a while longer. You see, he's in shock and her hands are larger and will give Mickey more warmth than yours. And you might, just accidentally, squeeze too much."

I sat in the bedroom rocker and nursed a gray mouse that seemed on the verge of having a heart attack—its heart beat so fiercely. It gasped and fluttered its eyelids. As I held it, I felt its small, warm body struggling to live on, I wanted it to live and be Cory's pet.

The door opened and the grandmother came in.

None of us was fully clothed; in fact, we still wore only our nightclothes, without robes to conceal what might be revealed. Our feet were bare, our hair was tousled, and our faces weren't washed.

One rule broken.

Cory cringed close at my side as the grandmother swept her discerning gaze over the disorganized, (well, truthfully,) really messy room. The beds weren't made, our clothes were draped on chairs, and socks were everywhere.

Two rules broken.

And Chris was in the bathroom washing Carrie's face, and helping her put on her clothes, and fasten the buttons of her pink coveralls.

Three rules broken. The two of them came out, with Carrie's hair up in a neat ponytail, tied with a pink ribbon.

Immediately, when she saw the grandmother, Carrie froze. Her blue eyes went wide and scared. She turned and clung to Chris for protection. He picked her up and carried her over to me and put her down in my lap. Then he went on to where the picnic basket was on the table and began to take out what she had brought up.

As Chris neared, the grandmother backed away. He ignored her, as he swiftly emptied the basket.

"Cory," he said, heading toward the closet, "I'll go up and find a suitable birdcage and while I'm gone, see if you can't put on all of your clothes, without Cathy's help, and wash your face and hands."

The grandmother remained silent. I sat in the rocker and nursed the ailing mouse, as my little children crowded in the seat with me, and all three of us fixed our eyes on her, until Carrie could bear it no longer and turned to hide her face against my shoulder. Her small body quivered all over.

It troubled me that she didn't reprimand us and speak of the unmade beds, the cluttered, messy room that I tried to keep neat and tidy—and why hadn't she scolded Chris for dressing Carrie? Why was she looking, and seeing, but saying nothing?

Chris came down from the attic with a birdcage and some wire screening he said would make the cage more secure.

Those were words to snap the grandmother's head in his direction. Then her stone eyes fixed on me, and the pale blue washcloth I held. "What do you hold in your hands, girl?" she fired in a glacial tone.

"An injured mouse," I answered, my voice as icy as hers.

"Do you intend to keep that mouse as a pet, and put it in that cage?"

"Yes, we do." I stared at her defiantly and dared her to do something about it. "Cory has never owned a pet, and it is time that he did."

She pursed her thin lips and her stone-cold eyes swept to Cory, who trembled on the verge of tears. "Go on," she said, "keep the mouse. A pet like that suits you." With that she slammed out the door.

Chris began to fiddle with the birdcage, and the screening, and spoke as he worked. "The wires are much too far apart to keep Mickey inside, Cory, so we'll have to wrap the cage with this screen, and then your little pet can't escape."

Cory smiled. He peeked to see if Mickey still lived. "It's hungry. I can tell, its nose is twitching."

The winning over of Mickey the attic mouse was quite a feat. First of all, he didn't trust us, though we'd set his foot free from the trap. He hated the confinement of the cage. He wobbled about in circles on the awkward thing we'd put on his foot and leg, seeking a way out. Cory dropped cheese and bread crumbs through the bars to entice him into eating and gaining strength. He ignored the cheese, the bread, and in the end, walked as far away as he could get, his tiny bead-black eyes wary with fear, his body atremble as Cory opened the rusty cage door, to put in a miniature soup tureen filled with water.

Then he put his hand in the cage and pushed a bit of cheese closer. "Good cheese," he said invitingly. He moved a bit of bread nearer to the trembling mouse whose whiskers twitched, "Good bread. It will make you strong and well."

It took two weeks before Cory had a mouse that adored him and would come when he whistled. Cory hid tidbits in his shirt pockets to tempt Mickey into them. When Cory wore a shirt with two breast pockets, and the right one held a bit of cheese, and the left a bit of peanut-butter-and-grape-jelly sandwich, Mickey would hesitate indecisively on Cory's shoulders, his nose twitching, his whiskers jerking. And only too plainly could you see we had not a gourmet mouse, but a gourmand who wanted what was in both pockets at the same time.

Then, when finally he could make up his mind as to which he would go for first, down he'd scamper into the peanut-butter pocket, and eat upside down, and in a squiggle he'd race back up to Cory's shoulder, around his neck, and down into the pocket with the cheese. It was laughable the way he never went directly over Cory's chest to the other pocket, but always up and around his neck, and then down, tickling every funnybone Cory had.

The little leg and foot healed, but the mouse never walked perfectly, nor could he run very fast. I think the mouse was clever enough to save the cheese for last, for that he could pick up and hold as he daintily nibbled, whereas the bit of sandwich was a messy meal.

And believe me, never was there a mouse better at smelling out food, no matter where it was hidden. Willingly, Mickey abandoned his mice friends to take up with humans who fed him so well, and petted him, and rocked him to sleep, though oddly enough, Carrie had no patience with Mickey at all. It could be just because that mouse was as charmed by her dollhouse as she was. The little stairways and halls fitted his size perfectly, and once on the loose, he headed directly for the dollhouse! In through a window he clambered, and tumbled down on the floor; and porcelain people, so delicately balanced, fell right and left, and the dining-room table turned over when he wanted a taste.

Carrie screamed at Cory, "Your Mickey is eating all the party food! Take him away! Take him out of my living room!"

Cory captured his lame mouse, which couldn't move too quickly, and he cuddled Mickey against his chest. "You must learn to behave, Mickey. Bad things happen in big houses. The lady who owns that house over there, she hits you for anything."

He made me giggle, for it was the first time I'd ever heard him make even the slightest disparaging remark about his twin sister.

It was a good thing Cory had a little, sweet gray mouse to delve deep into his pockets for the goodies his master hid there. It was a good thing all of us had something to do to occupy our time, and our minds, while we waited and waited for our mother to show up, when it was beginning to seem like she never would come to us again.

At Last, Momma

Chris and I never discussed what had happened between us on the bed the day of the whippings. Often I caught him staring at me, but just as soon as my eyes turned to meet his, his would shift away. When he turned suddenly to catch me watching him, mine were the eyes to flee.

We were growing more day by day, he and I. My breasts filled out fuller, my hips widened, my waist diminished, and the short hair above my forehead grew out longer and curled becomingly. Why hadn't I known before that it would curl without so much weight to pull the curls into waves only? As for Chris, his shoulders broadened, his chest became more manly, and his arms too. I caught him once in the attic staring down at that part of him he seemed so taken with—and measuring it too! "Why?" I asked, quite astonished to learn that the length mattered. He turned away before he told me once he'd seen Daddy naked, and what he had seemed so inadequate in size. Even the back of his neck was red as he explained this. Oh, golly—just like I wondered what size bra Momma wore! "Don't do it again," I whispered. Cory had such a small male organ, and what if he had seen and felt as Chris did, that *his* was inadequate?

Suddenly I stopped polishing the school desks, and stood very still, thinking of Cory. I turned to stare at him and Carrie. Oh, God, how too much closeness dims your perspective! Two years, and four months we had been locked away—and the twins were very much as they had been the night they came! Certainly their heads were larger and that should have diminished the size of their eyes. Yet their eyes appeared extraordinarily large. They sat listless on that stained and smelly old mattress we'd pulled close to the windows. Butterflies danced nervously in my stomach to view them objectively. Their bodies seemed frail flower stems too weak to support the blossoms of their heads.

I waited until they fell asleep in the weak sunlight, then said in an undertone to Chris, "Look at the buttercups, they don't grow. Only their heads are larger."

He sighed heavily, narrowed his eyes, and neared the twins, hovering above them, and bending to touch their transparent skins. "If only they would go outside on the roof with us to benefit from the sun and fresh air like we do. Cathy, no matter how much they fight and scream, we've got to force them outside!"

Foolishly, we thought if we carried them out on the roof while they were asleep, they would awaken in the sunlight, held safe in our arms, and they'd feel secure enough. Cautiously, Chris lifted up Cory, while I leaned to heft Carrie's slight weight. Stealthily, we approached an open attic window. It was Thursday, our day to enjoy outdoors on the roof, while the servants spent their day off in town. It was safe enough to use the back part of the roof.

Barely had Chris cleared the window ledge with Cory when the warm Indian summer air brought Cory suddenly out of sleep. He took one look around, seeing me with Carrie in my arms, obviously planning to take her out on the roof too, when he let out a howl! Carrie bolted out of sleep. She saw Chris with Cory on the steep roof, she saw me and where I was taking her, and she let out a scream that must have been heard a mile away!

Chris called to me through the racket, "Come on! For their own good, we have to do this!"

Not only did they scream, they kicked and beat at us with small fists! Carrie clamped her teeth down on my arm, so I screamed, too. Little as they were, they had the strength of those in extreme danger. Carrie was battering her fists into my face so I could hardly see, plus screaming in my ear! Hastily, I turned around and headed back toward the schoolroom window. Trembling and weak, I stood Carrie on her feet beside the teacher's desk. I leaned against that desk, gasping and panting, and thanking God for letting me get her safely back inside. Chris returned Cory to his sister. It was no use. To force them out on the roof endangered the lives of all four of us.

Now they were angry. Resentfully they struggled when we pulled them toward the markings on the wall, where we'd measured their height the first day in the schoolroom. Chris held them both in place, while I backed up to read the inches they'd grown.

I stared and I stared, shocked and disbelieving it was possible. In all this time to grow only two niches? Two inches, when Chris and I had gained many, many inches between the ages of five and seven, though they had been exceptionally small at birth, Cory weighing only five pounds and Carrie five pounds and one ounce.

Oh. I had to put my hands up to cover my face so they couldn't see my stunned and horrified expression. Then that wasn't enough. I spun around so they saw only my back as I choked on the sobs stuck in my throat.

"You can let them go now," I finally managed. I turned to catch a glimpse of them scurrying away like two small flaxen-haired mice, racing for the stairwell, heading toward the beloved television and the escape it offered, and the little mouse which was real and waiting for them to come and pleasure *his* imprisoned life.

Directly behind me Chris stood and waited. "Well," he asked when I just wilted, speechless, "how much have they grown?"

Quickly I brushed away the tears before I turned, so I could see his eyes when I told him. "Two inches," I said in a flat way, but the pain was in my eyes, and that was what he saw.

He stepped closer and put his arms about me, then held my head so it was against his chest, and I cried, really bawled. I hated Momma for doing this! Really hated her! She knew children were like plants—they had to have sunshine if they were to grow. I trembled in the embrace of my brother, trying to convince myself that as soon as we were freed, they'd be beautiful again. They would, of course they would; they'd catch up, make up the lost years, and as soon as the sunshine was upon them again, they'd shoot up like weeds—they would, yes, they would! It was only all the long days hidden indoors that made their cheeks so hollow, and their eyes so sunken. And all of that could be undone, couldn't it?

"Well," I began in my hoarse, choked voice, while clinging to the only one who seemed to care anymore, "does money make the world go around, or is it love? Enough love bestowed on the twins, and I would have read six or seven or maybe eight inches gain in height, not only two."

Chris and I headed for our dim sequestered prison to eat lunch, and as always I sent the twins into the bathroom to wash their hands, for they certainly didn't need mouse germs to imperil their health more.

As we sat quietly at the dining table, eating our sandwiches, and sipping our lukewarm soup and milk, and watching TV lovers meet and kiss and make plans to run away and leave their respective spouses, the door to our room opened. I hated to look away, and miss what would happen next, yet I did.

Gaily into our room strode our mother. She wore a beautiful, lightweight suit, with soft gray fur at the cuffs and around the neck of the jacket.

"Darlings!" she cried in enthusiastic greeting, then hesitated uncertainly when not one of us jumped up to welcome her back. "Here I am! Aren't you glad to see me? Oh, you just don't know how very glad I am to see all of you. I've missed you so much, and thought about you, and dreamed of you, and I've brought you all so many beautiful presents that I chose with such care. Just wait until you see them! And I had to be so sneaky—for how could I explain buying things for children? I wanted to make up for being away for so long. I did want to tell you why I was leaving, really I did, but it was so complicated. And I didn't know exactly how long I'd be gone, and though you missed me, you were cared for, weren't you? You didn't suffer, did you?"

Had we suffered? Had we only missed her? Who was she, anyway? Idiot thoughts while I stared at her and listened to how difficult four hidden children made the lives of others. And though I wanted to deny her, keep her from ever really being close again, I faltered, filling with hope, wanting so much to love her again, and trust her again.

Chris got up and spoke first, in a voice that had finally resolved from one that was high and squeaky at tunes into reliable, deep and masculine tones. "Momma, of course we're glad you're back! And yes, we missed you! But you were wrong to go away, and stay away for so long, no matter what complicated reasons you had."

"Christopher," she said, her eyes widening in surprise, "you don't sound like yourself." Her eyes flicked from him to me, then to the twins. Her vivaciousness simmered down. "Christopher, did anything go wrong?"

"Wrong?" he repeated. "Momma, what can be right about living in one room? You said I don't sound like myself—look me over good. Am I a little boy now? Look at Cathy—is she still a child? Look longest at the twins; notice in particular how tall they've grown. Then turn your eyes back on me, and tell me that Cathy and I are still children to be treated with condescension, and are incapable of understanding adult subjects. We haven't remained idle, twiddling our thumbs while you were off having a good time. Through books Cathy and I have lived a zillion lives . . . our vicarious way to feel alive."

Momma wanted to interrupt, but Chris overrode her small voice which faltered. He threw her many gifts a scornful glance. "So, you have come back bearing peace offerings, like you always do when you know you have done wrong. Why do you keep thinking your stupid gifts can make up for what we've lost, and what we are constantly losing? Sure, once we *were* delighted with the games and toys and clothes you brought up to our prison room, but we're older now, and gifts are just not enough!"

"Christopher, please," she begged, and looked uneasily at the twins again, and so quickly she averted her eyes. "Please don't speak as if you've stopped loving me. I couldn't bear that."

"I love you," was his reply. "I *make* myself keep on loving you, despite what you do. I've *got* to love you. We all have to love you, and believe in you, and think you are looking out for our best interests. But look at us, Momma, and really see us. Cathy feels, and I feel, that you close your eyes to what you are doing to us. You come to us smiling, and dangle before our eyes and our ears bright hopes for the future, but nothing ever materializes. Long ago, when you first told us about this house and your parents, you said we'd only be shut up in this room for *one* night, and then you changed it to a *few* days. And then it was another few weeks, and then another few months . . . and over two years have passed while we wait for an old man to die, who may never die from the skilled way his doctors keep pulling him back from the grave. This room is not improving *our* health. Can't you see that?" he almost shouted, his boyish face suffused with red as his limit of self-control was reached at last. I thought I would never live to see the day when he would attack our mother—*his* beloved mother.

The sound of his loud voice must have startled him, for he lowered his tone and spoke more calmly, and yet his words had the impact of bullets: "Momma, whether or not you inherit your father's immense fortune, we want out of this room! Not next

week, or tomorrow—but today! Now! This minute! You turn
that key over to me, and we'll go away, far away. And you can
send us money, if you care to, or send nothing, if that's what you
want, and you need never see us again, if that is your choice, and
that will solve all your problems, we'll be gone from your life,
and your father need never know we existed, and you can have
what he leaves you, all to yourself."

Momma went pale from shock.

I sat in my chair, with my lunch half-eaten. I felt sorry for
her, and I felt betrayed by my own compassion. I closed the
door, slammed it hard, just by thinking of those two weeks when
we were starved . . . four days of eating nothing else but crackers
and cheese, and three days without any food at all, and nothing
but water to drink. And then the whippings, the tar in my hair,
and, most of all, the way Chris had to slash his wrist to feed the
twins his nourishing blood.

And Chris, what he was saying to her, and the hard determined way he said it, was mostly my doing.

I think she guessed this, for she shot me a stabbing glance,
full of resentment.

"Say no more to me, Christopher—it's clear to see you are
not yourself."

Jumping to my feet, I stepped over to his side. "Look at us,
Momma! Observe our radiant, healthy complexions, just like
yours. Look especially long on your two youngest. They don't
look frail, do they? Their full cheeks don't look gaunt, do they?
Their hair isn't dull, is it? Their eyes—they're not dark and hollowed out, are they? When you look, and register, do you see
how much they've grown, how healthily they thrive? If you
can't have pity for Christopher and me, have pity for them."

"Stop!" she yelled, jumping up from the bed where she'd sat
to have us crowd cozily around, in our former way. She spun
on her heel so she wouldn't have to see us. Choking sobs were
in her voice that cried, "You have no right to talk to your mother
in this manner. But for me you would all be starving in the

streets." Her voice broke. She turned sideways, throwing Chris an appealing, woebegone look. "Haven't I done the best I could by you? Where did I go wrong? What do you lack? You knew how it would be until your grandfather died. You agreed to stay here until he did. And I've kept my word. You live in a warm, safe room. I bring to you the best of everything—books, toys, games, the best clothes that money can buy. You have good food to eat, a TV set." Fully she faced us now, spreading wide her hands in a supplicating gesture, appearing ready to fall down on her knees, pleading with her eyes at me now. "Listen to this— your grandfather is so ill now he is confined to bed all day long. He isn't even allowed to sit in the wheelchair. His doctors say he can't last long, a few days or the maximum of a few weeks. The day he dies, I'll come up and unlock your door and lead you down the stairs. I'll have money enough then to send all four of you to college, and Chris to medical school, and you, Cathy, can continue on with your ballet lessons. I'll find for Cory the best of musical teachers, and for Carrie, I'll do anything she wants. Are you going to throw away all the years you've suffered and endured without waiting for rewards—just when you're on the verge of reaching your goal! Remember how you used to laugh and talk of what you'd do when you were blessed with more money than you knew how to spend? Recall all the plans we made . . . our house where we could all live together again. Don't throw everything away by becoming impatient just when we're due to win! Tell me I've had pleasure while you've suffered, and I'll agree that I have. But I'll make up for that by tenfold!"

Oh, I admit I was touched, and wanted so much to step away from disbelief. I hovered near, trusting her again, and quivered with the suspicious fear that she was lying. Hadn't she told us from the very beginning that our grandfather was taking his last breath . . . years and years of his breathing his last breath? Should I yell out, *Momma, we just don't believe you anymore?* I wanted to wound her, make her bleed as we had bled with our tears, isolation, and loneliness—to say nothing of the punishments.

But Chris looked at me forbiddingly, making me ashamed. Could I be as chivalrous as he was? Would that I could open my mouth, ignore him, and shout all the grandmother had done to punish us for nothing. For some strange reason I stayed quiet. Maybe I was protecting the twins from knowing too much. Maybe I was waiting for Chris to tell her first.

He stood and gazed at her with soft compassion, forgetting the tar in my hair, and the weeks without food, and the dead mice he would make tasty with salt and pepper—and then the whippings. He was beside me, his arm brushing mine. He trembled with indecision, and in his eyes were tormented visions of hopes and despair as he watched our mother begin to cry.

The twins crept closer to cling to my skirt as Momma crumpled down on the nearest bed to sob and beat her fists into the pillow, just like a child.

"Oh, but you are heartless and ungrateful children," she wailed pitifully, "that you should do this to me, your own mother, the only person in this world who loves you! The only one who cares about you! I came so joyfully to you, so happy to be with you again, wanting to tell you my good news so you could rejoice with me. And what do you do? You attack me viciously, unjustly! Making me feel so guilty, and so ashamed, when all along I have done the best I could, and yet you won't believe!"

She was on our level now, crying, face down on the bed in the same way I would have done years ago, and Carrie would do this day.

Immediately, spontaneously, Chris and I were stricken contrite and sorry. Everything she said was only too true. She *was* the only person who loved us, who cared, and in her only lay our salvation, our lives, our futures, and our dreams. We ran to her, Chris and I, and threw our arms around her as best we could, pleading for forgiveness. The twins said nothing, only watched.

"Momma, please stop crying! We didn't mean to hurt your

feelings. We're sorry, we really are. We'll stay. We believe you. The grandfather is almost dead—he has to die sometime, doesn't he?"

On and on she wept, inconsolable.

"Talk to us, Momma, please! Tell us your good news. We want to know, we want to be glad and rejoice with you. We said those things only because we were hurt when you left us and didn't tell us why. Momma, please, please, Momma."

Our pleas, our tears, our anguish finally reached her. She somehow managed to sit up, and she dabbed at her eyes with a white linen handkerchief with five inches of fine lace all around, and monogrammed with a big white C.

She shoved Chris and me aside, then brushed off our hands as if they burned, and she got to her feet. Now she refused to meet our eyes which begged, pleaded, cajoled.

"Open your gifts that I selected with such care," she said in a cold voice filled with choked sobs, "and then tell me whether or not you are thought about and loved. Tell me then that I didn't think of your needs, and think of your best interests, and try to cater to your every whim. Tell me then I am selfish and that I don't care."

Dark mascara streaked her cheeks. Her bright red lipstick was smeared. Her hair, customarily worn on her head like a perfect hat, was mussed and displaced. She had strolled into our room a vision of perfection and now she appeared a broken mannequin.

And why did I have to go and think she was like an actress, playing her part for all she was worth?

She looked at Chris, and ignored me. And the twins—they could have been in Timbuktu for all the concern she showed for their welfare, and their sensitivities.

"I have ordered a new set of encyclopedias for your upcoming birthday, Christopher," she choked out, still dabbing at her face and trying to take off the mascara smudges. "The very set you always wanted—the best that is published, bound in genuine red leather, tooled in twenty-four-karat gold around all four sides, and hubbed-spined a full half-inch outward. I went directly to the publishing house, to order them for you especially. They'll bear your name, and the date, but they won't be mailed directly here, lest someone should see them." She swallowed heavily and put away her fancy handkerchief. "I thought and thought about a gift to please you the most, just like I have always given you the very best to educate yourself."

Chris appeared dumbfounded. The play of mixed emotions upon his face made his eyes look confused, bewildered, dazed, and sort of helpless. God, how he must have loved her, even after all she'd done.

My emotions were straightforward, with no indecision. I smoldered with rage. Now she was bringing up genuine, leather-bound, hubbed-spined, twenty-four-karat gold-tooled encyclopedias! Books like that must cost more than a thousand dollars—maybe two or three thousand! Why wasn't she putting that money into our escape fund? I wanted to yell out like Carrie and protest, but something broken in Chris's blue eyes kept my mouth shut. He'd always wanted a set of genuine red-leather-bound encyclopedias, and she'd already ordered them, and money was nothing to her now, and maybe, just maybe, the grandfather really would die today or tomorrow, and she wouldn't *need* to rent an apartment, or buy a house.

She sensed my doubts.

Momma raised her head regally high and turned toward the door. We had not opened our gifts, and she wasn't staying to watch our reactions. Why was I crying inside when I hated her? I didn't love her now. . . . I didn't.

She said when she reached the door and had it open, "When you have thought about the pain you have given me today, and when you can treat me with love and respect again, then I will come back. Not before."

So she came.

So she went.

So she had come and gone and left Carrie and Cory

untouched, unkissed, unspoken to, and hardly glanced at. And I knew why. She couldn't bear to look and see what gaining a fortune was costing the twins.

They jumped up from the table and came running to me, to cling to my skirts, and stare up into my face. Their small faces were fraught with anxieties, with fears, studying my expression to see if I were happy, so they, too, could feel happy. I knelt to lavish them with all the kisses and caresses she had overlooked—or just couldn't give to those she'd harmed so.

"Do we look funny?" asked Carrie worriedly, her small hands plucking at mine.

"No, of course not. You and Cory just look pale, because you stay inside too much."

"Did we grow much?"

"Yes, yes, of course you have." And I smiled, even as I lied. And with a pretense of joy, and keeping that false smile like a mask to wear, I sat down on the floor with the twins and Chris, and we all four began to open our gifts like it was Christmas Day. They were all beautifully wrapped in expensive paper, or gold or silver foil, and sporting huge satin bows of assorted colors.

Tear off the paper, toss away the ribbons, the bows, rip off the lids of boxes, pull out the inside tissue . . . see all the pretty clothes for each of us. Glance at the new books, hooray! See the new toys, the games, the puzzles, hurrah! My, oh, my, what a big, big box of maple sugar candy shaped like identical leaves!

Here before us was the display of her concern. She knew us well, I admit, our tastes, our hobbies—all but our sizes. With gifts she paid us for all those long empty months when we were left in the care of the witch grandmother who would quite willingly see us dead and buried.

And she knew what kind of mother she had—she knew!

With games and toys and puzzles, she sought to buy us off, and beg our forgiveness for doing what she knew in her heart was wrong.

With sweet maple sugar candy she hoped to take the sour gall of loneliness from our mouths, hearts, and minds. To her way of thinking, it was very obvious, we WERE still only children, though Chris needed to shave, and I needed to wear a bra . . . still children . . . and children she would keep us forever as the titles of the books she brought plainly indicated. *Little Men*. I'd read that years ago. Fairy tales by the brothers Grimm and Hans Christian Andersen—we knew them by heart. And *Wuthering Heights* and *Jane Eyre* again? Didn't she keep a list of what we'd already read? What we had?

I managed to smile though as I pulled over Carrie's head a new red dress, and in her hair I tied a purple ribbon. Now she was dressed as she'd always wanted to be, in her favorite colors. I put purple socks on her feet and new white sneakers. "You look beautiful, Carrie." And in a way she did, she was so happy to own bright, grown-up, royally colored clothes.

Next I helped Cory on with his bright red short pants, and a white shirt monogrammed on the pocket in red, and his tie had to be knotted by Chris, the way Daddy had shown him how a long time ago.

"Shall I dress you now, Christopher?" I asked sarcastically.

"If that is your heart's desire," he said wickedly, "you can dress me from skin out."

"Don't be vulgar!"

Cory had another new instrument to play—a shining banjo! Oh, golly day, he'd always wanted a banjo! She'd remembered. His eyes lit up. *Oh, Susannah, don't you cry for me, for I'm going to Louisiana with a banjo on my knee. . . .*

He played the tune, and Carrie sang the lyrics. It was one of his favorite happy songs, and one he could play on the guitar, though it never sounded right. On the banjo it sounded right, as it should. God blessed Cory with magic fingers.

God blessed me with mean thoughts to take the joy from everything. What good were pretty clothes when no one ever saw them? I wanted things that didn't come wrapped in fancy paper, and tied around with satin ribbons, and put in a box from

an expensive store. I wanted all the things money couldn't buy.
Had she noticed my hair cut so short on top? Had she seen how
thin we were? Did she think we looked healthy with our pale,
thin skins?

Bitter, ugly thoughts as I pushed a maple sugar leaf into
Carrie's eager mouth, and then a leaf into Cory's, and next one
into my own mouth. I glared at the beautiful clothes meant for
me. A blue velvet dress, such as should be worn to a party. A
pink and blue nightgown and peignoir set, with slippers to
match. I sat there with the candy melting on my tongue, and it
had the acrid taste of the iron lump in my throat. Encyclopedias!
Were we going to be here forever?

Yet candy made from maple sugar was my topmost favorite,
always had been. She brought this box of candy for me, *for me,*
and I could only swallow one piece, and that with great difficulty.

They sat on the floor with the candy box centered between
them, Cory, Carrie, and Chris. They stuffed the candy in, piece
after piece, laughing and pleased. "You should make that candy
last," I told them with sour hatefulness. "That may well be the
last box of candy you see for a long, long time."

Chris threw me a look, his blue eyes happy and shining.
Easy enough to see all *his* faith and trust was restored by just
one short visit from Momma. Why couldn't he see that gifts
were just a way of hiding the fact that she no longer cared
about us? Why didn't he know, as I did, that we weren't as real
to her now as once we'd been? We were another of those
unpleasant subjects that people don't like to talk about, like
mice in the attic.

"Sit there and act dumb," said Chris, sparkling his happiness
on me. "Deny yourself the candy, while we three satisfy our
sweet tooth all at once before the mice come down and eat it for
us. Cory, Carrie, and I will scrub our teeth clean, while you sit
and cry, and feel sorry for yourself, and pretend by self-sacrifice
you can change our circumstances. Go on, Cathy! Cry! Play the
martyr. Suffer! Pound your head on the wall! Scream! And we'll

still be here until the grandfather dies, and all the candy will be gone, gone, gone."

I hated him for making fun of me! I jumped to my feet, ran to the far side of the room, turned my back, and tried on my new clothes. Three beautiful dresses I yanked down over my head one by one. Easily they zipped up to the waist, and fitted there loosely. But try as I would, the zipper wouldn't close in back when it reached my bust. I tore off the last dress, looking for the darts in the bodice. None there! She was buying me little-girl dresses—silly, sweet little-girl garments that screamed out she *didn't* see! I threw those three dresses down on the floor and stomped on them, crushing the blue velvet so it could never be returned to the store.

And there sat Chris on the floor with the twins, looking devilish, and laughing with a raffishly wicked and boyish charm that would win me over to laughter, too—if I would let it. "Make out a shopping list," he joked. "It's time you started wearing bras and stopped bobbing up and down. And while you're at it, write down a girdle, too."

I could have slapped his grinning face! My abdomen was a hollowed out cave. And if my buttocks were rounded and firm, it was from exercise—not from fat! "Shut up!" I yelled. "Why should I have to write out a list and tell Momma anything? She'd know what clothes I have, and what I should be wearing, if she really looked at me! How do I know what size bra to order? And I don't need a girdle! What you need is a jock strap—and some sense in your head that doesn't come from a book!" I glared at him, happy to see his stunned expression.

"Christopher," I screamed, unable to control myself. "Sometimes I hate Momma! And not only that, sometimes I hate you, too! Sometimes I hate everybody—most of all myself! Sometimes I wish I were dead, because I think we would all be better off dead than buried alive up here! Just like rotting, walking, talking vegetables!"

My secret thoughts had been thrown out, spewed forth like

garbage to make both my brothers wince and go paler. And my small sister shrank even smaller as she began to tremble. Immediately after the cruel words were out of my mouth, I wanted them back in. I was drowning in shame, but unable to apologize and take it all back. I whirled about and ran for the closet, running for the tall, slender door that would take me up the stairs and into the attic. When I hurt, and I hurt often, I raced for the music, the costumes, the ballet shoes on which I could spin and twirl and dance away my troubles. And somewhere in that crimson-colored never-never land where I pirouetted madly, in a wild and crazy effort to exhaust myself into insensibility, I saw that man, shadowy and distant, half-hidden behind towering white columns that rose clear up to a purple sky. In a passionate *pas de deux* he danced with me, forever apart, no matter how hard I sought to draw nearer and leap into his arms, where I could feel them protective about me, supporting me . . . and with him I'd find, at last, a safe place to live and love.

Then, suddenly, the music was over. I was back in the dry and dusty attic, on the floor, with my right leg twisted beneath me. I had fallen! When I struggled to my feet, I could barely walk. My knee hurt so much, tears of another kind came to my eyes. I limped through the attic and on into the schoolroom, not caring if I ruined my knee forever. I opened up a window wider and stepped out onto the black roof. Painfully I eased my way down the steep incline, stopping only when I was at the very edge with the leaf-clogged gutters. Far below was the ground. With tears of self-pity and pain streaking my face and blurring my vision, I closed my eyes and let myself sway off balance. In a minute it would all be over. I'd be sprawled down there on top of the thorny rose bushes.

The grandmother and Momma could claim it was some idiot strange girl who climbed up on their roof and fell off accidentally, and Momma would cry when she saw me dead and broken and lying in a coffin, dressed in blue leotards and tulle tutu. Then she'd realize what she'd done, she'd want me back, she'd unlock the door to free Chris and the twins, and let them live real lives again.

And that was the golden side of my suicide coin.

But I had to turn it over, and see the tarnish. What if I didn't die? Suppose I just fell, and the rose bushes cushioned my fall, and I only ended up crippled and scarred for the rest of my life?

Then, again, suppose I really did die, and Momma didn't cry, or feel sorry, or any regret, and was only glad to be rid of a pest like me? Just how would Chris and the twins survive without me to take care of them? Who would mother the twins, and lavish them with the affection that was sometimes embarrassing for Chris to give as easily as I did? As for Chris—maybe he thought he didn't really need me, that books and red-leather, gold-tooled, hubbed-spined new encyclopedias were enough to take my place. When he got that M.D. behind his name, that would be enough to satisfy him all his life through. But when he was a doctor, I knew it still wouldn't be enough, never enough, if I wasn't there, too. And I was saved from death by my own ability to see both sides of the coin.

I stumbled away from the edge of the roof, feeling silly, childish, but still crying. My knee hurt so badly I ascended the roof by crawling to the special place near the back chimney, where two roofs met and made a safe corner. I lay on my back and stared up at that unseeing, uncaring sky. I doubted God lived up there; I doubted heaven was up there, too.

God and heaven were down there on the ground, in the gardens, in the forests, in the parks, on the seashores, on the lakes, and riding the highways, going somewhere!

Hell was right here, where I was, shadowing me persistently, trying to do me in, and make me into what the grandmother thought I was—the Devil's issue.

I lay on that hard, cold slate roof until darkness came on, and the moon came out, and the stars flashed angrily at me, as if knowing me for what I was. I wore only a ballet costume, leotards, and one of those silly frilly tutus.

Goosebumps came and chicken-skinned my arms, and still I stayed to plan all my revenge, my vengeance against those who had turned me from good to evil, and made of me what I was going to be from this day forward. I convinced myself there would come a day when both my mother and my grandmother would be under my thumb . . . and I'd snap the whip, and handle the tar, and control the food supply.

I tried to think of exactly what I would do to them. What was the right punishment? Should I lock them both up and throw away the key? Starve them, as we had been starved?

A soft noise interrupted the dark and twisted flow of my thoughts. In the gloom of early evening Chris spoke my name hesitatingly. No more, just my name. I didn't answer, I didn't need him—I didn't need anybody. He had let me down by not understanding, and I didn't need him, not now.

Nevertheless, he came and lay close by my side. He'd brought a warm woolen jacket with him that he spread over me without saying a word. He stared as I did up at the cold and forbidding sky. The longest, most fearful silence grew between us. There was nothing I really hated about Chris, or even disliked, and I wanted so much to turn on my side and say this to him, and thank him for bringing me the warm jacket, but I couldn't say a word. I wanted to let him know I was sorry that I struck out at him, and the twins, when God knows none of us needed another enemy. My arms, shivering under the warmth of the jacket, longed to slide around him, and comfort him as he so often comforted me when I woke up from another nightmare. But all I could do was lie there, and hope he understood that I was all tied up in knots.

Always he could raise the white flag first, and for that I'm forever grateful. In a stranger's husky, strained voice that seemed to span across a great distance, he told me he and the twins had already eaten dinner, but my share had been saved.

"And we only pretended to eat all of the candy, Cathy. There's plenty left for you."

Candy. He spoke of candy. Was he still in the child's world where candy stood for something sweet enough to hold back tears? I had grown older, and had lost enthusiasm for childish delights. I wanted what every teen-ager wants—freedom to develop into a woman, freedom to have full control over my life! Though I tried to tell him this, my voice had dried up along with my tears.

"Cathy . . . what you said . . . don't ever say ugly, hopeless things like that again."

"Why not?" I choked out. "Every word I said is true. I only expressed what I feel inside—I let out what *you* keep hidden deep. Well, keep on hiding from yourself, and you'll find all those truths turn into acid to eat up your insides!"

"Not once have I ever wished myself dead!" he cried out in the hoarse voice of one with an everlasting cold. "Don't you ever say such a thing again—or think about death! Sure I've got doubts and suspicions hidden away in me, but I smile and I laugh, and make myself believe because I want to survive. If you died by your own hand, you would take me down with you, and soon the twins would follow, for who would be their mother then?"

It made me laugh. Hard, brittle ugly laughter—duplicating my mother's way of laughing when *she* felt bitter. "Why, Christopher Doll, remember we have a dear, sweet, loving mother who thinks first of our needs, and she will be left to care for the twins."

Chris turned toward me then, reaching out to seize my shoulders. "I hate it when you talk that way, like she talks sometimes. Do you think I don't know that you are more a mother to Cory and Carrie than *she* is? Do you think I failed to see the twins only stared at their mother, like she was a stranger? Cathy, I'm not blind or stupid. I know Momma takes care of herself first, and us next." That old moon was out to sparkle the tears frozen in his eyes. His voice in my ear had been gritty, hushed and deep.

All of this he said without bitterness, only regret—just the flat, emotionless way a doctor tells his patient he has a terminal illness.

That's when it came over me in a cataclysmic flood—I loved Chris—and he was my brother. He made me whole, he gave me what I lacked, a stability when I would run off wild and frantic—and what a perfect way to strike back at Momma and the grandparents. God wouldn't see. He'd closed his eyes to everything the day Jesus was put on the cross. But Daddy was up there, looking down, and I cringed in shame.

"Look at me, Cathy, please look at me."

"I didn't mean any of it, Chris, really I didn't. You know how melodramatic I am—I want to live as much as anyone does, but I'm so afraid something terrible is going to happen to us, shut up all the time. So I say awful things just to shake you up, make you see. Oh, Chris, I just ache to be with lots of people. I want to see new faces, new rooms. I'm scared to death for the twins. I want to go shopping, and ride horses, and do all the things we can't do in here."

In the dark, on the roof, in the cold, we reached for each other intuitively. We clung as one, our hearts throbbing loud against each other. Not crying, not laughing. Hadn't we already cried an ocean of tears? And they hadn't helped. Hadn't we already said a zillion prayers and waited for deliverance that never came? And if tears didn't work, and prayers weren't heard, how were we to reach God and make him do something?

"Chris, I've said it before, and I'm saying it again. We've got to take the initiative. Didn't Daddy always say God helps those who help themselves?"

His cheek was tight against mine while he reflected for so darned long. "I'll give it some thought, though, as Momma said, we could come any day into that fortune."

Our Mother's Surprise

Each day of the ten that passed before Momma visited us again, Chris and I speculated for hours on end just why she had gone away to Europe and stayed so long, and most of all—what was the big news she had to tell us?

We thought of those ten days as just another form of punishment. For punishment was what it was, and it hurt to know she was in this same house, and yet she could ignore us and shut us out, as if we *were* only mice in the attic.

So, when she showed up, at long last, we were thoroughly chastised, and most fearful she would never come back if Chris and I showed more hostility or repeated our demands to be let out. We were quiet, timid and accepting of our fate. For what would we do if she never returned? We couldn't escape by using the ladder made of torn-up sheets—not when the twins went hysterical just to be on the roof.

So we smiled at Momma, and uttered not one word of complaint. We didn't ask why she had punished us again by staying away ten days, when already she'd been gone for months. We accepted what she was willing to give us. We were, as she had told us she had learned to be with her father, her dutiful, obedient, and passive children. And, what's more, she liked us this way. We were again, her sweet, her loving, her private "darlings."

Since we were so good, so sweet, so approving of her now, and so very respectful, and apparently trusting, this was the time she chose to drop her bombshell.

"Darlings, rejoice for me! I am so happy!" She laughed and spun around in a circle, hugging her arms over her chest, loving her own body, or so it seemed to me. "Guess what happened—go on, guess!"

Chris and I glanced at each other. "Our grandfather has died," he said cautiously, while my heart was doing pirouettes, preparing to really leap and bound if she gave us the glad tidings.

"No!" she said sharply, as if her happiness had dimmed some.

"He's been taken to the hospital," said I, guessing second best.

"No. I really don't hate him now, so I wouldn't come to you and say I was rejoicing over his death."

"Why don't you just tell us your good news, then," I said dully. "We'll never be able to guess; we don't know much about your life anymore."

She ignored what I implied and rhapsodized on: "The reason I was gone for so long, and what I found so difficult to explain—I've married a wonderful man, an attorney named Bart Winslow. You're going to like him. He's going to love all of you. He's dark-haired and so handsome, and tall and athletic. And he loves to ski, like you do, Christopher, and he plays tennis, and he's brilliant, like you are, darling," and she was looking at Chris, of course. "He's charming and everybody likes him, even my father. And we went to Europe on our honeymoon, and the gifts I brought to you all came from England, France, Spain or Italy." And on and on she raved about her new husband, while Chris and I sat silent.

Since the night of the Christmas party, Chris and I had voiced our suspicions many times. For as young as we had been back then, we were wise enough to know that a beautiful young woman who was as needing of a man as our mother, was not likely to remain a widow for long. But still, almost two years passed without a wedding, and that had given us reason enough to believe that the handsome, dark-haired man with the big moustache was of no real importance to Momma—just a passing fancy—one suitor amongst many. And deep down in our foolish hearts, we had convinced ourselves that she was going to be ever-faithful, ever-devoted to our dead father—our blond and blue-eyed Grecian god father whom she had to love beyond reason to have done what she did—marry a man so closely related.

I closed my eyes to try and shut out her hateful voice, telling us of another man who was taking our father's place. Now she was another man's wife, a totally different kind of man, and he'd been in her bed and sleeping with her now, and we'd see even less of her than we had. Oh, dear God, how long, how long?

Her news and her voice gave birth to a little gray bird of panic that fluttered wild in the cage of my ribs . . . wanting out, out, out!

"Please," Momma begged, her smiles and laughter, joy and happiness all struggling to survive in the bleak, sterile air of our reception to her news. "Try and understand, and be happy for me. I loved your father, you know that, but he's gone, and been gone for so long, and I need someone else to love, and someone to love me."

I saw Chris open his mouth to say he loved her, that we all loved her, but then he tightened his lips, realizing, as I did, that love from her children wasn't the kind of love she was speaking about. And *I* didn't love her anymore. I wasn't even sure I liked her now, but I could smile and pretend, and say the words just so the twins would not be frightened by my expression. "Yes, Momma, I'm glad for you. It's nice you found someone to love you again."

"He's been in love with me for a long time, Cathy," she rushed on, encouraged and smiling with confidence again, "though he did have his mind set on being a bachelor. It wasn't easy to convince him he needed a wife. And your grandfather never wanted me to marry a second time, just as another punishment for the evil I did when I married your father. But he likes Bart, and when I kept on begging and begging, he finally relented, and said yes, that I could marry Bart and still inherit." She paused to chew on her lower lip. Then she swallowed nervously. Her beringed fingers fluttered to her throat, to nervously work the string of genuine pearls she wore, and thus betrayed all the ways of a woman in distress, who could smile, even so. "Of course, I don't love Bart as much as I did your father."

Hah! How weakly she said this. Her glowing eyes and radiant complexion betrayed a love that loomed larger than any she'd known before. And I sighed. Poor Daddy.

"The gifts you brought us, Momma . . . they weren't all from Europe, or the British Isles. That box of maple sugar candy came from Vermont—did you go to Vermont, too? Is that where he's from?"

Her laughter came with lilting joy, uninhibited and even a little sensual, as if Vermont had given her much. "No, he isn't from Vermont, Cathy. But he has a sister living there and we visited her for a weekend after we came from Europe, and that's where I bought the box of candy, for I know how much you love maple sugar candy. He has two other sisters living down South. He's from some little town in South Carolina—Greenglena, Grenglenna, or something like that. But he stayed so long in New England, where he graduated from Harvard Law School, that he sounds more like a Yankee than a Southerner. And oh, it is so beautiful in Vermont in the autumn; it absolutely took my breath away. Of course, when you're on your honeymoon, you don't want to be with other people, so we visited his sister and her family only a short while, and then spent some time on the seashore." She flicked her eyes uneasily at the twins, and again her pearls were twisted so likely they'd break any second. Apparently, genuine pearls are more strongly strung than the simulated kind.

"Did you like the little boats I brought you, Cory?"

"Yes, ma'am," he answered, very politely, staring at her with his large, shadowed eyes, just as if she were a stranger.

"Carrie, sweetheart . . . the little dolls, I picked those up for you in England, to add to your collection. I hoped to find you another cradle, but they don't seem even to make dollhouse cradles anymore."

"It's all right, Momma," answered Carrie, her eyes on the floor. "Chris and Cathy made me a cradle out of cardboard, and I like it fine."

Oh, God, didn't she see?

They didn't know her now. They felt uncomfortable with her now.

"Does your new husband know about us?" I asked, dead serious. Chris glowered at me for asking, telling me mutely that of course our mother wouldn't be deceitful and not tell the man she'd married that she had four hidden children—that some considered the Devil's issue.

Shadows came to darken and pain Momma's happiness. Again I had asked a wrong question. "Not yet, Cathy, but just as soon as Daddy dies, I'll tell him about you four. I'll explain in minute detail. He'll understand; he's kind and gentle. You're going to like him."

She had already said that more than once. And here was another thing that had to wait until an old man died.

"Cathy, stop looking at me like that! I couldn't tell Bart before our marriage! He's your grandfather's attorney. I couldn't let him know about my children, not yet, not until the will is read, and I have the money in my name."

Words were on the tip of my tongue to say a man should know when his wife had four children by her first husband. Oh, how I wanted to say this! But Chris was glaring meanly at me, and the twins were huddled over, crouching small, with their large eyes fixed on the TV set. And I didn't know if I should speak, or stay silent. At least when you were silent, you didn't make any new enemies. Maybe she was right, too. *God, let her be right. Let my faith be renewed. Let me believe in her again. Let me believe that she is not just beautiful on the surface, but all the way through.*

God didn't reach down and lay a warm, reassuring hand on my shoulder. I sat there, realizing my suspicions were stretching the cord between her and me, very, very fine.

Love. How often that word came up in books. Over and over again. If you had wealth and health, and beauty and talent . . . you had nothing if you didn't have love. Love changed all that was ordinary into something giddy, powerful, drunken, enchanted.

Thus ran the course of my thoughts on a day early in winter, when rain pelted on the roof, and the twins sat on the floor in the bedroom, before the TV. Chris and I were in the attic, lying side by side on the old mattress, near the window in the schoolroom, reading together one of the antique books Momma had brought up from the big library downstairs. Soon the attic would again turn arctic winter, so we spent as much time up there as possible now, while we still could. Chris liked to scan a page, and then quickly leap to another. I liked to dawdle over the beautiful lines, going back to read through them twice, sometimes three times. We argued incessantly about this. "Read faster, Cathy! You try to absorb the words."

Today he was patient. He turned his back and stared up at the ceiling while I took my time, pursuing each beautifully written line, and soaking up the feel of Victorian times, when people wore such fancy clothes, and spoke in such elegant ways, and felt so deeply about love. From paragraph one, the story had captivated both of us with its mystical, romantic charm. Each slow page spinning out an involved tale of star-crossed lovers named Lily and Raymond, who had to overcome monumental obstacles to find and stand upon the magic place of purple grass, where all dreams are fulfilled. God, how

I wanted them to find that place! Then I discovered the tragedy of their lives. All along they had stood on the purple grass . . . can you imagine? On that special grass all the time, and they never looked down even once to see it. I hated unhappy endings! I slammed that hateful book shut and hurled it against the nearest wall. "If that isn't the most stupid, silly, ridiculous story!" I raged at Chris, as if he had written the book. "No matter whom I love, I'll learn to forgive and forget!" I continued to rail along with the storm outside, the weather and me beating out the same crescendo. "Now why couldn't it have been written differently? How is it possible for two intelligent people to float along with their heads in the clouds, not realizing happenstance can always bring about bad luck? Never, never am I going to be like Lily, or Raymond, either! Idealistic fools who don't know enough to look down at the ground on occasion!"

My brother seemed amused that I took a story so seriously, but then he reconsidered, and stared thoughtfully at the driving rain. "Perhaps lovers aren't supposed to look down at the ground. That kind of story is told in symbols—and earth represents reality, and reality represents frustrations, chance illnesses, death, murder, and all kinds of other tragedies. Lovers are meant to look up at the sky, for up there no beautiful illusions can be trampled upon."

Frowning, sulky, I gazed moodily at him. "And when I fall in love," I began, "I will build a mountain to touch the sky. Then, my lover and I will have the best of both worlds, reality firmly under our feet, while we have our heads in the clouds with all our illusions still intact. And the purple grass will grow all around, high enough to reach our eyes."

He laughed, he hugged me, he kissed me lightly, tenderly, and his eyes were so gentle and soft in the murky, cold gloom of the attic. "Oh, yes, my Cathy could do that. Keep all her fanciful illusions, dancing eye-high in purple grass, wearing clouds for gossamer clothes. She'd leap, she'd bound and pirouette until her clumsy-footed, awkward lover was dancing, too, just as gracefully."

Put on quicksand, I quickly jumped to where I was sure-footed. "It was a beautiful story though, in its own peculiar way. I feel so sorry that Lily and Raymond had to take their own lives, when it should have worked out differently. When Lily told Raymond the full truth, how she was virtually raped by that awful man, Raymond shouldn't have accused her of seducing him! Nobody in their right mind would want to seduce a man with eight children."

"Oh, Cathy, sometimes, really, you are just too much."

His voice sounded deeper than usual when he said that. His soft look traveled slowly over my face, lingering on my lips, then down to my bosom, to my legs, sheathed in white leotards. Over the leotards I wore a short wool skirt and a wool cardigan sweater. Then his eyes moved upward again, coming to lock with my surprised look. He flushed as I kept on staring at him, and turned aside his face for the second time today. I was close enough to hear his heart drumming fast, faster, racing, and all of a sudden my own heart caught the rhythm of his, in the only tempo hearts can have—thumpity-bump, thumpity-bump. He shot me a quick glance. Our eyes melded and held. He laughed nervously, trying to hide and pretend none of this could possibly be serious.

"You were right the first time, Cathy. It was a stupid, silly story. Ridiculous! Only insane people would die for the sake of love. I'll bet you a hundred to one a woman wrote that junky romantic trash!"

Just a minute ago I'd despised that author for bringing about such a miserable ending, then there I went, rushing to the defense. "T. M. Ellis could very well have been a man! Though I doubt any woman writer in the nineteenth century had much chance of being published, unless she used her initials, or a man's name. And why is it all men think everything a woman writes is trivial or trashy—or just plain silly drivel? Don't men have romantic notions? Don't men dream of finding the perfect love? And it seems to me, that Raymond was far more mushy-minded than Lily!"

"Don't ask me what men are like!" he stormed with such bitterness he didn't seem himself at all. He raged on: "Up here, living as we do, how am I ever going to know how it feels to be a man? Up here, I'm not allowed to have any romantic notions. It's don't do this, and don't do that, and keep your eyes averted, and don't see what's before your very eyes gliding about, show-ing off, pretending I'm just a brother, without feelings, without any emotions but childish ones. It seems some stupid girls think a gonna-be doctor is without sexuality!"

My eyes widened. Such a vehement outburst from one sel-dom upset took me completely by surprise. In all our lives he'd never spoken so fervently to me, and with such anger. No, I was the sour lemon, the bad apple in the barrel of good. I'd contami-nated him. He was acting now like he had when Momma went away and stayed so long. Oh, it was wicked of me to make him the troublesome thing *I* was. He should stay always what *he* was, the happy-go-lucky cheerful optimist. Had I robbed him of his greatest asset, besides his good looks and charm?

I put out my hand to touch his forearm. "Chris," I whispered, near tears. "I think I know exactly what you need to feel manly."

"Yeah," he bit out. "What can *you* do?"

Now he wouldn't even look at me. Instead, he fixed his gaze on the ceiling above. I ached for him. I knew what had him down; he was letting go of his dream, for my benefit, so he could be like me, and not care whether or not we inherited a for-tune. And to be like me, he had to be sour, bitter, hating every-one, and suspicious of their hidden motives.

Tentatively, I reached out to touch his hair. "A haircut, that's what you need. Your hair is much too long and pretty. To feel a man, you must have shorter hair. Right now, your hair looks like mine."

"And who has ever said your hair is pretty?" he asked in the tightest of voices. "Maybe once you had pretty hair, before the tarring."

Really? It seemed I could recall many times his eyes had told me my hair was more than just pretty. And I could recall the way he looked when he picked up the shiny shears to cut off that front hair, so delicate and brittle. He snipped with such reluctance it seemed he was cutting off fingers and not just hair that didn't feel pain. Then one day I caught him sitting in the attic sunshine, holding the long lengths of cut-off hair in his hands. He'd sniffed it, then put it to his cheek, and then to his lips, and then he hid it away in a box to keep under his pillow.

Not easily could I force laughter to deceive him and not let him know I'd seen. "Oh, Christopher Doll, you have the most expressive blue eyes. When we are free of this place, and out in the world, I pity all the girls who are going to fall for you. Most especially I'll feel sorry for your wife, with such a handsome husband to charm all his beautiful patients into wanting affairs. And if I were your wife I'd kill you if you even had one extra-marital affair! I'd love you so much, I'd be so jealous . . . I might even make you retire from medicine at age thirty-five."

"I never told you even once your hair was pretty," he said sharply, ignoring everything I'd said.

Ever so lightly I stroked his cheek, feeling the whiskers that needed shaving off.

"Sit right where you are. I'll run for the scissors. You know, I haven't given you a haircut for the longest time." Why should I bother cutting his hair and Cory's when the way our hair looked didn't seem important to our life-style? Not since we came had Carrie and I had our hair trimmed. Only the top of mine had been snipped off to signify our submission to a mean old woman made of steel.

And while I raced for the scissors, I thought how odd it was that none of our green plants would grow, yet each of us grew lots of hair. It seemed in all the fairy tales I'd read, the damsels in distress always had long, long blond hair. Had any brunette ever been locked away in a turret—if an attic could be considered a turret?

Chris sat on the floor, I knelt behind him, and though his hair hung below his shoulders, he didn't want much taken off. "Now go easy with those shears," he ordered nervously. "Don't cut off too much all at once. Feeling manly too suddenly, on a rainy afternoon in the attic, just might be dangerous," he teased, and grinned, and then he was laughing with a brilliant show of even, white teeth. I had charmed him back to how he should be.

Oh, I did love him as I crawled around and earnestly snipped and trimmed. Constantly I had to move backward for perspective, to check and see if his hair hung evenly, for most certainly, I wouldn't want to make his head lopsided.

I held his hair with a comb, as I'd seen barbers do, and I carefully snipped beneath that comb, not daring to take off more than a quarter of an inch a clip. I had a mental vision of how I wanted him to look—like someone I admired very much.

And when I'd finished, I brushed the bright hair snippings from his shoulders, and leaned back to see that I hadn't done a bad job at all.

"There!" I said in triumph, pleased with my unexpected mastery of what seemed to be a difficult art. "Not only do you look exceptionally handsome, but extremely manly, as well! Though, of course, you have been manly all along, it's a pity you didn't know it."

I thrust the silver-backed mirror with my initials into his hands. This mirror represented one-third of the sterling-silver set Momma had given me on my last birthday. Brush, comb, mirror: all three to be hidden away so the grandmother wouldn't know I had expensive items of vanity and pride.

Chris stared and stared into that mirror, and my heart faltered as he looked, for a moment, displeased and undecided. Then, slowly, a wide grin lit up his face.

"My God! You've made me look like a blond Prince Valiant! At first I didn't like it, but now I see you changed his style just a

bit, so it isn't squared off. You've curved it, and layered it to flatter my face like a loving cup. Thank you, Catherine Doll. I had
no idea you were so skilled at cutting hair."

"I have many skills you don't know about."

"I am beginning to suspect that."

"And Prince Valiant should be so lucky as to look like my
handsome, manly, blond brother," I teased, and couldn't help but
admire my own artistry. Oh, golly-gee, what a heartbreaker he'd
be one day.

He still had the mirror, and casually he laid it aside, and
before I knew what he was about, like a cat he pounced! He
wrestled with me, bearing me back to the floor, and reached for
the scissors at the same time! He yanked them from my hand,
and then grabbed a handful of my hair!

"Now, my lovely, let's see if I can't do the same thing for
you!"

Terrified, I yelped!

I thrust him away so he fell backward, and I jumped to my
feet. No one was going to shear off one-eighth of an inch of my
hair! Maybe it was too fine and too thin now, and maybe it
wasn't as sensational as it used to be, but it was all the hair I
had, and prettier even now than what most girls had. I took off
on the run from the schoolroom. I raced through the doorway
and into the immense attic, dodging behind posts, circling old
trunks, leaping over low tables, and bounding over sheet-
shrouded sofas and chairs. The paper flowers fanned frantically
as I ran, and he chased. The flames of the low fat candles that
we kept burning during the day just to cheer up and warm up a
dreary, vast and cold place, bent low in our wakes, and almost
guttered.

And no matter how swiftly I ran, or how cleverly I dodged, I
couldn't shake off my pursuer! I threw a glance over my shoulder, and I couldn't even recognize his face—and that scared me
even more. Lunging forward, he made an effort to seize hold of
my long hair which bannered out behind me, and seemed so
very intent on cutting it off!

Did he hate me now? Why had he spent one entire day so devotedly trying to save my hair, only to cut off my crowning glory for the sheer fun of it?

I fled back toward the schoolroom, planning on reaching there first. Then I'd slam the door, and lock it, and he'd come to his senses and realize the absurdity of it all.

Perhaps he sensed my purpose, and put some extra speed into his longer legs—he bounded forward, and caught hold of my long, streaming locks, causing me to scream as I tripped and fell forward!

Not only did I fall, but he fell too—straight on top of me! A sharp pain pierced my side! I screamed again—not in terror this time, but in shock.

He was over me, supported by his hands on the floor, staring down into my face, his face deadly white and frightened. "Are you hurt? Oh, God, Cathy, are you all right?"

Was I all right, was I? Lifting my head, I stared down at the heavy flow of blood quickly staining my sweater. Chris saw it, too. His blue eyes went stark, bleak, wild, distraught. With trembling fingers he began to unbutton my sweater, so he could spread it open and take a look at my wound.

"Oh, Lord . . ." he breathed, then expelled a low whistle of relief. "Wow! Thank God. I was so scared it would be a puncture. A deep puncture would be serious, but it's only a long cut, Cathy. Nasty, and you're losing a lot of blood. Now don't move a muscle! Stay right where you are, and I'll dash down to the bath and fetch medicine and bandages."

He kissed me first on the cheek, then was up and in a terrible hurry, racing madly toward the stairwell, whereas I thought I could have gone with him and saved time. Yet the twins were down there, and they'd see the blood. And all they had to do was see blood and they'd go to pieces and scream.

In a few minutes Chris came speeding back with our medical emergency kit. He fell down on his knees beside me, his hands still glistening with water from a fast scrub-up. He was in too much of a hurry to dry them well.

I was fascinated to see he knew so precisely what to do. First he folded a heavy towel, and used that to press down hard on the long cut. Looking very serious and intent, he bore down on the pad, checking every few seconds to see if the bleeding had stopped. When it did, he busied himself with antiseptic that stung like fire, and hurt worse than the injury itself.

"I know it stings, Cathy . . . can't help that . . . have to put it on to avoid infection. Wish I had sutures, but maybe it won't make a permanent scar; and I pray it doesn't. It would be so nice if people could go through all of their life without ever cutting into the perfect envelope they're born with. And here I am, the first one to really scar your skin. If you had died because of me—and you could have if the shears had been slanted differently—then I would want to die, too."

He had finished playing doctor, and was now winding the remaining gauze up in a neat roll before replacing it in the blue wrapping paper, and into a box. He stashed away the adhesive, closed the kit.

Leaning above me, his face hovered over mine, his serious eyes so delving, worried, and intense. His blue eyes were like the eyes we all had. Yet on this rainy day they were catching colors from the paper flowers, making them limpid dark pools of iridescence. A lump came in my throat as I wondered where the boy was I used to know. Where was that brother—and who was this young man with the blond whiskers, staring so long into my eyes? Just that look of his held me in thrall. And greater than any pain, or ache, or hurt I ever felt before, or since, was the pain caused me by the suffering I saw in the shifting kaleidescopic, rainbowed colors of his tortured eyes.

"Chris," I murmured, feeling unreal, "don't look like that. It wasn't your fault." I cupped his face in my palms first, then drew his head down to my breast as I'd seen Momma do in the past. "It's only a scratch, doesn't hurt a bit (though it hurt dreadfully), and I know you didn't do it deliberately."

Hoarsely he choked, "Why did you run? Because you ran, I

had to chase. And I was only teasing. I wouldn't cut one strand from your head; it was just something to do, to have fun. And you were wrong when you said I thought your hair was pretty. It's more than just pretty. I think you may grow on your head the most glorious hair in the world."

A little knife twisted in my heart as he lifted his head long enough to spread my hair fanlike and cover my bare breast. I could hear him breathing deeply my scent. We lay there quietly listening to the winter rain drumming on the slate roof not so far above. Deep silence all around. Always silence. Nature's voices were the only ones to reach us in the attic, and so seldom did nature speak in friendly, soft tones.

The rain on the roof pitter-pattered down into only drops, and the sun came out and shone down on us to shimmer his hair and mine like long glimmering strands of silken diamonds. "Look," I said to Chris, "one of the slats from a western window shutter has fallen out."

"Nice," he said, sounding sleepy and content, "Now we'll have sun where once there was none. See, I've made a rhyme." And then in a sleepy whisper, he said, "I'm thinking of Raymond and Lily and their quest for the purple grass where all dreams are fulfilled."

"Were you? In a way, I was kinda thinking the same thing," I answered, whispery, too. Over and over again I twirled a strand of his hair around my thumb, pretending not to notice one of his hands was ever so cautiously stroking my breast, the one his face didn't cover. Because I didn't object, he dared to kiss the nipple. I jumped, startled, wondering why that should feel so strange, and so extraordinarily thrilling. What was a nipple but a tannish-pink little peak? "I can picture Raymond kissing Lily, just where you kissed," I went on breathlessly, wanting him to stop, and wanting him to go on, "but I can't imagine them doing what comes next."

Words to make his head pop up. Just the right words to make him look at me intensely again, with strange lights flickering in his eyes which wouldn't stay only one color. "Cathy, do you know what comes next?"

A blush heated my face. "Yes, I know, sort of. Do *you* know?"

He laughed, one of those dry chuckles you read about in novels. "Sure I know. My very first day in school, I was told in the boy's restroom; that's all the older boys could talk about. They had four-letter words on the walls that I didn't understand. But they were soon explained, in detail. Girls, baseball, girls, football, girls, girls, girls were all they could talk about, and all the ways they were different from us. It's a fascinating subject for most boys, and, I suppose, men."

"But not fascinating for you?"

"Me? I don't think about girls, or sex, though I wish to God you weren't so damned pretty! And it would help if you weren't always so near, and so available."

"Then you do think about me? You do think I'm pretty?"

A smothered groan escaped his lips—more like a moan. He bolted up to sit straight, staring down at what my open sweater revealed, for the fan of my hair was displaced. If I hadn't cut off the top of my leotards, he wouldn't be seeing so much. But I had had to cut off the too-small bodice.

With trembling, clumsy fingers he fastened the buttons of my sweater, keeping his eyes averted from mine. "Get this straight in your head, Cathy. Of course you are pretty, but brothers don't think about sisters as girls—nor do they feel any sort of emotion for them other than tolerance and brotherly affection—and sometimes, hate."

"I hope God strikes me dead this second if you hate me, Christopher."

His hands lifted to cover his face, hiding, and when he came out from behind the shield, he was smiling, cheerful, clearing his throat. "Come on, it's time we went down to the twins before they burn their eyes into black holes from staring at the boob-tube for so long."

It hurt to rise, though he assisted me up. In his arms I was held close while my cheek was pressed against his heart. And though he would put me from him quickly, I clung tighter. "Chris—what we did just now—was it sinful?"

Again, he cleared his throat. "If you think it so, then it was."

What kind of an answer was that? If thoughts of sin stayed out of it, those moments lying on the floor when he touched me so tenderly with magical tingling fingers and lips were the sweetest moments since we'd come to live in this abominable house. I looked up to see what he was thinking and saw that strange look in his eyes. Paradoxically he seemed happier, sadder, older, younger, wiser . . . or was it he was feeling like a man now? And if he was, then I was glad, sinful or not.

We walked hand in hand down the steps to the twins, where Cory was plucking a tune on the banjo, while keeping his eyes glued to the TV. He picked up the guitar and began his own composition, as Carrie chanted simple lyrics he'd composed. The banjo was for happy tunes to move your feet. This melody was like rain on the roof, long, dreary, monotonous.

> Gonna see the sun,
> Gonna find my home,
> Gonna feel the wind,
> See the sun ag'in.

I sat on the floor near Cory, and took the guitar from his hands, for I could play a bit, too. He had taught me how—taught us all how. And I sang to him that special, wistful song that belonged to Dorothy in the movie *The Wizard of Oz*—a movie that the twins adored everytime they saw it. And when I had finished singing of bluebirds that flew over the rainbow, Cory asked, "Don't you like my song, Cathy?"

"You bet I like your song—but it's so sad. How about writing a few happy lyrics, with a little hope?"

The little mouse was in his pocket, just his tail poking out as

he fingered down there for bread crumbs. Mickey made a twisting movement, and then his head was out of the shirt pocket,
and in his forefeet he held a bit of bread and daintily began to
nibble. The look on Cory's face as he stared down at his first pet
touched me so deeply I had to turn away to keep from crying.

"Cathy, you know Momma, she never said nothing about my
pet."

"She hasn't noticed him, Cory."

"Why don't she notice?"

I sighed, not really knowing who and what my mother was
anymore, except a stranger we used to love. Death wasn't the
only thing that took away someone you loved and needed; I
knew that now.

"Momma's got a new husband," said Chris brightly, "and
when you're in love, you don't see anyone's happiness but your
own. Soon enough she'll notice you've got a friend."

Carrie was staring at my sweater. "Cathy, what's that stuff on
your sweater?"

"Paint," said I without the slighest hesitation. "Chris was trying to teach me how to paint, and he got mad when my picture
was better than anything he's ever done, so he picked up the little pan with red, and he threw it at me."

My older brother sat there with the darnedest look on his face.

"Chris, can Cathy paint better than you can?"

"If she says she can, then she must."

"Where is her painting?"

"In the attic."

"I want to see it."

"Then you go up and get it. I'm tired. I want to look at TV
while Cathy prepares dinner." He shot me a swift look. "My
dear sister, would you mind, for the sake of propriety, putting on
a clean sweater before we sit down to eat dinner? There's something about that red paint that makes me feel guilty."

"It looks like blood," said Cory. "It's stiff like blood when
you don't wash it off."

"Poster colors," said Chris, as I left to go into the bath to change into a sweater many sizes too large. "Poster colors stiffen up."

Satisfied, Cory began to tell Chris of how he'd missed seeing dinosaurs. "Chris, they were bigger than this house! They came up out of the water, and swallowed the boat, and two men! I knew you'd be sorry to miss seeing that!"

"Yeah," said Chris dreamily, "I sure would have liked to have seen that."

That night I felt strangely ill at ease, and restless, and my thoughts kept returning to the way Chris had looked at me in the attic.

I knew then what the secret was I'd been searching so long to find—that secret button that switched on love . . . physical, sexual desire. It wasn't just the viewing of naked bodies, for many a time I'd bathed Cory, and seen Chris naked, and I'd never felt any particular arousal because what he and Cory had was different from what Carrie and I had. It wasn't being naked at all.

It was the eyes. The secret of love was in the eyes, the way one person looked at another, the way eyes communicated and spoke when the lips never moved. Chris's eyes had said more than ten thousand words.

And it wasn't just the way he touched me, caressingly, tenderly; it was the way he touched, when he looked as he did, and that's why the grandmother made it a rule that we shouldn't look at the other sex. Oh, to think that old witch knew the secret of love. She couldn't have ever loved, no, not her, the iron-hearted, the steel-spined . . . never could her eyes have been soft.

And then, as I delved deeper into the subject, it was more than the eyes—it was what was behind the eyes, in the brain, wanting to please you, make you happy, give you joy, and take away the loneliness of never having anyone understand as you want to be understood.

Sin had nothing at all to do with love, real love. I turned my head and saw that Chris was awake, too, curled up on his side, staring over at me. He smiled the sweetest smile, and I could have cried for him, for me.

Our mother didn't visit us that day, nor had she visited us the day before, but we'd found a way to cheer ourselves by playing Cory's instruments and singing along. Despite the absence of a mother grown very negligent, we all went to bed more hopefully that night. Singing happy songs for several hours had convinced us all that sun, love, home and happiness were just around the bend, and our long days of traveling through a deep dark forest were almost over.

Into my bright dreams crept something dark and terrifying. Every day forms took on monstrous proportions. With my eyes closed, I saw the grandmother steal into the bedroom, and thinking me asleep, she shaved off all my hair! I screamed but she didn't hear me—nobody heard me. She took a long and shiny knife and sliced off my breasts and fed them into Chris's mouth. And there was more. I tossed, writhed, and made small whimpering sounds that awakened Chris as the twins slept on as children dead and buried. Sleepily, Chris stumbled over to sit on my bed, and asked as he fumbled to find my hand, "Another nightmare?"

Nooo! This was no ordinary nightmare! This was precognition, and psychic in nature. I felt it in my bone marrow, something dreadful was about to happen. Weak and trembling I told Chris what the grandmother had done. "And that wasn't all. It was Momma who came in and cut out my heart, and she was sparkled all over with diamonds!"

"Cathy, dreams don't mean anything."

"Yes, they do!"

Other dreams and other nightmares I'd willingly told my brother and he'd listened, and smiled, and expressed his belief that it must be wonderful to have nights like being in a movie theater, but it wasn't that way at all. In a movie, you sit and watch a big screen, and you know you are only watching a story that someone wrote. I participated in my dreams. I was in the dreams, feeling, hurting, suffering, and I'm sorry to say, very seldom did I really enjoy them.

Since he was so accustomed to me and my strange ways, why did Chris sit as still as a marble statue, as if this dream affected him more than any other? Had he been dreaming, too?

"Cathy, on my word of honor, we are going to escape this house! All four of us will run away! You've convinced me. Your dreams must mean something, or else you wouldn't keep having them. Women are more intuitive than men; it's been proven. The subconscious is at work at night. We won't wait any longer for Momma to inherit the fortune from a grandfather who lives on and on and never dies. Together, you and I, we'll find a way. From this second on, I vow on my life, we depend only on ourselves . . . and your dreams."

From the intense way he said this, I knew he wasn't joking, making fun—he meant what he said! I could have shouted, I felt so relieved. We were going to get away. This house wasn't going to do us in after all!

In the gloom and chill of that big shadowed and cluttered room, he stared down into my eyes. Maybe he was seeing me, as I saw him, looking larger than life, and softer than dreams. Slowly his head inclined toward mine, and he kissed me full on the lips as a way to seal his promise in a strong and meaningful way. Such a peculiar long kiss, to give me the sensation that I was falling down, down, down, when I was already lying down.

What we needed most was a key to our bedroom door. We knew it was the master key to every room in this house. We couldn't use the sheet-ladder because of the twins, and we didn't anticipate, either Chris or I, that our grandmother would be so thoughtlessly careless as to lay aside the key negligently. That just wasn't her way. Her way was to open the door, and immediately stash the key in her pocket. Always her hateful gray dresses had pockets.

Our mother's way was to be careless, forgetful, indifferent. And she didn't like pockets in her clothes to add extra bulk to her svelte figure. We counted on her.

And what did she have to fear from us—the passive, the meek, the quiet? Her private little captive "darlings," who were never going to grow up and be a threat. She was happy, in love; it lit up her eyes and made her laugh often. She was so damned unobservant you wanted to scream and make her see—make her see the twins so quiet and sick looking! She never mentioned the mouse—why wasn't she seeing the mouse? He was on Cory's shoulder, nibbling on Cory's ear, and she never said a word, not even when tears streamed down Cory's face because she wouldn't congratulate him on winning the affections of a very stubborn mouse that would have gone his way, if allowed.

She came a generous two or three times a month, and each time she bore with her the gifts that gave *her* solace if they gave us none. She came in gracefully to sit a while, wearing her beautiful, expensive clothes trimmed with furs, and decorated with jewels.

On her throne she sat as a queen and doled out the painting sets to Chris, the ballet slippers to me, and to each of us she brought sensational-looking clothes, well suited for attic wearing, for up here it didn't matter if they seldom fit, being too large, or too small, and our sneakers were sometimes comfortable, sometimes not, and I was still waiting for the bra she kept promising but always forgot.

"I'll bring you a dozen or so," she said with a benevolent cheerful smile, "all sizes, all colors, and you can try them on and see which you like best, and fit best, and I can give the ones you don't want to the maids." And on and on she chatted vivaciously, always true to her false facade, pretending we still mattered in her life.

I sat, I fixed my eyes on her, and I waited for her to ask me how the twins were. Had she forgotten that Cory had hay fever which kept his nose running all the time, and sometimes his nostrils stuffed up so he couldn't breathe except through his mouth? She knew he was supposed to be receiving allergy shots once a month, and years had passed since the last one. Didn't it hurt her to see Cory and Carrie clinging to me as if I were the one who had given them birth? Did one single thing reach out and tell her something was wrong?

If it did, in no way did she indicate that she saw us as less than perfectly normal, though I took pains to name our small illnesses: the way we threw up so often now, and how our heads ached from time to time, and we had stomach cramps, and sometimes very little energy.

"Keep your food in the attic, where it's cold," she said without flinching.

She had the nerve to speak to us of parties, of concerts, of the theater, of movies, and going to balls and on trips with her "Bart." "Bart and I are going on a shopping spree in New York," she said. "Tell me what you want me to bring you. Make out a list."

"Momma, after you Christmas-shop in New York, where will you go then?" I asked, careful not to turn my eyes on that key she had so casually tossed on the dresser top. She laughed, liking my question, and clasped her slender white hands together, and began to list her plans for the long dull days after the holidays. "A trip south, perhaps a cruise, or a month or so in Florida. And your grandmother will be here to take good care of you."

While she chatted on and on, Chris stole stealthily near to slip the key into his pants pocket. On into the bathroom he sauntered, excusing himself. He needn't have bothered; she didn't notice he was gone. She was doing her duty, visiting her children—and thank God she had chosen the right chair to sit in. In the bathroom I knew Chris was pressing the key into a bar of soap we kept ready for just this way to make a clear impression. Just one of the many things watching endless hours of television had taught us.

*   *   *

Once our mother had gone, Chris pulled out the piece of wood he had and began immediately to carve a rough wooden key. Though we had metal from the old trunk locks, we had nothing strong enough to cut and shape it. For hours and hours Chris slaved meticulously, carving that key, fitting and refitting it into the hardened soap impression. Purposefully, he had chosen very hard wood, fearing soft wood might break in the lock and give away our escape plan. It took three days of work before he had a key that worked.

Jubilance was ours! We threw our arms about each other and danced around the room, laughing, kissing, almost crying. The twins watched us, amazed we were so happy with a little key.

We had a key. We could open our prison door. Yet, strangely, we hadn't planned our future beyond the opening of the door.

"Money. We must have money," reasoned Chris, stopping in the middle of our wild dance of triumph. "With lots of money, all doors are open, and all roads are ours to travel."

"But where can we get money?" I asked, frowning and unhappy now. He had found another reason for stalling.

"There is no way but to steal it from Momma, her husband, and the grandmother."

He said this so pronounced, exactly as if thieving were an old and honored profession. And in dire need, perhaps it was, and still is.

"If we're caught, it will mean the whip for all of us, even the twins," I said, casting my eyes on their fearful expressions. "And when Momma goes on a trip with her husband, *she* could starve us again, and God alone knows what else *she* would do to us."

Chris fell down on the small chair before the dressing table. He propped his chin in his hand, thoughtful and considering for minutes. "One thing for sure, I don't want to see you or the twins punished. So I will be the one to steal out of here, and I alone will stand guilty if caught. But I'm not going to be caught; it *is* too risky to take from that old woman—she's too observant.

No doubt she knows to a penny exactly the amount of money in her purse. Momma never counts money. Remember how Daddy used to complain about that?" He grinned at me reassuringly. "I will be just like Robin Hood, stealing from the rich to give to the needy poor—us! And only on the nights Momma and her husband tell us they are going out."

"You mean *when* she tells us," I corrected. "And we can always watch from the window, on those days she doesn't come." When we dared, we had a fine view of the curved drive to watch the comings and goings.

Soon enough Momma told us she was going to a party. "Bart doesn't care much for the social life; he'd rather stay home. But I hate this house. He asks then why we don't move into our own home, and what can I say?"

What could she say? *Darling, I have a secret to tell you: upstairs, hidden away in the far northern wing, I have four children.*

It was easy enough for Chris to find money in his mother's grand, splendid bedroom. She was careless about money. Even he was shocked at how casually she left tens and twenties scattered over the dresser. It made him frown and put suspicions in his head. Wasn't she supposed to be saving up for that day when she could take us all out of our prison . . . even if she did have a husband now? More bills were in her many pocketbooks. Chris found change in her husband's trousers pockets. No, he was not as careless with *his* money. However, when Chris searched under the chair cushions, a dozen or more coins were there. He felt like a thief, an unwanted intruder in his mother's room. He saw her beautiful clothes, her satin mules, her negligees trimmed with fur, or marabou feathers, making his trust shrink even smaller.

Time after time that winter, he visited that bedroom, growing ever more careless since it was all so easy to steal. He came back to me, looking jubilant, looking sad. Day by day

our hidden cache was increasing—why did he look sad?
"Come with me next time," he said in way of reply. "See for
yourself."

I could go with a clear conscience now, knowing the twins
wouldn't awaken and find us gone. They slept so soundly, so
deeply, that even in the mornings they woke up blurry-eyed,
slow, reluctantly coming into reality. It scared me sometimes to
look at them asleep. Two small dolls, never growing, so sunken
into oblivion it seemed more a small death than normal nighttime rest.

Go away, run away, spring was approaching, we had to leave
soon, before it was too late. A voice inside, intuitive, kept drumming out this tune. Chris laughed when I told him. "Cathy, you
and your notions! We need money. At least five hundred. What
is the terrible hurry? We have food now, and we aren't being
whipped; even when *she* catches us half-undressed, she doesn't
say a word."

Why didn't the grandmother punish us now? We had not told
Momma of her other punishments, her sins against us, for to me,
they were sins, and not justified in any way. Yet, that old woman
stayed her hand. Daily she brought up the picnic basket, filled to
the brim with sandwiches, with lukewarm soups in thermos bottles, with milk, and always four powdered-sugar doughnuts.
Why couldn't she vary our menus and bring brownies, cookies,
slices of pie or cake?

"C'mon," urged Chris, dragging me along the corridors so
dark and sinister. "Lingering in one place is dangerous. We'll
take a quick look in the trophy room, then rush on into
Momma's bedroom suite."

All I needed was one glance in that trophy room. I hated—
actually detested that oil portrait over the stone fireplace—so
much like our father—and yet so very different. A man as cruel
and heartless as Malcolm Foxworth had no right to be handsome, even when he was young. Those cold blue eyes should
have corrupted the rest of him with sores, boils. I saw all those

heads of dead animals, and the tiger and bear skins on the floor, and I thought, how like him to want a room like this.

If Chris would let me, I would look into every room. But he insisted we pass by the closed doors, allowing me to peek in only a few. "Nosy!" he whispered. "There's nothing of interest in any of them." He was right. Right in so many things. I learned that night what Chris meant when he said this house was only grand and beautiful, not pretty or cozy. Nevertheless, I couldn't help being impressed. Our home in Gladstone shrank in the comparison.

When we had quietly traversed many a long and stingily lit dim hall, we came at last upon our mother's grand suite of rooms. Sure, Chris had told me in detail of the swan bed, and the infant bed at the foot—but hearing wasn't seeing! My breath pulled in. My dreams took off on wings of fancy! Oh, glory be to heaven! This wasn't a room, but a chamber fit for a queen or a princess! I couldn't believe the posh splendor, the opulence! Overwhelmed, I flitted from here to there, awed to touch the walls, covered with silk damask, colored a delicious strawberry pink, richer than the pale mauve of the two-inch-thick carpet I fingered the soft, furry coverlet and I threw myself upon it and rolled about. I touched the filmy bed curtains, and heavier drapes of purple velvet. I jumped up from the bed, to stand at the foot, and gazed in admiration at that marvelous swan that kept his observant, but sleepy red eye riveted on me.

Then I backed off, not liking a bed where Momma slept with a man not our father. I walked into her huge walk-in closet, drifting about in a dream of riches that could never be mine, *except* in dreams. She had more clothes than a department store. Plus shoes, hats, handbags. Four full-length fur coats, three fur stoles, a white mink cape, and a dark sable one, plus fur hats of a dozen different styles and made of different animal pelts, plus a leopard coat with green wool in between the fur trim. Then there were negligees, nightgowns, peignoir sets, flounced, beruffled, beribboned, feathered, furred, made of velvet, satin, chiffon, combinations—good glory be! She'd have to live a thousand years to wear all she owned just once!

What caught my eye most, I took from the closet and carried into the golden dressing room Chris showed me. I glanced in her bath, with the mirrors all around, live green plants, real flowers growing, two commodes—one didn't have a lid. (I know now one was a bidet.) A separate shower stall, too. "All this is new," explained Chris. "When I first came, you know, the night of the Christmas party, it wasn't so . . . well, so opulent as it is now."

I spun about to glare at him, guessing it had been all along, but he hadn't told me. He had been deliberately shielding her, not wanting me to know about all those clothes, the furs, plus the fabulous amount of jewelry she kept hidden in a secret compartment of her long dressing table. No, he hadn't lied—just omitted. It showed in his betraying, shifting eyes, his flushed face, and the quick way he hurried to escape more of my embarrassing questions—no wonder she didn't want to sleep in *our* room!

I was in the dressing room trying on the clothes from Momma's big closet. For the first time in my life I slipped on nylon hose, and, oh, did my legs look heavenly—divine! No wonder women liked these things! Next, I put on a bra for the first time, one that was much too large, to my dismay. I stuffed the cups full of tissues until they bulged way out. Next came the silver slippers, again, too large. And then I topped off the splendor of me with a black dress cut very low in front to show off what I didn't have much of.

Now came the fun part—what I used to do when I was little whenever I had the chance. I sat down at Momma's dressing table and began to apply her makeup with a lavish hand. She had ten carloads. On my face I slathered the whole works: foundation, rouge, powder, mascara, eyeshadow, lipstick. And then I swept my hair up in a way I considered sexy and stylish, stuck in hairpins and began to put on jewelry. And, last of all, perfume—lots of it.

Tottering awkwardly on the high heels, I teetered over to Chris. "How do I look?" I asked, flirtatiously smiling, and fluttering my sooty lashes. Truly, I was prepared for compliments. Hadn't the mirrors already told me I looked sensational?

He was carefully going through a drawer, putting everything back exactly as he had found it, but he turned to take a glance. Astonishment widened his eyes, and then he heavily scowled, while I rocked back and forth and sideways, seeking my balance on four-inch heels, and kept on batting my eyelids—maybe I didn't know how to put on false eyelashes right. I felt I was looking through spider legs.

"How do you look?" he began in a sarcastic way. "Let me tell you precisely. You look like a streetwalker—that's how!" He turned away in disgust, as if unable to bear the sight of me. "An adolescent whore—that's what! Now go wash your face, and put back all that stuff where you found it, and clean up the dressing table!"

I tottered over to the nearest full-length mirror. It had right and left wings so she could adjust them, and see herself from every angle, and in those three very revealing mirrors I took a fresh perspective—and what a fascinating mirror; it closed like a three-page book, and then there was a beautiful French pastoral scene to view.

Twisting and turning, I checked over my appearance. This wasn't the way my mother looked in the same dress—what had I done wrong? True, she didn't ladder so many bracelets up her arms. And she didn't wear three necklaces at once, while long, dangling diamond earrings brushed her shoulders, plus a tiara; nor did she ever wear two or three rings on each finger—including her thumbs.

Oh, but I did dazzle the eyes all right. And my jutting bosom was absolutely magnificent! Truthfully, I had to admit I'd overdone it.

I took off seventeen bracelets, twenty-six rings, the necklaces, the tiara, and the black chiffon formal gown that didn't look as elegant on me as when Momma wore it to a dinner party with only pearls at the throat. Oh, but the furs—nobody could help but feel beautiful in furs!

"Hurry up, Cathy. Leave that stuff alone and come help me search."

"Chris, I'd love to take a bath in her black marble tub."

"God Almighty! We don't have time for you to do that!"

I took off her clothes, her black lace bra, the nylon hose, and the silver slippers, and put on my own things. But on second thought, I sneaked a plain white bra from her drawer of many, and tucked it down inside my blouse. Chris didn't need my help. He'd been here so often, he could find money without my assistance. I wanted to see what was in every drawer, but I'd have to move fast. I pulled open a small drawer of her nightstand, expecting to find cold cream, tissues, but nothing of value for servants to steal. And there was night cream in the drawer, and tissues, plus two paperback books to read when sleep was evasive. (Were there nights when she tossed and turned and thought uneasily about us?) Underneath those paperbacks was a very large and thick book with a colorful dustjacket. *How to Create Your Own Needlework Designs.* Now, that was a title to really intrigue me. Momma had taught me to do some needlepoint stitches, and also crewelwork on my first birthday in that locked room. And how to create your own designs would indeed be inspiring.

Casually I lifted out the book and flipped through the pages at random. Behind me Chris was making soft noises as he opened and closed drawers, and moved on sneakered feet from here to there. I had expected to see flower designs—anything but what I actually saw. Silent, wide-eyed, full of stunned fascination, I stared down at the photographs in full color. Unbelievable pictures of naked men and women doing . . . did people really do such things as that? Was this lovemaking?

Chris wasn't the only one who'd heard whispered tales accompanied by much snickering from older children clustered in groups in the bathroom at school. Why, I had believed it was a sacred, reverent thing to do in complete privacy, behind locked doors. This book depicted many couples all in one room, all naked, and all into each other in one way or another. Against my will, or so I wanted to think, my hand stole out to slowly turn each page, growing ever more incredulous! So many ways to do it! So many positions! My God, was *this* what lovesick Raymond and Lily had in mind from page one of that Victorian novel? I lifted my head and stared blankly into space. From the beginning of life, were we all headed toward this?

Chris spoke my name, informing me he had found enough money. Couldn't steal too much all at once, or it might be noticed. He was taking only a few fives, and many ones, and all the change under chair cushions. "Cathy, what's the matter, are you deaf? Come on."

I couldn't move, couldn't leave, couldn't close that book without pursuing it from cover to cover. Because I stood so enthralled, unable to respond, he came up behind me to look over my shoulder at what held me so mesmerized. I heard his breath pull in sharply. After an eternal time, he exhaled a low whistle. He didn't say a single word until I reached the end and closed the book. Then he took over and began at the beginning, looking at each page he had missed as I stood beside him and looked again, too. There was small printed text opposite the full-page pictures. But the photographs didn't need explanations—not to my mind.

Chris closed the book. I glanced at his face quickly. He appeared stunned. I returned the book to the drawer, placing the paperbacks on top, just as I had found it. He took my hand and pulled me toward the door. Down all the long and dark halls we went silently back to the northern wing. Now I knew only too well why the witch-grandmother had wanted Chris and me put in separate beds, when that compelling call to human flesh was so strong, so demanding, and so thrilling it could make people act more like demons than saints. I leaned above Carrie, staring down in her sleeping face, which, in her sleep, regained the innocence and childishness that evaded her during her waking hours. She seemed a small cherub lying there on her side, curled up tight, her face rosy and flushed, her hair damp and curling on the nape of her neck and on her rounded forehead. I kissed her, and her cheek felt hot, and then I went over to Cory to touch his soft curls and kiss his flushed cheek. Children like the twins were made from a little of what I had just viewed in that erotic picture book, so it couldn't all be totally wicked, or else God wouldn't have made men and women the way He did. And yet I was so troubled, and so uncertain, and deep down really stunned and shocked, and still . . .

I closed my eyes and silently prayed: *God, keep the twins safe and healthy until we're out of here . . . let them live until we reach a bright and sunny place where doors are never locked . . . please.*

"You can use the bath first," said Chris, sitting on his side of the bed with his back toward me. His head was bowed down, and this was his night to take his bath first.

Under a kind of spell I drifted into the bath and did what I had to, then came out wearing my thickest, warmest, and most concealing granny-gown. My face was scrubbed clean of all makeup. My hair was shampooed and still a little damp as I sat down on the side of my bed to brush it into shining waves.

Chris rose silently and entered the bath without looking my way, and when he came out much later, and I was still sitting and brushing my hair, he didn't meet my eyes. Nor did I want him to look at me.

It was one of the grandmother's rules that we were to kneel down by our beds each night and say prayers. Yet, that night, neither of us knelt to say prayers. Often, I was on my knees by the bed, with my palms together under my chin, and I didn't know what to pray, since already I'd prayed so much, and none of it helped. I'd just kneel there, empty-minded, bleak-hearted, but my body and its nerve endings felt everything and screamed out what I couldn't bring myself to think, much less say.

I stretched out beside Carrie on my back, feeling soiled and changed by that big book that I wished to see again and would if I could, read every word of the text. Maybe it would have been the ladylike thing to just put the book back when I'd found out its subject—and most certainly I should have slammed it shut when Chris came to look over my shoulder. Already I knew I wasn't a saint, or an angel, or a puritan prude, and I felt in my bones that someday in the near future I was going to need to know all there was to know about how bodies were used in ways of love.

Slowly, slowly, I turned my head to peer through the rosy dimness and see what Chris was doing.

He was on his side, under the covers, gazing over at me. His eyes glimmered in some faint meandering light that filtered through the heavy draperies, for what light was in his eyes wasn't rosy-colored.

"Are you all right?" he asked.

"Yes, I'm surviving." And then I said good night in a voice that didn't even sound like me.

"Good night, Cathy," he said, using someone else's voice, too.

My Stepfather

That spring, Chris got sick. He looked greenish around his mouth and threw up every few minutes, staggering back from the bathroom to fall weakly on the bed. He wanted to study *Gray's Anatomy,* but threw it aside, irritated with himself. "Must have been something I ate," he grouched.

"Chris, I don't want to leave you alone," I said at the door, preparing to fit the wooden key into the lock.

"Look here, Cathy!" he yelled. "It's time you learned to stand on your own two feet! You don't need me at your side every livelong minute of the day! That was Momma's trouble. She thought she'd always have a man to lean on. Lean on yourself, Cathy, always."

Terror jumped into my heart, flooded up in my eyes. He saw, and he spoke more gently. "I'm all right, really. I can take care of myself. We need the money, Cathy, so go on alone. We might not have another chance."

I ran back to his bed, falling down on my knees, and pressing my face down on his pajamaed chest. Tenderly he caressed my hair. "Really, Cathy, I'll survive. It's not so bad you have to cry about it. But you've got to understand, no matter what happens to either one of us, the one left has to get the twins out."

"Don't say things like that!" I cried out. Just to think of him dying made me sick inside. And as I knelt there, staring at him, it fleetingly crossed my mind, how often one or the other of us was sick.

"Cathy, I want you to leave now. Stand up. Force yourself. And when you get there, take only ones and fives. Nothing larger. But take all the coins our stepfather lets fall from his pockets. And in the back of his closet, he keeps a big tin box full of change. Take a handful of the quarters."

He looked pale and weak, thinner, too. Quickly I kissed his cheek, loath to leave when he felt so unwell. Glancing at the sleeping twins, I backed off toward the door, clutching the wooden key in my hand. "I love you, Christopher Doll," I said in a joking way before opening the door.

"I love you too, Catherine Doll," he said. "Good hunting."

I threw him a kiss, then closed and locked the door behind me. It was safe enough to go stealing in Momma's room. Only this afternoon she had told us she and her husband were attending another party, at a friend's who lived down the road. And I thought to myself, as I stole quietly along the corridors clinging to the walls, keeping to the shadows, I *was* going to take at least one twenty, and one ten. I was going to risk somebody noticing. Maybe I'd even steal a few pieces of Momma's jewelry. Jewelry could be pawned, just as good as money, maybe better.

All business, all determination, I didn't waste time looking in the trophy room. Straight on to Momma's bedroom I crept, not expecting to see the grandmother, who retired very early, at nine. And the hour was ten.

With all brave determined confidence, I stole through the double doors to her rooms, and silently closed them behind me. One dim light was burning. Often she left lights burning in her rooms—sometimes every last one, according to Chris. For what was money to our mother now?

Hesitating uncertainly, I stood just inside the doors and looked around. Then I froze in terror.

There, in a chair, with his long legs stretched before him and crossed at the ankles, sprawled Momma's new husband! I was directly in front of him, wearing a transparent blue nightie that was very short, though little matching panties were underneath. My heart beat out a mad tune of panic as I waited for him to bellow out and demand to know who I was, and what the hell was I doing coming uninvited into his bedroom?

But he didn't speak.

He wore a black tuxedo, and his formal shirt was pink with black-edged ruffles down the front. He didn't bellow, he didn't question, because he was dozing. I almost turned about and left, I was so terrified he'd awaken and see me.

However, curiosity overcame my trepidations. On my toes I stole closer to peer down at him. I dared to go so close, up to his very chair, that I could reach out and touch him, if I chose. Close enough to put my hand in his pocket and rob him if I chose, which I didn't.

Robbery was the last thing I had in mind as I gazed down into his handsome sleeping face. I was amazed to see what was revealed now that I was so very close to my mother's dearly beloved Bart. I had viewed him from a distance a number of times: first, the night of the Christmas party, and another time when he was down there near the stairs, holding a coat for Momma to slip her arms in. He'd kissed the back of her neck, and behind her ear, and whispered something that made her smile, and so tenderly he'd drawn her against his chest before they both went out the door.

Yes, yes, I had seen him, and heard much about him, and knew where his sisters lived, and where he was born, and where he'd gone to school, but nothing had prepared me for what was so clearly revealed now.

Momma—how could you? You should be ashamed! This man is younger than you—years younger! She hadn't told us that.

A secret. How well she could keep such an important secret! And no wonder she adored him, worshipped him—he was the kind of man any woman would want. Just to look at him so casually, elegantly sprawled, I guessed he was both tender and passionate when he made love to her.

I wanted to hate that man dozing in the chair, but somehow I just couldn't. Even asleep, he appealed to me, and made my heart beat faster.

Bartholomew Winslow, smiling in his sleep, innocently, unknowingly responding to my admiration. A lawyer, one of those men who knew everything—like doctors—like Chris. Certainly he must be seeing and experiencing something exceptionally pleasing. What was going on behind his eyeballs? I wondered, too, if his eyes were blue or brown. His head was long and lean, his body slim, and hard and muscular. A deep cleft was near his lips, looking like a stretched vertical dimple to play games of hide and seek as it came and went with his vague sleepy smiles.

He wore a wide sculptured gold wedding band, and of course I recognized it as the twin to the slimmer one my mother wore. On the index finger of his right hand he wore a large square-cut diamond ring that sparkled even without much light. On a small finger he wore a fraternity ring. His long fingers had square nails buffed so they shone as much as mine. I remembered when Momma used to buff Daddy's nails, while they played teasing games with their eyes.

He was tall. . . . I already knew that. And of everything he had that pleased me well, it was his full and sensual lips beneath the moustache that intrigued me most. Such a beautifully shaped mouth—sensual lips that must kiss my mother . . . everywhere. That book of sexual pleasures had educated me well along that line of how adults gave and took when they were bare.

It came over me all of a sudden—the impulse to kiss him— just to see if the dark moustache tickled. Just to know also, what a kiss was like from a stranger who was no blood relation at all.

Not forbidden, this one. Not sinful to tentatively reach out and very lightly stroke his closely shaven cheek, so softly challenging him to wake up.

But he slept on.

I leaned above him and pressed my lips down on his ever so lightly, then drew away fast, my heart pounding in a paralyzing kind of fear. I was almost wishing that he would waken, but I was still fearful and afraid. I was too young and unsure of what I had to believe he would come rushing to my defense, when he had a woman like my mother madly in love with him. Would he, if I took his arm and shook him awake, sit and listen calmly to my story about four children sequestered in a lonely, isolated room year after year, waiting impatiently for their grandfather to die? Would he understand and sympathize with us, and would he force Momma to set us free, and give up hopes of inheriting that immense fortune?

My hands fluttered nervously to my throat, the way Momma's did when she was caught in a dilemma, not knowing which way to turn. My instinct was shouting loud: *Wake him up!* My suspicions whispered slyly, keep quiet, don't let him know; he won't want you, not four children he didn't father. He'll hate you for preventing his wife from inheriting all the riches and pleasures that money can buy. Look at him, so young, so handsome. And though our mother was exceptionally beautiful, and on the way to being one of the wealthiest women in the world, he could have had somebody younger. A fresh virgin who'd never loved anyone else, nor slept with another man.

And then my indecision was over. The answer was so simple. What were four unwanted children when compared to unbelievable riches?

They were nothing. Already Momma had taught me that. And a virgin would bore him.

Oh, it was unfair! Foul! Our mother had everything! Freedom to come and go as she wished; freedom to spend lavishly and buy out the world's best stores, if she chose. She even had the money to buy a much younger man to love, and sleep with—and what did Chris and I have but broken dreams, shattered promises, and unending frustrations?

And what did the twins have, but a dollhouse and a mouse and ever-declining health?

Back to that forlorn, locked room I went with tears in my eyes and a helpless, hopeless feeling heavy as stone in my chest. I found Chris sleeping with *Gray's Anatomy* lying face down and open on his chest. Carefully I marked his place, closed the book, and put it aside.

Then I lay beside him, and clung to him, and silent tears came to streak my cheeks and wet his pajama jacket.

"Cathy," he said, waking up, and coming sleepily into focus. "What's the matter? Why are you crying? Did someone see you?"

I couldn't meet his concerned look squarely, and for some inexplicable reason, I couldn't tell him what happened. I couldn't speak the words to say I'd found mother's new husband dozing in her room. Much less could I tell him I'd been so childishly romantic as to kiss him while he slept.

"And you didn't even find a single penny?" he asked with so much disbelief.

"Not even a penny," I whispered in return, and I tried to hide my face from his. But he cupped my chin and forced me to turn my head so he could delve deep into my eyes. Oh, why did we have to know each other so well? He stared at me, while I tried to keep my eyes blank, but it was no use. All I could do was close my eyes and snuggle closer in his arms. He bowed his face into my hair while his hands soothingly stroked my back. "It's all right. Don't cry. You don't know where to look like I do."

I had to get away, run away, and when I ran away, I would take all of this with me, no matter where I went, or who I ended up with.

"You can get in your own bed now," said Chris in his hoarse

voice. "The grandmother could open the door and catch us, you know."

"Chris, you didn't throw up again after I left, did you?"

"No. I'm better. Just go away, Cathy. Go away."

"You really feel better now? You're not just saying that?"

"Didn't I just say I was better?"

"Goodnight, Christopher Doll," I said, then put a kiss on his cheek before I left his bed and climbed into my own bed to snuggle up with Carrie.

"Good night, Catherine. You make a pretty good sister, and mother to the twins . . . but you're one helluva liar, and one damned no-good thief!"

Each of Chris's forays into Momma's room enriched our hidden cache. It was taking so long to reach our goal of five hundred dollars. And now summer was upon us again. Now I was fifteen, the twins recently turned eight. Soon August would mark the third year of our imprisonment. Before another winter set in, we had to escape. I looked at Cory, who was listlessly picking at black-eyed peas because they were "good luck" peas. First time on New Year's Day, he wouldn't eat them: didn't want any little brown eyes looking at his insides. Now he'd eat them because each pea gave one full day of happiness—so we'd told him. Chris and I had to make up tales like this or else he'd eat nothing but the doughnuts. As soon as that meal was over, he crouched down on the floor, picked up his banjo, and fixed his eyes on a silly cartoon. Carrie glued in beside him, as close as possible, watching her twin's face and not the TV. "Cathy," she said to me in her bird twitter. "Cory, he don't feel so good."

"How do you know?"

"Jus' know."

"Has he told you he feels sick?"

"He don't have to."

"And how do *you* feel?"

"Like always."

"And how is that?"

"Don't know."

Oh yes! We had to get out, and fast!

Later on I tucked the twins in one bed. When they were both asleep, I'd lift out Carrie, and put her in our bed, but for now, it was comforting for Cory to go to sleep with his sister by his side. "Don't like this pink sheet," complained Carrie, scowling at me. "We all like white sheets. Where are our white sheets?"

Oh, rue the day when Chris and I had made white the safest color of all! White chalk daisies drawn on the attic floor kept away evil demons, and monsters, and all the other things the twins feared would get them if white wasn't somewhere near to hide inside, or under, or behind. Lavender, blue or pink, or flower-strewn sheets and pillowcases were not to be tolerated . . . little colored places gave small imps a hole through which to drive a forked tail, or glare a mean eye, or stab with a wicked, tiny spear! Rituals, fetishes, habits, rules—Lord—we had them by the millions! Just to keep us safe.

"Cathy, why does Momma like black dresses so much?" asked Carrie, waiting as I took off the pink sheets and replaced them with plain white ones.

"Momma is blonde and very fair, and black makes her look even more fair, and exceptionally beautiful."

"She's not scared of black?"

"No."

"How old do you get before black doesn't bite you with long teeth?"

"Old enough to know such a question as that is absolutely silly."

"But all the black shadows in the attic have shiny, sharp teeth," said Cory, scooting backward so the pink sheets wouldn't touch his skin.

"Now look," I said, seeing Chris's laughing eyes watching as he anticipated some gem I would certainly deliver. "Black shadows don't have shiny sharp teeth unless your skin is emerald green, and your eyes are purple, and your hair is red, and you have three ears instead of two. Only then is black a threat."

Comforted, the twins scurried under the white sheet and white blankets, and were soon fast asleep. Then I had time to bathe, and shampoo my hair, and put on wispy baby-doll pajamas. I ran up into the attic to open a window wide, hopeful of catching a cool breeze to freshen the attic so I'd feel like dancing and not wilting. Why was it the wind could find its way inside only during a wintery blast? Why not now, when we needed it most?

Chris and I shared all our thoughts, our aspirations, our doubts, and our fears. If I had small problems, he was my doctor. Fortunately, my problems were never of much consequence, only those monthly cramps, and that womanly time never showed up on schedule, which he, my amateur doctor, said was only to be expected. Since I was of a quixotic nature, all my internal machinery would follow suit.

So I can write now of Chris and what happened one September night when I was in the attic, and he had gone stealing, just as if I were there, for later, when the shock of something totally unexpected had died down a bit, he told me in great detail of this particular trip to Momma's grand suite of luxurious rooms.

He told me it was that book in the nightstand drawer that drew him always; it lured him, beckoned to him, was to shipwreck him later, and me too. As soon as he found his quota of money— enough, but not too much—he drifted over to the bed and that table as if magnetized.

And I thought to myself, even as he told me: Why did he have to keep on looking, when each of those photographs was forever engraved on my brain?

"And there I was, reading the text, a few pages at a time," he said, "and thinking about right and wrong, and wondering about nature and all its strange exhilarating calls, and thinking about the circumstances of our lives. I thought about you and me, that these should be blossoming years for us, and I had to feel guilty and ashamed to be growing up, and wanting what other boys my age could take from girls who were willing.

"And, as I stood there, leafing through those pages, burning inside with so many frustrations, and wishing in a way you hadn't ever found that damned book that never drew my attention with its dull title, I heard voices approaching in the hall. You know who it was—it was our mother, and her husband, returning. Quickly I shoved the book back into the drawer and tossed in the two paperbacks which no one was ever going to finish reading, for the bookmarks were always in the same place. Next I dashed into Momma's closet—that big one, you know, the one nearest her bed—and way back near the shoe shelves I crouched down on the floor beneath her long formal gowns. I thought if she came in, she wouldn't see me and I doubt she would have. But no sooner did I feel this security, then I realized I'd forgotten to close the door.

"That's when I heard our mother's voice. 'Really, Bart,' she said as she came into the room and switched on a lamp, 'it's just plain carelessness for you to forget your wallet so often.'

"He answered, 'I can't help but forget it when it's never in the same place I put it down.' I heard him moving things about, opening and closing drawers and so forth. Then he explained, 'I'm certain I left it in this pair of trousers. . . . and damned if I'm going anywhere without my driver's license.'

" 'The way you drive, I can't say I blame you,' said our mother, 'but this is going to make us late again. No matter how fast you drive, we'll still miss the first act.'

" 'Hey!' exclaimed her husband, and I heard surprise in his voice, and inwardly I groaned, remembering what I'd done. 'Here's my wallet, on the dresser. Darned if I recall leaving it there. I could swear I put it in these trousers.'

"He really had hidden it in his chest of drawers," Chris explained, "under his shirts, and when I found it, I took out a few small bills, I just laid it down and went on to look at that book. And Momma, she said, 'Really, Bart!' as if she was out of patience with him.

"And then he said, 'Corrine, let's move out of this place. I believe those maids are stealing from us. You keep missing money, and so do I. For instance, I know I had four fives, and now I have only three.'

"I groaned again. I thought he had so much he never counted. And the fact that Momma knew what cash she carried in her purse really came as a shock.

" 'Just what difference does a five make?' questioned our mother, and that sounded like her, to be indifferent about money, just as she had been with Daddy. And then she went on to say the servants were underpaid, and she didn't blame them for taking what they could when it was left so opportunely before them, 'actually inviting them to steal.'

"And he answered, 'My dear wife, money may come easily to you, but I've always had to work hard to earn a buck, and don't want ten cents stolen from me. Besides, I can't say my day starts out right when I have your mother's grim face across the table from me every morning.' You know, I'd never given that any thought, how he felt about that old witch ironface.

"Apparently he feels just as we do, and Momma, she grew kind of irritated, and said, 'Let's not go through all that again.' And her voice had a hard edge to it; she didn't even sound like herself, Cathy. It never occurred to me before that she talked one way to us, and another way to other people. And then she said, 'You know I can't leave this house, not yet, so if we're going, come on, let's go—we're late already.'

"And that's when our stepfather said he didn't want to go if they'd already missed the first act, for that spoiled the whole show for him, and besides, he thought they could find something more entertaining to do than sit in an audience. And, of course, I guessed he meant they could go to bed and do a little lovemaking, and if you don't think that didn't make me feel sick, then you don't know me very well—darned if I wanted to be there when that was going on.

"However, our mother can be very strong-willed, and that surprised me. She's changed, Cathy, from the way she was with Daddy. It's like she is the boss now, and no man is going to tell her what to do. And she said to him then, 'Like last time? Now, that was really embarrassing, Bart! You came back to get your wallet, swearing to me you'd only be gone a few minutes and what did you do but fall asleep—and there I was at that party without an escort!'

"Now our stepfather sounded somewhat irritated, both by her words, and her tone, if I judged him correctly, and there's a lot you can read into voices even when you don't see facial expressions. 'Oh, how you must have suffered!' he replied, sounding sarcastic. But that didn't last long, for he must be basically a jovial fellow. 'As for me, I had the sweetest dream, and I'd come back every time if I knew that for certain, a lovely young girl with the long, golden hair would steal into the room and kiss me while I dozed. Oh, she was pretty, and she looked at me so longingly, yet, when I opened my eyes she was gone, and I thought she must have been a dream.'

"What he said made me gasp, Cathy—it was you, wasn't it? How could you be so bold, so indiscreet? I got so damned mad with you I felt ready to explode if just one more little thing happened to set me off. You think you're the only one wound up, right? You think you're the only one with frustrations, with doubts, suspicions, and fears. Well, take comfort from knowing I have them too—you've seen to that. And, boy, was I mad at you, madder than I've ever been before.

"And then Momma said sharply to her husband, 'God, I am sick of hearing about the girl and her kiss—why, to hear you tell it, you've never been kissed before!' And I thought that then and there they might have an argument. But Momma changed her voice, and sounded sweet and loving, like she used to sound with Daddy. But it proved she was more determined to leave this house than a would-be lover who would use the swan bed then and there, for Momma said, 'Come along, Bart, we'll stay overnight in a hotel, and then you won't have to see my mother's face in the morning.' And that solved my concern about how I was going to escape that room before they used that swan bed—for damned if I would stay and listen, or spy."

This was all happening while I was up in the attic, sitting on a windowsill, waiting for Chris to reappear. I was thinking of the silver music box Daddy had given me, and wishing I had it back. I didn't know then that the episode in Momma's room was to have its repercussions.

Something creaked behind me! A soft step on rotting wood! I jumped, startled, scared, and turned, expecting to see—God knows what! Then I sighed, for it was only Chris standing in the gloom, silently staring at me. Why? Did I look prettier than usual? Was it the moonlight, shining through my airy clothes?

All random doubts were cleared when he said in a voice gritty and low, "You look beautiful sitting there like that." He cleared the frog in his throat. "The moonlight is etching you with silver-blue, and I can see the shape of your body through your clothes."

Then, bewilderingly, he seized me by the shoulders, digging in his fingers, hard! They hurt. "Damn you, Cathy! You kissed that man! He could have awakened and seen you, and demanded to know who you were! And not thought you only a part of his dream!"

Scary the way he acted, the fright I felt for no reason at all. "How do you know what I did? You weren't there; you were sick that night."

He shook me, glaring his eyes, and again I thought he seemed a stranger. "He saw you, Cathy—he wasn't soundly asleep!"

"He saw me?" I cried, disbelieving. It wasn't possible . . . wasn't!

"Yes!" he yelled. This was Chris, who was usually in such control of his emotions. "He thought you a part of his dream! But don't you know that Momma can guess who it was, just by putting two and two together—just as I have? Damn you and your romantic notions! Now they're on to us! They won't leave money casually about as they did before. He's counting, she's counting, and we don't have enough—not yet!"

He yanked me down from the window sill! He appeared wild and furious enough to slap my face—and not once in all our lives had he ever struck me, though I'd given him reason to when I was younger. But he shook me until my eyes rolled, until I was dizzy and crying out: "Stop! Momma knows we can't pass through a locked door!"

This wasn't Chris . . . this was someone I'd never seen before . . . primitive, savage.

He yelled out something like, "You're mine, Cathy! Mine! You'll always be mine! No matter who comes into your future, you'll always belong to me! I'll make you mine . . . tonight . . . now!"

I didn't believe it, not Chris!

And I did not fully understand what he had in mind, nor, if I am to give him credit, do I think he really meant what he said, but passion has a way of taking over.

We fell to the floor, both of us. I tried to fight him off. We wrestled, turning over and over, writhing, silent, a frantic struggle of his strength against mine.

It wasn't much of a battle.

I had the strong dancer's legs; he had the biceps, the greater weight and height . . . and he had much more determination than I to use something hot, swollen and demanding, so much it stole reasoning and sanity from him.

And I loved him. I wanted what he wanted—if he wanted it *that* much, right or wrong.

Somehow we ended up on that old mattress—that filthy, smelly, stained mattress that must have known lovers long before this night. And that is where he took me, and forced in that swollen, rigid male sex part of him that had to be satisfied. It drove into my tight and resisting flesh which tore and bled.

Now we had done what we both swore we'd never do.

Now we were doomed through all eternity, damned to roast forever, hung upside down and naked over the everlasting fires of hell. Sinners, just as the grandmother had forecasted so long ago.

Now I had all the answers.

Now there might be a baby. A baby to make us pay in life and not wait for hell, and everlasting fires reserved for such as us.

We drew apart and stared at each other, our faces numb and pale from shock, and barely could we speak as we drew on our clothes.

He didn't have to say he was sorry . . . it was all over him . . . the way he quivered, the way his hands trembled and were so clumsy with his buttons.

Later, we went out on the roof.

Long strings of clouds blew across the face of the full moon, so it would duck and hide, then peek out again. And on the roof, on a night that was made for lovers, we cried in each other's arms. He hadn't meant to do it. And I had meant never to let him. The fear of the baby that might be the result of one single kiss on moustached lips rose high in my throat, and hesitated on my tongue. It was my worst fear. More than hell, or God's wrath, I feared giving birth to a monstrous baby, deformed, a freak, an idiot. But how could I speak of this? Already he was suffering enough. However, his thoughts were more knowledge-able than mine.

"The odds are all against a baby," he said fervently. "Just one time—there won't be a conception. I swear there won't be another time—no matter what! I'll castrate myself before I'll let it happen again!" Then he had pulled me tightly against him so I was crushed so hard it hurt my ribs. "Don't hate me, Cathy, please don't hate me. I didn't mean to rape you, I swear to God. There's been many a time when I've been tempted, and I was able to turn it off. I'd leave the room, go into the bathroom, or into the attic. I'd bury my nose in a book until I felt normal again."

Tight as I could, I wrapped my arms around him. "I don't hate you, Chris," I whispered, pressing my head tightly against his chest. "You didn't rape me. I could have stopped you if I'd really wanted to. All I had to do was bring my knee up hard, where you told me to. It was my fault, too." Oh yes, my fault too. I should have known better than to kiss Momma's handsome young husband. I shouldn't have worn skimpy little see-through garments around a brother who had all a man's strong physical needs, and a brother who was always so frustrated by everything, and everyone. I had played upon his needs, testing my femininity, having my own burning yearnings for fulfillment.

It was a peculiar kind of night, as if fate had planned this night, long ago, and this night was our destiny, right or wrong. It was darkness lit up by the moon so full and bright, and the stars seemed to flash Morse Code beams to one another . . . fate accomplished. . . .

The wind in the leaves rustled and made an eerie, melancholy music that was tuneless, yet music just the same. How could anything as human and loving be ugly on such a beautiful night as this one?

Perhaps we stayed too long on the roof.

The slate was cold, hard, rough. It was early September. Already the leaves were beginning to fall, so soon to be touched by the winter's frosty hand. Hot as hell in the attic. On the roof, it was beginning to turn very, very cold.

Closer Chris and I huddled, clinging to each other for safety and warmth. Youthful, sinful lovers of the worst kind. We had dropped ten miles in our own esteem, done in by yearnings stretched too thin by constant closeness. Just once too often we'd tempted fate, and our own sensuous natures . . . and I hadn't even known at the time that I was sensuous, much less that he was. I'd thought it was only beautiful music that made my heart ache and my loins crave; I hadn't known it was something far more tangible.

Like one heart shared between us, we drummed out a terrible tune of self-punishment for what we'd done.

A colder breeze lifted a dead leaf to the roof and sent it scuttling merrily on its way to catch in my hair. It crackled dry and brittle when Chris plucked it out and held it, just staring down at a dead maple leaf as if his very life depended on reading its secret for knowing how to blow in the wind. No arms, no legs, no wings . . . but it could fly when dead.

"Cathy," he began in a crackling, dry voice, "we now have exactly three hundred and ninety-six dollars and forty-four cents. Won't be long before the snow starts to fall. And we don't own winter coats or boots that fit, and the twins are already so weakened that they will catch cold easily, and might pass from colds into pneumonia. I wake up in the night, worrying about them, and I've seen you lying on your bed staring at Carrie, so you must be worrying, too. I doubt very much we'll be finding money lying about in Momma's suite of rooms now. They suspect a maid is stealing from them—or they did. Maybe now Momma suspects that it could be you . . . I don't know . . . I hope not.

"Regardless of what either of them thinks, the next time I play thief, I'm forced to steal her jewelry. I'll make a grand sweep, take it all—and then we'll run. We'll take the twins to a doctor as soon as we're far enough away, and we'll have enough money to pay their bills."

Take the jewelry—what I'd begged him to do all along! Finally he would do it, agree to steal the hard-won prizes Momma had struggled so to gain, and in the process, she was going to lose us. But would she care—would she?

That old owl that might be the same one that greeted us at the train depot on the first night we came, hooted in the far distance, sounding ghostly. While we watched, thin, slow, gray mists began to rise up from the damp ground, chilled by the night's sudden cold. The thick and billowing fog swelling up to the roof . . . undulating curling waves, rolling as a misty sea to shroud over us.

And all we could see in the murky-gray and cold, damp

clouds was that single great eye of God—shining up there in the moon.

I awakened before dawn. I stared over to where Cory and Chris slept. Even as my sleepy eyes opened, and my head turned, I sensed that Chris was awake, too, and had been for some time. He was already looking at me, and shiny, glistening tears sparkled the blue of his eyes and smeared the whites. The tears that rolled to fall on his pillow, I named as they fell: shame, guilt, blame.

"I love you, Christopher Doll. You don't have to cry. For I can forget, if you can forget, and there's nothing to forgive."

He nodded and said nothing. But I knew him well, right down to his bone marrow. I knew his thoughts, his feelings, and all the ways to wound his ego fatally. I knew that through me he had struck back at the one woman who had betrayed him in trust, faith and love. All I had to do was look in my hand mirror with the big C. L. F. on the back, and I could see my own mother's face, as she must have looked at my age.

And so it had come to pass, just as the grandmother predicted. Devil's issue. Created by evil seed sown in the wrong soil, shooting up new plants to repeat the sins of the fathers.

And the mothers.

Color All Days Blue,
But Save One for *Black*

We were leaving. Any day. As soon as Momma gave the word that she'd be out for the evening, she'd also be out of all her valuable, transportable possessions. We would not go back to Gladstone. There the winter came and lasted until May. We would go to Sarasota, where the circus people lived. They were known for having and showing kindness to those from strange backgrounds. Since Chris and I'd grown accustomed to high places, the roof, the many ropes attached to the rafter beams, I blithely said to Chris, "We'll be trapeze performers." He grinned, thinking it a ridiculous idea—at first—next calling it inspired.

"Golly, Cathy, you'll look great in spangled pink tights." He began to sing: "She flies through the air, with the greatest of ease, the daring young beauty on the flying trapeze. . . ."

Cory jerked up his blond head. Blue eyes wide with fear. *"No!"*

Said Carrie, his more proficient voice, "We don't like your plans. We don't want you to fall."

"We'll never fall," said Chris, "because Cathy and I are an unbeatable team." I stared over at him, recalling the night in the schoolroom, and on the roof afterward when he'd whispered, "I'm never going to love anyone but you, Cathy. I know it . . . I've got that kind of feeling . . . just us, always."

Casually I'd laughed. "Don't be silly, you know you don't really love me in *that* way. And you don't have to feel guilty, or ashamed. It was my fault, too. And we can pretend it never happened, and make sure it never happens again."

"But Cathy . . ."

"If there were others for you and me, never, never would we feel this way for each other."

"But I *want* to feel this way about you, and it's too late for me to love or trust anyone else."

How old I felt, looking at Chris, at the twins, making plans for all of us, speaking so confidently of how we would make our way. A consolation token for the twins, to give them peace, when I knew we would be forced to do anything, and everything to earn a living.

September had passed on into October. Soon the snow would fly.

"Tonight," said Chris after Momma took off, saying a hasty good-bye, not pausing in the doorway to look back at us. Now she could hardly bear to look at us. We put one pillowcase inside another, to make it strong. In that sack Chris would dump all Momma's precious jewelry. Already I had our two bags packed and hidden in the attic, where Momma never went now.

As the day wore on toward evening, Cory began to vomit, over and over again. In the medicine cabinet we had non-prescription drugs for abdominal upsets.

Nothing we used would stop the terrible retching that left him pale, trembling, crying. Then his arms encircled my neck and he whispered, "Momma, I don't feel so good."

"What can I do to make you feel better, Cory?" I asked, feeling so young and inexperienced.

"Mickey," he whispered weakly. "I want Mickey to sleep with me."

"But you might roll over on him and then he'd be dead. You wouldn't want him to die, would you?"

"No," he said, looking stricken at the thought, and then that terrible gagging began again, and in my arms he grew so cold. His hair was pasted to his sweaty brow. His blue eyes stared vacantly into my face as over and over again he called for his mother, "Momma, Momma, my bones hurt."

"It's all right," I soothed, picking him up and carrying him back to his bed, where I could change his soiled pajamas. How could he throw up again when there couldn't be anything left? "Chris is going to help you, don't worry." I lay beside him and held his weak and quivering body in my arms.

Chris was at his desk poring over medical reference books, using Cory's symptoms to name the mysterious illness that struck each one of us from time to time. He was almost eighteen now, but far from being a doctor.

"Don't go and leave me and Carrie behind," Cory pleaded. He cried out later, and louder, "Chris, don't go! Stay here!"

What did he mean? Didn't he want us to run away? Or did he mean never sneak into Momma's suite of rooms again to steal? Why was it Chris and I believed the twins seldom paid attention to what we did? Surely he and Carrie knew we'd never go away and leave them behind—we'd die before we did that.

A little shadowy thing wearing all white drifted over to the bed, and stood with big watery blue eyes staring and staring at her twin brother. She was barely three feet high. She was old, and she was young, she was a tender little plant brought up in a dark hothouse, stunted and withered.

"May I"—she began very properly (as we had tried to teach her, and she had consistently refused to use the grammar we tried to teach, but on this night of nights, she did the best she could)—"sleep with Cory? We won't do anything bad, or evil, or unholy. I just want to be close to him."

Let the grandmother come and do her worst! We put Carrie to bed with Cory, and then Chris and I perched on opposite sides of the big bed and watched, full of anxiety, as Cory tossed about restlessly, and gasped for breath, and cried out in his delirium. He wanted the mouse, he wanted his mother, his father, he wanted Chris, and he wanted me. Tears were pooling down on the collar of my nightgown, and I looked to see Chris with tears on his cheeks. "Carrie, Carrie . . . where is Carrie?" he asked repeatedly, long after she'd gone to sleep. Their wan faces were only inches apart, and he was looking directly at her, and still he didn't see her. When I took the time to look from him to Carrie, she seemed but a bit better off.

Punishment, I thought. God was punishing us, Chris and me, for what we'd done. The grandmother had warned us . . . every day she'd warned us up until the day we were whipped.

All through the night Chris read one medical book after another while I got up from the twins' bed and paced the room.

Finally Chris raised his red-rimmed, bloodshot eyes. "Food poisoning—the milk. It must have been sour."

"It didn't taste sour, or smell sour," I answered in a mumble. I was always careful to sniff and taste everything first before I'd give it to the twins or Chris. For some reason, I thought my tastebuds keener than Chris's, who liked everything, and would eat anything, even rancid butter.

"The hamburger, then. I thought it had a funny taste."

"It tasted all right to me." And it must have tasted fine to him, as well, for he'd eaten half of Carrie's hamburger on a bun, and all of Cory's. Cory hadn't wanted anything to eat all day.

"Cathy, I noticed you hardly ate anything yourself all day. You're almost as thin as the twins. She does bring us enough food, such as it is. You don't have to stint on yourself."

Whenever I was nervous, or frustrated, or worried—and I was all three now—I'd begin the ballet exercises, and holding lightly to the dresser that acted as a barre, I began to warm up by doing pliés.

"Do you have to do that, Cathy? You're already skin and bones. And why didn't you eat today—are you sick, too?"

"But Cory so loves the doughnuts, and that's all I want to eat too. And he needs them more than I do."

The night wore on. Chris returned to reading the medical books. I gave Cory water to drink—and right away he threw it up. I washed his face with cold water a dozen times, and changed his pajamas three times, and Carrie slept on and on and on.

Dawn.

The sun came up and we were still trying to figure out what made Cory ill, when the grandmother came in, bearing the picnic basket of food for today. Without a word she closed the door, locked it, put the key in her dress pocket, and advanced to the gaming table. From the basket she lifted the huge thermos of milk, the smaller thermos of soup, then the packets wrapped in foil, containing sandwiches, fried chicken, of bowls of potato salad or cole slaw—and, last of all, the packet of four powdered-sugar doughnuts. She turned to leave.

"Grandmother," I said tentatively. She had not looked Cory's way. Hadn't seen.

"I have not spoken to you," she said coldly. "Wait until I do."

"I can't wait," said I, growing angry, rising up from my place on the side of Cory's bed, and advancing. "Cory's sick! He's been throwing up all night, and all day yesterday. He needs a doctor, and his mother."

She didn't look at me, or at Cory. Out of the door she stalked, then clicked the lock behind her. No word of comfort. No word to say she'd tell our mother.

"I'll unlock the door and go and find Momma," said Chris, still wearing the clothes he put on yesterday, and hadn't taken off to go to bed.

"Then they'll know we have a key."

"Then they'll know."

Just then the door opened and Momma came in, with the

grandmother trailing behind her. Together they hovered over Cory, touching his clammy, cold face, their eyes meeting. In a corner they drifted to whisper and connive, glancing from time to time at Cory who lay quiet as one approaching death. Only his chest heaved in spasms. From his throat came gasping, choking noises. I went and wiped the beads of moisture from his brow. Funny how he could feel cool, and still sweat.

Cory rasped in, out, in, out.

And there was Momma—doing nothing. Unable to make a decision! Fearful still of letting someone know there was a child, when there shouldn't be any!

"Why are you standing there whispering?" I shouted out. "What choice do you have but to take Cory to a hospital, and get him the best doctor available?"

They glared at me—both of them. Grim faced, pale, trembling, Momma fixed her blue eyes on me, then anxiously they sidled over to Cory. What she saw on the bed made her lips tremble, made her hands shake and the muscles near her lips twitch. She blinked repeatedly, as if holding back tears.

Narrowly I watched each betraying sign of her calculating thoughts. She was weighing the risks of Cory being discovered, and causing her to lose that inheritance . . . for that old man downstairs just had to die one day, didn't he? He couldn't hold on forever!

I screamed out, "What's the matter with you, Momma? Are you just going to stand there and think about yourself, and that money while your youngest son lies there and dies? You *have* to help him! Don't you care what happens to him? Have you forgotten you are his mother? If you haven't, then, damn it, act like his mother! Stop hesitating! He needs attention now, not tomorrow!"

Sanguine color flooded her face. She snapped her eyes back to me. "You!" she spat. "Always it's you!" And with that she raised her heavily ringed hand, and she slapped my face, hard! Then again she slapped me.

The very first time in my life I'd been slapped by her—and for such a reason! Outraged, without thinking, I slapped back—just as hard!

The grandmother stood back and watched. Smug satisfaction twisted her ugly, thin mouth into a crooked line.

Chris hurried to seize hold of my arms when I would strike Momma again. "Cathy, you're not helping Cory by acting like this. Calm down. Momma will do the right thing."

It was a good thing he held my arms, for I wanted to slap her again, and make her see what she was doing!

My father's face flashed before my eyes. He was frowning, silently telling me I must always have respect for the woman who gave me birth. I knew that's how he would feel. He wouldn't want me to hit her.

"Damn you to hell, Corrine Foxworth," I shouted at the top of my lungs, "if you don't take your son to a hospital! You think you can do anything you want with us, and no one will find out! Well, you can throw away that security blanket, for I'll find a way for revenge, if it takes me the rest of my life, I'll see that you pay, and dearly pay, if you don't do something right now to save Cory's life. Go on, glare your eyes at me, and cry and plead, and talk to me about money and what it can buy. But it can't buy back a child once he's dead! And if that happens, don't think I won't find a way to get to your husband and tell him you have four children you have kept hidden in a locked room with their only playground an attic . . . and you've kept them there for years and years! See if he loves you then! Watch his face and wait to see how much respect and admiration he has for you then!" She winced, but her eyes shot deadly looks at me. "And what's more, I'll go to the grandfather and tell him, too!" I yelled even louder. "And you won't inherit one damned red penny—and I'll be glad, glad, glad!"

From the look on her face she could kill me, but oddly enough, it was that despicable old woman who spoke in a quiet way: "The girl is right, Corrine. The child must go to a hospital."

*   *   *

They came back that night. The two of them. After the servants retired to their quarters over the huge garage. Both of them were bundled up in heavy coats, for it had turned suddenly frigid-cold. The evening sky had gone gray, chilled with early winter that threatened snow. The two of them pulled Cory from my arms and wrapped him in a green blanket, and it was Momma who lifted him up. Carrie let out a scream of anguish. "Don't take Cory away!" she howled. "Don't take him, don't . . ." She threw herself into my arms wailing at me to stop them from taking away a twin from whom she'd never been separated.

I stared down in her small pale face, streaked with tears. "It's all right for Cory to go," I said as I met my mother's glare, "for I am going, too. I'll stay with Cory while he's in the hospital. Then he won't be afraid. When the nurses are too busy to wait on him, I'll be there. That will make him get well quicker, and Carrie will feel good knowing I'm with him." I spoke the truth. I knew Cory would recover quicker if I was there with him. *I* was his mother now—not her. He didn't love her now, it was me he needed and me he wanted. Children are very wise intuitively; they know who loves them most, and who only pretends.

"Cathy's right, Momma," Chris spoke up and he looked at her directly in the eye without warmth. "Cory depends on Cathy. Please let her go, for as she says, her presence there will help him get well sooner, and she can describe to his doctor all his symptoms better than you can."

Momma's glassy, blank stare turned his way, as if struggling to grasp his meaning. I admit she looked distraught, and her eyes jumped from me to Chris, and then to her mother, and then to Carrie, and back to Cory.

"Momma," said Chris more firmly, "let Cathy go with you. I can do for Carrie, if that's what you're worried about."

Of course they didn't let me go.

Our mother carried Cory out into the hall. His head was thrown back, his cowlick bobbing up and down as she strode

away with her child wrapped in a green blanket, the very color
of spring grass.

The grandmother gave me a cruel smile of derisive victory,
then closed and locked the door.

They left Carrie bereft, screaming, tears flowing. Her small
weak fists beat against me, as if I were to blame. "Cathy, I
wanna go, too! Make them let me go! Cory don't wanna go
nowhere I don't go . . . and he forgot his guitar."

Then all her anger dissipated, and she fell into my arms and
sobbed, "Why, Cathy, why?"

Why?

That was the biggest question in our lives.

By far it was the worst and longest day of our lives. We had
sinned, and how quickly God set about punishing us. He *did*
keep his sharpest eye turned on us, as if *He* knew all along
sooner or later we would prove ourselves unworthy, just as the
grandmother had known.

It was like it had been in the beginning, before the TV set
came to take over the better part of our days. All through the day
we sat quietly without turning on the television, just waiting to
hear how Cory was.

Chris sat in the rocker and held out his arms to Carrie and me.
We both sat on his lap as he rocked slowly back and forth, back
and forth, creaking the floorboards.

I don't know why Chris's legs didn't grow numb; we sat on
him for so long. Then I got up to take care of Mickey's cage, and
gave him food to eat and water to drink, and I held him, and petted him, and told him soon his master would be coming back. I
believe that mouse knew something was wrong. He didn't play
cheerfully in his cage, and even though I left the door open, he
didn't come out to scamper all over the room, and head for
Carrie's dollhouse that enchanted him the most.

I prepared the pre-cooked meals, which we hardly touched.
When the last meal of the day was over, and the dishes were put
away, and we were bathed and ready for bed, we all three knelt

in a row beside Cory's bed, and said our prayers to God. "Please, please let Cory get well, and come back to us." If we prayed for anything else, I don't recall what it was.

We slept, or tried to, all three in the same bed, with Carrie between Chris and me. Nothing gross was ever going to happen between us again . . . never, never again.

God, please don't punish Cory as a way to strike back at Chris and me and make us hurt, for already we hurt, and we didn't mean to do it, we didn't. It just happened, and only once. And it wasn't any pleasure, God, not really, not any.

A new day dawned, grim, gray, forbidding. Behind the drawn draperies life started up for those who lived on the outside, those unseen by us. We dragged ourselves into focus, and poked about, trying to fill our time, and trying to eat, and make Mickey happy when he seemed so sad without the little boy who laid down trails of bread crumbs for him to follow.

I changed the mattress covers, with the assistance of Chris, for that was a very hard thing to do, to slip a full-size mattress in and out of one of those heavy quilted things, and yet we had to do it often because of Cory's lack of control. Chris and I made the beds up with clean linens, and smoothed on the spreads, and tidied up the room, while Carrie sat alone in the rocker and stared off into space.

Around ten, there was nothing left to do but sit on the bed nearest the door to the hall, with our eyes riveted upon the knob, willing it to turn and admit Momma, who would bring us news.

Shortly thereafter, Momma came in with her eyes rimmed red from crying. Behind her was the steel-eyed grandmother, tall, stern, no tears.

Our mother faltered near the door as if her legs would give way and spill her to the floor. Chris and I jumped to our feet, but Carrie only stared at Momma's empty eyes.

"I drove Cory to a hospital miles away, the nearest one, really," explained our mother in a tight and hoarse voice that choked from time to time, "and I registered him under a false name, saying he was my nephew, my ward."

Lies! Always lies! "Momma—how is he?" I asked impatiently.

Her glazed blue eyes turned our way; void eyes, staring vacantly; lost eyes, seeking something gone forever—I guessed it was her humanity. "Cory had pneumonia," she intoned. "The doctors did all they could . . . but it was . . . too . . . too late."

Had pneumonia?

All they could?

Too late?

All past tenses!

Cory was dead! We were never going to see him again!

Chris said later the news hit him hard in the groin, like a kick, and I did see him stumble backward and spin around to hide his face as his shoulders sagged and he sobbed.

At first I didn't believe her. I stood and I stared, and I doubted. But the look on her face convinced me, and something big and hollow swelled up inside my chest. I sank down on the bed, numb, almost paralyzed, and didn't even know I was crying until my clothes were wet.

And even as I sat and cried, I still didn't want to believe Cory was gone from our lives. And Carrie, poor Carrie, she lifted up her head, threw it back, and opened up her mouth and screamed!

She screamed and screamed until her voice went, and she could scream no more. She drifted to the corner where Cory kept his guitar and his banjo, and neatly she lined up all his pairs of small worn tennis shoes. And that's where she chose to sit, with the shoes, with the musical instruments, and Mickey's cage nearby, and from that moment on, not a word escaped her lips.

"Will we go to his funeral?" Chris asked in a choked way with his back still turned.

"He's already been buried," said Momma. "I had a false name put on the tombstone." And then, very quickly, she escaped the room and our questions, and the grandmother followed, her lips set in a grim, thin line.

Right before our horrified eyes, Carrie shriveled more each day. I felt God might as well have taken Carrie, too, and buried her alongside Cory in that faraway grave with the wrong name that didn't even have the comfort of a father buried nearby.

None of us could eat much. We became listless and tired, always tired. Nothing held our interest. Tears—Chris and I cried five oceans of tears. We assumed all the blame. A long time ago we should have escaped. We should have used that wooden key and gone for help. We had *let* Cory die! He'd been our responsibility, our dear quiet little boy of many talents, and we had let him die. Now we had a small sister huddled in a corner, growing weaker each passing day.

Chris said in a low voice so Carrie wouldn't overhear, just in case she was listening, though I doubted she was (she was blind, deaf, mute . . . our babbling brook, damned), "We've got to run, Cathy, and quick. Or we are all going to die like Cory. Something is wrong with all of us. We've been locked up too long. We've lived abnormal lives, like being in a vacuum without germs, without the infections children usually come in contact with. We are without resistance to infections."

"I don't understand," I said.

"What I mean is," he whispered as we huddled in the same chair, "like the creatures from Mars in that book *The War of the Worlds* we could all die from a single cold germ."

Horrified, I could only stare at him. He knew so much more than I did. I turned my gaze on Carrie in the corner. Her sweet baby face, with eyes too large and shadowed underneath, stared blankly forward at nothing. I knew she had her vision fixed on eternity, where Cory was. All the love I'd given Cory, I put into Carrie now . . . so afraid for her. Such a tiny skeleton body, and her neck was so weak, too small for her head. Was this the way all the Dresden dolls were going to end?

"Chris, if we have to die, it's not going to be like mice in a trap. If germs can kill us, then let it be germs—so when you steal tonight, take everything of value you can find and we can carry! I'll pack a lunch to take along. With Cory's clothes taken from the suitcases, we'll have more room. Before the morning comes, we'll be gone."

"No," he said quietly. "Only if we know Momma and her husband have gone out—only then can I take all the money and leave, and all the jewelry in one fell swoop. Take only what we absolutely need—no toys, no games. And Cathy, Momma may not go out tonight. Certainly she can't attend parties in her time of mourning."

How could she mourn when she had to keep her husband always in the dark? And no one came but the grandmother to tell us what was going on. She refused to speak to us, or look at us. In my mind we were already on our way, and I looked at her as if she were already part of the past. Now that our time to depart was so near, I felt frightened. It was big out there. We'd be on our own. What would the world think of us now?

We weren't beautiful like we used to be, only pale and sickly attic mice with long flaxen hair, wearing expensive but ill-fitting clothes, and sneakers on our feet.

Chris and I had educated ourselves from reading so many books, and television had taught us much about violence, about greed, about imagination, but it had taught us hardly anything that was practical and useful in preparing us to face reality.

Survival. That's what TV should teach innocent children. How to live in a world that really doesn't give a damn about anyone but their own—and sometimes, not even their own.

Money. If there was one thing we'd learned during the years of our imprisonment, it was that money came first, and everything else came after. How well Momma had said it long ago: "It's not love that makes the world go 'round—it's money."

I took Cory's small clothes from the suitcase, his second-best sneakers, two pair of pajamas, and all the time tears fell and my nose ran. In one of the side pockets of the suitcase, I found sheet music he must have packed himself. Oh, it did hurt to pick up those sheets, and see the lines he had drawn by using a ruler, and his little black notes, and half-notes so crookedly done. And beneath the musical score (he had taught himself to write down the music from an encyclopedia Chris had found for him) Cory had written words to a half-completed song:

> I wish the night would end,
> I wish the day'd begin,
> I wish it would rain or snow,
> Or the wind would blow,
> Or the grass would grow,
> I wish I had yesterday,
> I wish there were games to play. . . .

Oh, God! Was there ever such a sad, melancholy song? So these were the lyrics to a tune I'd heard him play over and over. Wishing, always wishing for something he couldn't have. Something all other little boys accepted as a normal, unremarkable part of their lives.

I could have screamed the anguish I felt.

I went to sleep with Cory on my mind. And, like always, when I was most troubled, I fell into dreams. But this time I was only me. I found myself on a winding, dirt path with wide, flat pastures that grew wildflowers of crimson and pink on the left, and on the right, yellow and white blossoms swayed gently in the soft, warm kind breezes of eternal spring. A small child clung to my hand. I looked down, expecting to see Carrie—but it was Cory!

He was laughing and happy, and he skipped along beside me, his short legs trying to keep pace with mine, and in his hand he held a bouquet of the wildflowers. He smiled up at me and was about to speak when we heard the twitterings of many brightly colored birds in the parasol trees ahead.

A tall, slim man with golden hair, his skin deeply tanned, wearing white tennis clothes, came striding forward from a glorious garden of abundant trees and radiant flowers, including roses of all colors. He paused a dozen yards away and held his arms out to Cory.

My heart, even in my dream, pounded in excitement and joy! It was Daddy! Daddy had come to meet Cory so he wouldn't have to travel alone the rest of the way. And though I knew I should release Cory's small hot hand, I would hold him forever with me.

Daddy looked at me, not with pity, not with reprimand, but only with pride and admiration. And I let go of Cory's hand and stood to watch him joyfully run into Daddy's arms. He was swept up by powerful arms that once used to hold me and make me feel all the world was a wonderful thing. And I would step down the path, too, and feel those arms about me once again, and allow Daddy to take me where he would.

"Cathy, wake up!" said Chris, sitting on my bed and shaking me. "You're talking in your sleep, and laughing and crying, and saying hello, and then good-bye. Why is it you dream so much?"

My dream spilled from me so fast my words were garbled. Chris just sat there and stared at me, as did Carrie, who had awakened to hear as well. It had been so long since I last saw my father, his face had faded in my memory, but as I looked at Chris, I grew very confused. He was so very much like Daddy, only younger.

That dream was to haunt me many a day, pleasantly. It gave me peace. It gave me knowledge I hadn't had before. People never really died. They only went on to a better place, to wait a while for their loved ones to join them. And then once more they went back to the world, in the same way they had arrived the first time around.

Escape

November tenth. This was to be our last day in prison. God would not deliver us, we would deliver ourselves.

As soon as the hour passed ten, tonight, Chris would commit his final robbery. Our mother had visited to stay but a few minutes, ill at ease with us now, very obviously so. "Bart and I are going out tonight. I don't want to, but he insists. You see, he doesn't understand why I look so sad."

I bet he didn't understand. Chris slung over his shoulder the dual pillowcases in which to carry back heavy jewels. He stood in the open doorway and gave Carrie and me one long, long look before he closed the door and used his wooden key to lock us in, for he couldn't leave the door open, and in this way alert the grandmother, if she came to check. We couldn't hear Chris steal along the long dark northern corridor, for the walls were too thick, and the hall carpet too plush and sound-proofing.

Side by side Carrie and I lay, my arms protectively around her.

If that dream hadn't come to tell me Cory was well taken care of, I would have cried not to feel him close still. I couldn't help but ache for a little boy who had called me Momma whenever he was sure his older brother wouldn't overhear. Always he'd been so afraid Chris might consider him a sissy if he knew how much he missed and needed his mother, so much so, he had to make do with me. And though I'd told him Chris would never laugh, or jeer, for he had been very needing of a mother too, once upon a time, still Cory would keep it a secret just between him and me—and Carrie. He had to pretend to be manly, and convince himself it didn't matter if he had neither a mother, nor a father, when all along it did matter, a great deal.

I held Carrie tight, tight against me, vowing that if ever I had a child, or children, they'd never feel a need for me that I didn't sense and respond to. I'd be the best mother alive.

Hours dragged by like years, and still Chris didn't return from his last foray into our mother's grand suite of rooms. Why was it taking so long this time? Wide awake and miserable, I was filled with fears, and envisioned all the calamities that could stay him.

Bart Winslow . . . the suspicious husband . . . he'd catch Chris! Call the police! Have Chris thrown in jail! Momma would stand calmly by and mildly express shock and faint surprise that someone would dare steal from her. Oh, no, of course she didn't have a son. Everybody knew she was childless, for heaven's sake. Had they ever seen her with a child? She didn't know that blond boy with blue eyes so very much like her own. After all, she did have many cousins scattered about—and a thief was a thief, even if he were blood kin, some fifth or sixth distant relative.

And that grandmother! If she caught him—the worst possible punishment!

Dawn came up quickly, faint, shrilled by a cock's crow.

The sun lingered reluctantly on the horizon. Soon it would be too late to go. The morning train would pass on by the depot, and we needed several hours' head start before the grandmother opened the bedroom door and found us gone. Would she send out a search party? Notify the police? Or would she, more likely, just let us go, glad, at last, to be rid of us?

Despairing, I ascended the stairs to the attic to stare outside. Foggy, cold day. Last week's snow lay in patches here and there. A dull, mysterious day that seemed incapable of bringing us joy or freedom. I heard that rooster cockle-doodle-doo again; it sounded muffled and far away as I silently prayed that, whatever Chris was doing, and wherever he was, he heard it too, and would put some speed in his feet.

I remember, oh, how I remember that chilly early morning when Chris stole back into our room. Lying beside Carrie, I was tentatively on the edge of fretful sleep, so it was easy for me to bolt widely awake when the locked door to our room opened. I'd lain there, fully dressed, ready to go, waiting, even in the fitful dreams that came and went, for Chris to come back and save us all.

Just inside the door, Chris hesitated, his glazed eyes staring over at me. Then he drifted in my direction, in no great hurry, as he should be. All the while I could only stare at the pillowcases one inside the other—so flat! So empty looking! "Where are the jewels?" I cried. "Why did you stay so long? Look out the windows, the sun is rising! We'll never make it to the train depot on time!" My voice turned hard, accusing, angry. "You turned chivalrous again, didn't you? That's why you've come back without Momma's precious jewelry!"

He had reached the bed by this time, and he just stood there with the flat, empty pillowcases hanging from his hand.

"Gone," he said dully. "All the jewelry was gone."

"Gone?" I asked sharply, sure he was lying, covering up, still unwilling to take what his mother so cherished. Then I looked at his eyes. "Gone? Chris, the jewelry is always there. And what's the matter with you, anyway—why do you look so queer?"

He sagged down on his knees beside the bed, gone boneless and limp as his head drooped forward, and his face nestled down on my breast. Then he began to sob! Dear God! What had gone wrong? Why was he crying? It's terrible to hear a man cry, and I thought of him as a man now, not a boy.

My arms held him, my hands caressed and stroked his hair, his cheek, his arms, his back, and then I kissed him, all in an effort to soothe whatever awful thing had happened. I did what I had seen our mother do for him in times of distress, and intuitively I had no fears that his passions would be aroused into wanting more than just what I was willing to give.

Actually, I had to force him to talk, to explain.

He choked off his sobs, and swallowed them. He wiped away the tears and dried his face with the edge of the sheet. Then he turned his head so he could stare at those horrible paintings depicting hell and all its torment. His phrases came broken, disjointed, stopped often by sobs he had to hold back.

This was the way he told it, while on his knees beside my bed, while I held his shaky hands, and his body trembled, and his blue eyes were dark and bleak, warning me I was about to be shocked. Forewarned as I was, I still wasn't prepared for what I heard.

"Well," he began, breathing hard, "I realized that something was different the second I stepped into her suite of rooms. I beamed my flashlight around without turning on a lamp, and I just couldn't believe it! The irony of it . . . the hateful, despicable bitterness of making our move too late! Gone, Cathy— Momma and her husband have gone! Not just to some neighbor's party, but really gone! They had taken with them all those little mementos that made their rooms personal: the trinkets gone from the dresser, the geegaws from that dressing table, the creams, lotions, powders, and perfumes—everything that once was there, gone. Nothing was on her dressing table.

"It made me so mad, I ran about like someone demented, dashing from here to there, pulling open drawers and ransacking them, hoping to find something of value that we could pawn . . . and I didn't find anything! Oh, they did a very good job—not

even a little porcelain pillbox was left, or one of those heavy
Venetian-glass paperweights that cost a fortune. I ran into the
dressing room and yanked open all the drawers. Sure, she had
left *some* things—junk of no value to us, or anyone: lipsticks,
cold creams, and stuff like that. Then I pulled open that special
bottom drawer—you know the one she told us about a long time
ago, never thinking we'd be the ones to steal from her. I pulled
that drawer all the way out, like you have to, and set it aside
on the floor. Then I felt in back for the tiny little button you have
to push in a certain combination of numbers—her birthday
numbers, or else she would herself forget the combination.
Remember how she laughed when she told us that? The secret
compartment sprang open, and there were the velvet trays where
dozens of rings should have been fitted into small slots, and
there wasn't a ring there—not one! And the bracelets, necklaces,
and earrings gone, every last thing was gone, Cathy, even that
tiara you tried on. Oh, golly, you don't know how I felt! So
many times you pleaded with me to take just one little ring, and
I wouldn't, because I believed in her."

"Don't cry again, Chris," I begged when he choked up, and he
put his face down on my chest again. "You didn't know she'd
go, not so soon after Cory's death."

"Yeah, she grieves a lot, doesn't she?" he asked bitterly, and
my fingers twined in his hair.

"Really, Cathy," he went on, "I lost all control. I ran from
closet to closet, and threw out the winter clothes, and soon
found all the summer clothes were gone, along with two sets of
their fine luggage. I emptied shoe boxes, and rifled the closet
drawers, and looked for the tin of coins he keeps, but he'd taken
that, too, or hidden it away in a better place. I searched everything, and everywhere, feeling frantic. I even considered taking
one of the huge lamps, but I hefted one and it weighed a ton.
She'd left her mink coats, and I thought about stealing one of
those, but you'd tried them on, and all were too large—and
someone on the outside would be suspicious if an adolescent

girl was wearing a too-large coat of mink. The fur stoles were gone. And if I took one of the full-length fur coats, it would fill all of one suitcase, and then we wouldn't have room for our own things, and the paintings I might be able to sell—and we need what clothes we have. Really, I almost tore out my hair, I was that desperate to find something of value, for how would we ever manage without enough money? You know, at that minute, when I stood in the middle of her room and thought about our situation, and Carrie's poor health, it didn't matter a damn to me then whether or not I became a doctor. All I wanted was to get us out of here!

"Then, just when it seemed I wasn't going to find anything to steal, I looked in the lower drawer of the nightstand. I'd never checked that drawer before. And in it, Cathy, was a silver-framed photograph of Daddy, and their marriage license, and a small velvet box of green. Cathy, inside that little green velvet box, inside was Momma's wedding band, and her engagement diamond—the ones our father gave her. It hurt to think she would take everything, and leave his photograph as valueless, and the two rings he'd given her. And then the strangest thought fleeted through my mind. Maybe she knew who was stealing the money from her room, and she left those things there deliberately."

"No!" I scoffed, tossing that gracious consideration away. "She just doesn't care about him anymore—she has her *Bart.*"

"Regardless, I was grateful to find something. So the sack isn't as empty as it may appear. We've got Daddy's photograph, and her rings—but it's gonna take an awful, unbearable crisis to make me pawn either of those rings."

I heard the warning in his voice, and it didn't sound the least sincere, like it should have. It was as if he was putting on an act of being the same old trusting Christopher Doll, who saw good in everyone. "Go on. What happened next?" For he'd stayed away so long, what he'd just told me wouldn't have taken all the night.

"I figured if I couldn't rob our mother, then I would go on to the grandmother's room and rob her."

Oh, my God, I thought. He didn't . . . he couldn't have. And yet, what perfect revenge!

"You know she has jewels, lots of rings on her fingers, and that damned diamond brooch she wears every day of her life as part of her uniform, plus she has those diamonds and rubies we saw her wear at the Christmas party. And, of course, I figured she had more loot to be taken, as well. So, I stole down all the long dark halls, and I tiptoed right up to the grandmother's closed door."

Oh, the nerve to do that. I would never . . .

"A thin line of yellow light showed underneath, to warn me she was still awake. That made me bitter, for she should have been asleep. And under less driven circumstances, that light would have made me stay my hand, and act less foolhardy than I did—or maybe you could call it 'audacious' now that you're planning on being a woman of words one day, after you've been a woman of action."

"Chris! Don't meander from the subject! Go on! Tell me what crazy thing you did! If I had been you, I would have turned around and come straight back here!"

"Well, I am not you, Catherine Doll, I am *me*. . . . I used some caution, and very carefully eased open her door just a slot, though I feared every second it would creak or squeak and give me away. But someone keeps the hinges well-oiled, and I put an eye to the crack without fear of her being alerted, and I peered inside."

"You saw her naked!" I interrupted.

"No!" he answered impatiently, annoyed, "I didn't see her naked, and I'm glad I didn't. She was in the bed, under the covers, sitting up and wearing a long-sleeved nightgown of some heavy material, and it had a collar and was buttoned down the front to her waist. But I did catch her naked in a small way. You know that steel-blue hair we hate so much. It *wasn't* on her head! It was perched crookedly on a dummy head on her night-stand, as if she wanted the reassurance of having it near in case of an emergency during the night."

"She wears a wig?" I asked in total astonishment, though I should have known. Anybody who persistently took their hair and skinned it back from their face so tightly would sooner or later go bald.

"Yeah, you bet, she wears a wig, and that hair she had on during the Christmas party, that must have been a wig, too. What hair she's got left on her head is sparse and yellow-white, and there are wide pink places on her scalp with no hair at all, but short baby fuzz. She had rimless glasses perched on the end of that long nose, and you know we've never seen her with glasses on. Her thin lips were pursed up in a disapproving line as she moved her eyes slowly from line to line of the large black book she was holding—the Bible, of course. There she sat, reading of harlots and other wicked deeds, enough to put a terrible frown on her face. And as I watched, knowing I couldn't steal from her now, she laid aside the Bible and marked the place with a post-card, then put the Bible on the nightstand, then left the bed and knelt beside it. She bowed her head, templed her fingers under her chin, just the way we do, and she said silent prayers that lasted and lasted. Then she spoke aloud: 'Forgive me, Lord, for all my sins. I have always done what I thought best, and if I made mistakes, please believe I thought I was doing right. May I forever find grace in thine eyes. Amen.' She crawled back into bed, and then she reached to turn out the lamp. I stood in the hall and wondered what to do. I just couldn't come back to you empty-handed, for I hope we never have to pawn the rings our father gave our mother."

He continued, and now his hands were in my hair, cupping my head. "I went to that main rotunda, where the chest is near the staircase, and found our grandfather's room. I didn't know if I would have the nerve to open *his* door, and face up to that man who lies perpetually dying, year after year.

"But, this was my only chance, and I would make the most of it. Come what may, I raced down the stairs noiselessly like a real thief, carrying my pillowcase sack. I saw the big rich rooms, so grand and fine, and I wondered, just as you have wondered how it would be to grow up in a house like this one. I wondered how it felt to be waited on by many servants, and catered to hand and foot. Oh, Cathy, it is one beautiful house, and the furniture must have been imported from palaces. It looks too fragile to sit on, and too lovely to feel comfortable with, and there are original oil paintings, I know them when I see them, and sculptures and busts, mostly on top of pedestals, and rich Persian rugs and Oriental rugs. And, of course, I knew the way to the library, since you had asked so darned many questions of Momma. And you know what, Cathy? I was darned glad you had asked so many questions or else I may well have gotten lost; there's so many halls that shoot off right and left from the center stem.

"But it was easy enough to get to the library: a long, dark, really immense room, and it was quiet as a graveyard. The ceiling must have been twenty feet high. The shelves went all the way up, and there was a little stairway of iron that curved to a second level, and a balcony where you could reach books on that level. And on the lower level were two wooden ladders that slid along railings put there for that very purpose. Never have I seen so many books in a private home. No wonder the books Momma brought us had never been missed—though when I looked carefully, I could see the gaping spaces, like teeth, missing in the long rows of leather-bound, gold-tooled, hubbed-spined expensive books. A desk was there, dark and massive, must have weighed a ton, and a tall leather swivel chair was behind it, and I could just picture our grandfather sitting there, issuing orders right and left, and using the phones on his desk—there were six telephones, Cathy—six! Though when I checked, thinking I might have use for them, they were all disconnected. To the left of the desk was a row of tall narrow windows that looked out on a private garden—a really spectacular view, even at night. There was a dark mahogany filing system made to look like fine furniture. Two very long, soft, tan-colored sofas were set out from the walls about three feet, giving you plenty of room to move behind them. Chairs were placed near the fireplace, and, of course, there was a batch of tables and chairs and things to stumble against, and an awful lot of bric-a-brac."

I sighed, for he was telling me so much of what I'd longed to hear, and yet, I kept waiting for that terrible thing that kept me on edge, waiting for the knife to plunge.

"I thought that money could be hidden in that desk. I used my flashlight and set about pulling open each drawer. They were all unlocked. And it was no wonder, because they were all empty—completely empty! This sort of threw me—for why have a desk if you don't keep it full of junk? Important papers you lock away in a bank vault, or your own private vault; you don't leave them in locked desk drawers that a clever thief could force open. All those empty drawers without rubber bands, paper clips, pencils, pens, notepads, and other sorts of odds and ends—why have a desk if not for this? You just don't know the suspicions that jumped into my thoughts. And that's when I made up my mind. I could look across the long library and see the door to our grandfather's room. Slowly, I headed that way. I was going to see him at last . . . face to face with the detested grandfather, who was also our half-uncle.

"I pictured our encounter. He'd be on the bed, sick, but hard and still mean and cold as ice. I'd kick open the door, switch on the light, and he'd see me. He'd gasp! He'd recognize me . . . he'd have to know who I was, just one look and he'd know. And I'd say, 'Here I am, Grandfather—the grandson you never wanted to be born. Upstairs in a locked bedroom of the northern wing, I have two sisters. And once I had a younger brother, but he's dead now—and you helped kill him!' All that was in my mind, though I doubt I would really have said any of it. Although you no doubt would have screamed it out—just as Carrie would have if she had the words to express herself—which you do. Still maybe I would have said them, just for the joy of watching him wince, or maybe he would have shown sorrow, or grief, or pity . . . or, more likely, fierce indignation that we were living at all! I know this, I couldn't stand another minute of being kept a prisoner, and having Carrie pass away like Cory did."

I held my breath. Oh, the nerve of him, to face up to the detested grandfather, even if he was still lying on his deathbed, and that solid copper coffin was still waiting for him to fill it. I was waiting breathlessly for what came next.

"I turned the knob very cautiously, planning on taking him by surprise, and then I felt ashamed to be so timid, and I thought I would act boldly—and I lifted my foot and kicked open that door! It was so dark in there I couldn't see a damned thing. And I didn't want to use the flashlight. I reached inside the door and felt around for a wall switch, but I couldn't find one. I beamed the flashlight straight ahead and saw a hospital bed painted white. I stared and stared, for I was seeing something I hadn't expected to see—the blue-and-white-striped ticking of the mattress that was doubled over on itself. Empty bed, empty room. No dying grandfather there, gasping out his last breaths, and connected up to all kinds of machines to keep him alive—it was like a punch in the stomach, Cathy, not to see him there, when I'd prepared myself to meet him.

"In a corner not too far from the bed, was a walking cane, and not so far from the cane was that shiny wheelchair we'd seen him in. It still looked new—he must not have used it often. There was only one piece of furniture besides two chairs, and that was a single dresser . . . and not one item was on the top. No brush, comb, nothing. The room was as neat as the suite of rooms Momma had left, only this was a simple, plain room with paneled walls. And the grandfather's sickroom had the feel of not being used for a long, long time. The air was stale, musty. Dust was on the dresser top. I ran about, looking for something of value we could hock later on. Nothing—again nothing! I was so full of angry frustration that I dashed back into the library and sought out that special landscape painting Momma told us covered a wall safe.

"Now you know how many times we've watched thieves on TV open wall safes, and it seemed to me perfectly simple when you knew how. All you had to do was put your ear to the combination lock, and turn it slowly, slowly, and listen carefully for the betraying clicks . . . and count them . . . I thought. Then you would know the numbers, and dial them correctly—and next, violà! The safe would open."

I interrupted: "The grandfather—why wasn't he on the bed?"

He went on as if I hadn't spoken: "There I was, listening, hearing the clicks. I thought, if I lucked out, and the steel safe did open—it too would be empty. And you know what happened, Cathy? I heard the betraying clicks that told me the combination—hah-hah! I couldn't count fast enough! Nevertheless, I took the chance of turning the top wheel of the lock, thinking I just might by happenstance come up with the right choice of numbers, in the right sequence. The safe door didn't open. I heard the clicks, and I didn't understand. Encyclopedias don't give you good lessons on how to become a thief—that must come naturally. Then I looked about for something slim and strong to insert into the lock, hoping maybe I could trip a spring that would open the door. Cathy, that was when I heard footsteps!"

"Oh, hell and damnation!" I swore, frustrated for him.

"Right! I quickly ducked behind one of the sofas and fell flat on my stomach—and that's when I remembered I'd left my flashlight in the grandfather's small room."

"Oh, dear God!"

"Right! My goose was cooked, so I thought, but I lay perfectly still and quiet, and into the library strolled a man and a woman. She spoke first and had a sweet-girlish voice.

" 'John,' she said, 'I swear I'm not just hearin' things! I did hear noises comin' from this room.'

" 'You're always hearin' somethin',' complained a heavy, guttural voice. It was John, the butler with the bald head.

"And the bickering pair made a half-hearted search of the library, then the small bedroom beyond, and I held my breath, waiting for them to discover my flashlight, but for some reason they didn't. I suspect it was because John didn't want to look at anything but that woman. Just as I was about to get up and make my move to leave the library, they came back, and so help me God, they fell down on the very sofa I was hiding behind! I put my head down on my folded arms and prepared for a nap, guessing you'd be on edge up here, wondering why I didn't come back. But since you were locked in, I didn't fear you'd come looking for me. It's a good thing I didn't go to sleep."

"Why?"

"Let me tell it in my own way, Cathy, please. 'See,' said John, as they came back to the library and sat on the sofa, 'didn't I tell yuh nobody'd be in there or in here?' He sounded smug, pleased with himself. 'Really, Livvy,' he went on, 'you're so damned nervous all the time, it takes the pleasure out of this.'

" 'But, John,' she said, 'I *did* hear something.'

" 'Like I said before,' John answered, 'yuh hear too much of what ain't there. Hell's bells, jus' this mornin' you were speakin' of mice in the attic again, and how noisy they are.' John chuckled then, a soft and low chuckle, and he must have done something to that pretty girl to send her into peals of silly giggles, and if she was protesting, she didn't do a good job of it.

"Then that John, he murmured, 'That old bitch is killin' all the little mice in the attic. She carries up to them food in a picnic basket . . . enough food to kill a whole German army of mice.' "

You know, I heard Chris say that, and I didn't think anything unusual, that's how dumb I was, how innocent and still trusting.

Chris cleared his throat before he continued. "I got a queer feeling in my stomach, and my heart began to make so much noise, I thought that couple on the sofa would surely hear.

" 'Yeah,' said Livvy, 'she's a mean, hard old woman, and t' tell you the truth, I always took to the old man better—at least he knew how to smile. But her—she don't know how. Time and time ag'in, I come in this room to clean up, and I find her in *his* room . . . she's just standing there staring at his empty bed, and she's got this queer, little tight smile that I take for gloating because he's dead, and she's outlived him, and now she's free, and don't have nobody ridin' her back and tellin' her not to do this, and don't do that, and jump when I speak. God, sometimes I wonder how she stood him, and he stood her. But now that he's dead, she's got his money.'

" 'Yeah, sure, she's got some,' said John. 'She's got her own money that her family left her. But her daughter, she got all the millions old Malcolm Neal Foxworth left.'

" 'Well,' said Livvy, 'that old witch, she don't need no more. Don't blame the old man for leavin' his entire estate to his daughter. She put up with a lot of mess from him, makin' her wait on him hand and foot when he had nurses to hand him things. Still he treated her like some slave. But now she's free, too, and married to that handsome young husband, and she's still young and beautiful, and with loads of money. Wonder what it would feel like to be her? Some people, they get all the luck. Me . . . I never had any.'

" 'What about me, Livvy, honey? You got me—at least until the next pretty face comes along.'

"And there I was, behind the sofa, hearing all of this, and feeling numb with shock. I felt ready to throw up, but I lay very quiet and listened to that couple on the sofa talk on and on. I wanted to get up and run fast to you and Carrie, and take you out of this place before it was too late.

"But there I was, caught. If I moved they'd see me. And that John, he's related to our grandmother . . . third cousin, so Momma said . . . not that I think a third cousin matters one way or another, but apparently that John has our grandmother's confidence, or else she wouldn't allow him so much freedom to use her cars. You've seen him, Cathy, the bald-headed man who wears livery."

Sure, I knew who he meant, but I could only lie there, feeling my own sort of numb shock that made me speechless.

"So," Chris went on in that deadly monotone that didn't show that he was concerned, frightened, surprised, "while I hid behind the sofa, and put my head down on my arms and closed my eyes and tried to make my heart stop beating so damned loud, John and the maid began to get really serious with each other. I heard their little movements as he began to take off her clothes, and she began to work on his clothes."

"They undressed each other?" I asked. "She actually helped him off with his clothes?"

"It sounded to me that way," he said flatly.

"She didn't scream or protest?"

"Heck, no. She was all for it! And by golly, it took them so everlastingly long! Oh, the noises they made, Cathy—you wouldn't believe it. She moaned and screamed and gasped and panted, and he grunted like a stuck pig, but I guess he must have been pretty good at it, for she shrieked at the end like someone gone crazy. Then, when it was over, they had to lie and smoke cigarettes and gossip about what goes on in this house—and believe me, there's little they don't know. And then they made love a second time."

"Twice in the same night?"

"It's possible to do."

"Chris, why do you sound so funny?"

He hesitated, pulled away a bit, and studied my face. "Cathy, weren't you listening? I went to a great deal of pains to tell you everything just as it happened. Didn't you hear?"

Hear? Sure, I'd heard, everything.

He'd waited too long to rob Momma of her hoard of hard won jewelry. He should have been taking a little all along, like I'd begged him to do.

So, Momma and her husband were off on another vacation. What kind of news was that? They were always coming and going. They'd do anything to escape this house, and I can't say I blamed them. Weren't we prepared to do the same thing?

I screwed up my brows and gave Chris a long questioning

look. Obviously he knew something he wasn't telling me. He was still protecting her; he still loved her.

"Cathy," he began, his voice jagged and torn.

"It's all right, Chris. I'm not blaming you. So our dear, sweet, kind, loving mother and her handsome young husband have gone off on another vacation and taken all the jewelry with them. We'll still get by." Say good-bye to security in the outside world. But we were still going! We'd work, we'd find a way to support ourselves, and pay doctors to make Carrie well again. Never mind about jewelry; never mind about the callousness of our mother's act, to leave us without explaining where she was going, and when she was coming back. By now we were accustomed to ugly, harsh, thoughtless indifference. *Why so many tears, Chris—why so many?*

"Cathy!" he raged, turning his tear-streaked face to lock his eyes with mine. "Why aren't you listening and reacting? Where are your ears? Did you hear what I said? Our grandfather is dead! He's been dead for almost a year!"

Maybe I hadn't been truly listening, not carefully enough. Maybe his distress had kept me from hearing everything. Now it hit me fully for the first time. If the grandfather was truly dead—this was stunning good news! Now Momma would inherit! We'd be rich! She'd unlock the door, she'd set us free. Now we didn't have to run away.

Other thoughts came flooding, a torrent of devastating questions—Momma hadn't told us when her father died. When she knew how long these years had been for us, why had she kept us in the dark, waiting always? Why? Bewildered, confused, I didn't know which emotion to feel: happy, glad, sorry. A strange paralzying fear settled the indecision.

"Cathy," whispered Chris, though why he bothered to whisper I don't know. Carrie wouldn't hear. Her world was set apart from ours. Carrie was suspended between life and death, leaning more toward Cory every moment she starved herself and abandoned the will to live on without her other half. "Our mother deceived us deliberately, Cathy. Her father died, and months later his will was read, and all the while she kept quiet and left us here to wait and rot. Nine months ago we would all have been nine months healthier! Cory would be alive today if Momma had let us out the day her father died, or even the day after the will was read."

Overwhelmed, I fell into the deep well of betrayal Momma had dug to drown us in. I began to cry.

"Save your tears for later," said Chris, who had just cried himself. "You haven't heard everything. There's more . . . much more, and worse."

"More?" What more could he tell me? Our mother was proven a liar and a cheat, a thief who'd stolen our youth, and killed Cory in the process of acquiring a fortune she didn't want to share with children she no longer wanted, or loved. Oh, how well she explained to us what to expect that night when she gave us our lit- tle litany to say when we were unhappy. Did she know, or guess, way back then, that she would become the *thing* the grandfather would make of her? I toppled over into Chris's arms, and lay against his chest. "Don't tell me anymore! I've heard enough . . . don't make me hate her more!"

"Hate . . . you haven't begun to know what hate is yet. But before I tell you the rest, keep in mind we are leaving this place, no matter what. We will go on to Florida, just like we planned. We'll live in the sunshine and make our lives the very best we can. Not for one moment are we going to feel ashamed of what we are, or what we've done, for what we've shared between us is so small compared to what our mother has done. Even if you die before I do, I'll remember our lives up here and in the attic. I'll see us dancing beneath the paper flowers, with you so grace- ful, and me so clumsy. I'll smell the dust and the rotting wood, and I'll remember it as perfume sweet as roses, because without you it would have been so bleak, and so empty. You've given me my first taste of what love can be.

"We're going to change. We're going to throw out what's worse in us and keep what's best. But come hell or high water, we three will stick together, all for one, one for all. We're going to grow, Cathy, physically, mentally, and emotionally. Not only that, we're going to reach the goals we've set for ourselves. I'll be the best damned doctor the world's ever known and you will make Pavlova seem like an awkward country girl."

I grew weary of hearing talk of love, and what the future held, possibly, when we were still behind a locked door, and death was lying beside me curled up in fetal position, with small hands praying even in sleep.

"All right, Chris, you've given me a breather. I'm prepared for anything. And thank you for saying all of that, and for loving me, for you haven't gone unloved, or unadmired, yourself." I kissed him quickly on the lips, and told him to go on, to hit me with his knockout blow.

"Really, Chris, I know you must have something perfectly awful to tell me—so out with it. Keep holding me as you tell me, and I can stand anything you have to say."

How young I was. How unimaginative—and how confidently presuming.

Endings, Beginnings

"Guess what she told them," Chris continued on. "Name the reason she gave for not wanting this room cleaned on the last Friday of the month."

How could I guess? I'd need a mind like hers. I shook my head. So long ago the servants had stopped coming to this room, I had forgotten those first horrible weeks.

"Mice, Cathy," Chris said, his blue eyes cold, hard. "*Mice!* Hundreds of mice in the attic, our grandmother invented . . . clever little mice that used the stairs to steal down to the second floor. Devilish little mice that forced her to lock this door, leaving in the room—food covered over with arsenic."

I listened and thought that an ingenious, marvelous story for keeping the servants away. The attic *was* full of mice. They *did* use the stairs.

"Arsenic is white, Cathy, *white*. When mixed with powdered sugar, you cannot taste its bitterness."

My brain went spinning! Powdered sugar on the four daily doughnuts! One for each of us. Now only three in the basket!

"But, Chris, your story doesn't make any sense. Why would

the grandmother poison us bit by bit? Why not give us a sufficient amount to kill us immediately and have done with it?"

His long fingers went through my hair to cup my head
between his palms. He spoke in a low voice: "Think back to a
certain old movie we saw on TV. Remember that pretty woman
who would keep house for older gentlemen—rich gentlemen, of
course—and when she'd won their trust, and affection, and they
had written her into their wills, each day she fed them just a little arsenic? When you digest just a fraction of arsenic each day,
it is slowly absorbed by your entire system, and each day the
victim feels a little worse, but not too much so. The small
headaches, stomach upsets that can easily be explained away, so
that when the victim dies, say in a hospital, he already is thin,
anemic, and has a long history of illnesses, hay fever, colds, and
so forth. And doctors don't suspect poisoning—not when the
victim has all the manifestations of pneumonia, or just plain old
age, as was the case in that movie."

"Cory!" I gasped. "Cory died of arsenic poisoning? Momma
said it was pneumonia that killed him!"

"Can't she tell us anything she wants? How do we know
when she's telling the truth? Maybe she didn't even take him to
a hospital. And if she did, obviously the doctors didn't suspect
any unnatural cause of death, or else she'd be in jail by now."

"But, Chris," I objected, "Momma wouldn't allow the grandmother to feed us poison! I know she wants that money, and I
know she doesn't love us now as she did once—but still she
would never kill us!"

Chris turned aside his head. "Okay. We've got to make a test.
We're going to feed Cory's pet mouse a bit of powdered-sugar
doughnut"

No! Not Mickey, who trusted and loved us—we couldn't do
that. Cory had adored the little gray mouse. "Chris, let's catch
another mouse—a wild one that doesn't trust us."

"C'mon, Cathy, Mickey is an old mouse, and lame, too. It's
hard to catch a mouse alive, you know that. How many have

lived after the cheese was nibbled on? And when we leave, Mickey won't survive when we set him free—he's a pet now, dependent on us."

But I was planning on taking him with us.

"Look at it this way, Cathy—Cory's dead, and he hadn't even begun to live. If the doughnuts aren't poisonous, Mickey will live, and we can take him with us, if you insist. One thing for certain—we have to know. For Carrie's sake, we've got to be positive. Look at her. Can't you see she's dying, too? Day by day, she's losing ground—and so are we."

On three well legs, he came staggering to us, dragging the lame leg, our sweet little gray mouse that nibbled trustingly on Chris's finger before he bit into the doughnut. He took a small piece and ate it, trustingly, believing in us, his gods, his parents, his friends. It hurt to watch.

He didn't die, not right away. He grew slow, listless, apathetic. Later on he had small fits of pain that made him whimper. In several hours he was on his back, stiff, cold. Pink toes curled up into claws. Small black bead eyes, sunken and dull. So now we knew . . . for sure. God hadn't taken Cory.

"We could put the mouse in a paper sack along with two of the doughnuts and take it to the police," said Chris tentatively, keeping his eyes averted from mine. . . .

"They'd put the grandmother in jail."

"Yeah," he said, and then turned his back.

"Chris, you're holding something back—what is it?"

"Later . . . after we've gone. Right now I've said all I can say without throwing up. We'll leave early tomorrow morning," he said when I didn't speak. He caught both my hands in his and squeezed them tightly. "As soon as possible, we'll get Carrie to a doctor—and ourselves too."

Such a long day to live through. We had everything ready and nothing to do but stare at the TV for the last time. With Carrie in the corner, and the two of us on separate beds, we watched our favorite soap opera. When it was over I said, "Chris, soap people are like us—they seldom go outdoors. And when they do, we only hear about it, never see it. They loll about in living rooms, bedrooms, sit in the kitchens and sip coffee or stand up and drink martinis—but never, never go outside before our eyes. And whenever something good happens, whenever they think they're finally going to be happy, some catastrophe comes along to dash their hopes."

Somehow I sensed someone else in the room. My breath pulled in! There stood the grandmother. Something in her stance, in her cruel, hard, gray-stone eyes showed her mocking scornful contempt, and informed me she'd been there for some time.

She spoke, her voice cold: "How sophisticated the two of you have grown while locked away from the world. You think you jokingly exaggerated the way life is—but you didn't exaggerate. You forecast it correctly. Nothing ever works out the way you think it will. In the end, you are always disappointed."

Chris and I stared at her, both chilled. The hidden sun took a nose-dive into night. She'd had her say, so she left, locking the door behind her. We sat on our separate beds, with Carrie slouched over near the corner.

—"Cathy, don't look so defeated. She was only trying to put us down again. Maybe nothing did work out right for her, but that doesn't mean *we* are doomed. Let's go forth tomorrow with no great expectations of finding perfection. Then, expecting only a small share of happiness, we won't be disappointed."

If a little hill of happiness would satisfy Chris, good for him. But after all these years of striving, hoping, dreaming, long-ing—I wanted a mountain high! A hill wasn't enough. From this day forward, I vowed to myself, I was in control of my life. Not fate, not God, not even Chris was ever again going to tell me what to do, or dominate me in any way. From this day forward, I was my own person, to take what I would, when I would, and I would answer only to myself. I'd been kept prisoner, held captive by greed. I'd been betrayed, deceived, lied to, used, poisoned . . . but all that was over now.

I had been barely twelve years old when Momma led us through the dense piney woods on a starry, moonlit night, . . . just on the verge of becoming a woman, and in these three years and almost five months, I'd reached maturity. I was older than the mountains outside. The wisdom of the attic was in my bones, etched on my brain, part of my flesh.

The Bible said, as Chris quoted one memorable day, there was a time for everything. I figured my time for happiness was just ahead, waiting for me.

Where was that fragile, golden-fair Dresden doll I used to be? Gone. Gone like porcelain turned into steel—made into someone who would always get what she wanted, no matter who or what stood in her way. I turned my resolved gaze on Carrie, who slumped in the corner, her head so low her long hair covered her face. Only eight and a half years old, but she was so weak she shuffled like someone old; she didn't eat or speak. She didn't play with the sweet little baby who lived in the dollhouse. When I asked if she wanted to take along a few of those dolls, she kept on hanging her head.

Not even Carrie, with her stubborn, defiant ways would defeat me now. There was no one anywhere, much less an eight-year-old, who could resist the strength of my will now.

I strode over and picked her up, and though she fought weakly, her efforts to free herself were fruitless. I sat down at the table and forced food into her mouth, and made her swallow when she would spit it out. I held a glass of milk to her lips, and though she clamped those lips together, I pried them apart and forced her to swallow the milk too. She cried out that I was mean. I carried her into the bathroom, and used tissue when she refused even to do that.

In the tub I shampooed her hair. Then I dressed her in several layers of warm clothing, just as I dressed myself. And when her hair was dry, I brushed it until it shone and looked somewhat like it used to look, only far thinner, and less glorious.

All through the long hours of waiting, I held Carrie in my arms, whispering to her of the plans Chris and I had for our future—the happy lives we'd live in the golden, liquid sunshine of Florida.

Chris was in the rocker, fully clothed, and was strumming idly on Cory's guitar. "Dance, ballerina, dance," he softly chanted, and his singing voice wasn't bad at all. Maybe we could work as musicians—a trio—if Carrie ever recovered enough to want a voice again.

On my wrist was a fourteen-karat-gold watch, made in Switzerland, that must have cost Momma several hundred dollars, and Chris had his watch, too; we weren't penniless. We had the guitar, the banjo, Chris's Polaroid camera and his many watercolors to sell—and the rings our father had given our mother.

Tomorrow morning held escape for us—but why did I keep thinking I was overlooking something very important?

Then suddenly I realized something! Something both Chris and I had ignored. If the grandmother could open our locked door, and stand quietly for so long before we noticed her . . . had she done this on other occasions? If she had, she might now know of our plans! She might have made her own plans to prevent our escape!

I looked over at Chris, wondering if I should bring this up. He couldn't hesitate *this* time and find a reason to stay . . . so I voiced my suspicion. He kept picking on the guitar, apparently not disturbed in the least. "The minute I saw her there, that thought flashed into my mind," he said. "I know she puts a great deal of trust in that butler, John, and she might very well have him waiting at the bottom of the stairs to prevent us from leaving. Let him try—nothing and no one are going to stop us from leaving early tomorrow morning!"

But the thoughts of the grandmother and her butler waiting

at the bottom of the steps wouldn't go away and leave me peace. Leaving Carrie on the bed asleep, leaving Chris in the rocker and strumming the guitar, I wandered up to the attic to say good-bye.

Directly under the dangling lightbulb, I stood and looked around. My thoughts went flashing back to the first day we came up here. . . . I saw us, all four, holding hands, staring around, overwhelmed by the gargantuan attic and its ghostly furniture and clutter of dusty junk. I saw Chris up high, risking his life to hang two swings for Carrie and Cory to use. I ambled into the schoolroom, looking at the old desks where the twins had sat to learn to read and write. I didn't glance at the stained, smelly mattress to picture us sunbathing there. That mattress put other memories in my head. I stared at the flowers with sparkling centers—and the lopsided snail, the menacing purple worm, the signs Chris and I had lettered and through all the maze of our gardens and jungle, I saw myself dancing alone, always alone, except when Chris stood in the shadows watching, making his ache my ache. For when I waltzed with Chris, I'd made him someone else.

He called up the stairs. "It's time to go, Cathy."

Quickly I raced back to the schoolroom. On the blackboard I wrote very large, using white chalk:

> We lived in the attic,
> Christopher, Cory, Carrie, and me,
> Now there are only three.

I signed my name, and wrote down the date. In my heart I knew that the ghosts of the four of us would override all other ghosts of children shut away in an attic schoolroom. I left an enigma for someone in the future to unwind.

With Mickey in a paper sack along with two poisoned dough-nuts stored in Chris's pocket, he used that wooden key and opened our prison door for the last time. We'd fight to the death if the grandmother and the butler were below. Chris carried the two suitcases filled with our clothes and other possessions, and over his shoulder he slung both Cory's beloved guitar and his banjo. He led the way down all the dim halls, to the back stairs. Carrie was in my arms, partially asleep. She weighed but a bit more than she had the night we'd taken her up these same stairs more than three years ago. Those two suitcases my brother carried were the very same ones Momma had been burdened with on that terrible night so long ago, when we were young, so loving and trusting.

Pinned inside our clothes were two small bags holding bills stolen from Momma's room, divided equally just in case something unforseen separated Chris from me—then neither of us would be left penniless. And Carrie was sure to be with one of us, and taken care of. In the two suitcases were the heavy coins, also put into two bags, to weigh them evenly.

Both Chris and I were very much aware of what lay waiting for us on the outside. We hadn't looked at so much TV without learning the worldly and heartless lie in wait for the naïve and innocent. We were young and vulnerable, weak, half-sick, but no longer naïve, or innocent.

My heart stood still as I waited for Chris to unlock the back door, fearful every second someone would stop us. He stepped out, smiling back at me.

It was cold outside. Patches of snow lay melting on the ground. Soon enough the snow would fly again. The gray sky above foreboded that. Still, it was no colder than in the attic. The earth felt mushy beneath our feet. Strange feeling after walking so many years on hard, level wooden floors. I was not yet feeling safe, for John could follow . . . take us back, or try to.

I raised my head to sniff the clean, sharp mountain air. It was like sparkling wine to make one drunk. For a short way I kept Carrie in my arms. Then I set her on her feet. She wobbled uncertainly, stared around, disoriented and bedazed looking.

She sniffled, swiped at her reddened nose so small and finely shaped. Ohhh . . . was she going to catch cold so soon?

"Cathy," called back Chris, "you two have to hurry. We don't have much time, and it's a long, long way. Pick up Carrie when she tires."

I caught her small hand and pulled her along. "Take deep, long breaths, Carrie. Before you know it, the fresh air, good food, and sunshine will have you feeling strong and well again."

Her small pale face tilted upward to mine—was that hope sparking her eyes at last? "Are we going to meet Cory?"

The first question she'd asked since that tragic day when we learned Cory had died. I gazed down at her, knowing her deepest yearning was for Cory. I couldn't say no. I just couldn't put out that flicker of hope. "Cory is in a far-far place from here. Didn't you listen when I said I saw Daddy in a beautiful garden? Didn't you hear when I said Daddy took Cory up into his arms, and now Daddy is taking care of him? They're waiting for us, and someday we'll see them again, but not for a long, long time."

"But, Cathy," she complained, puckering her fault brows, "Cory won't like that garden if I'm not there, and if he comes back looking for us, he won't know where we are."

Earnestness like that put tears in my eyes. I picked her up and tried to hold her, but she struggled free to drag her feet and hang back, twisting halfway around so she could stare back at the huge house we were leaving.

"Come, Carrie, walk faster! Cory's watching us—he wants us to escape! He's down on his knees, praying we'll get away before the grandmother sends someone to take us back and lock us up again!"

Down all the winding trails we tagged along behind Chris, who set a very fast pace. And just as I knew he would, he led us unerringly to the same little train depot that was only a tin roof supported by four wooden posts, with a rickety green bench.

The rim of the dawning sun peeked over a mountaintop, chasing away the low morning mists. The sky turned lavender-rose as we drew nearer the depot.

"Hurry, Cathy!" called Chris. "If we miss this train, we'll have to wait until four o'clock!"

Oh, God, we couldn't miss this train! If we did, the grandmother might for sure have time to catch us again!

We saw a mail truck, with a tall, broomstraw man standing near three mailbags on the ground. He took off his cap, displaying a Brillo pad of reddish hair. Genially, he smiled in our direction., "You folks are sure up early," he called to us cheerfully. "On your way to Charlottesville?"

"Yep! On our way to Charlottesville," answered Chris, as, with relief, he put the two suitcases down.

"Pretty little girl you got there," said the tall mailman, sweeping his pitying gaze over Carrie, who clung fearfully to my skirt. "But if you don't mind my sayin' so, she seems kinda peaked."

"She's been sick," Chris confirmed. "But soon she'll be better."

The mailman nodded, seemingly believing this prognosis. "Got tickets?"

"Got money." Then Chris added sagaciously, practicing for less reliable strangers, "But just enough to pay for the tickets."

"Well, get it out, son, 'cause here comes the five-forty-five."

As we rode on that morning train, headed toward Charlottesville, we saw the Foxworth mansion sitting high on the hillside. Chris and I couldn't take our eyes from it, couldn't help but stare at our prison from the outside. Especially we fixed our gazes on the attic windows with the closed black shutters.

Then my attention was drawn to the northern wing, riveted on that end room on the second floor. I nudged Chris as the heavy draperies parted, and the shadowy, distant form of a large old woman appeared there, staring out, looking for us . . . then vanished.

Of course she could see the train, but we knew she couldn't see us, just as we'd never been able to see the passengers.

Nevertheless, Chris and I slipped down lower on our seat. "Wonder what she's doing up there so early?" I whispered to Chris. "Usually she doesn't carry up our food until six-thirty."

He laughed, sounding bitter. "Oh, just another of her efforts to catch us doing something sinful and forbidden."

Maybe so, but I wanted to know her thoughts, her feelings when she entered that room and found it empty, and the clothes gone from the closet and the drawers. And no voices, or steps overhead to come running—if she called.

In Charlottesville we bought bus tickets to Sarasota, and were told we had two hours to wait for the next Greyhound heading south. Two hours in which John could jump into a black limousine and overtake that slow train!

"Don't think about it," said Chris. "You don't know that he knows about us. She'd be a fool to tell him, though he's probably snoop enough to find out."

We thought the best way to keep him from finding us, if he was sent to follow, would be to keep on the move. We stored our two suitcases and the guitar and banjo in a rented locker. Hand in hand, Carrie in the middle, we strolled the main streets of that city, where we knew the servants of Foxworth Hall came to visit relatives on their day off, and to shop, go to the movies, or pleasure themselves in other ways. And if this were Thursday, we'd have really been fearful. But it was Sunday.

We must have looked like visitors from another planet in our ill-fitting bulky clothes, our sneakers, our clumsily cut hair, and our pale faces. But no one really stared as I feared they would. We were accepted as just a part of the human race, and no odder than most. It felt good to be back in crowds of people, each face different.

"Wonder where everyone's going in such a hurry?" asked Chris, just when I was speculating on the same thing.

We stopped on a corner, undecided. Cory was supposed to be buried not far from here. Oh, so much I wanted to go and find his grave and put flowers there. On another day we'd come back with yellow roses, and we'd kneel and say prayers, whether or not it did any good. For now, we had to get far, far away and not endanger Carrie more . . . out of Virginia before we took her to a doctor.

It was then that Chris took the paper sack with the dead mouse and the powdered-sugar doughnuts from his jacket pocket. His solemn eyes met mine. Loosely he held that bag in front of me, studying my expression, asking with his eyes: An eye for an eye?

That paper sack represented so much. All our lost years, the lost education, the playmates and friends, and the days we could have known laughter instead of tears. In that bag were all our frustrations, humiliations, tons of loneliness, plus the punishments and disappointments—and, most of all, that bag represented the loss of Cory.

"We can go to the police and tell our story," said Christopher, while he kept his eyes averted, "and the city will provide for you and Carrie, and you won't have to run. You two might be put in foster homes, or an orphanage. As for me, I don't know. . . ."

Chris never talked to me while he kept his eyes elsewhere unless he was hiding something—that special something that had to wait until we were outside of Foxworth Hall. "Okay, Chris. We've escaped, so out with it. What is it you keep holding back?"

His head bowed down as Carrie moved closer and clung to my skirt, though her eyes were wide with fascination as she watched the heavy flow of traffic, and the many people hurrying by, some who smiled at her.

"It's Momma," Chris said in a low voice. "Recall when she said she'd do anything to win back her father's approval so she could inherit? I don't know what he made her promise, but I did overhear the servants talking. Cathy, a few days before our grandfather died, he had a codicil added to his will. It states that if our mother is ever proven to have given birth to children by her first husband, she will have to forfeit everything she inherits—and return everything she's bought with the money, including her clothes, jewels, investments—everything. And that's not all; he even had it written in, that if she has children by her *second* marriage, she will lose everything too. And Momma thought he had forgiven her. He didn't forgive, or forget. He would keep on punishing her from his grave."

My eyes widened with shock as I added up the pieces. "You mean Momma . . . ? It was Momma, and not the grandmother?"

He shrugged, as if indifferent, when I knew he couldn't be. "I heard that old woman praying by her bed. She's evil, but I doubt she would put poison on the doughnuts herself. She would carry them up to us, and know we ate the sweets, when all along she warned us not to eat them."

"But, Chris, it couldn't have been Momma. She was on her honeymoon when the doughnuts started coming daily."

His smile came bitter, wry. "Yeah. But nine months ago the will was read; nine months ago Momma was back. Only Momma benefits from the grandfather's will—not our grandmother—she has her own money. She only brought up the baskets each day."

So many questions I had to ask—but there was Carrie, clinging to me, staring up at me. I didn't want her to know Cory had died from any but natural reasons. It was then Chris put the bag with the evidence in my hands. "It's up to you to decide. You and your intuition were right all along—if I'd have listened, Cory would be alive today."

There is no hate such as that born out of love betrayed—and my brain screamed out for revenge. Yes, I wanted to see Momma and the grandmother locked up in jail, put behind bars, convicted of premeditated murder—four counts, if intentions were counted, too. They'd be only gray mice in cages, shut up like us, only they'd have the benefit of being in the company of drug addicts, prostitutes, and other killers like themselves. Their clothes would be of gray prison cotton. No trips twice a week to

the beauty salon for Momma, no makeup, no professional mani-
cures—and a shower once a week. She'd even lose the privacy
of her most personal body places. Oh, she'd suffer without furs
to wear, and jewelry, and warm cruises in southern waters when
the winter rolled around. There wouldn't be a handsome, adoring young husband to romp with in a grand swan bed.

I stared up at the sky where God was supposed to be—could I
let Him in His own ways, balance the scales and take the burden
of justice from me?

I thought it cruel, unfair, that Chris should put all the burden
of decision on my shoulders. Why?

Was it because he would forgive her for anything—even the
death of Cory, and her efforts to kill all of us? Would he reason
that such parents as hers could pressure her into doing anything—even murder? Was there enough money in the whole
world to make *me* kill my four children?

Pictures flashed in my mind, taking me back to the days
before my father died. I saw us all in the back garden, laughing
and happy. I saw us at the beach, sailing, swimming, or in the
mountains skiing. And I saw Momma in the kitchen doing her
best to cook meals to please us all.

Yeah, surely her parents would know all the ways to kill her
love for us—they'd know. Or was Chris thinking, as I was, that
if we went to the police and told our story, our faces would be
splashed on the front pages of every newspaper in the country?
Would the glare of publicity make up for what we'd lose? Our
privacy—our need to stay together? Could we lose each other
just to get even?

I glanced up at the sky again.

God, He didn't write the scripts for the puny little players
down here. We wrote them ourselves—with each day we lived,
each word we spoke, each thought we etched on our brains. And
Momma had written her script, too. And a sorry one it was.

Once she'd had four children she considered perfect in every
way. Now she had none. Once she had four children who loved

her, and considered *her* perfect in every way—now she had none who saw her as perfect. Nor would she ever want to have others. Love for what money could buy would keep her forever faithful to that cruel codicil in her father's will.

Momma would grow old; her husband was years younger. She'd have time to feel lonely and wish she'd done it all differently. If her arms never ached to hold me again, they'd ache for Chris, and maybe Carrie . . . and, most certainly, she'd want those babies that would be ours one day.

From this city we'd flee southward on a bus to make of ourselves *somebodies*. When we saw Momma again—and to be certain fate would arrange it that way—we'd look her straight in the eyes, and turn our backs.

Into the nearest green trashcan I dropped the bag, saying good-bye to Mickey, and asking him to please forgive us for what we did.

"C'mon, Cathy," called Chris, stretching forth his hand. "What's done is done. Say good-bye to the past, and hello to the future. And we're wasting time, when already we've wasted enough. We've got everything ahead, waiting for us."

Just the right words to make me feel real, *alive, free!* Free enough to forget thoughts of revenge. I laughed and spun about to run back to where I could put my hand in his, stretched ready and waiting. With his free arm, Chris swooped down to pick up Carrie, and he hugged her close and kissed her wan cheek. "Did you hear all of that, Carrie? We are on our way to where the flowers bloom all through the winter—in fact, flowers bloom all year long down there. Does that make you want to smile?"

A tiny smile came and went on pale lips that seemed to have forgotten how to smile. But that was enough—for now.

Epilogue

It is with relief that I end the telling of our foundation years, on which we were to base the rest of our lives.

After we escaped Foxworth Hall, we made our way, and managed, somehow, to always keep striving toward our goals.

Our lives were always to be tempestuous, but it taught both Chris and me that we were survivors. For Carrie, it was far different. She had to be persuaded to want a life without Cory, even when she was surrounded by roses.

But how we managed to survive—that's another story.

Petals on the Wind

For Bill & Gene
Who remember when . . .

PART ONE

O'er the earth there comes a bloom;
Sunny light for sullen gloom;
Warm perfume for vapor cold—
I smell the rose above the mold!
                    —Thomas Hood

Free, at Last!

How young we were the day we escaped. How exuberantly alive we should have felt to be freed, at last, from such a grim, lonely and stifling place. How pitifully delighted we should have been to be riding on a bus that rumbled slowly southward. But if we felt joy, we didn't show it. We sat, all three, pale, silent, staring out the windows, very frightened by all we saw.

Free. Was ever a word more wonderful than that one? No, even though the cold and bony hands of death would reach out and drag us back, if God wasn't up there somewhere, or maybe down here on the bus, riding with us and looking out for us. At some time in our life we had to believe in someone.

The hours passed with the miles. Our nerves grew frazzled because the bus stopped often to pick up and let off passengers. It stopped for rest breaks, for breakfast, then to pick up a single huge black lady who stood alone where a dirt road met the concrete interstate. It took her forever to pull herself onto the bus, then lug inside the many bundles she carried with her. Just as she was finally seated, we passed over the state line between Virginia and North Carolina.

Oh! The relief to be gone from that state of our imprisonment! For the first time in years, I began to relax—a little.

We three were the youngest on the bus. Chris was seventeen years old and strikingly handsome with long,
waving blond hair that just touched his shoulders, then
curled upward. His darkly fringed blue eyes rivaled the color
of a summer sky, and he was in personality like a warm sunny
day—he put on a brave face despite the bleakness of our situation. His straight and finely shaped nose had just taken on
the strength and maturity that promised to make him all that
our father had been—the type of man to make every woman's
heart flutter when he looked her way, or even when he didn't.
His expression was confident; he almost looked happy. If he
hadn't looked at Carrie he might have even *been* happy. But
when he saw her sickly, pale face, he frowned and worry darkened his eyes. He began to pluck on the strings of the guitar
strapped to his shoulder. Chris played "Oh Susannah," singing softly in a sweet melancholy voice that touched my heart.
We looked at each other and felt sad with the memories the
tune brought back. Like one we were, he and I. I couldn't bear
to look at him for too long, for fear I would cry.

Curled up on my lap was my younger sister. She didn't
look older than three, but she was eight years old and small,
so pitifully small, and weak. In her large, shadowed blue
eyes lingered more dark secrets and sufferings than a child
her age should know. Carrie's eyes were old, very, very old.
She expected nothing: no happiness, no love, nothing—for all
that had been wonderful in her life had been taken from her.
Weakened by apathy, she seemed willing to pass from life into
death. It hurt to see her so alone, so terribly alone now that
Cory was gone.

I was fifteen. The year was 1960, and it was November. I
wanted everything, needed everything, and I was so terribly
afraid I'd never in all my life find enough to make up for what
I had already lost. I sat tense, ready to scream if one more bad

thing happened. Like a coiled fuse attached to a time bomb, I knew that sooner or later I would explode and bring down all those who lived in Foxworth Hall!

Chris laid his hand on mine, as if he could read my mind and knew I was already thinking about how I would bring hell to those who had tried to destroy us.

He said in a low voice, "Don't look like that, Cathy. It's going to be all right. We'll get by."

He was still the eternal cockeyed optimist, believing, despite everything, that whatever happened was for the best! God, how could he think so when Cory was dead? How could that possibly be for the best?

"Cathy," he whispered, "we have to make the most of what we have left, and that is each other. We have to accept what's happened and go on from there. We have to believe in ourselves, our talents, and if we do, we will get what we want. It works that way, Cathy, really it does. It has to!"

He wanted to be a dull, staid doctor who spent his days in small examination rooms, surrounded by human miseries. I wanted something far more fanciful—and a *mountain* of it! I wanted all my star-filled dreams of love and romance to be fulfilled—on the stage, where I'd be the world's *most* famous prima ballerina; nothing less would do! *That would show Momma!*

Damn you, Momma! I hope Foxworth Hall burns to the ground! I hope you never sleep a comfortable night in that grand swan bed, never again! I hope your young husband finds a mistress younger and more beautiful than you! I hope he gives you the hell you deserve!

Carrie turned to whisper: "Cathy, I don't feel so good. My stomach, it feels funny. . . ." I was seized by fear. Her small face seemed unnaturally pale; her hair, once so bright and shining, hung in dull, lank strings. Her voice was merely a weak whisper.

"Darling, darling." I comforted and then kissed her.

"Hang on. We're taking you to a doctor soon. It won't be so long before we reach Florida and there we'll never be locked up."

Carrie slumped in my arms as I miserably stared out at the dangling Spanish moss that indicated we were now in South Carolina. We still had to pass through Georgia. It would be a long time before we arrived in Sarasota. Violently Carrie jerked upright and began to choke and retch.

I'd judiciously stuffed my pockets with paper napkins during our last rest break, so I was able to clean up Carrie. I handed her over to Chris so I could kneel on the floor to clean up the rest. Chris slid over to the window and tried to force it open to throw out the sodden paper napkins. The window refused to budge no matter how hard he pushed and shoved. Carrie began to cry.

"Put the napkins in the crevice between the seat and the side of the bus," whispered Chris, but that keen-eyed bus driver must have been watching through his rear-view mirror, for he bellowed out, "You kids back there—get rid of that stinking mess some other way!" What other way but to take everything from the outside pocket of Chris's Polaroid camera case, which I was using as a purse, and stuff the smelly napkins in there.

"I'm sorry," sobbed Carrie as she clung desperately to Chris. "I didn't mean to do it. Will they put us in jail now?"

"No, of course not," said Chris in his fatherly way. "In less than two hours we'll be in Florida. Just try to hang on until then. If we get off now we'll lose the money we've paid for our tickets, and we don't have much money to waste."

Carrie began to whimper and tremble. I felt her forehead and it was clammy, and now her face wasn't just pale, but white! Like Cory's before he had died.

I prayed that just once God would have some mercy on us. Hadn't we endured enough? Did it have to go on and on? While I hesitated with the squeamish desire to vomit myself,

Carrie let go again. I couldn't believe she had anything left. I sagged against Chris while Carrie went limp in his arms and looked heartbreakingly near unconsciousness. "I think she's going into shock," whispered Chris, his face almost as pale as Carrie's.

This was when a mean, heartless passenger really began to complain, and loudly, so the compassionate ones looked embarrassed and undecided as to what to do to help us. Chris's eyes met mine. He asked a mute question—what were we to do next?

I was beginning to panic. Then, down the aisle, swaying from side to side as she advanced toward us, came that huge black woman smiling at us reassuringly. She had paper bags with her which she held for me to drop the smelly napkins in. With gestures but no words she patted my shoulder, chucked Carrie under the chin and then handed me a handful of rags taken from one of her bundles. "Thank you," I whispered, and smiled weakly as I did a better job of cleaning myself, Carrie and Chris. She took the rags and stuffed them in the bag, then stood back as if to protect us.

Full of gratitude, I smiled at the very, very fat woman who filled the aisle with her brilliantly gowned body. She winked, then smiled back.

"Cathy," said Chris, his expression more worried than before, "we've got to get Carrie to a doctor, and soon!"

"But we've paid our way to Sarasota!"

"I know, but this is an emergency."

Our benefactor smiled reassuringly, then she leaned over to peer into Carrie's face. She put her large black hand to Carrie's clammy brow, then put her fingers to her pulse. She made some gestures with her hands which puzzled me, but Chris said, "She must not be able to talk, Cathy. Those are the signs deaf people make." I shrugged to tell her we didn't understand her signs. She frowned, then whipped from a dress pocket beneath a heavy red sweater she wore a pad of multicolored sheets of notepaper and very swiftly she wrote a note which she handed to me.

My name Henrietta Beech, she'd written, *Can hear, but no talk. Little girl is very, very sick and need good doctor.* I read this, then looked at her hoping she'd have more information. "Do you know of a good doctor?" I asked. She nodded vigorously, then quickly dashed off another green note. *Your good fortune I be on your bus, and can take you to my own doctor-son, who is very best doctor.*

"Good golly," murmured Chris when I handed him the note, "we sure must be under a lucky star to have someone to direct us to such a doctor."

"Look here, driver," yelled the meanest man on the bus. "Get that sick kid to a hospital! Damned if I paid my good money to ride on a stinking bus!"

The other passengers looked at him with disapproval, and I could see in the rear-view mirror that the driver's face flushed with anger, or perhaps it was humiliation. In the mirror our eyes met. He lamely called to me. "I'm sorry but I've got a wife and five kids and if I don't keep my schedules, then my wife and kids won't eat, because I'll be out of a job." Mutely I pleaded with my eyes, making him mumble to himself, "Damn Sundays. Let the week days go by just fine, then comes Sunday, damn Sundays."

This was when Henrietta Beech seemed to have heard enough. Again she picked up her pencil and notepad and wrote. This note she showed to me.

Okay, man in driver's seat who hates Sundays. Keep on ignoring little sick girl, and her parents will sue big shot bus owners for two million!

No sooner had Chris had the chance to skim this note than she was waddling up the aisle and she pushed the note into the driver's face. Impatiently he shoved it away, but she thrust it forward again, and this time he made an attempt to read it while keeping one eye on the traffic.

"Oh, God," sighed the driver whose face I could clearly see in the mirror. "The nearest hospital is twenty miles off my route."

Both Chris and I watched, fascinated, as the mammoth black lady made gestures and signals that left the driver as frustrated as we had been. Once again she had to write a note, and whatever she wrote in that one soon had him turning the bus off the wide highway onto a side road that led into a city named Clairmont. Henrietta Beech stayed with the driver, obviously giving him instructions, but she took the time to look back at us and shine on us a brilliant smile, assuring us that everything would be just fine.

Soon we were rolling along quiet, wide streets with trees that arched gracefully overhead. The houses I stared at were large, aristocratic, with verandas and towering cupolas. Though in the mountains of Virginia it had already snowed once or twice, autumn had not yet laid a frosty hand here. The maples, beeches, oaks and magnolias still held most of their summer leaves, and a few flowers still bloomed.

The bus driver didn't think Henrietta Beech was directing him right, and to be honest I didn't think she was either. Really, they didn't put medical buildings on this kind of residential street. But just as I was beginning to get worried, the bus jerked to a sudden halt in front of a big white house perched on a low, gentle hill and surrounded by spacious lawns and flower beds.

"You kids!" the bus driver bellowed back to us, "pack your gear, turn in your tickets for a refund, or use them before the time limit expires!" Then quickly he was out of the bus and opening up the locked underbelly, and from there he pulled out forty or so suitcases before he came to our two. I slung Cory's guitar and banjo over my shoulders, as Chris very gently, and with a great deal of tenderness, lifted Carrie in his arms.

Like a fat mother hen, Henrietta Beech hustled us up the

long brick walk to the front veranda and there I hesitated, staring at the house, the double black doors. To the right a small sign read FOR PATIENTS ONLY. This was obviously a doctor who had offices in his own home. Our two suitcases were left back in the shade near the concrete sidewalk while I scanned the veranda to spy a man sleeping in a white wicker chair. Our good Samaritan approached him with a wide smile before she gently touched him on the arm, and when he still slept on she gestured for us to advance and speak for ourselves. Next she pointed to the house, and made signals to indicate she had to get inside and prepare a meal for us to eat.

I wished she'd stayed to introduce us, to explain why we were on his porch on Sunday. Even as Chris and I stole on cautious pussywillow feet toward him, even as I filled with fear I was sniffing the air filled with the scent of roses and feeling that I'd been here before and knew this place. This fresh air perfumed with roses was not the kind of air I'd grown to expect as the kind deemed worthy for such as me. "It's Sunday, damn Sunday," I whispered to Chris, "and that doctor may not appreciate our being here."

"He's a doctor," said Chris, "and he's used to having his spare time robbed . . . but *you* can wake him up."

Slowly I approached. He was a large man wearing a pale gray suit with a white carnation in his buttonhole. His long legs were stretched out and lifted to the top of the balustrade. He looked rather elegant, even sprawled out as he was with his hands dangling over the arms of the chair. He appeared so comfortable it seemed a terrible pity to awaken him and put him back on duty.

"Are you Dr. Paul Sheffield?" asked Chris who had read the sign with the doctor's name. Carrie lay in his arms with her neck arched backwards, her eyes closed and her long golden hair waving in the soft, warm breezes. Reluctantly the doctor came awake. He stared at us long moments, as if disbelieving his eyes. I knew we looked strange in our many layers of clothing. He shook his head as if trying to focus his eyes, and such beautiful hazel eyes they were, bejeweled with flecks of blue, green and gold on soft brown. Those remarkable eyes drank me in, then swallowed me down. He appeared dazzled, slightly drunk, and much too sleepy to put on his customary professional mask that would keep him from darting his eyes from my face to my breasts, then to my legs before he scanned slowly upward. And again he was hypnotized by my face, my hair. It was hair that was far too long, I knew that, and it was clumsily cut on top, and too pale and fragile on the ends.

"You are the doctor, aren't you?" demanded Chris.

"Yes, of course. I'm Dr. Sheffield," he finally said, now turning his attention to Chris and Carrie. Surprisingly graceful and quick, he lifted his legs from the railing, rose to his feet to tower above us, ran long fingers through the mop of his dark hair, and then stepped closer to peer down into Carrie's small, white face. He parted her closed lids with forefinger and thumb and looked for a moment at whatever was revealed in that blue eye. "How long has this child been unconscious?"

"A few minutes," said Chris. He was almost a doctor himself, he'd studied so much while we were locked away upstairs. "Carrie threw up on the bus three times, then began to tremble and feel clammy. There was a lady on the bus named Henrietta Beech, and she brought us here to you."

The doctor nodded, then explained that Mrs. Beech was his housekeeper-cook. He then led us to the door for patients only, and into a section of the house with two small examination rooms and an office, all while apologizing for not having his usual nurse available. "Take off all Carrie's clothes but her underpants," he ordered me. While I set about doing this, Chris dashed back to the sidewalk to fetch our suitcases.

Full of a thousand anxieties, Chris and I backed up against a wall and watched as the doctor checked Carrie's blood pressure, her pulse, her temperature and listened to her heart, front and back. By this time Carrie had come around so he could request her to cough. All I could do was wonder why everything bad had happened to us. Why was fate so persistently against us? Were we as evil as the grandmother had said? Did Carrie have to die too?

"Carrie," said Dr. Sheffield pleasantly after I had dressed her again, "we're going to leave you in this room for a while so you can rest." He covered her with a thin blanket. "Now don't be afraid. We'll be right down the hall in my office. I know that table isn't too soft, but do try and sleep while I talk to your brother and sister."

She gazed at him with wide, dull eyes, not really caring if the table was hard or soft.

A few minutes later Dr. Sheffield was seated behind his big impressive desk with his elbows on the blotter pad, and that's when he began to speak earnestly and with some concern. "The two of you look embarrassed and ill-at-ease. Don't be afraid you're depriving me of Sunday fun and games, for I don't do much of that. I'm a widower, and Sunday for me is no different than any other day. . . ."

Ah, yes. He could say that, but he looked tired, as if he worked too many long hours. I perched uneasily on the soft brown leather sofa, close by Chris. The sunlight filtering through the windows fell directly on our faces while the doctor was in the shadows. My clothes felt damp and miserable, and suddenly I remembered why. Quickly I stood to unzip and remove my filthy outer skirt. I felt quite pleased to see the doctor start in surprise. Since he'd left the room when I undressed Carrie, he didn't realize that I had two dresses on underneath. When I sat again next to Chris, I wore only one dress of blue, princess styled, and it was flattering and unsoiled.

"Do you always wear more than one outfit on Sundays?" he asked.

"Only on the Sundays I run away," I said. "And we have only two suitcases and need to save room for the valuables we can hock later on when we have to." Chris nudged me sharply, mutely signaling I was revealing too much. But I knew about doctors, from him mostly. That doctor behind the desk could be trusted—it was in his eyes. We could tell him anything, everything.

"Sooo," he drawled, "you three are running away. And just what are you running from? Parents who offended you by denying you some privileges?"

Oh, if he only knew! "It's a long story, Doctor," said Chris, "and right now all we want to hear about is Carrie."

"Yes," he agreed, "you're right. So we'll talk about Carrie." All professional now, he continued, "I don't know who you are, or where you're from, or why you feel you have to run. But that little girl is very, very ill. If this weren't Sunday, I'd admit her to a hospital today for further tests I can't make here. I suggest you contact your parents immediately."

Just the words to make me panic!

"We're orphans," said Chris. "But don't worry about not being paid. We can pay our own way."

"It's good you have money," said the doctor. "You're going to need it." He swept long, observant looks over both of us, sizing us up. "Two weeks in a hospital should be sufficient to discover the factor in your sister's illness I can't quite put my finger on." And while we gasped, stunned that Carrie was *that* sick, he made an approximate guess as to the amount of money it would cost. Again we were stunned. Dear God! Our stolen cache of money wouldn't even pay for one week, much less two.

My eyes clashed with the appalled look in Chris's blue eyes. What would we do now? We couldn't pay that much.

The doctor easily read our situation. "Are you still orphans?" he asked softly.

"Yes, we're *still* orphans," stated Chris defiantly, then glanced hard at me to let me know I was to keep my trap shut. "Once you're an orphan you stay that way. Now, tell us what you suspect is wrong with our sister, and what you can do to make her well again."

"Hold up there young man. First you have to answer a few questions." His was a soft voice, but firm enough to let us know *he* was in command here. "First, what is your last name?"

"I am Christopher Dollanganger, and this is my sister, Catherine Leigh Dollanganger, and Carrie is eight years old, whether or not you believe it!"

"Why shouldn't I believe it?" the doctor asked mildly, when just a few minutes ago in the cubelike examination room, he'd shown shock to hear her age.

"We realize Carrie is very small for her age," said Chris defensively.

"Indeed she is small." He flicked his eyes to me when he said this, then to my brother, and leaned forward on his crossed arms in a friendly, confidential manner that made me tense in preparation. "Now look. Let's stop being suspicious of one another. I'm a doctor, and anything you confide to me will remain in my confidence.

"If you really want to help your sister, you can't sit there and make up lies. You have to give me the truth, or else you're wasting my time and risking Carrie's life."

We both sat silent, holding hands, our shoulders pressed one against one other. I felt Chris shudder, so I shuddered too. We were so scared, so damned scared to speak the full truth—for who would believe? We'd trusted those who were supposedly honorable before so how could we trust again? And yet, that man behind the desk . . . he looked so familiar, like I'd seen him before. "All right," he said, "if it's that difficult, let me ask more questions. Tell me what all three of you ate last."

Chris sighed, relieved. "Our last meal was breakfast very early this morning. We all ate the same thing, hot dogs with everything, french fries dipped in catsup, and then chocolate milkshakes. Carrie ate only a little of her meal. She's very picky about food under the best of circumstances. I'd say she's never really had a healthy appetite."

Frowning, the doctor noted this down. "And all three of you ate exactly the very same things for *breakfast*? And only Carrie was nauseated?"

"Right. Only Carrie."

"Is Carrie often nauseated?"

"Occasionally, not often."

"How occasionally?"

"Well . . ." said Chris slowly, "Carrie threw up twice last week, and about five times last month. It's worried me a lot; her attacks seem to be growing more violent as they come more often."

Oh, the evasive way Chris was telling about Carrie made me really furious! He would protect our mother even now, after all she'd done. Maybe it was my expression that betrayed Chris and made the doctor lean my way, as if he knew he'd hear a more complete story from me. "Look, you came to me for help, and I'm willing to do what I can, but you aren't giving me a fair chance if you don't give me all the facts. If Carrie hurts inside, I can't look inside to see where it is—she has to tell me, or you have to tell me. I need information to work with—full information. Already I know Carrie is malnourished, underexercised and underdeveloped for her age. I see that all three of you have enlarged pupils. I see you are all pale, thin and weak looking. Nor can I understand why you hesitate about money when you wear watches that look quite expensive, and someone has chosen your clothes with taste and considerable cost—though why they fit so poorly is beyond my speculations. You sit there with gold and diamond watches, wearing rich clothes and shoddy sneakers, and tell me half-truths. So now I'm going to tell you a few *full truths*!" His voice grew stronger, more forceful. "I suspect your small sister is dangerously anemic. And because she is anemic she is susceptible to myriad infections. Her blood pressure is dangerously low. And there is some elusive factor I can't put my finger on. So, tomorrow Carrie will be admitted to a hospital, whether or not you call your parents, and you can hock those wristwatches to pay for her life. Now . . . if we admit her to the hospital this evening, the tests can begin early tomorrow morning."

"Do what you feel necessary," said Chris dully.

"Wait a minute!" I cried, jumping to my feet and moving swiftly to the doctor's desk. "My brother isn't telling you everything!" I threw Chris a hard glance over my shoulder, while he shot his fierce look to forbid me to reveal the whole truth. I thought bitterly, *don't worry, I'll protect our precious mother as much as I can!*

I think Chris understood, for tears came to his eyes. Oh, how much that woman had done to hurt him, hurt all of us, and he could still cry for her sake. His tears put tears in my heart too, not for her, but for him, who'd loved her so well, and for me who loved *him* so well, and tears for all we'd shared and suffered. . . .

He nodded, as if saying okay, go ahead, and then I began to tell what must have seemed to the doctor an incredible tale. At first I could tell he thought I was lying, or at least exaggerating. Why was that when every day the newspapers told terrible tales of what loving, caring parents did to their children?

". . . And so, after Daddy was in that fatal accident, Momma came and told us she was deeply in debt, and she had no way to earn a living for the five of us. She began writing letters to her parents in Virginia. At first they didn't reply, but then one day a letter came. She told us her parents lived in a fine, rich house in Virginia and were fabulously wealthy, but because she had married her half-uncle she'd been disinherited. Now we were going to lose everything we owned. We had to leave our bicycles in the garage, and she didn't even give us time to say good-bye to our friends, and that very evening we set off on a train headed for the Blue Ridge Mountains.

"We felt happy to be going to a fine, rich house, but not so happy about meeting a grandfather who sounded cruel. Our mother told us we'd have to hide away until she could win back his affections. Momma said *one* night only, or maybe two or three, then we could go downstairs and meet her father. He was dying of heart disease and never climbed the stairs so we were safe enough up there as long as we didn't make much noise. The grandmother gave us the attic to play in. It was huge—and dirty, and full of spiders, mice and insects. And that's where we played and tried to make the best of it until Momma won back her father's good will and we could go down and begin to enjoy living like rich children. But soon enough we found out that our grandfather was never going to forgive our mother for marrying his half-brother and we were going to remain 'Devil's issue.' We'd have to live up there until he was dead!"

I went on, despite the look of pained incredulity in the doctor's eyes. "And as if that weren't bad enough, being locked up in one room with our playground in the attic, we soon found out our grandmother hated us too! She gave us a long list of what we could do and what we couldn't do. We were never to look out of the front windows, or even open the heavy draperies to let in some light.

"At first the meals the grandmother brought up each morning in a picnic hamper were rather good, but gradually they worsened to only sandwiches, potato salad and fried chicken. Never any desserts, for they would rot our teeth and we couldn't go to a dentist. Of course, when our birthdays came around, Momma would sneak us up ice cream and a bakery cake, and plenty of presents. Oh, you bet she bought us everything to make up for what she was doing to us—as if books and games and toys could ever make up for all we were losing—our health, our belief in ourselves. And, worst of all, we began to lose faith in *her*!

"Another year came, and that summer Momma didn't even visit us at all! Then, in October she showed up again to tell us she'd married a second time and had spent the summer touring Europe on her honeymoon! I could have killed her! She could have told us, but she'd gone away and not said a word to explain! She brought us expensive gifts, clothes that didn't fit, and thought that made up for everything, when it didn't make up for *anything!* Finally I was able to convince Chris we should find a way to escape that house and forget about inheriting a fortune. He didn't want to go, because he thought that any day the grandfather might die, and he wanted to go to college, then medical school and become a doctor—like you."

"A doctor like me . . ." said Dr. Sheffield with a strange sigh. His eyes were soft with sympathy, and something darker too. "It's a strange story, Cathy, and hard to believe."

"Wait a minute!" I cried. "I haven't finished. I haven't told you the worst part! The grandfather did die, and he did write our mother into his will so she'd inherit his tremendous fortune—but he added a codicil that said she could never have children. If it were ever proven she'd given birth to children by her first husband, she'd have to forfeit everything she'd inherited and everything she'd bought with the money!"

I paused. I glanced at Chris who sat pale and weak looking, staring at me with hurt and pleading eyes. But he needn't have worried; I wasn't going to speak of Cory. I turned again to the doctor. "Now that mysterious, elusive factor you can't put your finger on—the thing wrong with Carrie that makes her throw up, and us too sometimes. It's really very simple. You see, once our mother knew she could never claim us and keep the fortune, she decided to get rid of us. The grandmother began to add sugared doughnuts to the basket. We ate them eagerly enough, not knowing that they were coated with arsenic."

And so I'd said it.

Poisoned doughnuts to sweeten our imprisoned days as we stole from our room by using the wooden key Chris had fashioned. Day by day dying for nine months while we sneaked into our mother's grand bedroom suite and took all the one- and five-dollar bills we could find. Almost a year we'd traversed those long, dim corridors, stealing into her room to take what money we could.

"In that one room, Doctor, we lived three years and four months and sixteen days."

When I'd concluded my long tale the doctor sat very quietly staring at me with compassion, shock, and concern. "So you see, Doctor," I said to finish, "you can't force us to go to the police and tell our story! They might throw the grandmother and our mother in jail, but we'd suffer too! Not only from the publicity, but also from being separated. They'd put us in foster homes, or make us wards of the court, and we've sworn to stay together, always!"

Chris was staring at the floor. He spoke without looking up. "Take care of our sister. Do whatever is needed to make her well again, and both Cathy and I will find a way to meet our obligations."

"Hold on, Chris," said the doctor in his slow, patient way. "You and Cathy have been fed arsenic too and will need to undergo many of the same tests I order for Carrie. Look at the two of you. You're thin, pale, weak. You need good food, rest and plenty of fresh air and sunshine. Maybe there is something I can do to help."

"You're a stranger to us, sir," Chris said respectfully, "and we don't expect or need anyone's charity or pity. Cathy and I are not that weak or sick. Carrie's the one most affected."

Full of indignation, I spun about to glare at Chris. We'd be fools to reject help from this kind man just so we could salvage some of our pride that had already gone down in defeat so many times before. What difference did one more time make?

". . . Yes," continued the doctor, as if both Chris and I had already agreed to his generous offer to help, "expenses are not as high for an 'out' patient as for an 'in' patient—no room and no board to pay. Now listen, this is only a suggestion which you're free to refuse, and travel on to wherever you have in mind—by the way, where are you going?"

"To Sarasota, Florida," Chris said weakly. "Cathy and I used to swing from the ropes we tied to the attic rafters, so she thought we could become aerialists, with some practice." It sounded silly when I heard him say it. I expected the doctor to laugh, but he didn't. He just looked sadder.

"Honestly, Chris, I would hate to see you and Cathy risk your lives like that, and as a doctor I feel I can't allow you to go as you are. Everything in my personal ethics and professional ones too refuses to let you go on without medical treatment. Common sense tells me I should keep my distance and not give a damn about what happens to three kids on their own. For all I know that horrendous story may just be a pack of lies to gain my sympathy." He smiled kindly to take the sting from his words. "Yet, my intuition tells me to believe your story. Your expensive clothes, your watches and the sneakers on your feet, your pale skin and the haunted look in your eyes all testify to the truth."

Such a voice he had, hypnotizing, soft and melodious, with just a bit of Southern accent. "Come," he said, charming me, if not Chris, "forget about pride and charity. Come live in my home of twelve lonely rooms. God must have put Henrietta Beech on that bus to lead you to me. Henny is a terrific worker and keeps my house spotless, but she constantly complains that twelve rooms and four baths are just too much for one woman to care for. Out in the back I have four acres of garden. I hire two gardeners to help, for I just can't devote as much time to the garden as I need to." At this point he riveted his brilliant eyes directly on Chris. "You can help earn your keep by mowing the lawns, clipping the hedges and preparing the gardens for winter. Cathy can help out in the house." He shot me a questioning, teasing look with his eyes twinkling. "Can you cook?"

Cook? Was he kidding? We'd been locked upstairs for more than three years, and we'd never even had a toaster to brown our bread in the mornings, and no butter, or even margarine!

"No!" I snapped. "I can't cook. I'm a dancer. When I'm a famous prima ballerina I'll hire a woman to do the cooking, like you do. I don't want to be stuck away in some man's kitchen, washing his dishes and fixing his meals and having his babies! That's not for me."

"I see," he said, his expression blank.

"I don't mean to sound ungrateful," I explained. "I will do what I can to help out Mrs. Beech. I'll even learn how to cook for her—and you."

"Good," he said. His eyes were laughing, full of sparkling lights as he templed his fingers beneath his chin and smiled. "You are going to be a prima ballerina, and Chris is going to be a famous doctor, and you are going to achieve all of this by running away to Florida to perform in the circus? Of course I'm of another stodgy generation and I can't fathom your reasoning. Does it really make good sense to you?"

Now that we were out of the locked room and the attic and in the full light of reality, no, it didn't make good sense. It sounded like foolish, childish and unrealistic folly.

"Do you realize what you'd be up against as professional aerialists?" the doctor asked. "You would have to compete against people who've trained from early childhood, people descended from long lines of circus performers. It wouldn't be easy. Still, I'll admit there's something in those blue eyes that tells me you two are very determined young people, and no doubt you'll get what you go after if you really want it badly enough. But what about school? What about Carrie? What's she going to do while the two of you swing from trapezes? Now don't bother to answer," he said quickly when my lips parted. "I'm sure you can come up with something to convince me, but I must dissuade you. First you have to tend to your health and Carrie's. Any day the two of you could come down as swiftly as Carrie and be just as sick. After all, didn't all three of you exist under the same miserable conditions?"

Four of us, not three, was the whisper in my ears, but I didn't speak of Cory.

"If you meant it about taking us in until Carrie is well," said Chris with his eyes shining suspiciously, "we're extremely grateful. We'll work hard, and when we can we'll leave and repay you every cent you spent on us."

"I meant it. And you don't have to repay me, except by helping out in the house and the yard. So, you see, it isn't pity, or charity, only a business arrangement to benefit all of us."

A New Home

That's the way it started. We moved quietly into the doctor's home and into his life. We took him over, I know that now. We made ourselves important to him, as if he hadn't had a life before we came. I know that now too. He made it seem we were doing him a favor by relieving him of a dreary, lonely life by adding our youthful presence. He made us feel that we were being generous to share *his* life, and oh, we did want to believe in someone.

He gave Carrie and me a grand bedroom to share, with twin beds and four tall windows facing south, and two windows facing east. Chris and I looked at each other with a terrible shared hurt. We were to sleep in different rooms for the first time in ever so long. I didn't want to part from him and face the night with only Carrie, who could never protect me as he had. I think our doctor may have sensed something that told him to fade into the background, for he excused himself and drifted toward the end of the hall. Only then did Chris speak. "We've got to be careful, Cathy. We wouldn't want him to suspect. . . ."

"There is nothing to suspect. It's over," I answered, but I

didn't meet his eyes, guessing, even then, that it would never be over. *Oh, Momma, look what you started by putting the four of us in one locked room, and leaving us there to grow up, knowing how it would be! You of all people should have known!*

"Don't," Chris whispered. "Kiss me good night, and there won't be any bedbugs here."

He kissed me, I kissed him, we said good night, and that was all. With tears in my eyes I watched my brother back down the hall, still holding his eyes on me.

In our room Carrie let out a loud howl. "I can't sleep in no little bed all by myself!" she wailed. "I'll fall off! Cathy, why is that bed so little?"

It ended up with Chris and the doctor coming back so they could take away the nightstand that separated the twin beds. Then they shoved the narrow beds so close they appeared one wide bed. This pleased Carrie enormously, but, as the nights passed, somehow the crack between our beds grew ever wider until I, the restless sleeper, finally woke up with one leg and one arm in the crack and Carrie being pulled along with me to the floor.

I loved that room Paul gave us. It was so beautiful with its pale blue wallpaper, and matching curtains. The rug was blue; each of us had a chair with lemon-yellow cushions and all the furniture was antique white. It was the kind of room a girl should have. No gloom. No pictures of hell on the wall. All the hell I had was in my mind, put there by thinking back much too often. Momma could have found another solution if she'd really wanted to! "She didn't have to lock us up! It was greed, avarice, that damned fortune . . . and Cory was in the ground because of her weakness!"

"Forget it, Cathy," said Chris when we were again saying good night.

I was terribly afraid to tell him what I suspected. My head bowed low against his chest. "Chris, it was a sinful thing we did, wasn't it?"

"It won't happen again," he said stiffly, then broke away and almost ran down the hall as if I were chasing. I wanted to lead a good life and hurt no one, especially Chris. Even so, I had to leave my bed around midnight and go to Chris. While he slept I crawled in the bed beside him. He wakened when he heard the bedsprings squeak. "Cathy, what the hell are you doing here?"

"It's raining outside," I whispered. "Just let me lie beside you for a moment or so, and then I'll go away." Neither of us moved, or even breathed. Then without even knowing how it came about, we were in each other's arms and he was kissing me. Kissing with such ardent fervor it made me respond when I didn't want to. It was evil and wrong! Yet I didn't really want him to stop. That sleeping woman inside of me woke up and took over, wanting what he felt he had to have, and I, the thinking, calculating part, pushed him away. "What are you doing? I thought you said this would never happen again."

"You came . . ." he said hoarsely.

"Not for this!"

"What do you think I'm made of? Steel? Cathy, don't do this again."

I left him and cried in my own bed, for he was down the hall and not there to waken me if I had a nightmare. No one to comfort me. No one to lend me strength. Then my mother's words came to haunt me with a horrible thought—was I so much like her? Was I going to be the kind of weak, clinging-vine female who always needed a man for protection? No! I was sufficient unto myself!

I believe it was the next day that Dr. Paul brought me four pictures to hang. Ballerinas in four different positions. For Carrie he brought a milk-glass vase filled with delicate plastic violets. Already he'd learned about Carrie's passion for all things purple or red. "Do what you can to make this room yours," he told us. "If you don't like the color scheme, we'll have it changed in the spring." I stared at him. We wouldn't be here, come spring.

Carrie sat holding her vase of fake violets while I forced myself to speak up and say what I had to. "Dr. Paul, we won't be here in the spring, so we can't afford to let ourselves become too attached to the rooms you've given us."

He was in the doorway, ready to depart, but he halted and turned to look back at me. He was tall, six two or more, and his shoulders were so wide they almost filled the doorway.

"I thought you liked it here," he said in a wistful tone, his dark eyes gone bleak.

"I do like it here!" I quickly answered. "We all like it here, but we can't take advantage of your good nature forever." He nodded without replying and left, and I turned to see Carrie staring at me with a great deal of animosity.

Daily the doctor took Carrie to the hospital with him. At first she'd wail and refuse to go unless I went along too. She made up fantastic stories about what they did to her in the hospital, and complained about all the questions they asked her.

"Carrie, we never tell lies; you know that. The three of us always tell the truth to each other—but we don't go around telling *everybody* about our past lives upstairs—understand?"

She stared up at me with those big, haunted eyes. "I don't tell nobody Cory went away to heaven and left me. I don't tell nobody but Dr. Paul."

"You told *him*?"

"I couldn't help it, Cathy," Carrie buried her head in her pillow and cried.

So now the doctor knew about Cory, and how he was supposed to have died in a hospital from pneumonia. How sad his eyes were that night when he questioned Chris and me, wanting all the details of Cory's illness that ended in his death.

Chris and I were huddled up close on the living room sofa when Paul said, "I'm very happy to report that arsenic has not done any permanent damage to any of Carrie's organs, as we all feared it might have. Now don't look like that. I haven't let out your secret but I had to tell the lab technicians what to look for. I made up a story about how you'd taken the poison accidentally, and your parents were good friends of mine, and I'm considering making you three my legal wards."

"Carrie's going to live?" I whispered, drowning in relief.

"Yes, she'll live—*if* she doesn't go swinging on trapezes." He smiled again. "I've made appointments for the two of you to be examined tomorrow—by me—unless you have some objections."

Oh, I had objections! I wasn't keen about taking off my clothes and having him go over me, even if a nurse was there. Chris told me I was silly to think a doctor of forty would get any erotic pleasure from looking at a girl of my age. But when he said it, he was looking the other way, so how could I tell what he was really thinking? Maybe Chris was right, for when I was on that examination table, naked and covered by a paper robe, Dr. Paul didn't seem the same man whose eyes followed me around when we were in the "home" side of his house. He did to me the same things he'd done to Carrie, but asked even more questions. Embarrassing questions.

"You haven't menstruated in more than two months?"

"I've never been regular, really! I started when I was twelve, and twice I skipped from three to six months. I used to worry about it, but Chris read up on the subject in one of the medical books Momma brought him, and he told me too many anxieties and too much stress can make a girl miss. You don't think . . . I mean . . . there isn't anything wrong with me, is there?"

"Not that I can tell. You seem normal enough. Too thin, too pale, and you're slightly anemic. Chris is too, but because of his sex not as much as you are. I'm going to prescribe special vitamins for all three of you."

I was glad when it was over and I could put on my clothes and escape that office where the women who worked for Dr. Paul looked at me so funny.

I raced back to the kitchen. Mrs. Beech was preparing dinner. Her smile shone big and wide when I came in, lighting up a moon face with skin as slick as oiled rubber. The teeth she displayed were the whitest, most perfect teeth I'd ever seen. "Golly, am I happy that's over!" I said, falling into a chair and picking up a knife to peel potatoes. "I don't like doctors poking me over. I like Dr. Paul better when he's just a man. When he puts on that long white jacket, he also puts a shade over his eyes. Then I can't see what he's thinking. And I'm very good at reading eyes, Mrs. Beech."

She grinned at me with teasing devilry, then whipped out a pink notepad from the huge square pocket of her starched white apron. With the apron tied about her middle she resembled nothing more than a rolled-up goosedown comforter, waddling about speechless. By now I knew she had a congenital speech defect. Though she was trying to teach Chris, Carrie and me to understand her sign language, as yet none of us had caught on enough to carry on a quick conversation. I think I enjoyed her notes too much—notes she could write lightning-fast in a very abbreviated style. *Doctor says*, she'd written, *young people need lots of good fresh fruit and vegetables, plenty of lean meat, but go easy on starches and desserts. He wants to put on you muscle not fat.*

Already we'd gained some weight in the two weeks of eating Mrs. Beech's delicious cooking, even Carrie who was so darn finicky. Now she ate with enthusiasm, and for her that was remarkable. So, as I peeled the red potatoes, Mrs. Beech wrote another note when her signals failed to communicate. *Fairy-Child, from now on call me only Henny. No Mrs. Beech.*

She was the first black person I'd known, and though at first I'd felt ill-at-ease with her and a little afraid of her, two weeks of intimacy had taught me much. She was just another human being of another race and color, with the same sensitivities, hopes and fears we all had.

I loved Henny, her broad smiles, her loose, flowing gowns

with flowers blooming riotously, and most of all I loved the wisdom that came from her small pastel paper sheets. Eventually, I did learn to understand her sign language, though I was never as good at it as her "doctor-son."

Paul Scott Sheffield was a strange man. So often he looked sad when there was no apparent reason for him to be sad. Then he'd smile and say, "Yes, God favored Henny and me that day he put you three on that bus. I lost one family, and grieved for them, and fate was kind enough to send me another, ready-made family."

"Chris," I said that evening when we had to reluctantly part, "when we lived in the room upstairs, you were the man, the head of the household. . . . Sometimes it feels funny to have Dr. Paul around, watching what we do and listening to what we say."

He blushed. "I know. He's taking my place. To be honest," and here he paused and blushed a deeper red, "I don't like him replacing me in your life, but I'm very grateful for what he's done for Carrie."

Somehow all that our doctor did for us made Momma seem a thousandfold worse in comparison. *Ten* thousandfold worse!

The next day was Chris's eighteenth birthday, and though *I'd* never forget, it surprised me that the doctor had planned a party with many fine gifts that sparkled Chris's eyes, and then saddened them with the guilt both he and I felt. Already we'd accepted so much. Already we had been making plans to leave soon. We just couldn't stay on and take advantage of Dr. Paul's good nature, now that Carrie was well enough to travel on.

After the party Chris and I sat on the back veranda, mulling this over. One look at his face and I could tell he didn't want to leave the one and only man who could, and would, help him reach his goal of becoming a doctor. "I really don't like the way he keeps looking at you, Cathy. His eyes follow you about all the time. Here you are, so available, and men his age find girls your age irresistible."

They did? How fascinating to know. "But doctors have plenty of pretty nurses available to them," I said lamely, knowing I would do anything short of murder, to see that Chris reached his goal. "Remember that day we first came? He spoke of the kind of competition we'd be up against in the circus. Chris, he's right. We can't go work for the circus; that's only a silly dream."

He stared off into space with knitted brows. "I know all of that."

"Chris, he's just lonely. Maybe he only watches me because there isn't anything else as interesting to watch as me." But how fascinating to know that men of forty were susceptible to girls of fifteen. How wonderful to wield over them the power that my mother had.

"Chris, if Dr. Paul says the right thing, I mean, if he really honestly wants us, would you stay on?"

He frowned and studied the hedges he'd so recently clipped. After long consideration he spoke slowly, "Let's give him a test. If we tell him we're leaving, and he doesn't say anything to prevent us, then that will be his polite way to let us know he doesn't really care."

"Is it fair to test him like that?"

"Yes. It's a good way to give him the chance to get rid of us and not feel guilty about it. You know, people like him often do nice things because they feel they should, not because they really want to."

"Oh."

We were not ones to procrastinate. The next evening after dinner, Paul came to join us on the back veranda. *Paul.* I was calling him that in my thoughts—getting familiar, liking him more and more because always he looked so casually elegant, so clean, so nice, sitting in his favorite white wicker rocker, wearing a red cable-knit sweater with gray slacks and slowly,

dreamily puffing on a c
the evening was chilly. (
while Carrie crouched
lous. Shallow marble
feet to other steps wh
small Japanese footl
stream. There were
random, which len
of worldly sensual
elegantly posed, ar
it was. For I'd bee

The doctor w
and started to blow dead leaves ....
eled abroad every other year to search out the beau....
ble statues he'd ship home and add to his collection. He'd
been so lucky the last time to come across a full-sized copy of
Rodin's *The Kiss*.

I sighed with the wind. I didn't want to go. I liked it here
with him, with Henny, with the gardens that held me in thrall
and made me feel enchanted, beautiful, desirable.

"So all my roses are old-fashioned roses that haven't had
the heady scent bred from them," said Dr. Paul. "Why have
roses at all if they don't reek of perfume?"

In the fading, purplish light of the failing day his glimmering eyes met with mine. My pulse quickened and forced
another sigh. I wondered what his wife had been like, and
how it felt to be loved by someone like him. Guiltily my eyes
fled from his long, searching look, afraid he'd see what I was
thinking. "You look disturbed, Cathy. Why?" His question
teased me, as if he knew already my secrets. Chris turned his
head to give me a hard look of warning.

"It's your red sweater," I said foolishly. "Did Henny knit
it for you?"

He chuckled softly, then glanced down at the handsome
sweater he wore. "No, not Henny. My older sister knitted the

, then mailed it to me parcel post. She
e of town."

our sister mail you a gift and not bring it
ked. "And why didn't you tell us you had a
would have given you gifts too."

he began, settling back comfortably and cross-
egs, "my birthday came and went shortly before you
d. I'm forty in case Henny hasn't told you. I've been a
ower thirteen years, and my sister, Amanda, has not spoken to me since the day my wife and young son died in an
accident." His voice faded away and he stared off into space,
moody, solemn, distant.

Dead leaves scuttled on the lawn, chased over the porch
and came to nestle near my feet, like brown, dried-up duck-
lings. All this took me back to a certain forbidden night when
Chris and I had so desperately prayed while we huddled on
the cold slate roof under a moon that looked like the scowling
eye of God. Would there be a price to pay for just one terrible sin committed? Would there? The grandmother would
quickly say, *yes! You deserve the worst punishment! Devil's spawn,
I knew it all along!*

And while I sat there floundering Chris spoke up.
"Doctor, Cathy and I have been talking this over, and we
feel now that Carrie is well we should be leaving. We deeply
appreciate everything you've done, and we intend to repay
you every cent, though it may take us a few years. . . ." His
fingers squeezed tight around mine, warning me not to say
anything different.

"Hold on there, Chris," interrupted the doctor, jerking
upright in his chair and planting both his feet solidly on the
floor. Clearly he meant business. "Don't think for one minute
I haven't seen this coming. I've dreaded each morning, fearful
I'd wake up to find you gone."

"I've been looking into the legal ramifications of making the three of you my wards. And I've found out it isn't as

complicated as I thought. It seems most children who run away say they're orphans, so you'll have to give me proof your father is really dead. If he's alive, I would need his consent, as well as your mother's."

My breath caught! My mother's consent? That meant we'd have to see her again! I didn't want to see her, not ever!

He went on, his eyes soft as they saw my distress. "The court would petition your mother to appear at a hearing. If she lived in this state she'd be forced to comply in three days, but since she's in Virginia, they'll give her three weeks. If she doesn't show up, then instead of having only temporary custody of you, I will be granted permanent custody—but only if you're willing to say I've done a good job as a guardian."

"You've been wonderful!" I cried out. "But she won't come! She wants to keep us a secret! If the world finds out about us, she'll lose all that money. Her husband might turn against her too if he knew she'd hidden us away. You can bet your life if you dare to try for permanent custody, you'll get it—and you might be sorry in the end!"

Chris's hand tightened more on mine, and Carrie looked up with huge, scared eyes.

"In a few weeks Christmas will be here. Are you going to leave me to spend another lonely holiday by myself? You've been here for almost three weeks, and I've explained to everyone who asked that you were the children of a relative of mine who died recently. I'm not going into this blindly. Henny and I have given this a great deal of thought. She feels, just as I feel, that the three of you are good for us. We both want you to stay on. Having young people in the house makes it more like a home. I feel healthier than I have in years, and happier too. Since the death of my wife and son, I've missed having a family. In all this time I've never gotten used to being a bachelor again." His persuasive tone grew wistful. "I feel fate *wants* me to have custody of you. I feel God *planned* for Henny to be on the bus, just so she could bring you to me. When fate steps in and makes the decisions, who am I to deny it? I accept the fact you three are godsent to help me make up for the mistakes I've made in the past."

Wow! Godsent! I was more than half-won. I knew people could always find the motivation to justify what they wanted; well enough I knew that. Even so, tears filled my eyes as I looked at Chris questioningly. He met my look and shook his head in bewilderment, confused as to what *I* wanted. His hand gripped mine like iron while he spoke, still looking at me, not at Dr. Paul. "We're sorry for the loss of your wife and son, sir. But we can't replace them, and I don't know if we'd be doing right to burden you with the expense of three kids not your own." Then he added, looking the doctor squarely in the eyes. "And you should think about this too. You'll have one hell of a time finding another wife when you assume guardianship of us."

"I don't intend to marry again," he replied in a strange way. Then he went on with an abstract air, "Julia was the name of my wife, and my son was named Scotty. He was only three when he died."

"Oh," I breathed, "how terrible to lose a son so young, and your wife too." His obvious grief and remorse reached out and touched me; I was very in tune with those who grieved. "Did they die in an accident, a car accident like our father?"

"An accident," he said sharply, "but not in a car."

"Our father was only thirty-six when he was killed, and we were having a surprise birthday party, with a cake, presents . . . and he never came, only two state policemen. . . ."

"Yes, Cathy," he said softly, "you've told me. The adolescent years aren't easy for anyone, and to be young and on your own, without the proper education, with little money, no family, no friends—"

"We've got each other!" said Chris staunchly, so as to test him more. "So, we will never truly be alone."

Paul went on. "If you don't want me, and what I have to give you isn't enough, then go on to Florida with my blessings.

Throw away all those long hours you studied, Chris, just when you're almost there. And you, Cathy, can forget your dream of being a prima ballerina. And don't you think for one moment that's going to be a healthy, happy life for Carrie. I'm not persuading you to stay, for you'll do what you want to and have to. So make up your minds—is it to be me and the chance to fulfill your aspirations, or is it to be the hard, unknown world?"

I sat there on the balustrade as close as possible to Chris, with my hand held in his. I wanted to stay. I wanted what the doctor could give to Chris, to say nothing of Carrie and myself.

The southern breezes kept blowing, caressing my cheek and whispering too convincingly that everything would work out right. I could hear Henny in the kitchen making fresh dough for the hot rolls we'd eat in the morning, made golden by dripping butter. Butter was one of the things denied us before, and the luxury Chris had missed most.

Everything here beguiled me, the air, the soft, warm glow in the doctor's eyes. Even the banging of Henny's pots and pans began to work magic, and my heart, so heavily burdened for so long, began to feel lighter. Maybe perfection did exist outside of fairy tales. Maybe we were good enough to walk upright and proud beneath God's blue sky; maybe we were not contaminated shoots grown from the wrong seed planted in the wrong soil.

And more than anything the doctor had said, or anything his sparkling eyes implied, I think it was the roses that still bloomed, though it was winter, that made me feel dizzy from the overwhelming sweetness of their perfume.

But it wasn't Chris and I who decided. It was Carrie. Suddenly she jumped up from the top step and went flying into the doctor's outstretched arms. She flung herself against him and wrapped her thin arms about his neck. "I don't want to go! I love you, Dr. Paul!" she cried out, almost frantic. "I don't want no Florida and no circus! I don't want to go anywhere!" Then she was crying, letting out all her grief for

Cory, withheld for so long. He picked her up and held her on
his lap, and put kisses on her wet cheeks before he used his
handkerchief to mop up the tears.

"I love you too, Carrie. I always wanted a little girl with
blond curls and big blue eyes, just like yours." But he wasn't
looking at Carrie. He was looking at me. "And I wanna be here
for Christmas," sobbed Carrie. "I've never seen Santa Claus,
not once." Of course she had, years ago, when our parents
took the twins to a department store and Daddy snapped a
picture of the two of them on Santa's lap, but maybe she'd
forgotten.

How could a stranger come so easily into our lives and
give us love, when our own blood kin had sought to give us
death?

Life's Second Chance

Carrie decided. We stayed. Even if she hadn't decided, still we would have stayed. How could we not?

We tried to give Dr. Paul what money we had left. He refused. "You keep that money for yourselves. You worked hard to get it, didn't you? And you might as well know I've seen my attorney so he can fill out the petitions that will bring your mother to Clairmont. I know you believe she won't come, but you can never tell. If I'm so lucky as to win permanent custody, I'll give each of you a weekly allowance. No one can feel free and happy without some money in his pocket. Most of my colleagues give their teenage children five dollars a week. Three dollars should be enough for a girl Carrie's age." He planned to buy all our clothes and everything else we needed for school. We could only stare at him, amazed he'd be so generous—again.

A few days before Christmas he drove us to a shopping mall that was carpeted in red; the ceiling was a glass dome; throngs of people swarmed about as pop Christmas music played. It was like fairyland! I glowed; so did Carrie and Chris—and our doctor. His huge hand held Carrie's small one as Chris and I held on to each other. I saw him watching us, enjoying our wide-eyed stares. We were charmed by everything. Awed, impressed, very wanting, fearful too he would see and try to satisfy all our yearnings.

I turned in circles when we reached the department that sold clothes for teenage girls. Dazzled and bewildered by so much, I looked at that, and looked at this, and couldn't decide what I wanted when everything was so pretty and I'd never had the chance to shop for myself before. Chris laughed at my indecision. "Go on," he urged, "now that you have the chance to fit yourself perfectly, try on what you like." I knew what he was thinking, for it had been my mean way to complain that Momma never brought me anything that fitted right.

With great care I selected parsimoniously the outfits I thought suitable for school that would begin for us in January. And I needed a coat, real shoes, and a raincoat and hat and umbrella. Everything that kind-hearted, generous man allowed me to buy made me feel guilty, as if we were taking advantage of him.

To reward me for my slowness and my reluctance to buy too much, Paul said impatiently, "For heaven's sake, Cathy, don't think we're going shopping like this every week. I want you to buy enough today to last you through the winter. Chris, while we finish up here, you dash on to the young men's section and begin picking out what you want. While you do that, Cathy and I can outfit Carrie with the clothes she needs."

I noticed that all the adolescent girls in the store were turning to stare at my brother as he made his way to the young men's department.

At last we were going to be normal kids. Then, when I felt tentatively secure, Carrie let out a howl to shatter crystal palaces in London! Her cries jolted the salespeople, startled the customers, and a lady bumped her baby-stroller into a dummy who went crashing down. The baby in the stroller added his screams to Carrie's!

Chris came on the run to see who was murdering his small sister. She stood, feet wide apart, head thrown back, with tears of frustration streaming her cheeks. "Good God, what's wrong now?" asked Chris as our doctor looked dumbfounded.

Men—what did they know? Obviously Carrie was outraged by the pretty little pastel dresses brought out for her approval. Baby clothes—that's what. Even so, all were too large, and none were red or purple—absolutely not Carrie's style at all! "Try the toddler department," suggested the heartless, haughty blonde with the beehive hair. She smiled graciously at our doctor who appeared embarrassed.

Carrie was *eight!* To even mention "toddler clothes" was insulting! She screwed her face into a puckered prune. "I can't wear toddler clothes to school!" she wailed. She pressed her face against my thigh and hugged my legs. "Cathy, don't make me wear pink and blue *baby* dresses! Everybody will laugh! I know they will! I want purple, red—no baby colors!"

Dr. Paul soothed her. "Darling, I adore blond girls with blue eyes in pastels, so why not wait until you're older to wear all those brilliant colors?"

Bittersweet milksop like this was something someone as stubborn as Carrie couldn't swallow. She glared her eyes, balled her fists, prepared her foot for kicking and readied her vocal cords for screaming when a middle-aged, plump woman who must have had someone like Carrie for a granddaughter suggested calmly that she could have her clothes custom made. Carrie hesitated uncertainly, looking from me to the doctor, then to Chris and back to the saleslady.

"A perfect solution!" said Dr. Paul enthusiastically, looking relieved. "I'll buy a sewing machine and Cathy can make you purple, red, and electric-blue clothes, and you'll be a knock-out."

"Don't wanna be no knock-out—just want bright colors." Carrie pouted while I was left with my mouth agape. I was a *dancer*, not a seamstress! (Something that didn't escape

Carrie's knowledge.) "Cathy don't know how to make good clothes," she said. "Cathy don't do nothing but dance."

That was loyalty. Me, who'd taught her and Cory to read, with a little help from Chris. "What's the matter with you, Carrie?" snapped Chris. "You're acting like a baby. Cathy can do anything she sets her mind to—remember that!" The doctor readily agreed. I said nothing as we shopped for an electric sewing machine.

"But in the meantime, let's buy a few pink, yellow and blue dresses, all right, Carrie?" Dr. Paul grinned mockingly. "And Cathy can save me tons of money by sewing her own clothes too."

Despite the sewing I'd have to learn, heaven was ours that day. We went home loaded, all of us made beautiful in barber shops and beauty salons; each of us had on new shoes with hard soles. I had my very first pair of high-heeled pumps—and a dozen pairs of nylons! My first nylons, my first bra—and to top it all off, a shopping bag full of cosmetics. I'd taken forever to select makeup while the doctor stood back and watched me with the queerest expression. Chris had grumbled, saying I didn't need rouge or lipstick, or eyeshadow, liner and mascara. "You don't know anything at all about being a girl," I answered with an air of superiority. This was my first shopping binge, and by heaven I was making the most of it! I had to have everything I'd seen on Momma's fabulous dressing table. Even her kind of wrinkle cream, plus a mud pack for firming.

No sooner were we out of the car and unloaded than Chris, Carrie and I dashed upstairs to try on all our new clothes. Funny how once new clothes had come to us so easily and hadn't made us happy like this. Not when no one would see us wear them. Yet, being what I was, when I slipped on the blue velvet dress with tiny buttons down the front, I thought of Momma. How ironic that I should want to cry for a mother we'd lost, who I was determined to hate forever. I sat on the edge of my twin bed and pondered this. Momma had given us new clothes, toys and games out of guilt for what she was doing, depriving us of a normal childhood. A childhood we'd never have the chance to recover. Lost years, some of the best years, and Cory was in a grave, no new suits for him.

His guitar was in the corner where Carrie could wake up and see it and the banjo. Why was it us who always had to suffer, why not her? Then, suddenly it hit me! Bart Winslow was from South Carolina! I ran down to our doctor's study and purloined his big atlas, then back I raced to the bedroom, and there I found the map of South Carolina. I found Clairmont . . . but didn't believe my eyes when I saw it was a twin city to Greenglenna! No, that was too much of a coincidence—or was it? I looked up and stared into space. God had meant for us to come here and live near Momma—if she ever visited her husband's home town. God wanted me to have the chance to inflict a little pain of my own. As soon as I could, I was going to Greenglenna and look up all the information I could about him and his family. I had five dollars a week— to order a subscription of the community paper that told of all the social activities of the wealthy people who lived near Foxworth Hall.

Yes, I was gone from Foxworth Hall, but I was going to know every move she made, and when she came this way I'd know that too! Sooner or later, Momma was going to hear from me, and know I would never, never forget or forgive. Somehow, in some way, she was going to hurt ten times more than we had!

With this decided, I could join Chris and Carrie in the living room to model all our new clothes for our doctor and Henny. Henny's smile beamed like a dazzling sun. I watched the bejeweled eyes of our benefactor, only to see them shadow over as he frowned reflectively. I saw no admiration or approval. Suddenly, he got up and left the room, offering a weak excuse of needing to do some paperwork.

Soon Henny became my mentor in all things domestic.

She taught me to bake biscuits from scratch, and tried to teach me how to make rolls light and fluffy.

Wham! went Henny's hand into the dough. Henny wiped her hands clean of flour and dashed off a note. *Henny got bad eyes for seeing small things like needle eyes. You have good eyes you sew on doctor son's missing shirt buttons—yes?*

"Sure," I agreed without enthusiasm, "I can sew holes, and I can also knit, crochet, needlepoint and do crewel work. My mother taught me how to do all those things as a way to keep busy." Suddenly I couldn't speak. I wanted to cry. I saw my mother's lovely face. I saw Daddy. I saw Chris and me as children hurrying home from school, rushing in with snow on our shoulders to find Momma knitting baby things for the twins. I couldn't help but bow my head into Henny's lap and begin to cry, really bawl. Henny couldn't speak, but her soft hand on my shoulder showed she understood. When I glanced upward, she was crying too. Big, fat tears that slid down to wet her bright red dress. "Don't cry, Henny. I'll be happy to sew on Dr. Paul's missing buttons. He's saved our lives, and there's nothing I wouldn't do for him." She gave me a strange look, then got up to fetch years of mending and perhaps a dozen shirts with missing buttons.

Chris spent every available moment with Dr. Paul who was coaching him so he could enter a special college-prep school in midterm. Carrie was our biggest problem. She could read and write but she was so very small. How would she manage in a public school where children were not always kind?

"It's a private school I have in mind for Carrie," explained our doctor. "A very good school for young girls, run by an excellent staff. Since I'm on the board of trustees, I think Carrie will be given special attention, and not subjected to any kind of stress." He eyed me meaningfully.

That was my worst fear, that Carrie would be ridiculed and made to feel ashamed because of her overlarge head and undersized body. Once Carrie had been so beautifully proportioned, so very perfect. It was all those lost years when the sun was denied us that made her so small. It was, I knew it was!

I was scared to death Momma would show up on that day she was supposed to appear at the court hearing. But I was certain, almost, that she wouldn't come. How could she? She had too much to lose and nothing to gain. What were we but burdens to bear? And there was jail too, a murder charge. . . .

We sat very quietly with Paul, dressed in our best to appear in the judge's chamber, and waited, and waited, and waited. I was a tight wire inside, stretched so taut I thought I might break and cry. She didn't want us. Again she told us by not showing up, how little she cared! The judge looked at us with too much pity, making me feel so sorry for all of us—and so angry with her! Oh, damn her to hell! She gave us birth, she claimed to have loved our father! How could she do this to his children—her own children? What kind of mother was she? I didn't want that judge's pity, or Paul's. I held my head high and bit down on my tongue to keep from screaming. I dared to glance at Chris and saw him sitting blank-eyed, though I knew his heart was being shredded, as mine was. Carrie crouched in a tight ball on the doctor's lap, as his hands soothed her, and he whispered something in her ear. I think he said, "Never mind, it's all right. You have me for a father and Henny for a mother. You'll never want for anything as long as I live."

I cried that night. I wet my pillow with tears shed for a mother I'd loved so much it hurt to think back to the days when Daddy was alive and our home life was perfect. I cried for all the good things she had done for us back then, and, most of all, for all the love she'd so generously given us—then. I cried more for Cory who was like my own child. And that's when I stopped crying and turned to bitter, hard thoughts of revenge. When you set out to defeat someone, the best way was to think as they did. What would hurt her most? She wouldn't want to think of us. She'd try to forget we ever existed. Well, she wouldn't forget. I'd see to it that she didn't. This very Christmas I would send her a card, and sign it with this, "From the four Dresden dolls you didn't want," and I had to change that to "The three alive Dresden dolls you didn't want, plus the dead one you carried away and never brought back." I could see her staring at that card, thinking to herself, *I only did what I had to.*

We had let down our shields and allowed ourselves to be vulnerable again. We allowed faith, hope and trust to come and dance like sugarplums in our heads.

Fairy tales could come true.

They were happening to us. The wicked queen was out of our lives, and Snow White would reign one day. She wouldn't be the one to eat the poisoned red apple. But every fairy tale had a dragon to slay, a witch to overcome or some obstacle to make things difficult. I tried to look ahead and figure out who would be the dragon, and what would be the obstacles. All along I knew who was the witch. And that was the saddest part of being me.

I got up and went out on the upper veranda to stare up at the moon. I saw Chris standing near the railing, gazing up at the moon too. From the slump of his shoulders, usually held so proud, I knew he was bleeding inside, just as I was. I tiptoed over to surprise him. But he turned as I neared and held out his arms. Without thought I went straight into them and put my arms up around his neck. He wore the warm robe Momma had given him last Christmas, though it was much too small. He'd have another from me when he looked under the tree Christmas morning, with his mono-gram—CFS—for he wanted never to be called Foxworth, but Sheffield.

His blue eyes gazed down into mine. Eyes so much alike. I loved him as I loved the better side of myself, the brighter, happier side.

"Cathy," he whispered, stroking my back, his eyes bright,

"if you feel like crying, go ahead, I'll understand. Cry enough for me too. I was hoping, praying that Momma would come and somehow give us a reasonable explanation for doing what she did."

"A reasonable excuse for murder?" I asked bitterly. "How could she dream up one clever enough? She's not that smart." He looked so miserable I tightened my arms about his neck. One hand stole into his hair and twined there. My other hand lowered to stroke his cheek. Love, it was such an encompassing word, different from sex and ten times more compelling. I felt full of love for him when he lowered his face into my hair and sobbed. He murmured my name over and over again, as if I were the only person in the world who would ever be real and solid, and dependable.

Somehow his lips found mine and we were kissing, kissing with so much passion he was aroused and tried to draw me into his room. "I just want to hold you, that's all. Nothing else. When I go away to school, I need to have something more to hold onto—give me just a little more, Cathy, please." Before I could answer he had me in his arms again, kissing me with such burning lips I became terrified—and excited too.

"Stop! Don't!" I cried, but he went on, touching my breasts and pushing my gown aside so he could kiss them. "Chris!" I hissed, angry then. "Don't love me, Chris. When you're gone, what you feel for me will fade away like it never happened. We'll force ourselves to love others so we can feel clean. We can't be our parents in duplicate. We can't make the same mistake."

He held me tighter and didn't say a word, yet I knew what he was thinking. There wouldn't be any others. He wouldn't let it come about. One woman had hurt him too deeply, betrayed him too monstrously when he was young and very, very vulnerable. There was only me he could trust.

He stepped back, two tears shining in the corners of his

eyes. It was up to me to slice the bond, now, here. And for his own good. Everybody always did everything for someone's good.

I couldn't go to sleep. I kept hearing him calling me, wanting me. I got up and drifted down the hall and again got in his bed, where he lay waiting. "You'll never be free of me, Cathy, never. As long as you live, it will be me and you."

"No!"

"Yes!"

"No!" But I kissed him, then jumped from his bed and raced back to my room, slamming and locking the door behind me. What was the matter with me? I should never have gone to his room and gotten into his bed. Was I as evil as the grandmother said?

No, I wasn't.

I couldn't be!

PART TWO

Visions of Sugarplums

It was Christmas. The tree touched the twelve-foot ceiling, and spread under it were gifts enough for ten children! Not that Chris and I were children anymore. Carrie was thrilled by everything Santa had brought for her. Chris and I had used the last of our stolen hoard of money to buy Paul a luscious red lounging robe, and a brilliant gown of ruby red velvet for Henny—size fifty-eight! Dazzled and pleased, she held it before her. Then she wrote a thank-you note, *Make good church dress. Make all friends jealous.*

Paul tried on his lavish new lounging robe. He looked divine in that color and it fitted him beautifully.

Next came the biggest surprise of all. Paul strode over to me and hunkered down on his heels. From his wallet he pulled five large yellow tickets. If he had sat down for a year and thought about nothing but a way to please me most, he couldn't have been more successful. There, fanned in his large, finely shaped hand, were tickets to *The Nutcracker*, performed by the Rosencoff School of Ballet.

"It's a very professional company, I hear," explained

Paul. "I don't know much about ballet myself, but I've asked around, and they say it is one of the best. They also teach beginner, intermediate and advanced lessons. Which level are you?"

"Advanced!" proclaimed Chris while I could only stare at Paul, too happy to speak. "Cathy was a beginner when she went upstairs to live. But something wonderful happened to her in the attic—the ghost of Anna Pavlova came and took over her body. And Cathy taught herself how to go on *pointe*."

That night all of us, including Henny, sat enthralled in the third row, center section. Those dancers on stage weren't just good—they were superb! Especially the handsome man named Julian Marquet who danced the lead. As in a dream I followed Paul backstage during intermission, for I was going to meet the dancers!

He led us toward a couple standing in the wings. "Madame, Georges," he said to a tiny woman sleek as a seal and a not much larger man by her side, "this is my ward, Catherine Doll, who I was telling you about. This is her brother Christopher, and this younger beauty is Carrie, and you have met Henrietta Beech before. . . ."

"Yah, of course," said the lady who looked like a dancer, talked like a dancer, and wore her black hair just like a dancer would, drawn back from her face and pinned up in a huge chignon. Over black leotards she wore a floating chiffon dress of black, and over that a bolero of leopard skins. Her husband, Georges, was a quiet man, sinewy, pale-faced, with startlingly black hair, and lips so red they seemed made of congealed blood. They were a pair, all right, for her lips were scarlet slashed too, and her eyes were charcoaled smudges in pale pastry dough. Two pairs of black eyes scanned me and then Chris. "You too are a dancer?" they asked of my brother. My, did they always speak simultaneously?

"No! I don't dance," said Chris, appearing embarrassed.

"Ah, the pity of that," sighed the madame regretfully.

"What a glorious pair the two of you would make on stage. People would flock to stare at beauty such as you and your sister possess." She glanced down at small Carrie, clinging fearfully to my hand, and casually disregarded her.

"Chris plans to be a doctor," explained Dr. Paul.

"Ha!" Madame Rosencoff scoffed, as if Chris must have taken leave of his senses. Both she and her husband turned their ebony eyes on me, concentrating with such intensity I began to feel hot, sweaty, self-conscious.

"You have studied the daunce?" (Always she said "daunce," as if it had a "u.")

"Yes," I said in a small voice.

"Your age when you started?"

"I was four years old."

"And you are now . . . ?"

"In April I will be sixteen."

"Good. Very, very good." She rubbed the palms of her long, bony hands together. "Eleven years and more of professional training. At what age did you go on *pointe*?"

"Twelve."

"Wonderful!" she cried. "I never put girls on full *pointe* until they are thirteen, unless they are excellent. Then she frowned suspiciously. "Are you excellent, or only mediocre?"

"I don't know."

"You mean no one has ever told you?"

"No."

"Then you must be only mediocre." She half-sneered, turned toward her husband and waved her hand arrogantly to dismiss us.

"Now you wait a minute!" flared Chris, looking red and very angry. "There's not a dancer on that stage tonight who is as good as Cathy! Not one! That girl out there, playing the lead role of Clara—sometimes she is out of time with the music—Cathy is *never* out of time. *Her* timing is perfect; her *ear* is perfect. Even when Cathy dances to the same melody, each time she varies it just a little, so she never duplicates, always improvises to make it better, and more beautiful, and more touching. You'd be lucky to get a dancer like Cathy in your company!"

Those slanted, jet eyes turned to him, savoring the intensity of his report. "*You* are an authority on the subject of ballet?" she asked with some scorn. "*You* know how to separate the gifted dancers from the horde?"

Chris stood as if in a dream, and spoke as if his feet were firmly rooted there, and even his voice had a huskiness to betray his feelings. "I only know what I see, and what emotions Cathy makes me feel when she dances. I know when the music turns on, and she begins to move with it, my heart stands still, and when her dance is over, I know I am left aching because such beauty has gone. She doesn't just dance a role, she is that character; she makes you believe—because *she* believes—and there's not a girl in your company who reaches out and grabs my heart and squeezes it until it throbs. So go on and turn her away, and let some other dance company benefit from your stupidity."

The Madame's jet eyes fixed on Chris long and penetratingly, as did our doctor's eyes. Then slowly Madame Rosencoff turned to me, and from head to toe I was assessed, weighed, measured. "Tomorrow, one o'clock sharp. At my studio you will audition for me." It was not a request, but a command—not to be disobeyed—and for some reason when I should have been happy, I was angry.

"Tomorrow is too soon," I said. "I have no costumes, no leotards, no *pointes*." All of those things had been left behind in the attic of Foxworth Hall.

"Trifles," she dismissed, with an arrogant wave of her shapely hand. "We will supply what you need—just be there—and don't be late, for we demand that our dancers be disciplined in *all* things, including punctuality!" With a queenly gesture we were dismissed, and gracefully she drifted off with her husband in tow, leaving me stunned. Mouth agape, speechless, I caught the strong study of the dancer, Julian Marquet, who must have overheard every word. His dark eyes shone with a glow of interest and admiration. "Feel flattered, Catherine," he said to me. "Customarily she and Georges won't take anyone unless they've waited months, or sometimes years, for an audition."

I cried that night in Chris's embrace. "I'm out of practice," I sobbed. "I know I'm going to make a fool of myself tomorrow. It isn't fair that she won't let me have more time to prepare! I need to limber up. I'm going to be stiff, clumsy, and they won't want me, I know they won't!"

"Aw, come off it, Cathy," he said, tightening his arms about me. "I've seen you in here holding to the bedpost, and doing your *pliés* and *tendus*. You are *not* out of practice, or stiff, or clumsy—you're just scared. You've got a great big case of stage fright, that's all. And you don't need to worry, you're terrific. *I* know it, *you* know it."

He brushed a light good-night kiss on my lips, dropped his arms and backed toward the door. "Tonight I'll go down on my knees and pray for you. I'll ask God to let you wow them tomorrow. And I'll be there to gloat when I see their stunned expressions—for no one is gonna believe the dancing wonder of you."

With that he was gone. And I was left aching and wanting. I crawled under my covers to lie wide awake and full of trepidations.

Tomorrow was my big day, my chance to prove what I was and if I had that special something you had to have if you were to reach the top. I had to be *the* best, nothing else would do. I had to show Momma, the grandmother, Paul, Chris, everybody! I wasn't evil, or corrupt, or the Devil's issue. I was only me—the best ballerina in the world!

I tossed, turned, fretted in and out of nightmares while Carrie slept on peacefully. In my dreams I did everything wrong at the audition, and, what was worse, I did everything wrong throughout my whole lifetime! I ended up a withered old lady begging on the streets of some huge city. In the dark I passed by my mother and begged for alms. She was still young and beautiful, richly gowned, bejeweled and furred, and escorted by forever-young and faithful Bart Winslow.

I awoke. It was still night. What a long night. I stole down the stairs to find the Christmas tree lights burning, and on the floor, Chris was lying and staring up into the tree branches. It was what the two of us used to do when we were children. Though I should have known better, I was irresistibly drawn toward him, and I lay down beside him. I gazed up into the sparkling other-worldliness of the Christmas tree.

"I thought you'd forgotten," Chris murmured without looking my way. "Remember when we were in Foxworth Hall, the tree was so small and it was on a table and we couldn't lie under it like this—and look what happened. Let's never forget again. Even if our future trees are only one foot high, we will hang it up high, so we can lie underneath."

It worried me the way he said that. Slowly I turned my head to stare at his profile. He was so beautiful, lying there with his fair hair changing colors. Each strand seemed to catch a different rainbowed hue, and when he turned his head to meet my eyes his eyes were glowing too. "You look . . . so divine," I said in a tight voice. "I see candy in your eyes and the crown jewels of England too."

"No—that's what I am seeing in your eyes, Cathy. You're so very beautiful in that white nightgown. I love you in white nightgowns with blue satin ribbons. I love the way your hair spreads like a fan, and you turn your cheek so it rests on a satin pillow." He moved closer, so his head was on my hair too. Even closer he inclined his head until our foreheads met. His warm breath was on my face. I moved so my head tilted backward and my neck arched. I didn't feel quite real when his warm lips kissed the hollow of my throat and stayed there.

My breath caught. For long, long moments I waited for him to move away. I wanted to pull back myself, but somehow I couldn't. A sweet peace stole over me, quivering my flesh with a tingling sensation. "Don't kiss me again," I whispered, clinging harder to him and pressing his head to my throat.

"I love you," he choked. "There will never be anyone for me but you. When I'm an old, old man, I'll look back to this night with you under the Christmas tree, and remember how sweet it was of you to let me hold you like this."

"Chris, do you have to go away and be a doctor? Couldn't you stay on here and decide on something else?"

He lifted his head to stare down into my eyes. "Cathy—do you have to ask? All my life it's been the only thing I've wanted, but you . . ."

Again I sobbed. I didn't want him to go! I tickled his face with a tress of my hair, until he cried out and kissed my lips. Such a soft kiss, wanting to grow bolder, and afraid I'd turn away if he did. He began to say wild and crazy things when our kiss was over, about how much I looked like an angel. "Cathy—look at me! Don't turn your head and pretend you don't know what I'm doing, what I'm saying! Look and see the torment you've put me in! How can I find anyone else, when you've been bred into my bones—and are part of my flesh? Your blood runs fast when mine does! Your eyes burn when mine do—don't deny it!" His trembling hands began to fumble with the tiny, lace-covered buttons that opened my nightgown to the waist. I closed my eyes and was again in the attic, when he'd accidentally stabbed me in the side with the scissors, so now I was hurting, bleeding, and I needed his lips to kiss and take away the pain.

"How beautiful your breasts are," he said with a low sigh, leaning to nuzzle them. "I remember when you were flat, and then when you began to grow. You were so shy about them, always wanting to wear loose sweaters so I couldn't see. Why were you ashamed?"

Somewhere above I hovered, watching him tenderly kiss my breasts, and somewhere deep inside me I shivered. Why was I letting him do this? My arms drew his body tighter against me, and when my lips again met his, maybe it was my fingers that had unbuttoned his pajama jacket so his bare chest was against mine. We melded in a hot blend of unsatisfied desire—before I suddenly cried out, "No—it would be sinful!"

"Then let us sin!"

"Then don't ever leave me! Forget about being a doctor! Stay with me! Don't go and leave me! I'm afraid of myself without you! Sometimes I do crazy things. Chris, please don't leave me alone. I've never been alone, please stay!"

"I *have* to be a doctor," he said, then groaned. "Ask me to give up anything else, and I'd say yes. But don't ask me to give up the only thing that's held me together. You wouldn't give up dancing—would you?"

I didn't know, as I responded to his demanding kisses, the fire between us growing larger, overwhelming us both and taking us to the brinks of hell. "I love you so much sometimes I don't know how to handle it," he cried. "If only I could have you just once, and there would be no pain for you, only joy."

The unexpected parting of his hot lips, his tongue that forced my lips open, shot through me with a jolt of electricity! "I love you, oh, how I love you! I dream of you, think of you all day." And on and on he went, while his breath came faster, until he was panting and I was overcome by my body ready and willing to be satisfied. While my thoughts wanted to deny him, I wanted him! I gasped with the shame of it!

"Not here," he said between kisses. "Upstairs in my room."

"No! I'm your sister—and your room is too near Paul's. He'd hear us."

"Then we'll use your room. Carrie can sleep through a war."

Before I knew what was happening he had me in his arms
and was racing up the back stairs and into my room where he
fell with me on my bed. He had my gown off and his pajamas
too when he fell down beside me and started again to complete what he had begun. I didn't want this. I didn't want it
ever to happen again! "Stop!" I cried, then rolled away from
under him. I fell to the floor. In a flash he was on the floor
with me, wrestling. Over and over we turned, two naked bodies that suddenly collided with something hard.

That was what stopped him. He stared at the box with
Oreo cookies, a loaf of bread, apples, oranges, a pound of
cheddar cheese, a stick of butter, several cans of tuna fish,
beans and tomato juice. Out spilled a can opener, dishes,
glasses and silverware. "Cathy! Why are you stealing Paul's
food and hiding it under your bed?"

I shook my head, fuzzy about why I had taken the food
and hidden it away. Then I sat up and reached for the gown
he'd tugged off, and modestly I held it before me. "Get
out! Leave me alone! I don't love you except as a brother,
Christopher!"

He came to put his arms about me, and bowed his head
on my shoulder. "I'm sorry. Oh, darling, I know why you took
the food. You feel you have to keep food handy—you're afraid
someday we will be punished again. Don't you know I'm the
only one who will understand? Let me love you just one more
time, Cathy, just one more time to last us our whole lives. Let
me just once give you the pleasure I didn't before, just once to
last us both all our lives through."

I slapped his face! "No!" I spat. "Never again! You promised, and I thought you would keep that promise! If you have
to be a doctor, and go away and leave me—then it will always
be no!" I stopped short. I didn't mean that. "Chris . . . don't
look at me like that, please!"

Slowly he drew on his pajamas. He flashed me a hurt look.
"There is no life for me if I'm not a doctor, Cathy."

I put both hands over my mouth to keep from screaming. What was wrong with me? I couldn't demand him to abandon his dream. I wasn't like my mother, making everyone else suffer so she could have her way. I sobbed in his arms. In my brother I had already found my everlasting, forever-green, springtime love that could never, never blossom. Later, as I lay alone on my bed with my eyes open, I realized from the hopeless, flat way I felt that even in a valley without mountains the wind could still blow.

The Audition

It was the day after Christmas. At one o'clock I had to be in Greenglenna, the home of Bart Winslow and Rosencoff School of Ballet.

We all crowded into Dr. Paul's car and we arrived with five minutes to spare.

Madame Rosencoff told me to call her Madame Marisha, if I was accepted. If I failed, I need never address her again, by any name. She wore only black leotards, which showed up every hill and valley of her superb body, kept trim and slim though she must be nearing fifty. Her nipples poked through the black knit material hard as metal points. Her husband, Georges, was also wearing black to show off his sinewy body which was just beginning to show age with the small protrusion of his belly. Twenty girls and three boys were to audition.

"What music do you choose?" she asked. (It seemed her husband was never going to speak, though he kept his bright bird eyes on me constantly.)

"Sleeping Beauty," I said meekly, believing the role of Princess Aurora the greatest of all testing pieces in the

classical repertory—so why choose a less demanding part? "I can dance *The Rose Adagio* all alone," I boasted.

"Wonderful," she said sarcastically. Then added with additional scorn, "I guessed, just by your looks, you would want *The Sleeping Beauty*."

That made me wish I'd chosen something lesser.

"What color leotards do you want?"

"Pink."

"I thought so."

She tossed me a pair of faded pink leotards and then, just as casually, picked at random from a triple row of many dozens *pointe* shoes. She threw me a pair that fitted perfectly, unbelievable as it sounds. When I'd undressed and donned my leotards and slippers, I sat before a long dressing table with a mirror to equal its length and began to bind up my hair. I didn't have to be told Madame would want to see my neck cords, and any *épaulement* I'd perform was sure to displease her. I knew that already.

Hardly had I finished dressing and doing my hair, with a gaggle of giggling girls surrounding me, when Madame Marisha put her head through a partially opened door to see if I was ready. Critically her jet black eyes scanned me. "Not bad. Follow me," she ordered, and off she strode, her strong legs heavily muscled. How had she let that come about? I was never going to be on *pointe* so much my legs would look lumpy like hers—never!

She led me out into a big arena with a polished floor that really wasn't as slick as it appeared. Seats for onlookers were lined against the walls, and I saw Chris, Carrie, Henny and Dr. Paul. Now I wished I hadn't asked them to come. If I failed, they'd witness my humiliation. Eight or ten other people were there too, though I didn't pay much attention to them. The girls and boys of the company gathered in the wings to watch. I was more afraid than I'd thought I'd be. Sure, I'd practiced some since I escaped Foxworth Hall, but not with the same dedication as in the attic. I should have stayed up all night and exercised, and arrived at dawn to warm up more—then maybe I wouldn't feel nervous enough to be sick.

It was my desire to be last, to watch all the others and see the mistakes they made and learn from them, or to see their accomplishments and benefit from those. In this way I could size up what I should do.

Georges himself sat down to play the piano. I swallowed over the lump in my throat; my mouth felt dry, and butterflies panicked in my chest as my eyes raked over the spectators to find the lodestone I needed in the blue of Chris's eyes. And as always, he was there to smile, and telegraph his pride and confidence and undying admiration. My dear, beloved Christopher Doll, always there when I needed him, always giving to me and making me better than I would have been without him. God, I prayed, let me be good. Let me live up to his expectations!

I couldn't look at Paul. He wanted to be my father, not my touchstone. If I failed and embarrassed him, certainly he'd see me differently. I'd lose what charm I had for him. I'd be nobody special.

A touch on my arm made me jump. Whirling about I confronted Julian Marquet. "Break a leg," he whispered, then smiled to show his very white and perfect teeth. His dark eyes sparkled wickedly. He was taller than most male dancers, almost six feet, and soon I'd learn he was nineteen. His skin was as fair as mine, though in contrast to his dark hair it made him look too pale. His strong chin sported a devil's cleft and another dimple in his right check teased in and out at his will. I thanked him for his wish of good luck, very much taken by his astonishing good looks. "Wow!" he said when I smiled, his voice husky. "You're sure a beautiful girl. Too bad you're only a kid."

"I'm not a kid!"

"What are you then, some old lady of eighteen?"

I smiled, very pleased to think I looked *that* old. "Maybe so, maybe not."

He grinned as if he had all the answers. From the way he bragged of being one of the hottest dancers in a New York company, maybe he *did* have all the answers. "I'm only here for the holidays—to do Madame a favor. Soon I'll go back to New York where I belong." He looked around, as if the "provinces" bored him beyond belief, while my heart did a flip-flop. I was hoping he was one of the dancers I'd work with.

We exchanged a few more words and then my musical cue sounded. Suddenly I was alone in the attic, with colored paper flowers dangling on long strings; nobody but me and that secret lover who danced always just ahead, never letting me get near enough to see his face. I danced out, fearful at first, and did all the right things, the *entrachets*, the arm flutters, the *pirouettes*. I was sure to keep my eyes open and my face always toward the viewers I didn't see. Then the magic came and took me. I didn't have to plan and count, the music told me what to do, and how to do it, for I was its voice and could do no wrong. And as always that man appeared to dance with me—only this time I saw his face! His beautiful pale, pale face, with the dark and, and the blue-black hair and the ruby lips.

Julian!

I saw him as in a dream, stretching out his strong arms as he went down on one knee, and the other leg pointed backward gracefully. With his eyes he signaled I was to run, then leap into his receiving arms.

Enchanted to see him there, a professional, I was halfway to him when a terrible pain seized my abdomen! I doubled over and cried out! At my feet was a huge pool of blood! Blood streamed down my legs; it stained my pink shoes, my leotards. I slipped and fell to the floor, and grew so weak I could only lie there and hear the screams. Not my screams, but Carrie's. I closed my eyes not caring who it was who came to pick me up. From a far distance I heard Paul's voice and Chris's. Chris's concerned face hovered above me, with his love for me too clearly revealed; it both comforted me and frightened me, for I didn't want Paul to see. Chris said something about not being afraid as blackness came and took me to a far, far place where nobody wanted me.

And my dancing career, not yet begun, was over, over.

Out of a dream of witches I emerged to find Chris sitting on the hospital bed, holding my limp hand . . . and those blue eyes, oh, God, those eyes . . . "Hi," he said softly, squeezing my fingers. "I've been waiting for you to come around."

"Hi yourself."

He smiled and leaned to kiss my cheek. "I'll tell you this, Catherine Doll, you sure know how to end a dance dramatically."

"Yeah, that's talent. Real talent. I guess I'd better go into acting."

He shrugged indifferently. "You could, I guess, though I doubt you will."

"Oh, Chris," I stormed weakly, "you know I've ruined what chance I had! Why did I bleed like that?" I knew my eyes were full of fear. Fear that he saw and knew the cause. He leaned to draw me up into his embrace and held me fast against his chest.

"Life offers more than one chance, Cathy, you know that. You needed a D & C. You'll be fine and on your feet by tomorrow."

"What's a D & C?"

He smiled and stroked my cheek tenderly, always forgetting I wasn't as medically sophisticated as he was. "It's short for a procedure in which a woman is dilated, and an instrument called a curette is used to scrape waste material from the lining of the uterus. Those missed periods of yours must have clotted and then broke free."

Our eyes met. "That's all it was, Cathy . . . *all*, nothing else."

"Who did the scraping?" I whispered, scared it was Paul.

"A gynecologist named Dr. Jarvis, a friend of our doctor. Paul says he's the best gyn. around."

I lay back on the pillows, not knowing what to think. Of all times for something like that to happen—in front of everyone I was trying to impress. My God, why was life so cruel to me?

"Open your eyes, my lady Catherine," said Chris. "You're making too much out of this, when it doesn't matter. Take a look at that dresser over there and see all the pretty flowers, real flowers, not paper ones. I hope you don't mind if I took a peek at the cards." Of course I didn't mind what *he* did, and soon he was back from the dresser and putting a small white envelope in my flaccid hand. I stared at the huge floral bouquet, thinking it was from Paul, and only then did my eyes flick to the card in my hand. My fingers shook as I extracted from the envelope the small note that read:

Hope you recover soon. I expect to see you next Monday, three o'clock sharp.

Madame Marisha.

Marisha! I was accepted! "Chris, the Rosencoffs want me!"

"Of course they do," he said mildly. "They'd be just plain dumb if they didn't, but that woman scares the hell out of me! I wouldn't want her controlling my life, even if she is little. But, I guess you can handle her fine; you can always bleed on her feet."

I sat up and threw my arms about him. "Is it going to work out for us, Chris? Do you really think it will? Can we be that lucky?"

He nodded, smiled and then pointed to another bouquet, one from Julian Marquet with another short note. *I'll be seeing you when I fly down from New York again, Catherine Doll, so don't forget me.*

And over Chris's shoulder, while his arms held me tight, Paul came into the room and hesitated near the doorway, frowning as he stared at the two of us, then he put on a smile and came forward. Quickly Chris and I drew apart.

School Days Renewed

There came a day in January when we had to part. We'd taken exams to grade our abilities, and, much to Chris's surprise, and mine, we'd all done extremely well. I qualified for the tenth grade, Carrie for the third, and Chris for a college-prep school. But there was no happiness on Carrie's face when she screamed out, "No! No!" Her foot was ready for kicking, her fists balled to do battle with anyone who tried to force her. "Don't want no private ole school for funny lookin' lil girls! I won't go! You can't make me go! I'm gonna tell Dr. Paul, Cathy!" Her face was red with fury and her weeping voice was a siren's wail.

I wasn't overjoyed by the idea of putting Carrie in a private school ten miles outside the city. The day after she left, Chris would be leaving too. I'd be left alone to attend high school—and we'd sworn a solemn vow never, never to part. (I'd forced myself to put back the hidden cache of food—and no one knew about that but Chris.) I lifted Carrie onto my lap to explain to her how Dr. Paul had selected this very special school and had already paid an enormous tuition. She squinched her eyes shut and tried not to hear. "And it is *not* a school for funny little girls, Carrie," I said soothingly and then kissed her forehead. "It's a school for *rich* girls with parents who can afford the best. You should feel proud and very lucky to have Dr. Paul as our legal guardian." Did I convince her? Had I ever convinced her of anything?

"I still don't wanna go," she wailed stubbornly. "Why can't I go to *your* school, Cathy? Why do I have to go off all alone with nobody?"

"Nobody?" I laughed to hide what I was feeling, a reflection of her own fears. "You won't be alone, darling. You'll be with hundreds of other girls near your own age. Your school is an elementary one; I have to go on to high school." I rocked her to and fro in my arms, and stroked her long, shining cascade of hair, then tilted her piquant dollface to mine. Oh, she was a pretty little thing. Such a beauty she'd be if only her body would grow in proportion to her large head. "Carrie you have four people who love you very much. Dr. Paul, Henny, Chris and me. We all want what's best for you, and even though a few miles separate us, you'll be in our hearts, in our thoughts, and you can come home every weekend. And, believe it or not, school is not such a dreary place, it's fun, really. You'll share a lovely room with a girl your own age. You'll have expert teachers and, best of all, you'll be with girls who will think you're the prettiest thing they've ever seen. And you must want to be with other children. I know that being with a great many girls is loads of fun. You play games, and have secret societies and parties, and whisper and giggle all through the night. You'll love it." Yeah. Sure. She'd love it.

Carrie acquiesced only after she'd shed a waterfall of tears, her pleading eyes telling me she was going only to please me and her big benefactor whom she loved well. She'd sleep on nails to please him. And to her that school for girls was a bed of nails to endure. Just in time to hear, "Am I gonna stay there a long, long time?" Paul and Chris entered the living room. The two of them had been sequestered in Paul's study for hours, with Paul coaching Chris on some of the chemistry he'd neglected studying while locked away. Paul gave Carrie just one glance, saw her misery, then headed for the hall closet. Shortly, he was back with a big box wrapped in purple paper and tied with red satin ribbon three inches wide. "This is for my favorite blond," he said kindly.

Carrie's big, haunted eyes stared up at him before she smiled thinly. "Oh!" she cried in delight to open her gift and see the bright red leather luggage, complete with a cosmetic case outfitted with a gold comb, brush, mirror and little plastic jars and bottles, and a leather stationery case for writing letters home to us. "It's bea-u-ti-ful!" she exclaimed, won over at once by everything red and so fine. "I never knew they made red suitcases and put gold mirrors and things in them."

I had to look at Paul, who certainly didn't think a little girl needed makeup.

As if he read my thoughts, he said, "I know it's rather adult, but I wanted to give her something she can use for many, many years. When she sees it years from now, she'll think of me."

"That's the prettiest luggage I ever saw," I said cheerily. "You can put your toothbrushes, your toothpaste, your bath powder and your toilet water in your makeup case."

"I'm not gonna put no nasty toilet water in my suitcases!"

That made all of us laugh. Then I was up and running toward the stairs, hurrying to my room to fetch a small box that I rushed back to Carrie. Gingerly I held that box in my hands, wondering if I should give it to her and awaken old memories. "Inside this box are some old friends of yours, Carrie. When you're in Miss Emily Dean Calhoun's School for Properly Bred Young Ladies and feel a little lonely, just open this box and see what's inside. Don't show the contents to everybody, just to very special friends."

Her eyes grew large when she saw the tiny porcelain

people and the baby she'd loved so much, all stolen by me from that huge, fabulous doll house that she'd spent so many hours playing with in the attic. I'd even taken the crib.

"Mr. and Mrs. Parkins," breathed Carrie, tears of happiness shining in her big, blue eyes, "and little baby Clara! Where did they come from, Cathy?"

"You know where they came from."

She looked at me, holding the box full of cotton to cushion the fragile dolls and handmade wooden crib, all priceless heirlooms. "Cathy, where is Momma?"

Oh, God! Just what I didn't want her to ask. "Carrie, you know we are supposed to tell everybody both our parents are dead."

"*Is* Momma dead?"

"No . . . but we have to pretend she is."

"Why?"

Once again I had to explain to Carrie why we could never tell anyone who we really were, and that our mother still lived, or else we'd end up back in that dreary northern room. She sat on the floor near her shiny new red luggage, with the box of dolls in her lap, and stared at me with haunted eyes and no comprehension at all.

"I mean this, Carrie! You are *never* to mention any family but Chris and me, and Dr. Paul and Henny. Do you understand?"

She nodded, but she didn't understand. It was in her lips that quivered and in her wishful expression—she still wanted Momma!

Then came the terrible day when we drove Carrie ten miles outside the city limits of Clairmont to enter her in that fancy private school for the daughters of the affluent. The building was large, painted white, with a portico in front and the customary white columns. A brass plaque near the front door read, ESTABLISHED IN 1824.

We were received in a warm and cozy-looking office

by a descendant of the school founder, Miss Emily Dean Dewhurst. A stately, handsome woman with startling, white hair and not a wrinkle to betray her age. "She's a lovely child, Dr. Sheffield. Of course we'll do what we can to make her happy and comfortable while she learns."

I leaned to embrace Carrie who trembled and I whispered, "Cheer up, make an effort to enjoy yourself. Don't feel abandoned. Every weekend we'll come to take you home with us. Now is that so bad?"

She brightened and forced a smile. "Yes, I can do it," she murmured weakly.

It wasn't easy to drive away and leave Carrie in that beautiful, white, plantation house.

The very next day was Chris's time to depart for the boy's prep-school, and oh, how I hurt to see him pack up his things. I watched but couldn't speak. Chris and I couldn't even bear to look at one another.

His school was even farther away. Paul drove thirty miles before we reached the campus with buildings of rose-colored bricks and, again, the obligatory white columns. Sensing we needed to be alone, Paul made some flimsy excuse of wanting to inspect the gardens. Chris and I weren't really alone, but in an alcove with big bay windows. Young men were constantly passing by to glance in and stare at us. I wanted to be in his arms, with my cheek against his. I wanted this to be a farewell to love, so complete we'd know it was forever gone, at least forever gone from being wrong. "Chris," I stammered, near tears, "whatever am I going to do without you?"

His blue eyes kept changing colors, jumbling his kaleidoscope emotions. "Cathy, nothing will change," he whispered hoarsely, clinging to my hands. "When next we see each other, we'll still feel the same. I love you. I always will—right or wrong, I can't help it. I'll study so diligently I won't have time to think about you, and miss you, and wonder what's going on in your life."

"And you'll end up the youngest graduate from med school in the history of mankind," I chided, though my voice was as hoarse as his. "Save a little love for me, and store it away in the deepest part of your heart, the same as I'm going to store my love for you. We can't make the same mistake our parents did."

He sighed heavily and hung his head, studying the floor at his feet, or maybe he was studying my feet in the high heels that made my legs look so much prettier. "You'll take care of yourself."

"Of course. You take care of yourself. Don't study too much. Have some fun, and write me at least once a day; I don't think we should run up phone bills."

"Cathy, you're awfully pretty. Maybe too pretty. I look at you and see our mother all over again, the way you move your hands, and the way you tilt your head to the side. Don't enchant our doctor too much. I mean, after all, he's a man. He has no wife—and you'll be living in the same house with him." He looked up, his eyes suddenly sharp. "Don't rush into anything trying to escape what you feel for me. I mean it, Cathy."

"I promise to behave myself." It was such a weak promise when *he'd* awakened that primitive urge in me that should have been held back until I was old enough to handle it. Now all I wanted was to be fulfilled and loved by someone I could feel good about.

"Paul," Chris said tentatively, "he's a great guy. I love him. Carrie loves him. What do you feel for him?"

"Love, the same as you and Carrie. Gratitude. That's not wrong."

"He hasn't done anything out of the way?"

"No. He's honorable, decent."

"I see him looking at you, Cathy. You're so young, so beautiful, and so . . . needing." He paused and flushed, looking away guiltily before he went on. "I feel ugly asking you, when he's done so much to help us, but still, sometimes I think he took us in only because, well, only because of you. Because he wants you!"

"Chris, he's twenty-five years older than me. How can you think like that?"

Chris looked relieved. "You're right," he said. "You are his ward, and much too young. There must be plenty of beauties in those hospitals who'd be happy to be with him. I guess you're safe enough."

Smiling now, he pulled me gently into his embrace and lowered his lips to mine. Just a soft, tender kiss of good-bye-for-a-while. "I'm sorry about Christmas night," he said when our kiss was over.

My heart was an aching ruin as I backed off to leave him. How was I going to live without him nearby? Another thing *she'd* done to us. Made us care too much, when we should never have cared in the way we did. Her fault, always her fault! Everything gone wrong in our lives could be laid at her door!

"Don't overwork yourself, Chris, or soon you will be needing to wear glasses." He grinned, promised, made a reluctant gesture of farewell. Neither of us could manage to speak the word "good-bye." I spun about to run out, with tears in my eyes as I raced down the long halls, and then out into the bright sunshine. In Paul's white car I crouched down low and really sobbed, like Carrie when she bawled.

Suddenly Paul showed up from nowhere and silently took his place behind the wheel. He switched on the ignition, backed the car out and turned to head for the highway again. He didn't mention my reddened eyes or the sodden handkerchief I clutched in my hand to dab at the tears that kept coming. He didn't ask why I sat so silently when usually I teased, and gibed, and rattled on nonsensically just to keep from hearing silence. *Quiet, silence. Hear the feathers fall, listen to the house squeal. That was the attic gloom.*

Paul's strong, well-cared-for hands guided the car with an easy, casual skill, while he sat back relaxed. I studied his hands, for, next to a man's eyes, I noticed his hands. Then I moved my glance to his legs. Strong, well-shaped thighs which his tight, blue knit trousers showed up well, perhaps too well, for all of a sudden I wasn't sad, or gloomy, but felt an onrush of sensuality.

Giant trees lined the wide, black road, trees gnarled and dark, thick and ancient. "Bull Bay magnolias," said Paul. "It's a pity they aren't in bloom now, but it won't be too long. Our winters are short. One thing you must remember: never breathe on a magnolia blossom, or touch one; if you do it will wither and die." He threw me a teasing look so I couldn't tell whether or not he was speaking the truth.

"I used to dread turning onto my street, before you came with your brother and sister. I was always so alone. Now I drive home happily. It's good to feel happy again. Thank you, Cathy, for running south instead of north or west."

As soon as we got home Paul headed for his office and I headed upstairs to try to work off my loneliness by exercising at the barre. Paul didn't come home for dinner, and that made it even worse. He didn't show up after dinner either, so I went to bed early. All alone. I was all alone. Carrie was gone. My steadfast Christopher Doll, gone too. For the first time we were to sleep under separate roofs. I missed Carrie. I felt awful, afraid. I needed someone. The silence of the house and the deep dark of the night were screaming all about me. *Alone, alone, you are alone, and nobody cares, nobody cares.* I thought about food. I'd worried that I hadn't kept a big supply at hand. Then I remembered I needed some warm milk. Warm milk was supposed to help you fall asleep—and sleep was what I needed.

Enchantress . . . Me?

Soft firelight glowed in the living room. The gray logs had guttered into ashes in the hearth, and Paul, wrapped in his warm red robe, sat in a wing-backed chair and slowly drew on a pipe.

I gazed at his smoke-haloed head and saw someone warm, needing, wistful and yearning, as I yearned, and I wished. And being the fool I often was, I drifted toward him on bare feet that didn't make a sound. How nice he'd wear our gift so soon. I wore a gift from him—a soft, turquoise peignoir of airy fabric that floated over a gown of the same color.

He started to see me there, so near his chair, in the middle of the night, though he didn't speak to break the spell that was somehow binding us together in a mutual need.

There was a lot I didn't know about myself, nor did I understand what impulse lifted my hand to caress his cheek. His skin felt raspy, as if he needed a shave. He put his head back against the chair and tilted his face to mine.

"Why are you touching me, Catherine?"

His question was asked in a tight, cold voice, and I could

have felt rebuked and hurt, but his eyes were soft, limpid pools of desire, and I had seen desire before, only not in the kind of eyes he had. "Don't you like to be touched?"

"Not by a seductive young girl wearing flimsy clothes who is twenty-five years my junior."

"Twenty-four and seven months your junior," I corrected, "and my maternal grandmother married a man of fifty-five, when she was only sixteen."

"She was a fool and so was he."

"My mother said she made him a good wife," I added lamely.

"Why aren't you up in your bed asleep?" he snapped.

"I can't sleep. I guess I'm too excited about school tomorrow."

"Then you'd better go to bed so you'll be at your best."

I started to go, really I did, for the thought of warm milk was still in my head, but I had other thoughts, too, more seductive. "Dr. Paul . . ."

"I hate it when you call me that!" he interrupted. "Use my first name or don't speak to me at all."

"I feel I should show you the respect you deserve."

"A fig for respect! I'm not any different than other men. A doctor isn't infallible, Catherine."

"Why are you calling me Catherine?"

"Why shouldn't I call you Catherine? It's your name, and it sounds more grown up than Cathy."

"A moment or so ago, when I touched your cheek, you flared your eyes at me, as if you didn't want me to be grown up."

"You're a witch. In a second you change from a naive girl into a seductive, provocative woman—a woman who seems to know exactly what she's doing when she lays her hand on my face."

My eyes fled before the onslaught of his. I felt hot, uneasy, and wished now I'd gone directly to the kitchen. I stared at the fine books on the shelves and the miniature objects d'art he seemed to crave. Everywhere I looked was something to remind me that what he needed most was beauty.

"Catherine, I'm going to ask you something now that is none of my business, but I must ask. Just what is there between you and your brother?"

My knees began to click together nervously. *Oh, dear God, did it show on our faces?* Why did he have to ask? It wasn't any of his business. He had no right to ask such a question. Common sense and good judgment should have glued my tongue to the roof of my mouth and kept me from saying what I did in a shamed, lame way. "Would you be shocked to hear that when we were locked up in one room, always together, four of us, and each day was an eternity, that sometimes Chris and I didn't always think of ourselves as brother and sister? He attached a barre in the attic for me, so I could keep my muscles supple, so I could keep on believing someday I'd be a ballerina. And while I danced on that soft, rotten wood, he'd study in the attic schoolroom, poring for hours over old encyclopedias. He'd hear my dance music and come and stand in the shadows to watch. . . ."

"Go on," he urged when I paused. I stood with my head bowed, thinking backward, forgetting him. Then he suddenly leaned forward, seized hold of me and yanked me down onto his lap. "Tell me the rest."

I didn't want to tell him, yet his eyes were hot, demanding, making him seem a different person.

Swallowing first, I continued with reluctance, "Music has always done something special for me, even when I was small. It takes me over and lifts me up and makes me dance. And when I'm up there's no way to come down except by feeling love for someone. If you come down and feel your feet on the floor, and there's no one there to love, then you feel empty and lost. And I don't like to feel lost or empty."

"And so you danced in the attic, and dwelled in your fanciful imagination, and came back to the floor and found the only one there to love was your brother?" he said with icy heat, burning his eyes into mine. "Right? You had another kind of love you reserved for your little twins, didn't you? You were mother to them. I know that. I see that every time you look at Carrie and speak Cory's name. But what kind of love do you have for Christopher? Is it *motherly*? Sisterly? Or is it—" He paused, flushed, and shook me. "What did you do with your brother when you were locked up there, when you were alone?"

Seized by panic, I shook my head, and pushed his hands from my shoulders. "Chris and I were decent! We did the best we could!"

"'The best you could'?" he fired, looking hard and belligerent, as if the kindly, gentle man I knew had been only a disguise. "What the hell does that tell me?"

"All you need to know!" I flared back and flashed my eyes with temper as hot and red as his. "You accuse me of seducing you. That's what you're doing; you sit and you watch every move I make! You undress me with your eyes. You take me to bed with you with your eyes. You talk about ballet classes, and sending my brother to college and medical school, and all the while you imply that sooner or later you are going to demand your payment, and I know what kind of payment you want!" I took my hands and ripped open the peignoir so the skimpy bodice of the aqua nightgown was revealed. "Look at the kind of gift you gave me. Is this the kind of nightgown a girl of fifteen wears? No! It's the kind of gown a bride wears on her wedding night! And you gave it to me, and you saw Chris frown, and you didn't even have the decency to blush!"

His laughter mocked me. I smelled the strong red wine he liked to drink before retiring. His breath was hot on my face, his face very close to mine so I could see each strong dark hair that poked from his skin. It was the wine that made him act as he did, I thought. Only the wine. Any woman on his lap would serve—*any woman!* Teasingly he touched the peaks of both my nipples, skipping from one to the other, and then he dared to slip his hand beneath my bodice so he could fondle the young breasts that were fired with heat from his unexpected caresses. Then my nipples rose up hard and I was breathing just as heavily and fast as he was. "Would you undress for me, Catherine?" he whispered in a mocking way. "Would you sit naked on my lap and let me have my way with you? Or would you pick up that Venetian glass ashtray and crash it down on my head?"

He stared at me then, suddenly shocked to find his hand where it was, cupping my left breast, and he yanked his hand away as if my flesh burned him. He pulled the fabric of my frail peignoir together and hid what his hungry eyes had devoured before. He stared at my lips that were slightly parted and waiting to be kissed, and I think he planned to kiss me just before he gained control and shoved me away. At that moment thunder crashed overhead, and a lightning bolt sizzled jaggedly to crackle with fire as it struck a telephone wire outside. I jumped! Cried out!

As suddenly as he had withdrawn his hand, he snapped out of his fog and into what he was customarily—a detached, lonely man who was determined to keep himself aloof. How wise I was in my innocence to know this even before he snapped, "What the hell are you doing sitting on my lap half naked? Why did you let me do what I did?"

I didn't say anything. He was ashamed; I could see that now in the glow of the dying fire, and in the intermittent flashes of lightning. He was thinking all sorts of self condemning thoughts, chastising, berating, whipping himself—I knew it was my fault; as always it was my fault.

"I'm sorry, Catherine. I don't know what possessed me to do what I did."

"I forgive you."

"Why do you forgive me?"

"Because I love you."

Again he jerked his head into profile, and I couldn't see his eyes well enough to read them. "You don't love me," he said calmly, "you're only grateful for what I've done."

"I love you—and I'm yours, when, or if, you want me. And you can say you don't love me, but you'll be lying, for I see it in your eyes each time you look at me." I pressed closer against him and turned his face to mine. "When I was put away by Momma, I swore that when I was free, if love came and demanded of me I'd open my door and let it in. The first day I came I found love in your eyes. You don't have to marry me, just love me, when you need me."

He held me and we watched the storm. Winter fought with spring and finally conquered. Now it only hailed, and the thunder and lightning were gone, and I felt so . . . so right. We were much alike, he and I. "Why aren't you afraid of me?" he softly asked, as his big, gentle hands stroked my back, my hair. "You know you shouldn't be here, letting me hold you, touch you."

"Paul . . ." I began tentatively, "I'm not bad; neither is Chris. When we were locked away, we did do the best we could, honest. But we were locked in one room and growing up. The grandmother had a list of rules that forbade us to even look at each other and now I think I know why. Our eyes used to meet so often and without a word spoken he could comfort me, and he said my eyes did that for him too. That wasn't bad, was it?"

"I shouldn't have asked, and of course you had to look at each other. That's why we have eyes."

"Living like we did for so long, I don't know a lot about other girls my age, but ever since I was only table high, any kind of beauty has made me light up. Just to see the sun falling on the petals of a rose, or the way light shines through tree leaves and shows the veins, and the way rain on the road turns the oil iridescent, all that makes me feel beautiful. More than anything, when music is playing, especially my kind, ballet music, I don't need the sun or flowers or fresh air. I light up inside and wherever I am magically turns into marble palaces, or I am wild and free in the woods. I used to do that in the attic, and always just ahead a dark-haired man danced with me. We never touched, though we tried to.

I never saw his face, though I wanted to. I said his name once, but when I woke up I couldn't remember what it was. So, I guess I'm really in love with him, whoever he is. Every time I see a man with dark hair who moves gracefully I suspect he's the one."

He chuckled and twined his long fingers into my unbound hair. "My, what a romantic you are."

"You're making fun of me. You think I'm only a child. You think if you kissed me it wouldn't be exciting."

He grinned, accepted the challenge and slowly, slowly his head inclined until his lips met mine. Oh! So this was what it was like, a kiss from a stranger. Electric tingles sizzled madly up and down my arms, and all those nerves that a "child" my age wasn't supposed to have burned with fire! I drew away sharply, afraid. I was wicked, unholy, still the Devil's spawn!

And Chris would be shocked!

"What the hell are we doing?" he barked, coming out of the spell I'd cast. "What kind of little devil are you to let me handle you intimately and kiss you? You are very beautiful, Catherine, but you are only a child." Some realization darkened his eyes as he guessed at my motives. "Now get this straight in your pretty head—you don't owe me, not anything! What I do for you, for your brother and sister, I do willingly, gladly, without expecting any repayment—of any kind—do you understand?"

"But . . . but . . ." I sputtered. "I've always hated it when the rain beats hard and the wind blows at night. This is the first time I've felt warm and protected, here, with you, before the fire."

"Safe?" he teased lightly. "You think you're safe with me, as you sit on my lap, and kiss me like that? What do you think I'm made of?"

"The same as other men, only better."

"Catherine," Paul said, his voice softer and kinder now, "I've made so many mistakes in my life, and you three give me an opportunity to redeem myself. If I so much as lay a hand on you again, I want you to scream for help. If no one is here, then run to your room, or pick up something and bash me over the head."

"Ooh," I whispered, "and I thought you loved me!" Tears trickled down my cheeks. I felt like a child again, chastised for presuming too much. How foolish to have believed love was already knocking on my door. I sulked as he lifted me away from him. Then he gently lifted me to my feet, but kept his hands on my waist as he looked up into my face.

"My God, but you are beautiful and desirable," he said with a sigh. "Don't tempt me too much, Catherine—for your own good."

"You don't have to love me." My head bowed to hide my face and my hair was something to hide behind as I shamelessly said, "Just use me when you need me, and that will be enough."

He leaned back in the chair and took his hands from my waist. "Catherine, don't ever let me hear you offer such a thing again. You live in fairyland, not reality. Little girls get hurt when they play grown-up games. You save yourself for the man you marry—but for God's sake, wait to grow up first. Don't rush into having sex with the first man who desires you."

I backed off, scared of him now, while he stood to come within arm's reach. "Beautiful child, the eyes of Clairmont are fixed upon you and me, wondering, speculating. I don't have a gilt-edged reputation. So, for the health of my medical practice and the good of my soul and conscience stay away from me. I'm only a man, not a saint."

Again I backed off, scared. I flew up the stairs as if pursued. For he wasn't, after all, the kind of man I wanted. Not him, a doctor, perhaps a womanizer—the last kind of man who could fulfill my dreams of faithful, devoted and forever-green-springtime-romantic love!

The school Paul sent me to was big and modern with an indoor swimming pool. My schoolmates thought I looked good and talked funny, like a Yankee. They laughed at the way I said "water, father, farther" or any word that had an "a" in it. I didn't like being laughed at. I didn't like being different. I wanted to be like the others, and though I tried I found out I was different. How could it be otherwise? She had made me different. I knew Chris was feeling lonely in his school because he too was an alien in a world that had gone on without us. I was fearful for Carrie in her school, all alone, made different too. Damn Momma for doing so much to set us apart, so we couldn't blend into the crowd and talk as they did and believe as they did. I was an outsider, and in every way they could all my schoolmates made me feel it.

Only one place made me feel I belonged. Straight from my high school classes I'd catch a bus and ride to ballet class, toting my bag with leotards, *pointes*, and a small handbag tucked inside. In the dressing room the girls shared all their secrets. They told ridiculous jokes, sexy stories, some of them even lewd. Sex was in the air, all around us, breathing hotly and demandingly down our necks. Girlishly, foolishly, they discussed whether they should save their bodies for their husbands. Should they pet with clothes on or off—or go "all the way"—and how did they stop a guy after they had "innocently" turned him on?

Because I felt so much wiser than the others I didn't contribute anything. If I dared to speak of my past, of those years when I was living "nowhere" and the love that had sprung up from barren soil, I could imagine how their eyes would pop! I couldn't blame them. No, I didn't blame anyone but the one who'd made it all happen! Momma!

One day I ran home from the bus stop and dashed off a long, venomous letter to my mother—and then I didn't know where to send it. I put it aside until I found out the address in Greenglenna. One thing for sure, I didn't want her to know where we lived. Though she had received the petition, it didn't have Paul's name on it, or our address, only the address of the judge. Sooner or later though, she'd hear from me and be sorry she did.

Each day we began bundled up in heavy, woolen, knitted leg-warmers, and at the barre we exercised until our blood flowed fast and hot and we could discard the woolens as we began to sweat. Our hair, screwed up tight as old ladies' who scrubbed floors, soon became wet too, so we showered two or three times a day—when we worked out eight or ten hours on Saturdays. The barre was not meant for holding onto tightly, but was meant only for balance, to help us develop control, grace. We did the *plié's*, the *tendus*, and *glissés*, the *fondus*, the *ronds de jambe a terre*—and none of it was easy. Sometimes the pain of rotating the hips in the turnouts could make me scream. Then came the *frappes* on three-quarter *pointe*, the *ronds de jambe en l'air*, the *petite* and *grande battlements*, the *developpes* and all the warm-up exercises to make our muscles long, strong and supple. Then we left the barre and used the center arena to repeat all of that without the aid of the barre.

And that was the easy part—from there on the work became increasingly difficult, demanding technical skills awesomely painful to do.

To hear I was good, even excellent, lifted me sky-high . . . so there had been some benefits gained from dancing in the attic, dancing even when I was dying, so I thought as *pliéd un, deux,* and on and on as Georges pounded on the old upright piano. And then there was Julian.

Something kept drawing him back to Clairmont. I thought his visits were only ego trips so we could sit in a circle on the floor and watch him perform in the center, showing off his superior virtuosity, his spinning turns that were blurrily fast. His incredible, leaping elevations defied gravity, and from these *grand jetés* he'd land goose-down soft. He cornered me to tell me it was "his" kind of dancing that added so much excitement to the performance.

"Really, Cathy, you haven't seen ballet until you see it done in New York." He yawned as if bored and turned his bold, jet eyes on Norma Belle in her skimpy see-through, white leotards. Quickly I asked why, if New York was the best place to be, he kept coming back to Clairmont so often.

"To visit with my mother and father," he said with a certain indifference. "Madame is my mother, you know."

"Oh, I didn't know that."

"Of course not. I don't like to boast about it." He smiled then, devastatingly wicked. "Are you still a virgin?" I told him it was none of his business and that made him laugh again. "You're too good for this hick place, Cathy. You're different. I can't put my finger on it, but you make the other girls look clumsy, dull. What's your secret?"

"What's yours?"

He grinned and put his hand flat on my breast. "I'm great, that's all. The best there is. Soon all the world will know it." Angry, I slapped his hand away. I stomped down on his foot and backed away. "Stop it!"

Suddenly, as quickly as he'd cornered me, he lost all interest and walked away to leave me staring.

Most days I'd go straight home from class and spend the evening with Paul. He was so much fun to be with when he wasn't tired. He told me about his patients without naming them, and told tales of his childhood, and how he'd always wanted to be a doctor, just like Chris. Soon after dinner he'd have to leave to make his rounds at three local hospitals, including one in Greenglenna. I'd try and help Henny after dinner while I waited for Paul to come back. Sometimes we watched TV, and sometimes he took me to a movie. "Before you came, I never went to movies."

"Never?" I asked.

"Well, almost never," he said. "I did have a few dates before you came, but since you've been here my time just seems to disappear. I don't know what uses it all up."

"Talking to me," I told him, teasing with my finger that I trailed along his closely shaven cheek. "I think I know more about you than I know about anyone else in the world, except Chris and Carrie."

"No," he said in a tight voice, "I don't tell you everything."

"Why not?"

"You don't need to know all my dark secrets."

"I've told you all my dark secrets, and you haven't turned away from me."

"Go to bed, Catherine!"

I jumped up and ran over to him and kissed his cheek, which was very red. Then I dashed for the stairs. When I was at the top, I turned to see him at the newel post, staring upward, as if the sight of my legs under the short, rose, baby-doll nightie fascinated him.

"And don't run around the house in such things!" he called to me. "You should wear a robe."

"Doctor, you brought this outfit to me. I didn't think you'd want me to cover myself. I thought you wanted to see me with it on."

"You think too much."

In the mornings I was up early, before six, so I could eat breakfast with him. He liked me to be there, though he didn't say so. Nevertheless, I could tell. I had him bewitched, charmed. I was learning more and more how to be like Momma.

I think he tried to avoid me, but I didn't let him. He was the one to teach me what I needed to know.

His room was down the hall from mine, but I never dared to go to him at night as I had to Chris. I longed for Chris and for Carrie. When I woke up, I ached not to see them in the room beside me; I ached more not to see them at the breakfast table, and if Paul hadn't been there, I think I might have started off each and every day with tears instead of forced smiles.

"Smile for me, my Catherine," Paul said one morning when I sat staring down at my plate of grits and scrambled eggs and bacon. I looked up, caught by something I heard in his voice, something wistful, as if he needed me.

"Don't ever say my name like that again," I said hoarsely. "Chris used to call me his lady Cath-er-ine, and I don't like to hear anyone else call me his Catherine."

He didn't say anything more, just laid aside the newspaper, got up and went out to the garage. From there he'd drive to the hospitals, then back to his home offices, and I wouldn't see him again until dinner time. I didn't see enough of him, never enough of anyone I cared about.

Only on the weekends, when Chris and Carrie were home, did he seem really at ease with me. And yet, when Chris and Carrie were back in their schools, something would come between us, some subtle spark that revealed that he was just as attracted to me as I was to him. I wondered if the real reason was the same as my own. Was he trying to escape memories of his Julia by letting me into his heart? Just as I was trying to escape Chris?

But my shame was worse than his, or so I thought then. I thought I was the only one with a dark, ugly past. I never dreamed anyone as fine and noble as Paul could have ugliness in his life too.

Only two weeks passed and Julian flew down from New York again. This time he made it very obvious he'd come just to see me. I felt flattered and a little awkward, for he'd already gained success, while I was still only hoping. He had an old ricky-tin car he said had cost him nothing but his time, for all the pieces had come from the junkyard. "Next to dancing, I love to tinker with cars," he explained as he drove me home from dance class. "Someday, when I'm rich, I'm going to have luxury cars, three or four, or maybe seven, one for each day of the week."

I laughed; it sounded so outrageous and ostentatious. "Does dancing pay that much?"

"It will when I hit the big-time money," he answered confidentially. I had to turn my head and stare at his handsome profile. If you took his features apart one by one, you could find fault with them, for his nose could have been better, and his skin needed more color, and perhaps his lips were too full and red, and too sensual. But when he was put all together, he was sensational looking. "Cathy," he began, throwing me a long look as his tinny car chugged and choked along, "you'd love New York. There's so much to do, so much to see and experience. That doctor you live with isn't your real father, you shouldn't stick around just to please him. Think about moving to New York as soon as possible." He put his arm about my shoulders to draw me closer to his side. "What a team we'd make, you and I," he said softly, cajolingly, and painted for me bright pictures of what our life would be like in New York. Clearly he made me understand I'd be under his wing, and in his bed.

"I don't know you," I answered, pulling away to sit as far from him as possible. "I don't know your past, and you don't know mine. We're nothing at all alike, and though you flatter me with your attention you also scare me."

"Why? I won't rape you."

I hated him for saying that. It wasn't rape I was afraid of. In fact I didn't know what made me afraid of him, unless I was more afraid of myself when I was with him. "Tell me who you are, Julian Marquet. Tell me about your childhood, your parents. Tell me why you think you are God's gift to the dance world and to every woman you meet."

Casually he lit up a cigarette, which he wasn't supposed to do. "Let me take you out tonight and I'll give you all the answers you want."

We'd reached the big house on Bellefair Drive. He parked in front, while I stared toward the windows softly lit in the rosy twilight glow. I could barely discern the dark shadow of Henny who peered out to see who was parking in front of her home. I thought of Paul, but more than anyone else I thought of Chris, my better half. Would Chris approve of Julian? I didn't think he would, and still I said yes, I'd date him that night. And what a night it turned out to be.

My First Date

I was hesitant about bringing up the subject of Julian to Paul. It was Saturday night; Chris and Carrie were home, and, truthfully, I'd just as soon have gone to a movie with them and Paul. It was with great reluctance that I brought up the fact I had a date with Julian Marquet. "Tonight, Paul, you don't mind, do you?"

He flashed me a tired look and a weak smile. "I think it's about time you started dating. He's not too much older, is he?"

"No," I whispered, feeling a little disappointed that he didn't object.

Julian showed up promptly at eight. He was slicked up in a new suit, with his shoes shined, his unruly hair tamed, his manners so perfect he didn't seem himself. He shook hands with Paul, leaned to kiss Carrie's cheek. Chris glared at him. The two had been bicycling when I'd told Paul about my first date, and even as Julian held my new spring coat I felt Chris's disapproval.

He drove to a very elegant restaurant where colored lights churned and rock music played. With surprising confidence Julian read the wine list, then tasted what the waiter brought and nodded, saying it was fine. This was all so new to me I felt on edge, afraid of making a mistake. Julian handed me a menu. My hands trembled so much I turned it over to him and asked him to select. I couldn't read French, and it seemed he could from the speedy way he chose our meal. When the salad and main course came it was just as good as he'd promised.

I was wearing a new dress, cut low in front and much too old for a girl of my age. I wanted to appear sophisticated, even though I wasn't.

"You're beautiful," he said, while I was thinking the same thing about him. My heart felt funny, as if I were betraying someone. "Much too beautiful to be stuck here in Hicktown for years on end while my mother exploits your talents. I'm not a male lead like I told you before, Cathy; I'm second string in the *corps*. I wanted to impress you, but I know if I had you with me, as my partner, both of us could make it big. There's a certain magic between us I've never had with another dancer. Of course you'd have to begin in the *corps*. But soon enough Madame Zolta would see your talent far surpasses your age and experience. She's an old crow, but no dummy. Cathy, I've danced my head off to get where I am—but I could make it easier for you. With me to back you up you'll make it quicker than I did. Together we'd make a sensational team. Your fairness complements my darkness; it's the perfect foil." And on and on he talked, half-convincing me I was great already, when a certain part of me knew deep down I wasn't that sensational, and not nearly good enough for New York. And there was Chris whom I couldn't see if I went to New York, and Carrie who needed me on the weekends. And Paul, he fit in my life somewhere, I knew he fit somewhere. The problem was— where?

Julian wined and dined me, then danced me out onto the

floor. Soon we were dancing to rock like no one else in the place could. Everyone drew back just to watch, then applaud. I was giddy with the nearness of him and the amount of wine I'd consumed. On the way home Julian drove onto a secluded lane where lovers parked to make out. I'd never made out and wasn't ready for someone as overwhelming as Julian.

"Cathy, Cathy, Cathy," he murmured, kissing my neck, behind my ears, while his hand sought to stroke my upper thigh.

"Stop!" I cried. "Don't! I don't know you well enough! You go too fast!"

"You're acting so childish," he said with annoyance. "I fly all the way from New York just to be with you, and you can't even let me kiss you."

"Julian!" I stormed, "take me home!"

"A kid," he muttered angrily and turned on the ignition. "Just a damned beautiful kid who tantalizes but won't come through. Wise up, Cathy. I'm not going to hang around forever."

He was in my world, my dancing, glamorous world, and suddenly I was afraid of losing him. "Why do you call yourself Marquet when your father's name is Rosencoff?" I asked, reaching to turn off the ignition.

He smiled and leaned back, then turned to me. "Okay, if you want to talk. I think you and I are a lot alike, even if you won't admit it. Madame and Georges are my mother and father, but they have never seen me as a son, especially my father. My father sees me as an extension of himself. If I become a great dancer, it won't be to my credit; it will be just because I am *his* son and bear *his* name. So I put an end to that idea by changing my name. I made it up, just like any performer does when he wants to change his name.

"You know how many baseball games I've played? None! They wouldn't let me. Football was out of the question. Besides, they kept me so busy practicing ballet positions,

I was too tired for anything else. Georges never let me call him Father when I was little. After a while I wouldn't call him Father if he got down on his knees and begged. I tried my damndest to please him, and I never could. He'd always find some flaw, some minute mistake I'd made to keep any performance from being perfect. So, when I make it, I'm making it on my own steam, and nobody is going to know he is my father! Or that Marisha is my mother. So don't go shooting off your mouth to the rest of the class. They don't know. Isn't it funny? I throw a tantrum if he even dares to mention he has a son, and I refuse to dance. That kills him, so he let me go on to New York, thinking I wouldn't make it without his name. But I have made it, and without his help. I think that kills him. Now tell me about you. Why are you living with that doctor and not your own parents?"

"My parents are dead," I said, annoyed he'd ask. "Dr. Paul was a friend of my father, so he took us in. He felt sorry for us and didn't want us to go into an orphanage."

"Lucky you," he said with a certain sourness. "*I'd* never be so lucky." Then he leaned over until his forehead was pressed against mine and our lips were only inches apart. I could feel his breath hot on my face. "Cathy, I don't want to say and do anything wrong with you. I want to make you the best thing that's ever happened to me. I am thirteenth in a long line of male dancers who have married ballerinas, most of them. How do you think that makes me feel? Not lucky, you can bet. I've been in New York since I was eighteen, and last February I turned twenty. That's two years, and still I'm not a star. With you I could be. I've got to prove to Georges I'm the best, and better than he ever was. I've never told anyone this before, but I hurt my back when I was a kid, trying to lift an engine that was too heavy. It bothers me all the time, but still I dance on. And it's not just because you're small and don't weigh much. I know other dancers who are smaller and lighter, but something about your proportions seems to balance just right when I lift. Or maybe it's what you do to your body that adjusts to my hands. . . . Whatever it is you do, you fit me to a tee. Cathy, come with me to New York, please."

"You wouldn't take advantage of me if I did?"

"I'd be your guardian angel."

"New York is so big. . . ."

"I know it like the palm of my hand. Soon you'll know it just as well."

"There's my sister and my brother. I don't want to leave them yet."

"Eventually you'll have to. The longer you stay the harder it will be to make the break. Grow up, Cathy, be your own person. You never are when you stay home and let others dominate you." He looked away, his scowl bitter. I felt sorry for him, and touched too.

"Maybe. Let me think about it more."

Chris was on the upper veranda outside my bedroom when I went in to undress. When I saw him out there in his pajamas, his slouched shoulders drew me to him.

"How'd it go?" he asked without looking at me.

Nervously my hands fluttered around. "Okay, I guess. We had wine with dinner. Julian got a little drunk, I think. Maybe I did too."

He turned to stare in my eyes. "I don't like him, Cathy! I wish he'd stay in New York and leave you alone! From what I hear from all the girls or boys in your dance company, Julian has claimed you so now no other dancer will ask you out. Cathy, he's from New York. Those guys up there move fast, and you're only fifteen!" He moved to cradle me in his arms.

"Who are you dating?" I asked with a sob in my throat. "Don't tell me you're not seeing any girls."

His cheek was against mine when he answered slowly, "There's no girl I've met who can compare to you."

"How are your studies going?" I asked, hoping to take his mind off me.

"Great. When I'm not thinking of all I have to do in the first year of med school—gross anatomy, micro-anatomy and neuroanatomy—I get around to prepping for college."

"What do you do in your spare time?"

"What spare time? There's none left when I finish worrying about what's happening to you! I like school, Cathy. I'd really enjoy it if you weren't constantly on my mind. I wait for the weekends when I can see you and Carrie again."

"Oh, Chris . . . you've got to try to forget me and find someone else."

But just one long look into his tortured eyes revealed that what had been started so long ago wasn't going to be easy to stop.

I had to try to find someone else and then he'd know it was over, forever over. My thoughts took wing to Julian who was striving so to prove himself a better dancer than his father. How like me, who had to be better in all ways than my mother.

I was ready the next time Julian flew down. When he asked me for a date, this time I didn't hedge. It might as well be him; we did have the same goals. Then, after the movie and a soft drink in a club for me, and beer for him, he again drove to the lover's lane every city seemed to have. I allowed him this time to do a bit more than just kiss me, but too soon he was breathing hot and fast, and touching me with so much expertise that soon I was responding even when I didn't want to. He pushed me back on the seat. Suddenly I realized what he was about to do—and I grabbed up my handbag and began to beat him on his face. "Stop! I told you before, go slower!"

"You asked for it!" he raged. "You can't lead me on, then turn me off. I despise a tease."

I thought of Chris and began to cry. "Julian, please. I like you, honest I do. But you don't give me a chance to fall in love with you. Please stop coming at me so fast."

He seized my arm and ruthlessly twisted it behind my back until I cried out from the pain. I thought he meant to break it. But he released it just when I was about to scream.

"Look, Cathy. I'm half in love with you already. But no girl strings me along like I'm some country bumpkin. There are plenty of girls willing to give out—so I don't need you as much as I thought—not for anything!"

Of course he didn't need me. Nobody really needed me but Chris and Carrie, though Chris needed me in the wrong way. Momma had twisted and warped him, and turned him toward me, and now he couldn't turn away. I couldn't forgive her for that. She had to pay for everything wrong she'd caused. If he and I had sinned, *she had made us.*

I thought and thought that night of how I could make Momma pay, and I came up with the exact price that would hurt most. It wouldn't be money, she had too much of that. It would have to be something she prized more than money. Two things—her honorable reputation which was a bit tarnished from marrying her half-uncle, and her young husband. Both would be gone when I was through with her.

Then I was crying. Crying for Chris, for Carrie who didn't grow and for Cory who was by now, probably, only bones in his grave.

I turned over to grope for Carrie, reaching to draw her into my arms. But Carrie was in a private school for girls, ten miles outside the city limits. Chris was thirty miles away.

It began to rain hard. The staccato beats on the roof overhead were military drums to take me into dreams and back to exactly where I didn't want to go. I was dumped down in a locked room cluttered with toys and games and massive, dark furniture, and pictures of hell on the walls. I sat in an old wooden rocker, half coming apart, and on my lap I held a ghostly, small brother who called me Momma, and on and on we rocked, and the floorboards creaked, and the wind blew, and the rain pelted down, and below us, around us, above us, the enormous house of countless rooms was waiting to eat us up.

I hated the rain so close above my head, like it used to be when we were upstairs. How much worse our lives had been when it rained, and the room was damp and chill, and in the attic there was nothing but miserable gloom and dead faces that lined the wall. Bands like the grandmother's gray iron came to tighten about my head, smothering my thoughts, making me confused and terrified.

Unable to sleep, I left the bed and slipped on a filmy negligee. For some curious reason I stole to Paul's bedroom and cautiously eased open his closed door. The alarm clock on his nightstand read two o'clock—and still he wasn't home! Nobody in the house but Henny who was so far, far away—way at the other end of the house in her room adjacent to the kitchen.

I shook my head and stared again at Paul's smoothly made bed. Oh, Chris was crazy to want to be a doctor! He'd never have a full night's rest. And it was raining. Accidents happened so often on rainy nights. What if Paul should be killed? What would we do then! *Paul, Paul*, I screamed to myself as I raced toward the stairs and flew down them, then sped on to where I could peer out the French windows in the living room. I hoped to see a white car parked in the drive, or turning into the drive. God, I prayed, don't let him have an accident! Please, please—don't take him like you took Daddy!

"Cathy, why aren't you in bed?"

I whirled about. There was Paul sitting comfortably in his favorite chair, puffing on a cigarette in the dark. There was just enough light to see he wore the red robe we'd given him for Christmas. I was so overwhelmed with relief to see him safe and not spread out dead on a morgue slab. Morbid thoughts. *Daddy, I can barely remember how you looked, or how your voice sounded, and the special smell of you has faded away.*

"Is something wrong, Catherine?"

Wrong? Why did he call me Catherine at night when we

were alone, and only Cathy during the day? *Everything* was wrong! The Greenglenna newspapers and the Virginia one I'd subscribed to and had delivered to my ballet school both told stories of how Mrs. Bartholomew Winslow would make her second "winter" home in Greenglenna. Extensive renovation was being done so her husband's home would be as it was when it was new. Only the best for my mother! For some reason I couldn't fathom I lit into Paul like a shrew. "How long have you been home?" I demanded sharply. "I've been upstairs worrying about you so much I can't sleep! And here you were, all the time! You missed your dinner; you missed last night's dinner; you were supposed to take me out to a movie last night and you forgot all about it! I finished my homework early, dressed in my best clothes and sat around waiting for you to show up, and you forgot it! Why do you let your patients make so many demands on your time so you don't have a life of your own?"

For a long time he didn't answer. Then when my lips parted to speak again, he said in a mild tone, "You really do sound upset. I guess the only excuse I can offer is to say I'm a doctor, and a doctor's time is never his own. I'm sorry I forgot about the movie. I apologize for not calling and telling you there was an emergency and I couldn't leave."

"Forget—how could you forget? Yesterday you forgot to bring the things I had on my list, so after I waited for hours on end for you to come home I sat around thinking you might come home and bring me the shampoo I wanted, *but you didn't!"*

"I'm sorry again. Sometimes I have things on my mind other than movies and the cosmetics you need."

"Are you being sarcastic?"

"I am trying to control my temper. It would be nice if you could control yours."

"I'm not mad!" I shouted. He was so like Momma, so much in control, so poised, when I never was! He didn't care. That's why he could sit there and look at me like that! He didn't really care if he made promises and broke them—like her! I ran forward as if to strike him, but he caught my fists and stared up at me in utter surprise. "Would you hit me, Catherine? Does missing a movie mean so much to you that you can't understand how I could forget? Now say you're sorry for screaming at me, as I said I was sorry for disappointing you."

What tortured me was more than mere disappointment! Nowhere was there anyone I could depend on—only Chris who was forbidden to me. Only Chris who would never forget anything I needed or wanted.

I shuddered. Oh, what kind of person was I? Was I so like Momma I had to have what I wanted, when I wanted, no matter what the cost to others? Was I going to make Paul pay for what she'd done? None of it was his fault. "Paul, I am sorry I yelled at you. I do understand."

"You must be very tired. Perhaps you take your ballet classes too seriously. Maybe you should let up a little."

How could I tell him I couldn't let up? I had to be the best, and to be the best at anything meant hours and hours of work. I fully intended to give up all the pastimes other girls my age enjoyed. I didn't want a boyfriend who wasn't a dancer. I didn't want any girlfriends who didn't dance. I didn't want anything to come between me and my goal, and yet, and yet . . . sitting there, looking up at me, was a man who said he needed me, and who was hurt by the hateful way I'd acted.

"I read about my mother today," I said lamely, "and a house she's having remodeled and redecorated. She always gets what she wants. I never get anything. So I act ugly to you and forget all that you've done." I backed off a few feet, aching with the shame I felt. "How long have you been home?"

"Since eleven-thirty," he answered. "I ate the salad and the steak Henny left for me in the warming oven. But I don't sleep well when I'm exceptionally tired. And I don't like the sound of the rain on the roof."

"Because the rain shuts you off and makes you feel lonely?"

He half-smiled. "Yeah, something like that. How did you know?"

How he felt was all over his face as dim as it was in that big room. He was thinking of her, his Julia, his dead wife. Always he looked sad when Julia was on his mind. I approached his chair and impulsively reached out to touch his cheek. "Why do you have to smoke? How can you tell your patients to quit the habit and keep on smoking yourself?"

"How do you know what I tell my patients?" he asked in that soft voice, in a way that tingled my spine. Nervously I laughed, telling him he didn't always close his office door tight, and if I happened to be in the back hall, sometimes, despite my will, I couldn't help overhearing a few things. He told me to go to bed and stop hanging around in the back hall where I didn't belong—and he'd smoke if he wanted to smoke.

"Sometimes you act like a wife, asking such questions, getting angry at me for forgetting to stop at the drugstore for you. Are you sure you didn't desperately need that shampoo?"

Now he had me feeling a fool, and again I was angry. "I only asked you to get those things because you pass by a discount store where everything is cheaper! I was just trying to save money! From now on I'll never ask you to pick up anything I need! When you invite me to dinner in a restaurant, or to a movie, I'll be prepared to be disappointed, and that way I won't be disappointed. I might as well get used to expecting the worst from everyone."

"Catherine! You can hate me if that's what you want make me pay for everything you have suffered, and then, perhaps, you can go to sleep at night and not toss and turn and cry out in your sleep, and call for your mother like a child of three."

Stunned, I stared at him. "I call out for *her*?"

"Yes," he said, "many, many times I've heard you call for your mother." I saw the pity in his eyes. "Don't be ashamed of being human, Catherine. We all expect only the best from our mothers."

I didn't want to talk about her, so I stepped nearer. "Julian is back in town. I went out with him tonight since you stood me up last night. Julian thinks I'm ready for New York. He thinks his dance instructor, Madame Zolta, would develop me quicker than his mother. He thinks together we'd make a brilliant team."

"And what do *you* think?"

"I think I'm not ready for New York yet," I whispered, "but he comes on so strong, sometimes he makes me believe, because he seems so convinced."

"Go slowly, Catherine. Julian is a handsome young man, with arrogance enough for ten men. Use your own good common sense and don't be influenced by someone who might only want to use you."

"I dream every night of being in New York, on stage. I see my mother in the audience staring up at me with disbelieving eyes. She wanted to kill me. I want her to see me dance and realize I have more to give the world than she does."

He winced. "Why do you need revenge so much? I thought if I took you three in and did the best I could for you, you'd find peace and forgiveness. Can't you forgive and forget? If there's one chance we poor humans have of reaching godliness, it's in learning to forgive and forget."

"*You* and Chris," I said bitterly. "It's easy for you to talk about forgiving and forgetting—because you haven't been a victim, and I have. I've lost my younger brother who was like my own son. I loved Cory, and she stole away his life. *I hate her for that!* I hate her for ten million reasons—so don't talk to me about forgiving and forgetting—when she's got to pay for what she did! She lied to us, betrayed us in the worse possible way! She said nothing to let us know our grandfather had died, and kept right on letting us stay locked up—for nine long, long months—and in those long months we were eating poisoned doughnuts! So don't you dare talk to me of forgiving and forgetting! I don't know how to forgive and forget! All I know how to do is hate! And you don't know what it's like to hate as I do!"

"Don't I?" he asked in a flat voice.

"*No*, you don't know!"

He drew me down on his lap when I sobbed and tears streamed down my face. He comforted me as a father would, with little kisses and kind, stroking hands. "Catherine, I've got a story of my own to tell. Maybe in some ways it equals the horror of yours. Maybe if I tell you you'll be able to use some of what I've learned."

I stared up into his face. His arms held me lightly as I leaned back. "Are you going to tell me about Julia and Scotty?"

"Yes." A hard edge toned his voice. His eyes fixed on the rain-washed windows, and his hand that found mine squeezed tight. "You think only your mother commits crimes against those she loves—well, you're wrong. It's done every day. Sometimes it's done to gain money, but there are other reasons." He paused, sighed, then went on. "I hope when you've heard my story, you can go to bed tonight and forget about vengeance. If you don't you'll hurt yourself more than anyone else."

I didn't believe that because I didn't want to believe that. But I was eager enough to hear the tale of how Julia and Scotty both died on the same day.

When Paul began to speak of Julia, I feared the ending. I squeezed my eyelids closed, wishing now my ears didn't have to hear, for I didn't need more to add to the anguish I already felt for one little dead boy. But he did it for my sake, to save me, as if anything could.

"Julia and I were childhood sweethearts. She never had another boyfriend; I never had another girlfriend. Julia belonged to me, and I let every other boy know it. I never gave myself, or her, the chance to experience what others were like—and that was a terrible mistake. We were foolish enough to believe our love would last forever.

"We went steady, we wrote love letters to each other though she lived only a few blocks away. The older Julia grew, the more beautiful she became. I thought I was the luckiest guy in the world, and she thought I was perfect. We both had each other up on pedestals. She was going to be the perfect doctor's wife, and I was going to be the perfect husband, and we'd have three children. Julia was an only child, and her parents doted on her. She adored her father; she used to say I was like him." His voice deepened here, as if what he had to say was very painful.

"I put an engagement ring on Julia's finger the day she was eighteen. I was nineteen at the time. When I was in college, I'd think of her back here and wonder what man had his eye on her. I was afraid I'd lose her to someone else if we didn't marry. So at age nineteen she married me. I was twenty."

His voice turned bitter while his eyes went blank, and his arms tightened about me. "Julia and I had kissed many times, and we always held hands, but she would never let me do anything truly intimate—that had to wait until she had a wedding band on her finger. I'd had a few sexual encounters, not many. She was a virgin and thought I was. I didn't take my marriage vows lightly, and I meant to be exactly the kind of husband who'd make her happy. I loved her very much. So, on our wedding night, she took two hours to undress in the bathroom. She came out of the bathroom wearing a long white gown, and her face was as white as that gown. I could tell she was terrified. I convinced myself I would be so tender, so loving, she would enjoy being my wife.

"She didn't enjoy sex, Cathy. I did the best I could to arouse her, while she cringed back with her eyes wide and full of shock, and then she screamed when I tried to take off her nightgown. I stopped and thought I'd try again the next night, after she pleaded for me to give her more time. The next night it was the same thing all over again, only worse. 'Why, why can't you just lie here and hold me?' she asked tearfully. 'Why does it have to be so ugly?'

"I was just a kid myself, and didn't know how to handle a situation like that. I loved her, and I wanted her, and in the end I raped her—or so she said time and again. Still I loved her. I'd loved her most of my life and couldn't believe I'd made the wrong choice. So I began to read every book on love-making I could find, and I tried all the techniques to arouse her and make her want me—and she was only repulsed. I took to drinking after I graduated from medical school, and when I felt like it I found some other woman who was glad to have me in her bed. The years passed while she held herself aloof, cleaned my house, washed my clothes, ironed my shirts and sewed on my missing buttons. She was so lovely, so desirable and so near that sometimes I'd force her, even if she cried afterward. Then, she found out she was pregnant. I was delighted, and I think she was too. Never was a child more loved and pampered than my son, and, fortunately, he was the kind of child who couldn't be spoiled by too much love."

His voice took on an even deeper register while I huddled closer in his arms, fearing what was to come, for I knew it would be terrible.

"After Scotty's birth Julia told me flatly she'd done her duty and given me a son, and that from now on I was to leave her alone. Gladly I left her alone, but I was deeply wounded. I talked to her mother about our problem, and her mother hinted at some dark secret in Julia's past, a cousin of hers who'd done something to Julia when she was only four. I never learned just what he'd done, but whatever it was, it spoiled sex forever for my wife. I suggested to Julia we should both visit a marriage counselor or a psychologist but she'd have none of that—it would be too embarrassing—why couldn't I leave her alone?

"I did leave her alone after that," he went on. "There are always women around willing to accommodate a man, and in my office I had a lovely receptionist who let me know she was more than available, anytime anyplace. We had an affair that lasted several years. I thought we were both very discreet, and no one knew. Then one day she came and told me she was pregnant with my child. I couldn't believe her, for she'd told me she was on the pill. I couldn't even believe the child was mine since I knew she had other lovers. So I said no, I couldn't divorce my wife and risk losing Scotty to father a child who might not be mine. She blew up.

"I went home that evening to confront a wife I'd never known before. Julia lashed out at me for being unfaithful, when she'd done the best she could and given me the son I wanted. And now I'd betrayed her, broken my vow and made her the laughing stock of the town! She threatened to kill herself. I pitied her as she screamed out *she'd make me hurt!* She'd threatened suicide before but she'd never done anything.

"I thought this blow-up would clear the air between us. Julia never spoke to me again about my affair. In fact she stopped speaking to me at all except when Scotty was around, for she wanted him to have a normal home with ostensibly happy parents. I had given her a son she loved beyond reason.

"Then came June and Scotty's third birthday. She planned a party for him and invited six small guests, who naturally had to bring along their mothers as well. It was on a Saturday. I was home, and to help calm Scotty, who was very excited about his party, I gave him a sailboat to go with the sailor suit he was going to wear. Julia came down the stairs with him, dressed in blue voile. Her lovely dark hair was bound back with a blue satin ribbon. Scotty clung to his mother's hand, and in his free hand he carried the sailboat. Julia told me she was afraid she hadn't bought enough candy for party, and it was such a beautiful day that she and Scotty would walk to the nearest drugstore and buy some more. I offered to drive her there. She refused. I offered to walk along with them. She said she didn't want me to. She wanted me to wait and be there in case any of the guests arrived early. I sat down on the front veranda and waited. Inside, the dining table was all set for the for party, with balloons suspended from the chandelier, and snappers, hats and other favors, and Henny had made a huge cake.

"The guests began to arrive around two. And still Julia and Scotty didn't return. I began to worry so I got in my car and drove to the drugstore, expecting to see them on the sidewalk leading home. I didn't see them. I asked the druggist if they'd been there; none of the clerks had seen them. That's when I began to feel really frightened. I cruised the streets looking for them, and stopped to ask passers-by if they'd seen a lady dressed in blue with a little boy in a sailor suit. I guess I'd questioned four or five before a boy on a bicycle told me yes, he'd seen such a lady in blue, with a little boy carrying a sailboat, and he pointed out the direction they'd taken.

"They were headed for the river! I drove as far as I could then jumped out of the car and ran down the dirt path, fearing every moment I'd get there too late. I couldn't bring myself to believe she'd really do it. I kept calming myself by thinking Scotty only wanted to float his boat on the water, like I used to do. I ran so fast my heart hurt, and then I reached the grassy river bank. And there they were, the two of them, both in the water floating face upward. Julia had her arms locked around Scotty who'd clearly tried to free himself from her hold, and his little boat was sailing with the tide. The blue ribbon had come unbound from her hair, and it floated too, and all about her hair streamed like dark ribbons to twine in the weeds. The water was only knee-high."

I made some small sound that choked my throat, feeling his terrible anguish, but he didn't hear. He went on, "In no time at all I had them both in my arms and I carried them to shore. Julia was barely alive, but Scotty seemed dead, so it was him I worked over first in a futile effort to bring him around. I did everything possible to pump the water from his lungs, but he was dead. I then turned to Julia and did the same for her. She coughed and choked out the water. She didn't open her eyes but at least she was breathing. I put both of them in my car and drove them to the nearest hospital where they slaved to bring Julia back, but they couldn't. No more than I could bring Scotty back to life."

Paul paused and stared deep into my eyes. "That is my story for a girl who thinks she's the only one who has suffered, and the only one who has lost, and the only one who grieves. Oh, I grieve just as much as you do but I also bear the guilt. I should have known how unstable Julia was. We had watched *Medea* on TV only a few nights before Scotty's birthday and she showed unusual interest in it, and she didn't care for television. I was stupid not to know what she was thinking and planning. Yet, even now, I cannot understand how she could kill our son when she loved him so much. She could have divorced me and kept him. I wouldn't have taken him from her. But that wasn't enough revenge for Julia. She had to kill the thing I loved best, my son."

I couldn't speak. What kind of woman had Julia been? Like my own mother? My mother killed to gain a fortune. Julia killed for revenge. Was I going to do the same thing? No, no, of course not. My way would be better, much better, for she'd live to suffer on, and on, and on.

"I'm sorry," I said brokenly, so sorry I had to kiss his cheek. "But you can have other children. You can marry again." I put my arms about him when he shook his head.

"Forget Julia!" I cried, throwing my arms about his neck and snuggling closer in his arms. "Don't you tell me all the time to forgive and forget? Forgive yourself, and forget what happened to Julia. I remember my mother and father; they were always loving and kissing. I've known since I was a little girl that men need to be loved and touched. I used to watch my mother to see how she tamed Daddy down when he was angry. She did it with kisses, with soft looks and small touches." I tilted my head back and smiled at him as I'd seen my mother smile at my father. "Tell me how a wife should be on her wedding night. I wouldn't want to disappoint bridegroom."

"I will tell you no such thing!"

"Then I'll just pretend you're my bridegroom, and I have just come from the bathroom after getting un-dressed. Or maybe I should undress in front of you. What do you think?"

He cleared his throat and tried to shove me away, but clung like a burr. "I think you ought to go to bed and forget games of pretending."

I stayed where I was. Over and over again I kissed him and soon he was responding. I felt his flesh grow warmer but then his lips beneath mine tightened into a thin line as his hands went under my knees and shoulders. He stood with me in his arms and headed toward the stairs. I thought he was going to take me to his room and make love to me and I was frightened, ashamed—and excited and eager too. But he headed straight for my room and there by my narrow bed he hesitated. He held me close against his heart for an excruciatingly long time as the rain pelted down and beat on the window glass. Paul seemed to forget who I was as his raspy cheek rubbed against mine, caressing with his cheek, not his hands this time. And again, as always, I had to speak and spoil it all.

"Paul." My timid voice drew him out of some deep reverie that might, if I'd stayed silent, have led me sooner toward that forever-withheld ecstasy my body yearned for. "When we were locked away upstairs our grandmother always called us Devil's spawn. She told us we were evil seed planted in the wrong soil, that nothing good would ever come of us. She made us all unsure of what we were, or whether we had the right to be alive. Was it so terrible what our mother did to marry her half-uncle when he was only three years older than she? No woman with a heart could have resisted him. I know I couldn't have. He was like you. Our grandparents believed our parents had committed an unholy sin so they despised us, even the twins who were so little and adorable. They called us unwholesome. Were they right? Were they right to try to kill us?"

I'd said exactly the right words to snap him back into focus. Quickly he dropped me. He turned his head sideways so I couldn't read his eyes. I hated for people to hide their eyes from me so I couldn't see the truth.

"I think your parents were very much in love and very young," he said in a strange, tight voice, "so much in love they didn't pause to consider the future and the consequences."

"Oh!" I cried, outraged. "You think the grandparents were right—and we are evil!"

He spun about to face me, his full, sensual lips open, his expression furious. "Don't take what I say and twist it about to suit your need for revenge. There's no reason, ever, to justify murder, unless it's a case of self-defense. You're not evil. Your grandparents were bigoted fools who should have learned to accept what was and make the best of it. And they had much to be proud of in the four grandchildren your parents gave them. And if your parents took a calculated gamble when they decided to have children, I say they won. God and the odds were on your side and gave you too much beauty and appreciation of it, and perhaps too many talents. Most certainly there is one very young girl who smolders with adult emotions too large for her size and age."

"Paul . . . ?"

"Don't look at me like that, Catherine."

"I don't know how I'm looking."

"Go to sleep, Catherine Sheffield, this instant!"

"What did you call me?" I asked as he backed off toward the door.

He smiled at me. "It wasn't a Freudian slip, if that's what you're thinking. Dollanganger is too long a name. Sheffield would be a much better choice. Legally we can arrange to have your surname changed."

"Oh." He made me feel sick with disappointment.

"Look here, Catherine," he said from the doorway. He was so large he blocked out the light from the hall. "You're playing a dangerous game. You're trying to seduce me and you're very lovely and very hard to resist. But your place in my life is as my daughter—nothing else."

"Was it raining that day in June when you put Julia and Scotty in the ground?"

"What difference does that make? *Any day* you put someone you love underground it's raining!" And he was gone from my door, striding quickly down the hall to his room where he slammed the door hard.

So, I'd tried twice and he'd rejected me twice. Now I was free to go on my merry, destructive way to dance and dance until I reached the top. And that would show Momma, who could do nothing but embroider and knit, just who had the most talent and brains. She would see who could make a fortune on her own without selling her body, and without stooping to murder to inherit it!

The whole world was going to know about me! They'd compare me to Anna Pavlova and say I was better. She'd come to a party they threw in my honor, and with her would be her husband. She'd look old, jaded, tired, while I'd be fresh and young, and her darling Bart would come straight to me, his eyes dazzled as he kissed my hand. "You are the most beautiful woman I've ever seen," he'd say, "and the most talented." And with his eyes alone I'd know he loved me, loved me ten times more than he had ever loved her. And then when I had him and she was alone, I'd tell him who I was, and he'd not believe at first. Then he would. And he'd hate her! He'd take all her money from her. Where would it go? I paused, stumped. Where would the money go if it were taken from Momma? Would it go back to the grandmother? It wouldn't come to us, not Chris, Carrie or me, for we just didn't exist as Foxworths. Then I smiled to myself, thinking of the four birth certificates I'd found sewn under the lining of one of our old suitcases. I began to laugh. Oh, Momma, what stupid things you do! Imagine, hiding the birth certificates. With those I could prove Cory existed, and without them it would be her word against mine, unless the police went back to Gladstone and found the doctor who had delivered the twins. And then there was our old babysitter, Mrs. Simpson—and Jim Johnston. Oh, I hoped none had moved away and that they could still remember the four Dresden dolls.

I knew I was evil, just like the grandmother said from the beginning, born to be bad. I'd been punished before I'd even done anything evil, so why not let the punishment fit the crime that was to be? There was no reason why I should be haunted and ruined just because once upon a miserable time, I had turned for refuge into the arms of my brother. I'd go to the man who needed me most. If that was evil, to give what his words denied and his eyes pleaded for, then let me be evil!

I began, as I grew sleepy, to plan how it would be. He wouldn't turn away and put me off, for I'd make it impossible. He wouldn't want to hurt me. He'd take me and then he'd think to himself he had to, and then he wouldn't feel guilty, not guilty at all.

The guilt would all be mine. And Chris would hate me and turn, as he had to, to someone else.

Sweeter Than All the Roses

I was sixteen in April of 1961. There I was, at the blossoming, ripe age when all men, young and old, and most of all those past forty, turned to stare at me on the streets. When I waited on the corner for a bus, cars slowed because male drivers couldn't keep from gaping at me.

And if they were enraptured, I was even more so. I preened before the many mirrors in Paul's home and saw, sometimes by surprise, a lovely, even breathtakingly beautiful girl—and then that glorious revelation—that was *me!* I was dazzling and I knew it. Julian flew down often to turn his desiring eyes upon me, telling me he knew what he wanted even if I didn't. I saw Chris only on the weekends and I knew he still wanted me, still loved me more than he'd ever love anyone again.

Chris and Carrie came home for my birthday weekend and we laughed and hugged and talked so fast, as if we'd never have the time to say enough, especially Chris and I. I wanted to tell Chris that Momma would be living in Greenglenna soon but I was afraid he'd try to stop me from doing what I had planned so I never mentioned it. After a

while Carrie drew away to sit with big, sad eyes and stare at
our kind benefactor. That big, handsome man who ordered
me to dress up in my very best. "Why not wear that dress
you've been saving for a special occasion? For your birthday I'm treating all of you to a gourmet feast at my favorite
restaurant The Plantation House."

Right away I had to rush upstairs and begin dressing. I
was going to make the most of my birthday. My face didn't
really need makeup, yet I put it on, the whole works, including mascara black as ink, and then I used tongs to curl my
lashes. My nails gleamed like lustrous pearls and the gown
I wore was Paris pink. Oh, did I feel pretty as I preened and
primped before a cheval glass bought for my vanity.

"My lady Catherine," said Chris from the open doorway.
"You do look gorgeous but it is in appallingly bad taste to
admire yourself so much you have to kiss your own reflection.
Really, Cathy, wait for compliments from others—don't give
them to yourself."

"I'm afraid no one will tell me," I said defensively, "so
I tell it to myself to give myself more confidence. Do I look
beautiful and not just pretty?"

"Yeah," he said in a funny, tight voice, "I doubt I'll ever
see another girl as beautiful as you look right now."

"Would you say I'm improving with age?"

"I'm not going to compliment you anymore! It's no wonder the grandmother broke all the mirrors. I've got a good
mind to do that myself. Such conceit!"

I frowned, not liking to be reminded of that old woman.
"*You* look fantastic, Chris," I said, giving him a big, warm
smile. "I'm not ashamed or embarrassed to hand out compliments when they're deserved. You're as handsome as Daddy."

Every time he came home from his school he looked more
mature and more handsome. Though, when I peered closer, wisdom was putting something strange in his eyes, something that
made him seem much, much older than I was. He also appeared

sadder than me, more vulnerable, and the combination was extremely appealing. "Why aren't you happy, Chris?" I asked. "Is life disappointing you? Is it less than you thought it would be when we were locked away and we had so many dreams for the future? Are you sorry now that you decided on being a doctor? Are you wishing instead to be a dancer like me?"

I had neared to watch his oh, so revealing eyes, but he lowered them to hide away and his hands tried to span my waist, but my waist wasn't that small or his hands weren't that large. Or was he just doing something to touch me? Making a game out of what was serious. Was that it? I ducked to peer into his face and I saw the love I was looking for and then wished I didn't know.

"Chris, you haven't answered."

"What did you ask?"

"Life, medical training, is it living up to your expectations?"

"What does?"

"That sounds cynical. My style, not yours."

He raised his head and smiled brightly. *Oh, God!* "Yes," he said, "life on the outside is what I thought it would be. I was realistic, unlike you. I like school and the friends I've made. But I still miss you; it's hard being separated from you, always wondering what you're up to." His eyes shifted again and became shadowed as he yearned for the impossible. "Happy birthday, my lady Cath-er-ine," he softly said, and then brushed my lips with his. Just a feathery little kiss that didn't dare much. "Let's go," he said resolutely, taking hold of my hand. "Everyone is ready but fussy, prissy you."

We descended the stairs hand in hand. Paul and Carrie were all dressed and waiting, with Henny too.

The house felt strange, so hushed and expectant—so weirdly dark, with all the lights off but in the hall. How funny.

Then, suddenly, out of the dark came, *"Sur-prise! Sur-prise!"* Screamed by a chorus of voices as the lights all came on, and members of my ballet class, thronging about Chris and me.

Henny carried in a birthday cake of three layers, each smaller than the one underneath and proudly said she'd I made it and decorated it herself. *Let me always succeed at what I set out to do*, I wished with my eyes closed when I blew out all the candles. *I'm gaining on you, Momma—getting older and wiser each day, so when the time comes, I'll be ready—your match.*

I blew so well the melted pink wax smeared the sugary pink roses nestled sweetly on pale green leaves. Across from me was Julian. His ebony eyes riveted as mutely he asked the same question over and over.

Whenever I tried to meet eyes with Chris he had his turned another way or lowered to stare at the floor. Carrie crowded close beside Paul, who sat some distance away from the boisterous revelry and tried not to look stern. As soon as I had all the presents opened Paul got up, picked Carrie up in his arms, and both disappeared up the stairs.

"Good night, Cathy," called Carrie, her small face happy and flushed with sleepiness, "this is the best birthday party I've ever been to."

I could have cried from the pain of that, for she was almost nine years old and the birthday parties she could remember, except Chris's last November, had been pitiful attempts to make much out of little.

"Why are you looking sad?" asked Julian who came up and swung me into his embrace. "Rejoice—for now you have me at your feet, ready to set your heart on fire along with your body."

Truly I hated him when he acted like that. He tried to demonstrate in every way possible that I belonged to him and him alone. His gift had been a leather tote to carry my ballet leotards, shoes, etc. I danced away from him, not wanting to be claimed tonight. All the girls who weren't already infatuated with Julian immediately fell for Chris, and this in no way enhanced Julian's liking for my brother. I don't know what happened to put the match to the grass but suddenly Chris and Julian were in a corner arguing and about to exchange

blows. "I don't give a damn what you think!" stormed Chris
in his eye-of-the-hurricane calm way. "My sister is too young
for a lover and not ready for New York!"

"You! You—" fired Julian back. "What do you know about
the dance? You know nothing! You can't even manage to move
your feet without stepping on yourself!"

"That may be true," said Chris in an icy voice, "but I have
other skills. And we're talking about my sister and the fact
that she is still underaged. I won't have you persuading her
to accompany you to New York when she hasn't even finished
high school yet!"

My head swiveled from one to the other and between the
two it was hard to say which was the better looking. I felt sick
that they would show everyone their hostility, and sick because
I wanted so much for them to like each other. I trembled on
the brink of crying out, *stop, don't do this!* But I said nothing.

"Cathy," called Chris, not moving his eyes for one second
from Julian who appeared ready to throw a blow or deliver
a kick, "do you honestly believe you are ready to make your
debut in New York?"

"No . . ." I said in a near whisper.

Julian's eyes raged my way, for he was at me, demanding of
me every second we were together, wanting me to accompany
him to New York and be his mistress and dance partner. I knew
why he wanted me—my weight, my height, my balance suited
his abilities perfectly. It was of utmost importance to find the
perfect partner when you wanted to impress in a *pas de deux.*

"May all your birthdays be hell on earth!" Julian said as he
headed for the front door, and he slammed it hard behind him.
That's how my party ended, with everyone going home looking embarrassed. Chris stalked up to his room without wishing me good night. With tears in my eyes I began to pick up
the trash from the living room carpet. I found a hole burned
in the plushy green from a carelessly held cigarette. Someone
had broken one of Paul's prized pieces of hand-blown glass—

a transparent rose of shimmering crystal. I held it, thinking about buying glue that would put it back I together again, even as I planned a way, for there had to be a way, to cover up the holes in the carpet and take the white rings from the tables.

"Don't worry about the rose," Paul's voice came from behind me, "it's just a cheap knickknack. I can always buy another."

I turned to look at him. He was standing so casually in the archway of the foyer, meeting my teary look with his soft, kind eyes. "It was a beautiful rose," I choked, "and I know it was expensive. I'll buy you another if I can find a duplicate, and if I can't I'll buy you something better when I can. . . ."

"Forget it."

"Thank you again for the beautiful music box." Nervously my hands fluttered to my daring decolletage and sought to hide the cleavage. "My father gave me a silver music box with a ballerina inside once but I had to leave it. . . ." My voice trailed off and I could speak no more, for thoughts of my father always left me in childish ruins of bleakness without hope.

"Chris told me about the music box your father gave you and I tried to find one just like it. Did I succeed?"

"Yes," I said, though it wasn't the same.

"Good. Now go to bed. Forget the mess—Henny will clean up. You look sleepy."

I was soon up the stairs and into my room, where to my surprise Chris was waiting for me.

"What is going on between you and Julian?" he shot out fiercely.

"Nothing is going on!"

"Don't lie to me, Cathy! He doesn't fly down here so often for *nothing!*"

"Mind your own damned business, Christopher!" I said viciously. "I don't try to tell you what to do and I demand the same from you! You are not a saint and I am not an angel! The trouble is you're just another man who thinks you can do anything *you* want while I have to sit prim and prissy on the sidelines and wait for someone to come along and marry me! Well, I'm not that kind of woman! Nobody is going to push me around and make me do what I don't want to—never again! Not Paul! Not Madame! Not Julian—and not you either!" His face paled as he listened and restrained himself from interrupting. "I want you to stay out of my life, Christopher. I'll do what I have to, anything I have to, to get to the top!"

He glared at me with his heavenly blue eyes shooting devilish electric sparks. "I take it you'll sleep with just any man if that's necessary."

"I'll do what I have to!" I raged back, though I hadn't given that any thought.

He seemed on the verge of slapping me, and the control it took to keep his hands at his sides made him clench them into fists. A white line etched about his tightened lips. "Cathy," he began in a hurt voice, "what's come over you? I didn't think you'd ever become another opportunist."

Bitterly I met his eyes. What did *he* think he was doing? We'd stumbled fortunately upon an unhappy, lonely man and we were using him, and sooner or later there'd be a price to pay. Our grandmother had always told us nobody did anything for nothing. But somehow I couldn't hurt him more, and I couldn't speak a word against Paul who'd taken us in and was doing everything he could. Truthfully, I had reason enough for knowing he didn't expect any reward.

"Cathy," he pleaded, "I hate every word you just said. How can you talk to me like that when you know how much I love and respect you? There isn't a day that passes that I don't long for you. I live for the weekends when I can see you and Carrie. Don't turn from me, Cathy, I need you. I'll always need you. It scares the hell out of me to think I'm not nearly that necessary in *your* life." He had hold of my arms and would have pulled me against his chest, but I yanked away and turned my back. How could I tell what was wrong and what was right when nobody seemed to care anymore?

"Chris," I began brokenly, "I'm sorry I spoke like that. It matters to me very much what you think. But I'm all torn up inside. I think I have to have everything immediately to help make up for all I've lost and suffered. Julian wants me to go with him to New York. I don't think I'm ready yet and I don't have the discipline I need—Madame tells me that all the time and she's right. Julian says he loves me and will take care of me. But I'm not sure what love is, or if he loves me at all or only wants me to help him reach his goal. But his goal is my goal. So tell me how I can tell if he loves me or if he only wants to use me?"

"Have you let him make love to you?" he asked flatly, his eyes dead looking.

"*No!* Of course not!"

His arms encircled me and held me fast. "Wait at least one more year, Cathy. Trust Madame Marisha, not Julian. She knows more than he does." He paused and forced me to lift my bowed head. I studied his handsome face and wondered why he hesitated and didn't go on.

I was an instrument of yearning, filled with a ravenous desire for romantic fulfillment. I was scared too of what was inside me. So scared I was like Momma. When I looked in the mirrors I saw my mother's face beginning to emerge more definitely. I was exalted that I looked like her, and paradoxically I hated myself for being her reflection. No, no, I wasn't like her inside, only on the outside. My beauty was not only skin deep.

I kept telling myself this as I made a special trip to Greenglenna downtown. In the city hall there I made some flimsy excuse about looking up my mother's birth certificate just so I could look up the birth certificate of Bart Winslow. I found out he was eight years younger than my mother and I also discovered exactly where he lived. I walked fifteen blocks until I came to a quiet, elm-lined street where old mansions were in a state of decaying disrepair. All but the home of Bart Winslow! His home had scaffolding all around. Dozens of workmen were putting up storm windows on a freshly painted brick home with white trim around the windows and a white portico.

Another day found me in the Greenglenna library where I read up on the Winslow family. Much to my delight, when I searched back through the old newspapers I found a society editor who seemed to devote most of her column to Bart Winslow and his fabulously wealthy and very beautiful wife with her aristocratic background. "The heiress to one of the country's greatest fortunes."

That column I snipped out furtively and sneaked home to Chris. I didn't want him to know Momma would live in Greenglenna. He showed some distress as he scanned the column. "Cathy, where did you find this article?"

I shrugged. "Oh, it was in some Virginia paper they sell in a newsstand."

"She's in Europe again," he said in a queer way. "I wonder why she keeps going to Europe." He turned his blue eyes my way and a dreamy expression softened his features. "Remember the summer she went on her honeymoon?"

Remember? As if I could ever forget. As if I would ever *let* myself forget. Someday, someday when I was rich and famous too, Momma was going to hear from me and when she did, she'd better be well prepared, for bit by bit I was forming my strategy.

Julian didn't come to Greenglenna as much as he had before my sixteenth birthday party. I figured Chris had scared him off. I didn't know if that made me happy or not. When he did visit his parents he ignored me. He began to pay attention to Lorraine DuVal, my best friend. For some reason I felt hurt and resentment, not only against him but also against Lorraine. In the wings I half-hid myself and watched them dance a passionate *pas de deux*. That was when I determined I'd study twice as hard as I had before, for I was going to show Julian too! I was going to show everyone just what I was made of!

Steel, covered over with frilly, silly tulle tutus!

Owl on the Roof

Now I'm going to recount an event in Carrie's life, for this is her story and Chris's as well as mine. When I look back now and reflect on how life turned out for Carrie, I truthfully believe what happened to Carrie in Miss Emily Dean Calhoun's School for Properly Bred Young Ladies had a great deal to do with how she thought of herself in the future.

Ah, dig me a well to cry in before I begin, for I loved her so, and what pain she had to bear I bear, even now.

From the jigsaw pieces that I've gathered from Carrie herself and from Miss Dewhurst, and from several other students at that school, this was Carrie's nightmare to endure, and I will report it as honestly as possible.

Carrie spent her weekends with us but she had retreated into that quiet, little apathetic creature who'd grieved so when her twin died. Everything about Carrie worried me. Though when I asked her questions she insisted everything was all right and refused to say anything against that school or the student body or the faculty. She said one thing, and one thing only, to express her feelings—and what a clue it was. "I like the carpet—it's colored like grass." That was it. She left me wondering, worried, trying to guess what was troubling her. Something was wrong, I knew it, and she wouldn't tell me what it was.

Each Friday at about four Paul would drive to fetch Carrie and Chris and bring them back home. He did his best to make all our weekends memorable. Though Carrie appeared happy enough with us, she seldom laughed. Try as we would, all we could pull from her was a weak smile.

"What's wrong with Carrie?" whispered Chris. I could only shrug. Somewhere along the way I'd lost Carrie's confidence. Her big, blue eyes fastened on Paul. They mutely pleaded with him. But he was looking at me, not Carrie.

As the time approached for her to be driven back to school Carrie would grow very quiet; her eyes would become blank and resigned. We'd kiss her good-bye and tell her to be good, make friends, "and if you need us, you know how to call."

"Yes," she said weakly, her eyes downcast. I pressed her against me telling her again how much I loved her, and if she was unhappy she had to speak up and say so. "I'm not unhappy," she answered with her eyes fixed sadly on Paul.

It was truly a beautiful school. I'd have loved to attend such a school. Each girl was allowed to decorate her side of a double room as she saw fit. Miss Dewhurst had only one restriction, and that was each girl had to choose "proper, ladylike" appointments. Soft, passive femininity was greatly stressed in the South. Soft, whispering clothes, drifting chiffon, dulcet voices, shy, downcast eyes, weak, fluttery hands to express helplessness, and absolutely no opinions that would conflict with male ones—and never, never let a man know you had a brain that might be better than his. And I'm afraid, after reconsidering, it wouldn't be the proper school for me after all.

Carrie's bed was twin size, covered by a bright purple spread. On it she had decorator pillows of rose, red, purple, violet and green. Beside her bed was a night-stand with the milk-glass vase filled with plastic violets given to her by Paul. Whenever he could he brought her real flowers. Strangely, she adored that little pot of violets more than the real flowers that soon withered and died.

Since Carrie was the smallest girl in the school of one hundred students, she was given as a roommate the next smallest girl, named Sissy Towers. Sissy had brick-red hair, emerald eyes that were long and narrow, thin, paper-white skin, and a spiteful, mean temper which she never displayed to any adult, but saved for the girls she knew how to intimidate. Worst of all, though she was the second smallest, she towered over Carrie by six inches!

Carrie had celebrated her ninth birthday with a party the week before her ordeal began. It was May, and it began on a Thursday.

The school days ended at three. The girls had two hours to play outside before dinner at five-thirty. All the students wore uniforms of colors determined by what grade they were in. Carrie was in the third grade; her uniform was of yellow broadcloth with a dainty- white organdy pinafore to top it off. Carrie had a strong dislike for the color yellow. Yellow represented to her, as it did to Chris and me, the color of all the best things we couldn't have when we'd been locked away and made to feel unwholesome, unwanted and unloved. Yellow was also the color of the sun that was denied us. The sun was what Cory had wanted most to see, and now that all yellow things were so easily accessible, and Cory wasn't, yellow was a hateful thing.

Sissy Towers adored yellow. She envied Carrie's long, golden locks and despised her own head of crinkly rust. Perhaps too she envied the beauty of Carrie's doll-like face, and those big, blue eyes with the long, dark, curling lashes, and her lips ripe as strawberries.

Oh, yes, our Carrie was a doll with an exquisite face,

sensational Goldilocks hair and, the pity of it all, this beauty hovered above a body much too thin, too small, and a neck too delicate to support a head that belonged on someone bigger and taller.

Yellow dominated Sissy's side of the room; yellow spread, yellow slip-covered chairs; her dolls were blondes wearing yellow, her books wore yellow jackets, homemade. Sissy even wore yellow sweaters and skirts when she went home. The fact that Sissy looked unbecomingly sallow in yellow did not lessen her determination to annoy Carrie with the color— come what may. And on this day, for some trifling reason that was never explained, she began to taunt Carrie in a mean, spiteful way.

"Carrie is a dwarf . . . a dwarf . . . a dwarf," sang Sissy in a sing-song chant.

"Carrie should be in a circus . . . a circus . . . a circus," Sissy chanted on and on. Then she jumped up on the top of her desk and in the loud, brassy manner of a barker touting a freak show at a carnival Sissy really began to shout, *"Come one! Come all! Come pay your quarter to see the living sister of Tom Thumb! Come see the world's smallest woman! Come, pay your money and see the little one with the huge, huge eyes—like an owl's! Come view the huge, huge head on the little, scrawny neck! Come pay your quarter to see our little freak naked!"*

Dozens of little girls crowded into the room to stare at Carrie who crouched in a corner on the floor, with her head hanging low and her long hair hiding her shamed, terrified face.

Sissy opened up her small purse to receive the quarters the affluent little girls dropped in willingly. "Now take off your clothes, little dwarf-freak," ordered Sissy. "Give the customers their money's worth!"

Quivering and beginning to cry, Carrie crouched into a tighter ball and pulled up her knees and prayed that God would somehow open up the floor. But floors never graciously

open up and swallow you when they should. It remained hard
and unyielding beneath her as the taunting voice of Sissy
went on and on.

"Look at her tremble . . . look at her shake . . . she's gonna
make . . . an earthquake!"

All the girls giggled, except one average-sized girl of ten
who looked on Carrie with pity and sympathy. "I think she's
cute," said Lacy St. John. "Leave her alone, Sissy. It's not nice
what you're doing."

"Of course it's not nice!" Sissy said with a laugh. "But
it's such fun! She's such a timid little mouse! You know, she
never says anything. I don't think she *can* talk!" Down from
the chair Sissy jumped to run to where Carrie was, and there
she prodded Carrie with her foot. "Have you got a tongue,
little freak? Come, little big-eyes, tell us how you got to be so
funny-looking. Did the cat steal your tongue? Do you have a
tongue? Stick it out!"

Carrie hung her head even lower.

"See, she doesn't have a tongue!" proclaimed Sissy, jumping up and down. Sissy whirled around and spread her arms
wide. "Look at what they gave me for a roomy—an owl without a tongue! What can we do to make her talk?"

Lacy moved protectively closer to Carrie. "Come on,
Sissy, enough is enough, leave her alone."

Pivoting, Sissy stomped down hard on Lacy's foot. "*Shut
up!* This is my room! When you're in my room, you do as I
say! And I'm just as big as you are, Lacy St. John, and my
daddy's got more money too!"

"I think you are a mean, nasty, ugly girl to torment
Carrie!" said Lacy.

Sissy raised her fist in the manner of a professional boxer,
dancing around to take quick jabs at Lacy. "You wanna fight?
C'mon, put up your dukes! Just see if you can get me before I
blacken your eyes!" And before Lacy could raise her hands for
protection, Sissy shot out a right that caught Lacy squarely

on the left eye. Then Sissy's left hook smashed Lacy's fine straight nose! Blood spurted everywhere!

This was when Carrie lifted her head, saw the only girl who'd shown her the least bit of kindness being beaten to a pulp, and that was cause enough for Carrie to use her most formidable weapon—her voice. She began to scream. Full blast, using every bit of vocal power she had, Carrie threw back her head and let go!

Down in her study on the first floor, Miss Emily Dean Dewhurst bolted upright and smeared the ink in her ledger. She ran to sound an alarm in the hall to bring each and every female teacher on the run.

It was eight o'clock in the evening. Most of the faculty had retired to their rooms. Clad in bathrobes, negligees, and one in a scarlet evening gown, apparently ready to slip out on the sly, the teachers raced toward the clamor. They burst into the room Carrie shared with Sissy and found a frightful scene. Twelve girls all doing battle, while others stood back and watched. One girl, like Carrie, only screamed, but the others were yelling, kicking, wrestling on the floor, pulling hair, biting and tearing off clothes—and above all the racket of the fray resounded the blaring trumpet of one small human in terror.

"Where is the man—the man?" cried out Miss Longhurst, the one in the scarlet evening gown with her bosom about to fall out of the lowcut bodice.

"Miss Longhurst, control yourself!" ordered Miss Dewhurst, who promptly assessed the situation and planned her strategy. "There is no man here. *Girls!*" she boomed, "*stop this fracas this very second, or every one of you will be denied liberty this weekend!*" Then she said in a low voice to the sexy Longhurst, "You report to my office when this is under control."

Every girl in that room about to have her hair pulled or her face scratched jerked abruptly still and quiet. With horrified eyes they looked around and saw the room full of teachers—

and worst of all Miss Dewhurst, who was not known for showing mercy once bedlam broke loose, as it often did. All hushed.
All but Carrie who kept right on screaming, her eyes squeezed
shut, her small, pale hands in tight fists.

"Why is that child screaming?" asked Miss Dewhurst as
a guilty-looking Miss Longhurst sneaked away to take off her
incriminating evidence—that somewhere a man *was* hiding
and waiting.

Naturally, it was Sissy Towers who recovered first. "She's
the one who started it all, Miss Dewhurst. It's *all* Carrie's
fault. She's like a baby. You've just got to give me a new roomy
or I'll die living so close to a baby."

"Repeat what you just said, Miss Towers. Tell me again
what I *must* do."

Intimidated, Sissy smiled uneasily. "I mean, I would like
to have a new roomy; I don't feel good living so close to someone so unnaturally small."

Coldly Miss Dewhurst eyed Sissy. "Miss Towers, *you* are
unnaturally cruel. From now on you will room on the first
floor in the room next to mine where I can keep an eye on
you." She flashed her sharp gaze around the room. "As for
the rest of you, I'm going to notify your parents that your
weekend leaves are canceled! Now, each of you report to Miss
Littleton so she may mark your records with demerits."
The girls groaned and one by one they drifted out to have
their names recorded with minus marks. Only then did Miss
Dewhurst advance to where Carrie was on her hands and
knees, her voice faded to a whimper, but her head kept moving from side to side in a hysterical way. "Miss Dollanganger,
are you calm enough now to tell me what happened?"

Carrie was beyond speech. Terror and the sight of blood
had taken her back to the locked room, to a hungry day when
she had been forced to drink blood or starve to death. Miss
Dewhurst was touched and bewildered. Forty years she'd
seen girls come and go, and she knew girls could be just as

devastatingly ugly and cruel as boys. "Miss Dollanganger, unless you respond to me, you will not visit your family this weekend. I know you've had a hard time of it and I want to be kind to you. Can't you please explain what happened?"

Fallen flat on the floor now, Carrie looked up. She saw the older woman towering above her, and the blue skirt she wore was almost gray. Gray was the color the grandmother always wore. And the grandmother did terrible things; somehow the grandmother had caused Cory to die—and now she had come to get Carrie too!

"I hate you! I hate you!" screamed Carrie over and over, until finally Miss Dewhurst was driven from the room and the school nurse was sent in to give Carrie a sedative.

That Friday, I answered the telephone when Miss Dewhurst called to say twelve of her girls had broken her rules and disobeyed her orders, and Carrie was one of them. "I'm sorry, really I am. But I can't give your sister privileges and still punish the others. She was in the room and she refused to quiet when I ordered her to."

I waited until evening at the dinner table to discuss it with Paul. "It's a terrible mistake to leave Carrie over the weekend, Paul. You know we promised her, she could come home every weekend. She's too little to be the cause of anything, so it's not fair she should be punished too!"

"Really, Cathy," he said, putting down his fork, "Miss Dewhurst called me right after she talked to you. She does have rules, and if Carrie misbehaved then she has to suffer along with the rest of the girls. And I respect Miss Dewhurst even if you don't."

Chris, home for the weekend, spoke up and agreed with Paul. "Sure, Cathy, you know as well as I do that Carrie can cut up when she wants to. If she did nothing but scream she could drive you batty—and deaf."

That weekend was a flop without Carrie. I couldn't get her

off my mind. I stewed, fretted, worried over Carrie. I seemed to hear her calling to me. I closed my eyes and I saw her small, white face with her eyes huge and haunted by fear. She *was* all right! She had to be, didn't she? What could happen to a little girl in an expensive school controlled by such a responsible, respectable woman as Miss Emily Dean Dewhurst?

When Carrie was hurting and at odds with herself and all the world, and there was no one near who loved her, she retreated to yesterdays and the safe comfort of the tiny porcelain dolls she'd carefully hidden away beneath all of her clothes. Now she was the only girl in the school with a room all to herself. She'd never been alone before. Not once in all her nine years had Carrie I spent a night in a room alone. She was alone now and she knew it. Every girl in the school had turned against her, even pretty Lacy St. John.

From her very secret place Carrie would take her dolls, Mr. and Mrs. Parkins and dear little baby Clara, and she'd talk to them as she used to do when she was locked away in the attic. "And Cathy," she told me later, "I thought maybe Momma was up in God's heaven, in the garden with Cory and Daddy, and I felt so mean at you and Chris because you let Dr. Paul put me in that place, and you know how much I liked to be with all of you. And I hated you, Cathy! I hated everybody! I hated God for making me so small so people laugh at my big head and little body!"

In the short halls and long corridors of green carpeting Carrie heard the girls whispering. Furtively they shifted their eyes when she looked their way. "I told myself I didn't care," whispered Carrie hoarsely to me, "but I did care. I told myself I could be brave like you wanted and Chris wanted and Dr. Paul wanted. I kept on making myself feel brave but I wasn't really brave. I don't like dark. And I told myself God was gonna hear my prayers and make me grow taller, 'cause everybody grows taller when they grow older, and so would I.

"It was so dark, Cathy, and the room felt so big and scary. You know I don't like night and darkness with no lamp burning, with nobody there but me. I even wanted Sissy back, she seemed better than nobody. Something in the shadows moved and I was terrified, and though we're not supposed to I turned on a lamp. I wanted to take all my little dolls to bed with me so I'd have company. I was gonna be so careful not to toss and turn and break off their heads.

"I always put Mr. and Mrs. Parkins left and right with baby Clara in the middle in the bottom drawer of my dresser. I picked up the cotton wadding that was in the middle first and felt something hard. But when I looked, Cathy, when I looked there was no baby, only a little stick! I unwrapped Mr. and Mrs. Parkins, and they were only sticks too—bigger ones! It hurt so bad not to find them I began to cry. All my little dolls gone all turned to wood, so I knew God was never gonna let me grow tall when he would make my pretty dolls into only sticks.

"Something funny happened to me then, like I turned into wood too. I felt stiff and couldn't see too good. I went and crouched in a corner and waited for something bad to happen. The grandmother said something terrible would happen if I broke a doll, didn't she?" Not another word would she say, but I learned from others what happened after that.

In the dark, long after midnight, the twelve little rich girls Miss Dewhurst had denied liberty all stole furtively into Carrie's room. It was Lacy St. John who had the integrity to tell me, but only when Miss Dewhurst was out of hearing.

Twelve girls, all wearing long white cotton nightgowns, the official sleeping garments of the school, filed into Carrie's room, each bearing a single candle held so her face was lit up under her chin. Such lighting made their eyes appear sunken, dark hollows and lent their youthful faces an eerie, ghoulish appearance—enough to terrify a little girl still crouched in the corner, already in a trance of haunted fear.

They came to form a semicircle around Carrie, to stare

down at her as each put over her head a pillowcase with holes for eyes. Then came the ritual of weaving the candles intricately in formalized patterns as they chanted in the way of real witches. They sought to drive the smallness out of Carrie. They sought to set her "free" and themselves "free" from whatever evil they were driven to do for self-protection from someone so "unnaturally small and strange."

One voice shrilled above all the others and Carrie knew it was Sissy Towers. To Carrie, all those shrouded girls in their long nightgowns with white hoods over their heads and the black holes for eyes were devils straight from hell! She began to whimper, to tremble, and oh, she was so scared, as if once more the grandmother were in the room, only this time she had multiplied until there were twelve of her!

"Don't you cry, don't you fear," soothed the nightmarish voice from a mouthless hood. "If you live through this night, through this initiation, you, Carrie Dollanganger, will become a member of our most private and very exclusive society. If you succeed from this night forward, you will share in our secret rituals, our secret parties, our secret hoards of goodies."

"Ohhh," moaned Carrie, "go away, leave me alone, go away, leave me alone."

"*Quiet!*" ordered the shrill voice of the hidden speaker, "you have no chance to become one of us unless you sacrifice your *most* beloved and precious possessions. It is either that or suffer our trial."

Crouched in the corner, Carrie could only stare at the moving shadows behind the white witches who threatened her. The glows from the candles grew larger, larger, turning her world into one of yellow and scarlet fire.

"Give to us what you dearly cherish or you must suffer, suffer, suffer."

"I have nothing," whispered Carrie honestly.

"The dolls, the pretty little china dolls, give us those," intoned the austere voice of the speaker. "Your little clothes won't fit us; we don't want those; give us your dolls, your pretty man, woman and child dolls."

They're gone," cried Carrie, fearful they would set fire to her. "They turned to wooden sticks."

"Ho-ho! A likely story! You lie! So now you must suffer, little owl, to become one of us—or die. Take your choice."

It was an easy decision. Carrie nodded and tried not to sniffle.

"All right, from this night forward you, Carrie Dollanganger, funny name, funny face, will be one of *us*."

It hurts to write of how they took Carrie and blindfolded her, then tied her small hands behind her back, then pushed her out into the hall, then up a flight of steep stairs, and suddenly they were outside. Carrie felt the cool night air, the slant of the support beneath her bare feet, and guessed correctly the girls had taken her onto the roof! There was only one thing she feared more than the grandmother and that was the roof—any roof! Anticipating her bellowing screams the girls had gagged Carrie. "Now lie or sit still as a proper owl should," said the same harsh voice. "Perch here on the roof, near the chimney under the moon, and in the morning you will be one of *us*."

Struggling and frantic now, Carrie tried to resist the pull of so many who forced her to sit. Then, even worse, they suddenly took away their hands and left her there in the darkness on the roof—all alone. Far away she heard the whispering titters of their retreat and the slight click of a door latching down.

Cathy, Cathy, she screamed to herself, *Chris, come save me! Dr. Paul, why did you put me here? Don't nobody want me?* Sobbing, making small mewing sounds while blindfolded, gagged and bound, Carrie braved the steep incline of the huge, strange roof and began to move toward where the latching sound had come from. Inch by inch, sitting up and sliding along on her bottom, Carrie moved forward, praying every time she moved an inch not to fall. It seemed from her faltering report that she gave me much, much later that she was not only guided by instinct, but she could hear, above and from behind the oncoming spring thunderstorm, the sweet and distant voice of Cory singing as he strummed his melancholy song of finding his home and the sun again.

"Oh, Cathy, it was so strange way up there high, and the wind started to blow, and the rain began to fall, and the thunder rumbled and the lightning struck so I could see the brightness through the blindfold—and all the time Cory was singing and leading me to the trapdoor that opened when I used my feet to force it upward, and somehow I wiggled through. Then I fell down the stairs! I fell into blackness and I heard a bone break. And the pain, it came like teeth and bit me so I couldn't see or feel anything or even hear the rain anymore. And Cory, he went away."

Sunday morning came and Paul, Chris and I were at the breakfast table eating brunch.

Chris had a hot, homemade buttery roll in his hand, his lips parted wide to put at least half inside with one bite, when the telephone in the hall rang. Paul groaned as he put down his fork. I groaned too, for I had made my first cheese soufflé and it had to be eaten right away. "Would you mind getting that, Cathy?" he asked. "I really want to dig into your soufflé. It looks delicious and it smells heavenly."

"You sit right there and eat," I said, jumping up and hurrying to answer, "and I'll do what I can to protect you from the pesky Mrs. Williamson. . . ."

He softly laughed and flashed me an amused look as he picked his fork up again. "It may not be my lonely widow lady with another of her minor afflictions." Chris went right on eating.

I picked up the phone and in my most adult and gracious way I said, "Dr. Paul Sheffield's residence."

"This is Emily Dean Dewhurst calling," said the stern voice on the other end. "Please put Dr. Sheffield on the phone immediately!"

"Miss Dewhurst!" I said, already alarmed. "This is Cathy, Carrie's sister. Is Carrie all right?"

"You and Dr. Sheffield are needed here immediately!"

"Miss Dewhurst—"

But she didn't let me finish. "It seems that your younger sister has disappeared rather mysteriously. On Sundays those girls who are being punished by weekend liberty denial are required to attend chapel services. I myself called the roll and Carrie did not respond to her name." My heart beat faster, apprehensive of what I was to hear next, but my finger moved to push a button that would put Miss Dewhurst's message onto the attached microphone so Chris and Paul would hear even as they ate.

"Where was she?" I asked in a small voice, already terrified.

She spoke calmly. "A strange hush came in the air this morning when your sister's name was called and when I asked where she was. I sent a teacher to check your sister's room and she wasn't there. I then ordered a thorough search of the grounds and the entire school building from basement to attic, and still your sister wasn't found. I would, if your sister was of a different character, presume she'd run off and was on her way home. But something in the atmosphere warns that at least twelve of the girls here know what has happened to Carrie and they refuse to talk and incriminate themselves."

My eyes widened. "You mean you still don't know where Carrie is?"

Paul and Chris had stopped eating. Now both stared at me with mounting concern. "I'm sorry to say I don't. Carrie hasn't been seen since nine o'clock last night. Even if she walked all the way home she should have reached there by now. It's almost noon. If she is not there and she is not here, then she is either injured, lost or some other accident has befallen her. . . ."

I could have screamed. How could she speak so dispassionately! Why, why every time something terrible came into our lives was it a flat, uncaring voice that told us the bad news?

Paul's white car sped down Overland Highway toward Carrie's school. I was sandwiched in the front seat between Paul and Chris. My brother had his bag so he could catch a bus and go on to his school after he found out what had happened to Carrie. He had my hand squeezed tight in his to reassure me that *this* child of ours was going to live! "Stop looking so worried, Cathy," said Chris as he put an arm about my shoulder and drew my head to his shoulder. "You know how Carrie is. She's probably hiding and just won't answer. Remember how she was in the attic? She wouldn't stay even when Cory wanted to. Carrie'd take off to do her own thing. She hasn't run away. She'd be too afraid of the dark. She's hiding somewhere. Somebody did something to hurt her feelings and she's punishing them by letting them worry. She couldn't face the world in the dead of night."

Dead of night! Oh, God! I wished Chris hadn't mentioned the attic where Cory had almost died in a trunk before he went on to meet Daddy in heaven. Chris kissed my cheek and wiped away my tears. "Come now, don't cry. I said all of that wrong. She'll be all right."

"What do you mean you don't know where my ward is?" fired Paul in a hard voice as he coldly eyed Miss Dewhurst. "It was my understanding the girls in this school were properly supervised twenty-four hours a day!"

We were in the posh office of Miss Emily Dean Dewhurst. She was not seated behind her impressive, large desk, but restlessly pacing the floor. "Really, Dr. Sheffield, nothing like this has ever happened before. Never have we *lost* a girl. We make a room check every night to see the girls are tucked in bed with lights out, and Carrie *was* in her bed. I myself looked in on her, wanting to comfort her if she'd let me, but she refused to look at me or to speak. Of course it all began with I that fight in your ward's room and the demerits that resulted in their loss of their weekend liberty. Every member of the faculty has helped me search and we've questioned our girls who profess to know nothing about it—which I imagine they do—but if they won't talk, I don't know what to do next."

"Why didn't you notify me when you first found her missing?" Paul asked. I spoke up then and asked to be taken to Carrie's room. Miss Dewhurst turned eagerly to me, anxious to escape the doctor's wrath. As we three followed her up the stairs she spilled forth lengthy excuses so we'd understand how difficult it was to handle so many mischievous girls. When we finally entered Carrie's room several students trailed behind us, whispering back and forth about how much Chris and I looked like Carrie, only we weren't "so freakishly small."

Chris turned to scowl at them. "No wonder she hates it here if you can say things like that!"

"We'll find her," assured Chris. "If we have to stay all week and torture each little witch here we'll make them tell us where she is."

"Young man," shot out Miss Dewhurst, "nobody tortures my girls but me!"

I knew Carrie better than anyone and around the grooves of her brain I ambled. Now, if I were Carrie's age, would I try to escape a school that had unjustly kept me from going home? Yes! *I* would do exactly that. But I was not Carrie; I would not run away in only a nightgown. All her little uniforms were there, custom sewn by Henny, and her small sweaters, skirts and blouses, and pretty dresses, all there. Everything she'd brought to this school was in its proper place. Only the porcelain dolls were missing.

Still on my knees before Carrie's dresser, I sat back on my

heels and looked up at Paul and showed him the box that contained nothing but cotton wadding and sticks of wood. "Her dolls aren't here," I said dully, not comprehending the sticks at all, "and as far as I can tell the only article of her clothing that's missing is one of her nightgowns. Carrie wouldn't go outside wearing only her nightgown. She's got to be here—someplace no one has looked."

"We have looked *everywhere!*" Miss Dewhurst spoke impatiently, as if I had no voice in this matter, only the guardian, the doctor, whose favor she sought even while Paul turned on her another of his stern, hard looks.

For some reason I can't explain I swiveled my head about and caught a cat-who's-eaten-the-canary look on the pale and sickly face of a frizzled, rust-haired, skinny girl whom I detested merely from hearing the little Carrie had told me about her roommate. Maybe it was just her eyes, or the way she kept fingering the big square pocket of her organdy pinafore that narrowed my own eyes as I tried to pierce the depths of hers. She blanched and shifted her green eyes toward the windows, shuffled her feet about uneasily and quickly yanked her hand from her pocket. It was a lined pocket and it bulged suspiciously.

"You," I said, "you're Carrie's roommate, aren't you?"

"I was," she murmured.

"What is that you have in your pocket?"

Her head jerked toward me. Her eyes sparked green fire as the muscles near her lips twitched. "None of your business!"

"Miss Towers!" whiplashed Miss Dewhurst. "Answer Miss Dollanganger's question!"

"It's my purse," said Sissy Towers, glaring at me defiantly.

"It's a very lumpy purse," I said, and suddenly I lunged forward and seized Sissy Towers about the knees. With my free hand, as she struggled and howled, I pulled from her pocket a blue scarf. From that scarf tumbled Mr. and Mrs. Parkins and baby Clara. I held the three porcelain dolls in my hand and demanded, "What are you doing with my sister's dolls?"

"They're my dolls!" said the girl, her gimlet eyes narrowing to slits. The girls gathered around began to snicker and made whispering remarks to one another.

"Your dolls? These dolls belong to my sister."

"*You* lie!" she fired back. "You are stealing from me and my father can have you thrown in jail!"

"Miss Dewhurst," ordered the small demon, her hand reaching for the dolls, "you make this person leave me alone! I don't like her, no more than her *dwarf* sister!"

I got to my feet and towered threateningly above her. Protectively I put the dolls behind my back. She'd have to kill me to get to them!

"Miss Dewhurst!" shrieked the imp as she attacked me. *"My mommy and daddy gave me those dolls for my Christmas!"*

"You lying little devil!" I said, itching to slap her defiant face. "You stole those dolls and the crib from my sister. And because you did Carrie is at this very moment in extreme danger!" I knew it. I felt it. Carrie needed help and fast. "Where is my sister?" I raged.

I stared hard at that red-haired girl named Sissy, knowing she had the answer to where Carrie was but knowing she'd never tell me. It was in her eyes, her mean, spiteful eyes. It was then that Lacy St. John spoke up and told us what they'd done to Carrie the night before.

Oh, God! There was no place in the world more terrifying to Carrie than a roof—any roof! I went reeling back into the past, when Chris and I had tried to take the twins out on the roof of Foxworth Hall so we could hold them in the sunlight and keep them in the fresh air so they'd grow. And like children out of their minds from fright they'd screamed and kicked.

I squeezed my eyelids very tight, concentrating fully on Carrie, where, where, where? And behind my eyes I saw her crouched in a dark corner in what seemed a canyon rising tall on either side of her.

"I want to look in the attic myself," I said to Miss Dewhurst, and she quickly said they'd already thoroughly searched the attic and called and called Carrie's name. But they didn't know Carrie like I did. They didn't know my small sister could go off to a never-never land where speech didn't exist, not when she was in shock.

Up the attic stairs all the teachers, Chris, Paul and I climbed. It was so much like it used to be, a huge, dim and dusty place. But not full of old furniture covered with dusty gray sheets or remnants of the past. Up here were only stacks upon stacks of heavy wooden crates.

Carrie was here. I could sense it. I felt her presence as if she reached out and touched me, though when I looked around I saw nothing but the crates. "Carrie!" I called as loudly as possible. "It's me, Cathy. Don't hide and keep quiet because you're afraid! I've got your dolls and Dr. Paul is with me and so is Chris. We've come to take you home, and never again are we going to send you away to school!" I nudged Paul, "Now you tell her that too."

He abandoned his soft voice and boomed, "Carrie, if you can hear me, it's just as your sister says. We want you to come home with us to stay. I'm sorry, Carrie. I thought you'd like it here. Now I know you couldn't possibly have been happy. Carrie, please come out, we need you."

Then I thought I heard a soft whimper. I raced in that direction with Chris close at my heels. I knew about attics, how to search, how to find.

Abruptly I drew to a halt and Chris collided with me. Just ahead, in the dim shadows created by the towers of heavy wooden crates, still in her nightgown, all torn, dirty and bloody, gagged and still blindfolded, I spied Carrie. Her spill of blond hair gleamed in the faint light. Beneath her a leg was twisted in a grotesque way. "Oh, God," whispered Chris and Paul at the same time, "her leg looks broken."

"Wait a minute," Paul cautioned in a low voice, clamping

both his hands down on my shoulders when I would heedlessly run forward and rescue Carrie. "Look at those crates, Cathy. Just one careless move on your part and they will all come crashing down on both you and Carrie."

Somewhere behind me a teacher moaned and began to pray. How Carrie had managed to drag herself down that close passageway while blind and bound was unbelievable. A fully adult person couldn't have done it—but I could do it—I was still small enough.

Even as I spoke I planned the way. "Carrie, do exactly as I say. Don't lean to the right or to the left. Lie flat on your stomach, aim for my voice. I'm going to crawl in to you and take hold of you under your arms. Raise your head high so your face won't be scraped. Dr. Paul will grab hold of my ankles and pull us both out."

"Tell her it's going to hurt her leg."

"Did you hear Dr. Paul, Carrie? It's going to hurt your leg so please don't thrash about if you feel pain, everything will be over in a second or two and Dr. Paul will make your leg well again."

It seemed to take hours for me to inch down that tunnel while the crates teetered and rocked, and when I had her by the shoulders I heard Dr. Paul cry out "Okay, Cathy!" Then he pulled, fast and hard! Down thundered the wooden crates! Dust flew everywhere. In the confusion I was at Carrie's side, removing the gag and blindfold while the doctor untied her bonds.

Then Carrie was clinging to me, blinking because the light hurt, crying from the pain, terrified to see the teachers and her leg so crooked.

In the ambulance that came to take Carrie to the hospital Chris and I rode and shared the same stool, each of us holding one of Carrie's hands. Paul followed in his white car so he'd be there to supervise the orthopedist who would set Carrie's broken leg. Lying face upward on the pillow near her head with fixed smiles and rigid bodies were Carrie's three dolls.

That's when I remembered. Now the crib was missing too, just as the cradle had disappeared years ago.

Carrie's broken leg spoiled the long summer vacation trip our doctor had planned for all of us. Again I raged inwardly at Momma. Her fault; always we were punished for what she'd caused! It wasn't fair that Carrie had to be laid up and we couldn't journey north—while our mother gallivanted from here to there, going to parties, hobnobbing with the jet set and the movie stars as if we didn't exist at all! On the French Riviera now. I cut that item from Greenglenna's society column and pasted it into my huge scrapbook of revenge. That was one article I showed to Chris before I put it into the book. I didn't show him all of them. I didn't want him to know I had subscribed to the Virginia newspaper that reported on everything the Foxworths did.

"Where did you get this?" he demanded, looking up from the clipping he handed back to me.

"The Greenglenna newspaper—it's more concerned with high society than Clairmont's *Daily News*. Our mother is a hot item, didn't you know?"

"I try to forget, unlike you!" he said sharply. "*We* don't have it so bad now, do we? We're lucky to be with Paul, and Carrie's leg will mend and be as good as ever. And other summers will come when we can go to New England."

How did he know that? Nothing ever was offered twice. Maybe in other summers to come we'd be too busy or Paul would. "You realize, being an 'almost' doctor, don't you, that her leg might not grow while she's in that cast?"

He looked strangely ill-at-ease. "If she grew like average kids I guess there might be that risk. But, Cathy, she doesn't grow very much, so there's little chance one leg will be shorter than the other."

"Oh, go bury your nose in *Gray's Anatomy*!" I flared, angry because he'd always make light of anything I said that made Momma the fault of anything. He knew why Carrie didn't grow as well as I did. Deprived of love, of sunshine and freedom, it was a marvel she'd lived to survive! Arsenic too! Damn Momma to hell!

Busily, day by day, I added to my collection of news clippings and blurry photographs cut from many newspapers. That's where most of my "pin money" went. Though I stared at all the pictures of Momma with hate and loathing, I looked at her husband with admiration. How very handsome, how powerfully built her young husband was with his long, lean, darkly bronzed skin. I stared at the photograph that showed him lifting a champagne glass high as he toasted his wife on their second wedding anniversary.

I decided that night to send Momma a short note. Sent first class, it would be forwarded.

Dear Mrs. Winslow,

How well I remember the summer of your honeymoon. It was a wonderful summer, so refreshingly pleasant in the mountains in a locked room with windows that were never opened.

Congratulations and my very best wishes, Mrs. Winslow, and I do hope all your future summers, winters, springs and falls will be haunted by the memory of the kind of summers, winters, springs and falls your Dresden dolls used to have.

Not yours anymore,
The doctor doll,
The ballerina doll,
The praying-to-grow-taller doll,
And the dead doll.

I ran to post the letter and no sooner had I dropped it in the mailbox on the corner than I was wishing I had it back. Chris would hate me for doing this.

It rained that night and I got up to watch the storm. Tears streaked my face as much as the rain streaked the window glass. Because it was Saturday Chris was home. He was out there on the veranda, allowing the wind-driven rain to wet his pajamas and glue them to his skin.

He saw me just about the time I saw him, and he stepped into my room without saying a word. We clung together, me crying and him trying hard not to. I wanted him to go, even as I held hard to him and cried on his shoulder. "Why, Cathy, why all the tears?" he asked as I sobbed on and on.

"Chris," I asked when I could, "you don't still love *her*, do you?"

He hesitated before he answered. That made anger simmer my blood into a rolling boil. "*You do!*" I cried. "How can you after what she did to Cory and to Carrie? Chris, what's wrong with you that you can go on loving when you should hate as I do?"

Still he didn't say anything. And his very silence gave me the answer. He went on loving her because he had to if he were to go on loving me. Every time he looked in my face he saw her and what she'd been like in her early youth. Chris was just like Daddy, who had been just as vulnerable to the kind of beauty I had. But it was only a surface resemblance. I wasn't weak! I wasn't without abilities! I could have thought of one thousand ways to earn a living, rather than lock my four children in a miserable room and leave them in care of an evil old woman who wanted to see them suffer for sins that weren't even theirs!

While I thought my vengeful thoughts and made my plans to ruin her life when I could, Chris was tenderly kissing me. I hadn't even noticed. "Stop!" I cried when I felt his lips pressing down on mine. "Leave me alone! You don't love me like I want to be loved, for what I am. You love me because my face is like hers! Sometimes I hate my face!"

He looked terribly wounded as he backed toward the door. "I was only trying to comfort you," he said in a broken voice. "Don't turn it into something ugly."

My fear that Carrie's leg would come out of the cast shorter than the other proved groundless. In no time at all after her leg was cut free from the plaster she was walking around as good as ever.

As fall neared, Chris, Paul and I conferred and decided that a public school where Carrie could come home every afternoon would be best for her after all. All she'd have to do was board a bus three blocks from home; the same bus would bring her home at three in the afternoon. In Paul's big homey kitchen she'd stay with Henny while I attended ballet class.

Soon September was upon us again, then November had gone by, and still Carrie hadn't made a single friend. She wanted most desperately to belong, but always she was an outsider. She wanted someone as dear as a sister but she found only suspicion, hostility and ridicule. It seemed Carrie would walk the long halls of that elementary school forever before she found a friend.

"Cathy," Carrie would tell me, "nobody likes me."

"They will. Sooner or later they will know how sweet and wonderful you are. And you have all of us who love and admire you so don't let others worry you. Don't care what they think!" She sniffed, for she did care, she did!

Carrie slept on her twin bed pushed close beside mine, and every night I saw her kneel beside her bed, temple her small hands under her chin, and with lowered head she prayed, "And please, God, let me find my mother again. My real mother. And most of all, Lord God, let me grow just a little bit taller. You don't have to make me as tall as Momma, but almost as tall as Cathy, please God, please, please."

Lying on my bed and hearing this, I stared bleakly up at the ceiling and I hated Momma, really despised and loathed her! How could Carrie still want a mother who'd been so cruel? Had Chris and I done right in sparing her the grim truth of how our own mother had tried to kill us? How she'd caused Carrie to be as small as she was?

Upon her smallness Carrie placed all her unhappiness and loneliness. She knew she had a pretty face and sensational hair, but what did they matter when the face and the hair were on a head much too large for the thin little body? Carrie's beauty did nothing at all to win her friends and admiration, just the opposite. "Doll face, Angel Hair. Hey you, midget, or are you a dwarf? Are you gonna join a circus and be their littlest freak?" And home she'd run, all three blocks from the bus stop, scared and crying, tormented again by children without sensitivity.

"I'm no good, Cathy!" she wailed with her face buried in my lap. "Nobody likes me. They don't like my body 'cause it's too little, and they don't like my head 'cause it's too big, and they don't even like what is pretty 'cause they think it's wasted on somebody too little like me!"

I said what I could to comfort her but I felt so inadequate. I knew she watched my every movement and compared my proportions to hers. She realized I was very much in proportion and how much she was constructed grotesquely.

If I could have given her a part of my height, gladly I would have done so. Instead, I gave her my prayers. Night after night, I too went down on my knees and prayed to God, "Please let Carrie grow! Please, God, she's so young, and it hurts her so much, and she's been through so much. Be kind. Look down, God! See us! Hear us!"

One afternoon Carrie went to the only one who could deliver almost everything—so why not size?

Paul was sitting on his back veranda, sipping wine, nibbling cheese and crackers. I was at ballet class, so I heard only Paul's version of what happened.

"She came to me, Cathy, and asked if I didn't have a stretching machine to pull her out longer."

I sighed when he told me.

"'If I had such a machine,' I told her"—and I knew he'd done it with love, kindness and understanding, not with mockery—"'it would be a very painful process. Have patience, darling, you're taller than you were when you came. Time will make you grow. Why, I've seen the shortest young people suddenly just shoot up overnight after they reach puberty.' She stared at me with those big blue haunted eyes and I saw her disappointment. I had failed her. I could tell from the way she ambled off with her shoulders drooping and her head hung so low. Her hopes must have ridden high when those cruel kids at her school chided her about finding a 'stretching machine.'"

"Isn't there one thing modern medicine can do to help her grow?" I asked Paul.

"I'm looking into it," he said in a tight voice. "I'd give my soul to see Carrie reach the height she wants. I'd give her inches of my height, if only I could."

Momma's Shadow

We had been with our doctor for one year and a half, and what exhilarating and baffling days they were. I was like a mole coming out of darkness only to find the brilliant days weren't at all like I had supposed they would be.

I'd thought once we were free of Foxworth Hall and I was almost an adult life would lead me down a clear and straight path to fame, fortune and happiness. I had the talent; I saw that in the admiring eyes of Madame and Georges. Madame especially harped on every little flaw of technique, of control. Every criticism told me I was worth all her efforts to make me not only an excellent dancer but a sensational one.

During summer vacation Chris obtained a job as a waiter in a café from seven in the mornings to seven in the evenings. In August he would leave again for Duke University where he would begin his second year in college. Carrie fiddled away her time playing on the swing, playing with her little girl toys, though she was ten now and should be outgrowing dolls. I spent five days a week in ballet class, and half of Saturday. My small sister was like a shadow tagging after me when I was at home. When I wasn't she was Henny's shadow. She needed a playmate of her own age but she couldn't find one. She had only the porcelain dolls to confide in now that she felt too old to act the baby with Chris and me, and suddenly she stopped complaining about her size. But her eyes, those sad, sad yearning eyes, told how she longed to be as tall as the girls we saw walking in the shopping malls.

Carrie's loneliness hurt so much that again I thought of Momma and damned her to everlasting hell! I hoped she was hung over the eternal fires by her heels and prodded by imps with spears.

More and more often I was writing Momma short notes to torment her sunny life wherever she was. She never settled down in one place long enough to receive my letters, or if she did she didn't respond. I waited for the letters to come back stamped ADDRESS UNKNOWN but none ever did.

I read the Greenglenna newspaper carefully every evening, trying to find out just what my mother was up to and where she was. Sometimes there was news.

Mrs. Bartholomew Winslow left Paris and flew on to Rome to visit Italy's new chic couturier. I cut out that clipping and added it to my scrapbook. Oh, would do when I met up with her! Sooner or later she'd have to come to Greenglenna and live in that home of Bart Winslow's which was newly repaired, redecorated and refurbished. I cut out that news article too and stared long and hard at a photograph which was not flattering. This was unusual. Customarily she could put on a brilliant smile to show the world how happy and contented she was with her life.

Chris left for college in August, two weeks before I went back to high school. In late January I would graduate. I couldn't wait to be finished with high school so I studied like mad.

The autumn days flew swiftly by, so much in contrast to other autumns when time had crept monotonously while we grew older and youth was stolen from us. Just keeping track of my mother's activities kept me busy, and then when I really put my nose on the trail of Bart's family history I used up more of my precious time.

In Greenglenna I pored for hours over old books written about the founding families of Greenglenna. His ancestors had arrived just about the same time mine had, back in the eighteenth century, and they too had been from England, settling down in Virginia in the part that was now North Carolina. I looked up and stared into space. Was it just a coincidence that his ancestors and mine had been part of that "Lost Colony"? Some of the husbands had sailed back to England for more supplies only to return much later and find their colony abandoned, with not one single survivor to tell why. After the Revolution the Winslows had moved to South Carolina. How odd. Now the Foxworths too were in South Carolina.

Not a day passed as I shopped and traveled on the busy streets of Greenglenna that I didn't expect to see my mother. I stared after every blond I saw. I went into expensive shops looking for her. Snobbish salesladies would come up silently behind me and inquire if they could help. Of course they couldn't help. I was looking for my mother, and she wasn't hanging from a clothes rack. But she was in town! The society column had given me this information. Any day I would see her!

One sunny Saturday I was rushing to do an errand for Madame Marisha when I suddenly spotted on the sidewalk ahead of me a man and a woman so familiar my heart almost stopped beating! It was them! Just to see her strolling so casually at his side, enjoying herself, put me in a state of panic! Sour gall rose in my throat. I dared to draw nearer, so I was very close behind them. If she turned she'd be sure to see me—and what would I do then? Spit in her face? Yes, I would like to do that. I could trip her and make her fall and watch how she lost her dignity. That would be nice. But I didn't do anything but tremble and feel ill as I listened to them talk.

Her voice was so soft and sweet, so cultivated and genteel. I marveled at how svelte she still was, how lovely her pale, gleaming hair that waved softly back from her face. When she turned her head to speak again to the man at her side I saw her profile. I sighed. Oh, God, my mother in that expensive, rose-colored suit. The beautiful mother I had loved so well. My murdering mother who could still take my heart and wring it dry, for once I had loved her so very much and trusted her . . . and deep inside of me was that little girl, like Carrie, who still wanted a mother to love. Why, Momma? Why did you have to love money more than you loved your children?

I stifled the sob that she might have heard. My emotions raged out of control. I wanted to run up and scream accusations before her husband, and shock him and terrify her! I also wanted to run up and throw my arms about her, cry out her name and plead that she love me again. But all the tempestuous emotions I felt were submerged in the tidal wave of spite and vengeance I felt. I didn't accost her, for I wasn't ready to face her yet. I wasn't rich or famous. I wasn't anybody special and she was still a great beauty. She was one of the wealthiest women in the area and also one of the luckiest.

I dared much that day but they didn't turn to see me. My mother was not the type to look behind her or stare at passersby. She was accustomed to being the one who drew all the admiring glances. Like a queen among peasants she strolled as if no one was on the street but her and her young husband.

When I had my fill of viewing her, I looked at her husband and drank up the special kind of virile, pantherlike handsomeness that was his. He no longer sported a huge thick mustache. His dark hair was waved smoothly back and was styled modishly. He reminded me a bit of Julian.

The words my mother and her husband exchanged weren't particularly revealing. They were discussing what restaurant

they should dine in, and did he think the furniture they'd
shopped for this afternoon could be bettered if they shopped
in New York? "I do love the breakfront we chose," she said in
a voice that brought back my childhood. "It reminds me so
much of the one I bought just before Chris was killed."

Oh, yes. That breakfront had cost two thousand five hundred dollars and was so needed to balance one end of the living room. Then Daddy died on the highway and everything
unpaid for was repossessed, including the breakfront.

I followed where they led, daring fate to let them see me.
They were here, living in the home of Bart Winslow. As I
tagged along, full of vengeful schemes, despising her, admiring him, I planned which way to hurt her most. And what
did I do—I chickened out! I did nothing, absolutely nothing!
Furious with myself I went home and raged in front of the
mirror, hating my image because it was her all over! Damn
her to hell! I picked up a heavy paperweight from the special
little French provincial desk Paul had bought me and I hurled
it straight at the mirror! *There, Momma! You're broken in pieces
now! Gone, gone, gone!* Then I was crying, and later a workman
came and replaced the glass in the mirror frame. Fool, that's
what I was. Now I'd wasted some of the money I was planning
to use for a wonderful gift for Paul's forty-second birthday.

Someday I'd get even, and in a way in which I wouldn't
be hurt. It would be more than just a broken mirror. Much,
much more.

A Birthday Gift

Medical conventions ruined many a plan of mine, as did patients. On this unique day I skipped ballet class to rush straight home from high school. I found Henny in the kitchen slaving over a gourmet menu I had planned—all Paul's favorite dishes. A Creole jambalaya with shrimp, crabmeat, rice, green bell peppers, onions, garlic, mushrooms and so many other things I thought I'd never finish measuring out half teaspoons of this and that. Then all the mushrooms and other vegetables had to be sautéed. It was a troublesome dish I wasn't likely to make again.

No sooner was this in the oven than I began another cake from scratch. The first was sunk in the middle and was soggy. I covered up the hollow with thick frosting and gave it to the neighborhood kids. Henny bustled and bumbled around, shaking her head and throwing me critical glances.

I had the last rose squeezed from the pastry tube when Chris dashed in the back door bearing his gift. "Am I late?" he asked breathlessly. "I can't stay longer than nine o'clock; I have to be back at Duke before roll call."

"You're just in time," I said, all flustered and in a flurry to get upstairs and bathe and dress. "You set the table while Henny finishes up with the salad." It was beneath his dignity, of course, to set a table, but for once he obliged without complaint.

I shampooed my hair and set it on large rollers, and polished my nails a glowing, silvery pink, my toenails too. I painted my face with an expertise born of hours of practice and long consultations with Madame Marisha and the beauty assistants in the department stores. When I was done no one would have guessed I was only seventeen. Down the stairs I drifted, borne aloft by the admiration that shone from my brother's eyes and by the envy from Carrie's and a big grin that split Henny's face from ear to ear.

Fussily I arranged the table again, changing around the noise-makers, the snappers and the colorful, ridiculous paper clown hats. Chris blew up a few balloons and suspended them from the chandelier. And then we all sat down to wait for Paul to come and enjoy his "surprise party."

When he didn't show up and the hours passed, I got up to pace the floor as Momma had done on Daddy's thirty-sixth birthday party when he never came home, not ever.

Finally Chris had to leave. Then Carrie began to yawn and complain. We fed her and let her go to bed. She slept in her own room now, especially decorated in purple and red. Next it was only Henny and me watching TV as the Creole casserole kept warming and drying out, and our salad was wilting, and then Henny yawned and left for bed. Now I was left alone to pace and worry, my party ruined.

At ten I heard Paul's car turn into the drive and through the back door he strode, bearing with him the two suitcases he'd taken to Chicago. He tossed me a casual greeting before he noticed my fancy attire.

"Hey, . . ." he said, throwing a suspicious glance into the dining room and seeing the party decorations, "have I somehow managed to spoil something you planned?"

He was so damned casual about being three hours late I could have killed him if I hadn't loved him so much. Like those who always try to hide the truth, I lit into him, "Why did you have to go to that medical convention in the first place? You might have guessed we'd have special plans for your birthday! And then you go and call us up and tell us what time to expect you home, and then you're three hours late—"

"My flight was delayed—" he started to explain.

"I've been slaving to make you a cake that tastes as good as your mother's," I interrupted, *"and then you don't show up!"* I brushed past him and pulled the casserole from the oven.

"I'm ravenous," said Paul humbly, apologetically. "If you haven't eaten, we might as well make the most of what looks like it could have been a very festive and happy occasion. Have mercy on me, Cathy. I don't control the weather."

I nodded stiffly to indicate I was at least a little understanding. He smiled and lightly brushed the back of his hand over my cheek. "You look absolutely exquisite," he breathed softly, "so take the frown off your face and get things ready, and I'll be down in ten minutes."

In ten minutes he had showered and shaved and changed into fresh clothes. By the light of four candles the two of us sat down at the long dining table with me to his left. I had arranged this meal so I wouldn't have to hop up and down to serve him. Everything that was needed was put upon a serving cart. The dishes that had to be served hot were on electrical heating units, and the champagne was cooling in a bucket. "The champagne is from Chris," I explained. "He's developed a liking for it."

He lifted the champagne bottle from the ice and glanced at the label. "It's a good year and must have been expensive; your brother has developed gourmet taste."

We ate slowly and it seemed whenever I lifted my eyes

they met with his. He'd come home looking tired, mussy; now he looked completely refreshed. He'd been gone two long, long weeks. Dead weeks that made me miss his presence in the open doorway of my bedroom as I practiced at the barre, doing my warm-up exercises before breakfast to beautiful music that sent my soul soaring.

When our meal was over I dashed into the kitchen, then glided back bearing a gorgeous coconut cake with miniature green candles fitted into red roses made of icing. Across the top I'd written as skillfully as I could with that pastry tube, *Happy Birthday to Paul.*

"What do you think?" Paul asked after he blew out the candles.

"Think about what?" I questioned back, carefully setting down the cake with twenty-six candles, for that was the age he appeared to me, and the age I wanted him to be. I felt very much an adolescent, floundering in the world of adult quicksand. My short, formal gown was flame-colored chiffon, with shoestring straps and lots of cleavage showing. But if my attempts to look sophisticated had succeeded, inside I was in a daze as I tried to play the role of seductress.

"My mustache—surely you've noticed. You've been staring at it for half an hour."

"It's nice," I stammered, blushing as red as my gown. "It becomes you."

"Now ever since you came you've been hinting how much more handsome and appealing I'd be with a mustache. And now that I've taken the trouble to grow one you say it's *nice.* Nice is such a weak word, Catherine."

"It's because . . . because you do look so handsome," I stumbled, "that I can find only weak words. I fear that Thelma Murkel has already found all the strong words to flatter you."

"How the hell do you know about her?" He fired this at me as he narrowed his beautiful eyes.

Gosh, he should know—gossip—and so I told him this:

"I went to that hospital where Thelma Murkel is the head nurse on the third floor. And I sat just beyond the nurse's station and watched her for a couple of hours. In my opinion she's not quite beautiful, but handsome, and she seemed to me terribly bossy. And she flirts with all the doctors, in case you don't know that."

I left him laughing with his eyes lit up. Thelma Murkel was a head nurse in the Clairmont Memorial Hospital and everyone there seemed to know she had her mind set on becoming the second Mrs. Paul Scott Sheffield. But she was only a nurse in a sterile white uniform, miles and miles away, and I was under his nose, with my intoxicating new perfume tickling his senses (as the advertisement had said, a bewitching, beguiling, seductive scent no man could resist). What chance did Thelma Murkel, age twenty-nine, have against the likes of me?

I was giddy from three glasses of Chris's imported champagne and hardly alert at all when Paul began to open the gifts Carrie, Chris and I had saved up to buy for him. I'd embroidered for him a crewel painting of his gingerbread white house with trees showing above the roof and a part of the brick wall to the sides with a little of the flowers showing. Chris had sketched it for me and I'd slaved many hours to make it perfect.

"It's a stunningly beautiful work of art!" he said with impressed awe. I couldn't help but think of the grandmother, and how she'd cruelly rejected our tedious and hopeful gesture to win her friendship. "Thank you very much, Catherine, for thinking so much of me. I'm going to hang it in my office where all my patients can see it."

Tears flooded my eyes, smeared my mascara as I furtively tried to blot them away before he realized it wasn't just the candlelight making me this beautiful, but three hours of preparation. He didn't notice the tears or my handkerchief that came from the cleavage of my low-cut gown. He was still admiring the small stitches I'd so carefully made. He put the gift aside, caught my glance with his own shining eyes and stood to help me up. "It's too beautiful a night to go to bed," he said as he glanced at his watch. "I've got a yearning to walk in the garden by moonlight. Do you ever have yearnings like that?"

Yearnings? I was made of yearnings, half of them adolescent and too fanciful to ever come true. Yet as I strolled by his side through the magic of his Japanese garden and over the little red-lacquered footbridge, and as we ascended marble steps and walked on hand in hand, I felt we'd both entered a magical never-never land. It was the marble statues, of course, life-size marble statues standing in their cold and perfect nudity.

The breezes were blowing the Spanish moss, and Paul had to duck to escape it, while I could stand straight and smile because having height did cause a few problems I could escape. "You're laughing at me, Cath-er-ine," he said, just as Chris used to tease, and separate my name into slow and distinct syllables. *My lady, Cath-er-ine.*

I ran on ahead and down the marble steps to the center where Rodin's *The Kiss* dominated the garden. Everything seemed silvery bluish and unreal, and the moon was big and bright, full and smiling, with long dark clouds streaking its face and making it seem sinister one moment and gay the next. I sighed, for it was like that strange night that put Chris and me up on the roof of Foxworth Hall, both of us fearful we'd roast over the eternal fires of hell.

"It's a pity you are here with me and not with that beautiful boy you dance with," said Paul, yanking me back from thoughts of yesterday.

"Julian?" I asked in surprise. "He's in New York this week—but I suspect he'll be back again next week."

"Oh," he said. "Then next week will belong to him, and not me."

"That all depends. . . ."

"On what?"

"Sometimes I want him and sometimes I don't. Sometimes he seems just a boy and I want a man. Then again, sometimes he's very sophisticated and that impresses me. And when I dance with him I fall madly in love with the prince he's supposed to be. He looks so splendid in those costumes."

"Yeah," he said, "I've noticed that myself."

"His hair is jet black, while yours is sort of brownish smoky black."

"I suppose jet black is more romantic than brownish smoky black?" he teased.

"That all depends."

"Catherine, you are female through and through—stop giving me enigmatic answers."

"I'm not enigmatic, I'm just telling you love isn't enough, nor romance. I want skills to see me through life so I'll never have to lock away my children to inherit a fortune I didn't earn. I want to know how to earn a buck and see us through, even if we don't have a man to lean on and support us."

"Catherine, Catherine," he said softly, taking both my hands in his and holding them tight. "How hurt you've been by your mother. You sound so adult, so hard. Don't let bitter memories deprive you of one of your greatest assets—your soft, loving ways. A man likes to take care of the woman he loves and his children. A man likes to be leaned on, looked up to, respected. An aggressive, domineering woman is one of God's most fearsome creatures."

I yanked free of him and ran on to the swing and threw myself down on the seat. I pushed myself high, higher, fast, faster, flying so high it took me back to the attic and the swings there when the nights were long and stuffy. Now here I was, free, on the outside and swinging crazily to put myself *back* into the attic! It was seeing Momma and her husband again that was making me desperate, making me want what should be put off until I was older.

I flew so high, so wild, so abandoned my skirts fanned up

into my face and made me blind. Dizzy, I suddenly fell to the ground! Paul came running to my side, falling down on his knees to lift me up in his arms. "Are you hurt?" he asked, and kissed me before I could answer. No, not hurt. I was a dancer who knew how to fall. He started murmuring the love words I needed to hear between his kisses that came slower and lasted longer, and the look in his eyes made me fill with a drunkenness far headier and far more sparkling than any imported French champagne.

My lips parted beneath his prolonged kiss. I gasped because his tongue touched mine. His kisses came hot, soft, moist on my eyelids, my cheeks, my chin, neck, shoulders, cleavage as his hands endlessly roamed and sought all my most intimate places.

"Catherine," he gasped, pulling away and gazing down at me with his eyes on fire, "you're only a child. We can't let this happen. I swore I'd never let this happen, not with you." Useless words that I snuffed out by encircling his neck with my arms. My fingers sank into the thickness of his dark hair as I murmured huskily, "I wanted to give you a shiny silver Cadillac for your birthday, but I didn't have enough money. So I thought I'd give you second best—me."

He moaned softly. "I can't let you do this—*you don't* owe *me.*" I laughed and kissed him, shamelessly kissed him long and deep.

"Paul, it's *you* who owes me! You've given me too many long, desiring looks to tell me you don't want me now. If you say that you're lying. You think of me as a child. But I grew up a long time ago. Don't love me, I don't care. For I love you and that's enough. I know you'll love me the way I want to be loved, because even though you won't admit it, you do love me and want me."

The moon lit up his eyes and made them shine. Even as he said, "No, you're a fool to think it will work," his eyes were speaking differently.

To my way of thinking, his very restraint proved exactly how very much he *did* love me. If he had loved me less he would have eagerly taken long ago what I wouldn't have denied. So when he made a move to rise, to leave me and have done with temptation, I took his hand and put it where it would pleasure me most. He groaned. And groaned even louder when I put *my* hand where it would pleasure *him* most. Shameless what I did, I knew it. I shut off my thoughts of what Chris would think, of how the grandmother would consider me a scarlet harlot. Oh, was it fortunate or just the opposite that that book in Momma's nightstand drawer had shown me well what to do to pleasure a man and how to respond?

I thought he would take me there on the grass under the stars, but he picked me up and carried me back into the house. Up the back stairs he stole quietly. Neither of us spoke though my lips traveled over his neck and face. Far off, in the room to the rear of the kitchen, I could hear Henny's TV as she listened to a late-night talkshow.

On his bed he laid me down and with his eyes alone he began his lovemaking, and in his eyes I drowned, and things grew blurry as my emotions swelled higher like a tidal wave engulfing both of us. Skin to skin we pressed, just holding close at first and thrilling in the exaltation of sharing what the other had to give. With each touch of his lips, of his hands I was shot through with electrifying sensations, until at last I was wild to have him enter me, no longer tender, but fervent with his own fierce, demanding need to reach the same heights I was seeking.

"Catherine! Hurry, hurry, *come!*"

What was he talking about? I was there beneath him, doing what I could. Come where? He was slippery and wet with sweat. My legs were raised and clutched about his waist and I could feel the terrible effort of his restraint as he kept telling me to come, come, come! Then he groaned and gave up.

Hot juices spurted forth to warm up my insides pleasantly five or six times, and then it was over, all over, and he
was pulling out. And I hadn't reached any mountain high,
or heard bells ringing, or felt myself exploding—not as he
had. It was all over his face, relaxed and at peace now, vaguely
smeared with joy. How easy for men, I thought, while I still
wanted more. There I was on the verge of Fourth-of-July fire-
works and it was all over. All over but for his sleepy hands that
roamed over my body, exploring all hills and crevices before
he fell asleep. Now his heavy leg was thrown over mine. I was
left staring up at the ceiling with tears in my eyes. *Good-bye,
Christopher Doll—now you are set free.*

Sunlight through the window wakened me early. Paul was
propped up on an elbow gazing dreamily down at me. "You
are so beautiful, so young, so desirable. You aren't sorry, are
you? I hope you don't wish now you had done it differently?"

I snuggled closer against his bare skin. "Explain one
thing, please. Why did you keep asking me to come?" He
roared with laughter.

"Catherine, my love," he finally managed. "I nearly killed
myself trying to hold back until you could climax. And now
you lie there with those big innocent blue eyes and ask what
I meant! I thought those dancing playmates of yours had
explained everything to you. Don't tell me there is one subject
you haven't read about in a book!"

"Well, there was a book I found in Momma's night table
drawer. . . . But I just looked at the photographs. I never read
the text, though Chris did, but then he stole more often to her
bedroom suite than I did."

He cleared his throat. "I could tell you what I meant by
what I said, but demonstrating would be more fun. Really,
you don't have the least idea?"

"Yes," I said defensively, "of course I do. I'm supposed
to feel stunned by lightning bolts so I stiffen out and go

unconscious and then I'm split wide apart into atoms that float around in space and then gather together and sizzle me with tingles so I can float back to reality with dream-stars in my eyes—like you had."

"Catherine, don't make me love you too much." He sounded serious, as if I'd hurt him if he did.

"I'll try to love you the way you want."

"I'll shave first," he said, throwing back the covers and making ready to get up.

I reached to pull him back. "I like the way you look now, so dark and dangerous."

Eagerly I surrendered to all Paul's desires. We developed delicate ways of keeping our trysts secret from Henny. On Henny's day off I washed the bed linens that were duplicates of the ones soiled that I hid away until they could be washed. Carrie could have been in another world she was so unobservant. But when Chris was home we had to be more discreet and not even look at each other, lest we betray ourselves. I felt strange with Chris now, like I'd betrayed him.

I didn't know how long the rapture between Paul and me would last. I longed for passion undying, for ecstasy everlasting. Yet my suspicious self guessed nothing as glorious as what Paul and I had could go on indefinitely. He would soon tire of me, a child whose mental capacities couldn't compete with his, and he'd go back to his old ways—maybe with Thelma Murkel. Maybe Thelma Murkel had gone with him to that medical convention, though I was wise enough not to question him ever about what he did when I wasn't with him. I wanted to give him everything Julia had denied, and give gladly with no recriminations when we parted.

But in the moment of our flaming obsession with each other I felt so large, so generous, and I gloated in our selfless abandonment. And I think the grandmother with her talk of evil and sin had made it ten times more exciting because it was so very, very wicked.

And then again I'd flounder, not wanting Chris to think I was wicked. Oh, it mattered so much to me what Chris would think. *Please, God, let Chris know why I'm doing this. And I do love Paul, I do!*

After Thanksgiving Chris still had a few days of vacation, and while we were at the dinner table with Henny hovering nearby, Paul asked all of us what we wanted for Christmas. This would be our third Christmas with Paul. In late January I'd be graduating from high school. I didn't have much time to go, for my next step, I hoped, would be New York.

I spoke up and told Paul what I wanted for Christmas. I wanted to go to Foxworth Hall. Chris's eyes widened and Carrie began to cry. "No!" said Chris firmly. "We will not open healed wounds!"

"My wounds are not healed!" I stated just as firmly. *"They will never be healed until justice is done!"*

Foxworth Hall, from the Outside

The minute the words left my mouth he shouted, "*No!* Why can't you let bygones be bygones?"

"*Because I am not like you, Christopher!* You like to pretend that Cory didn't die of arsenic poisoning, but of pneumonia, because you feel more comfortable with that! Yet you were the one who convinced me she was the one who did it! So why can't we go up there and see for ourselves if any hospital has a record of Cory's death?"

"Cory could have died of pneumonia. He had all the symptoms." How lamely he said that, knowing full well he was protecting her.

"Now wait a minute," said Paul who had kept quiet, and spoke only when he saw the fire blazing from my eyes. "If Cathy feels she must do this thing, why not, Chris? Though if your mother admitted Cory to a hospital under a false name it won't be easy to check up."

"She had a fake name put on his tombstone too," said Chris, giving me a long, hateful look. Paul gave that some thought, wondering aloud how we could find a grave when we didn't know the name. I believed I had all the answers. If she registered Cory in a hospital for treatment under a certain name, then naturally she'd use the same name when he was buried. "And Paul since you're a doctor you can gain entry to all the hospital records, right?"

"You really want to do this?" he asked. "It's sure to bring back a lot of unhappy memories and, like Chris just said, open up healed wounds."

"My wounds are not healed, and will never be healed! I want to put flowers on Cory's grave. I think it will comfort Carrie to know where he's buried, then we can visit him from time to time. Chris, *you don't have to go* if you are so dead set against it!"

What I wanted Paul tried to deliver, despite Chris's opposition. Chris did travel with us to Charlottesville, riding in the back seat with Carrie. Paul went inside several hospitals and charmed the nurses into giving him the records he wanted. He looked and I looked while Carrie and Chris stayed outside. Not one eight-year-old boy had died of pneumonia two years ago in late October! Not only that, the cemeteries didn't have a record of a child his age being buried! Still stubbornly determined, I had to trek through all the cemeteries, feeling Momma might have lied and put Dollanganger on his headstone after all. Carrie cried, for Cory was supposed to be in heaven, not in the ground lightly frosted with a recent snowfall.

Fruitless, time-consuming, unrewarding waste! As far as the world was concerned, no male child of eight years had died in the months of October and November 1960! Chris insisted we go back to Paul's. He tried to persuade me that I didn't really want to see Foxworth Hall.

I whirled to glare at Chris. *"I do want to go there! We do have time!* Why come this far and turn back without seeing that house? At least once in the daylight, on the outside—why not?"

It was Paul who reasoned with Chris by telling him I needed to see the house. "And to be honest, Chris, I'd like to see it myself."

Brooding sullenly in the back seat beside Carrie, Chris relented. Carrie cried as Paul headed his car toward the climbing mountain roads that Momma and her husband must have traversed thousands of times. Paul stopped at a gas station to ask directions to Foxworth Hall. Easily we could have guided Paul to Foxworth Hall, if we knew where the train tracks were and could find the mail depot that was a stop-off point.

"Beautiful country," said Paul as he drove. Eventually we did come upon that grand house that sat all alone on a mountainside. "That's the one!" I cried, terribly excited. It was huge as a hotel, with double wings that jutted out front and back from the long main stem constructed of pink brick with black shutters at all the windows. The black slate roof was so sharply pitched it looked scary—how had we ever dared to walk up there? I counted the eight chimneys, the four sets of dormer windows in the attic.

"Look over there, Paul," I directed, pointing out the two windows on the northern wing where we had been held prisoners for so long, waiting endlessly for our grandfather to die.

While Paul stared at those two windows, I looked up at the dormer windows of the attic and saw that the fallen slat from one of the black shutters had been replaced. There wasn't a scorch mark anywhere or signs of a fire. The house hadn't burned! God hadn't sent an errant breeze to blow the candle flame until it caught a dangling paper flower on fire. God wasn't going to punish our mother or the grandmother, not for anything!

All of a sudden Carrie let out a loud howl. "I want Momma!" she screamed. "Cathy, Chris, that's where we used to live with Cory! Let's go inside! I want Momma, please let me see my real momma!"

It was frightful the way she cried and pleaded. How

could she remember the house? It had been dark the night we arrived, with the twins so sleepy they couldn't have seen anything. The morning we stole away it was before dawn and we'd left by the back door. What was it that told Carrie this was our prison of yesteryears? Then I knew. It was the houses lower down the street. We were at the end of the cul-de-sac and up much higher. We'd often peeked out the windows of our locked room and gazed down on all the fine houses. Forbidden to look out of the windows—and yet we dared, on occasion.

What had been accomplished by our long journey? Nothing, nothing at all except more proof that our mother was a liar beyond belief. I mulled it over, day after day, even when I was perched on one of the built-in shower seats as Paul lathered my hair and carefully began to wash it. The long length couldn't be piled on top and screwed around or I'd never get out the tangles. He did it the way I'd taught him, working the soapy lather from scalp to ends, and when it was over, he'd dry it, brush it free of tangles and all around me it would fall like a silken shawl to cover my nakedness, like Eve must have covered hers.

"Paul," I asked, my eyes downcast, "it's not sinful what we're doing, is it? I keep thinking of the grandmother and all her talk of evil. Tell me that love makes this all right."

"Open your eyes, Cathy," he said softly, using a washcloth to wipe away the suds before I did. "Look at what you see—a naked man, the way God planned him to be." When I'd looked, he tilted my face upwards and then lifted me so he could hold me close. Holding me in his tight embrace, he began to talk, and every word he said told me our love was beautiful and right.

I couldn't speak. Silently I cried inside, for so easily I could have ended up the prude the grandmother wanted to make of me.

Like a young child I allowed him to dry me off and brush my hair, and do what he would with his kisses and caresses, until the embers always ready between us caught fire and he picked me up and carried me to his bed.

When our passion was sated, I lay in the circle of his arms and thought of all I could do. Things that would have shocked me as a child. Things that once I would have considered terribly gross, ugly, for I had thought then only of the acts and not of the feelings of giving. How strange that people were born so sensual and had to be stifled for so many years. I recalled the first time his tongue had touched me *there* and the electrifying jolt I'd felt.

Oh, I could kiss Paul everywhere and feel no shame, for loving him was better than smelling roses on a sunny summer day, better than dancing to beautiful music with the best of all partners.

That was what loving Paul was like for me when I was seventeen and he was forty-two.

He had restored me and made me whole, and deeper down I shoved the remorse I felt for Cory.

There was hope for Chris, he was alive.

There was hope for Carrie, that she could grow and find love too.

And maybe, if things turned out right—there was hope for me too.

Toward the Top

Julian didn't fly down as often as he used to, and his mother and father complained about this. When he did come, he danced better than ever, but not once did I see him glance my way. I had the suspicion though, he did plenty of looking when he knew I couldn't see him. I was getting better, more disciplined, more controlled . . . and I worked. Oh, how I worked!

From the very first I'd been included in the professional group of the Rosencoff Ballet Company, but only as a member of the *corps de ballet*. This Christmas we were to alternate performances of *The Nutcracker* and *Cinderella*.

Long after the others had gone home I had the dance studio all to myself on a Friday afternoon, and I was lost in the world of the Sugarplum Fairy, intent upon giving this role something different, when suddenly Julian was dancing with me. He was like my shadow, doing what I did, even pirouetting, making a mockery of what I did.

He frowned, then grabbed up a towel to dry his face and hair. I wiggled my toes and started toward the dressing room. I was going out to dinner with Paul that evening.

"Cathy, hold up!" he called. "I know you don't like me—"

"I don't."

He grinned wickedly, leaning forward to stare into my eyes. His lips brushed my cheek as I cringed away, then he had me pinioned in his arms, with his palms flat against the wall to prevent my running away. "You know what, I think you should be the one to dance Clara, or Cinderella." He tickled under my chin, then kissed near my ear. "If you're nice to me I could see to it that you dance both lead roles."

I ducked and ran. "Come off it, Julian!" I flared. "Your favors would demand a price . . . and you don't interest me."

Ten minutes later I had showered and dressed and was ready to leave the building when Julian showed up in his street clothes. "Cathy, seriously, I think you're ready for New York now. Marisha thinks so too." His smile was wry, as if his mother's opinion wasn't as worthy as his own. "No strings attached. Not unless someday you decide you want strings."

Now I didn't know what to say, so I said nothing. I did get chosen for both the roles for the Rosencoff performances. I thought the other girls would be jealous and resentful, but instead they applauded when it was announced. We all worked well together, making it one merry, hectic time. Then came my debut as Cinderella!

Julian didn't even knock before he entered the girl's dressing room to survey me in my costume of rags and tatters. "Stop being so damned nervous. They're only people out there. You don't think I'd come back here to dance with a girl who wasn't sensational, do you?"

As we stood in the wings his arm stayed about my shoulders, lending me confidence as we both counted toward my cue to go on. His part didn't come until much later. I couldn't see Paul, Chris, Carrie or Henny out in the darkened audience. I trembled more as the footlights dimmed and the overture was played, and then the curtain rose. My mounting anxiety disappeared and took all my insecurity along with it, as some astonishing kinesthetic memory took over and I allowed the music to control and direct me. I wasn't Cathy, or Catherine, or anybody but Cinderella! I swept ashes from the hearth and enviously watched two hateful stepsisters prepare for the ball, feeling love and romance would never come into my life.

If I made mistakes, if my technique wasn't perfect, I didn't know it. I was in love with the dance, with performing before a large audience, with being young and pretty, and most of all I was in love with life and all it had to offer outside of Foxworth Hall.

Red, yellow and pink roses came to fill my arms. I thrilled when the audience rose to give us a standing ovation. Three times I handed Julian a rose of a different color; each time our eyes met and clung. See, his were saying to me mutely, we *do* create magic together! We *are* the perfect dancing partners!

He cornered me again during the buffet party. "Now you've had a taste of what it's like," he said softly and persuasively, his dark eyes pleading. "Can you give up the applause? Can you keep on staying here, in a hick town, when New York is waiting for you? Cathy, as a team we'll be sensational! We look so right together. I dance with you better than I dance with any other ballerina. Oh, Cathy, you and I could reach the top so much sooner together. I swear to take good care of you. I'll look out for you and never let you feel lonely."

"I don't know," I said miserably, though I was lit up inside. "I have to finish high school first—but do you really think I'm good enough? Up there they expect the best."

"You *are* the best! Trust me, believe in me. Madame Zolta's company isn't the largest, or top rank, but she's got what it takes to make our company rate as high as the larger and older ones—once she has a couple of fantastic dancers like us!"

I asked what Madame Zolta was like. Somehow that made him confident I'd already agreed and, laughing first, he managed to plant a kiss on my lips. "You're going to adore

Madame Zolta! She's Russian and the sweetest, kindest, most
gentle little old lady you ever met. She'll be like your mother.
[Good God!] She knows everything there is about dance. She's
our doctor sometimes, our psychologist; whatever we need,
she's it. Life in New York is like living on Mars compared to
here, another world, a better world. In no time at all you'll
love it. I'll take you to famous restaurants where you'll eat
food such as you've never tasted before. I'll introduce you to
movie stars, TV celebrities, actors, actresses, authors."

I tried to resist him by fastening my eyes on Chris, Carrie
and Paul, but Julian moved so he blocked out my view. All
I could see was him. "It's the kind of life you were born for,
Cathy," and this time he sounded sincere and deeply earnest.
"Why have you studied and put yourself through so much
torture, if not for success? Can you achieve the kind of fame
you want here?"

No. I couldn't.

But Paul was here. Chris and Carrie were here. How could
I leave them?

"Cathy, come with me to where you belong, behind the
footlights, on stage, with roses in your arms. Come with me,
Cathy, and make my dreams come true too."

Oh, he was winning that night, and I was heady with my
first success, and even when I wanted to say no, I nodded and
said, "Yes . . . I'll go, but only if you come down here and
fly with me. I've never been on a plane, and I wouldn't know
where to go once I landed."

He took me in his arms then, tenderly, and held me as
his lips brushed my hair. Over his shoulder, I could see both
Chris and Paul staring our way, both of them looking astonished and more than a little hurt.

In January of 1963 I graduated from high school. I wasn't
particularly brilliant, like Chris, but I'd made it through.

Chris was so smart it was more than likely he'd finish college in three years rather than four. Already he'd won several

scholarships to help take the financial burden of his education from Paul's shoulders, though he never mentioned a word about any of us paying him back—for anything. It was understood, though, that Chris would become an associate with Paul when he had his M.D. I marveled that Paul could keep spending on us and never complain, and when I asked, he explained. "I enjoy knowing I'm helping to contribute to the world the wonderful doctor Chris will make—and the super ballerina you will be one day." He looked so sad when he said that, so terribly sad. "As for Carrie, I hope she decides to stay home with me and marry a local boy, so I can see her often."

"When I'm gone it will be Thelma Murkel for you again, won't it?" I asked with some bitterness, for I wanted him to stay faithful, no matter how many miles I put between us.

"Maybe," he said.

"You won't love anyone else as much as you love me, say you won't."

He smiled. "No. How could I love anyone as much as I love you? No other could dance into my heart the way you did, could she?"

"Paul, don't mock me. Say the word and I won't go. I'll stay."

"How can I say the words to make you stay when you have to fulfill your destiny? You were born to dance, not to be the wife of a stodgy, small-town doctor."

Marriage! He'd said wife! He'd never mentioned marriage before.

It was more than awful to tell Carrie I was leaving. Her screams were deafening and pitiful. *"You cannot go!"* she bellowed, tears streaming. *"You promised we would all stay together, and now you and Chris both go away and leave me! Take me too! Take me!"* She beat at me with small fists, kicked at my legs, determined to inflict some pain for what Chris and I were giving her—and already I felt pain enough for the world in leaving her. "Please try and understand, Carrie, I will be coming back, and Chris will too—you won't be forgotten."

"I hate you!" she screamed. "I hate both you and Chris! I hope you die in New York! I hope you both fall down and die!" It was Paul who came to save me.

"You've still got me every day, and Henny," he said, hefting Carrie's slight weight up in his arms. "We're not going anywhere. And you'll be the only daughter we have when Cathy is gone. Come, dry your tears, put a smile on your face and be happy for your sister. Remember this is what she'd been striving for all those long years when you were locked up."

I ached inside as I wondered if I really wanted a dance career as much as I had always thought. Chris threw me a long, sad look then bent to pick up my new blue suitcases. He hurried out the front door trying not to let me see the tears in his eyes. When we all went out, he stood near Paul's white car, his shoulders squared off, his face set, determined not to show any emotion.

Henny had to pile in with the rest of us; she didn't want to be left home to cry alone. Her so eloquent brown eyes spoke to me, wishing me good luck as her hands were kept busy wiping the tears from Carrie's face.

At the airport Julian paced back and forth, constantly glancing at his watch. He was afraid I'd back out and wouldn't show up. He looked very handsome in his new suit as his eyes lit up when he saw me approach. "Thank God, I was thinking I flew down here for nothing—and I wouldn't do this twice."

The evening before, I'd already said a private good-bye to Paul. His words rang in my ears to haunt me even as I boarded the plane. "We both knew it couldn't last, Catherine. From the beginning I warned you, April just can't marry with September."

Chris and Paul followed us up the ramp to help with the many pieces of hand luggage I wouldn't trust to the baggage compartment, and once more I had to hug Paul close. "Thank you, Catherine," he whispered so neither Chris nor Julian could overhear, "for everything. Don't look back with any regrets. Forget about me. Forget all the past. Concentrate on your dancing and wait before you fall in love with anyone— and let it be someone near your own age."

Choking, I asked, "And what about you?"

He forced a smile and then a chuckle. "Don't worry about me. I've got my memories of a beautiful ballerina and that's enough."

I burst into tears! Memories! What were they? Just something to torture yourself with, that's all! Blindly I turned to find myself locked in Chris's arms. My Christopher Doll who was six feet tall now, my knight so gallant, chivalrous and sensitive. Finally I could pull away and then he took my hands, both of them, as our gazes met and locked. We too had shared a great deal, even more than Paul and I. *Good-bye my walking, talking, cheerful, chiding, and living set of encyclopedias, my fellow prisoner of hope. . . . You don't need to cry for me. . . . Cry for yourself . . . or don't cry at all. It's over. Accept it, Chris, like I have, like you have to. You're only my brother. I'm only a sister, and the world is full of beautiful women who'd love you better than I can, or could.*

Every word I didn't speak I knew he heard, and still he kept on looking at me with his heart in his eyes, making me hurt all over.

"Cathy," he said hoarsely, loud enough for Julian to hear, "it's not that I'm afraid you won't make it, I'm sure you will if you don't get so damned impulsive! Please don't do anything reckless that you'll regret later on. Promise to think of all the ramifications first before you jump in with both feet. Go easy on sex and love. Wait until you're old enough to know what you want in a man before you choose one."

I'm sure my smile was crooked, for already I'd chosen Paul. I flicked my eyes from Paul who looked serious, to

Julian who was frowning and glaring at Chris, then at Paul. "You go easy on sex and love too," I said jokingly to Chris, making sure my tone was light. I hugged him tight once more, hurting to let him go. "And write to me often, and come to New York with Paul, Carrie and Henny whenever you can—or come alone, but come—promise?"

Solemnly he promised. Our lips met briefly, and then I turned to take my seat near the window. Since this was my first plane trip, Julian graciously gave up that privilege. I waved like mad to my family who I couldn't even see from the plane window.

Julian, so adroit and adept on stage, was at a loss when it came to handling a girl who sobbed on his shoulder, trembling, already homesick, wishing she wasn't going even before the plane was five thousand feet up. "You've got me," he said smoothly. "Didn't I swear to take care of you? And I will, honest to God. I'll do everything possible to make you happy." He grinned at me and kissed me lightly. "And, my love, I'm afraid I exaggerated the charms of Madame Zolta just a wee, wee bit, as you'll soon find out."

I stared at him. "What do you mean?"

He cleared his throat and without the slightest embarrassment he told me about his first meeting with the once-famous Russian dancer. "I don't want to spoil the surprise in store when you meet up with this great beauty, so I'll save that and let you see for yourself. But I'll warn you about this, Madame Z. is a toucher. She likes to feel you, your muscles, how hard and firm they are. Would you believe she put her hand directly on my fly to find out the size of what was underneath?"

"No! I don't believe that!"

He laughed merrily and threw his arm about me. "Oh, Cathy, what a life we're going to live, you and I! What heaven will be ours when you find out you've got sole property rights to the handsomest and most gifted and graceful *danseur* ever born." He drew me even closer and whispered in my ear, "And I haven't said a word about the talented lover I am."

I laughed too—and shoved him away. "If you aren't the most conceited, arrogant person I've ever met. And I suspect you can be quite ruthless too when it comes to getting what you want."

"Right on!" he said with a following laugh. "I'm all of that and more too, as you'll soon find out. After all, wasn't I ruthlessly determined to get you where I want you?"

New York, New York

It was snowing hell-bent when our plane landed in New York. The cold in my nostrils stunned me. I'd forgotten bitter winters like this. The wind howling down those narrow canyonways seemed to want to rip the skin from my face. Ice seemed to enter my lungs and shrivel them with constricting pain. I gasped, laughed, turned to glance at Julian who was paying the cab driver, and then I pulled from my coat pocket a red knitted scarf Henny had made for me. Julian took it and helped me swath it about my head and neck so it half-covered my face. Then I shocked him by pulling from the other pocket a red scarf I had knitted for him.

"Gosh, thanks. I never thought you cared." He seemed very pleased as he wrapped his neck and ears.

On this day of days the cold had made his cheeks as red as his lips, and with that blue-black hair that curled just above his coat collar and those sparkling dark eyes the sheer beauty of him was enough to steal anyone's breath. "Okay," he said, "pull yourself together, and prepare to meet ballet personified—my sweet, delicate, delicious dance instructor whom you will positively adore."

Just to be here had me on edge, so I clung as close as possible to Julian, staring at all the people who dared to brave such ferocious weather.

The luggage we'd brought was left in a waiting room of the huge building, and in the flurry of scurrying after Julian I didn't notice much of anything until we were in the office of our ballet mistress, Madame Zolta Korovenskov. Her stance, her arrogance immediately reminded me of Madame Marisha. But this woman was much older, if all those wrinkles could be counted as tree-rings to indicate her age.

Queenly stiff she rose from behind a desk that was impressively wide. Coolly, all business, she stalked over to us and looked us over with bead-black eyes as small as those of a mouse. What hair she had was skinned back from her dry brittle face like fine white floss. She wasn't five feet tall, but radiated six feet of authority. Her half-moon glasses perched precariously on the end of an astonishingly long thin nose. Above those half-disks she peered at us, squinting, so her minute eyes almost disappeared in the crow's feet. Julian was so unlucky as to gain her scrutiny first.

Her puckered little prune mouth drew up like a drawstring purse. I watched and waited for a smile to come and break her parchment skin. I expected her voice to crackle, cackle, witchlike.

"So!" she spat at Julian. "You take off *when* you want, and come back *when* you want and you expect me to say I'm glad to see you! Bah! Do that one more time and out you go! Who is this girl with you?"

Julian gave the old hag a charming smile, and quickly put his arm about her. "Madame Zolta Korovenskov, may I introduce you to Miss Catherine Doll, the wonderful dancer I've been telling you about for months and months—and she is the reason why I left without your permission."

She looked me over with very interested gimlet eyes. "You come from some nowhere too?" she whiplashed. "You've got the look of another place, like my black devil here does. He's a very good dancer, but not as good as he thinks. Can I believe him about you?"

"I guess, Madame, you'll just have to watch me dance and judge for yourself."

"Can you dance?"

"As I said before, Madame, wait and judge for yourself."

"See, Madame," Julian said eagerly, "Cathy's got spirit, fire! You should see her whip her leg doing *fouettés*. She's so fast she's a blur!"

"Ha!" she snorted, then came to encircle me and next she gave my face such a close scrutiny I was blushing. She felt my arms, my chest, even my breasts, then put her bony hands on my neck and felt the cords. Those audacious hands roamed down the length of my body while I wanted to scream out I wasn't a slave to be sold in the marketplace. I was grateful she didn't put her hand on my crotch as she'd done to Julian. I stood still and endured the inspection and felt all the while a deep, hot blush. She looked up to see it and smiled sarcastically.

When she'd done and I'd been physically appraised and evaluated, she delved the depths of my eyes to drink up my essence. I felt she was trying to absorb my youth with her eyes and drain it from me. Then she was touching my hair. "When do you plan to marry?" she shot out.

"Sometime when I'm near thirty, maybe, or maybe never." I answered uneasily. "But most certainly I'm going to wait until after I'm rich and famous, and the world's best prima ballerina."

"Hah! You have many illusions about yourself. Beautiful faces don't usually go with great dancers. Beauty thinks it needs no talent and can feed on itself, so it soon dies. Look at me. Once I was young and a great beauty. What do you see now?"

She was hideous! And she couldn't have ever been beautiful, or there'd be some evidence.

As if sensing my doubt to her claim, she gestured arrogantly to all the photographs on the walls, on her desk, on the tables, bookshelves. All showed the same lovely young ballerina. "Me," she proudly informed. I couldn't believe it. They were old photos, brownish in color, the costumes outdated, and yet she had been lovely. She gave me a wide, amused smile, patted my shoulder and said, "Good. Age comes to everyone and makes everyone equal.

"Who did you study with before Marisha Rosencoff?"

"Miss Denise Danielle." I hesitated, fearful of telling her about all the years I'd danced alone and been my own instructor.

"Ah," she sighed, looking very sad, "I saw Denise Danielle dance many times, such a brilliant performer but she made the old mistake and fell in luv. End of promising career. Now, all she do is teach." Her voice rose and fell, quivering, gaining strength, then losing it. She pronounced "luv" with a long "u," making the word sound foreign and silly. "Big-head Julian says you are a great dancer, but I have to see you dance before I believe, and then I will decide if beauty is its own excuse for being." Once more she sighed. "You drink?"

"No."

"Why is your skin so pale? Do you never go in sun?"

"Too much sun burns me."

"Ah . . . you and your lover boy—afraid of the sun."

"Julian is *not* my lover!" I said between clenched teeth, shooting him a fierce look, for he must have told her we were.

Not an element of our expressions missed the keen observation of those ebony-bead eyes. "Julian, did you or did you not tell me you were in luv with this girl?"

He flushed and lowered his eyes, and had the decency to look embarrassed for once. "Madame, the love is all on my side, I'm ashamed to admit. Cathy feels nothing for me . . . but she will, sooner or later."

"Fine," the old witch said with a birdlike nod. "You have a big passion for her, she has none for you—that makes for sizzling, sensational dancing on your part. Our box office will overflow. *I see it coming!*"

That was, of course, the reason she took me on, knowing Julian had his unsatisfied lust and knowing I had a smoldering desire to find someone else offstage. Onstage, he was everything beautiful, romantic and sensual—my dream lover. If we could have danced through all our days and nights, we could have set the world on fire. As it was, when he was only himself, with his glib and often smutty tongue, I ran from him. I went to bed each night thinking of Paul prowling his lonely gardens, and refused to let myself dream of Chris.

I was soon ensconced in a small apartment twelve blocks from the dance studio. Two other dancers shared the three small rooms and one tiny bath with me. Two floors above, Julian shared an apartment with two male dancers in rooms no bigger than those we three girls had. His roommates were Alexis Tarrell and Michael Michelle, both in their early twenties, and both just as determined as Julian to become the best male *danseur* of their generation. I was astonished to find out Madame Zolta considered Alexis the best, and Michael next, and Julian third. I soon found out why she held him back—he had no respect for her authority. He wanted to do everything in his own way, and because of this she punished him.

My roommates were as different as night and day. Yolanda Lange was half British, half Arab, and the strange combination made for one of the most exotic, dark-haired, sloe-eyed beauties I'd ever seen. She was tall for a dancer, five eight, the same height as my mother. Her breasts, when I saw them, were small hard lumps, all large dark nipples, but she wasn't ashamed of their size. She delighted in walking about naked, showing off, and soon I found out her breasts mirrored her personality—small, hard and mean. Yolanda wanted what she wanted when she wanted it and she'd do anything to get it. She asked me a thousand questions in less than an hour, and in that same hour told me her life story. Her father was a British diplomat who'd married a belly dancer. She'd lived everywhere, done everything. I immediately disliked Yolanda Lange.

April Summers was from Kansas City, Missouri. She had soft brown hair, blue-green eyes; we were both the same height, five feet four and a half inches. She was shy and seldom did she raise her voice above a whisper. When loud, raucous Yolanda was around, April seemed to have no voice at all. Yolanda liked noise; at all times the record player or the television had to be turned on. April spoke of her family with love, respect and pride, while Yolanda professed hatred for parents who'd pushed her into boarding schools and left her alone on holidays.

April and I became fast friends before our first day together was over. She was eighteen and pretty enough to please any man, but for some strange reason the boys of the academy didn't pay April one whit of attention. It was Yolanda who made them hot and panting, and soon enough I learned why—she was the one who gave out.

As for me, the boys saw me, they asked for dates, but Julian made it clear I wasn't available—I was *his*. He told everyone we were lovers. Though I persistently denied this, he would tell them in private I was old-fashioned and ashamed to admit we were "living in sin." He chidingly explained in my very presence, "It's that old southern-belle tradition. Gals down south like guys to think they're sweet, shy, demure, but underneath that cool magnolia exterior—sexpots—every one!" Of course they believed him and not me. Why should they believe the truth when a lie was so much more exciting?

I was happy enough though. I adapted to New York as one native born, rushing about as every New Yorker had to—get there fast, don't waste a second, there was so much to prove before someone else with a pretty face and more talent showed up to knock you off the board. But while I was ahead in the game, it was wild and heady stuff, exhausting and demanding. How grateful I was that Paul kept sending me a weekly check, for what I earned at the dance company, wouldn't have paid for my cosmetics.

The three of us who shared rooms 416 required at least ten hours of sleep. We got up at dawn to limber up at our home barre before breakfast. Breakfast had to be very light, as was lunch. Only during the last meal of the day, after a performance, could we really satisfy our ravenous appetites. It seemed I was always hungry, that I never had enough to eat. In just one performance in the *corps de ballet* I lost five or six pounds.

Julian was with me constantly, shadowing me too closely, keeping me from dating anyone else. Depending on my mood or state of exhaustion, I was resentful of this, and other times happy to have someone around who wasn't a stranger.

Madame Zolta said one day in June, "Your name is silly! Change it! Catherine Doll—what kind of name for dancer? An inane, unexciting name—it doesn't suit you at all!"

"Now you wait a minute, Madame!" I snapped back, abandoning my attitude position. "I chose that name when I was seven and my father liked it. *He* thought it suited me fine, so I'm going to use it, stupid or not!" I longed to tell her Madame Naverena Zolta Korovenskov wasn't exactly what I'd call a lyrical name either.

"Don't argue with me, girl, change it!" She used her ivory walking cane to pound on the floor. But, if I changed my name, how would my mother know when I reached the top? She had to know! Still that wretched little witch in her outdated, silly costume could narrow her fierce dark eyes and lift that cane and brandish it so I was forced to yield, or else! Julian slouched nearby and grinned.

I agreed I would change the spelling of my last name from

Doll to Dahl. "That is better," she said sourly, "somewhat."

Madame Z. rode my back. She nagged. She criticized. She complained if I was innovative and complained when I wasn't. She didn't like the way I wore my hair and said I had too much. "Cut it off!" she ordered but I refused to snip off even an inch, for I believed my long hair a great asset for the role of Sleeping Beauty. She snorted when I said this. (Snorting was one of her favorite means of expression.) If she hadn't been a wonderfully gifted instructor we'd have all hated her. Her very dour nature forced the best from us, for we so wanted to see her smile. She was also a choreographer, but we had another too who came and went and supervised when he wasn't in Hollywood, in Europe, or off in some remote spot dreaming up new dancing scores.

One afternoon after class, when we dancers were playing about foolishly, I jumped up to dance wildly to a popular song. Madame came in and caught me, then exploded, "We dance *classical* here! No modern dance here!" Her dry, wrinkled face screwed into a dried headhunter's belt ornament. "You, Dahl, explain the difference between classical and modern."

Julian winked at me, then fell backward to rest on his elbows and cross an elegant ankle over a knee, as he delighted in my discomfort. "Succinctly, Madame," I began with my mother's poise, "the modern form of ballet consists mostly of groveling about on the floor and posturing, while classical stands up on its toes, whirls, spins, and is never too seductive or awkward. And it tells a story."

"How right you are," she said icily. "Now get you home to bed and posture and grovel there if you feel the need to express yourself in such a manner. Never let me catch you doing such before my eyes again!"

Modern and classical could be blended and made beautiful. The tightness of that small shrew enraged me, and I screamed back, "I hate you, Madame! I despise your ratty old gray costumes that should have been thrown away thirty years ago! I hate your face, your voice, your walk and your talk! Find yourself another dancer. *I'm going home!*" I flounced off toward the dressing room, leaving all the dancers standing in shock staring after me.

I ripped off my practice clothes and yanked on underwear. Into the dressing room stalked the grim-faced witch, her eyes mean, her lips pressed tightly together. "If you go home *you never come back!*"

"I don't want to come back!"

"You will wither away and die!"

"You're a fool if you think that!" I snapped without regard to her age or respect for her talent. "I can live my life without dancing, and happily too—*so go to hell, Madame Zolta!*"

As if a spell had been broken that old hag smiled at me, and sweetly too. "Ah . . . you have spirit. I was wondering if you did. Tell me to go to hell, it is nice to hear. Hell is better than heaven anyway. Now, seriously, Catherine," she said in a kind tone, kinder than I'd ever heard from her, "you are a wonderfully gifted dancer, the best I have, but you are so impulsive you abandon the classical and toss in whatever comes to your mind. I only try to teach you. Invent all you want, but keep it classical, elegant, beautiful." Tears glistened her eyes. "You are my delight, did you know? I think you are the daughter I never had; you take me back to when I was young and thought all life was one big romantic adventure. I'm so afraid life will steal your look of enchantment, your childish wonderment. If you can hang onto that expression, you'll soon have the world at your feet."

It was my attic face she was speaking of. That enchanted expression that used to so enthrall Chris. "I'm sorry, Madame," I said humbly. "I was rude. I was wrong to scream, but you pick on me all the time, and I'm tired, homesick too."

"I know, I know," she crooned as she came to embrace me, then rocked with me back and forth. "To be young and in a strange city is hard on the nerves and confidence. But remember, I only needed to know what you are made of. A dancer without fire is no dancer at all."

I'd been living in New York seven months, working even on the weekends until I fell into bed dead tired, before Madame Zolta thought I should be given a chance to dance a lead role with Julian to partner me. It was Madame's rule to alternate lead roles, so that there would be no stars in her company, and though she'd hinted many times she wanted me for Clara in *The Nutcracker*, I thought she just used that to dangle before me, like a rich plum I'd never be allowed to eat. Then it became a reality. Our company was in competition with much larger and better-known companies, so it was an absolute stroke of genius that she was able to sell a television producer on the notion that people who couldn't afford to buy ballet tickets could be reached by television.

I called Paul long distance to tell him my great news. "Paul, I'm going to appear on TV in *The Nutcracker*, I'll be Clara!" He laughed and congratulated me. "I guess that means you won't be coming home this summer," he said rather sadly. "Carrie misses you an awful lot, Cathy. You've only paid us one short visit since you went away."

"I'm sorry, I want to come but I need this chance to star, Paul. Please explain to Carrie so her feelings won't be hurt. Is she there?"

"No, she's finally made a friend and is 'sleeping-over.' But call again tomorrow night and reverse the charges, and tell her yourself."

"And Chris, how is he?" I asked.

"Fine, fine. He gets nothing but A's, and if he can manage to keep that up, he'll be accepted for an accelerated program and can finish out his fourth year of college while starting his first year in medical school."

"Simultaneously?" I asked, marveling that anyone, even Chris, could be that smart and accomplish so much.

"Sure, it can be done."

"Paul, what about you? Are you well? Are you working too much, too many long hours?"

"I'm healthy and yes, I do work long hours, as every doctor does. And since you can't come to visit us, I think it would be nice for Carrie if we came to visit you."

Oh, that was the best idea I'd heard in months and months. "And bring Chris," I said. "He'll love to meet all the pretty ballerinas I can introduce him to. But you, Paul, you'd better not look at anyone but me."

He made a strange sound in his throat before he chuckled. "Don't worry, Catherine, there's not a day that passes that I don't see your face before me."

In early August the television production of *The Nutcracker* was taped for Christmastime release. Julian and I sat close together and watched the rushes, and when it was over he turned to take me in his arms, and for the first time he told me with the kind of sincerity I could believe, "I love you, Cathy. Please stop taking me so lightly!"

Hardly had we rested up from *The Nutcracker* when Yolly fell and sprained her ankle, and April was visiting her parents, so I had the chance to be Sleeping Beauty! Since Julian had played two roles in the TV production, both Alexis and Michael thought it should be their turn to partner me. Madame Zolta frowned and looked at Julian, then at me. "Alexis, Michael, I promise you the very next lead roles, but let Julian dance with Catherine. They have a rare magic between them that is spellbinding. I want to see how they do in a really lavish production like *The Sleeping Beauty*."

Oh, the thoughts I had on stage as I lay so still on the purple velvet couch, waiting for my lover to come and put on my lips an arousing, come-alive kiss. The glorious music made me feel more real on that couch than when I was just me with no royal blood at all. I felt enchanted, surrounded by an aura of beauty as I quietly, gracefully lay with my arms folded on my breasts and my heart pulsated in rhythm with the glorious music. Out in the dark audience, Paul, Chris and Carrie and Henny were watching for the first time a New York performance. Truly, I felt in my bones I was that mystical medieval princess.

I saw him dreamily from beneath almost closed eyes, my prince. He danced about me, then down on one knee he knelt to tenderly gaze upon my face before he dared to put a hesitant kiss upon my closed lips. I awakened, shy, disoriented, fluttering my eyelids. I feigned love on sight, but was so frightened, so maidenly virtuous, he had to woo me with more dancing and coax me to dance too, and in the most passionate *pas de deux* I soon succumbed to his charms and in conquest he lifted me high and up on the flat of his palm that knew well the exact spot to balance my weight just right, and I was carried offstage.

The last act ended; the applause thundered and resounded as time and again the curtain rose and came down. Julian and I took eight curtain calls of our very own! Red roses were thrust again and again into my arms, and flowers were tossed onto the stage. I looked down to see one single yellow buttercup weighted down by a folded slip of paper. I bent to pick it up and knew it was from Chris even before I had the chance to read his note. Daddy's four yellow buttercups—and here was one put in a freezer to keep it fresh until it could be thrown to me as a tribute to what we used to be.

Blindly I stared out into an audience of blurred faces, searching to see those I loved. All I could see was the attic, the gloomy, awesomely huge attic with its paper flowers, and over there, near the stairwell, was Chris standing in the shadows, near the shrouded sofa and the big trunk and his yearning desire was on his face as he watched me dance on and on.

I was crying, and the audience loved it. They gave me a standing ovation. I turned to hand a red rose to Julian, and again they thundered their applause. And he kissed me! Right in front of thousands—he dared to kiss me—and it wasn't respectful, it was possessive. "Damn you for doing that!" I hissed, feeling humiliated.

"Damn you for not wanting me!" he hissed back.

"I'm not yours!"

"You will be!"

My family came backstage to lavish me with praise. Chris had grown taller but Carrie was very much the same—maybe a bit taller, not much. I kissed Henny's firm, round cheek. Only then could I look at Paul. Our eyes locked and held. Did he still love me, want me, need me? He hadn't answered my last letter. Easily hurt, I'd written only to Carrie to tell her of the upcoming performances, and only then did Paul call to say he was bringing my family to New York.

After the performance came the buffet party given for us by the rich patrons Madame Z. cultivated. "Wear the costumes you have on," she instructed. "The aficionados get a big thrill seeing dancers up close in costumes—but take off the stage makeup, use what you wear every day to look stunning. Never for one second give the public the idea you are less than glamorous!"

Music was playing and Chris took me into his arms for a waltz, the dance I had taught him so many years ago. "This is still the way you dance?" I chided.

He grinned in a self-effacing way. "Can't help it if you got all the dancing talent and I got all the brains."

"Remarks like that could easily make me think you have no brains."

He laughed again and I was drawn closer. "Besides, I don't have to dance and posture to win over the girls. Just take a look at your friend Yolanda. She's quite a beauty, and she's been giving me the eye all evening."

"She gives every good-looking guy the eye, so don't feel so flattered. She'll sleep with you tonight if you want that, and tomorrow night with someone else."

"Are you like her too?" he shot back, narrowing his eyes.

I smiled at him wickedly, thinking, no, I was like Momma, sweet and cool and able to handle men—at least, I was learning. To prove this I winked at Paul, seeing if he'd come over and cut in. Swiftly Paul was on his feet, moving gracefully across the dance floor to take me from Chris. My brother's lips tightened, then he strolled straight from me to Yolanda. In a minute or two they disappeared.

"I guess you think I'm all hands and clumsy feet, after dancing with Julian," said Paul, who could dance better than Chris. Even when the music changed into a faster rhythm with a jungle beat he followed along, surprising me that he could let go of his dignity and jiggle around almost as abandoned as a college kid. "Paul, you're wonderful!" He laughed and said I made him feel young again. It was so much fun to see him like this, relaxed, that I went a bit wild with my dancing.

Carrie and Henny looked tired and ill-at-ease. "I'm sleepy," complained Carrie, rubbing her eyes. "Can't we go to bed now?" It was twelve o'clock when we dropped Henny and Carrie off at their hotel, then Paul and I sat in a quiet Italian café and looked at one another. He still wore the mustache— not a neat, dandy one, but a thick brush above his sensual lips. He'd gained a few pounds, but it didn't detract from his looks or his appeal. He reached across the table to gather both my hands in his, then lifted them to his face so he could rub his cheek against them. And all the while he did this, his eyes asked a burning question, forcing a question from me. "Paul, have you found someone else?"

"Have you?"

"I asked first."

"I'm not looking for anyone else."

It was an answer to make my heartbeats quicken, for it had been so long and I loved him too much. I watched him pay the check, pick up my coat and hold it, and then his own for me to hold. Our eyes met—and then we almost ran from the restaurant to the nearest hotel where he registered us as Mr. and Mrs. Paul Sheffield. In a room painted dark red, he took off my clothes with such seductive slowness I was ready even before he went down on his knees to kiss me everywhere. Then he held me close, caressed and cherished me, kissed and pleasured until we were again made one.

After we were spent, he traced his finger along my lips, looking at me so tenderly. "Catherine, what I wrote on that hotel register I meant," he said, kissing me softly.

I stared at him, disbelieving. "Paul, don't tease me."

"I'm not teasing, Catherine. I've missed you so much since you've been away. I realized what a fool I've been to deny you and myself the chance to find happiness. Life is too short to have so many doubts. Now you're finding success in New York; I want to share it with you. I don't want us to have to sneak around behind Chris's back, I don't want to have to worry about the small-town gossips. I want to be with you, I want you forever, I want you to be my wife."

"Oh Paul," I cried, throwing my arms about his neck, "I'll love you forever, I promise!" My eyes filled with tears, I was so relieved he'd asked me to marry him at last. "I'll make you the best wife any man has ever known." I meant it too.

We didn't sleep that night. We stayed awake, planning how it would be when we were married. I would stay with the company, somehow we'd work it out. The only shadow that darkened our joy was Chris. How would we tell Chris? We decided to wait until Christmas, when I would be in Clairmont. Until then I had to keep my happiness a secret, hide it from the world, so no one would guess I was about to become Mrs. Paul Scott Sheffield.

A Fighting Chance

That was the autumn of my happiness, of my burgeoning success, of my love for Paul. I thought I had fate fully under my control; I dared it to stop me, for I was free and running true on my course. Almost on top now. I had nothing to fear now, nothing at all. I couldn't wait to tell the world about my engagement to Paul. But stealthily I protected my secret. I told no one, not Julian, nor Madame Zolta, for there was much at stake, and I had to bide my time, to make sure everything would continue to go my way. Right now I still needed Julian to partner me, just as much as he needed me. And I needed Madame Zolta to have complete confidence in me. If she knew I was going to be married, something she did not highly approve of, she might not give me all the lead roles, she might think I was a lost cause and not worth her time. And I still had to be famous. I still had to show Momma how much better I was than she.

Now that Julian and I were achieving a little recognition, Madame Zolta began to pay us more money. Julian came running to me one Saturday morning, terribly excited as he grabbed me up and swung me off my feet in a circle. "Guess what? The old witch said I could buy her Cadillac on a time payment plan! It's only two and a half years old, Cathy." He looked wistful. "Of course, I always hoped my first Cadillac would be a brand new one, but when a certain ballet mistress is scared to death a certain sensational *danseur* might join another ballet company and take along with him her best ballerina—how can that certain someone refuse to almost give away her Cadillac?"

"Blackmail!" I cried. He laughed and grabbed my hand, and we dashed to look at his new car parked outside our apartment building. My breath pulled in, it looked so new! "Oh, Julian, I love it! You couldn't blackmail her if she didn't want you to have one of her pets—she knows you will pamper it—and don't ever, ever sell it."

"Oh, Cathy," his eyes shone brilliantly with unused tears. "Can't you see why I love you so? We're alike—why can't you love me, just a little?" Proudly he swung open the door to give me the rare privilege of being the first girl to ride in his first Cadillac.

We had a wild and crazy kind of day from there on. We drove through Central Park and all the way up through Harlem, to the George Washington Bridge and back. It was raining but I didn't mind. It was warm and cozy in the car.

Then Julian started in again. "Cathy . . . you're never going to love me, are you?" It was a question he put to me at least once or twice a day, in one form or another. I longed to tell him of my engagement to Paul, to put an end to his questions once and for all. But I steadfastly kept my secret.

"It's because you're still a virgin, isn't it? I'll be so gentle, so tender, Cathy . . . give me a chance, please."

"Good God, Julian, is that all you ever have on your mind?"

"Yeah!" he snarled. "You're damned right it is! And I'm sick and tired of the game you play with me!" He guided the car out into a heavy stream of traffic. "You're a cockteaser. You lead me on while we dance, then kick me in the groin when we're not!"

"Take me home, Julian! I find that kind of talk disgusting!"

"Right! You bet I'll take you home!" he spat at me as I crouched near the passenger door he had locked. He shot me a fierce, distraught look then bore down hard on the gas pedal! We sped down all those rain-slick streets, and every so often he'd glance my way to see how I was enjoying the terrifying ride! He laughed, wild and crazy, then braked so fast I was flung forward so my forehead struck the windshield! Blood trickled from the cut. Next he snatched the purse from my lap, leaned to unlock my door, then he shoved me out into the pouring rain!

"To hell with you, Catherine Dahl!" he shouted as I stood there in the rain, refusing to beg. My coat pockets were empty. No money. "You've had your first and your last ride in my car. I hope you know your way around!" He saluted me with an evil smile. "Get home the best way you can, puritan saint," he spat out, "if you can!"

He drove off leaving me on the street corner in the downpour, in Brooklyn where I'd never been before. I didn't have even a nickel. I couldn't make a phone call, or use a subway, and the rain came down strong. My lightweight coat was soaked through. I knew I was in an unsavory district where anything could happen . . . and he'd left me here, when he'd sworn to take care of me!

I began to walk, not knowing north from south, east from west, and then I saw a cab cruising by and hailed it. Nervously I leaned forward to watch the meter click away the miles—and the dollars. *Damn you again, Julian, for taking me so far!* Finally we reached my apartment building—at the cost of fifteen dollars!

"What do you mean you ain't got it on yuh?" the cab driver flared. "I'll drive ya straight to the police precinct!"

We bickered back and forth, with me trying to explain

he couldn't be paid unless he let me out to go for money, and all the while the meter was running. Finally he agreed. "But you'd better be back, chicky, in five minutes—or else!"

An English fox chased by a hundred hounds couldn't have run faster than I did. The elevator crawled upward, creaking all the way. Never did I step in that thing when I wasn't afraid it would stop between floors and I'd be trapped. Finally, the door opened, and I raced down the hall to bang on the door, praying April or Yolanda would be there to let me in. Crazy Julian had my hand bag and my key!

"Take it easy!" bellowed Yolanda. "I'm comin'. Who is it anyway?"

"Cathy! Let me in quick! I've got a taxi driver waiting with his meter running!"

"If you think you're going to put the bite on me, forget it!" she said, swinging open the door. She wore only nylon briefs, and her freshly shampooed head was wrapped with a red towel. "You look like something the sea coughed up," she said invitingly. I wasn't one to pay much attention to Yolanda. I shoved her aside, ran to where I hid my secret cache of emergency money—then I went slack. The small key to my locked treasure chest was in the bag Julian had—if he hadn't thrown it away. "Please, Yolly, loan me fifteen and a buck for a tip."

Shrewdly she looked me over while she removed the towel and began to comb her long dark hair. "What yah got to trade for small favors like that?"

"I'll give you anything you want. Just give me the money."

"Okay—you just keep your promise to repay." Slowly she took a twenty from her fat billfold. "Give the driver a fiver; that will cool him down—and anything I want—right?" I agreed and raced off.

No sooner did the driver grab the twenty, than he was smiling, friendly as he tipped his cap. "See you around, chicky." I hoped he'd drop dead!

I was so chilled the first thing I did was to run a tub of

hot water, but only after I'd scrubbed off the dirty ring Yolly had left.

My hair was still wet as I pulled on clothes, planning to go to Julian and demand my purse back, when Yolly blocked my way. "Come on, Cathy . . . I want you to keep your bargain—anything I want, right?"

"Right," I said, disgusted. "What do you want?"

She smiled and leaned provocatively against a wall.

"Your brother . . . I want you to invite him up next weekend."

"Don't be ridiculous! Chris is in college. He can't come up here any time he wants."

"You get him up here any way you have to. Say you're sick, say you desperately need him, but get him up here! And then you can keep the twenty."

I turned to stare at her with hostility. "No! I've got the money to pay you back. . . . I'm not going to let Chris get involved with the likes of you!"

Still wearing only the briefs, she smeared on scarlet lipstick without looking in a mirror. "Cathy, love, your dear, precious brother is already involved with the likes of me."

"I don't believe you! You're not his type!"

"Nooo," she purred, her eyes narrowing as she watched me finish dressing, "let me tell you something, dollface, there isn't a guy alive who doesn't go for *my* type. Including your dear brother and your lover-boy Julian!"

"You lie!" I cried. "Chris wouldn't touch you with a ten-foot pole—and as for Julian, I don't give a damn if he sleeps with ten whores like you!"

Suddenly her face flamed red, she stiffened and came at me with her hands raised and her fingers curled into claws with long red fingernails! "Bitch!" she snarled. "Don't you dare call me a whore! I don't take pay for what I want to give out—and your brother likes what I give out—go and ask him how many times he's—"

"Shut up!" I yelled, not letting her finish. "I don't believe anything you say! He's too smart to do anything but use you for physical needs. . . . Beyond that, you couldn't mean more than dirt to him!"

She grabbed me and I belted her back, hard. Hard enough so she fell to the floor. "You're nothing but a shallow, mean tramp, Yolanda Lange!" I screamed with fury. "Not nearly good enough for my brother to wipe his feet on! You've slept with every dancer in the company. I don't care what you do . . . just leave *me*, and leave *my brother* alone!"

Her nose was bleeding. . . . Oh, I didn't know I'd hit that hard, and her nose was also beginning to swell. Quickly she jumped to her feet, but for some reason she backed off from me. "Nobody talks to me like that and gets away with it. . . . You're gonna regret this day, Catherine Dahl! I'll get your brother. And what's more, I'll take Julian from you too! And when he's mine, you'll find out that without him you're nothing! Nothing but a hick dancer Madame Z. would throw out if Julian didn't insist on keeping you on because he's got the hots for a virgin."

What she screamed out could be so true. Maybe she was right, that without Julian I wouldn't be anything special. I felt sick and I hated her—hated her for soiling Chris and my image of him. I began to throw my clothes in my suitcases, determined I'd go back to Clairmont before I'd live another hour near Yolanda!

"Go on!" she hissed between her clenched teeth. "Run away, little prude—what a fool you are. I'm not a whore! It's just I'm not the tease you are—and between the two, I choose my kind!"

Heedless of what she said, I finished packing, then strapped the handles of my three bags together so I could drag them out into the hall, and under my arm I carried a soft leather satchel stuffed full. I turned at the door to look back at Yolanda who had sprawled on the bed like a sleek cat. "You really do terrify me, Yolanda. I'm so scared I could laugh. I've faced up to bigger and better than you, and still I'm alive . . . so don't you come near me again, or it will be *you* who lives to regret this day!"

Shortly after I slammed the door I was on Julian's floor. Dragging along my tied-together luggage, I banged on the door to Julian's apartment with both fists! "Julian!" I cried, "if you're in there, open this door and give me back my purse. Open this door or you'll never have me for a dance partner again!"

He opened the door quickly enough, wearing nothing but a bath towel wrapped about his narrow hips. Before I knew what was happening he dragged me into the room and threw me down on the bed. I looked around frantically, hoping to see Alexis or Michael, but it was my bad luck he had the apartment to himself. "Sure," he barked, "you can have your damned purse back—after you answer a few questions!"

I jumped up from the bed—and he shoved me down again, then knelt so he straddled my body, and in no way could I escape! "You let me go, you beast!" I yelled. "I walked six blocks in the rain and was freezing cold—now let me up and give me my purse!"

"Why can't you love me?" he shot out, holding me down with both hands as I struggled to free myself. "Is it because you're in love with someone else? Who is it? It's that big doctor who took you in, isn't it?"

I shook my head, terribly afraid of him. I couldn't tell him the truth. He looked almost insane with jealousy. His hair was so wet from his recent shower he dripped water on me. "Cathy, I've had about all I can take from you! It's been about three years since we met, and I'm not getting anywhere. It can't be me that's wrong—so it must be you! Who is it?"

"Nobody!" I lied. "And you are all wrong for me! The only thing I like about you, Julian Marquet, is the way you dance!"

Blood flooded his face. "You think I'm blind and stupid, don't you?" he asked, so furious he could likely explode.

"But I'm not blind, I'm not stupid and I've seen the way you look at that doctor—and so help me God if I haven't seen you look at your own brother in the same way! So don't go getting up on your high horse of morals, Catherine Dahl, for I've never seen a brother and sister so fascinated with each other before!"

I slapped him then! He slapped back, twice as hard! I tried to fight him off, but he was like an eel as he wrestled me down to the floor where I feared he'd soon rip off my clothes and rape me—but he didn't do that. He only held me beneath him and breathed heavily until he had some control of his raging emotions, and only then did he speak. "You're mine, Cathy, whether you know it or not . . . you belong to me. And if any man comes between us, I'll kill him—and you too. So remember that before you turn your eyes on anyone but me."

He gave me my purse then, and told me to count my money to see if he'd stolen any. I had forty-two dollars and sixty-two cents, it was all there.

Shakily I gained my feet, when he allowed me to, and I trembled as I backed to the door, opened it, and stepped out into the hall clutching my purse tight. Only then did I dare to speak what I thought.

"There are institutions for madmen like you, Julian. You can't tell me whom to love, and you can't force me to love you. If you had deliberately set out to make yourself repugnant to me, you couldn't have done a better job of it. Now I can't even like you—and as for dancing together again, forget it!" I slammed the door in his face, then hurried away.

But as I reached the elevator, he had the door open again, and he cursed something so terrible I can't repeat it, except it ended with, "Damn you to hell, Cathy. . . . I've said it before, and I'll say it again . . . and you'll wish to God you were in hell before I'm done with you!"

After that terrible scene with Yolanda, then Julian, I sought out Madame Zolta and told her I just couldn't live any longer in an apartment with a girl determined to ruin my career.

"She afraid of you, Catherine, that's all. Yolanda was the superstar in my small company until you came along. Now she feels threatened. Make up with her. . . . Be a good girl, and go and say you're sorry for whatever it was."

"No, Madame. I don't like her, and I refuse to live in the same apartment with her. So if you don't give me more money, I'll have to go to another company and see if they will, and if they won't then I'll go back to Clairmont."

She groaned, bowed her skeleton head into her bony hands and moaned some more. Oh, how grand Russians were at expressing emotions! "Okay . . . you blackmail me, and I give in. I'll give you a small raise, and tell you where to find cheap apartment—but it won't be so nice as one you left."

Hah! That had been nice? But she was right. The only apartment I could find would fit in Paul's smallest bedroom, all two rooms of it. But it was my own . . . the very first place I'd had all to myself, and for a few days I exalted in fixing it up as best I could. Then I really began to sleep restlessly, waking up every few minutes to listen to all the squeaks and squeals the old building made. I longed for Paul. I longed for Chris. I heard the wind blow, and there was no one in another bed three feet from mine to comfort me with soft words and sparkling blue eyes.

Chris's eyes were in front of me as I got up and sat at my kitchen table to write a note to "Mrs. Winslow." I sent her my first rave review, one with a sensational photo of Julian and me in *The Sleeping Beauty*. And I wrote at the bottom of my letter,

> It won't be long now, Mrs. Winslow. Think about that every night before you fall asleep. Remember somewhere I'm still alive, and I'm thinking of you, and planning.

I even mailed off that letter in the middle of the night before I had the chance to reconsider and tear it up. I raced home, threw myself on my bed and sobbed. Oh God, I was never going to be set free! Never! And despite all my tears I woke up again, thinking of how I could hurt her so she'd never be the same. *Be happy now, Momma, for it won't be long!*

I bought six copies of all papers that had anything to say about me. Unfortunately, most often my name was coupled with Julian's. Paul and Chris were also favored with my reviews; the others I kept for myself—or Momma. I pictured how she'd look when she opened the envelope, though it was my fear she'd just pitch it in the trashcan after she'd torn up the envelope with its contents unread. Not once did I call her Mother or Momma, but kept my salutations always formal and cold. There would come a day when she would see me face to face and I would call her Mother and I would watch her pale, then shudder.

One morning I was awakened by someone banging on my door. "Cathy, let me in! I have terrific news!" It was Julian's voice.

"Go way!" I said sleepily, getting up and pulling on a robe before I stumbled over to make him stop pounding on the door. "Stop that!" I yelled. "I haven't forgiven you—I never will—so stay out of my life!"

"Let me in or I'll kick the door down!" he bellowed. I unlocked the deadbolts, and swung the door open a crack. Julian barged in to sweep me up in his arms and plant on my lips a long, hot kiss while I was half yawning. "Madame Zolta . . . yesterday after you left, she broke the news! We're going on tour in London! Two weeks there! I've never been to London, Cathy, and Madame is so delighted they've taken official notice of us over there!"

"Really?" I asked, catching his excitement. Then I staggered off toward my minute kitchen. . . . Coffee, had to have coffee before I could think straight.

"God, are you always so disoriented in the mornings?" he asked, following me into the kitchen where he straddled a chair backwards and leaned on his elbows to watch my every move.

"Wake up, Cathy! Forgive me, kiss me, be my friend again. Hate me all you want tomorrow, but love me this day—for I was born for this day, you too—Cathy, we're going to make it! I know we are! Madame Zolta's company was never noticed before we became a team! It isn't her success—it's ours!"

His modesty deserved a medal. "You've eaten breakfast?" I asked, and hoped. I had only two slices of bacon and wanted both for myself.

"Sure I have; I grabbed a bite before I came over, but I can eat again."

Naturally he could eat again! He could always eat . . . and that's when it hit me . . . London! Our company going to London! I spun around, crying, "Julian, what you said, you're not kidding? We're going over there—all of us?"

He jumped up. "Yes, all of us! It's a big break, our chance to make it big! We'll make the world sit up and take notice! And you and I, we'll be the stars! Because together we're the best, and you know it as well as I do."

I shared my meal and listened to him rhapsodize on the long and fantastic career we had just ahead. We'd be rich, and when we grew older, we'd settle down and have a couple of kids, and then teach ballet, I'd like that, wouldn't I? I hated to spoil his plans, but I had to say it. "Julian, I don't love you, so we can never be married. We'll go to London and dance together, and I'll do my best—but I plan to marry someone else. I'm already engaged. I have been for a long time now."

His long, glaring look of disbelief and pure hatred delivered and redelivered a series of visual slaps on my face. "You're lying!" he screamed. I shook my head to deny it. "Goddamn you to hell for leading me on!" he raged, then hurled himself out of my apartment. I'd never led him on, except when we were dancing, and that was my role to play. . . . That was all, all there was between us.

Winter Dreams

I was going home for Christmas. The unpleasantness with Julian was forgotten in my happy anticipation of seeing Paul, and bringing with me such good news. Thank God I had Paul to escape to. And I wasn't going to let Julian take the joy from this Christmas. For this was the time Paul and I had agreed to announce our engagement, and the only person who could ruin my happiness now was Chris.

At two o'clock in the morning Chris and Paul met me at the airport. It was bitterly cold even in South Carolina. It was Chris who reached me first to catch me up in his strong arms, and he tried to put a kiss on my lips but I turned my face so his kiss landed on my cheek. "Hail to the conquering ballerina!" he cried, hugging me tight and looking at me with so much pride. "Oh, Cathy, you are so beautiful! Each time I see you, you make my heart hurt."

He made my heart hurt too, to see him more handsome than even Daddy had been. Quickly I looked in another direction. I tore away from my brother's embrace and ran toward Paul who stood and watched. He stretched out his hands to take mine in them. *Careful, careful*, warned his long look, mustn't let *our news escape too soon*.

That was our best Christmas ever, from beginning to end—or almost to the end. Carrie had grown half an inch, and to see her sitting on the floor on Christmas morning with her big blue eyes happy and glowing as she exclaimed over the red velvet dress I'd bought her, found after hours and hours of searching almost every shop in New York. She looked like a radiant, small princess when she tried the dress on. I tried to picture Cory seated cross-legged on the floor looking at his gifts too. It was impossible for me to leave the memory of him out of any happy occasion. Oh, many a time I'd glimpsed a small boy with blond curls and blue eyes on the streets of New York, and I'd run to chase after, hoping by some miracle it would be him—and it never was, never was.

Chris put a small box into my hands. Inside was a tiny gold heart-locket and in the center of the lid was a genuine diamond, a small one, but a diamond nevertheless. "Paid for by my own hard-earned cash," he said as he fastened the chain about my neck. "Waiting on tables pays well when you give good service with a smile." Then, furtively, he slipped a folded note in my hand. An hour later, when I had the chance, I read a note that made me cry:

> To my lady Catherine,
>
> I give you gold with a diamond you can barely
>   see,
> But the gem would be castle-sized if it expressed all I feel for
>   thee.
> I give you gold because it endures, and love like
>   the eternal sea.
> Only your brother, Christopher.

I hadn't read that note when Paul gave me his gift wrapped in gold foil and topped by a huge red satin bow. My hands trembled as I fumbled with the many layers of tissue, all while he watched expectantly. A *grey fox* coat! "The kind of coat you really need for New York winters," he said, his eyes shining with all the warmth and love he felt.

"It's too much," I choked, "but I love it, absolutely love it!"

He smiled, made happy so easily. "Every time you wear it, it's essential you think of me, and it should keep you warm on those cold, foggy days in London too."

I told him it was the most beautiful coat I'd ever seen, though I felt uneasy. It brought back thoughts of Momma and her closet full of many furs, gained only because she had the heartless cruelty to lock us away, and thus gain a fortune, and furs, and jewelry, and everything else money could buy.

Chris jerked his head around to catch something on my face that must have betrayed my love for Paul. His brows drew together in a scowl before he shot a glance at Paul. Then he got up and left the room. Somewhere upstairs a door slammed violently. Paul pretended not to notice. "Look over in the corner, Catherine—that's a gift for all of us to enjoy."

I stared at the huge cabinet TV set that Carrie jumped up and ran to turn on. "He bought it just so we could watch you dance in *The Nutcracker* in *color*, Cathy. Now he won't let me touch it."

"It's only because it is the devil to tune in correctly," Paul apologized.

Throughout the rest of Christmas Day I saw very little of Chris, except at mealtimes. He wore the bright blue sweater I'd knitted for him—and it did fit—and under it the shirt and tie I'd given him as well. But none of my gifts to him could equal that gold and diamond locket with the small poem that left my heart bleeding. I hated it that he kept caring so much, and yet—when I thought about it later—I would hate it more if he didn't.

That evening we all settled down comfortably before the new color TV. I curled up on the floor near Paul's leg as he sat in a chair, with Carrie close at my side. Chris sat far away, deep in a mood that took him even farther away than the actual feet that separated us. So I didn't feel as happy as I should have as I watched the credits roll by on the colorful screen. A tape which had been made in August and only now was to be seen in hundreds of cities across the country. How beautiful the sets looked in color; they hadn't appeared nearly so ethereal in reality. I gazed at myself as Clara—did I really look like that? I forgot myself and leaned unconsciously against Paul's thigh, and I felt his fingers twine into my hair—and then I didn't know where I was, except on stage, with Julian now transformed by magic from the ugly nutcracker into the handsome prince.

When it was over I came back to myself and the first thing I thought of was my mother. *God, let her be home this night, and let her have seen me. Let her know what she tried to kill! Let her hurt, cry, grieve . . . please, please!*

"What can I say, Cathy," said Paul in an awed way. "No dancer could have performed that role better than you did. And Julian was superb too."

"Yeah," said Chris coldly, getting to his feet and coming to lift Carrie up in his arms. "You both were sensational— but it sure wasn't the kiddy performance I remember seeing when *I* was a child. The two of you made it seem a romance. Really, Cathy, turn that guy off, and quickly!" With those words he strode from the room and up the stairs to tuck Carrie into bed.

"I think your brother is suspicious," said Paul mildly, "not only of Julian, but also of me. All day he has treated me as a rival. He's not going to be happy when he hears our news."

Because like others I wanted to put off what was unpleasant, I suggested we not tell him until the next day. Then, when I was curled up on Paul's lap and we had our arms wrapped about each other, we exchanged the kind of passionate kisses held back until now. I was aching for him. After we'd turned off all the lights we stole up the back stairs and with the zeal born of starvation made love on his bed. Later on we slept, then woke up to make love again. At dawn I kissed him once more, then slipped on a robe to sneak down the hall to my own room. To my utter dismay, just as I stepped from Paul's room into the hall, Chris opened his door and came out! Abruptly he jerked to a stop and stared at me with astonished, hurt eyes. I cringed backward, so ashamed I could cry! Neither of us said a word. His eyes were the first to break from the frozen stare that also stilled our limbs. He ran for the stairs, but halfway there he turned to throw me a look of outraged disgust. I wanted to die! I went in to look at Carrie who was sound asleep with her red velvet dress clutched in her arms. And on my bed I lay trying to think of what to say to Chris to make it right between us again. Why did I feel in my heart that I was betraying him?

The day after Christmas was for returning the gifts you hated, didn't want, or those that didn't fit. I forced myself to approach Chris who was in the garden, fiercely snipping at the rose bushes with hedge clippers. "Chris, I need to talk to you and explain a few things."

He exploded. "Paul had no right to give you a fur coat! A gift like that makes you seem a kept woman! Cathy, give him back that coat! And, most of all, stop what you are doing with him!"

First I took the clippers from his hands before he ruined Paul's beloved roses. "Chris, it isn't as bad as you believe. You see . . . Paul and I . . . well, we are planning to marry in the spring. We love each other, so it isn't wrong what we do together. It's not an affair to be forgotten tomorrow; he needs me and I need him." I stepped closer when he turned his back to hide his expression. "It's better this way for me and for you too," I said softly. I encircled his waist and twisted about to stare up in his face. He seemed stunned, like a healthy man who learns suddenly he has a terminal illness—and all hope had fled from him.

"He's too old for you!"

"I love him."

"So, you love him. What about your career? Are you throwing away all those years of dreaming, of working? Are you going to break your word? You know we swore to each other to go after our goals and not let those lost years make a difference."

"Paul and I have discussed that. He understands. He thinks we can work it out. . . ."

"*He* thinks? What does a doctor know about the dancer's life? You'll never be with him. He'll be here; you'll be God knows where, with men your own age. You don't owe him anything, Cathy, you don't! We'll pay him back every cent he's spent on us. We'll give him the respect he deserves, and the love—but you don't owe him your life."

"Don't I?" I asked in a whisper, aching inside for Chris. "I think I do owe him my life. You know how I felt when I came here. I thought no one could be trusted or depended on. I expected the worst to happen to us, and it would have too without him. And I don't love him just for what he's done. I love him because of who and what he is. Chris, you don't see him as I do."

He whirled about, seizing the shears from my hands. "And what about Julian? You are going to be married to Paul and dance with Julian? You know Julian is mad for you. It's all over him, the way he looks at you, the way he touches you."

I backed off, stricken. Chris wasn't talking *just* of Julian. "I'm sorry if this has ruined your holiday," I said, "but you'll find someone too. You love Paul, I know you do. And when you've thought about this, you'll know we are right for each other, despite our age difference, despite everything." I went off, leaving Chris in the garden with the hedge clippers.

Paul drove me to Greenglenna while Carrie stayed home to enjoy the new color TV set and all her new clothes and games. Paul chatted happily of the party he planned for all of us tonight at his favorite restaurant. "I wish I could be selfish and leave Chris and Carrie at home. But I want them there when I put the ring on your finger." I fixed my eyes on the winter landscape rolling by, the trees bare, the grass brown, the pretty houses with decorations and outdoor lights turned on after dark. Now I was part of the show, no longer just a spectator locked away—and yet I felt so torn, so miserable.

"Cathy, you are seated beside the happiest man in the world!"

And back in his garden, I'd left a man just as miserable as I felt.

In my purse I had a ring I'd bought for Carrie in New York. A tiny ruby for a very small finger, and even so, it was too large for anything but her thumb. As I stood there, in the better jewelry department of the best store in town, discussing just how the ring could be reduced in size without ruining the setting, I suddenly heard a very familiar voice! A sweet, husky, dulcet-toned voice. As in slow motion, I cautiously turned my head.

Momma! Standing right next to me! If she'd been alone, perhaps she would have seen me, but she was absorbed in chatting to her female companion who was dressed just as elegantly as she was. I'd changed considerably since she saw me last—still if she looked, she would have to know who I was. The two of them were discussing the party they had attended last night. "Really, Corrine, Elsie does carry the festive theme through to an outrageous extreme—all that red!"

Parties! Was that all she did, go to parties! My heart went pounding in fox-trot time. My spirits went limp, sagged out by disappointment. A party—I should have known! She never stayed at home and watched TV! She hadn't seen me! Oh, but

I was angry! I turned to *make* her see me! A small standing mirror on the glass jewelry showcase reflected her profile, and showed me how lovely she was still. A bit older looking, but striking nonetheless. Her flaxen hair was drawn back to emphasize the perfection of her small gem of a nose, her pouting red lips, her long and naturally dark lashes that were made thicker by mascara. Her ears glittered with gold and diamonds, the real things—and she was speaking.

"Can't you show me something just right for a lovely young girl?" she asked the saleslady. "Something in good taste, not gaudy, or too large, but something a young girl can keep all her life and be proud of."

Who? What girl did she have to give gifts to? I felt jealous and watched her select a lovely gold locket very much like the one Chris had given me! Three hundred dollars! Now our dear mother was spending money on a girl not her own, forgetting about us. Didn't she think of us, wonder how we were faring? How could she sleep at night when the world could be so cold, ugly and cruel to children on their own?

As far as I could tell, she was completely without guilt or regrets. Maybe that was what millions could do—nail a satisfied smirk to one's face—despite what it covered. I wanted to speak and see her poise collapse! I wanted her smiles to peel off like bark from a tree and she'd be revealed before her friend for what she was—a monster without a heart! A killer! A fraud! But I said nothing.

"Cathy," said Paul, coming up behind me and putting his hands on my shoulders, "I've returned everything—how about you? Ready to go now?"

I wanted desperately for my mother to see me with Paul, a man every bit as handsome as her darling "Bart." I wanted to shout it out. *See, I too can attract intelligent, kind, educated and handsome men!* So quickly I glanced to see if Momma had heard Paul speak my name, hoping to delight in her stunned surprise, her guilt, her shame. But she'd moved on farther down the counter, and if she heard the name, Cathy, it didn't cause her to turn her head.

For some reason I didn't understand, I sobbed.

"Are you all right, darling?" asked Paul. He saw something on my face that puzzled him and put concern in his eyes. "You're not having second thoughts about us, are you?"

"No, of course not!" I denied. But I was having second thoughts about *me*. Why hadn't I done something? Why hadn't I put out my foot this time and tripped her? Then I could have seen her sprawled on the floor, her poise vanished—maybe. It would be like her to fall gracefully and have all the men in the store hurry to assist her up—even Paul.

I was dressing for the big affair at The Plantation House when Chris came into my bedroom and sent Carrie away. "Go watch TV," he said with more sharpness than I'd ever heard him use with her. "I want to speak to your sister." Carrie threw him, then me, an odd look before she skipped out of the room.

No sooner had Carrie closed the door behind her, than Chris was at my side and seizing my shoulders. He shook me violently. "Are you going through with this farce? You don't love him! You still love me! I know you do! Cathy, please, don't do this to me! I know you're trying to set me free by marrying Paul, but that's not a good reason for marrying a man." He hung his head, released my shoulders, and looked terribly ashamed. His voice came so low I had to keen my ears to hear his words. "I know it's wrong what I feel for you. I know I should try and find someone else, like you try to do . . . but I can't stop loving you and wanting you. I think about you all during my days, every day. I dream about you at night. I want to wake up and see you in the room with me. I want to go to bed and know you're there, very close, where I can see you, touch you." A sob tore from his throat before he could go on. "I can't bear to think of you with another man!

Damn it, Cathy, I want you! You don't plan to have children anyway, so *why can't it be me?*"

I'd drawn away when he released my shoulders. When his words stopped I ran to fling my arms about him, as he clutched at me, as if I were the one and only woman who could save him from drowning. And we'd both drown if I did as he wanted. "Oh, Chris, what can I say? Momma and Daddy made their mistake in marrying each other—and we were the ones to pay the price. We can't risk repeating their mistake!"

"Yes we can!" he fervently cried. "We don't have to have a sexual relationship! We can just live together, be together, just brother and sister, with Carrie too. Please, please, *I beg you not to marry Paul!*"

"*Shut up!*" I screamed. "*Leave me alone!*" I struck at him then, wanting to hurt him, as every word he said hurt me. "You make me feel so guilty, so ashamed! Chris, I did the best I could for you when we were prisoners. Maybe we did turn to each other, but only because we had no others! If there had been, you would never have wanted me, and I would never have given you a second glance! You are only a *brother* to me, Chris, and I want to keep you where you should be . . . which isn't in my bed!"

Then he had me in his arms, and I couldn't help but cling to him with my cheek pressed against his thudding heart. He was having a hard time controlling his tears. I wanted him to forget . . . but every second he held me hard against him raised his hopes, and he was aroused! And he was the one who thought we could live platonically together! "Let me go, Chris. If you love me for the rest of your life, keep it to yourself; I never want to hear about it again! I love Paul, and nothing you say will keep me from marrying him!"

"You're lying to yourself," he choked, holding me tighter. "I see you watching me before you turn your eyes his way. You want me, and you want him. You want everyone, and everything! Don't ruin Paul's life when already he's suffered enough! He's too old for you—and age *does* count! He'll be old and dried up sexually when you're at your peak! Why even Julian would be better!"

"You are one big fool if you believe that!"

"Then I'm a fool! I've always been a fool, haven't I? When I put my love and trust in you that was the biggest mistake of my life, wasn't it? You are just as heartless, in your own way, as our mother! You want every man who appeals to you, regardless of the consequences . . . but I would let you have whomever you wanted, as long as you always came back to me."

"Christopher, you're jealous because I found someone to love before you did! And don't stand there and glare your icy blue eyes at me—for you've had plenty of affairs! I know you've slept with Yolanda Lange, and God knows how many others. And what did you tell them? You told them you loved them too! Well I don't love you now! I love Paul, and there's not one thing you can do to stop us from marrying each other!"

He stood there, pale faced and quivering all over, and then he said in a hoarse whisper, "Yes there is. I could tell him about us . . . he wouldn't want you then."

"You wouldn't tell him that. You're much too honorable, and besides, he already knows."

For long, long moments we glared at each other . . . and then he ran from the room, slamming the door so hard behind him it put a long crack in the ceiling plaster.

Only Carrie accompanied Paul and me to The Plantation House. "It's too bad Chris doesn't feel well. I hope he doesn't have the flu. . . . Everyone else does."

I didn't say anything, just sat and listened to Carrie chatter on and on about how much she loved Christmas and the way it made everything ordinary look so pretty.

Paul slipped a two-carat diamond ring on my finger while a huge fire crackled the Yule log, and soft music played. I did my best to make it a joyous occasion, laughing, smiling, exchanging long, romantic looks while we sipped champagne and toasted each other and our long and happy future together. I danced with him under the giant crystal chandeliers and kept my eyes closed, picturing Chris home alone, sulking in his room and hating me.

"We're going to be so happy, Paul," I whispered, standing on the toes of my high-heeled silver slippers. Yes, this was the way our life together would be. Easy. Sweet. Effortless. Just like the lilting, old-fashioned waltz we danced to. Because when you truly loved there were no problems that love couldn't overcome.

Me . . . and my ideas.

April's Fool

Drive. Dedication. Desire. Determination. The four D's of the ballet world we had to live by. If Madame Z. had been tough on us before Christmas, now she clamped down on us such a heavy schedule of practice all we did was work. She lectured on how perfect The Royal Ballet was, strictly classical—but we were to do everything in our own unique American way, classical . . . but more beautiful and innovative.

Julian was absolutely ruthless, even demonic. I began to really despise him! We were both wet with sweat and our hair hung in strings. My leotard was glued to my skin. Julian wore only a loin cloth. He yelled as if I were deaf, "Do it right this time, damn it! I don't want to be here all night!"

"Stop yelling at me, Julian! I can hear perfectly well!"

"Then *do it right!* First take three steps and then you kick, then jump for me to catch, and for God's sake this time lay back immediately! Don't stay upright and stiff, the moment I catch you fall backwards and go limp—if you can manage to do anything right or graceful today."

That was my trouble. I didn't trust him now. I was afraid

he was going to try to hurt me. "Julian, you yell at me as if I'm deliberately doing everything wrong!"

"It seems to me you are! If you really wanted to do it right you could. All you have to do is take three steps, kick, then jump, and I lift and you fall back. Now see if you can get it right at least one time out of fifty tries!"

"Do you think I like this? Look at my armpits," I said as I lifted my arms to show him. "See how raw they are, how you've rubbed the skin off? And tomorrow I'll be black and blue all over from the bruises you make with your hard grasps!"

"Then *do it right!*" He raged not only with his voice, but with his jet eyes, and I was terribly afraid he was just waiting for the opportunity to let me fall—on purpose—for revenge. But I got up, and we did it again. And again I failed to fall back and fully trust him. This time he threw me to the floor where I lay panting, gasping, and wondering why the hell I kept this up.

"You're gasping for breath?" he asked sarcastically, towering above me, his bare feet wide apart and straddling my legs. His bare chest glistened with perspiration that dripped down to fall on me. "I do all the hard work, and you lie there sprawled out and exhausted looking. What happened to you down there? Did you use all your energy making it with your doctor?"

"Shut up! I'm tired from twelve hours of continuous practice, that's all!"

"If you're tired, I'm ten times more so—so get up, and let's do it again—and get it right this time, goddamn you!"

"Don't you swear at me! Get yourself another partner! You tripped me up and made me fall so my knee hurt for three days afterward—so how can I run and jump into your arms— you're mean enough to cripple me permanently!"

"Even if I hated you, I wouldn't let you fall. And, Cathy, I don't hate you. *Not yet.*"

After practicing over and over again to the piano music,

counting, timing, repeating the same series of steps, at last I
got it right, and even Julian could smile and congratulate me.
Then came the final dress rehearsal and the performance of
Romeo and Juliet.

It was the stunning sets and dazzling costumes that
brought out the best in all of us when combined with a full
orchestra. Now I could give to the role of Juliet all the little
nuances that would make her real, and not some wooden stick
that Yolanda appeared tonight, as she did her *pliés* while her
eyes seemed glassy, unfocused. Madame Z. came up to peer
closely into her face, and then she sniffed Yolly's breath. "By
God . . . you been smoking grass! No dancer of mine goes
spaced out onto the stage and cheats my audience—get home
and to bed. Catherine, get ready to play Juliet!"

Yolanda staggered past me, then tried to give me a savage
kick as she hissed, "Why did you have to come back? Why
didn't you stay down there where you belong?"

I didn't think of Yolanda and her threats as I stood on the
flimsy balcony and gazed dreamily down into Julian's pale
face that tilted upward to mine. He appeared so beautiful
under the bluish lights, wearing white tights, with his dark
hair gleaming, his jet eyes glittering along with the fake jewels on his medieval costume. He seemed to be my attic lover
who would ever bound away from me, and never let me near
enough to see the features of his face.

The applause thundered as the curtain lowered. And
behind it, out of breath Julian sprang up to hug me close. "You
were sensational tonight! How do you manage to frustrate me
right up until the moment of performance?" The curtain rose
for our bows—then he kissed me full on the lips. "Bravo,"
they cried, for this was the sort of drama and passion all
balletomanes craved.

It was our night, the best yet, and drunk with success I
dashed past photographers, and autograph hounds toward
my dressing room, for there was a big bash afterward, a

celebration before our company took off for London. Quickly I lathered on cold cream to take off the makeup, then I changed from my last act costume into a short formal of periwinkle blue. Madame Zolta rapped on my door and called out, "Catherine, a lady here says she has flown all the way from your home town to watch you dance. Come, open your door and we will hold up the party until you arrive."

A tall attractive woman entered. Dark-haired, dark-eyed, her clothes were expensive and flattering to her figure. For some strange reason, it seemed I'd met her before, or she reminded me of someone. She looked me over from head to toe, and only then did she turn to stare around the small dressing room filled with plastic bags jammed with all the costumes I was taking with me to England, each labeled with my name and the name of the ballet the costumes were designed for. I waited impatiently for her to have her say, then go, so I could get on to putting on my coat.

"I don't think I know you," I said to hurry her up.

She smiled crookedly, then sat down uninvited to cross her nicely shaped legs. Rhythmically she swung one foot in a high-heeled black pump back and forth.

"Of course you don't know me, my dear child . . . but I know a great deal about you."

There was something in her sweet and too-smooth tongue to warn me, and I stiffened, prepared for whatever she'd come to deliver—and it would be bad. I could tell from the mean look that hid beneath the false sweet one.

"You're very pretty, maybe even beautiful."

"Thank you."

"You dance exceptionally well—that surprised me. Though of course you would have to dance well to be with this company which I've heard is fast becoming an important one."

"Thank you again," I said, thinking she'd never come to the point.

She took a long time before she spoke again, keeping me

in suspense, on edge. I picked up my coat, trying to signal to her that I was trying to leave.

"Nice fur coat," she commented. "I suppose my brother gave you that. I've heard he's throwing away his money like a drunken sailor. Giving all he's saved to three nobodies who came on a bus and took over his life." She laughed low and sarcastically, the way women of culture know how to laugh. "Now I know why, seeing you; though I've heard from others you were pretty enough to make any man foolish. Still, I had no idea a child such as you could look so voluptuous, so sensual and skinny all at the same time. You're a peculiar blend, Miss Dahl. All innocence and sophistication too. Such a brew must be heady intoxication for a man of my brother's type." She chortled. "There's nothing like the combination of youth, long blond hair, a beautiful face and full breasts to bring out the beast even in the best of men." She sighed, as if pitying me. "Yes, that's the trouble with being too young and beautiful. Men are made their worst selves. Paul's made an ass of himself before, you know. You're not his first little playmate; though he's never given one a fur coat before, and a diamond ring. Just as *if* he could possibly marry you."

So this was Paul's sister, Amanda—the queer sister who knitted him sweaters and mailed them off Parcel Post, but refused to speak to him on the streets.

Amanda got up and prowled around me. A cat on the stalk, ready to spring. Her perfume was Oriental, musky, heavy, as she moved in on what she must think a timid prey. "Such flawless skin you have," she said, reaching to stroke my cheek, "so firm, like porcelain. You won't keep that skin, or all that hair once you're thirty-five or so, and long before then he'll have tired of you. He likes his women young, very young. He likes them pretty, intelligent and talented. I have to acknowledge he has good taste, if not good sense. You see," she smiled again that hateful smile, "I really don't give a damn what he does as long as it stays within the limits of decency and doesn't reflect on *my* life."

"Get out of here," I managed to say. "You don't know your brother at all. He's an honorable, generous man and in no way could he harm *your* life." Pityingly she smiled.

"My dear child, don't you realize you are ruining his career? Are you fool enough to think this affair has gone unnoticed? In a town the size of Clairmont everybody knows everything. Though Henny can't talk, the neighbors do have eyes and ears. Gossip, that's all I hear, gossip—throwing away his money on juvenile delinquents who take advantage of his good nature, and soon enough he'll be broke, and he won't have a medical practice left!" She was heating up now, and I feared any moment she'd rake my face with her long red nails.

"Get out of here!" I ordered hotly. "I know all about you, Amanda, for gossip has reached my ears too! Your trouble is you think your brother owes you the rest of his life because you worked to help put him through college and medical school. But I used to keep his books, and he's paid you back, plus ten percent interest—so he doesn't owe you anything! You're a liar to try and make him seem small in my eyes—for you can't do that! I love him, and he loves me, and nothing you say can stop our marriage!"

She laughed again, hard and mirthless, then her face turned hard, determined. "Don't order *me* to do anything! When I'm ready to go, I'll leave—and that's when I've had my say! I flew up here just to see his newest little paramour, his dancing doll . . . and believe me you won't be his last. Why Julia used to tell me he—"

I hotly interrupted, *"Get out! Don't you dare say one word more about him!* I know about Julia. He's told me. If she drove him to others, I don't blame him; she wasn't a real wife; she was a housekeeper, a cook—not a wife!"

Merrily she laughed—God how she liked to laugh! She was enjoying this, someone competitive enough to fight back, someone she could claw. "Fool girl! That's the same old line every married man passes on to his newest conquest. Julia was one of the dearest, sweetest, kindest and most wonderful women who ever lived. She did everything she could to please him. Her one fault lay in the fact she couldn't give him all the sex he wanted, or the kind of sex he demanded, so yes, in a way, he did have to turn to others—like you. I'll admit most married men fool around, but they still don't do what he did!"

I hated the spiteful witch now, really detested her. "What's he done that was so terrible? Julia drowned his three-year-old son—there's nothing on earth that would make *me* take the life of my child! I don't need revenge that much!"

"I agree," she said, back to mild tone now. "That was an insane thing for Julia to do. Scotty was such a handsome, lovely boy—but Paul drove her to do what she did. I understand her reasoning. Scotty was the thing Paul loved most. When you seek to destroy someone emotionally, you kill what he loves best."

Oh! The horror of her!

"He wears a hair shirt, doesn't he?" she asked in a gloating way, her dark, pretty eyes glowing with satisfaction. "He tortures himself, blames himself, longs for his son, and then you came along, and he put a baby in you. Don't think the whole town doesn't know about your abortion! We know! We know everything!"

"You lie!" I shrieked. "It wasn't an abortion! I had a D & C because my periods weren't regular!"

"It's on the hospital records," she said to me smugly. "You miscarried a two-headed embryo with three legs—twins who didn't separate properly. You poor thing, don't you know a D & C is an abortion procedure?"

Drowning, drowning, I was going under, black swirls of water all around . . . two headed? Three legs? Oh, God—the monster baby I so dreaded! But Paul hadn't touched me then, not Paul. "Don't cry," she soothed, and I yanked from the touch of her large hand that flashed with diamonds, "all men are beasts, and I guess he didn't tell you. But don't you see, you can't marry him. I'm doing this for your own good. You're beautiful, young, gifted, and to live in sin with a married man is a pure waste. Save yourself while you can."

Tears blurred my vision. I rubbed at my eyes as a child would, feeling a child in a crazy adult world as I stared dully at her bland, smooth face. "Paul's not a married man. Paul's a widower. Julia's dead. She killed herself the day she drowned Scotty."

Like a mother she patted my shoulder. "No, child, Julia is *not* dead. Julia lives in an institution where my brother put her after she drowned Scotty. She's still his legal wife, insane or not."

She thrust into my slack hand several snapshots, pictures of a thin, pitiful-looking woman lying on a hospital bed, her face in profile in both. A woman ravaged by suffering. Her eyes wide open and staring blankly into space, and her dark hair lay like strings on the pillows. Yet I'd seen too many pictures of Julia not to recognize her, even as changed as she was.

"By the way," said Paul's sister, leaving me with the snapshots, "I enjoyed the performance. You're a marvelous dancer. And that young man—he's spectacular. Take *him*. He's obviously in love with you." She left then. Left me in a daze of broken dreams and floundering in despair. How was I ever going to learn to swim in an ocean of deceit?

Julian took me to the big bash which was being thrown in our honor. Hordes of people surrounded us, congratulated us, said so many flattering words. They meant nothing to me. All I could think was Paul had lied to me, lied to me, took me when he knew he was married—*lies*, I hated lies!

Never had Julian been sweeter or more considerate. He held me close in one of those slow, old-fashioned dances, so close I could feel every hard muscle of his lean body, and the maleness of him pressed hard, hard. "I love you, Cathy," he whispered. "I want you so much I can't sleep at night. I want to hold you, make love to you. If you don't let me soon, I'll go mad." He buried his face in my piled up hair. "I've never had anyone brand new, like you. Cathy, please, please love me, love me."

His face swam before me. He seemed dream-godlike, perfect, and yet, and yet . . . "Julian, what if I told you I wasn't *brand new?*"

"But you are! I know you are!"

"How can you tell?" I giggled drunkenly. "Is there something written on my face that says I am still a virgin?"

"Yes," he said firmly. "Your eyes. Your eyes tell me you don't know what it's like to be loved."

"Julian, I fear *you* don't know much."

"You underestimate me, Cathy. You treat me like a little boy one minute, and the next like some hungry wolf who will eat you up. Let me make love to you, then you'll know no man has ever touched you before."

I laughed. "All right—but one night only."

"If you have me for one night, you will never, never want me to go," he warned, and his eyes glowed and sparkled, black as coal.

"Julian . . . I don't love you."

"But you will—after tonight."

"Oh, Julian," I said with a long yawn, "I'm tired, and partially drunk—go away, leave me alone."

"Not on your life, kiddo. You said yes, and I'm holding you to it. It's me tonight . . . and every night for the rest of your life—or mine."

On a rainy Saturday morning, with all our luggage already piled into the taxies that would take our company to the airport, Julian and I stood in the city hall with our best friends to support us, and a judge said the words that would bind us

together until "death do you part." When it came my turn to
speak my vows, I hesitated, wanting to run away and fly to
Paul. He would be crushed when he found out. Then there
was Chris. But Chris would rather see me marry Julian than
Paul; that's what he'd told me.

Julian held tight to me, his dark eyes soft and shining
with love and pride. I couldn't run. I could only say what I was
supposed to, and then I was married to the one man I'd sworn
I would never allow to touch me intimately. Not only Julian
was happy and proud, but also Madame Zolta who beamed
at us and gave us her blessings, kissed our cheeks and shed
motherly tears. "You've done the right thing, Catherine. You
will be so happy together, such a beautiful couple . . . but
remember not to make any babies!"

"Darling, sweetheart, love," Julian whispered when we
were on the plane flying over the Atlantic, "don't look so
sad. This is our day for rejoicing! I swear you will never
be sorry. I'll make you a fantastic husband. I'll never love
anyone but you."

My head bowed down on his shoulder, then I bawled! Crying for everything that should have been mine on my wedding
day. Where were my birdsongs, the bells that should chime?
Where was the green grass, and the love that was mine?
And where was my mother who was the cause of everything
gone wrong? *Where?* Did she cry when she thought of us?
Or did she, more likely, just take my notes with the news-
clippings and tear them up? Yes, that would be like her, never
to face up to what she'd done. How easily she tripped away on
her second honeymoon and left us in the care of a merciless
grandmother, and back she came, all smiling and happy, telling us of what a wonderful time she had. While we, locked up,
had been brutalized and starved, and she'd never even looked
at Cory and Carrie who didn't grow. Never noticed how shadowed their hollow eyes, how thin their weak legs and arms.
Never noticed anything she didn't want to see.

The rain kept coming down, down, forecasting what was ahead. That cold blasting torrent of freezing water put ice on the wings of the plane that was carrying me farther and farther from all those I loved. That ice was in my heart too. And tonight I had to sleep with a man I didn't even like when he wasn't on stage, and dressed in costume, and playing the role of a prince.

But to give Julian his due, he was all he boasted of being in bed. I forgot who he was, and pretended he was someone else as his kisses played over my body, and not one inch went unexplored, unkissed or un-caressed. Before he finished, I wanted him. I was more than willing to have him take me . . . and try to erase the persistent thought that I had just made the worst mistake of my life.

And I had made many mistakes.

Labyrinth of Lies

Before our bodies had adjusted to jet lag, we went into rehearsals with The Royal Ballet looking on, comparing our style to theirs. Already Madame Z. had told us their way was strictly classical, but we were to do everything in our own way, and were not to be intimidated. "Stick to your guns, keep it pure, but make each dance your very own. Julian, Catherine, as newlyweds, all eyes will be upon you two—so make every scene as romantic as you can. The two of you together touch my heart and make it cry . . . and if you keep it up, what you're doing, you may make ballet history."

She smiled, and tears filled the deep furrows about her tiny eyes. "Let us all prove that America too can produce the very best!" She broke then and turned her back, so we couldn't see her face crumple. "I luv all of you so much," she sobbed. "Now go away . . . leave me be . . . and make me proud of you."

We were determined to do our very damndest to make Madame Zolta's name famous once more, not as a dancer, but as a teacher. We practiced until we fell exhausted into our beds.

The Royal Opera House, Covent Gardens shared its space with the ballet company, and when I first saw it I sucked in my breath and held fast to Julian's hand. The red and gold auditorium seated more than two thousand people. Its sparkling swirl of balconies that rose up to a high dome with a sunburst design in the middle stunned me with its old-fashioned splendor. Soon we were to find out that backstage was far less opulent, with no charm in its crowded dressing rooms and a rabbit warren of tiny offices and workrooms; worst of all, no rehearsal studios at all! Try as I would to find something admirable about British plumbing and heating facilities, I failed utterly. I was forever cold, except under the duress of dancing. I hated the stingy supply of hot water in the bathrooms, forcing me to take the quickest bath possible before I froze to death.

And all the time Julian stayed glued to my side. Privacy was something he'd never heard of and had no respect for. Even when I was in the bathroom he had to be there, so I'd race to lock the door and leave him pounding. "Let me in! I know what you're doing, why all the secrecy?"

Not only that, he wanted to crawl into my mind and know all my past, all my thoughts, everything I'd done. "And so your mother and father were killed in an auto crash, what happened next?" he asked, holding me in an iron embrace. Why did he have to hear it again? I swallowed. By now I had concocted a believable story about the law wanting to put us in an orphanage, so Chris, Carrie and I had to run away. "We had a little money saved up, you know, from birthdays, Christmas, and such. We caught a bus that would take us to Florida, but Carrie was sick and threw up, and this huge fat black lady came and took us to her 'doctor son.' I guess he felt sorry for us; he took us in . . . and that's all there is to it."

"All there is to it," he repeated slowly. "There's a hell of a lot you're not telling me! Though I can guess the rest. He saw a rich plum in a young beautiful girl, and that's why he was so damned generous. Cathy—just how intimate were you with him?"

"I loved him, and I planned to marry him."

"Then why didn't you?" he shot out. "Why did you finally say yes to me?"

Tact and subtlety were never among my virtues. I grew angry because he was making me explain, when I didn't want to explain. "You were at me all the time!" I stormed. "You made me believe I could learn to love you—but I don't think I can! We've made a mistake, Julian! A horrible mistake!"

"Don't you say anything like that again, you hear!" Julian sobbed as if I'd wounded him terribly, and I was reminded of Chris. I couldn't go through my life damaging everyone I met, so my rage vanished as I allowed him to take me in his arms. His dark head lowered so he could kiss my neck. "Cathy, I love you so much. More than I ever wanted to love any woman. I've never had anyone love me for myself. Thank you for trying to love me, even though you say you don't."

It hurt to hear the quiver in his voice. He seemed a small boy who was pleading for the impossible to happen, and perhaps I was doing him an injustice. I turned and wrapped my arms around his neck. "I do want to love you, Jule. I did marry you, and I am committed, so I'll try and make you the best wife I can. But don't push at me! Don't make demands—just let love come as I learn more about you. You're almost a stranger to me, even though we've known each other for three years."

He winced, as if I ever really knew him, then love would be, indeed, impossible. He doubted himself so much. Oh, God, what had I done? What kind of person was I, that I could turn from an honest, sincere, honorable man and rush head-long into the arms of someone I suspected was a brute?

Momma had a way of acting impulsively, and being sorry when it was too late. I *wasn't* like her underneath; I couldn't be! I had too many talents to be like someone who had none . . . none but for making every man fall in love with her, and that wasn't intelligence. No, I wanted to be like Chris . . . and then I floundered again, caught, as always, in the quicksand of *her* making. All of it was her fault, even my marriage to Julian!

"Cathy, you're going to have to learn to overlook a lot of flaws," said Julian. "Don't put me up on a pedestal, don't expect perfection. I have feet of clay, as you already know, and if you try to make me into the Prince Charming I think you want . . . you are going to fail. You have that doctor of yours on a pedestal too; I think you might be the kind to put all the men you love up so high they are bound to come tumbling down. Just love me and try not to see what doesn't please you."

I wasn't good at overlooking faults. I'd always seen Momma's when Chris never had. I always flipped over the brightest coin and looked for the tarnish. Funny. Paul's tarnish had seemed all Julia's fault until Amanda came with her horror story. Another reason to hate Momma, making me doubt my instinct!

Long after Julian returned to bed I sat by the windows and contemplated myself, my eyes fixed on the long shiverlets of ice striking the glass. The weather was only telling me what lay ahead. Spring was back there in the garden with Paul . . . and I'd done it myself. I didn't have to believe Amanda. God help me if I turned out to be like Momma inside, as well as out!

Our weeks in London were busy, exciting and exhausting—but I dreaded the time when we returned to New York. How long could I keep putting off telling Paul? Not forever. Sooner or later he had to know.

Shortly before the first day of spring, we flew back to Clairmont, and we taxied to Paul's house. It was the place of our deliverance, and it seemed nothing there had changed. Only I had, for I was coming to devastate a man who didn't need to be hurt again.

I stared at the boxwoods neatly clipped into cones and spheres, and the wisteria trees that were blooming; azaleas rioted colorfully everywhere, and the big magnolias were ripe and soon to flower, and over everything emerald draped the dangling gray Spanish moss, misting and fogging, to create shreds of living lace. I sighed. If at twilight there was anything more beautiful and somehow romantically, sadly mystical than a live oak dripping with Spanish moss that would in the end kill its host, I'd yet to see it. Love that clung and killed.

I thought I could take Julian inside, then tell Paul our news—but I couldn't. "Would you mind waiting on the veranda until I tell Paul?" I asked. For some reason he only nodded. I'd expected an argument. Agreeably, for a change, he sat in a white wicker rocker, the same one Paul had been in when first we found him dozing on that Sunday afternoon, after the bus put us off. He'd been forty then. He was now forty-three.

Quivering a little, I went on alone to open the front door with my own key. I could have telephoned or sent a cable. But I had to see his face and watch his eyes, and try to read his thoughts. I needed to know if I'd really injured his heart, or only wounded his pride and ego.

No one heard me open the door. No one heard my footsteps on the hard parquet of the foyer. Paul was sprawled in his favorite chair before the color television and the fireplace, dozing. His long legs were stretched to rest on the matching ottoman, his ankles crossed and his shoes off. Carrie was sitting cross-legged on the floor near his chair, as needing as always to be near someone who loved her. She was deeply engrossed in her play with the small porcelain dolls. She wore a white sweater banded at the neck and wrists with purple, and over this her red corduroy jumper. She looked like a pretty little doll.

My eyes went again to Paul. In his light dozing sleep he

had the expression of someone anxiously waiting. Even his feet moved often to cross and uncross, while his fingers flexed into fists, then unflexed. His head was thrown back to rest on the high back of his chair, but that too kept moving from side to side . . . dreaming, I thought, maybe of me. Then his face turned in my direction. Did he sense my presence even in his sleep?

Ever so slowly his eyelids fluttered open. He yawned and lifted a hand to cover his mouth . . . then stared at me fuzzily. As if I were merely an apparition. "Catherine," he murmured, "is that you?"

Carrie heard his question, jumped up and came flying to me, crying out my name as I caught her and swung her high. I lavished on her small face a dozen or so kisses, and hugged her so tight she cried out, "Ouch, that hurts!" She looked so pretty, so fresh and well fed. "Oh, Cathy, why did you stay away *so long?* We wait every day for you to come home, and you never do. We make plans for your wedding, but when you don't write, Dr. Paul says we should wait. Why did you send only postcards? Didn't you have time to write long letters? Chris said you must be awfully busy." She had pulled out of my arms and was back on the floor near Paul's chair, and staring at me reproachfully. "Cathy . . . you forgot all about us, didn't you? All you care about is dancing. You don't need no family when you dance."

"Yes, I do need a family, Carrie," I said absently, with my eyes fixed on Paul, trying to read what he was thinking.

Paul got up and came toward me, his eyes locked with mine. We embraced and Carrie sat quietly on the floor and watched, as if studying the way a woman should act with the man she loved. His lips only brushed over mine. Yet his touch shivered me as Julian's never did. "You look different," he said to me in his slow, soft way. "You've lost weight. You look tired too. Why didn't you telephone or telegraph to let me know you were on the way? I would have met you at the airport."

"You look thinner too," I said in a hoarse whisper. His weight loss was far more becoming than mine. His mustache seemed darker, thicker. I touched it tentatively, longingly, knowing it wasn't mine to feel now—and he had grown it just to please me.

"It hurt when you stopped writing to me every day. Did you stop when your schedule became too crowded?"

"Something like that. It's tiring to dance every day, and try to see as much as possible at the same time. . . . I got so busy, I never had enough time."

"I subscribe to *Variety* now."

"Oh . . ." was all I could say, praying they didn't write about my marriage to Julian. "I've nominated myself as your clipping service, though Chris is keeping a scrapbook too. Whenever he's home, we compare clippings; if one of us has something the other doesn't, we have it photocopied." He paused as if puzzled by my expression, my demeanor, something. "They are all rave reviews, Catherine, why do you look so . . . so . . . emotionless?"

"Tired, like you said." I hung my head not knowing what to say, or how to meet his eyes. "And how've you been?"

"Catherine, is something the matter? You act strange." Carrie was staring at me . . . as if Paul had expressed her thoughts too. I gazed around the big room filled with the beauty of all that Paul had collected. Sunlight through the ivory sheers shone on the miniatures in his tall étagère with the glass shelves, the black, gold-veined mirror behind them, and lit from the top and bottom. How easy to hide away in looking around, pretending everything was all right, when everything was all wrong.

"Catherine, speak to me!" Paul cried. "There is something wrong!"

I sat down, knees weak, my throat tight. Why couldn't I ever do anything right? How could he have lied to me, deceived me, when he knew I'd had enough of lying and deceit? And how could he look so trustworthy still?

"When will Chris be home?"

"Friday, for Easter vacation." His long look was reflective, as if he thought it strange when usually Chris and I kept in constant communication. Then there was Henny to greet and hug and kiss . . . and I could put it off no longer . . . though I found a way. "Paul, I brought Julian home with me. . . . He's out on the veranda waiting. Is that all right?"

He gave me the strangest look, and then nodded. "Of course. Ask him in." Then he turned to Henny. "Set two more places, Henny."

Julian came in, and, as I'd cautioned him, he didn't say a word to let anyone know we were married. Both of us had taken off our wedding rings and had them in our pockets. It was the strangest of quiet meals, and even when Julian and I handed out the gifts the stiffness grew, and Carrie only glanced at her bracelet of rubies and amethysts, though Henny beamed a broad smile when she put on her solid gold bracelet.

"Thank you for the lovely figurine of yourself, Cathy," said Paul, putting it carefully aside on the closest table. "Julian, would you please excuse Cathy and me for a while? I'd like to have a private talk with her." He said this as a doctor requesting a private interview with the responsible family member of a critically ill patient. Julian nodded and smiled at Carrie. She glared back at him.

"I'm going to bed," stated Carrie defiantly. "Good night, Mr. Marquet. I don't know why you had to help Cathy buy me that bracelet, but thank you anyway."

Julian was left in the living room to stare at the TV as Paul and I took off for a stroll in his magnificent gardens. Already his fruit trees were in bloom, and climbing red, pink and white roses made a brilliant display on the white trellises.

"What's wrong, Catherine?" Paul asked. "You come home to me and bring along another man, so maybe you don't have to explain at all. I can guess."

Quickly I put out my hand to seize hold of his. "Stop! Don't say anything!" Falteringly and very slowly I began to tell him about his sister's visit. I told him I knew now that Julia was still alive, and though I could understand his motivation, he *should* have told me the truth. "Why did you lead me to believe she was dead, Paul? Did you think me such a child I couldn't bear to hear it? I could have understood if you had told me. I loved you, don't you ever doubt that I did! I didn't give to you because I thought I owed you anything. I gave because I wanted to give, because I desperately needed you. I knew better than to expect marriage, and I was happy enough in the relationship we had. I would have been your mistress forever—but you should have told me about Julia! You should have known me well enough to realize I'm impulsive, I act without thought when I'm hurt—and it hurt terribly that night Amanda came and told me your wife was still alive!

"Lies!" I cried. "Oh, how I hate liars! *You* of all people to lie to me! Besides Chris, there was no one I trusted more than you."

He'd stopped strolling, as I had. The nude marble statues were all around, mocking us. Laughing at love gone awry. For now we were like them, frozen and cold.

"Amanda," he said, rolling her name on his tongue as something bitter and fit to be spit out. "Amanda and her half-truths. You ask why—why didn't you ask *why* before you flew to London? Why didn't you give me the chance to defend myself?"

"How can you defend lies!" I bit back meanly, wanting him to hurt as I'd hurt that night when Amanda slammed out of the theater.

He walked away to lean against the oldest oak, and from his pocket he drew a pack of cigarettes.

"Paul, I'm sorry. Tell me now what your defense would have been."

Slowly he puffed on the cigarette, and exhaled smoke. That smoke came my way and weaved around my head, neck, body—and chased off the scent of roses. "Remember when you came," he began, taking his time, "you were so bitter from your loss of Cory, to say nothing of how you felt about your mother. How could I tell you my own sordid story when already you'd known too much pain? How was I to know you and I would become lovers? You seemed to me only a beautiful, haunted child—though you've touched me deeply— always you've touched me. You touch me now, standing there with your accusing eyes. Though you are right. I *should* have told you." He sighed heavily.

"I told you about the day Scotty was three, and how Julia took him down to the river and held him under the water until he was dead. But what I didn't tell you was she lived on. . . . A whole team of doctors worked on her for hours on end trying to bring her out of the coma, but she never came out."

"Coma," I whispered. "She's alive now, and still in the same coma?"

He smiled so bitterly, and then looked up at the moon that was smiling too, sarcastically, I thought. He turned his head and allowed his eyes to meet with mine. "Yes, Julia lived on, with her heart beating, and before you came along with your brother and sister I drove every day to visit her in a private institution. I'd sit beside her bed, hold her hand, and force myself to look at her gaunt face and skeleton body. . . . It was the best way I had to torment myself and try to wash away the guilt I felt. I watched her hair become thinner each day—the pillows, covers, everything covered by her hair as she withered away before my very eyes. She was connected to tubes that helped her to breathe, and a tube was in her arm through which she was fed. Her brain waves were flat, but her heart kept on beating. Mentally she was dead, physically she was alive. If she ever came out of the coma, she'd never speak, move, or even be able to think. She'd have been a living dead

woman at the age of twenty-six. That's how old she was when
she took my son down to the river to hold him under the shallow water. It was hard for me to believe a woman who loved
her child so much could drown him and feel his struggles to
live . . . and yet she did it just to get back at me." He paused,
flicked the ash from his cigarette and turned his shadowed
eyes to me. "Julia reminds me of your mother. . . . Both could
do anything when they felt justified."

I sighed, he sighed, and the wind and flowers sighed too. I
think those marble statues sighed along as well, in their lack
of understanding the human condition. "Paul, when did you
see Julia last? Doesn't she have any chance at all for a full
recovery?" I began to cry.

He gathered me in his arms and kissed the top of my
head. "Don't cry for her, my beautiful Catherine. It's all over
for Julia now; she is finally at peace. The year we became lovers, she died less than a month after we started. Quietly she
just slipped away. I remember at the time you looked at me
as if you sensed something was wrong. It wasn't that I felt
less for you that made me stand back and look at myself. It
was a blend of painful guilt and sorrow that someone as sweet
and lovely as Julia, my childhood sweetheart, had to leave life
without once experiencing all the wonderful, beautiful things
it had to give." He cupped my face between his palms, and
tenderly kissed away my tears. "Now smile and say the words
I see in your eyes, say you love me. When you brought Julian
home with you, I thought it was over between us, but now I
can tell it will never be over. You've given me the best you
have within you, and I'll know that even when you're off thousands of miles, dancing with younger and handsomer men . . .
you'll be faithful to me, as I'll be faithful to you. We'll make it
work, because two people who are sincerely in love can always
overcome obstacles no matter what they are."

Oh . . . how could I tell him now? "Julia's dead?" I
asked, quivering, deep in shock, hating myself and Amanda!

"Amanda lied to me. . . . She knew Julia was dead, and yet she flew to New York to tell me a lie? Paul, what kind of woman is she?"

He held me so tight I felt my ribs ache, but I clung just as fast to him, knowing this was the last time I could. I kissed him wild and passionately, knowing I'd never feel his lips again on mine. He laughed jubilantly, sensing all the love and passion I had for him, and in a happy, lighter voice he said, "Yes, my sister knew when Julia died; she was at her funeral. Though she didn't speak to me. Now please stop crying. Let me dry your tears." He used his handkerchief to touch to my cheeks and the corners of my eyes, then held it so I could blow my nose.

I'd acted the child, the impulsive, impatient child Chris had warned me not to be—and I had betrayed Paul who trusted me. "I still don't understand Amanda," I said in a mournful wail, still putting off that moment of truth I didn't know if I could face. He held me and stroked my back, my hair, as I clung with my arms about his waist, staring up into his face.

"Sweetheart, Catherine, why do you look and act so strange?" he said in his voice that had gone back to normal. "Nothing my sister said should rob us of taking what joy we can from life. Amanda wants to drive me out of Clairmont. She wants to take over this house so she can leave it to her son, so she does her best to ruin my reputation. She's very active socially and fills the ears of her friends with lies about me. And if there were women before Julia drowned my son, that was lesson enough for me to change my ways. There was no other woman until *you!* I've even heard it rumored that Amanda has spread it about that I made you pregnant and your D & C was actually an abortion. You see what a spiteful woman can do—anything!"

Now it was too late, too late. He asked me again to stop crying. "Amanda," I said stiffly, my control about to break.

"She said that D & C was the same as an abortion. She said you kept the embryo, one with two heads. I've seen that thing in your office in a bottle. Paul, how could you keep it? Why didn't you have it buried? A monster baby! It isn't fair—it isn't—why, why?"

He groaned and wiped his hand over his eyes, to quickly deny everything. "I could kill her for telling you that! A lie, Catherine, all a lie!"

"Was it a lie? It could have been mine, you know that. For God's sake, Chris doesn't know—he didn't lie to me too, did he?"

He sounded frantic as he denied everything, and sought once more to embrace me, but I jumped backward, and thrust forth both arms to ward him off. "There *is* a bottle in your office with a baby like that inside! I saw it! Paul, how could you? *You*, of all people, to save something like *that*!"

"No!" he flared immediately. "That thing was given to me years ago when I was in med school—a joke, really—med students play all sorts of jokes you'd find gruesome, and I'm telling you the truth, Catherine, you *didn't* abort." Then he stopped abruptly, just as I did, with my thoughts reeling. I'd betrayed myself!

I began to cry. *Chris, Chris, there was a baby, there was a monster just like we feared.*

"No," said Paul again and again, "it's not yours, and even if it were, it wouldn't make any difference to me. I know you and Chris love each other in a special way. I've always known it, and I do understand."

"Once," I whispered through my sobs, "only once on one terrible night."

"I'm sorry it was terrible."

I stared up at him then, marveling that he could look at me with so much softness and so much respect, even knowing the full truth. "Paul," I asked tremulously, timidly, "was it an unforgivable sin?"

"No . . . an understandable act of love, I'd call it."

He held me, he kissed me, he stroked my back and began telling me his plans for our wedding. ". . . and Chris will give you away, and Carrie will be your bridesmaid. Chris was very hesitant and wouldn't meet my eyes when I discussed this with him. He said he thought you weren't mature enough to handle a complicated marriage like ours will be. I know it's not going to be easy for you, or for me. You'll be touring the world, dancing with young, handsome men. However, I'm looking forward to accompanying you on a few of those tours. To be the husband of a prima ballerina will be inspiring, exciting. Why, I could even be your company doctor. Surely dancers need doctors on occasion?"

I went dead inside. "Paul," I began dully, "I can't marry you." Then, quite out of context, I went on, "You know, wasn't it stupid of Momma to hide our birth certificates inside the linings of our two suitcases? She didn't do too good a job and the linings ripped and I found them. Without my birth certificate I couldn't have applied for a passport, and I also needed that certificate to prove I was of age to apply for a marriage license. You see, several days before our company flew to London Julian and I had blood tests and our marriage ceremony was just a simple one, with Madame Zolta and the company dancers there, and even as I said my marriage vows, and swore fidelity to Julian . . . I was thinking of you, and Chris, and hating myself, and knowing I was doing the wrong thing."

Paul didn't say anything. He reeled backward, then staggered over to fall upon a marble bench. For moments he just sat, and then his head drooped into his hands and hid his face.

I stood. He sat. He lost himself somewhere, while I waited for him to come back and rail at me. But his voice when it came was as soft as a whisper, "Come, sit beside me for a while. Hold my hand. Give me time to realize it's all over between us." I did as he said and held his hand, while both of us stared up at the sky full of diamonds and dark clouds.

"I'll never hear your kind of music again without thinking of you. . . ."

"Paul, I'm sorry! I wish to God I'd have listened to my instinct that told me Amanda was lying. But the music was playing where I was too and you were far away, and Julian was there, pleading with me, telling me he loved and needed me, and I believed him, and convinced myself you didn't really love me. I can't bear to be without someone who loves me."

"I'm very happy he loves you," he said, then got up quickly and started for the house, his strides so long and fast I'd never catch up even if I ran. "Don't say another word! Leave me alone, Catherine! Don't follow me! You did the right thing—don't doubt that! I was an old fool, playing with a young one, and you don't have to tell me I should have known better—I already know that!"

Too Many Loves To Lose

Gone as deaf and stony as one of Paul's marble statues, I sat on the veranda and stared up at the night sky that was turning stormy and black with clouds. Julian came out to sit beside me and in his embrace I began to softly cry. "Why?" he asked. "You do love me a little, don't you? Your doctor can't be really hurt; he was very kind to me, and told me to come out and comfort you."

It was then that Henny came out to signal with her lightning-fast signs that her doctor-son was packing for a trip and I was to stay here. "What's she saying to you?" asked Julian with annoyance. "Damn, it's like hearing someone talk in a foreign tongue. I feel so left out."

"Stay here and wait!" I ordered, then jumped up to race into the house and fly up the back stairs, then on into Paul's room where he was flinging his clothes into an open suitcase on his bed. "Look," I cried in distress, "there's no reason why you have to leave! This is your home. *I'll* go. I'll take Carrie with me, so you need never see my face again!" He turned to give me a long and bitter look as he went on putting shirts in his bag.

"Cathy, you've taken the wife I expected to have, and now you want to take away my daughter. Carrie is like my own flesh and blood, and she wouldn't fit into your kind of life. Let her stay with me and Henny. Let me have something to call my own. I'll be back before you go . . . and you should know that Julian's father is very, very ill."

"Georges is ill?"

"Yes. Perhaps you don't know that he's had kidney disease for several years, and has been on a dialysis machine for months. I don't think he'll live much longer. He's not my patient, but I stop in to visit him as often as I can, more or less to hear about you and Julian. Now will you please get out, Cathy, and not force me to say things I'd regret."

I cried face down on my bed until Henny came into my room.

Strong, motherly, dark hands patted my back. Henny's misting, liquid brown eyes spoke when her tongue couldn't. She talked to me with her gestures, and then took from her apron pocket a clipping from the local newspaper. An announcement of my marriage to Julian! "Henny," I wailed, "what am I going to do? I'm married to Julian, and I can't demand a divorce; he depends on me, believes in me!"

Henny shrugged her broad shoulders, expressing that people were as complex to her as they were to me. Then quickly she signaled, "Big sister always been big trouble maker. One man already hurt, no good hurting two. Doctor good man, strong man, will survive disappointment, but young dancing man might not. Wipe away tears, cry no more, put on big smile and go downstairs and take hand of new husband. For everything work out for the best. You see."

I did as Henny directed, and joined Julian in the living room, and there I told him about his father being in the hospital, and not expected to live. His pale face went even whiter. Nervously he chewed on his lower lip. "It's really that serious?"

It had been my opinion that Julian didn't care much for his father, so I was surprised to see his reaction. At that moment Paul came into the living room with his suitcase and offered to drive us to the hospital. "And remember, my house has plenty of rooms, and there is no reason at all why the two of you should even consider a hotel. Stay as long as you like. I'll be back in a few days."

He backed his car out of the garage so Julian and I could join him on the front seat. Hardly a word was said until he let us out in front of the hospital, and sadly I hesitated before the steps, watching Paul drive away into the night.

They had Georges in a private room, and with him was Madame Marisha. When I saw Georges in the bed, I drew in my breath! Oh! To be like that! He was so thin he seemed already dead. His face had a grayish pallor, and every bone he had jutted forward to make jagged peaks beneath the thin skin. Madame M. was crouched at his side, staring down into his gaunt face pleading with her eyes, commanding him to hold on and live! "My love, my love, my love," she crooned as to a baby, "do not go, do not leave me alone. We have so much to do yet, to experience yet. . . . Our son has to reach fame before you die. . . . Hold on, my love, hold on."

Only then did Madame Marisha glance up to see us there, and with her same old authority she snapped, *"Well, Julian. You did finally come!* And after all the cables I sent you! What did you do, tear them up and dance on, as if nothing matters?"

I blanched, very surprised, and looked from him to Madame. "My dear mother," he said coldly, "we were on tour, you know that. We had engagements and contracts, so my wife and I kept our commitments."

"You heartless brute!" she snarled, then gestured for him to come closer. "Now you say something kind and loving to that man on the bed," she hissed in a whisper, "or so help me *God I'll make you wish you were never born!"*

Julian had a great deal of trouble making the effort to approach the bed, so much so I had to give him a shove, while his mother sobbed into a handful of pink tissues. "Hello, Father," was all he could manage, along with, "I'm sorry you are so ill." Quickly he came back to me, and held me hard against him. I felt his whole body trembling.

"See, my love, my sweetheart, my darling," crooned Madame Marisha again, once more bending above her husband and smoothing back his damp, dark hair. "Open your dear eyes and see who has flown thousands of miles to be at your side. Your own Julian and his wife. All the way from London they flew the moment they knew you were so sick. Open your eyes, my heart, see him again, see them together, such a beautiful pair of newlyweds—please open your eyes, please look."

On the bed the pale, thin wraith of a man slitted his dark eyes and they moved slowly, trying to focus on Julian and me. We were at the foot of his bed, but he didn't seem to see us. Madame got up to push us closer, and then held Julian there so he couldn't back off. Georges opened his eyes a bit wider and thinly smiled. "Ah, Julian," he sighed. "Thank you for coming. I have so much to say to you—things I should have said before. . . ." He faltered, stammered, "I should have—" and then he broke off. I waited for him to continue—and I waited. I saw his wide open eyes glaze and go blank and his head stayed so still. Madame screamed! A doctor and nurse came on the run, and shooed us out as they began to work over Georges.

We formed a pitiful group in the hall outside his room, and in only a short while the gray-haired doctor came out to say he was sorry, all had been done that could be done. It was over. "It is better so," he added. "Death can be a good friend to those in extreme pain. I wondered how he held on so long. . . ."

I stared and stared at Julian, for we could have come back

sooner. But Julian made his eyes blank and refused to speak. "He was your father!" screamed Madame as tears streaked her cheeks. "For two weeks he suffered, waiting to see you before he could let himself die and escape the hell of living on!"

Julian whirled, his pale skin flamed with bright red fury, as he lashed out at his mother, "Madame Mother, just what *did* my father give me? All I was to him was an extension of himself! All he was to me was a dance instructor! Work, dance, that's all he ever said! He never discussed what I wanted besides the dance; he didn't give a damn what else I wanted, or what else I needed! I wanted him to love me for myself; I wanted him to see me as his son, not just as a dancer. I loved him; I wanted him to see I loved him, and say he loved me in return . . . but he never did! And try as I would to dance perfectly, he never gave me a compliment—for I didn't do anything nearly as well as he could have done it when he was my age! So, that is what I was to him, somebody to step into his shoes and carry on his name! But, damn him, and you, I've got my own legal name . . . Julian Marquet, not Georges Rosencoff, and his name will not live on and steal from me what fame I achieve!"

I held Julian in my arms that night, understanding him as I hadn't before. When he broke and cried, I cried along with him, for a father he'd professed to despise, when underneath he loved him. And I thought of Georges, and how sad it was that he tried, too late, to say what he should have years and years ago.

So we'd come from a honeymoon where we had achieved a certain amount of fame and publicity, and given many, many hours of hard work, only to attend the funeral of a father who wouldn't live to know about his son's accomplishments. All the glory of London now seemed shrouded in funeral mists.

Madame Marisha held out her arms to me when the graveside ceremony was over. She held me in her thin arms, as she might have once held Julian, and in a sort of hypnotic trance we rocked back and forth, both of us crying. "Be good to my son, Catherine," she sobbed and sniffled. "Have patience with him when he acts wild. His has not been an easy life, for much of what he says is true. Always he felt himself in competition with his father, and never could he surpass his father's abilities. Now I will tell you something. My Julian has a love for you that is almost holy. He thinks you are the best thing that has ever happened in his life, and to him you are without flaw. If you have flaws, hide them. He won't understand. A hundred times he's been in then out of love, all within the space of a few months. For years you frustrated him. So now that he's your husband, give to him generously all the love that's been denied, for I am not a demonstrative woman. I have always wanted to be, but somehow I could never humble myself to touch first. Touch him often, Catherine. Take his hand when he would pull from you and go off and sulk alone. Understand why he's moody, and love him three times as much. That way you will bring out the best in him, for he does have admirable qualities. He has to, for he is Georges's son."

She kissed me, and said good-bye for a while, and made me swear to come with Julian often on visits. "Fit me in the corners of your life," she said with sadness making her face long and hollow eyed. But when I promised, and turned to look, Julian was glaring hard at the both of us.

Chris came home for his Easter vacation, and less than eagerly he greeted Julian. I noticed Julian glaring at him with narrowed, suspicious eyes.

No sooner were Chris and I alone when he bellowed, "You married *him?* Why couldn't you wait? How could you be so intuitive when we were locked away and so damned dumb now that we're out! I was wrong not wanting you to marry Paul only because he is so much older. And I admit it, I was jealous, and didn't want you to marry anyone. I had a dream of you and me . . . someday. Well . . . you know what I dreamed.

But if it had to be a choice between Paul and Julian, then it should have been Paul! He's the one who took us in, and fed and clothed us, and gave us the best of everything. I don't like Julian. He'll destroy you."

He hesitated, turning his back so I couldn't see his face. He was twenty-one and beginning to take on the virile strength of a man. In him I could see so much of our father—and our mother. And when I wanted to, I could take things and twist them to suit my purpose, and so I thought he was more like Momma in some ways than like Daddy. I started to say this, and then I too floundered, for I couldn't. He wasn't anything at all like our mother!

Chris was strong . . . she was weak. He was noble, she was without any honor at all. "Chris . . . don't make it harder for me. Let's be friends again. Julian is hot-headed and arrogant and a lot of things that irritate on the surface, but underneath he's a little boy."

"But you don't love him," he said without meeting my eyes.

In a few hours Julian and I would be leaving. I asked Carrie if she would like to come and live in New York with us, but I had lost her trust; I had betrayed her too many times already and she let me know it. "You go on back to New York, Cathy, where it snows all the time, and muggers get you in the park, and killers get you in the subway—*but you leave me here! I used to want to be with you, now I don't care!* You went and married that ole Julian with the black eyes when you could have been Dr. Paul's wife, and my real mother. *I'll marry him!* You think he won't want me 'cause I'm too little—but he will. You think he's too old for me, but I won't be able to get any-body else, so he'll feel sorry and marry me, and we'll have six children—*you just wait and see!*"

"Carrie—"

"Shut up! I don't like you now*! Go away! Stay away! Dance until you die! Chris and me don't want you! Nobody here wants you!*"

Those screamed words hurt! My Carrie, yelling at me to
go away, when I'd been like a mother to her most of her life.
Then I looked over to where Chris was standing before the
pink sweetheart roses, his shoulders sagging, and in his eyes,
oh, those blue, blue eyes . . . that look would always follow me.
Never, never was his love going to set me free to love anyone
without reservations as long as he kept loving me.

Just an hour before we had to leave for the airport Paul's
car turned into the drive. He smiled at me as he always
smiled, as if nothing between us had changed. He had some
tale to tell Julian of a medical convention that had kept him
away, and he was terribly sad and sorry to hear his father had
died. He shook hands with Chris, then slapped him heartily
on the back, the way men so commonly showed affection to
one another. He greeted Henny, kissed Carrie and gave her a
little box of candy, and only then did he look at me.

"Hello, Cathy."

That told me so much. I was no longer Catherine, a
woman he could love as an equal, I had been moved back to
only a daughter. "And, Cathy, you can't take Carrie with you
to New York. She belongs with me and Henny so she can see
her brother from time to time, and I'd hate for her to change
schools too."

"I wouldn't leave you for nothing," said Carrie staunchly.
Julian went upstairs to finish packing his things, and I dared
to follow Paul out into the garden, despite the forbidding look
Chris gave me. He was down on his knees, still wearing a good
suit, pulling up a few weeds someone had overlooked. He got
up quickly when he heard my steps and brushed the grass
from his trousers, then he stared off into space as if the last
thing he wanted to do was to look at me.

"Paul . . . this would have been our wedding day."

"Would it? I'd forgotten."

"You haven't forgotten," I said, drawing closer, " 'The first

day of spring, a fresh start' you said. I'm so sorry I spoiled everything. I was a fool to have believed Amanda. I was a double fool
not to have waited to talk to you first before I married Julian."

"Let's not talk about it anymore," he said with a heavy sigh.
"It's all over now, and finished." Voluntarily he stepped close
enough to draw me into his arms. "Cathy, I went away to be
alone. I needed that time to think. When you lost faith in me,
you turned impulsively, but truthfully, to the man who has loved
you for a number of years. Any fool with eyes could see that. And
if you can be honest with yourself, you have been in love with
Julian almost as long as he's loved you. I believe you put your
love for him on a shelf because you thought you owed me. . . ."

"Stop saying that! I love you, not him. I'll always love
you!"

"You're all mixed up, Cathy. . . . You want me, you want
him, you want security, you want adventure. You think you
can have everything, and you can't. I told you a long time ago
April wasn't meant for September. We did and said a lot of
things to convince ourselves that the years between us didn't
matter, but they do matter. And it isn't only the years, it's the
space that would separate us. You'd be somewhere dancing
and I'd be here, rooted and tied down but for a few weeks a
year. I'm a doctor first and a husband second—sooner or later
you'd find that out and you'd turn to Julian eventually anyway." He smiled, and tenderly kissed away the tears I always
had to shed, and he told me fate always dealt out the right
cards. "And we'll still see each other—it isn't as if we're forever lost to one another—and I have my memories of how
wonderfully sweet and exciting it was between us."

"You don't love me!" I cried accusingly. "You never loved
me, or you wouldn't be taking this so agreeably!"

Softly he chuckled and cuddled me close again, as a father
would. "Dear Catherine, my hot-blooded, feisty dancer, what
man wouldn't love you? How did you learn so much about loving locked away in a cold, dim, northern room?"

"From books," I said, but the lessons taught were not all from books.

His hands were in my hair and his lips were near mine. "I'll never forget the best birthday gift I ever had." His breath was warm on my cheeks. "Now here's the way it's going to be from now on," he said firmly. "You and Julian will go back to New York, and you will make him the best wife you are capable of being. The two of you will do your damndest to set the world on fire with your dancing, and you've got to determine never to look back with regrets, and forget about me."

"And you—what about you?"

He lifted his hand and fingered his mustache. "You'd be surprised what this mustache has done for my sex appeal. I might never shave it off."

We both laughed, real laugher, not faked. I took then the two-carat diamond ring he'd given me and tried to return it to him. "No! I want you to keep that ring. Save it to hock, when or if you ever need a bit of extra cash."

Julian and I flew back to New York and hunted for weeks before we found just the right cozy apartment. He wanted something much more elegant, but between us we didn't earn enough for the penthouse apartment he thought was our due. "Sooner or later though, I'll see we live in that kind of place, near Central Park, in rooms filled with real flowers."

"We don't have time to baby along real plants and flowers," I said, having experienced all the time and trouble it took to keep flowers and plants alive and healthy. "And when we go to visit Carrie, we can always enjoy Paul's gardens."

"I don't like that doctor of yours."

"He's not *my* doctor!" I felt fluttery inside, afraid for no reason at all. "Why don't you like Paul? Everybody else likes him well enough."

"Yeah, I know," he answered shortly, pausing with his fork held midway between his plate and his mouth. He gave me a heavy, solemn look. "That's the trouble, my darling wife, I think you like him *too* much, even now. And what's more, I'm not crazy about your brother, either. Your sister is okay. You can ask her up for visits once in a while—but don't you ever forget, not for one second, that I come first in your life now. Not Chris, not Carrie, and, most of all, not that doctor you were engaged to. I'm not blind or stupid, Cathy. I've seen him look at you, and though I don't know how far you went with him before you'd better let it be dead now!"

My head bowed with the panic I felt. My brother and sister were like extensions of myself! I needed them in my life, not just on the fringes. What had I done? I had the blinding precognition that he was going to be my loving keeper, my jailor, and I'd be as imprisoned with him as I'd been in the locked room in Foxworth Hall! Only this time I'd be as free to come and go as far as his invisible chain would allow. "I love you like crazy," he said, polishing off the last of his meal. "You are the best thing that's ever happened to me. I want you at my side all the time, *never* out of sight. I need you to keep me straight. I drink too much sometimes, and then I get mean, real mean, Cathy. I want you to make me over into what you think I am on stage; I don't want to hurt you."

He touched me then, for I knew he'd been terribly hurt, as I'd been hurt, and he'd been so disappointed in his father, as my mother had disappointed me. And he needed me. Maybe Paul was right. Fate had used Amanda to deal out the right cards so Julian and I would be winners, not losers. Youth did call to its own age, and he was young, handsome, a talented dancer—and charming when he wanted to be. He had a cruel, dark side, I knew that. I'd experienced some of that . . . but I could tame him. I wouldn't let him be my ruler and my judge, my superior or my master. We'd make it fifty-fifty, share and be equals, and eventually, one bright and sunny morning, I'd wake up and see his darkly stubbled face and know I loved him. Know I loved him better than anyone I'd loved before—anyone.

PART THREE

Dreams Come True

While Julian and I worked slavishly to reach the top of the ballet world, Chris whizzed his way through college, and in his fourth year he entered an accelerated program for medical students, completing his fourth year of college while simultaneously beginning his first year of medical school.

He flew to New York and explained it to me while we strolled hand in hand in Central Park. It was spring and the birds were chirping and merrily collecting the trash they needed to build nests.

"Chris, Julian doesn't know you're here, and I'd rather he didn't find out. He's terribly jealous of you, and Paul too. Would you feel insulted if I didn't ask you over for dinner?"

"Yes," he said stubbornly. "I came up to visit my sister, and visit my sister I will. Not furtively either. You can tell him I came to visit Yolanda. Besides, I only intend to stay for the weekend."

Julian was obsessively possessive of me. He was like an only child who needed constant pampering, and I didn't mind, except when he tried to keep me from my family. "Okay. He's rehearsing now, and he thinks I'm home doing housework before I join him this afternoon. But stay away from Yolanda, Chris. She's nothing but trouble. Whatever she does with any man is news for the class the next day."

He gave me a strange look. "Cathy, I don't give a damn about Yolanda. She was just my excuse to see you; I know your husband hates me."

"I wouldn't call it hate . . . not exactly."

"All right, call it jealousy, but whatever it is, he's not keeping me from you." His tone and his look grew serious. "Cathy, always you and Julian seem just on the verge of making it big, and then something happens, and you never become the stars you should be. What is it?"

I shrugged. I didn't know what it was. I thought Julian and I were as dedicated to the dance as any others, and even more so, and still Chris was right . . . we'd put on a spectacular performance and draw rave reviews, and then we'd slide backwards. Perhaps Madame Zolta didn't want us to become superstars, lest we leave her company and join another.

"How is Paul?" I asked as we sat on a bench dappled with sunlight and shade.

Chris had my hand in his and tightly he held it. "Paul's Paul . . . he never changes. Carrie adores him; he adores her. He treats me like a younger brother he's very proud of. And really, Cathy, I don't think I would have made it as well without all the tutoring he gave me."

"He hasn't found anyone else to love?" I asked in a tight voice. I didn't fully believe Paul's letters that said there weren't any women he cared for.

"Cathy," said Chris, putting his fingers tenderly under my chin to tilt my face upward to his, "how can Paul find anyone to equal you?" I could have cried from the expression in his eyes. Would the past never set me free?

No sooner did Julian see Chris than the two of them were at it. "I don't want you sleeping under my roof!" stormed

Julian. "I don't like you and I never have and never will—so get the hell out and forget you've got a sister!" Chris left to stay at a hotel, and on the sly we met once or twice before he went back to his school. Dully I went back to attend class with Julian, then the afternoon rehearsal and the evening performance. Sometimes we had the lead roles, sometimes only minor ones, and sometimes, as punishment for some sarcastic remark Julian would make to Madame Zolta, we both had to dance in the *corps*. Chris didn't visit New York again for three years.

When Carrie was fifteen she came to spend her first summer with us in New York. Hesitating and frightened-looking from the long flight she'd made all alone, she ambled slowly through the bustling, noisy crowds at the airport terminal. Julian spotted her first and he cried out, then bounded forward to sweep her up in his arms. "Hi there, gorgeous sister-in-law!" he greeted, planting a hearty kiss on her cheek. "My, how much you've grown to look like Cathy—first thing you know I won't even know the difference—so watch out! Are you positively sure the dancing life isn't for you?"

She was made happy and secure by his pleasure to see her again, and quickly she responded by throwing her arms about his neck. In the three years Julian and I had been married, she'd learned to love him for what he appeared to be. "Don't you dare call me Tinkerbell!" she said, laughing. It was our standing joke, for Julian thought Carrie just the right size to play a fairy—and kept telling her it still wasn't too late for her to become a dancer. If someone else had even suggested such a thing, she would have been deeply insulted, but for Julian, someone she deeply admired, she would be a fairy only by flitting around and fluttering her arms. She knew he meant "fairy" as a compliment, and not a criticism of her small size.

Then it was my turn to have Carrie in my arms. I loved her so much I was overwhelmed by the force that swept over me and made me feel I was holding a child born of my own flesh. Though there was never a time I could look at Carrie and not long for Cory who should be at her side. I wondered too, if he had lived, would he too stand only four feet six inches tall? Carrie and I laughed and cried, exchanged news and then she whispered so Julian wouldn't overhear. "I don't wear a training bra anymore. I've got on a *real* one."

"I know," I whispered back. "The first thing I noticed was your bosom."

"Really?" She appeared delighted. "You can see them? I didn't think they showed that much."

"Well of course they show," said Julian, who shouldn't have sneaked so close to eavesdrop on this sisterly confidence. "That's the first thing my eyes go for once they get past a fabulous face. Carrie, do you realize you have a fabulous face? I just might kick out my wife and marry you."

It was a remark that didn't sit well with me. Many an argument we'd have because he cared too much for very young girls. However I was determined to let nothing spoil Carrie's vacation in New York, the first time she'd come alone, and Julian and I had mapped out a schedule so we could show her everything. At least there was one member of my family Julian would accept.

The months flew swiftly by, and then the spring we'd waited for so long was upon us.

Julian and I were in Barcelona, enjoying our first real vacation since we'd married. Five years and three months of married life, and still there were times when Julian seemed a stranger. Madame Zolta had suggested the vacation, thinking it a good idea if we visited Spain so we could study the Flamenco style of dancing. In a hired car we drove from one town to another, loving the beautiful countryside. We liked the late evening meals, the sleepy siesta afternoons lying on the rocky shores of the Côte d'Azur—but, most of all, we loved Spanish music and dancing.

Madame Z. had mapped our tour throughout Spain, list-ing all the villas that charged nominal rates. She was thrifty and taught all her dancers her tricks. If one occupied one of the small cottages near a hotel, and cooked their own meals, the fee was even less. So this was where Julian and I were on the day Chris's graduation invitation arrived. It had followed us all over Spain, to catch up with us here.

My heart jumped when I spied the thick creamy enve-lope, knowing it contained the graduation announcement of Chris's achievement—his medical degree—at long last! It was almost as if I myself had completed college, then medical school all within seven years.

Very carefully I used a letter opener so I could put this souvenir in my scrapbook of dreams, some of which were coming true. Inside was not only the formal announcement, but also a note on which Chris had written modestly:

I am embarrassed to tell you this, but I am the top grad in a class of two hundred. Don't you dare find an excuse to keep away. You have to be there to bask in the glow of my excitement, as I bask in the radiance of your admiration. I cannot possibly accept my M.D. if you aren't there to see. And you can tell Julian this when he tries to prevent your coming.

The bothersome thing about this was Julian and I had signed a contract some time ago to tape a TV production of *Giselle*. It was set for June, but now in May they wanted us both. We were sure the television exposure would make us the stars we'd strived so long to be.

It seemed a perfect time to approach Julian with the news. We had returned to our cottage after touring old castles. As soon as our evening meal was over we sat out on the terrace sipping glasses of a red wine he was nuts about, but that gave me a headache. Only then did I dare to timidly approach going back to the States in time for Chris's May graduation. "Really, we do have the time to fly there, and be back in plenty of time to go into rehearsals for *Giselle*."

"Oh, come off it, Cathy!" he said impatiently. "It's a difficult role for you, and you'll be tired, and you'll need to rest up."

I objected. Two weeks was plenty of time . . . and a TV taping didn't take too long. "Please, darling, let's go. I'd be sick not to see my brother become a doctor, just as you'd be if your brother was reaching the goal he'd strived for year after year."

"Hell, no!" he flared, narrowing his dark eyes and shooting sparks my way. "I get so damned sick and tired of hearing Chris this, and Chris that, and if it isn't his name you drum in my ears, then it's Paul this and that! *You are not going!*"

I pleaded with him to be reasonable. "He's my only brother, his graduation day is as important to me as it is to him. You can't understand how much this means not only to him, but to me as well! You think he and I lived lives of luxury compared to yours, but you can rest assured, it was no picnic!"

"Your past is something you don't talk about to me," he snapped. "It's exactly as if you were born the day you found your precious Dr. Paul! Cathy, you are my wife now, and your place is with me. Your Paul has Carrie, and they'll be there, so your brother won't lack applause when he gets that damned M.D.!"

"You can't tell me what I can do and what I can't do! I'm your wife, not your slave!"

"I don't want to talk about this anymore," he said, standing and seizing hold of my arm. "C'mon, let's hit the sack. I'm tired." Without speaking I allowed him to tug me into the bedroom where I began to undress. But he came over to help, and in this way I was informed it was to be a night of love, or rather sex. I shoved his hands away. Scowling, he put them back on my shoulders and leaned to nibble on my neck; he fondled my breasts before he reached to unhook my bra. I slapped his hands away, screamed *no!* But he persisted in taking off my bra. Easy as a mask to take off, he threw away his anger and put on his dreamy-eyed romantic look.

There had been a time when Julian had appeared to me the epitome of everything sophisticated, worldly, elegant, but compared to the way he was now, since his father's death, he'd been only a country-bumpkin. There were times I actually detested him. This was such a time. "I *am* going, Julian. You may come with me, or you may meet me in New York after I fly back from the graduation ceremony. Or you can stay on here and sulk. Whatever—*I am going.* I want you to come with me and share in the family celebration, for you never share in anything—you hold me back, so I don't share either—*but this time you can't stop me!* It's too important!"

Quietly he listened and he smiled in a way that sent chills down my spine. Oh, how wicked he could look. "Hear this, beloved wife, when you married me, I became your ruler, and by my side you will stay until I kick you out. And I'm not yet ready to do that. You are not leaving me alone in Spain when I don't speak Spanish. Maybe you can learn from records, but I can't."

"Don't threaten me, Julian." I said coolly, though I backed off and felt a terrible pounding of panic. "Without me you don't have anyone who cares, except your mother, and since you don't care for her, who have you got left?"

Lightly he reached out to slap both my cheeks. I closed my eyes, resigned to accept anything he did, as long as I could go to Chris. I allowed him to undress me and do what he would, even though he clutched my buttocks so hard they hurt. I could, when I chose, withdraw until I was outside of myself, looking on, and what he did to me that was appalling didn't really matter—for I wasn't truthfully there—unless the pain was great—as sometimes it was.

"Don't try and sneak away," he warned, his words muffled

because he was kissing everywhere, teasing me as a cat who plays with a mouse when it's not hungry. "Swear on your word of honor that you will stay and miss your dearly beloved brother's graduation—stay with the husband who needs you, who adores you, who can't live without you."

He was mocking me, though his need for me was that of a child needing his mother. That was what I had become—his mother, in everything but sex. I had to choose his suits, his socks and shirts, his costumes, his practice outfits, though he consistently refused to let me handle the household accounts.

"I will not swear to anything so unfair. Chris has come to see you perform and you have gloried in showing off to him. Now let him have his turn. He's worked hard for it." I pulled free from him then, and strolled to pick up a black lace nightgown he liked me to wear. I hated black nightgowns and underwear; they reminded me of whores and call girls—and my own mother who'd had a fancy for black lingerie. "Get up off your knees, Julian. You look ludicrous. You can't do anything to me if I choose to go. A bruise would show, and besides, you've grown so accustomed to my weight and balance you can't even lift another dancer properly."

He came at me angrily. "You're mad because we haven't made it to the top, aren't you? You're blaming me because our booking was canceled. And now Madame Z. has given us a leave so I can sober up and come back refreshed, made wholesome by playing games with my wife. Cathy, I don't know how to entertain myself except by dancing; I'm not interested in books or museums like you are, and there are ways of hurting and humiliating you that won't leave any bruises—except on your ego—and you should know that by now."

Foolishly I smiled, when I should have known better than to challenge him when he was feeling less than confident. "What's the matter, Jule? Didn't your sex break satisfy your lust for perversion? Why don't you go out and find a school-girl, for I'm not going to cooperate."

I'd never before thrown in his face that I knew about his debaucheries with very young girls. It had hurt at first when I found out, but now I knew he used those girls like he used paper napkins, to casually toss away when soiled, and back he'd come to me, to say he loved me, needed me, and I was the *only* one.

Slowly he advanced, using his pantherlike stalk that told me he would be ruthless, but I held my head high, knowing I could escape by shutting off my mind, and he couldn't afford to hit me. He paused one foot away. I heard the clock on the nightstand ticking.

"Cathy, you will do as I say if you know what's good for you."

He was cruel that night, evil and spiteful; he forced upon me what should only be given in love. He dared me to bite. And this time I wouldn't have just one black eye, but two, and maybe worse. "And I'll tell everybody you are sick. Your period has you so badly cramped you can't dance—and you won't skip out on me, or make any phone calls, for I'll bind you to the bed and hide your passport." He grinned and slapped my face lightly. "Now, honey-chile, whatcha gonna do this time?"

Smiling and himself again, Julian sauntered naked to the breakfast table, flung himself down, sprawled out his long, beautifully shaped legs and asked casually, "What's for breakfast?" He held out his arms so I could come and kiss his lips, which I did. I smiled, brushed the lock of dangling hair from his forehead, poured his coffee, and then said, "Good morning, darling. Same old breakfast for you. Fried eggs and fried ham. I'm having a cheese omelet."

"I'm sorry, Cathy," he murmured. "Why do you try to bring out the worst in me? I only use those girls to spare you."

"If they don't mind, then I don't mind . . . but don't ever force me to do what I did last night. I'm very good at hating,

Julian. Just as good as you are at forcing. And at harboring revenge I'm an expert!"

I slid onto his plate two fried eggs and two slices of ham. No toast and no butter. Both of us ate in silence. He sat across the checkered red and white tablecloth, closely shaven, clean and smelling of soap and shaving lotion. In his own dark and light exotic way he was the most beautiful man I'd ever seen.

"Cathy . . . you haven't said you love me today."

"I love you, Julian."

An hour after breakfast I was madly searching every room to find my passport, while Julian slept on the bed, where I'd dragged him from the kitchen after he fell asleep from all the sedatives I'd dumped in his coffee.

He wasn't nearly as good at hiding as I was at finding. Under the bed, and under the blue rug, I found my passport. Quickly I threw clothes into my suitcases. When I was packed, dressed and ready to go, I leaned above him and kissed him good-bye. He was breathing deep and regularly, and smiling slightly; perhaps the drugs were giving him pleasant dreams. Though I'd drugged him, I hesitated, wondering if I'd done the right thing. Shrugging off my indecision, I headed toward the garage. Yes, I did what I had to do. If he were awake now, he'd be burred to my side all through the day, with my passport in his pocket. I'd left a note telling him where I was going.

Paul and Carrie met me at the airport in North Carolina. I hadn't seen Paul in three years. Down the ramp I went, my eyes locked with his. His face tilted up to mine, the sun in his eyes so he had to squint. "I'm glad you could come," he said, "though I'm sorry Julian couldn't make it."

"He's sorry too," I said, looking up into his face. He was the type of man who improved with age. The mustache I'd persuaded him to grow was still there, and when he smiled dimples showed in both his cheeks.

"Are you searching to find gray hair?" he teased when I stared too long and perhaps with too much admiration. "If you see any let me know and I'll have my barber touch them up. I'm not ready for gray hair yet. I like your new hair style; it makes you even more beautiful. But you're much too thin. What you need is lots of Henny's home cooking. She's here, you know, in a motel's small kitchen, whipping up homemade rolls your brother so loves. It's her gift to him for becoming another doctor-son."

"Did Chris get my telegram? He does know I'm coming?"

"Oh, indeed yes! He was fretting through every moment, afraid Julian would refuse to let you leave him, and knowing Julian wouldn't come. Honestly, Cathy, if you hadn't shown up, I don't think Chris *would* accept his degree."

To sit beside Paul, with Henny on his far side and Carrie next to me, and watch my Christopher stride down the aisle and up the steps to accept his diploma, and then stand behind the podium and make the valedictory speech, put tears in my eyes and a swelling happiness in my heart. He did it so beautifully I cried. Paul, Henny and Carrie also had tears to shed. Even my success on stage couldn't compare to the pride I felt now. And Julian, he should be here too, making himself a part of my family and not stubbornly resisting all the time.

I thought of our mother too, who should be here to witness this. I knew she was in London, for I was still following her movements about the world. Waiting, always waiting to see her again. What would I do when I did? Would I chicken out and let her get away again? I knew one thing, she'd learn that her eldest son was now a doctor—for I'd be sure she knew— just as I kept her informed about what Julian and I were doing.

Of course I knew by now why my mother kept always on the move—she was afraid, so afraid I'd catch up with her! She'd been in Spain when Julian and I arrived. The news had been published in several papers, and not long after that I picked up a Spanish paper to see the lovely face of Mrs.

Bartholomew Winslow, flying to London as fast as she could.

Tearing my thoughts from her, I glanced around at the thousands of relatives crowded into the huge auditorium. When I looked back at the stage I saw Chris up there, ready to step behind the podium. I don't know how he managed to find me, but somehow he did. Our gazes met and locked, and across all the heads of those who sat between us, we met in silent communication and shared an overwhelming jubilation! We'd done it! Both of us! Reached our goals; become what we'd set out to be when we were children. It wouldn't have mattered at all about those years and months we'd lost— if Cory hadn't died, if our mother hadn't betrayed us, if Carrie had gained the height that should have been hers, and would have been if Momma had found another solution. Maybe I wasn't a prima ballerina yet—but I would be one day, and Chris would be the finest doctor alive.

Watching Chris, I believed we shared the same thoughts. I saw him swinging a bat when he was ten to smash a ball over the fence, and then he'd run like mad to touch all bases in the quickest possible time, when he could have walked and made his home run. But that wasn't his way, to make it look too easy. I saw him racing on his bike yards ahead of me, then slowing down deliberately so I could catch up and we'd both reach home at the same time. I saw him in the locked room, in his bed three feet from mine, smiling encouragingly. I saw him again in the attic shadows, almost hidden in the immense space, looking so lost and bewildered as he turned away from the mother he loved . . . to me. Vicariously we'd shared so many romances while lying on a dirty old mattress in the attic while the rain pelted down and separated us from all humanity. Was that what did it? Was that why he couldn't see any girl but me? How sad for him, for me.

The university planned a huge luncheon celebration, and at our table Carrie babbled away, but Chris and I could only stare at each other, each of us trying to find the right words to say.

"Dr. Paul has moved into a new office building, Cathy," gushed Carrie breathlessly. "I'd hate him being so far away, but I am going to be his secretary! I am going to have a brand new electric typewriter colored red! Dr. Paul thought a custom-painted typewriter of purple might look a little garish, but I didn't think it would, so I settled for second best. And nobody ever is gonna have a better secretary than I'll be! I'll answer his phone, make his appointments, keep his filing system, do his bookkeeping, and every day he and I will eat lunch together!" She beamed on Paul a bright smile. It seemed he'd given her the security to regain the exuberant self-confidence that she'd lost. But I was to find out later, sadly, this was Carrie's false facade, one for Paul, Chris and me to see, and when she was alone, it was far different.

Then Chris frowned and asked why Julian hadn't come. "He wanted to come, Chris, really he did," I lied. "But he has obligations that keep him so busy he couldn't spare the time. He asked me to give you his congratulations. We do have very tight schedules. Actually, I can only stay two days. We're going to do a TV production of *Giselle* next month."

Later we celebrated again in a fine hotel restaurant. This was our chance to give Chris the gifts each of us had for him. It had been our childish habit to always shake a present before it was opened, but the big box Paul gave Chris was too heavy to shake. "Books!" said Chris rightly. Six huge, fat medical reference volumes to represent an entire set that must have cost Paul a fortune. "I couldn't carry more than six," he explained. "The remainder of the set will be waiting for you at home." I stared at him, realizing his home was the only real home we had.

Deliberately Chris saved my gift for last, anticipating this would be the best and in that way, just as we used to, we could stretch out the enjoyment. It was too large and much too heavy to shake and besides I cautioned him it was fragile, but he laughed, for we used to always try and trick the other, "No, it's more books—nothing else could be as heavy." He gave me a funny, wistful smile that made him seem a boy again.

"I give you one guess, my Christopher Doll, and one hint. Inside that box is the one thing you said you wanted more than anything else—and our father said he would give it to you the day you got your black doctor's bag." Why had I used that kind of soft voice, to make Paul turn his eyes and narrow them, and see the blood that rose to stain my brother's cheeks? *Were we never to forget, and change? Were we forever going to feel too much?* Chris fiddled with the ribbons, careful not to tear the fancy paper. When he stripped off the paper, tears of remembrance welled in his eyes. His hands trembled as he carefully lifted from the cushioned box a French mahogany case with a gleaming brass lock, key and carrying handle. He gave me a tortured look even as his lips quivered, seeming incredulous that after all these years I'd remembered.

"Oh, damn it, Cathy," he said all choked up with emotion, "I never really hoped to own one of these. You shouldn't have spent so much . . . it must have cost a fortune . . . and you shouldn't have!"

"But I wanted to, and it's not an original, Chris, only a replica of a John Cuff Side Pillar Microscope. But the man in the shop said it was an exact duplicate of the original and a collector's item nevertheless. And it works too." He shook his head as he handled the solid brass and ivory accessory instruments, and the optical lens, the tweezers, and the leather-bound book titled *Antique Microscopes, 1675-1840*.

I said faintly, "In case you decide to play around in your spare time, you can do your own research on germs and viruses."

"Some toy you give," he said, gritty-voiced, and now the two tears in the corners of his eyes began to slide down his cheeks. "You remembered the day Daddy said he would give me this when I became a doctor."

"How could I forget? That little catalog was the one thing you took of yours that wasn't clothes, when we went to Foxworth Hall. And every time he swatted a fly, or killed a spider, Paul, Chris would long to have a John Cuff microscope. And once he said he wanted to be the Mouseman of the Attic, and discover for himself why mice die so young."

"Do mice die young?" asked Paul seriously. "How did you know they were young? Did you capture baby ones, and mark them in some way?"

Chris and I met eyes. Yeah, we'd lived in another world back when we were young and imprisoned, so that we could look at the mice who came to steal and nibble on our food, especially the one named Mickey.

Now I had to go back to New York and face Julian's wrath. But first I had to have a little time alone with my brother. Paul took Henny and Carrie to a movie while Chris and I strolled the campus of his university. "And you see that window up there on the second floor, the fifth from the end there—that was my room I shared with Hank. We had a study group of eight guys, and all through college and med school we stuck together, and studied together, and when we dated, we dated together."

"Oh," I sighed. "Did you date a lot?"

"Only on the weekends. The study schedule was too heavy for socializing during the week. None of it was easy, Cathy. There's so much to know, physics, biology, anatomy, chemistry, and I could go on and on."

"You're not telling me what I want to hear. Who did you date? Was there, or is there, someone special?"

He caught my hand and drew me closer to his side. "Well, should I begin to list them one by one, and by name? If I did it would take several hours. If there had been someone special, all I would do is name one—and I can't do that. I liked them all . . . but I didn't like any well enough to love, if that's what you want to know."

Yes, that was exactly what I wanted to know. "I'm sure

you didn't live a celibate life, even though you didn't fall in love . . . ?"

"That's none of your business," he said lightly.

"I think it is. It would give me peace to know you had a girl you loved."

"I do have a girl I love," he answered. "I've known her all my life. When I go to sleep at night, I dream of her, dancing overhead, calling my name, kissing my cheek, screaming when she has nightmares, and I wake up to take the tar from her hair. There are times when I wake up to ache all over, as she aches all over, and I dream I kiss the marks the whip made . . . and I dream of a certain night when she and I went out on the cold slate roof and stared up at the sky, and she said the moon was the eye of God looking down and condemning us for what we were. So there, Cathy, is the girl who haunts me and rules me, and fills me with frustrations, and darkens all the hours I spend with other girls who just can't live up to the standards she set. And I hope to God you're satisfied."

I turned to move as in a dream, and in that dream I put my arms about him and stared up into his face, his beautiful face that haunted me too. "Don't love me, Chris. Forget about me. Do as I do, take whomever knocks first on your door, and let her in."

He smiled ironically and put me quickly from him. "I did exactly what you did, Catherine Doll, the first who knocked on my door *was* let in—and now I can't drive her out. But that's my problem—not yours."

"I don't deserve to be there. I'm not an angel, not a saint . . . you should know that."

"Angel, saint, Devil's spawn, good or evil, you've got me pinned to the wall and labeled as yours until the day I die. And if you die first, then it won't be long before I follow."

Gathering Shadows

Both Chris and Paul, to say nothing of Carrie, persuaded me to go back to Clairmont and spend a few days with my family. When I was there, surrounded by all the cozy comforts, the charm of the house and the gardens had their chance to beguile me again. I told myself this was the way it would have been if I'd married Paul. No problems. A sweet, easy life. Then, when I let myself wonder how Julian was faring, I thought of all the mean and spiteful ways he had of annoying me by opening my mail from Paul or Chris, as if he were looking for incriminating evidence. No doubt when he flew back from Spain, he'd deliberately let my house plants die as a way to punish me.

There must be something weird about me, I was thinking as I stood on the balcony overlooking Paul's magnificent gardens. I wasn't that beautiful, or that unforgettable, or that indispensable, to any man. I stayed there and let Chris come up behind me and put his arm about my shoulders. I leaned my head against him and sighed, staring up at the moon. The same old moon that had known our shame before, still there to witness more. I didn't do anything; I swear I didn't, just let his arm stay about me. Maybe I moved a little to contour myself against him when he had me in a tight embrace. "Cathy, Cathy," he groaned, pressing his lips down into my hair, "sometimes life just doesn't have any meaning without you. I'd throw away my M.D. and set out for the South Pacific if you'd go with me. . . ."

"And leave Carrie?"

"We could take her with us." I thought he was playing a game of wishing, like we had when children. "I'd buy a sail boat and take out tourists, and if they cut themselves I'd have all the training to bandage their cuts." He kissed me then with the fervor of a man gone wild from denial. I didn't want to respond, yet I did, making him gasp as he tried to coax me into his room.

"Stop!" I cried. "I don't want you except as a brother! Leave me alone! Go find someone else!"

Dazed and hurt-looking, he backed off. "What kind of woman are you anyway, Cathy? You returned my kisses—you responded in every way you could—and now you draw away and pull the virtuous act!"

"Hate me then!"

"Cathy, I could never hate you." He smiled at me bitterly. "There are times when I want to hate you, times when I think you are just the same as our mother, but I don't ever stop loving once I start!" He entered his room and slammed the door, leaving me speechless, staring after him.

No! I wasn't like Momma, I wasn't! I'd responded only because I was still seeking my lost identity. Julian stole my reflection and made it his. Julian wanted to steal my strength and call it his own; he wanted me to make all the decisions, so he couldn't be blamed when a mistake was made. I was still trying to prove my worth, so in the end I could disprove the grandmother's condemnation. *See, Grandmother, I am not bad or evil. Or else everyone wouldn't love me so much.* I was still that selfish, ravenous, demanding attic mouse who had to have it proven time and time again that I was worthy enough to live in the sunlight.

I was thinking about this one day when I was on the back veranda, and Carrie was planting pansies she'd grown from seed, and beside her were little pots with tiny petunia settings. Chris came out from the house and tossed me the evening newspaper. "There's an article in there that might be of some interest to you," he said in an off-hand way. "I thought about not showing it to you, but then I decided I should."

The husband and wife ballet team of Julian Marquet and Catherine Dahl, our own local celebrities, seems to have parted company. For the first time Julian Marquet will partner a ballerina other than his wife in a major television production of *Giselle*. It has been rumored about that Miss Dahl is ill, and also rumored that the ballet team are about to split.

There was more to read, including the fact that Yolanda Lange was to replace me! This was our big chance—another of many, to make stars of ourselves, and he was putting Yolanda in my part! Damn him! Why didn't he grow up? Every chance we had he blew it. He couldn't lift Yolanda easily, not with his bad back.

Chris threw me a strange look before he asked, "What are you going to do about it?" I yelled back, "Nothing!" For a second or two he didn't say anything.

"Cathy, he didn't want you to come to my graduation, did he? And that's why he's put Yolanda in your role. I warned you not to let him be your manager. Madame Zolta would have treated you more fairly."

I got up to pace the porch. Our original contract with Madame Z. had expired two years ago, and all we owed her now was twelve performances a year. The rest of the time Julian and I were freelance, and could dance with whatever company we chose.

Let Julian have Yolanda. Let him make a fool of himself—I

hoped to God he dropped her! Let him have all his teeny-bopper playmates for sex games . . . I didn't care. Then I was running in the house and up to my bedroom where I flung myself face down and bawled.

Everything was made worse by the fact that I had made a secret trip to the gynecologist the day before. Two missed periods didn't really mean anything for a woman like me, who was so irregular. I might not be pregnant; it might be just another false alarm . . . and if it wasn't, I prayed I'd have the strength to go through with an abortion! I didn't need a baby in my life. I knew once I had a child, he or she would become the center of my world, and *luv* would again spoil a ballerina who could have been the best.

Ballet music was in my head when I drove Chris's car to visit Madame Marisha one hot spring day when all the world seemed sleepy and lazy except for those idiot children being instructed by a shrill little bat wearing black, as always. I sat in the shadows near the far wall of a huge auditorium and watched the large class of boys and girls dance. It was scary to think of how soon those girls would grow up to replace the stars of the present. Then I too would become another Madame Marisha and the years would flow like seconds, until I was Madame Zolta, and all my beauty would be preserved only in old, faded photographs.

"Catherine!" called Madame M. joyfully when she spied me. She came striding swiftly, gracefully my way. "Why do you sit in shadows?" she asked. "How nice to see your lovely face again. And don't think I don't know why you look so sad! You're one big fool to leave Julian! He's a big baby; you know he can't be left alone or he does things to hurt himself, and when he hurts himself, he hurts you too! Why did you let him get control of management? Why did you let him burn up your money as fast as it hits your pockets? I tell you this, in your place, I would never, never have let him put another in my role of *Giselle!*"

God, what a blabbermouth he was!

"Don't worry about me, Madame," I said coolly, "if my husband doesn't want me for his partner anymore, I'm sure there will be others who will."

She scowled, advanced. She put those bony hands on me and shook me as if to wake me up. Up close, I could see she'd aged terribly since Georges had died. Her ebony hair was almost white now, and streaked with charcoal. She snarled then, baring teeth whiter than they used to be and far more perfect. "You gonna let my son make a fool of you? You let him put another dancer in your place? I gave you credit for having more backbone! Now you hightail it back to New York and push that Yolanda out of his life! Marriage is sacred, and wedding vows are meant to be kept!"

Then she softened and said, "Come now, Catherine," and led me into her small cluttered office. "Now you tell me about this foolishness going on between you and your husband!"

"It is really none of your business!"

She swung another straight chair to where she could straddle it. Leaning forward upon her arms, she stabbed me with her hard penetrating glare. "Anything, and everything concerning my son is my business!" she snapped. "Now you just sit there and keep quiet, and let me tell you what you don't know about your husband." Her voice turned a little kinder. "I was older than Georges when we were married, and even so I dared putting off having a child until I believed the best of my career was behind me, and then I became pregnant. Georges never wanted a child to hold him down, and back, and so, from the beginning Julian had two strikes against him.

"I tell myself we didn't force the dance upon our son, but we did keep him with us, so the ballet became part of his world, the most important part." She sighed heavily and wiped a bony hand over her troubled brow. "We were strict with him, I admit that. We did everything we could to make him what was perfect in our eyes, but the more we tried, the more determined he became to be everything we didn't want him to be. We tried to teach him perfect diction, so he ended up mocking us with all kinds of vulgar street language—gutter talk, Georges called it. You know," she went on with a wistful expression, "only after my husband was dead and buried did I realize that he never spoke to our son unless it was an order not to do something, or an order to improve his dancing technique. I never realized that Georges could have been jealous of his own son, seeing that he was a better dancer and would achieve more fame. It wasn't easy for me to become only a ballet mistress, and for Georges to be only an instructor. Many a night we lay on our bed and held to each other, craving the applause, the adulation. . . . It was a hunger that would not be satisfied until we heard the applause for our son."

Again she paused, and birdlike craned her neck to peer at me and see if I was paying full attention. Oh, yes, she had my attention. She was telling me so much I needed to know.

"Julian tried to hurt Georges and Georges got hurt because Julian made light of his father's reputation. One day he called him only a second-class performer. Georges didn't speak to his own son for a whole month! They never got back together after that. Farther and farther they drifted apart . . . until one fine Christmas Day when another prodigy drifted into our lives, and offered herself. *You!* Julian had flown back to visit us, only because I had pleaded with him to try and make it up with his father . . . and Julian saw you.

"It is our responsibility to pass along our skills of technique to the younger generation, and still I felt some apprehension in taking you on, mostly because I thought you would hurt my son. I don't know why I thought that, but it seemed obvious from the very start, it was that older doctor you loved. Then I thought you had something very rare, a passion for the dance that is seldom seen. You were, in your own way, equal to what Julian was, and the two of you together were so sensational I couldn't believe my eyes. My son felt it too, the rapport between you two. You turned those big, soft, admiring blue eyes on him, so later he came and told me you were a sex kitten who would fall easily under his spell and into his arms. He and I always had a close relationship, and he confessed to me what other boys would have kept secret."

She paused, flicked her stony eyes over me and went on breathlessly, "You came, you admired him, you loved him when you were dancing with him, and when you weren't, you were indifferent. The harder you were to win, the more determined he was to have you. I thought you clever, playing a skillful woman's game when you were only a child! And now you, you . . . you go and leave him when he was in a foreign country, when he couldn't speak the language, when you should have learned he has weaknesses, many of them, and that he cannot bear to be alone!"

She jumped up like a black, scrawny alleycat and stood above me. "Without Julian to give you inspiration and enhance your talent with his own, where would you be? Without him would you be in New York, dancing with what is fast becoming one of the leading ballet companies? No! You'd be here, raising babies for that doctor. God knows why you said yes to Julian, and how you can keep from loving him. For he tells me you don't, and never have! So you drug him. You leave him. You take off to see your brother become a doctor, when you know damn well your place is at your husband's side, making him happy and taking care of his wants!

"Yes! Yes!" she shrilled, "he called me long distance and told me everything! Now he thinks he hates you! Now he wants to cut you off. And when he does, he won't have a heart left to keep him alive! For he gave you his heart years and years ago!"

Slowly I rose to my feet; my legs felt weak and trembly. I brushed a hand over my aching forehead, and held back tired tears. All of a sudden it hit me hard, I did love Julian! Now I saw how very much we were alike, him with his hate for his father who had denied him as a son. And me with my hatred for

my mother, making me do crazy things, like sending off hateful letters and Christmas cards to sadden her life and never,
never let her find peace. Julian in competition with his father,
never knowing he'd won, and was better . . . and me in competition with my mother—but I had yet to prove myself better.
"Madame, I am going to tell you something Julian might not
know, and I didn't really know until today; I do love your son.
Perhaps I always loved him, and just couldn't accept it."

She shook her head, then fired her words like bullets. "If
you love him, why did you leave him? Answer me that! You
left him because you found out he has a liking for young girls?
Fool! All men have yearnings for young girls—but still they
go on loving their wives! If you let his desire for young flesh
drive you away, you are crazy! Slap his face; kick his behind—
tell him to leave those girls alone or you will divorce him! Say
all of that, and he will be what you want. But when you say
nothing, and act like you don't care, you tell him plainly you
don't love him, or want him, or need him!"

"I'm not his mother, or a priest, or God," I said wearily,
sick of all the passion she used. Backing toward the door, I
tried to leave. "I don't know if I can keep Julian from young
girls, but I'm willing to go back and try. I promise to do better.
I'll be more understanding, and I'll let him know I love him so
much, I can't abide the thought of him making love to anyone
but me."

She came to take me in her arms. She soothed, "Poor baby,
if I have been hard on you, it was for your own good. You have
to keep my son from destroying himself. When you save him,
you save yourself, for I lied when I said you would be nothing without Julian. *He* is the one who would be nothing without you! He has a death wish, always I've known it. He thinks
he's not good enough to live on because his father could never
convince him he was, and that was my fault too, as well as
Georges's. Julian waited for years and years for his father to
see him as a son, worthy of being loved for himself. He waited

equally as long for Georges to say yes, you will be even a better dancer than I was, and I'm proud of what and who you are.
But Georges kept his silence. But you go back and tell Julian
Georges did love him. To me he said it many times. Tell him
too that his father was proud of him. Tell him, Catherine. Go
back and convince him of how much you need and love him.
Tell him how sorry you are to have left him alone. Go quickly
before he does something terrible to himself!"

It was time to say good-bye to Carrie, Paul and Henny
again. Only this time I didn't have to bid adieu to Chris. He
put his foot down. "No! I'm coming with you! I'm not letting
you go back to a crazy man. When you've made your peace with
him, and I know everything is all right—only then will I leave."
Carrie cried, as she always did, and Paul stood back and
let only his eyes speak and say yes, I could find a place in his
heart again.
I looked down as the plane began to lift, and saw Paul
holding Carrie's small hand, as she tilted her face to stare up
at us and waved, and waved until we could see her no more.
I squirmed into a comfortable position and put my head on
Chris's shoulder, and told him to wake me when we reached
New York. "A fine traveling companion you make," he grumbled, but soon his cheek was on my hair as he dozed off too.
"Chris," I said sleepily, "remember that book about Raymond
and Lily who were always seeking the magical place where
purple grass grew that would fulfill all their wishes? Wouldn't
it be wonderful to look down and see purple grass?"
"Yeah," he said as sleepily as I. "I keep looking for it too."

The plane set down at La Guardia around three. A hot,
sultry day. The sun played coy, darting in and out of gathering
storm clouds. We were both tired. "At this hour Julian will be
in the theater rehearsing. They'll use the rehearsals as a pro-
motion film. There have to be a lot of rehearsals; we've never

danced in this theater before and it's important to get the feel
of the space you have to move in."

Chris was lugging along my two heavy suitcases, while I
carried his much lighter bag. I laughed and smiled his way,
glad he was with me, though Julian would be furious. "Now
you stay in the background . . . and don't let him even see you
if everything goes all right. Really, Chris, I'm sure he'll be
glad to see me. He's not dangerous."

"Sure," he said glumly.

We sauntered on into the darkened theater. The stage up
ahead was very brightly lit. The TV cameras were in position,
ready to shoot the warm-ups. The director, producer and a
few others were lined up in the front-row seats.

The heat of the day was chased by the chill of the huge
space. Chris opened up one of my bags and spread a sweater
about my shoulders after we both sat down near the aisle,
midway back in the center section. Automatically I lifted both
my legs to stretch them on top of the seat just ahead. Though
I shivered, the *corps de ballet* were sweating from the hot klieg
lights. The eye was down and a few flats were up. I looked for
Julian but didn't see him.

Just to think of Julian was to bring him out of the wings,
onto the stage in a series of whirling *jetés*. Oh, he looked terrific in that snug, white leotard with bright green leg warmers.

"Wow!" whispered Chris in my ear. "Sometimes I forget
how sensational he is on stage. No wonder every ballet critic
thinks he will be the star of this decade when he learns some
discipline. Let it be soon . . . and I mean you too, Cathy." I
smiled, for I too needed discipline. "Yes," I said, "I too, of
course."

No sooner had Julian finished his solo performance than
Yolanda Lange pirouetted out from the wings, wearing red. She
was more beautiful than ever! She danced extraordinarily well
for a girl so tall. That was, she danced well until Julian came
to partner her, and then everything went wrong. He reached

for her waist and got her buttocks, then he had to quickly shift his hold, so she slipped and nearly fell and again he adjusted to save her. A male dancer who let a ballerina fall would soon never have a partner to lift. They tried again the same jump, lift, and fall back, and this time it went almost as awkwardly, making Yolanda seem ungainly, and Julian unskilled.

Even I, sitting halfway down the row of seats, could hear her loud curse. "Damn you!" she screeched. "You make me look gauche—if you let me fall, *I'll see you never dance again!*"

"Cut!" called the director, getting to his feet and looking impatiently from one to the other.

The *corps de ballet* milled about, grumbling, throwing angry looks at the pair center stage that was wasting so much time. Obviously, from the sweaty, hot looks of all of them, this had been going on for some time, and badly. "Marquet!" called the director, well known for having little patience for those who required two, or even more takes. "What the hell is wrong with your timing? I thought you said you knew this ballet. I can't think of one thing you've done right in the past three days."

"Me?" Julian railed back. "It's not *me* . . . it's *her*—she jumps too soon!"

"Okay," the director said sarcastically, "it's always *her* fault and never yours." He tried to control his impatience, knowing Julian would walk out in a second if criticized too much. "When is your wife going to be well enough to dance again?"

Yolanda screamed out, "Hey, wait a minute! I came all the way from Los Angeles and now you're sounding as if you're going to replace me with Catherine! I won't have it! I'm written into that contract now! I'll sue!"

"Miss Lange," said the director smoothly, "you are the *cover* only—but while you are, let's attempt it again. Marquet, listen for your cue—Lange, make ready—and pray to God this time it will be fit to show an audience who might expect better from professionals."

I smiled to hear she was only the cover; I had thought I was really written out.

I perversely enjoyed watching Julian make a fool out of himself and Yolanda as well. Yet, when the dancers on stage groaned, I groaned along with them, feeling their exhaustion, and despite myself I began to feel pity for Julian who was diligently trying to balance Yolanda. Any second the director could call "take ten" and that's when I would make my move.

Up ahead, first row, Madame Zolta suddenly turned her wizened giraffe neck to crane my way, and those sharp little beady eyes saw me sitting tensely, watching like an eagle. "Hey, you, Catherine," she called with great enthusiasm. *Come*, she gestured, *sit by my side.*

"Excuse me a minute, Chris," I whispered. "I've got to go up there and save Julian before he ruins both our careers. I'll be all right. There's not much he can do with an audience—is there?"

Once I was seated beside Madame Zolta, she hissed, "Sooo, you not so sss-ick after all! Thank God for small favors. Your husband up there is ruining my reputation along with his and yours. I should have known better than to always let him partner you, so now he can dance with no one as well."

"Madame," I asked, "who arranged for Yolanda to be my stand-in?"

"Your husband, my luv," she whispered cruelly. "You let him get control—you were a fool to do that. He is *impossible!* He is a tempest, a devil, so unreasonable! Soon he will go mad, if he doesn't see your face—or *we* will go *mad.* Now run fast and put on dance clothes and save me from extinction!"

It was only a matter of seconds before I had on a practice outfit and, as soon as I had my hair bound up and securely fastened in place, I strapped on my *pointes.* At the dressing room barre I warmed up quickly. Doing my *pliés*, and the *rond de jambes* to pump blood into each limb. Soon enough I was ready. Not a day passed I didn't do my exercises for several hours.

In the darkened wings I hesitated. I was prepared, I thought, for most anything when Julian saw me—what would he do? While I watched him on stage, suddenly from behind I was brutally shoved aside! "You've been replaced," hissed Yolanda. "Sssooo, get out—and stay out! You had your chance and loused it up—now Julian is *mine!* You hear that—he's *mine!* I have slept in your bed, and used your makeup and worn your jewelry—I have taken your place in everything."

I wanted to ignore her and not believe anything she said. When the cue came for Giselle to go on, Yolanda tried to hold me—that's when I turned savagely upon her and pushed her so hard she fell. She blanched with pain, while I went on *pointe* and glided onto the stage, making my perfect little string of pearls. . . . Each tiny step could have been measured and proven to be of an exact distance. I was the shy, young village girl, sweetly, sincerely falling in love with Loys. Others on stage gasped to see me. Relief lit up Julian's dark eyes—for an instant. "Hi," he said coolly as I neared him, and fluttered my dark lashes to enchant him more. "Why'd you come back? Your doctors kick you out? Sick of you already?"

"You are a nasty, inconsiderate brute, Julian, to replace me with Yolanda! You know I despise her!"

His back was to the lookers as he sneered wickedly, all the while keeping time, "Yeah, I *know* you hate her; that's why I wanted her." He curled his beautiful red lips so they looked ugly. "Listen to this, dancing doll. *Nobody* runs out on me, especially my wife, and comes back and thinks she can still fit in my life. My love, my dearest heart, I don't want you now, I don't *need* you now, and you can go and play bitch to any man you want! Get the hell out of my life!"

"You don't mean that," I said, as we both performed perfectly, and no one called cut. How could they when we did everything so exquisitely right?

"You don't love me," he said bitterly. "You've never loved me. No matter what I did, or what I said, and now I don't give a damn! I gave you the best I had to give, and it wasn't enough. So, dear Cath-er-ine—*I give you this!*" And with those sudden words, he broke the routine, jumped high into the air, to come down forcefully and directly onto my feet. All his weight, brought down like a battering ram to crush my toes!

I uttered some small cry of pain, then Julian was whirling back to chuck me under the chin. "Now, *luv,* see who will dance Giselle with me. Certainly it won't be you, will it?"

"Take ten!" bellowed the director, too late to save me.

Julian gripped my shoulders and shook me like a rag doll. I stared at him rattle-eyed, expecting anything. Then suddenly he whirled away leaving me center stage, alone, on two damaged feet that hurt so badly I could have screamed. Instead, I sank to the floor and sat there staring at my rapidly swelling feet.

From out of the darkened auditorium Chris came running to my assistance. "Damn him to hell for doing this!" he cried, falling on his knees to take off my *pointe* shoes and examine my feet. Tenderly he tried to move my toes, but I cried out from the awful pain. Then he picked me up easily and held me tight against him. "You'll be all right, Cathy. I'll see that your toes heal properly. I fear a few are broken on each foot. You'll need an orthopedist."

"Take Catherine to our orthopedist," ordered Madame Zolta who teetered forward and stared at my darkening, enlarging feet. She peered more closely at Chris, having seen him only a few times before. "You're Catherine's brother who caused all this trouble?" she asked. "Take her quick to the doctor. We have insurance. But that fool husband, this is it. I *fire* him!"

The Thirteenth Dancer

Both of my feet were X-rayed, disclosing three broken toes on my left foot, and one broken small toe on my right. Thank God both my big toes were spared, or else I *might* never dance again! An hour later Chris was carrying me out of the doctor's office with a plaster cast drying on one foot that reached to my knee, while the small toe was only taped and left to heal without such protection. Each of the toes in the cast was nestled securely in its own little padded compartment so I couldn't move a one, and left exposed for everyone to admire the lovely shades of black, blue and purple. In my thoughts the sour lemon-drops of the doctor's last words failed to melt and sweeten the future. "You may, or you may not dance again, it all depends." On what it depended, he didn't say.

So I asked Chris. "Sure," he said confidently, "of course you'll dance again. Sometimes a doctor likes to be overly pessimistic so you can think how great he was when everything works out fine—due to his special skill." Clumsily he tried to support me while he used my key to open the door of the apartment Julian and I shared. Then he carefully lifted me up again, carried me inside and kicked the door closed behind him. He tried to make me as comfortable as possible on one of the soft couches. I had my eyes squeezed tightly together, trying to suppress the pain I felt at every move.

Chris tenderly supported both legs so he could stuff pillows under and keep them elevated to reduce the swelling. Another fat pillow was carefully eased under my back and head . . . and he never said one word . . . not one word.

Because he was so silent, I opened my eyes and studied his face that loomed above me. He tried to look professional, detached, but he failed. He showed shock each time his eyes moved from one object to another. Fearful I looked around. My eyes bulged. My mouth opened. This room! The mess! Oh, God, it was awful!

Our apartment was a wreck! Every painting Julian and I had so carefully selected was torn down from the walls, smashed on the floor. Even the two watercolors Chris had painted especially for me, portraits with me in costume. All the expensive bric-a-brac lay broken on the hearth. Lamps were on the floor, the shades slashed to ribbons and the wire frames bent. Needlepoint pillows I'd made during the long tedious flights from here to there while on tour were ripped, destroyed! Houseplants had been dumped from their pots and left with roots exposed to die. Two cloisonné vases that Paul had given as a wedding gift, gone too. Everything fine and costly, and very cherished, things he and I had planned to keep all our lives and leave to our children—all beyond restoration.

"Vandals," said Chris softly. "Just vandals." He smiled and kissed my forehead and squeezed my hand as tears came to my eyes. "Stay calm," he said, then he went to check the other three rooms, while I sank back on the pillows and sniffed back my sobs. Oh, how he must hate me to do this! Shortly Chris was back with his expression very composed, in that same eye-of-the-hurricane way I'd seen a few times on his face. "Cathy," he began, settling cautiously down on the edge of the sofa and reaching for my hand, "I don't know what to think. All your clothes and shoes have been ruined. Your jewelry is scattered all over the bedroom floor, the chains ripped apart, the rings stepped on, bracelets hammered out of shape. It looks as if somebody set out deliberately to ruin all of your things and left Julian's in perfect condition." He gave me a baffled, troubled look, and maybe the tears I tried to hold back jumped from my eyes to his. With glistening blue eyes he extended his palm to show me the setting of a once exquisite diamond engagement ring, given to me by Paul. The platinum band was now a crooked oval. The prongs had released their clasp on the clear and perfect two-carat diamond.

Sedatives had been shot into my arm so I couldn't feel the pain of my broken toes. I felt fuzzy and disoriented, and rather detached. Someone inside me was screaming, screaming—hatred was near again—the wind was blowing, and when I closed my eyes, I saw the blue-misted mountains all around me, shutting out the sun—like upstairs, like in the attic.

"Julian," I said weakly, "he must have done this. He must have come back and vented his rage on all my belongings. See the things left whole—they are things he chose for himself."

"Damn him to hell!" cried Chris. "How many times has he vented his rage on you? How many black eyes—I've seen one—but how many others?"

"Please don't," I said sleepily, hazily. "He never hit me that he didn't cry afterward, and he'd say he was sorry." *Yes, so sorry, my sweetheart, my only love . . . I don't know what makes me act as I do when I love you so much!*

"Cathy," began Chris tentatively, tucking the platinum band in his pocket, "are you all right? You look close to fainting. I'll go in and straighten up the bed, so you can rest in that. Soon you'll fall asleep and forget all of this, and when you wake up, I'm taking you away. Don't cry for the clothes and things *he* gave you, for I'll give you better and more. As for this ring Paul gave you, I'll search around the bedroom until I find the diamond."

He looked, but he didn't find the diamond, and when I drifted into sleep, he must have carried me to the bed he'd made up with clean sheets. I was under a sheet and a thin blanket when I opened my eyes, and he was sitting on the edge of the bed, watching my face. I glanced toward the windows and saw it was getting dark. Any moment Julian would come home, and find Chris with me—and there'd be hell to pay!

"Chris . . . did you undress me and put on this gown?" I asked dully, seeing the sleeve of a blue gown that was one of my favorites.

"Yes. I thought you'd be more comfortable than wearing that pantsuit with the leg split up the seam. And I'm a doctor, remember? I'm used to seeing all there is—and I took care not to look."

The darkness of late twilight was in the room, turning all the shadows soft and purplish. Fuzzily I saw him as he used to be, when the attic atmosphere was like this, purplish, dim, scary, and we were alone and facing some unknown horror ahead. Always he gave me comfort when nothing else could. Always he was there when I needed him to do and say the right thing.

"Remember the day Momma received the letter from the grandmother saying we could stay in her home? We thought wonderful things were ahead of us then; we later thought all joy lay in the past. Never, never in the present."

"Yes," he said softly, "I remember. We believed we'd be rich as King Midas, and everything we touched would turn to gold. Only we'd have more self-control, enough to keep those we loved still made of flesh and blood. We were young and silly then, and so trusting."

"Silly? I don't think we were silly, only normal. You've achieved your goal of being a doctor. But I'm still not a prima ballerina." I said this last bitterly.

"Cathy, don't belittle yourself. You will be a prima ballerina yet!" he said fervently. "You would have been a long time
ago, if Julian could control his fits of temper that makes every
company manager afraid to sign the pair of you on. You get
stuck in a minor company just because you won't leave him."

I sighed, wishing he hadn't said that. It was true enough
Julian's fiery temper tantrums had scared off more than one
offer that would have placed us in a more prestigious company. "You've got to leave, Chris. I don't want him to come
home and find you here. He doesn't want you near me. And
I can't leave him. In his own way he loves me and needs me.
Without me to keep him steady he would be ten times more
violent, and I do love him after all. If he struck out sometimes, he was just trying to make me see that. Now I do see."

"*See?*" he cried. "You're not seeing! You're letting pity for
him rob you of good common sense! Look around you, Cathy!
Only a crazy man could have done this. I'm not leaving you
alone to face a madman! I'm staying to protect you. Tell me
what you could do if he decides to make you pay again for
leaving him alone in Spain? Could you get up and run? No!
I'm not leaving you here, unprotected, when he might come
home drunk, or on drugs—"

"He doesn't use drugs!" I defended, protective of the good
that was in Julian, and for some reason, wanting to forget all
that wasn't.

"He jumped on your toes, when you need those toes to
dance on—so don't tell me you will have a sane man to deal
with. When you were putting on your clothes, I overheard
someone say that since Julian started running around with
Yolanda he's been an entirely different man. Everyone else
suspects he's on drugs—that's why I said it," and here he
paused, "and besides, I know for a fact that Yolanda takes
anything she can get."

I was sleepy, in pain and worried about Julian who should
be home by now, and there was an *incipient* baby in me whose

fate I had to decide. "Chris, stay then. But when he comes home, let me do the talking—just fade into the background— promise?"

He nodded, while I began to drift off again, feeling as if nothing was real but the bed underneath me and the sleep I needed. Lazily, without thought, I tried to turn on my side, and my legs slipped from the heaped pillows, making me cry out. "Cathy . . . don't move," said Chris, quickly adjusting my legs back on the pillows. "Let me lie beside you, and hold you until he comes. I promise not to sleep, and the minute he comes through that door, I'll jump up and fade away." He smiled to charm me into cheer again, so I too nodded and welcomed the warm, strong arms he put around me as again I sought the sweet relief of sleep.

As in a dream I felt soft lips move on my cheek, in my hair, then lightly over my eyelids, and finally my lips. "I love you so much, oh, God, how much I love you," I heard him say, and I thought for a disoriented moment it was Julian who'd come home to say he was sorry for hurting and humiliating me . . . for this was his way, to give me pain, and then apologize, and make love with passionate abandon. So I turned a bit on my side and responded to his kisses, and put my arms around him, and twined my fingers into his strong dark hair. That's when I knew. The hair I felt wasn't strong and crisp, but silky and fine, like my own. "Chris!" I cried out, "stop!" But he was out of control as he lavished my face, my neck, and the bosom he bared with his ardent kisses.

"Don't cry stop," he murmured, caressing and stroking me, "all my life I've had nothing but frustrations. I try to love others, but it's always you . . . you, whom I can never have! Cathy . . . leave Julian! Come away with me! We'll go to some distant place, where no one knows us, and together we can live as man and wife. We won't have any children . . . I'll see to that. We can adopt babies. You know we make good parents . . . you know we love each other and always will!

Nothing can change that! You can run from me and marry twelve other men, but your heart is in your eyes when you look at me—it's me you want—as I want you!"

He was carried away with his own persuasions and wouldn't listen to my weak words. "Cathy, just to hold you, to have you again! This time I'll know how to give you the pleasure I couldn't before—please, if you ever loved me—leave Julian before he destroys us both!"

I shook my head, trying to focus on what he was saying and what he was doing. His blond hair was beneath my chin, nuzzling at my breasts, and he didn't see my denial, but he did hear my voice. "Christopher—I'm going to have Julian's baby. I went to a gynecologist while I was in Clairmont—it's the reason I stayed longer than I originally intended. Julian and I are having a baby."

I could have slapped him from the way he moved backward, abandoning the sweet ecstasy of kissing forbidden places that had aroused me. He sat up on the side of the bed and bowed his head into his hands. Then he sobbed, "Always you manage to defeat me, Cathy! First Paul, then Julian . . . and now a baby." Then suddenly he faced me. "Come away and let me be the father to that child! Julian isn't fit! If you never let me touch you, let me live near enough so I can see you every day and hear your voice. Sometimes I want it back like it used to be . . . just you and I, and our twins."

Silence that we both knew well came and took us, and shut us away in our own secret world where sin lived and unholy thoughts dwelled, and we'd pay, pay, pay, if ever . . . but no, there wouldn't be any "if ever". . . .

"Chris, I'm going to have the baby with Julian." I said with a firm resolution that surprised me. "I want Julian's child—for I do love him, Chris—and I've failed him in so many ways. Failed him because you and Paul got in my eyes, and I didn't appreciate what I could have had in him. I should have been a better wife, and then he wouldn't have needed those girls. I'll always love you—but it's a love that can't go anywhere, so I give it up. You give it up! Say good-bye to yesterdays and a Catherine Doll who doesn't exist anymore."

"You forgive him for breaking your toes?" he asked, astonished.

"He kept begging me to say I loved him, and I never would. I kept a deceptive parasol over my head, to keep dark doubts in my mind, and I refused to see anything that was noble and fine about him but his dancing. I didn't realize that to love me, even when I denied him, was noble and fine in itself. So, let me go, Chris—even if I never dance again, I'll have his child . . . and he will go on to fame without me."

He slammed the door and left me, and I soon fell asleep to dream of Bart Winslow, my mother's second husband. We were waltzing in the grand ballroom of Foxworth Hall, and upstairs, near the balcony balustrade, two children were hidden inside the massive chest with the wire screen backing. The Christmas tree over in the corner towered up to heaven, and hundreds of people danced with us, but they were made of transparent cellophane, not of the healthy flesh, blood and muscle that was the beauty of Bart and I. Bart suddenly stopped dancing, and picked me up to carry me up the broad stairs, and down on the sumptuous swan bed he laid me. My beautiful gown of green velvet and softer green chiffon melted beneath the touch of his burning hands—and then that powerful male shaft that entered me and wound about me started shrieking, screaming, and each loud cry sounded exactly like a telephone ringing.

I bolted awake . . . why did a telephone ringing in the dead of night always have such a threatening sound? I sleepily reached for the receiver. "Hello?"

"Mrs. Julian Marquet?"

I came awake a bit more, and rubbed at my eyes. "Yes, this is she."

She named a hospital on the other side of town. "Mrs.

Marquet, would you please come as quickly as possible? If
you can, have someone else drive you. Your husband was in an
auto accident, and is even now in surgery. Bring with you his
insurance papers, identification, and any medical history you
have. . . . Mrs. Marquet . . . are you there?"

No. I wasn't there. I was back in Gladstone, Pennsylvania,
and I was twelve years old. Two state troopers were in the
driveway, with a white car parked . . . and swiftly they were
striding to interrupt a birthday party to tell us all that Daddy
was dead. Killed in an accident on Greenfield Highway.

"Chris! Chris!" I screamed, terrified he might have gone.

"I'm here. I'm coming. I knew you'd need me."

In that dim and lonely hour that comes before dawn, Chris
and I arrived at the hospital. In one of those sterile waiting
rooms we sat down to wait and find out if Julian would survive the accident and the surgery. Finally, around noon, after
hours in the recovery room, they brought him down.

They had him laid out on what they called a "fracture
bed"—a torturous looking device that strung up his right leg
which wore a cast from his toes to his hip. His left arm was broken, and in a cast, and strung up in a peculiar way too. His pale
face was lacerated and bruised. His lips, usually so full and red,
were as pale as his skin. But all of that was nothing compared
to his head! I shivered to look! His head had been shaved and
small holes drilled for metal calipers to be hooked in to pull
his head up and backward! A leather collar lined with fleece
was fastened about his neck. *A broken neck!* Plus a leg fracture,
and a compound fracture of his forearm—to say nothing of the
internal injuries that had kept him on the operating table three
hours!

I cried out, "Will he live?"

"He is on the critical list, Mrs. Marquet," they answered so
calmly. "If he has other close relatives, we suggest you contact
them."

Chris made the call to Madame Marisha, for I was deathly afraid he'd pass away any moment, and I might miss the only chance to tell him I loved him. And if that happened, I'd be cursed and haunted all through the rest of my life.

Days passed. Julian flitted in and out of consciousness. He stared at me with eyes lackluster, unfocused. He spoke but his voice came so thick, heavy and unintelligible I couldn't understand. I forgave him for all the little sins, and the big ones too, as you are apt to when death is around the corner. I rented a room in the hospital next to his where I could catch naps, but I never had a full night's rest. I had to be there when he came to, where he could see and know me, so I could plead with him to fight, to live, and, most of all, say all the words I'd so stingily kept from his ears. "Julian," I whispered, my voice hoarse from saying it so often, "please don't die!"

Our dancing friends and musicians flocked to the hospital to offer what consolation they could. His room filled with flowers from hundreds of fans. Madame Marisha flew up from South Carolina and stalked into the room wearing a dreary black dress. She gazed down on the unconscious face of her only child without any expression of grief. "Better he die now," she said flatly, "than to wake up and find himself a cripple for life."

"How dare you say that?" I flared, ready to strike her. "He's alive—and he's not doomed. His spinal cord wasn't injured! He'll walk again, and dance again too!"

Then came the pity and disbelief to shimmer her jet eyes—and then she was in tears. She who'd boasted she never cried, never showed grief, wept in my arms. "Say it again, that he'll dance—oh, don't lie, he's got to dance again!"

Five horrible days came and went before Julian could focus his eyes enough to really see. Unable to turn his head, he rolled his eyes my way. "Hi."

"Hello, dreamer. I thought you were never going to wake up," I said.

He smiled, a thin ironic smile. "No such luck, Cathy love." His eyes flicked downward to his strung-up leg. "I'd rather be dead than like this"

I got up and went to his fracture bed that was made with two wide strips of rough canvas slipped over strong rods, and a mattress was beneath this that could be lowered enough to allow a bedpan to be placed in position. It was a hard, unyielding bed to lie on, yet I stretched beside him very carefully, and curled my fingers into his tangle of uncombed hair—what he had left. My free hand stroked his chest. "Jule, you're not paralyzed. Your spinal cord was not severed, crushed, or even bruised. It's just in shock, so to speak."

He had an uninjured arm that could have reached to hold me, but it stayed straight at his side. "You're lying," he said bitterly. "I can't feel one damn thing from my waist down. Not your hand on my chest either. Now get the hell out of here! You don't love me! You wait until you think I'm ready to kick off, and then you come with your sweet words! I don't want or need your pity—*so get the hell out, and stay out!*"

I left his bed and reached for my purse. Crying, even as he cried and stared at the ceiling. "Damn you for wrecking our apartment!" I stormed when I could talk. "You tore up my clothes!" I rampaged, angry now, and wanting to slap his face that was already bruised and swollen. "Damn you for breaking all our beautiful things! You knew how painstakingly we chose all those lamps, the accessories that cost a fortune. You know we wanted to leave them as heirlooms for our children. Now we've got nothing left to leave anyone!"

He grinned, satisfied. "Yeah, nothing left for nobody." He yawned, as if dismissing me, but I was unwilling to be dismissed. "Got no kids, thank God. Never gonna have any. You can get a divorce. Marry some son of a bitch and make his life miserable too."

"Julian," I said with such heavy sadness. "Have I made your life miserable?"

He blinked, as if not wanting to answer that, but I asked him again, and again, until I forced him to say, "Not altogether miserable—we had a few moments."

"Only a few?"

"Well . . . maybe more than a few. But you don't have to stay on and take care of an invalid. Get the hell out while you can. I'm no good, you know that. I've been unfaithful to you time and again."

"If you are again, I'll cut your heart out!"

"Go 'way, Cathy. I'm tired." He sounded sleepy from the many sedatives they fed into him and shot into him. "Kids are not good for people like us anyway."

"People like us . . . ?"

"Yeah, people like us."

"How are we different?"

He mockingly, sleepily laughed, bitterly too. "We're not real. We don't belong to the human race."

"What are we then?"

"Dancing dolls, that's all. Dancing fools, afraid to be real people and live in the real world. That's why we prefer fantasy. Didn't you know?"

"No, I didn't know. I always thought we were real."

"It wasn't me who ruined your things, it was Yolanda. I watched, though."

I felt sick, scared he was telling the truth. Was I only a dancing doll? Couldn't I make my way in the real world, outside the theater? Wasn't I, after all, any better at coping than Momma?

"Julian . . . I do love you, honest I do. I used to think I loved someone else, because it seemed so unnatural to go from one love to another. When I was a little girl, I used to believe love came only once in a lifetime, and that was the best kind. I thought once you loved one person, you never could love another. But I was wrong."

"Get out and leave me alone. I don't want to hear what you've got to say, not now. Now I don't give a damn."

Tears coursed my face and dropped down on him. He closed his eyes and refused to see, or listen. I leaned to kiss his lips, and they stayed tight, hard, unresponding. Next he spat, *"Stop! You sicken me!"*

"I love you, Julian," I sobbed, "and I'm sorry if I realized it too late, and said it too late—but don't let it *be* too late. I'm expecting your baby, the fourteenth in a long line of dancers . . . and that baby is a lot to live for, even if you don't love *me* anymore. Don't close your eyes and pretend not to hear, because you are going to be a father, whether or not you want to be." He rolled his dark, shining eyes my way, and I saw why they shone, for they were full of tears. Tears of self-pity, or tears of frustration, I didn't know. But he spoke more kindly, and there was a tone of love in his voice. "I advise you to get rid of it, Cathy. Fourteen is no luckier a number than thirteen."

In the room next door, Chris held me in his arms all through the night.

I woke up early in the morning. Yolanda had been thrown from the car in that accident, and today she would be buried. Cautiously I eased from the fold of Chris's arms, and I arranged his nodding head more comfortably before I stole away to take a peek into Julian's room. He had a night nurse on duty, and she was sound asleep beside his bed. I stood in the doorway and watched him in the dim, greenish light from the lamp covered by a green towel. He was asleep, deeply asleep. The intravenous tube that led to his arm ran under the sheet and into his vein. For some reason I fixed my eyes upon that bottle with the pale yellow liquid that seemed more water than anything else, so quickly it was being depleted. I ran back to shake Chris awake. "Chris," I said, as he tried to pull himself together, "isn't that IV supposed to just trickle into his arm? It's running out very quickly—too quickly, I think."

Hardly were the words out of my mouth when Chris was up and running toward Julian's room. He snapped on the ceiling light as he entered, then wakened the sleeping nurse. "Damn you for falling asleep! You were in here to watch him!" By the time he had that said, he'd pulled back the covers and there was Julian's casted arm with the opening for the needle—and the needle was still inserted, and taped in position—but the tube had been cut! "Oh, God," sighed Chris, "an air bubble must have reached his heart."

I stared at the shiny scissors held so loosely in Julian's slack right hand. "He cut the tube himself," I whispered, "he cut the tube himself, and now he's dead, dead, dead. . . ."

"Where did he get the scissors?" snapped Chris, while the nurse began to tremble. They were her small embroidery scissors she used to cut her crochet thread. "They must have fallen out of my pocket," she said weakly. "I swear I don't remember losing them—or maybe he took them when I was leaning over. . . ."

"It's all right," I said dully. "If he hadn't done it this way, it would have been another. I should have known and warned you. There was no life for him if he could never dance again. No life at all."

Julian was buried next to his father. On the headstone, I made sure Madame Marisha agreed to the name I added: *Julian Marquet Rosencoff, beloved husband of Catherine, and thirteenth in a long line of Russian male ballet stars.* Maybe it was ostentatious and gave away my own failure to love him enough while he lived, but I had to let him have it the way he wanted—or as I thought he wanted.

Chris, Paul, Carrie and I paused at the foot of Georges's grave too, and I bowed my head to show respect to Julian's father. Respect I should have given him too. Graveyards with their marble saints, angels, all so sweetly smiling, so pious or sober—how I hated them! They patronized we who lived; we who were made of fragile tissue and blood, who could grieve and cry while they would stand there for centuries, smiling piously down on all. And I was right back where I'd started.

* * *

"Catherine," said Paul when we were all seated in the long black limousine, "your room is still as it was, all yours. Come home and live with Carrie and me until your baby is born. Chris will be there too, doing his internship at Clairmont Hospital."

I stared over at Chris who was seated on the jumpseat, knowing he'd won a much better position in a very important hospital—and he was interning in a small, unimportant one. "Duke is so far away, Cathy," he said with his eyes avoiding mine. "It was bad enough traveling when I was in college and med school . . . so if you don't mind, let me be somewhere near so I can be here the day my nephew or niece arrives in the world."

Madame Marisha jolted so her head almost struck the ceiling of the car. "You carry Julian's child?" she cried. "Why didn't you tell me before? How wonderful!" She glowed, so the sadness dropped from her like a gloomy cloak. "Now Julian's not dead at all—for he will father a son, who will be exactly like him!"

"It may be a girl, Madame," Paul said softly, while he reached for my hand. "I know you long for a boy like your son, but I long for a little girl like Cathy and Carrie . . . but if it's a boy, I won't object."

"Object?" cried Madame. "God in his infinite wisdom and mercy will send to Catherine the exact duplicate of Julian! And he will dance, and he will reach the fame that was waiting just around the corner for the son of my Georges!"

Midnight found me all alone on the back veranda, rocking back and forth in Paul's favorite chair. My head was full of thoughts for the future. Thoughts of the past conflicted and nearly drowned me. The floorboards squeaked faintly; they were old and had known grief like mine before; they sympathized. The stars and moon were out; even a few fireflies came to bob about in the garden darkness.

The door behind me opened and closed quietly. I didn't look to see who it was, for I knew. I was good at sensing people, even in the dark. He sat in the chair next to mine, and rocked his chair in the same rhythm as I rocked.

"Cathy," he said softly. "I hate to see you sitting there with that lost and drained expression. Don't think all the good things in your life have passed you by and nothing is left. You're still very young, very beautiful, and after your baby is born, you can quickly whip yourself back into shape, and dance until you feel you're ready to retire and teach."

I didn't turn my head. Dance again? How could I dance when Julian lay in the ground? All I had was the baby. I would make the baby the center of my life. I would teach my child to dance, and he or she would reach the fame that should have been Julian's and mine. Everything that Momma failed to give us I would bestow on my child. Never would my child be neglected. When my child reached for me, I would be there. When my child cried out for Momma, he wouldn't have to make do with only an older sister. No . . . I'd be like Momma was when she had Daddy. That was what hurt the most, that she could change from someone loving and kind into what she was, a monster. Never, never would I treat my child as she'd treated hers!

"Good night, Paul," I said as I stood to go. "Don't stay out here too long. You have to get up early, and you looked tired at dinner."

"Catherine . . . ?"

"Not now. Later. I need time."

Slowly I ascended the back stairs, thinking of the baby in my womb, how I had to be careful and not eat junk food; I had to drink plenty of milk, take vitamins, and think happy thoughts . . . not vengeful ones. Every day from now on I would play ballet music. Inside me my baby would hear, and even before he or she was born a small living soul would be indoctrinated to the dance. I smiled, thinking of all the pretty tutus I could buy for my little girl. I smiled even more to think of a boy like his father with a wild tumble of dark curls. Julian Janus Marquet would be his name. Janus for looking both ways, ahead and behind.

I passed Chris who was ready to come down the stairs. He touched me. I shivered, knowing what he wanted. He didn't have to say the words. I knew them backward and forward, inside and out, upside down, or right side up; I knew them . . . as I knew him.

Though I tried diligently to think only of the innocent child growing within me, still my thoughts would steal to my mother, filling me with hate, filling me with unwanted plans for revenge. For somehow she had caused Julian's death too. If we'd never been locked away in the first place and needed to escape and run, then I would never have loved Chris, or Paul, and perhaps Julian and I would have met inevitably in New York. Then I could have loved him as he needed and wanted to be loved. I could have gone to him "virgin pure, brand new."

And would that have made any difference, I asked over and over. . . . Yes! Yes! I convinced myself it would have made *all* the difference!

Interlude for Three

As my baby grew within me, I began to find the identity I had lost, for the ballet kept the real me always in an embryo state, enclosed by my desire to dance and succeed. I was now standing firmly on the ground with the fantasy of glamorous life pushed to the background. Not that I didn't still crave the stage and the applause now and then. Oh, I had my sorrowful moments—but I had one sure way to shut them out. I turned my thoughts on my mother, on what she'd done to us. Another death on your record, Momma!

Dear Mrs. Winslow,

Are you still running away from me? Don't you know yet you can never run fast enough or far enough? Someday I will catch up, and we will meet again. Perhaps this time you will suffer as you made me suffer, and, hopefully, thrice the amount.

My husband has just died as the result of a car accident, just as your husband died many years ago. I am expecting his baby, but I won't do anything as desperate as you did. I will find a way to support him or her, even if I have triplets—or quadruplets!

I mailed that letter off, addressed to her home in Greenglenna, but the newspapers later informed me she was in Japan. Japan! Wow, she did get about.

I was turning into a woman I'd never seen before. Mirrors showed I wasn't slim and supple anymore. That terrified me. I saw my breasts become rounder, fuller, as my middle swelled outward. I hated to move less than gracefully, but my hands loved to caress the swell of my baby's small rump.

One day I realized I was luckier than most widows, I had two men needing me. Men who let me know in subtle ways they were ready to take Julian's place. And I had Carrie, Carrie who considered me a model by which she could mold her own life. Dear, sweet little Carrie who was now sixteen, and had never had a date, or a boyfriend, or been to a prom. Not that she couldn't have, if she'd forget her smallness. Chris persuaded his friends to date a younger sister who was dying on the vine for want of romance. She complained to me: "Chris doesn't have to make dates for *you!* That college student, he doesn't want me. He just comes to worm in closer to you." I laughed at how ridiculous that was. Nobody would want me in the condition I was, pregnant, a widow, and too old for a college boy.

Carrie heard this, but sulked near the window. "Since you came back, Dr. Paul doesn't take me out to the movies and to dinner like he used to. I used to pretend he wasn't my guardian, but my sweetheart, and that made me feel good inside, because all the ladies look at him, Cathy. He is handsome, even if he is old."

I sighed, for to me Paul would never be old. He was wonderfully young looking for his age of forty-eight. I took Carrie in my arms and consoled her, saying love was waiting for her just around the corner. "He'll be young too, Carrie, near your own age. And once he sees you, and really knows what you are, he won't have to be coerced, he'll be more than willing to love you." Quietly she got up and entered her own room, not convinced by anything I'd said.

Madame Marisha came often to check on my condition, and filled me with authoritative advice. "Now you keep up your practicing; play the ballet music to fill Julian's baby with love for beauty before he is born; inside you he'll know the dance is waiting for him." She glanced down at my feet that had finally healed. "How do those toes feel now?"

"Fine," I answered dully, though they ached when it rained.

Henny was there to wait on me hand and foot when Carrie wasn't around. She was growing old amazingly fast. I worried about her. She diligently tried to keep to the rigid diet both her "doctor-sons" insisted on, but she ate what she wanted to, never counting calories or cholesterol.

The long days of grief sped by more quickly because I had Julian's baby, part of him to keep with me. Soon Christmas was upon us, and I was so large I didn't feel I should show myself. Chris insisted, along with Paul, that it would be good therapy to go shopping.

I bought an antique gold locket to send to Madame Zolta, and inside I put two small photos of Julian and I, in our *Romeo and Juliet* costumes.

Shortly after Christmas her thank-you note arrived.

Dear Catherine, my own luv,

Yours is the best gift of all. I grieve for your beautiful dancing husband. I grieve for you most of all if you decide not to dance again just because you are to become mother! Long ago you would have been a prima ballerina if your

husband had shown less arrogance and more respect for
those in authority. Keep in shape, do exercises, bring your
baby with you and we will all live together in my place until
you find new *danseur* to luv. Life offers many chances, not
just one. Come back.

Her note put a wistful smile on my face. She even spelled
love "luv." "What is it that makes you smile like that?"
asked Paul, laying aside the medical journal that must have
held only a part of his interest. Awkwardly I leaned forward
to hand the note to him. He read it, then held out his arms,
inviting me to come and cuddle on his lap and in his arms.
Eagerly I accepted his invitation, I was hungry for affection.
Life seemed to me nothing without a man.

"You could go on with your career," he said softly.
"Though I pray to God you won't go back to New York and
leave me again."

"Once upon a time," I began, "there was a beautiful set of
blond parents who gave life to four children who should never
have been. And they adored them beyond reason. Then one day
the father was killed, and the mother changed, and forgot all
about the love, affection and attention those four children so
desperately needed. So, now that another beautiful husband is
dead, I will not have my child feel neglected, or fatherless, or
unwanted and unnecessary. When my child cries, I'll be there.
I'll be there always to make my child feel secure, and very
loved, and I'll read to him, and sing to him, and he'll never
feel left out, or betrayed—as Chris felt betrayed by the one he
loved most."

"He? You sound as if you know." His iridescent eyes
looked sad. "And are you going to be both mother and father
to this child? Are you going to close the gates to any man
who might want to share your life? Catherine, I hope you're
not going to be one of those women who lets herself go sour
because life doesn't always fulfill her wishes."

I leaned my head backward to stare into his eyes. "You don't still love me, do you?"

"Don't I?"

"That's no answer."

"I didn't think I needed to answer. I thought you could tell. I thought too, from the way you look at me, that you would turn to me again. I love you, Catherine. . . . Since the day you first came up my veranda steps, I've loved you. I love the way you talk, the way you smile, the way you walk—that is, before you became pregnant and started leaning backward and holding to your back—does it hurt that much?"

"Oh," I said in disgust, "why did you have to stop saying all those sweet words to ask if my back hurts? Of course it bothers me. I'm not used to carrying an extra nineteen pounds in front—go on with what you were saying before you remembered you're a doctor."

He slowly lowered his lips to brush mine, just lightly, before passion came and he pressed them hard with his own. My arms found their way around his neck and ardently I returned kiss for kiss.

The front door opened and then banged shut. I pulled quickly away from Paul and tried to stand up before Chris came into the room—but I wasn't quick enough. He strode in, his overcoat covering his white intern suit. He carried a bag with a quart of pistachio ice cream that I had expressed a desire for at dinner. "I thought you were on duty tonight," I said too quickly to hide my distress and surprise. He thrust the ice cream into my hands and looked at me coldly.

"I *am* on duty. But it's a dull night, so I thought I could take a few minutes off to drive and get you the dessert you seemed to want so much." He flicked his glance to Paul. "I'm sorry I arrived at the wrong time. Go on with what you were doing." He spun on his heel and left the room, then slammed the front door a second time.

"Cathy," said Paul who got up to take the ice cream from me. "We have to do something about Chris. What he wants can never be. I've tried to talk to him about it, but he won't listen. He closes his ears and walks away. You must make him understand that he's ruining his life by refusing to let any other girl into his heart." He went on into the kitchen, coming back in a few minutes with two sherbet dishes of the green ice cream I didn't want now.

He was right. Something did have to be done about Chris—but what? I couldn't hurt him; I couldn't hurt Paul. I was like a battlefield wanting both sides to win.

"Catherine," said Paul softly, as if he'd been watching my reaction, "you don't owe me if you don't love me. Cut Chris off, make it clear that he has to let go and find someone else. Anyone else but you . . ."

"I find it so difficult to tell him that," I said in a low voice, ashamed to admit I didn't want Chris to find anyone else. I wanted him with me always—just the nearness of him, the confidence he gave me—nothing else. I was trying to balance my time between Chris and Paul, to give each of them enough, but not too much. I watched the jealousy between them grow, and felt it was none of my fault—only Momma's! As everything wrong in my life was her fault.

It was a cold February night when I felt my first contraction. I gasped from the sharp pain—I had known it would hurt, but not so much! I glanced at the clock—two in the morning of St. Valentine's Day. Oh, how marvelous, my baby would be born on what would have been our sixth wedding anniversary! "Julian," I cried out, as if he could hear me, "you are about to become a father!"

I got up and dressed as speedily as I could before I crossed the hall to rap on Paul's door. He mumbled something in way of a question. "Paul," I called, "I think I just had my first contraction."

"Thank God!" he cried from the other side, instantly wide awake. "Are you all set to go?"

"Of course. I've been ready for a month."

"I'll call your doctor, then alert Chris—you sit down and take it easy!"

"Would it be all right if I came in?"

He swung open the door, wearing only his trousers. His chest was bare. "You're the calmest mother-to-be I've ever seen," he said as he helped me sit. He raced next to swipe at his face with an electric razor, then he was running to put on a shirt and tie. "Had any more contractions?" It was on the tip of my tongue to say no, when another seized me. I doubled over. "Fifteen minutes since the last." I gasped. He looked pale as he pulled on his jacket, then came to help me up. "Okay, I'll put you in the car first, then go for your suitcase. Keep calm, don't worry, this baby will have three doctors doing their very best . . ."

"To get in each other's way," I concluded.

"To see you have the best medical attention possible," he corrected, then he bellowed toward the kitchen. "Henny, I'm taking Catherine to the hospital! Tell Carrie when she wakes up. Then call Madame Marisha and put on that tape we made for her."

We'd thought of everything. When Paul opened the front door after he'd backed his car out, I heard behind me the tape playing for Madame M., my own voice speaking "Madame," I'd taped weeks ago, "your grandchild is on the way."

It seemed forever before the hospital loomed up ahead. Under a protective canopy at the emergency entrance, a solitary intern paced restlessly back and forth. Chris, who said "Thank God you're here! I was picturing all sorts of calamities," even as he assisted me out, while someone else rushed up with a wheelchair, and without any of the preliminaries other patients had to endure, I was snug in bed in no time at all—and gasping from another contraction.

Three hours later, my son was born. Chris and Paul were

there, both of them with tears in their eyes, but it was Chris who picked up my son, still with the cord attached, messy and bloody. He put him upon my belly and held him there while another doctor did what he had to. "Cathy . . . can you see him?"

"He's beautiful," I breathed in awe, seeing all the dark, curling hair, the perfect little red body. With a fierce anger so like his father's he waved his tiny fists and flailed his thin legs, screaming at all the indignities inflicted upon him—and all the light that came so suddenly to shine in his eyes, and put him center stage, so to speak.

"His name is Julian Janus Marquet, but I'm going to call him Jory."

Both Chris and Paul heard my thin whisper. I was so tired, so sleepy.

"Why would you call him Jory?" asked Paul, but it wasn't me who had the strength to answer. It was Chris who understood my reasoning.

"If he had been blond, she would have named him Cory—but the J will stand for Julian, and the rest for Cory."

Our eyes met and I smiled. How wonderful to be understood, and never have to explain.

PART FOUR

My Sweet Small Prince

If ever a child was born into a palace of adoring worshipers, it was my Jory with his blue-black curls, his pale creamy skin, and his dark, dark blue eyes. He was Julian all over, and to him I could give the lavish affection I'd been unable to give his father.

From the very first Jory seemed to know I was his mother. He seemed to know my voice, my touch, even the sound of my footsteps. Yet he had almost as great a love for Carrie who ran home every night straight from Paul's office to gather him in her arms and play with him for hours.

"We should find our own place," said Chris, who wanted to establish himself firmly as Jory's father. In Paul's home, this wasn't possible.

I didn't know what to say to that. I loved Paul's big house, and being with him and Henny. I wanted Jory to have the garden paths where I could push him in his carriage and he'd be surrounded by beauty. And in no way could Chris and I give him as much. Chris didn't know about my sky-high debts.

Upstairs Paul had made a nursery, completely refurbished

with crib, playpen, bassinet and dozens of soft plushy stuffed animals a baby could enjoy without harming himself. There were times when both Paul and Chris would rush home with the same toy. They'd look at each other, and both would force a smile to hide the embarrassment. Then I had to rush forward and exclaim, "Two men with the same idea." And one would have to be taken back . . . but never, never did I let either one know whose gift it was that I returned.

Carrie graduated from high school the June she was seventeen. She didn't want college; she was very much contented to be Paul's private secretary. Her small fingers could fly over the typewriter keyboard; she took dictation with remarkable speed and accuracy—but still she kept wishing for someone to love her, despite her small size.

To see her unhappy made me furious with my mother—again! I began to dwell on what I would do when I had my chance. Now I was free, no husband to hold me back—make her pay, as Carrie was paying!

Each day she saw Paul and Chris battling for my attention, each desiring me, each beginning to look at the other with enmity. I had to settle something that should have been settled a long time ago. If only Julian hadn't put himself in the way, I would now be Paul's wife, and Jory would be Paul's son, and yet, and yet . . . I loved Jory for who he was, and on second thought I was glad I'd had Julian for a while. I was no longer a sweet, innocent virgin—two men had taught me well. I would have the knowledge to hold my own when it came time to steal my mother's husband away from her. I'd be like she'd been with Daddy. I'd cast Bart Winslow shy glances, meaningful long, long looks. I'd reach to caress his cheek. . . . And my biggest asset of all was I looked like her, but I was years younger! How could he resist? I'd put on a few pounds to make myself curvier—like her.

Christmas came and Jory, less than a year old, sat amidst his presents, wide-eyed and bewildered, not knowing what to do, or which toy to pick up first. Snap, snap, snap went the click of three cameras. But Paul had the movie camera, not Chris, Carrie or I.

"Lullabye and good night," sang Carrie softly to my son, rocking him to sleep on Christmas night, ". . . may heaven's sweet charms hold you safe in its arms."

I couldn't help but cry to see her there, like a child herself, but so longing to have a child of her own. Chris came up behind me and put his arms around my waist as I leaned back against him. "I should run for a camera," he whispered, "they look so sweet together, but I don't want to break the spell. Carrie is so much like you, Cathy, except in size."

One little word, "except." One little word that kept Carrie from ever feeling really happy.

Footsteps sounded on the stairs. Quickly I jerked from Chris's arms and went in to tuck my small son into his crib. I sensed Paul in the doorway now that Chris had gone on to his room. "Cathy," whispered Carrie so Jory wouldn't awaken, "do you think I'll ever have a baby?"

"Yes, of course you will."

"*I* don't think I will," she said, and then ambled away, leaving me to stare after her.

Paul came into the nursery, kissed Jory good night, then turned as if to take me in his arms. "No," I said in a small voice, "not while Chris is in the house." He nodded stiffly, then said good night, and I went to lie awake until almost dawn—wondering how I could solve the dilemma I was in.

Jory seemed quite happy with his situation; he wasn't spoiled; he didn't whine and cry or make unnecessary demands, he just accepted. He could sit for minutes staring from one to the other of us, as if sizing us up, and our relationship to him. He had the patience of Chris; the quiet sweetness of Cory, and only occasionally the brashness of his father—and his mother. But nothing at all about Jory reminded me of Carrie; he smiled so much more than she. Nevertheless, when Carrie strolled through Paul's gardens with Jory in her arms, she pointed out the differences between this tree and that. Incessantly explaining. She forced Jory to imitate speech sooner than he would have otherwise.

"Regard this oak leaf," said Carrie one day after Jory had learned to walk, and spring breezes stirred the air. "Each tree leaf has its own shape, texture and smell. All flowers open up easily for a bee to enter, except the rose. But daisies don't smell as pretty as roses, so the bees fly right on by, and head for the roses that are so stingy with their nectar, and hold their heads high on tall stems." She pointed to a rose, then glanced at me. Next she was showing Jory the daisies and the pansies.

"Now, if I were a bee, you could bet I'd go straight for the violets and pansies too, even though they don't stand as tall." She lifted her eyes to meet mine and said in a strange, tight small voice. "You are like a rose, Cathy. All the bees come to you, and they don't even see me down so low. Please don't get married again before I have my chance. Please don't be around if ever some man looks my way. . . . Don't you smile at him, please."

Oh, how fast the years go when you have a baby to fill all the hours. All of us took snapshots like crazy: Jory's first smile; his first tooth; his first crawl from me to Chris, and then over to Paul, and to Carrie.

Paul began his courtship that was to last two years; the same two years Chris interned in the Clairmont Hospital. They couldn't hurt each other when each loved and respected the other. They couldn't even speak of the barrier between them, except through me.

"It's this town," said Chris. "I think Carrie would fare better in another city. All of us together."

It was twilight in the gardens, our favorite time there. Paul was off making his rounds in three hospitals, and Carrie was entertaining Jory before she put him to bed. Henny rattled pots and pans to let us know she was still up—and still busy.

Chris had completed his two years of internship, and had started on his residency which would take another three years. When he told me he was considering another hospital, far more famous, to further his training, I felt a deep shock. He was leaving me!

"I'm sorry, Cathy, the Mayo Clinic has accepted me, and that's an honor. I'll only be there nine months, and then back here to complete my training. Why don't you and Jory come with me?" His eyes were very bright and lambent. "Carrie can stay to keep Paul company."

"Chris! You know I can't do that!"

"You are going to stay on here after I'm gone?" he asked bitterly.

"If Julian's insurance company would pay off, I could afford a house of my own, and start my own dance school. But they keep insisting his death was suicide. I know that policy has a two-year suicide clause, and we paid on it since the day we married—so it was not in effect when he died. Yet, they won't pay."

"What you need is a good attorney."

My heart jumped. "Yes. Yes I do. Chris, go on to the Mayo Clinic without me. I'll make out fine, and I swear not to marry anyone until you are back and give your approval. Worry about finding someone yourself. After all, I'm not the only woman who resembles our mother."

He flared. "Why the hell do you put it like that? It's *you*, not *her*! It's everything about you that's not like her that makes me need and want you so!

"Chris, I want a man I can sleep with, who will hold me when I feel afraid, and kiss me, and make me believe I am not evil or unworthy." My voice broke as tears came. "I wanted to show Momma what I could do, and be the best prima ballerina, but now that Julian's gone all I want to do is cry when I hear ballet music. I miss him so, Chris." I put my head on his chest and sobbed. "I could have been nicer to him—then he wouldn't have struck out in anger. He needed me and I failed him. You don't need me. You're stronger than he was. Paul doesn't really need me either, or he would insist on marrying me right away. . . ."

"We could live together, and, and . . ." And here he faltered as his face turned red.

I finished for him, "No! Can't you see it just wouldn't work?"

"No, I guess it wouldn't work for you," he said stiffly. "But I'm a fool; I've always been a fool, wanting the impossible. I'm even fool enough to want us locked up again, the way we were—with me the only male available to you!"

"You don't mean that!"

He seized me in his arms. "Don't I? God help me but I do mean it! You belonged to me then, and in its own peculiar way our life together made me better than I would have been . . . and you made me want you, Cathy. You could have made me hate you, instead you made me love you."

I shook my head, denying this; I'd only done what came naturally from watching my mother with men. I stared at him, trembling as he released me. I stumbled as I turned to run toward the house. Before me Paul loomed up! Startled I faltered guiltily and stared at him as he turned abruptly and strode in the opposite direction. Oh! He'd been watching and listening! I pivoted about, then raced back to where Chris had his head resting against the trunk of the oldest oak. "See what you've done!" I cried out. "*Forget me, Chris!* I'm not the one and only woman alive!"

He appeared blind as he turned his head and he said, "You are for me the only woman alive."

October came, the time for Chris's departure. To see him pack, to know he was going, to say good-bye as if I didn't care when he came back made me deathly ill while I smiled.

I cried in the rose arbor. It would be easier now. I wouldn't have to keep putting Paul off so Chris wouldn't be hurt. No longer would I have to weigh each smile and balance it off against what I'd given the other. Now I had a clear, straight path to Paul—but something got in my eyes. The vision of my mother as she stepped off the plane with her husband on the step behind her. She was coming back to Greenglenna! I clipped out the newsphoto and the caption and put that in my scrapbook. Perhaps if she'd stayed away, I would have married Paul then and there. As it was, I did something entirely unplanned.

Madame Marisha was "getting along" and needed an assistant, so I went to convince her I should be the one to keep her school running—if ever, well, you could never tell. . . .

"I don't intend to die," she snapped. Then begrudgingly she nodded, her ebony eyes suspicious. "Yes, I suppose *you* would think of me as old, though I never do. But don't you try and take over, and try to run *me*. I am still the boss here, and will be until I am in my grave!"

By the time November rolled around I realized working with Madame M. was impossible. She had fixed ideas about everything, while I had a few ideas of my own. But I needed money, I needed a place of my own. I wasn't ready to marry Paul, and if I stayed there, that's just what would happen. I had spent enough years plotting and planning. It was time to make my move. The first pawn to play would be Mr. Attorney at Law. It wouldn't work if I stayed with Paul, and though he objected, saying it was an unnecessary expense, I explained I had to have a chance to be my own person, and in my own home to find out what I really wanted. He gave me a puzzled look, then a more shrewd one. "All right, Catherine, do what you must. You will anyway."

"It's only because Chris insisted that I not marry again until Carrie had her chance, and Chris objects to my staying here with you . . . when he isn't here. . . ." My ending was lame, and oh, such a lie!

"I understand," he said with a wry smile. "Since the day Julian died, it has been very clear that I am in competition with your brother for your affection. I've tried to talk to him about it, but *he* won't let me. I try to talk to you about it, and *you* won't let me. So go live in your own home, and be your own person, and find your own self, and when you feel grown up enough to act adult, come back to me."

Opening Gambit

As soon as I was installed in a small, rented cottage, halfway between Clairmont and Greenglenna, I sat down to draft a blackmail letter to my mother. I was deeply in debt, with one child, but I had Carrie too. The enormous bills Julian had run up in New York stores were still unpaid; there was also his hospital bill, his funeral bill, plus my own hospital bills made when Jory was born. Credit cards just didn't solve everything. Not for one moment was I going to accept more from Paul. He'd done enough. I needed to prove I was better than Momma, more able, smarter . . . and what did I do but write her a letter, as she'd written to her mother after Daddy died. Why not ask for just one paltry million? Why not? She owed us! It was ours too! With that money I could pay off all the debts I owed, pay back Paul and do something to make Carrie happier. And if I felt some shame to do the same thing she'd done—in a way—I rationalized it away by thinking it was her own fault! She'd asked for it! Jory was not going to live his life in need, when she had so much!

Finally, after many futile attempts, I came up with what I believed the perfect letter of extortion:

Dear Mrs. Winslow:

Once upon a Gladstone, Pennsylvania time, there lived a man and wife who had four children everyone referred to as the Dresden dolls. Now one of those dolls lies in a lonely grave and another of those dolls fails to grow to the height that should have been hers if she'd have been given sunlight and fresh air, and the love that a mother owed her when she needed it most.

Now the ballerina doll has a small son of her own, and not much money. I know, Mrs. Winslow, you don't have much compassion for children who might cast a shadow over your sunny days, so I will come directly to the point. The ballerina doll *demands* payment of one million dollars—if you are to keep any of *your* millions— or billions. You may send that amount to the post office box I name, and be assured, Mrs. Winslow, that if you fail to do so, the ears of Mr. Bartholomew Winslow, Attorney at Law, will be filled with horror tales I'm sure you'd rather he not hear.

Cordially yours, the ballerina doll,
Catherine Dollanganger Marquet

Each day I waited for a check to come in the mail. Each day I was disappointed. I wrote another letter, then another, and another. Each day for seven days I mailed off a letter to her, with a fierce anger growing in my heart. What was one measly million to her who had so many? I wasn't asking for too much. Part of that money belonged to us anyway.

Then, after fruitless months of waiting while Christmas and the New Year came and went, I decided I'd waited long enough. She was going to ignore me. I looked up a number in the Greenglenna telephone book, and in no time at all I had an appointment to see Bartholomew Winslow, Attorney at Law.

It was February and Jory was three. He was to spend the afternoon with Henny and Carrie as I, dressed in my very best with my hair becomingly styled, sauntered into the posh office to gaze upon my mother's husband. At last I was looking at him up close—and this time he had his eyes open. Slowly he rose to his feet, wearing a bemused expression—as if he'd seen me before and couldn't quite remember where. I thought back to the night I had stolen to Momma's grand suite of rooms in Foxworth Hall and found Bart Winslow asleep in the chair. He'd had a big dark mustache then, and I had dared to kiss him while he dozed. Believing as I did that he was fully asleep . . . and he hadn't been! He'd seen me and thought me part of his dream. Because of one stolen kiss that Chris was to hear about later, the repercussions had led Chris and I down a path we'd determined never to follow. Now we were paying the price—and it was *her* fault that Chris was now living apart from me, trying to deny what she'd started. I could not accept Paul as my husband until I had made her pay—and not just in money.

He smiled at me then, my mother's ruggedly handsome husband, and I saw for the first time the dazzling charisma of him. A light of recognition came into his dark brown eyes. "As I live and breathe, if it isn't Miss Catherine Dahl, the lovely ballerina who takes my breath away even before she dances. I'm enchanted you have need of a lawyer and you chose me, though I cannot possibly imagine why you are here."

"You've seen me dance?" I asked, stunned to hear he had. If he had seen me, then Momma must have too! Oh, and I never knew! Never knew! I glowed, I dimmed, saddened, became confused. Somewhere deep within me, despite all the hate on top, I still felt some of the love I'd had for her when I was young and trusting.

"My wife is a ballet buff," he went on. "Actually, I didn't care much for it when she first started dragging me to every one of your performances. But soon I learned to enjoy it, especially when you and your husband were featured in the lead roles. In fact, my wife seemed to have no interest in ballet at all unless you and your husband *were* featured. I used to fear she had a crush on your husband—he looks a little like me." He took my hand and lifted it to his lips, flashing his eyes upward and smiling with the easy charm of a man who knew what he was, a ladies' man used to putting notches on his belt. "You are even more beautiful off stage than on. But what are you doing in this part of the country?"

"I live here."

He pulled out a chair for me, sat me down so close he could watch my legs when I crossed them. He perched on the edge of his desk to offer me a cigarette, which I refused. He lit one for himself, then asked, "You're on vacation? Visiting your husband's mother?"

I realized he didn't know about Julian. "Mr. Winslow, my husband died from injuries sustained in an auto accident more than three years ago—didn't you hear about it?"

He appeared shocked and a bit embarrassed. "No, I didn't hear. I'm very sorry. Please accept my belated condolences." He sighed and ground out his half-smoked cigarette. "The two of you were sensational on stage—it's a terrible pity. I've seen my wife cry she was so impressed."

Yeah! I'll bet she was impressed. I shrugged off more questions and came directly to the object of my visit by handing him Julian's insurance policy. "He took out this policy shortly after we were married and now they won't pay because they think he cut the intravenous tube that was feeding him. But, as you can see, after two years the suicide clause is no longer in effect."

He sat down to read it carefully, and then looked up at me again. "I'll see what I can do. Are you in immediate need of this money?"

"Who isn't in need of money, Mr. Winslow, unless they are millionaires?" I smiled and tilted my head in the manner of my mother. "I have hundreds of bills and I have a small son to support."

He asked the age of my son; I told him. He appeared puzzled and confounded in more ways than one as I looked at him with sleepy, half-closed eyes, my head tilted backward and slightly to one side, in a mannerism that was my mother's way of looking at a man. I was only fifteen when I'd kissed him. He was far more handsome now. His mature face was long and lean, his bones too prominent, but in a very virile, masculine way he was strikingly good looking. Something about him suggested an exaggerated sensuality. And no wonder my mother hadn't sent a check. Probably all my blackmail letters were still following her from place to place.

Bart Winslow asked a dozen or more questions, then he said he'd see what he could do. "I'm a pretty good lawyer once my wife allows me to stay home and get my hand into a practice."

"Your wife is very rich, isn't she?"

This appeared to annoy him. "I suppose you could say she is," he answered stiffly, letting me know he didn't like discussing the subject.

I stood to leave. "I'll bet your rich wife leads you around like a pet poodle on a jeweled leash, Mr. Winslow. That's the way rich women are. They don't know the least thing about working for a living, and I wonder if *you* do."

"Well, by God," he said, jumping off the desk and standing with feet wide apart, "why did you come if you feel that way? Go to another attorney, Miss Dahl. I don't want a client who insults me and has no regard for my abilities."

"No, Mr. Winslow, I want *you*. I want *you* to prove you know your business as you claim to. Maybe, in a way, you can then prove something to yourself as well—that you aren't after all, just a rich woman's bought little plaything."

"You have the face of an angel, Miss Dahl, but a bitch's

tongue! I'll see your husband's insurance firm pays off. I'll petition them to appear in court, and threaten to sue. Ten to one they'll settle within ten days."

"Good," I said. "Let me know, for as soon as I have the money, I'm moving."

"Where?" he asked, striding forward to take hold of my arm.

I laughed, looking up into his face and using the ways a woman had to make a man interested, "I'll let you know where I go, in case you want to keep *in touch*."

In ten days, true to his word, Bartholomew Winslow came by the dance school to hand me the check for one hundred thousand dollars, "Your fee?" I asked, waving off the girls and boys who came running to surround me. I was wearing a tight practice outfit, and he was all eyes.

"Dinner at eight, next Tuesday night. Wear blue to match your eyes, and we'll discuss the fee then," he said, then turned to leave, not even waiting for my answer.

When he was gone, I turned around and looked at the children doing their warm-up positions, and somewhere above I hovered, looking down, and feeling scorn for the pitiful thing I was that innocence should admire me so much. I felt sad for them, for me.

"Who was that man who came to give you check?" Madame Marisha asked me when class was over.

"An attorney I hired to force Julian's insurance company to pay off—and they did."

"Ah," she said, falling into her old swivel desk chair, "now you have money and can pay off bills—I suppose you will quit working for me and go off somewhere, yah?"

"I'm not sure just what I plan to do yet. But you must admit, Madame, you and I don't get along very well, do we?"

"You have too many ideas I don't like. You think you know more than me! You think now that you work here few months, you can go away and start new school of your own!" She smiled evilly to see my start of surprise, revealing the truth she only guessed at. "So . . . you think me stupid too! You'll look all your life before you find another as smart as me. I read your mind, Catherine. You don't like me, never have, never will . . . yet you come to work for me to learn the business, right again? I don't care. Dancing schools come and dancing schools go, but the Rosencoff School of Ballet go on forever! Once I thought I'd leave it to Julian, but he's dead, then I thought when I die, I'd leave it to you—but I won't if you take your son away so I can't teach him!"

"Madame, that is your choice, but I am taking Jory away."

"Why? You think you can teach him as well as I can?"

"I don't know for certain, but I think I can. My son may not choose to be a dancer," I continued, ignoring her hard stony eyes. "If he does decide one day, I think I will make an able teacher—as good as any."

"If he choose to dance!" Words like cannonshot. "What other choice does Julian's son have *but to dance*? It is in his bones, in his brain—and most of all in his blood and in his heart! *He dances—or he dies!"*

I got up to leave. It was in my heart to be kind to her, to let her share in Jory's life . . . but the meanness in her hard eyes changed my mind. She would take my son and make of him what she'd made of Julian, someone who could never find fulfillment because life offered to him but one choice.

"I didn't expect to say this today, Madame, but you force me. You made Julian believe if he couldn't dance, then life held nothing. He would have recovered from that broken neck and his internal injuries, except you said he would never dance again—and he overheard you. He wasn't sleeping. So, he chose to die! The very fact that he could move the arm that wasn't strapped down, enough to steal the scissors from that nurse's pocket, proved he was already recovering but all he could see was a bleak desert where the ballet didn't exist!

Well, Madame . . . you *are not doing that to my son!* My son will
have the chance to choose for himself what kind of life he
wants—and I hope to God it is *not* the ballet!"

"You fool!" she spat at me, jumping up to pace back and
forth in front of her old, beat-up desk, "there is nothing better than adulation from your fans, the sound of thundering
applause, the feel of roses in your arms! And soon enough
you will find that out for yourself! You think to take my husband's grandson away, and hide him from the stage? *Jory will
dance, and before I die I will live to see him on stage—doing what
he must—or he too will die!*

"You wanna play 'mommy,'" she sneered, curling her lip
scornfully, "and 'wifey' to that big handsome doctor too, perhaps? And make another child for him, yah? *Well . . . to hell
with you, Catherine, if that is all you want out of life.*" She broke
then, and sobs came from deep down in her depths, to make
her voice when she spoke again harsh and husky, when before
it had been high and shrill. "Yess, go on . . . marry that big
doctor you've had a yen for since you came starry-eyed and
fresh faced as a kid to me—and ruin his life too!"

"Ruin his life too?" I repeated dully.

She spun about. *"You got something eating at you, Catherine,
Something gnawing at your guts. Something so bitter it simmers in
your eyes and grits your teeth together! I know your kind. You ruin
everyone who touches your life and God help the next man who loves
you as much as my son did!"*

Unexpectedly, some enigmatic, invisible cloak dropped
down to wrap me in my mother's cool, detached poise. Never
before had I felt so untouchable. "Thank you for enlightening
me, Madame. Good-bye and good luck. You won't be seeing
me again, or Jory." I turned and left. Left for good.

Tuesday night Bart Winslow showed up at my cottage door.
He was dressed in his best, and I was wearing blue; he smiled,
pleased I'd obeyed. He took me to a Chinese restaurant where

we ate with chopsticks, and everything was black or red.

"You are the most beautiful woman I have ever seen, with the exception of my wife," he said while I read my fortune cookie slip. *"Beware of impulsive actions."*

"Most men don't mention their wives when they take another woman out—"

He interrupted: "I am not an ordinary man. I'm just letting you know, you are not the most beautiful woman I know."

I smiled at him sweetly, closely watching his eyes. I saw I irritated him, charmed him, but most of all intrigued him, and when we danced, I also learned I excited him. "What is beauty without brains?" I asked, my lips brushing his ear as I stood on tiptoes. "What is beauty that is growing old, and overweight, and no challenge at all?"

"You are the damndest female I've ever known!" His dark eyes flashed. "How dare you imply my wife is stupid, old and fat? She looks very young for her age!"

"So do you," I said with a small mocking laugh. His face reddened. "But don't worry, Mr. Attorney . . . I'm not competing with her—I don't want a pet poodle."

"Lady," he said coldly, "you won't have one, not in me. I'm leaving soon to set up my offices in Virginia. My wife's mother isn't well and needs some attendants. As soon as you've settled your account with me, you can say good-bye to a man who obviously brings out the worst in you."

"You haven't mentioned your fee."

"I haven't decided yet."

Now I knew where I was going—back to Virginia to live somewhere near Foxworth Hall.

Now I could begin the real revenge.

"But Cathy," wailed Carrie tearfully, very upset because we were leaving Paul and Henny. "I don't want to leave! I love Dr. Paul and Henny! You go anywhere you want to, but leave me here! Can't you see Dr. Paul doesn't want us to go? Don't

you care when you hurt him? You're always hurting him! I
don't want to!"

"I care very much about Dr. Paul, Carrie, and I don't want
to hurt him. However, there are certain things I must do, and
I must do now. And Carrie, you belong with me and Jory. Paul
needs his chance to find a wife without so many dependents.
Don't *you* see, we are an encumbrance to him?"

She backed off and glared at me. "Cathy, he wants *you* for
his wife!"

"He hasn't said so in a long, long time."

"That's because you got your mind set on going and doing
something else. He told me he wants you to have what you
want. He loves you too much. If I were him, I'd make you stay,
and wouldn't care what you wanted!" She sobbed then, and
ran from me to slam her bedroom door.

I went to Paul and told him where I was going and why. His
happy expression turned sad, and then his eyes went vague.
"Yes, I suspected all along you would feel it necessary to go
back there and confront your mother face to face. I've seen you
making your plans and I hoped you'd ask me to go with
you."

"It's something I have to do myself," I said, holding to both
his hands now. "Understand, please understand I still love you
and always will."

"I understand," he said simply. "I wish you luck, my
Catherine. I wish you happiness. I wish all your days are bright
and sunny and you get what you want—whether or not I am
included in your plans. When you need me, *if* you ever need me,
I'll be here, waiting to do what I can. Every minute I'll be loving
you and missing you. . . . Just remember, when you want me I'll
be there."

I didn't deserve him. He was much too fine for the likes
of me.

I didn't want Chris or Carrie to know what part of
Virginia I was headed for. Chris wrote to me once or twice a week

and I responded letter for letter—but not one word did I tell him . . . he'd find out when he saw the change of address.

The month was May, and the day after Carrie's twentieth birthday party, celebrated without Chris there, Carrie, Jory and I set off in my car, backing out of Paul's driveway where we had come to say good-bye. Paul waved and when I looked in the rear-view mirror I saw him reach in his breast pocket for his handkerchief. He touched the tears in the corners of his eyes even as he kept on waving.

Henny stared after us. I thought I saw written in her expressive brown eyes. *Fool, fool, fool to go away and leave good man!*

Nothing proved more what a fool I was than the sunny day I set out for the mountains of Virginia with my small sister and son in the front seat next to me. But I had to do it—compelled by my own nature to seek the revenge in the place of our incarceration.

The Siren Call of the Mountains

At the last moment I decided I couldn't risk seeing Bart Winslow even long enough to pay his fee, so I dropped a check for two hundred dollars in a mailbox and considered that enough—whether or not it was.

With Carrie beside me and Jory on her lap I headed straight for the Blue Ridge Mountains. Carrie was very excited now that we were on our way, her big blue eyes wide as she commented on everything we passed. "Oh, I love to travel!" she said happily. When Jory grew sleepy, she carefully made a bed for him on the back seat and sat with him to be sure he didn't roll off and fall to the floor. "He's so beautiful, Cathy. I am going to have at least six children, or maybe even more. I want half to look just like Jory, and half like you and Chris, and two or three like Paul."

"I love you, Carrie, and I pity you too. You're planning on a dozen children, not just six."

"Don't worry," she said, settling back to take a nap herself. "Nobody is gonna want me, so I won't ever have any children but yours to love."

"That's not true. I've got the feeling, once we are in our new home, Miss Carrie Dollanganger Sheffield is going to have a love of her own. I'll even bet you five dollars—is it a bet?" She smiled, but she refused to take on the bet.

As I drove on northwest and the night began to descend Carrie grew very quiet. She stared out the windows and then back at me, and her large blue eyes held a look of fear. "Cathy, are we going back *there*?"

"No, not exactly." That's all I'd say until we'd found a hotel and settled in for the night.

The first thing in the morning a real estate woman I'd contacted in advance came to drive us in her car to look over the "properties for sale." She was a large, mannish woman and all business. "What you need is something compact, utilitarian and not too expensive. In this neighborhood all the houses run into big money. But there are a few small houses that the rich people used to use for guest homes, or they housed their servants in some. There's one that's very pretty with a nice flower garden."

She showed us that five-room cottage first and immediately I was won over. I think Carrie was too, but I'd warned her to show no signs of approval. I picked at small details to lead the agent astray. "The chimney looks like it won't work."

"It's a fine chimney, a good draft."

"The furnace—does it use oil or gas?"

"Natural gas was installed five years ago and the bath has been remodeled, the kitchen too. A couple used to live here who worked for the Foxworths on the hill, but they sold out and went down to Florida. But you can tell they loved this house."

Of course they had. Only a house that had been very beloved would have all the nice little details that made it exceptional. I bought it and signed all the papers without a lawyer, though I'd read up on the subject and insisted on having the deed checked.

"We'll have a wall oven put in with a glass door," I said

to Carrie who loved to cook—thank God, for I'd hardly have the time. "And we'll repaint the whole interior of the house ourselves and save the money."

Already I was finding out that one hundred thousand, after paying all the accounts I had to settle and putting the down payment on the cottage, was not going to last long. But I hadn't gone into this venture blindfolded. While Carrie stayed with Jory in a motel, I visited the ballet instructor who was selling her school and retiring. She was blond and very small, and nearing seventy. She seemed pleased to see me as we shook hands and settled on the amount she wanted. "I've seen you and your husband dance and really, Miss Dahl, though I'm delighted you want my school, it's a shame you are retiring at such an early age. I couldn't have given up performing at twenty-seven, never!"

She wasn't me. She didn't have my past or my kind of childhood. When she saw my determination to go through with the deal, she gave me the list of her students. "Most of these children belong to the wealthy people who live around here, and I don't think any of them seriously intend to become professional dancers. They come to please their parents who like to see them looking pretty in little tutus during the recitals. I have failed to turn out one gifted performer."

All three bedrooms in our cottage were very small, but the living room was L-shaped and of reasonable proportions, with a fireplace sided by bookcases. The short part of the L could be used as a dining room. Carrie and I set to with paint brushes and in one week we had painted every room a soft green. With the white woodwork it looked delicious. The space opened up and everything seemed larger. Carrie, of course, would have to have red and purple accessories for "her" room.

In three weeks we had both settled into a new routine, with me teaching the ballet school located over the local pharmacy and Carrie doing the housework and most of the cooking while she looked out for Jory. As often as possible I took Jory with me to class, not only to relieve Carrie of the responsibility, but also to have him near me. I was remembering Madame Marisha's talk of letting him look and listen and get the feel of the dance.

I sat one Saturday morning in early June staring out the windows at the blue-misted mountains that never changed. The Foxworth mansion was still the same. I could have turned back the clock to 1957 and on this night taken Jory and Carrie by the hand and followed those meandering trails from the train depot. It would have been the same as when Momma led her four children up to their prison of hope and despair, then left them to be tortured, whipped and starved. I went over and over everything that had happened: the wooden key we'd made to escape our prison room, the money we'd stolen from our mother's grand bedroom, that night when we found a large book of sexual pleasures in the nightstand drawer. Maybe if we'd never seen that book . . . maybe then things would have turned out differently.

"What are you thinking of?" asked Carrie. "Are you thinking we should go back to visit Dr. Paul and Henny—I hope that's what you're thinking."

"Really, Carrie, you know I can't do that. It's recital time and the little girls and boys in my class will be rehearsing every day. It's the recitals the parents pay to see. Without them they have nothing to boast of to their friends. But maybe we could ask Paul and Henny to visit us."

Carrie pouted and then for some reason brightened. "You know, Cathy, the day the man came to put in the new oven he was young and good looking, and when he saw me with Jory he asked if that was my son. That made me giggle, and he smiled too. His name was Theodore Alexander Rockingham, but he asked me to call him Alex." Here she paused and looked at me fearfully, with hope trembling her all over. "Cathy, he asked me for a date."

"Did you accept?"

"No."

"Why not?"

"I don't know him well enough. He said he's going to college and works part-time doing electrical work to help pay his tuition. He says he's going to be an electrical engineer or maybe a minister. . . . He hasn't decided yet which one." She gave me a small smile of both pride and embarrassment. "Cathy, he didn't seem to notice how little I am."

The way she said that made me smile too. "Carrie—you're blushing! You tell me one moment you don't know this fella very well, and then you come up with all sorts of pertinent facts. Let's invite him to dinner. Then I can find out if he's good enough for my sister."

"But, but . . ." she stammered, her small face flushed red. "Alex asked me to go home with him to Maryland for a weekend. He told his parents about me . . . but Cathy, I'm not ready to meet his parents!" Her blue eyes were full of panic. That's when I realized that Carrie must have seen this young man many, many times while I was teaching my ballet classes.

"Look, darling, invite Alex here to dinner and let him fly home alone. I think I should know him better before you go off with him alone."

She gave me the strangest long look, then lowered her eyes to the floor. "Will you be here if he comes to dinner?"

"Why, of course I will." Only then did it dawn on me. Oh God! I drew her into my arms. "Look, sweetheart, I'll ask Paul to come up this weekend, so when Alex sees I go for older men he won't even glance my way. Besides, you saw him first and he saw you first. He won't want an older woman with a child."

Happily she threw her thin arms about my neck. "Cathy, I love you! And Alex can fix toasters, steam irons. Alex can fix *anything!*"

*   *   *

One week later Alex and Paul were at our dinner table. Alex was a nice-looking young man of twenty-three who complimented my cooking. I was quick to point out that Carrie had prepared most of the meal. "No," she denied modestly, "Cathy did most of it. I only stuffed the chicken, made the dressing, mashed the potatoes, made the hot rolls and the lemon meringue pie—Cathy did the rest." Suddenly I felt I'd done nothing but set the table. Paul winked to show he understood.

When Alex took Carrie to the movies and Jory was snug in bed with his favorite stuffed toys, Paul and I settled down before the fire like an old married couple.

"Have you seen your mother yet?" he asked.

"They're here, my mother and her husband," I said quietly. "Staying in Foxworth Hall. The local newspaper is full of their comings and goings. It seems my dear, stone-eyed grandmother has suffered a slight stroke, so the Bartholomew Winslows will now make their home with her—that is, until she is dead."

Paul didn't say anything for the longest time. We sat before the fire and watched the red coals burn down to gray ashes. "I like what you've done with this house," he said finally. "It's very cozy."

He got up then and came to sit close by my side on the sofa. Tenderly he drew me into his arms. He just held me, with our eyes locked. "Where do I fit in?" he whispered. "Or don't I fit anywhere now?"

My arms tightened about him. I'd never stopped loving him, even when Julian was my husband. It seemed there wasn't any one man who could give me everything.

"I want to make love with you, Catherine, before Carrie comes back."

Quickly we shed our clothes. Our passion for each other had not lessened in all the years since we'd first met in this most intimate way. It didn't seem wrong. Not when he could murmer, "Oh, Catherine, if there is one thing I wish for, it is to have you as mine all my life through, and when I die, let it be after such as this, with you in my arms, your arms about me, and you will be looking at me as you are now."

"How beautiful and poetic," I said. "But you won't be fifty-two until September. I know you'll live to be eighty or ninety. And when you are, I pray passion will still rule both of us as it does now."

He shook his head. "I don't want to live to eighty unless you're with me and still love me. When you don't love me, let my time on earth be over." I didn't know what to say. But my arms spoke for me, drawing him closer so I could kiss him again and again. Then the phone was ringing. Lazily I reached for it—then bolted straight up in the bed.

"Hello, my lady Cath-er-ine!" It was Chris. "Henny had a friend over when I called Paul, and her friend gave me your phone number. Cathy, what the hell are you doing in Virginia? I know Paul is with you—and I hope to God he can persuade you not to do whatever it is you've got on your mind!"

"Paul is much more understanding than you are. And you are the one who should know best why I'm here!"

He made some noise of disgust. "I do understand, that's the worst of it. But you'll be hurt, I know that. And there's Momma. I don't want you to hurt her more than she already hurts, and you know she does. But more than anything I don't want you to be hurt again, and you will be. You're always running from me, Cathy, and you can't ever run far enough or fast enough, because I'll be right at your heels, loving you. Whenever anything good happens to me I sense you by my side, clinging to my hand, loving me as I love you, but refusing to recognize it because you think it's sin. If it is a sin, then hell would be heaven with you."

I felt a terrible sense of panic, as I nastily said good-bye and hung up, then turned to cuddle close to Paul, hoping he wouldn't know why I trembled.

*   *   *

In the dead of night, with Paul deeply asleep in the tiny third bedroom, I woke suddenly. I thought I heard the mountains calling out, Devil's spawn! The wind through the hills whistled and shrieked and added its voice to call me unholy, wicked, evil and everything else the grandmother had named us.

I got up and padded over to the windows to stare at the shadowy, dark peaks in the distance. The same mountain peaks I'd gazed on so often from the attic windows. And yes, just like Cory, I could hear the wind blowing and howling like a wolf searching for me, wanting to blow me away too, just as it had blown Cory and made him into only dry dust.

Quickly I ran to Carrie's room and crouched by her bed, wanting to protect her. For it seemed to me, in my nightmarish state, it was more likely the wind would take her before it got me.

Carrie's Bittersweet Romance

Carrie was twenty now, I was twenty-seven, and this November Chris would be thirty. That seemed an impossible age for him to be. But when I looked at my Jory it hit me hard how quickly time moves as you get older.

Time that had once moved so slowly speeded up, for our Carrie was in love with Alex! It sparkled from her blue eyes and danced her tiny feet around the room as she dusted, ran the vacuum, washed the dishes or planned menus for the next day. "Isn't he handsome, Cathy?" she asked and I agreed, though honestly he was just an average, nice-looking boy of five eight or nine with light brown hair that ruffled up easily and gave him a shaggy-dog appearance that was somehow appealing, for he was so neat in other ways. His eyes were turquoise and his expression that of someone who has never once had an ugly, unkind thought.

Carrie thrilled to hear the phone ring. She bubbled with excitement for so often the call was for her. She wrote Alex long, passionate love poems, then gave them to me to read and stored them away without mailing them off to the one who should read them.

I was happy for her and for myself too, for my ballet school was progressing nicely and any day Chris would be coming home! "Carrie, can you believe it? Chris's extended course is almost up!" She laughed and came running to me, as she had when she was a little girl, and in my outstretched arms she flung herself. "I know!" she cried. "Soon we will be a whole family again! Like we used to be. Cathy, if I have a little boy with blond hair and blue eyes, guess who I'll name him after." I didn't have to guess, I knew. Her firstborn, blond, blue-eyed son would be called Cory.

Carrie in love was pure enchantment to watch. She stopped talking of her small size and even began to feel she wasn't inadequate. For the first time in her young life she began to use makeup. Her hair was naturally wavy, like mine, but she had it cut shoulder length and there it curled upward in a wild tumble.

"Look, Cathy!" she cried when she came home from the beauty parlor with her new, smarter hair style. "Now my head doesn't look so big, does it? And have you noticed how much taller I've grown?"

I laughed. She was wearing shoes with three-inch heels and two inches of platform! But she was right. The shorter hair did make her head look smaller.

Her youth, her loveliness, her joy all touched me so much my heart ached in the awful apprehension that something might happen to spoil it for her.

"Oh, Cathy," said Carrie, "I would want to die if Alex didn't love me! I want to make him the best possible wife. I'll keep his house so clean dust motes won't dance in the sunlight. Every night he'll eat the gourmet meals I prepare—never frozen TV junk. I'll make my own clothes and his and our children's. I'll save him loads of money in lots of ways. He doesn't say much; he just sits and looks at me in that special, soft way. So, I take what I can from that and not what words he says—or he hardly says any."

I laughed and hugged her close. Oh, I did so long for her to be happy. "Men don't talk as freely about love as women do, Carrie. Some like to tease you, and that's a pretty good indication you've got their interest, and it can grow into something larger. And the way you find out how much they care is by looking into the eyes—eyes never learn how to lie."

It was easy to see that Alex was enchanted with Carrie. He was still working part-time as an electrician for a local appliance store while he took summer courses at the university, but he spent every spare minute with Carrie. I suspected he either had asked or was about to ask her to marry him.

I woke suddenly a week later to see Carrie sitting before the bedroom windows and staring off toward the shadowy mountains. Carrie who never had insomnia as I often did. Carrie who could sleep through thunderstorms, a tornado, telephone shrills a foot from her ears and a fire across the street. So naturally I was alarmed to see her there. I got up and went to her.

"Darling, are you all right? Why aren't you asleep?"

"I wanted to be with you near," she whispered, her eyes still riveted on the distant mountains, dark and mysterious in the night. They were all around us, boxing us in like they used to do. "Alex asked me to marry him tonight." She told me this in a flat, dull tone and I cried out, "How wonderful! I'm so happy for you, Carrie, and for him!"

"He told me something, Cathy. He's decided he wants to be a minister." Pain and sorrow were in her voice, and I didn't understand at all.

"Don't you want to be a minister's wife?" I asked, while I was so frightened underneath. She seemed so remote.

"Ministers expect people to be perfect," she said in that deadly, scary tone, "especially their wives. I remember all the things the grandmother used to say about us. About us being Devil's issue and evil and sinful. I didn't used to understand what she meant, but I remember the words. And she was always saying we were wicked, unholy children who should never have been born. *Should* we have been born, Cathy?"

I choked, overwhelmingly frightened, and swallowed over the lump that rose in my throat. "Carrie, if God hadn't wanted us to be born He wouldn't have given us life in the first place."

"But . . . Cathy, Alex wants a perfect woman—and I'm *not* perfect."

"Nobody is, Carrie. Absolutely nobody. Only the dead are perfect."

"Alex is perfect. He has never done even one bad thing."

"How would you know? Would he tell you if he had?"

Her lovely young face was darkly shadowed. Falteringly she explained. "It seems Alex and I have known each other for a long, long time, and until recently he didn't tell me much about himself. I've talked my head off to him, but I've never told him about our past, except how we became wards of Dr. Paul's after our parents died in an auto accident. And that's a lie, Cathy. We aren't orphans. We still have a mother who is alive."

"Lies are not deadly sins, Carrie. Everyone tells little lies now and then."

"Alex doesn't. Alex has always felt drawn toward God and religion. When he was younger he wanted to become a Catholic so he could be a priest. He grew older and learned priests have to live lives of celibacy, so he decided against being a priest. He wants a wife and children. He told me he's never had sex with anyone because he's been looking all his adult life for just the right girl to marry—somebody perfect, like me. Somebody godly, like him. And *Cath-eee,*" she wailed pitifully, *"I'm not perfect! I'm bad!* Like the grandmother was always telling us, I'm evil and unholy too! I have ugly thoughts! I hated those mean little girls who put me on the roof and said I was like an owl! I wished them all to die! And Sissy Towers, I hated her more than any other! And Cathy, did you know Sissy Towers drowned when she was twelve? I never wrote and told you, but I felt it was my fault for hating her so much! I hated Julian too for taking you away from Paul, and he died too! You see how it is; how can I tell Alex all of that and then tell him our mother married her half-uncle too? He'd hate me, Cathy. He wouldn't want me then, I know he wouldn't. He'd think I would give birth to deformed children, like me—and I love him so much!"

I knelt by the side of her chair and held her close as a mother would. I didn't know what to say, and how to say it. I longed for Chris and his support, and for Paul who always knew how to say everything just right. And remembering this I took his words, said to me, and I repeated them to Carrie, even as I felt a terrible wrath against the grandmother who'd implanted all these crazy notions in the head of a five-year-old child. "Darling, darling, I don't know how to say everything right, but I'm going to try. I want you to understand that what is black to one person is white to another. And nothing in this world is so perfect that it is pure white, or so bad it is pure black. Everything concerning human beings comes in shades of gray, Carrie. None of us is perfect, without flaws. I've had the same doubts about myself as you have."

Her teary eyes widened to hear this, as if she considered me, of all people, perfect. "It was our doctor Paul who set me straight, Carrie. He told me long ago, if a sin was committed when our parents married and conceived children, it was *their* sin and not ours. He said God didn't intend to make us pay the price for what our parents did. And they weren't that closely related, Carrie. Do you know in ancient Egypt the pharaoh would only allow his sons and daughters to marry a brother or sister? So you see, society makes the rules; and never forget, our parents had four children and not one of us is a freak—so God didn't punish them, or us."

She glued her huge blue eyes to my face, desperately wanting to believe. And never, never should I have mentioned "freak."

"Cathy, maybe God did punish me. I don't grow; that is punishment."

I laughed shakily and drew her closer. "Look around you, Carrie. Many other people are smaller than you. You aren't a midget or a dwarf, you know that. Even if you were, which you aren't, still you would have to accept it and make the best of it, just as many do who consider themselves too tall, or too fat, or too thin, or too something. You have a beautiful face, sensational hair, a lovely complexion, an adorable figure with everything where it should be. You have a beautiful singing voice, and you've got a brilliant mind; look at how fast you can type and how well you take shorthand and keep Paul's books, and you can cook twice as well as I can. You are also a much better housekeeper than I am, and look at the dresses you sew. They look better than anything I see in a store. When you add all that up, Carrie, how can you think you aren't good enough for Alex or any other man!"

"But, Cathy," she wailed, stubbornly unappeased by what I'd said, "you don't know him like I do. We went by an X-rated movie theater and he said anybody who did any of those things was evil and perverted! And you and Dr. Paul told me sex and making babies was a natural, loving part of living—and I'm bad, Cathy. Once I did something very wicked."

I stared at her, taken by surprise. With whom? It was as if she read my mind, for she shook her head while tears streamed down her cheeks. "No . . . I've never had . . . had . . . intercourse, not with anybody. But I did other things that were wicked, Alex would think so, and I should have known it was evil."

"What did you do, darling, that was so terrible?" She gulped and bowed her head in shame. "It was Julian. One day when I was visiting and you weren't home he wanted to do . . . do something with me. He said it would be fun and wasn't real sex, the kind that made babies—so I did what he wanted, and he kissed me and said next to you he loved me best. I didn't know it was wicked just to do what I did."

I swallowed over the huge, aching lump in my throat, smoothed her silken hair from her fevered forehead and wiped away her tears. "Don't cry and feel ashamed, darling. There are all kinds of love and ways to express love. You love Dr. Paul and Jory and Chris in three different ways, and me in another—and if Julian convinced you to do something you feel was wicked, that was *his* sin, not yours. And mine too, for I should have told you what he might want. He promised me never to touch you or do anything sexual with you, and I believed him. But if you did it, don't be ashamed any longer— *and Alex doesn't have to know.* Nobody will tell him."

Very slowly her head lifted, and the moon that suddenly came into view from behind dark clouds shone in her eyes full of self-torture. "But *I'll* know." She began to sob, wild, hysterical sobs. "That's not the worst thing, Cathy," she screamed, "I liked doing what I did! I liked him wanting me to do it—I tried not to let my face show I was feeling any pleasure for God might have been watching. So you see why Alex won't understand? He'd hate me, he would, I know he would! And even if he never knows, I'll still hate myself for doing it and liking it!"

"Please stop crying. What you did isn't that bad, really. Forget our grandmother who kept talking about our evil blood. She's a bigoted, narrow-minded hypocrite who can't tell right from wrong. She did all kinds of horrible things in the name of righteousness and nothing at all in the name of love. You're not bad, Carrie. You wanted Julian to love you, and if what you did gave him pleasure and you pleasure, then that's normal too. People are made to feel sensual pleasure, made to enjoy sex. Julian was wrong and he shouldn't have asked you, but that was *his sin*, not yours."

"I remember lots of things you don't think I do," she whispered. "I remember the funny way Cory and I used to talk to each other, so you and Chris couldn't understand. We knew we were the Devil's issue. We heard the grandmother.

We talked about it. We knew we were locked up because we weren't good enough to be out in the world with people better than us."

"Stop!" I cried. "Don't remember! Forget! We did get out, didn't we? We were four children not responsible for the actions of our parents. That hateful old woman tried to steal our confidence and our pride in ourselves—don't let her succeed! Look at Chris, aren't you proud of him? Weren't you proud of *me* when I was on stage dancing? And one day, after you and Alex are married, he will change his mind about what is perverted and what isn't—for I did. Alex will grow up and stop being overly righteous. He doesn't know yet the pleasures love can give."

Carrie pulled from my arms and went to stare out of the windows at the dark and distant mountains, and at the quarter moon that sailed as an uptilted Viking ship through the black seas of night. "Alex won't change," she said dully. "He's gonna be a minister. Religious people think everything is bad, just like grandmother. When he told me he was going to give up the idea of being an electrical engineer, I knew it was all over between us."

"Everybody changes! Look at the world about us, Carrie. Look at the magazines and the movies that decent people go to and enjoy, and the stage plays with everyone naked, and the kind of books being published. I don't know if it's for the better, but I do know people aren't static. We all change from day to day. Maybe twenty years from now our children will look back to our time and be shocked, and maybe they will look back and smile and call us innocents. Nobody knows how the world will change—so if the world can change, *so can one man named Alex.*"

"Alex won't change. He hates today's lack of morals, hates the kinds of books being published, the movies that are dirty and the magazines with couples doing wicked things. I don't think he even approves of the kind of dancing you used to do with Julian."

I wanted to yell out, *To hell with Alex and his prudery!* Yet I couldn't slander the only man Carrie had found to love. "Carrie, sweetheart, go to bed. Go to sleep and remember in the morning that the world is full of all sorts of men who would be delighted to love someone as pretty, sweet and domestically oriented as you are. Think of what Chris tells us always, 'things always happen for the best.' And if it doesn't work out for you and Alex, then it will work out for you and someone else."

She threw me a quick glance of deepest despair. "How was it for the best when God made Cory die?"

Dear Lord, how to answer a question like that?

"Was it for the best when Daddy was killed on the highway?"

"You don't remember that day."

"Yes I do. I've got a good memory."

"Carrie, absolutely no one is perfect, not me, not you, not Chris, not Alex. Not anybody."

"I know," she said, crawling into her bed like a good little girl obeying her mother. "People do bad things and God sees them and punishes them later on. Sometimes he uses a grandmother with her whip, like she beat you and Chris. I'm not dumb, Cathy. I know you and Chris look at each other in the way Alex and I look at each other. I think you and Dr. Paul were lovers too—and maybe that's why Julian died, to punish you. But you're the kind of woman men like and I'm not. I don't dance; I don't know how to make everybody love me. Only my family loves me, and Alex. And when I tell Alex he won't love me or want me."

"You won't tell him!" I ordered sternly. She lay with her eyes fixed on the ceiling until finally she drifted off to sleep. Then I was the one left to lie awake, hurting inside, still astonished by the effect one old woman had on the lives of so many. I hated Momma for taking us to Foxworth Hall. She'd known what her mother was like and still she took us there. She'd known her mother and father better than anyone and still she married a second time and left us alone, so she had the fun and we had the torture. And it was us who were still suffering while she had the fun!

Fun that would soon be over, for I was here and Bart was here, and sooner or later we would meet. Though how he had managed to avoid me so far I wasn't to learn until later.

I comforted myself with the thoughts of how Momma would be suffering soon too, like we had suffered. Pain for pain, she'd learn how we had felt when *she* was left alone and unloved. She wouldn't be able to cope . . . not again. One more blow would be her undoing. Somehow I knew that perhaps because I was so much like her.

"Are you sure you're all right?" I asked Carrie a few days later. "You haven't been eating well. Where has your appetite gone?"

She said quietly, her face expressionless. "I'm just fine. I just don't feel like eating much. Don't take Jory with you today to your dance studio. Let me keep him all day. I miss him when he goes away with you."

I felt uneasy about leaving her all day with Jory who could be a handful, and Carrie didn't look like she was feeling well. "Carrie, be honest with me, please. If you feel unwell, let me take you to a doctor."

"It's my time of the month," she said with her eyes downcast, "I just feel crampy in my middle three or four days before it starts."

Only the blues of the month—and when you were her age you did feel more cramps than at mine. I kissed my small son good-bye while he set up a terrible wail, wanting to go with me and watch the dancers.

"Wanna hear the music, Mommy," objected Jory who knew very well what he wanted and what he didn't. "Wanna watch the dancers!"

"We'll go for a walk in the park. I'll push you in the swing and we'll play in the sandbox," said Carrie hastily, picking up my son and holding him close. "Stay with me, Jory. I love you so much and I never see enough of you. . . . Don't you love your aunt Carrie?"

He smiled and threw his arms about her neck, for yes, Jory loved everyone.

It was a terribly long day. Several times I called to check on Carrie to see if she was all right. "I'm fine, Cathy. Jory and I had a wonderful time in the park. I'm going to lie down now and take a nap—so don't call and wake me up again."

Four o'clock came, and my last class of the day, when my six- and seven-year-olds moved on out into the center of the studio. While the music played I counted, *"Un, deux, pliés, un, deux, pliés,* and now, *un, deux, tendu,* close up, *un, deux, tendu,* close up."* And on and on I instructed, when suddenly I felt that prickly rise of my neck hackles to inform me that someone was staring at me intently. I whirled about to see a man standing far to the rear of the studio. Bart Winslow—my mother's husband!

The minute he saw I recognized him he came striding toward me. "You do look sensational in purple tights, Miss Dahl. May I have a moment of your time?"

"I'm busy!" I snapped, annoyed that he could ask when I had twelve little dancers I couldn't take my eyes off of. "My day will be over at five. If you care to you can sit over there and wait."

"Miss Dahl, I've had one devil of a time finding you, and you've been right here under my nose all the time."

"Mr. Winslow," I said coolly, "if I didn't mail you an adequate fee you could have written a letter and it would have been forwarded to me."

He knitted his dark, thick brows together. "I'm not here about the fee—though you didn't pay me the price I had in mind." Smiling and assured, he slipped a hand inside his jacket and pulled from the breast pocket a letter. I gasped to see my own handwriting and all the postmarks and cancellation marks on that letter that had followed my mother all about Europe! "I see you recognize this letter," he said with his keen brown eyes watching my every flicker of expression.

"Look, Mr. Winslow," I said, very much in a state of flurry, "my sister isn't feeling well today and she's taking care of my son who is hardly more than a baby. And you can see I've got my hands full here. Can we talk about this some other time?"

"At your convenience, Miss Dahl, any time." He bowed and then handed me a small business card. "Make it as soon as possible. I've many questions to ask you—and don't try skipping out. This time I'm keeping close tabs on you. You don't think one dinner date was enough, do you?"

It upset me so much to see him with that letter that the moment he was gone I dismissed my class and went into my office. There I sat down to pore over my green ledger, totaling the figures and seeing I was still in the red. Forty students I'd been assured when I bought out this school, but I hadn't been told most of them went away during the summers and didn't return until fall. All the spoiled little rich kids in the winter and the middle-class children in the summer who could only come once or twice a week. No matter how I stretched the money I earned it didn't cover all my costs of redecorating and installing new mirrors behind the long barre.

I glanced then at my watch, saw it was almost six o'clock, then changed into my street clothes and ran the two blocks to my small house. Carrie should have been in the kitchen preparing dinner while Jory played in the fenced-in yard. But I didn't see Jory, nor was Carrie in the kitchen!

"Carrie," I called, "I'm home—where are you and Jory hiding?"

"In here," she responded in a thin whisper.

All the way I ran to find her still in bed. Weakly she explained Jory was staying with the next-door neighbor.

"Cathy . . . I don't really feel very good. I've thrown up four or five times; I can't remember how many . . . and I'm so crampy. I feel funny, real funny. . . ."

I put my hand to her head and found it strangely cold, though the day was very warm. "I'm going to call a doctor." No sooner were the words out of my mouth than I had to laugh bitterly at myself. There wasn't a doctor in this town who made house calls. I ran back to Carrie and stuck a thermometer in her mouth, then gasped to read the figures.

"Carrie, I'm going to get Jory and then I'm driving you to the nearest hospital. You have a temperature of one hundred and three point six!"

Listlessly she nodded, then drifted off to sleep. I rushed next door to check on my son who was happily playing with a little girl a month older than he was. "Look, Mrs. Marquet," said Mrs. Townsend, a sweet, motherly woman in her early forties who was taking care of her granddaughter, "if Carrie is sick, let me keep Jory until you come home. I do hope Carrie isn't seriously ill. She's such a dear little thing. But I've noticed she's been looking pale and miserable for a day or so."

I'd noticed the same thing and had tied it all to her romance with Alex that was going awry.

How wrong I was!

The very next day I called Paul. "Catherine, what's wrong?" he said when he heard the panic in my voice.

I spilled it all out, how Carrie was sick and in the hospital where they had already made several tests, and still they didn't know what was wrong with her. "Paul, she looks dreadful! And she's losing weight fast, unbelievably fast! She's vomiting, can't keep any food down and has diarrhea too. She keeps calling for you and Chris too."

"I'll have another doctor fill in for me here and fly right up there," he said without hesitation. "But wait before you try and get in touch with Chris. The symptoms you name are so common to a number of minor ailments."

I took him at his word and didn't try and contact Chris who was enjoying a two-week tour of the West Coast before he came home and continued his residency. In three hours Paul was with me in the hospital room staring down at Carrie. She smiled weakly to see him there and held out her thin arms. "Hello," she whispered thinly, "I'll bet you didn't think you'd see me in an ole hospital bed, did you?"

Immediately he took her in his arms and began to ask questions. What were her first signs that something was wrong?

"About a week ago, I started feeling very tired. I didn't tell Cathy 'cause she worries so much about me anyway. Then I had headaches and I felt sleepy all the time, and I got big bruises and didn't know how I got them. Then I combed my hair and lots and lots of it came out, and then I just started throwing up . . . and other things that other doctors have already asked me and I told them." Her thin, whispering voice drifted off. "I wish I could see Chris," she mumbled before her eyes closed and she was asleep.

Paul had already seen Carrie's chart and talked to her doctors. Now he turned to me with that blank expression that put dread in my heart . . . it was so fraught with meaning. "Maybe you ought to send for Chris."

"Paul! Do you mean . . . ?"

"No, I don't mean that. But if she wants him, he should be here with her."

I was in the hall, waiting for the doctors to do certain tests on Carrie. They had chased me from the room. As I paced back and forth before the closed door to her room, I sensed him before I saw him. I whirled about, catching my breath to see Chris striding down the long corridor, bypassing nurses carrying bedpans and trays of medicines who gaped to see him in all his splendid glory.

Time rolled backward and I saw Daddy, Daddy as I best

remembered him, dressed in white tennis clothes. I couldn't speak when Chris took me in his arms and bowed his tanned face down into my hair. I heard the thud of his heart beating strong and regular. I sobbed, so near a deluge of tears, "It didn't take you long to get here." His face was in my hair and his voice was husky. "Cathy," he asked, raising his head and looking me directly in the eyes, "what is wrong with Carrie?"

His question stunned me—for he should know! "Can't you guess? It's that damned arsenic, I know it is! What else could it be? She was fine until a week ago, then all of a sudden she's sick." I broke then and sobbed, "She wants to see you." But before I led him to Carrie's small room, I put in his hand a note I'd found in the diary she'd started the day she met Alex. "Chris, Carrie knew for a long time something was going wrong, but she kept it to herself. Read this and tell me what you think." While he read, my eyes stayed glued to his face.

Dear Cathy and Chris,

Sometimes I think you two are my real parents, but then I remember my real momma and daddy, and she seems like a dream that never was, and I can't picture Daddy unless I have his photograph in my hand—though I can picture Cory just like he was.

I've been hiding something. So if I don't write this you are going to blame yourselves. For a long time I've felt I was going to die soon, and I don't care anymore, like I used to. I can't be a minister's wife. I wouldn't have lived this long if you two, and Jory, and Dr. Paul and Henny hadn't loved me so much. Without all of you to hold me here, I would have gone on to Cory a long time ago. Everybody has somebody special to love, except me. Everybody has something special to do, except me. I've always known I'd never get married. I knew I was fooling myself about having children, for my hips are too narrow, and I think too I'm too small to make a good wife. I'd never be anybody special, like you, Cathy, who can dance and have babies and everything else. I can't be a doctor like Chris, so I'd just be nothing much, just somebody to get in the way and worry everybody because I'm unhappy.

So, right now, before you read on further, promise in your heart you won't let the doctors do anything to make me live on. Just let me die, and don't cry. Don't feel sad and miss me after I'm buried. Nothing has been right, or felt right since Cory went away and left me. What I regret most is I won't be around to watch Jory dance on stage like Julian used to. Now I have to confess the truth, I loved Julian, the same as I love Alex. Julian never thought I was too little, and he was the only one who made me feel a normal woman, for a short time. Though it was sinful, even when you say it was not, I know it was, Cathy.

Last week I started thinking about the grandmother and what she used to say to us all the time about being the Devil's spawn. The more I thought about it, the more I knew she was right—I shouldn't have been born! I am evil! When Cory died because of the arsenic on the sugared doughnuts the grandmother gave us, I should have died too! You didn't think I knew, did you? You thought all the time I was sitting on the floor, in the corner, I couldn't hear and didn't take notice, but I was seeing and hearing, but I didn't believe, back then. Now I believe.

Thank you, Cathy, for being like my mother and the best sister alive. And thank you, Chris, for being my substitute father and my second best brother, and thank you, Dr. Paul, for loving me even though I didn't grow. Thank all of you for never being ashamed to be seen with

me, and tell Henny I love her. I think maybe God won't
want me either, until I grow taller, and then I think about
Alex, who thinks God loves everybody, even when they
aren't so tall.

She'd signed that letter in a huge scrawl to make up for
her small size. "Oh, dear God!" cried Chris. "Cathy, what does
this mean?"

Only then could I open my purse and take from it something I'd found hidden away in the dark, far end of the closet in
Carrie's room. His blue eyes grew wide and the color seemed
to fade as he read the name of the rat poison bottle, then saw
the package of sugared doughnuts with only one left. One left.
It had been bitten into just once. Tears began to course down
his cheeks, then he was really sobbing on my shoulder. "Oh,
God . . . she put that arsenic on the doughnuts, didn't she, so
she could die in the same way Cory did?"

I broke free from his clutching arms and backed a few
feet away, feeling I was drained of all blood. "Chris! Read that
letter over again! Didn't you notice what she wrote, how she
didn't believe, and 'Now I believe.' Why wouldn't she believe
back then, and believe now? Something happened! Something happened to make her believe that our mother could
poison us!"

He shook his head in a bewildered fashion, the tears still
eking from his eyes. "But if she knew all along, how could
anything more happen to convince her, when overhearing us
talking and seeing Mickey die didn't?"

"How can I tell you?" I cried out desperately. "But the
doughnuts have been liberally coated with arsenic! Paul had
them tested. Carrie ate those, knowing they would kill her.
Can't you see this is another murder our mother committed?"

"She isn't dead yet!" Chris cried. "We'll save her! We
won't let her die. We'll talk to her, tell her she has to hold on!"

I ran to hold him, fearing it was too late and desperately

hoping it wasn't. Even as we clung together, made parents
again by our common suffering, Paul came from Carrie's room.
The solemn expression on his drawn face told me everything.

"Chris," said Paul calmly, "how wonderful to see you
again. I'm sorry the circumstances are so sad."

"There's hope, isn't there?" cried Chris.

"There's always hope. We are doing what we can. You look
so tan and vibrant. Hurry in to see your sister and pass along
some of that vitality to her. Catherine and I have said all we
can think of to try to make her fight back and gain her will to
live. But she has given up. Alex is in there on his knees by her
bed, praying for her to live, but Carrie has her head turned
toward the windows. I don't think she realizes what is said
or what is done. She's gone off somewhere out of our reach."

Paul and I trailed along behind Chris who ran to Carrie.
She lay thin as a rail beneath a pile of heavy covers, when it
was still summer. It just didn't seem possible she could age
so quickly! All the firm, ripe, rosy roundness of youth had
fled, leaving her small face gaunt and hollow. Her eyes were
deep pits to make her cheekbones very prominent. She even
seemed to have lost some of her height. Chris cried out to see
her so. He leaned to gather her in his arms, called her name
repeatedly, stroked her long hair. To his horror hundreds of
the golden strands clung to his fingers when he drew them
away. "Good God in heaven—what's being done for her?"

When he brushed the hair from his fingers I hurried forward to pluck them from his hands, and in a plastic box I
carefully laid them out. The electric static of the box kept
them in place. An idiot notion, but I couldn't bear to see her
beautiful hair swept up and thrown away. Her hair glinted on
the pillows, on the bedspread, on the white lace of her bed-
jacket. As in a trance of nightmares unending I gathered up
the long hairs and arranged them neatly while Alex prayed on
and on. Even as he was introduced to Chris he paused only
long enough to nod.

"Paul, answer me! What is being done to help Carrie?"

"Everything we know how to do," answered Paul, his voice low and soft, the way people speak when death is near. "A team of good doctors are working around the clock to save her. But her red blood cells are being destroyed faster than we can replace them with transfusions."

Three days and nights all of us lingered beside Carrie's bedside while my neighbor took care of Jory. Each of us who loved her prayed that she'd live. I called Henny and told her to go to church and have all her family and church members pray for Carrie too. She tapped over the line her signal for "Yes, Yes!"

Flowers arrived daily to fill her room. I didn't look to see who sent them. I sat beside Chris or Paul, or between both, and held to their hands and silently prayed. I looked with distaste upon Alex, whom I believed responsible for much of what was wrong with Carrie. Finally I could keep my question to myself no longer; I got up and stalked Alex and backed him into a corner. "Alex, why would Carrie want to die during the happiest days of her life? What did she tell you and what did you say?"

He turned his bewildered, unshaven, grief-stricken face to mine. "What did I say?" he asked, his eyes red-rimmed from lack of sleep. I repeated my question with an even harder edge to my voice. He shook his head as if to clear it, looking hurt and sleepy as he ran long fingers through the tumble of his uncombed brown curls. "Cathy, God knows I've done everything I can to convince her I love her! But she won't listen to me. She turns her face aside and says nothing. I asked her to marry me and she said yes. She threw her arms about my neck and said yes over and over again. Then she said, 'Oh, Alex, I'm not nearly good enough for you.' And I laughed and said she was perfect, just exactly what I wanted. Where did I go wrong, Cathy? What did I do to make her turn against me so now she won't even look my way?"

Alex had the kind of sweet, pious face you expect to

see carved only on marble saints. Yet, as he stood there, so humbled, so racked by grief and torn by love turned against him, I reached out and soothed him as best I could, for he did love Carrie. In his own way he loved her. "Alex, I'm sorry if I sounded harsh; forgive me for that. But did Carrie confess anything to you?"

Again his eyes clouded. "I called and asked to see her a week ago and her voice sounded strange, as if something terrible had happened and she couldn't speak about it. I drove as fast as I could to be with her, but she wouldn't let me in. Cathy, I love her! She's told me she's too small and her head is too large, but in my eyes her proportions are just right. To me she was a dainty doll who didn't know she was beautiful. And if God lets her die I will never in this life find my credence again!" That's when he buried his face in his hands and began to cry.

It was the fourth night after Chris arrived. I dozed beside Carrie. The others were trying to catch a catnap before they too were ill and Alex was napping in the hall on a cot when I heard Carrie call my name. I ran to her bed and knelt beside it, then reached for her small hand under the covers. It was only a bony hand now, with skin so translucent her veins and arteries could be seen.

"Darling, I've been waiting for you to wake up," I whispered in a hoarse voice. "Alex is in the hall and Chris and Paul are napping in the doctor's quarters—shall I call them in?"

"No," she whispered. "I want to talk only to you. I'm gonna die, Cathy." She said it so calmly, as if it didn't matter, as if she accepted it and was glad. "No!" I objected strongly. "You are *not* going to die! I'm not going to let you die! I love you as my own child. Many people love and need you, Carrie! Alex loves you so much and he wants to marry you, and he won't be a minister now, Carrie; I've told him it makes you uncomfortable. He doesn't really care what his career as long as you stay alive and love him. He doesn't care if you are small or if you have children. Let me call him in so he can tell you all . . ."

"Nooo," she whispered thinly. "I've got something secret to tell you. Her voice was so faint it seemed to come from over hundreds of soft, rounded, little hills far, far away. "I saw a lady on the street." Her voice was so low I had to lean to hear. "She looked so much like Momma I had to run up. I caught hold of her hand. She snatched hers away and turned cold hard eyes on me. 'I don't know you' she said. Cathy, that was our mother! She looks like she used to almost, only a little older. She even had on the pearl necklace with the diamond butterfly clasp that I remember. And, Cathy, when your own mother doesn't want you—don't that mean nobody can want you? She looked at me and she knew who I was; I saw it in her eyes, and still she didn't want me because she knows I'm bad. That's why she said what she did—that she didn't have any children. She doesn't want you or Chris either, Cathy, and all mothers love and want their children unless they're evil, unholy children . . . like us."

"Oh, Carrie! Don't let her do this to you! It's the love of money that made her deny you . . . not that you are bad or wicked or unholy. You haven't done anything evil! It's money that matters to her, Carrie, not us. But we don't need her. Not when you have Alex and Chris, Paul and me . . . and Jory too, and Henny. . . . Don't break our hearts, Carrie, hang on long enough to let the doctors help you. Don't give up. Jory wants his aunt back; every day he asks where you are. What am I going to tell him—that you didn't care enough to live?"

"Jory don't need me," she said in the manner she'd spoken when she was a child. "Jory's got lots of people besides me to love and care for him . . . but Cory, he's waiting for me, Cathy. I can see him right now. Look over there behind your shoulder; he's standing next to Daddy and they want me more than anyone here."

"Carrie, don't!"

"It's nice where I'm going, Cathy, flowers everywhere, and beautiful birds, and I can feel myself growing taller. . . . Look, I'm almost as tall as Momma, like I always wanted to be. And when I get there nobody's ever gonna say again I got eyes big and scary as an owl's. Nobody will ever call me 'dwarf' again, and tell me to use a stretching machine . . . 'cause I'm just as tall as I want to be."

Her weak and trembling voice faded away. Her eyes rolled heavenward and stayed open without blinking. Her lips stayed parted, as if she had something else to tell me. *Dear God, she was dead!*

Momma had started all of this. Momma who got out of everything scot-free! Scar-free! And rich, rich, rich! All she had to do was shed a few tears of self-pity after she went home. That's when I screamed! I know I screamed. I wailed and wanted to rip the hair from my head and tear the skin from my face—for I looked too much like that woman who had to pay, pay, pay . . . and then pay some more!

On a hot August day we buried Carrie in the Sheffield family plot, a few miles outside the city limits of Clairmont. No rain this time. No snow on the ground. Now death had claimed every season but winter and left only that cold, blustery weather for me to rejoice in. We covered Carrie over with the crimson flowers she so loved, and purple ones too. The sun above was a rich saffron color, almost orange before it turned to vermilion as it sank to the horizon and turned the heavens rosy-red.

My thoughts were like the dry leaves blowing in the strong wind of hate as I sat on and on and on, though the marble bench beneath me was hard and uncomfortable. I made those dry leaves, after I gathered them together and twisted them, into a cruel witch's stick, a thing to stir up a neglected brew of revenge!

Out of the four Dresden dolls only two were left. And *one*

would do nothing. He had taken an oath to do what he could to preserve life and keep alive even those who didn't deserve to live.

I was loath to leave Carrie alone in the night, the first one she'd spend in the ground. I had to spend this one night with her and comfort her in some unknown way. I threw a glance at where Julia and Scotty lay asleep too, near Paul's parents, and an older brother who had died even before Amanda was born. I wondered what we, the Foxworths, were doing in the Sheffield family plot? What meaning was there to any of this?

If Alex hadn't come into Carrie's life when he did and given her love, would she have been better off? If Carrie hadn't spied Momma on the street and raced to catch up with her, happy enough to take hold of her hand and call her Momma, would that have made a difference? It must have made *all* the difference! It must have! Straight from her mother's denial she had gone to purchase rat poison because she didn't feel fit to live, not when even her mother could deny her. And the poison on her doughnuts hadn't been just a trace, but heavily laced—pure arsenic!

Someone spoke my name softly. Someone reached with tenderness to lift me up by my elbows. With his arm about my waist, supporting me, he led me from the cemetery where I would have stayed until dawn to see the sun come up. "No, darling," said Chris. "Carrie doesn't need you now. But others do. Cathy, you must forget the past and your plans for revenge. I see the look on your face and read your mind. I'll share with you my secret for finding peace. I've tried to give it to you before but you refuse to listen. *Now this time listen and believe!* Do as I do and force yourself to forget everything that gives you pain, and remember only what gives you joy. It is the whole secret to happy living, Cathy. Forgetting and forgiving."

Bitter, bleak eyes I turned upon him and scornfully I said, "You are indeed very good at forgiving, Christopher—but at forgetting, now that is another matter."

He flushed as red as the dying sun. "Cathy, please! Isn't forgiving the better half? I only remember the sweeter part."

"No! No!" But I clung to him as one who approaches hell holds tight to salvation.

Though I'm not sure, I thought I saw a woman dressed in black, with her head and face covered by a black veil, duck behind a tree as we approached the road and the parked car. Hiding so we wouldn't see her. But I caught a glimpse, enough to reveal the rope of lustrous pearls she wore. Pearls that were there for a thin white hand to lift and nervously, out of long habit, twist and untwist into a knot.

Only one woman I knew did that—and she was the perfect one to wear black, and should run to hide! *Forever hide!*

Color all her days black! Every last one!

I'd see to it that all her remaining days on earth were black. Blacker than the tar put on my hair. Blacker than anything in that locked room and in the darkest shadows in the attic that had been given to us when we were fearful and young and needing so much to be loved enough. Blacker than the deepest pit in hell.

I'd waited long enough to deliver what I must. Long enough. And even with Chris here to try and stop me—even he wouldn't be enough to prevent what I had to do!

PART FIVE

The Time for Vengeance

The untimely death of Carrie left a hole in the lives of all of us who loved her. Now the little porcelain dolls were mine to cherish and keep. Chris went away to be a resident at the University of Virginia just so he wouldn't be too far from me.

"Stay, Catherine," pleaded Paul when I told him I was going back to my place in the mountains to pick up my life as dance instructor. "Don't go and leave me alone again! Jory needs a father; I need a wife; he needs a man to emulate. I'm sick to death of having you to love only once in a while."

"Later," I said with hard determination, backing off from his arms. "I'll come to you one day and we will be married, but I have some unfinished business to attend to first."

Soon I was back into my routine of work, not far from where the Foxworths lived in their mansion. I settled down to scheming. Jory was a problem now that I didn't have Carrie. He grew tired at the dance school and wanted to play with children his own age. I enrolled him in a special preschool and hired a maid to help out with the housework and stay with

Jory when I wasn't there. At night I went on the prowl, looking, of course, for one particular man. So far he had eluded
me, but sooner or later fate would see that we met—God help
you then, Momma!

The local newspaper gave Bartholomew Winslow a big
write-up when he opened his second law office in Hillendale
while his junior partner ran his first office in Greenglenna.
Two offices, I thought. What money couldn't buy! I didn't
plan or, being so bold as to approach him directly; ours would
be an "accidental" confrontation. Leaving Jory in the care of
Emma Lindstrom, as he played in our fenced-in yard with
two other children, I drove my car to the woods that weren't
so far from Foxworth Hall.

Bart Winslow was a celebrity of sorts, with all the details
of his life explored, so I knew from the news story that it was
his habit to jog a few miles each day before breakfast. Indeed,
he would need a strong heart for what was coming up in his
near future. For days on end I jogged myself, using dirt paths
that twisted and turned, cluttered by dead, dry and crackling
leaves. It was September and Carrie had been dead a month.
Sad thoughts while I sniffed the pungent aroma of wood-fires
burning and heard the noise of wood being chopped. Sounds
and smells Carrie should be enjoying—they'll pay, Carrie! I'll
make them pay, and somehow I forgot, Bart Winslow didn't
have anything to do with it. Not him, only *her*! How quickly
time passed and I was getting nowhere! Where was he? I
couldn't prowl the singles' bars; that was too commonplace
and too obvious. When we met, and someday we had to, he'd
say something that was a cliché, or I would, and that would
be the beginning—or the ending I had in mind since the first
time I laid eyes on Bartholomew Winslow dancing with my
mother on Christmas night.

As contrary as life would be, I didn't meet him jogging.
One Saturday noon I sat in a sleazy café and suddenly Bart
Winslow sauntered in the door! He glanced around, spied me

seated by the windows and came toward me in his three-piece
lawyer's suit that must have cost a fortune. With attaché case
in hand, he actually swaggered! His smile was wide, his lean,
tanned face slightly sinister—or maybe it was me scaring
myself.

"We-ll," he drawled, "as I live and breathe, if it isn't
Catherine Dahl, the very woman I've been hoping to run into
for months." He set down his attaché case, sat across from me
without my invitation, then leaned on his elbows to peer into
my eyes with intense interest. "Where the hell have you hidden yourself?" he asked, using his foot to draw his case nearer
and guard it.

"I haven't hidden myself," I said, feeling nervous and
hoping it wouldn't show.

He laughed as his dark eyes scanned over my tight sweater
and skirt and what he could see of my foot that nervously
swung. Then his face grew solemn. "I read in the newspaper
about your sister's death. I am very sorry. It always hurts to
read of someone so young dying. If it's not too personal, may
I ask what killed her? A disease? An accident?"

My eyes opened wide. What killed her? Oh, I could write
a book about that!

"Why don't you ask your wife what killed my sister?" I
said stiffly.

He appeared startled, then shot out, "How can she know
when she doesn't know you or your sister? Yet, I saw her with
the clipping cut from the obituary page, and she was crying
when I snatched it from her hand. I demanded an explanation; she got up and ran upstairs. She still refuses to answer
my questions. Just who the hell are you, anyway?"

I bit again into my ham, tomato and lettuce sandwich and
chewed irritatingly slowly just to watch his vexation. "Why
not ask *her*?" I said again.

"I do hate people who answer questions with questions,"
he snapped, then motioned to a red-haired waitress who

hovered nearby and gave her his order to have the same as I. "Now," he said, scooting his chair forward. "Some time ago I came to your dance studio and showed you those blackmail letters you keep writing to my wife." He reached into his pocket and pulled out three I'd written years ago. From the dog-eared look of them, and the many stamps and cancellations, they had followed her about the world to end up again in my hands, with him almost shouting again, "Who the hell are you?"

I smiled to charm him. My mother's smile. I tilted my head as she did hers and fluttered one hand up to play with my simulated pearls. "Do you really have to ask—can't you guess?"

"Don't play coy with me! Who are you really? What is your relationship to my wife? I know you look like her, same hair, same eyes, and even some of your mannerisms are the same. You must be some kind of relative . . . ?"

"Yes. You could say that."

"Then why haven't I met you before? A niece, cousin?" He had a strong animal magnetism that almost frightened me from playing the kind of game I had in mind. This was no adolescent boy who would be timidly impressed with a former ballerina. His dark appeal was strong, almost overwhelming me. Oh, what a wild lover he'd make. I could drown in his eyes and, making love with him, I'd be forever lost to any other man. He was too confidently masculine, too assured. He could smile and be at ease while I fidgeted and longed to escape before he led me down the trail I thought I'd wanted up until this very moment.

"Come," he said, reaching to forcefully restrain my departure when I rose to go, "stop looking frightened and play the game you've had in mind for some time." He picked up the letters and held them before my eyes. I looked away, unhappy with myself. "Don't turn away your eyes. Five or six of your letters came while my wife and I were in Europe, and she'd see them and paled. She'd swallow nervously—as you are swallowing nervously now. Her hand would lift to play with her necklace, just as you are playing with your beads now. Twice I saw her write on the envelope, 'Address unknown.' Then one day I collected the mail and I found these three letters you'd written to her. I opened them. I read them." He paused, leaned forward so his lips were only inches from mine. His voice came hard and cold and fully in control of any savagery he might feel. "What right have you to try and blackmail my wife?"

I'm sure the color left my cheeks. I know I felt sick and weak and wanted to flee this place and him. I imagined I heard Chris's voice saying, *Let the past rest in peace. Let it go, Cathy. God in his own way will eventually work the vengeance you want. In his own way, at his own speed He will take the responsibility from your shoulders.*

Here was my chance to spill it forth—*all of it!* Let him know just what kind of woman he'd married! Why couldn't my lips part and my tongue speak the truth? "Why don't you ask your wife who I am? Why come to me when she has *all* the answers?"

He leaned back against the gaudy, bright orange, plastic-covered chair and took out a silver cigarette case with his monogram in diamonds. That just had to be a gift to him from my mother—it looked like her. He offered that case to me. I shook my head. He tapped the loose tobacco from one end and then lit the other with a silver lighter with diamonds too. All the while his dark, narrowed eyes held mine and, like a fly caught in a web of my own making, I waited to be pounced upon.

"Each letter you write says you need desperately a million dollars," he said in a flat monotone, then blew smoke directly into my face. I coughed and fanned the air. All around the walls bore signs reading NO SMOKING. "Why do you need a million?"

I watched the smoke; it circled and came directly to me, wreathed about my head and neck. "Look," I said, struggling to regain my control, "you know my husband died. I was expecting his child and I was inundated with bills I couldn't pay, and even after the insurance paid off, with *some* assistance from you, still I'm going under. My dance school is in the red. I have a child to support, and I need things for him, to save for his college education, and your wife has so many millions. I thought she could part with just one."

His smile was faint, cynical. He blew smoke rings to make me dodge and cough again. "Why would an intelligent woman like you presume to think my wife would be so generous as to turn over one dime to a relative she doesn't even claim?"

"Ask her why!"

"I have asked her. I took your letters and pushed them in her face and demanded to know what it was all about. A dozen times I've asked just who you are and how you are connected to her. Each time she says she doesn't know you, except as a ballerina she's seen dance. This time I want straight answers from you." To assure that I didn't turn my face and hide my eyes, he reached forward to firmly grip my chin so I couldn't turn my head. *"Who the hell are you?* How are you connected to my wife? Why should you think she would pay you blackmail money? Why should your letters send her running upstairs to take out a picture album she keeps locked in her desk drawer or in a safe? An album she quickly hides and locks away whenever I come into the room."

"She took the album—the blue album with a gold eagle on the leather cover?" I whispered, shocked that she would do that.

"Everywhere we go the blue album goes with her in one of her locked trunks." His dark eyes narrowed dangerously. "You described that blue and gold album exactly, though it's old and worn shabby now. While my wife looks in a picture album, my mother-in-law reads her Bible to rags. Sometimes

I catch my wife crying over the photographs that blue album holds, which I presume are pictures of her first husband."

I sighed heavily and closed my eyes. *I didn't want to know she cried!*

"Answer me, Cathy. *Who are you?*" I felt he would grip my chin and hold me there throughout eternity if I didn't speak up and say something, and for some stupid reason I lied. "Henrietta Beech was your wife's half-sister. You see, Malcolm Foxworth had an extramarital affair, and three children were the result. I am one. Your wife is my half-aunt."

"Ahhh," he sighed, releasing my chin and leaning back in his chair, as if satisfied I was telling the truth. "Malcolm had an affair with Henrietta Beech who gave him three illegitimate children. What extraordinary information." He laughed mockingly. "I never thought the old devil had it in him, especially after that heart attack soon after my wife married the first time. Gives a man inspiration to know that." He sobered then to give me a long and searching look. "Where is your mother now? I'd like to see and talk to her."

"Dead," I said, hiding my hands under the table and keeping my fingers crossed like a superstitious, silly child. "She's been dead a long, long time."

"Okay. I get the picture. Three young, illegitimate Foxworth children hoping to cash in on their bloodline by blackmailing my wife—right?"

"Wrong! It was only me. Not my brother or my sister. I only want what is due us! At the time I wrote those letters I was in a desperate situation, and even now I'm not much better off. The hundred thousand the insurance paid didn't go very far. My husband had run up huge bills and we were behind in our rent and car payments; plus I owed hospital bills for him, the money for his funeral, and then the costs of having my baby. I could go on all night telling you my dance school's problems and how I was tricked into believing it was a profitable, going concern."

"And it's not?"

"Not when it consists of so many little rich girls who take off and go on vacations two or three times a year and aren't really serious about dancing anyway. All they want to do is look pretty and feel graceful. If I had one really good student it would be worth all my efforts. But I don't have one, not one."

He drummed his strong fingertips on the tablecloth, looking deeply reflective. Next he had a cigarette lit again, not as if he truly enjoyed smoking, but more as if he had to have something to keep his restless fingers busy. He inhaled deeply, then looked me straight in the eyes. "I'm going to speak very frankly to you, Catherine Dahl. First, I don't know if you are lying or telling the truth, but you do look like a member of the Foxworth clan. Second, I don't like you trying to blackmail my wife. Third, I don't like to see her unhappy, so much so that she cries. Fourth, I happen to be very much in love with her, though there are times, I admit, I'd like to choke the past from her throat. She never speaks of it; she is full of secrets my ears will never hear. And one great big secret I've never heard before is that Malcolm Neal Foxworth, the good, pious, saintly gentleman, had a love affair after he had heart trouble. Now before his heart trouble, I happen to know he had at least one, possibly, but no more."

Oh! He knew more than I. I had shot an arrow into the sky, not knowing it would hit a bulls-eye!

Bart Winslow glanced about the café. Families were coming in to dine early, and I suppose he feared someone might recognize him and report back to his wife, my mother.

"C'mon, Cathy, let's get out of here," he urged, getting to his feet and reaching to pull me on mine. "You can invite me to have a drink in your home, then we can sit and talk and you can tell me everything in more detail."

Twilight came like a quickly dropped shade to the mountains—suddenly it was evening—and we'd been hours in that café. We were on the sidewalk when he held my cardigan sweater for my arms to fill the sleeves, though the air was so brisk I needed a jacket or coat.

"Your home, where is it?"

I told him and he looked disconcerted. "We'd better not go there . . . too many people might see me go inside." (He didn't know then, of course, I had chosen that cottage mainly because it backed up to a wooded area, and there was plenty of privacy for a man to come and go on the sly.) "My face is in the newspapers so often," he continued, "I'm sure your neighbors would see me. Could you call your babysitter and have her stay on awhile longer?"

I did just that, speaking first to Emma Lindstrom, and then to Jory, telling him to be a good boy until Mommy was home again.

Bart's car was sleek and black, a Mercedes. It purred along like one of Julian's sleek luxury cars, so heavy it didn't rattle or clank, and firmly it gripped the curved mountain roads. "Where are you taking me, Mr. Winslow?"

"To a place where we can talk and no one will see us or hear us." He looked my way and grinned. "You've been studying my profile. How do I rate?"

A hot rush of blood heated my face. Knowing I was blushing made me blush again, so then I felt damp. My life was full of handsome men, but this man was far different from any I had known. A rakish, bandit type of man who was filling me with alarm signals—go slow with this one! My intuitiveness warned as I studied his face and took note. Everything, his expensive, beautifully fitted suit, shouted that he should be as determined as I was in getting what he wanted, when he wanted.

"Well-ll," I drawled to make a mockery of this, "your looks tell me to run fast and lock the door behind me!"

Wickedly he grinned again, seemingly satisfied. "So, you find me exciting and a bit dangerous. Nice. To be handsome but boring would be worse than being ugly and charming, wouldn't it?"

"I wouldn't know. If a man is charming and intelligent enough, I often forget how he actually looks and think he's handsome regardless."

"Then you must be easily pleased."

I shifted my eyes and sat up primly. "Truthfully, Mr. Winslow—"

"Bart."

"Truthfully, Bart, I am very difficult to please. I'm inclined to put men up on a pedestal and think of them as perfect. As soon as I find out they have feet of clay, I fall out of love, become indifferent."

"Not many women know themselves so well," he mused. "Most go around never knowing what they are beneath the facade. At least I know where I stand—a sex symbol not on a pedestal."

Nooo! I'd never put *him* on a pedestal. I knew him for what he was, a womanizer, a skirt-chaser, wind and fire, enough to drive a jealous wife crazy! Certainly my mother had never bought that sex manual to instruct him how to or when to and where to! He'd know everything. Abruptly he pulled his car to a stop, then turned to meet my gaze. Even in the darkness the whites of his dark eyes shone. Too virile, too vibrant for a man who should be showing signs of aging. He was eight years younger than my mother. That made him forty years old, a man's most attractive time, his most vulnerable time, his time to think youth would soon be over. He'd have to make his new conquests now, before the sweet and fleeting bird of youth had flown away and taken with it all the young and pretty girls that could have been his. And he must be tired of the wife he knew so well, though he professed to love her. Why then were his eyes gleaming, challenging me? *Oh, Momma, wherever you are, you should be down on your knees praying! For I'm not going to show you mercy, no more than you showed us!*

Yet as I sat there summing him up I realized he was no self-sacrificing, quiet man like Paul. This one wouldn't need seducing. He'd do that himself, staccato time. He'd stalk like a black panther until he had what he wanted, and then he'd walk out and leave me and it would be all over. He was not going to give up his chance to inherit millions and the pleasures millions gave for some chance mistress who came his way. Red lights were flashing behind my eyes . . . go easy . . . do it right, for there's danger if you do it wrong.

As I measured him, he was measuring me in just about the same way. Did I remind him too much of his wife so there would be no real difference? Or was my likeness to her an advantage? After all, didn't men always fall over and over again for the same type?

"Beautiful night," he said. "This is my favorite season. Fall is so passionate, even more than spring. Come walk with me, Cathy. This place puts me in a strange, melancholy mood, as if I've got to run fast to catch up with the best thing in my life, which up until now has always eluded me."

"You sound poetic," I said as we left his car and he caught hold of my hand. We began to stroll, with him deftly guiding me—would you believe it—alongside a railroad track in the country! It seemed so familiar. Yet it couldn't be, could it? Not the same railroad track that had taken us as children to Foxworth Hall fifteen years ago when I was twelve!

"Bart, I don't know about you, but I've got the weirdest feeling that I have walked this path with you before, on some other night before this."

"Déjà vu," he said. "I have that same feeling. As if once you and I were deeply in love, and we walked through those woods over there. We sat on that green bench beside these train tracks. I was compelled to bring you here, even when I didn't know where it was I was driving to."

This forced me to stare up into his face to see if he could be serious. From his bemused and slightly discomforted look, I believe he was surprising himself. "I like to ponder all things considered impossible or implausible," I said. "I want everything impossible to become possible, and everything implausible to reverse and become reality. Then when everything is explainable I want new mysteries to confront me so I always have something inexplicable to think about."

"You are a romantic."

"Aren't you?"

"I don't know. I used to be when I was a boy." "What made you change?"

"You can't stay a boy with romantic notions when you go to law school and you are faced with the harsh realities of murder, rape, robbery, corruption. You have professors pounding dogmatic ideas into your head to drive out the romance. You go into law fresh and young, and you come out tough and hard, and you know every step of the way ahead you've got to fight and fight hard to be any good. Soon enough you learn you are not the best, and the competition is astounding."

He turned to smile with a great deal of winsome charm. "I think, though, you and I have much in common, Catherine Dahl. I too had that need of the mysterious, the need to be confounded, and the need to have someone to worship. So I fell in love with an heiress to millions, but those millions she wanted to inherit got in my way. They put me off and scared me. I knew everyone would think I was marrying her just for her money. I think she thought it too, until I convinced her otherwise. I fell for her hard, before I knew who she was. In fact I used to think she was like you."

"How could you think that?" I asked, all tight inside from hearing his revelations.

"Because she *was* like you, Cathy, for a while. But then she inherited millions, and in great orgies of shopping she'd buy everything her heart desired. Soon there was nothing to wish for at all—but a baby. And she couldn't have a baby. You can't imagine all the time we spent in front of shops that sold infant clothes, toys and furniture. I married her knowing we couldn't have children and I thought I didn't care. Soon I began to care too much. Those infant shops held a fascination for me too."

The faint path we followed led straight to the green bench stretched between two of the four rickety old green posts that supported a rusty tin roof. There we sat in the cold mountain air, with the moon bright, the stars flickering on and off; bugs were humming, just as my blood was singing.

"This used to be a mail pick-up and drop-off station, Cathy." He lit another cigarette. "They don't run the trains by here anymore. The wealthy people who live nearby finally won their petition against the railroad company and put an end to trains that so inconsiderately blew their whistles at night and disturbed their rest. I was very fond of hearing the train whistles at night. But I was only twenty-seven, a bridegroom living in Foxworth Hall. I'd lie on my bed near my wife, with a swan overhead—can you believe that? She would sleep with her head on my shoulder or we'd hold hands all through the night. She took pills so she'd sleep soundly. Too soundly, for she never heard the beautiful music coming from overhead. It puzzled me so—and she said, when I told her, it was my imagination. Then one day it stopped, and I guessed she was right, it was only my imagination. When the music ended I missed it. I longed to hear it again. The music had given that old dry house some enchantment. I used to fall asleep and dream of a lovely young girl who danced overhead. I thought I was dreaming of my wife when she was young. She told me that often, as a way of punishment, her parents would send her into the attic schoolroom and force her to stay there all day, even in the summers when the temperature up there must have been over a hundred degrees. And they sent her up there in the winters too—she said it was frigidly cold and her fingers would turn blue. She said she spent her time crouched on the floor near the window, crying because she was missing out on some fun thing her parents considered wicked."

"Did you ever go and take a look in the attic?"

"No. I wanted to, but the double doors at the top of the stairs were always locked. And besides, all attics are alike; see one and you've seen them all." He flashed me a wicked smile. "And now that I've revealed so much about myself—tell me about you. Where were you born? Where did you go to school? What made you take up dancing—and why haven't you ever attended one of those balls the Foxworths throw on Christmas night?"

I sweated, though I was cold. "Why should I tell you everything about myself. Just because you sat there and revealed a *little* about yourself? You didn't tell me anything of real importance. Where were *you* born? What made *you* decide to become an attorney? How did you meet your wife? Was it in the summer, the winter, what year? Did you know she'd been married before, or did she tell you only after you were married?"

"Nosy little thing, aren't you? What difference does it make where I was born. I haven't led an exciting life like you have. I was born in the nothing little town called Greenglenna, South Carolina. The Civil War ended the prosperous days of my ancestors, and we went steadily downhill, as did all the friends of the family. But it's an old story, told so many times. Then I married a Foxworth lady and prosperity reigned again in the South. My wife took my ancestral home and practically had it reconstructed, and refurbished, and spent more than if she had bought a new place. And what was I doing during all of this? A top grad from Harvard running around the world with his wife. I've done very little with my education; I've become a social butterfly. I've had a few court cases and I helped you with your difficulties. And, by the way, you never paid the fee I had in mind."

"I mailed you a check for two hundred dollars!" I objected hotly. "If that wasn't enough, please don't tell me now; I don't have another two hundred to give away."

"Have I mentioned money? Money means little to me now that I have so much of it at my disposal. In your special case I had another kind of fee in mind."

"Oh, come off it, Bart Winslow! You've brought me way out into the country. Now do you want to make love on the grass? Is it your lifelong ambition to make love to a former ballerina? I don't give sex away and I don't pay any bills that way. And what's so attractive about you, a lap dog for a pampered, spoiled, rich woman who can buy anything she wants—including a much younger husband! Why, it's a wonder she didn't put a ring through your nose to lead you around and make you sit up and beg!"

He seized me then hard and ruthlessly, then pressed his lips down on mine with a savagery that hurt! I fought him off with my fists, battering his arms as I tried to twist my head from beneath his, but whichever way my head went, right or left, up or down, he kept his kiss, demanding my lips to separate and yield to his tongue! Then, realizing I couldn't escape the arms of steel he banded about me to mold my form to his, against my will, my arms stole up around his neck. My unruly fingers betrayed me and twined into his thick, dark hair, and that kiss lasted, and lasted, and lasted until both of us were hot and panting—and then he thrust me from him so cruelly I almost fell from the bench.

"Well, little Miss Muffet—what kind of lap dog do you call me now? Or are you Little Red Riding Hood who has just met the wolf?"

"Take me home!"

"I'll take you home—but not until I've enjoyed a little more of what you just gave." He lunged again to seize me, but I was up and running, running for his car, running to seize my purse so that when he got there I held my manicuring scissors ready to stab with.

He grinned, reached out and wrested them from me. "They would deliver a nasty scratch," he mocked. "But I don't like scratches except on my back. When I let you out you can have your little two-inch scissors back again."

In front of my cottage he handed me the scissors. "Now, do your worst. Cut out my eyes; stab me in the heart—you might as well. Your kiss has begun it, but I still demand my total payment."

Tiger by the Tail

Early on a Sunday morning a few days later I was warming up at the barre in my bedroom. My small son was earnestly trying to do as I did. It was sweet to watch him in the mirror I'd moved from the dresser over to the barre.

"Am I dancing?" asked Jory.

"Yes, Jory. *You are dancing!*"

"Am I good?"

"Yes, Jory. *You are wonderful!*"

He laughed and hugged my legs and looked up into my face with that ecstatic rapture only the very young can express—all the wonder of being alive was in his eyes, all the wonder of learning something new every day. "I love you, Mommy!" It was something we said to each other a dozen or more times each day. "Mary's got a daddy. Why don't I have a daddy?"

That really hurt. "You did have a daddy, Jory, but he went away to heaven. And maybe someday Mommy will find you a new daddy."

He smiled because he was pleased. Daddy's were big in his

world, for all the children in the nursery school had one . . . all but Jory.

Just then I heard the front door bang. A familiar voice called my name. Chris! He strode through the small house as I hurried toward him in my blue tights, leotards and *pointe* shoes. Our eyes met and locked. Without a word he held out his arms and I ran unhesitatingly into them, and though he sought my lips to kiss he found only my cheek. Jory was pulling on his gray flannel trousers, eager to be swept up in strong, manly arms. "How's my Jory?" asked Chris after he kissed both round, rosy cheeks. My son's eyes were huge as they stared at him. "Uncle Chris, are you my daddy?"

"No," he said gruffly, putting Jory again on his small feet, "but I sure wish I had a son like you." This made me shift around uncomfortably so he couldn't see my eyes, and then I asked what he was doing here when he should be attending his patients.

"Got the weekend off, so I thought I'd spend it with you; that is, if you'll let me." I nodded weakly, thinking of someone else who was likely to come this weekend. "I was as good as a resident can be and was rewarded and given a weekend without duty." He gave me one of his most winning smiles. "Have you heard from Paul?" I asked. "He doesn't come as often as he used to, and he doesn't write much either."

"He's away on another medical convention. I thought he always kept in touch with you."

He put just a little stress on the "you." "Chris, I'm worried about Paul. It isn't like him not to answer every letter I write."

He laughed and fell into a chair, then lifted Jory up on his lap. "Maybe, dear sister, you have finally met a man who can get over loving you."

Now I didn't know what to say or what to do with my legs and hands. I sat and stared down at the floor, feeling Chris's long, steady gaze trying to read my intentions. No sooner did I think that than he was asking, "Cathy, what are you doing here in the mountains? What are you planning? Is it your scheme to take Bart Winslow from our mother?"

My head jerked up. I met his narrowed blue eyes and felt the heat that sprang up from my heart. "Don't question me like I'm some ten-year-old without a brain. I do what I have to—just as you do."

"Sure, you do. I didn't have to ask, I know. It doesn't take a crystal ball to read you. I know what makes you tick and how your thoughts range—but leave Bart Winslow alone! He'll never leave her for you! She's got the millions and all you have is youth. There are thousands of younger women he can choose from—why should he choose you?"

I didn't say anything, just met his scowling look with my own confident smile, making him flush, then turn aside his face. I felt mean, cruel and ashamed. "Chris, let's not argue. Let's be friends and allies. You and I are all that's left out of four."

His blue eyes grew soft as they studied me. "I was only trying, as I am always trying." He looked around, then back to me. "I share a room with another resident at the hospital. It would be nice if I could live here with you and Jory. It would be like it used to be, just us."

What he said made me stiffen. "It would be a long drive for you every morning, and you couldn't be on immediate call."

He sighed. "I know—but how about the weekends? Every other weekend I have off-duty time—would that bug you too much?"

"Yes, it would bug me too much. I have a life of my own, Christopher."

I watched him bite down on his lower lip before he forced a smile. "Okay, have it your way . . . do what you must, and I hope to God you won't be sorry."

"Will you please drop the subject?" I smiled and went to him and hugged him close. "Be good. Take me as I am, obstinate as Carrie. Now, what would you like for lunch?"

"I haven't had breakfast yet."

"Then we'll eat brunch—and that can do for two meals." From then on the day went swiftly. On Sunday morning he came to the table ready for the cheese omelet he favored. Jory, thank God, would eat anything. Despite myself I thought of Chris as a father to Jory. It seemed so right to have him at the table, like it used to be . . . him and I playing at being parents. Doing the best we could, all we could, and we had been only children ourselves.

We ambled through the woods after breakfast, using all the trails I followed when I jogged. Jory rode on Chris's shoulder. We looked at the world that was just outside Foxworth Hall, all the places we hadn't been able to see when we were on the roof or locked away. Together we stood and stared at that huge mansion. "Is Momma in there?" he asked in a tight thick voice.

"No. I've heard she's down in Texas in one of those beauty spas for very wealthy women, trying to lose fifteen extra pounds."

Alerted, he swiveled his head. "Who told you that?"

"Who do you think?"

He shook his head violently, then lifted Jory down and set him on his feet. "Damn you for playing with him, Cathy! I've seen him. He's dangerous—leave him alone. Go back to Paul and marry him if you must have a man in your life. Let our mother live out her life in peace. You don't believe for one moment, do you, that she doesn't suffer? Do you think she can be happy knowing what she did? All the money in the world can't give her back what she's lost—and that is *us*! Let that be enough revenge."

"It isn't enough. I want to confront her in front of Bart with the truth. And you can stay one hundred years and get down on your knees and plead until your tongue falls out—I will still go ahead and do what I must!"

The time Chris stayed with me he slept in the room that had been Carrie's. We did very little talking, though his eyes followed my every movement. He looked drained, lost ... and, most of all, hurt. I wanted to tell him that when I'd finished what I had to do I'd go back to Paul and have a safe life with him, and Jory would have the father he needed, but I said nothing.

Mountain nights were cold, even in September when the days were warm still. In that attic we'd nearly melted from the sweltering heat, and I guess this was on both our minds as we sat before the guttering log fire on the night before Chris had to leave. My son had been in bed for hours when I rose, yawned, stretched wide my arms, then glanced at the clock on the mantel which read eleven. "It's time for bed, Chris. Especially for you who has to get up so early tomorrow."

He followed me toward Jory's room without speaking and together we looked down on Jory, sleeping on his side, his dark curls damp and his face flushed. In his arms he cuddled a stuffed, plushy pony, much like the real one he said he had to have when he was four.

"When he's sleeping he looks more like you than Julian," whispered Chris. Paul had said the same thing.

"Good night, Christopher Doll," I said as we paused by the door of Carrie's room, "sleep tight, don't let the bed bugs bite."

What I said made his face contort in pain. He turned from me, opened the door to Carrie's room, then swung back to face me. "That's the way we used to say good night when we slept in the same room," he said, then he turned and closed the door behind him.

Chris was gone by the time I got up at seven o'clock. I cried a little. Jory stared at me with widened, surprised eyes. "Mommy ... ?" he asked fearfully.

"It's all right. Mommy just misses your uncle Chris. And Mommy is not going to work today." No, why should I? Only three students were due and I could teach them tomorrow when the class would be full.

My plans were moving too slowly. To speed them up I asked Emma to come and stay with Jory while I jogged through the woods. "I won't be gone longer than an hour. Let him play outside until lunchtime, and by then I'll be back."

Dressed in a bright blue jogging outfit trimmed with white, I set off down the dirt trails. This time I used a right fork I'd never tried before and into a denser pine forest I ran. The trail was faint and jaggedly crooked, so I had to keep a keen eye on the ground for tree roots that might trip me up. The mountain trees that grew between the pines were a brilliant blaze of fall colors, like fire against the emerald green of the pines, firs and spruces. And it was, as I'd told myself long ago, the year's last passionate love affair before it grew old and died from the frosty bite of winter.

Someone was jogging behind me. I didn't turn to look. The crispy crackle of the dead leaves pleased my ears, so I ran faster, faster, letting the wind take my loose hair just as I let the beauty of the day take my grief, remorse, shame and guilt and make them transparent shadows that didn't hold up beneath the sun.

"Cathy, hold up!" called a man's strong voice. "You run too fast!"

It was Bart Winslow, of course. As it had to be sooner or later. Fate couldn't always outwit me, and my mother couldn't always win. I threw a glance over my shoulder, smiling to see him panting as he ran in his stylish jogging costume of maple-sugar tan, trimmed with bands of orange and yellow knit at the cuffs, neck and waistband. Two vertical lines of yellow and orange ran down the sides of the loose pants. Just what a local runner should wear when on the prowl.

"Hello, Mr. Winslow," I called back as I speeded up. "A man who can't catch a woman *is no man at all!*"

He took the challenge and put more speed into his long

legs and I really had to put out to keep ahead! I flew, my long hair bannering behind. Squirrels on the ground scrounging around for nuts had to scamper to get out of my way. I laughed with the power I felt, then threw out my arms and pirouetted, feeling I was on stage playing out the best role of my life. Then from nowhere a knobby tree root caught beneath the toe of my dirty sneaker and down I fell, flat on my face. Luckily, the dead leaves cushioned me.

In a flash I was up and running again, but my fall had given Bart the chance to draw nearer. Panting, gasping, clearly indicating he didn't have nearly the stamina I had, despite the advantage of his longer legs, he cried out again, "Stop running, Cathy! Have mercy! This is killing me! There are other ways I can prove my manhood!"

I had no mercy! It was catch me if you can, or else I'd never be taken. I shouted this back to him and ran on, rejoicing in my powerful dancer's legs, my supple, long muscles and all that ballet training had done to make me feel a blue streak of light.

No sooner did this self-conceit flash through my mind than my stupid knee suddenly gave way and down I went again, on my face in the dead leaves. And this time I was hurt, really hurt. Had I broken a bone? Sprained an ankle, torn a ligament—again?

In a few moments Bart was beside me, down on his knees, rolling me over so he could see my face before he asked with a great deal of concern, "Are you hurt? You look so pale—what's paining?"

I wanted to say of course I was all right, for dancers knew how to fall, except when they didn't know they were going to fall—and why was my knee aching so badly? I stared down at it, feeling betrayed by a knee that was always the one to foul me up and hurt me in more than one way. "It was my stupid knee. If I bump my elbow on the shower door, my right knee hurts. When I have a headache, my knee hurts along with it to keep it company. Once I had a tooth filled, and the dentist was careless enough to let the drill slip and cut my gum, and my right knee shot right out and kicked him in the stomach."

"You're kidding."

"I'm serious—don't you have anything peculiar about your physical makeup?"

"Nothing I'm going to speak of." He smiled and the devil made his dark eyes sparkle, then he assisted me to my feet and felt my knee as if he knew what he was doing. "Seems a good, functional knee to me."

"How would you know?"

"My knees are functionally good, so I know one when I feel one—but if I could see the knee I could tell more."

"Go home and look at your wife's functional knee."

"Why are you being so hateful to me?" He narrowed his eyes. "Here I was, delighted to see you again, and you act so antagonistic."

"Pain always makes me antagonistic—are you any different?"

"I'm sweet and humble when I'm suffering, which isn't often. You get more attention that way—and remember you threw down the challenge, not me."

"You didn't have to accept it. You could have gone along your merry way and let me go along mine."

"Now we're arguing," he said, disappointed. "You want to fight when I want to be friendly. Be nice to me. Say you're glad to see me. Tell me how much better looking I've grown since you saw me last, and how exciting you find me. Even if I don't run like the wind I have my own bag of tricks."

"I'll bet you do."

"My wife is still in that beauty spa and I've been all by my lonesome for long, long months, bored to death by living with an old lady who can't talk and can't walk, but manages to scowl every time she sees me. One evening I was just sitting before the fire, wishing someone around here would commit murder so I'd have an interesting case for a change. It's damn frustrating to be an attorney and be surrounded by nothing but happy, normal people with no suppressed emotions to erupt suddenly."

"Congratulations, Bart! Before you stands someone full of aggressive resentment and mean, hateful spite seeking revenge that will erupt—you can count on that!"

He thought I was joking, playing a cat and mouse, man and woman game, and willingly he rose to that challenge too, not at all suspicious of my real purpose. He looked me over good, stripping off my sapphire jogging suit with the sensual eyes of a man starving for what I could give. "Why did you come to live up here near me?"

I laughed. "Arrogant, aren't you? I came to take over a dance school."

"Sure you did. . . . There's New York and your home town, wherever that is, and you come here—to enjoy the winter sports as well?" His eyes insinuated the kind of indoor winter sport he had in mind, if I didn't.

"Yes, I do like all kinds of sports, inside and outside," I said innocently.

Confidently he chuckled, assuming as all conceited men do that already he'd scored a point in the only intimate game a man really wanted to play with women.

"That old lady who can't talk, does she get around at all?" I asked.

"A little. She's my wife's mother. She speaks but her words come out jumbled and unintelligible to anyone but my wife."

"You leave her there all alone—is that safe?"

"She's not alone. There's a private duty nurse there with her all the time, and a staff of servants." He frowned as if he didn't like my questions, but I persisted. "Why stay there at all then, why not go and have fun while the cat's away?"

"You do have a shrewish way about you. Though I've never cared much for my mother-in-law, as she is now I feel sorry for her. And human nature being what it is, I don't trust servants to take proper care of her without a family member in the house to keep check on what's done to keep her comfortable.

She's helpless and can't rise from a chair without assistance, or get out of bed unless she's lifted out. So, until my wife is home again, I'm in charge to see that Mrs. Malcolm Foxworth is not abused or neglected or stolen from."

An overwhelming curiosity came over me then. I wanted to know her first name, for I'd never heard it. "Do you call her Mrs. Foxworth?"

He hadn't understood my interest in an old lady, and tried to turn the conversation elsewhere, but I persisted. "Olivia, that's what I call her!" he said shortly. "When I was first married, I tried not to speak to her at all, to try to forget she existed. Now I use her first name; I think it pleases her, but I can't be sure. Her face is of stone, fixed in one expression—icy."

I could picture her, unmoving but for her flintstone eyes of gray. He'd told me enough. Now I could make my plans— just as soon as I found out one more small thing. "Your wife, when is she due back?"

"Why should you know?"

"I too get lonely, Bart. I have only my small son after Emma, his babysitter, goes home. So . . . I thought maybe some evening you might like to have dinner with us. . . ."

"I'll come tonight," he said immediately, his dark eyes aglow.

"Our schedule revolves around my son. We eat at five-thirty in the summer, but now that the days are shorter five is dinner time."

"Great. Feed him at five and put him to bed. I'll be there at seven-thirty for cocktails. After dinner we can get to know each other better." He met my considering look with grave intensity, as a proper attorney should. Then, because of that look we held too long, simultaneously we both broke into laughter.

"And incidentally, Mr. Winslow, if you cut through the woods back of your place, you can reach mine and no one will see you unless, of course, you make a big show of yourself."

He put his palm up and nodded, as if we were both conspiring. "Discretion is the password, Miss Dahl."

The Spider and the Fly

Exactly at seven-thirty the door chimes sounded, punched by an impatient finger, forcing me to hurry lest he waken Jory who hadn't liked being put to bed at such an early hour.

If I had taken pains to look my best, so had Bart. He strode in as if he already owned the place and me. He left behind a drift of shaving lotion with a piney forest scent, and every hair on his head was carefully in place, making me wonder if he had a thinning spot—which I'd find out for myself sooner or later. I took his coat and hung it in the hall closet, then sashayed over to the bar where I busied myself as he sat down before the log fire I had burning (nothing had been over-looked; I even had soft music playing). By this time I knew enough about men and the ways of pleasing them best. There wasn't a man alive who wasn't charmed by a lovely woman bustling about, eager to wait on him, pamper and wine and dine him. "Name your weakness, Bart."

"Scotch."

"On the rocks?"

"Neat."

He watched my every movement, which was deliberately graceful and deft. Then, turning my back I mixed a fruity drink for myself, lacing it lightly with vodka. And with my two little stemmed goblets on a silver tray, I seductively ambled his way, leaning to give him an enticing view of my braless bosom. I sat across from him and swung one leg over the other to allow the long slit of my rose-colored dress to open and expose one leg from silver sandal midway to the hip. He couldn't take his eyes off it. "Sorry about the glasses," I said smoothly, well pleased with his expression, "I don't have room in this cottage to unpack everything I own. Most of my crystal is in storage and I have here only wine glasses and water goblets."

"Scotch is scotch no matter how it's served. And what in the world is that thing you're sipping?" By this time he'd shifted his gaze to the low V of my gown.

"Well, you take orange juice freshly squeezed, a dab of lemon juice too, a dash of vodka, bit of coconut oil, and drop in a cherry to dive after. I call it A Maiden's Delight."

After a few minutes of conversation, we drifted to the dining table, not so far from the fireplace, to eat by candlelight. Every so often he'd drop his fork, or spoon, or I would, and both of us would go for it, then laugh to see who was fastest. I was, every time. He was much too distracted to spot a missing fork or spoon when a neckline opened up so obligingly.

"This is delicious chicken," he said after demolishing five hours of hard labor in about ten minutes. "Usually I don't like chicken—where'd you learn to prepare this dish?"

I told him the truth. "A Russian dancer taught me, she was on tour over here, and we liked each other. She and her husband stayed with Julian and me, and we'd cook together whenever we weren't dancing or shopping or touring. It took four chickens to feed four people. Now you know the nasty truth about dancers; when it comes to eating we are not in the least dainty. That is, after a performance. Before we go on we have to eat very lightly."

He smiled and leaned across the small drop-leaf table.

Candlelight was in his eyes, sparkling them devilishly. "Cathy, tell me honestly why you came to live in this hick town and why you've got your heart set on me for a lover."

"You flatter yourself," I said in my most aloof manner, thinking I was very successful in appearing cool on the outside while inside I was a web of conflicting emotions. It was almost as if I had stage fright and was in the wings waiting to go on. And this was the most important performance of my life.

Then almost magically I felt I *was* on stage. I didn't have to think of how to act or what to say to charm him and make him forever mine. The script had been written a long time ago when I was fifteen and locked away upstairs. *Yes, Momma, it's first act time.* Expertly written by someone who knew him well from all the answers to her many questions. How could I fail?

After dinner I challenged Bart to a game of chess, and he accepted. I hurried to bring out the chessboard as soon as the table was cleared and the dishes were stacked in the sink. We began to set up the two armies of medieval warriors. "Exactly what I came for," he said, darting me a hard look, "to play chess! I showered, shaved and put on my best suit—so I could play chess!" Then he smiled, devastatingly winsome. "If I win—what reward?"

"A second game."

"When I win the second game—what reward?"

"If you win two games, then comes the playoff. And don't sit there and grin at me so smugly. I was taught this game by a master." Chris, of course.

"*After I* win the playoff—what reward?" he insisted. "You can go home and fall asleep very satisfied with yourself."

Very deliberately he picked up the chessboard with its hand carved ivory chessmen and put it on top of the refrigerator. He caught my hand and drew me into the living room. "Put on the music, ballerina," he said softly, "and let's dance. No fancy footwork, just something easy and romantic."

Popular music I could listen to only on the car radio to

cheer up a long, lonely drive, but when it came to spending my money on records I bought classical or ballet. However, today I'd made a special purchase of "The Night Was Made for Love." And, as we danced in the dimness of the living room with only the fire for light, I was reminded of the dry and dusty attic and Chris.

"Why are you crying, Cathy?" he asked softly, then turned my head so his cheek was smeared by my tears. "I don't know," I sobbed. And I didn't. . . .

"Of course you know," he said, rubbing his smooth cheek against mine as we danced on and on. "You are an intriguing combination, half child, half seductress, half angel."

I laughed short and bitterly. "That's what all men like to think about women. Little girls they have to take care of—when I know for a fact it is the male who is more boy than man."

"Then say hello to the first grown-up man in your life."

"You're not the first arrogant, opinionated man in my life!"

"But I'll be the last. The most important one—the one you will never forget." Oh! Why did he have to say that? Chris was right. I was over my head with this one.

"Cathy, did you really think you could blackmail my wife?"

"No, but I gave it a try. I'm a fool. I expect too much, then I'm angry because nothing ever works out the way I want. When I was young and full of hopes and aspirations, I didn't know I would get hurt so often. I think I'll get tough and won't ache again, then my fragile shell shatters, and again, symbolically, my blood is spilled with the tears I shed. I pull myself back together again, go on, convince myself there is a reason for everything, and at some point in my life it will be disclosed. And when I have what I want, I hope to God it stays long enough to let me know I have it, and it won't hurt when it goes, for I don't expect it to stay, not now. I'm like a doughnut, always being punched out in the middle, and constantly I go around searching for the missing piece, and on and on it goes, never ending, only beginning. . . ."

"You're not being honest with yourself," Bart said softly. "You know better than anyone where that missing piece is, or I wouldn't be here."

His voice was so low and seductive I put my head on his shoulder as we went on dancing. "You're wrong, Bart, I don't know why you're here. I don't know how to fill my days. When I'm teaching class and when I'm with my son, then I'm alive—but when he's in bed and I'm alone, I don't know what to do with myself. I know Jory needs a father, and when I think of his father I realize I've always managed to do the wrong thing. I've read my reviews that rave about the potential I had . . . but in my personal life I've made only mistakes, so what I accomplished professionally doesn't matter at all." I stopped moving my feet and sniffled, then tried to hide my face—but he tilted it upward, then dried my tears and held his handkerchief so I could blow my nose.

Then came the silence. The long, long silence. Our eyes met and clung and my heart started a faster thumping. "Your problems are all so simple, Cathy," he began, "all you need is someone like me, who needs someone like you. If Jory needs a father, then I need a son. See how simply all complicated matters are solved?"

Too simply, I thought, when he had a wife and I was discerning and cynical enough to know he couldn't possibly care for me enough. "You have a wife *you love*," I said bitterly. I shoved him away. I didn't want to get him too easily, but only after long and difficult struggles against my mother, and she wasn't here to know.

"Men are liars too," he said flatly, with some of the zest gone from his eyes. "I have a wife and occasionally we sleep together, but the fire has gone out. I don't know her. I don't think anyone knows her. She's a bundle of secrets, wound up tight, and she won't let me inside. It's gone on so long I don't care to be let in now. She can keep her secrets and her tears, and eat her way out of her anxieties and whatever it is that makes her wake up in the night and go and look in that damned blue album! Now she's overweight and she's written she's just had plastic surgery—face lift—and I won't know her when she comes back. As if I ever really knew her!"

I panicked inside—he had to care! How could I break up a marriage that was already coming apart? I needed to feel I'd accomplished this against overwhelming odds! "Go home!" I said, pushing at him. "Get out of my house! I don't know you well enough to even listen to your problems—and I don't believe you. I don't trust you!"

He laughed, mocking me, aroused by my puny efforts to push him away. His libido was fired. . . . It flamed in his eyes as he grabbed my upper arms and drew me hard against him. "Now you come off it! Look at the way you're dressed. You had me come here for a reason. So here I am, ready to be seduced. You seduced me the first time I saw you—and for the life of me it seems I've known you much longer than I actually have. Nobody plays games with me, then calls it a draw. You win or I win, but if we go to bed together we might wake up in the morning and find out we've both won."

Red lights flashed, *Stop! Resist! Fight!* I did none of those things. I beat on his chest with ineffectual small fists as he laughed and picked me up and threw me over his shoulder. With one hand he gripped both of my legs to keep them from kicking, and with the other he turned out the lamps. In the dark, with me still beating on his back, he carried me into my bedroom and threw me down on the coverlet. I scrambled to get up, but he came at me fast! There wasn't a chance to use the knee I had ready. He sensed my dancer's ability could defeat him so he lunged, caught me about the waist so we both tumbled to the floor! I opened my mouth to scream. He clamped his hand upon my open lips, then pinioned my arms with his iron strength and sat on the legs that tried to kick myself free.

"Cathy, my lovely seductress, you went to such a lot of trouble. You seduced me long ago, ballerina. Until the week before Christmas you are mine, and then my wife will be home—and I won't need you."

His hand eased away from my lips and I thought I would scream, but instead I bit out, "At least *I* didn't have to buy you with my father's millions!" That did it. He crushed his lips brutally hard down on mine before I realized what was happening. This wasn't the way I wanted it! I wanted to tempt him, set him on fire, make him chase me, and give in only after a long and arduous pursuit that my mother could watch and suffer through, knowing she could do nothing or I'd talk. And yet he was taking me heartlessly, more ruthless than Julian at his worst! Savagely he bore down on me. He squirmed and writhed to grind in, even as his hands ripped and tore off my clinging rose dress. All I had on then was pantyhose, and soon he had those pulled down so my silver slippers came off and stayed inside of them.

With his lips still crushed brutally hard on mine, he carried my resisting hand to his zipper and squeezed until my knuckles cracked. It was either tug it down or have my fingers broken! How he managed to wiggle out of his clothes, even as he held me naked beneath him, I'll never know. When he was naked, but for his socks, I kept on wiggling, writhing, squirming, butting and trying to scratch or bite while he kissed, fondled and explored. I had my chance to scream several times—but I too was breathing fast and hard, and jerking upward to force him off. But he took this as a welcoming arch of invitation. He entered, and had his too-quick satisfaction, then pulled out before I had any!

"Get out of here." I screamed. "I'm calling the police! I'll have you thrown in jail, charged with assault and rape!"

He laughed scornfully, chucked me under the chin playfully, then stood up to pull on his clothes. "Oh," he said, mocking me with an imitation of my own voice, "I am so frightened." Then his voice was deeply earnest. "You aren't happy, are you? It didn't work out the way you planned it, but don't you worry, tomorrow night I'll be back, and maybe then you can please me enough, so I'll feel like taking the time to please you."

"I've got a gun!" (I didn't.) "And if you dare set foot in this house again you're a dead man! Not that you are a man. You are more brute than human!"

"My wife often says the same thing," he said casually, zipping up his trousers shamelessly, without the decency to even turn his back. "But she likes it just the same, just as you did. Beef Wellington, you can have that tomorrow night, plus a tossed salad and a chocolate mousse for dessert. If you make me fat, we can burn off the calories in the most pleasant way possible—and I don't mean jogging." He grinned, saluted me, put one foot behind the other to turn smartly, military fashion, then paused at the doorway as I sat up and clutched the remnants of my gown to my breasts. "Same time tomorrow night, and I'll stay the night—that is, if you treat me right."

He left, and slammed the front door behind him. *Damn him to hell!* I began to cry, not from pity for myself. It was frustration so huge I could have torn him limb from limb! *Beef Wellington!* I'd lace it with arsenic!

A small timid sound came from outside my door. "Mommy . . . I'm scared. Are you cryin', Mommy?"

Hastily I pulled on a robe and called him in, then held him close in my arms. "Darling, darling, Mommy is all right. You had a bad dream. Mommy isn't crying . . . see?" I brushed away the tears—for I'd get even.

Three dozen red roses arrived while Jory and I were eating breakfast—the long-stemmed variety from the florist. A small white card read:

I'm sending you a big bouquet of roses,
One for every night you'll have my heart.

No name. And what the devil was I supposed to do with three dozen roses in a matchbox house? I couldn't send them to a children's ward; the hospital was miles and miles away. Jory decided what to do with them. "Oh, Mommy, how pretty! Uncle Paul's roses!"

For Jory I kept the roses instead of throwing them out, and in many vases I scattered them throughout the house. He was delighted, and when I took him with me to dancing school he told all my students roses were all over his home—even in the bathroom.

After lunch I drove Jory to the nursery school he so loved. It was a Montessori school that was inspiring him to want to learn by appealing to his senses. Already he could print his name, and he was only three! He was like Chris, I told myself, brilliant, handsome, talented—oh, my Jory had everything—but a father. From his bright blue eyes shone the quick intelligence of someone who would have a lifetime curiosity about everything. "Jory, I love you."

"I know that, Mommy." He waved good-bye as I drove off.

I was there to meet him when he came from his school, his small face flushed and troubled. "Mommy," he said as soon as he was beside me in the car, "Johnny Stoneman, he said his mommy slapped him when he touched her—there." And he shyly pointed at my breast. "You don't slap me when I touch you there."

"But you don't touch me there, not since you were a little baby and Mommy nursed you for a short while."

"Did you slap me then?" He looked so worried. "No, of course not. Babies are meant to suckle their mother's breasts—and I would never slap you for touching there—so if you want to try me, go ahead and touch." His small hand reached out tentatively while he watched my face to see if I'd be shocked. Oh, how fast the young learned all the taboos! And when he'd touched and God's lightning hadn't struck him down, he smiled, very relieved. "Oh, it's just a soft place." He'd made a pleasant discovery, and around my neck he threw his arms. "I love you too, Mommy. 'Cause you love me even when I'm bad."

"I'll always love you, Jory. And if you're bad sometimes, I'll try and understand." Yes, I was not going to be like my grandmother—nor my mother. I was going to be the perfect mother, and someday he'd have a father too. How was it that little children, such young ones, would already be talking of sin and being slapped for only touching? Was it because it was too high here, too near God's eyes? So that everyone lived under his spell, living afraid, acting righteous, while they committed every sin in the book? *Honor thy father and thy mother. Do unto others as thou wouldst have done unto you. An eye for an eye.*

Yes . . . *an eye for an eye*—that's why I was here.

I stopped to buy stamps before I reached my cottage, and left Jory dozing on the front seat. *He* was in the post office, which was no larger than my living room, buying stamps too. Charmingly he smiled at me, as if nothing untoward had happened between us the night before. He even had the nerve to follow me to my car so he could ask how I liked the roses. "Not your kind of roses," I snapped, then got primly into my car and slammed the door in his face. I left him staring after me without a smile—in fact, he looked rather miserable.

At five-thirty a special-delivery man brought a small package to our front door. It was certified so I had to sign for it. Inside a larger box was another box, and inside of that was a velvet jewelry case which I quickly opened while Jory watched, all eyes. On black velvet lay a single rose comprised of many diamonds. Also a card with a note that read, "Perhaps this kind of rose is more to your liking." I put the thing away as a trifle bought with *her* money, so it wasn't really from him—no more than the real roses.

He had the nerve to come that night at seven-thirty just as he'd said he would. Nevertheless, I readily let him in, then led him silently to the dining table with no to do about cocktails or other niceties. The table was set even more elaborately than the night before. I'd hauled out some boxes and done some unpacking, and on the table were my best lace mats and covered silver serving dishes. Neither of us had as yet spoken. All his forgive-me roses I'd gathered together and they were in the box near his plate. On his empty plate was the jeweler's velvet container with the diamond rose brooch inside. I sat to watch his expression as he put the jewelry box aside casually, and just as casually moved the flower box out of his way. He then took from his breast pocket a folded note that he handed to me. He'd written in a bold hand:

> I love you for reasons that have no beginning and no ending. I loved you even before I knew you, so that my love is without reason or design. Tell me to go and I will. But know first, if you turn me away, I will remember all my life that love that should have been ours, and when I'm stretched out cold, I will but love you better after death.

I glanced upward to meet his eyes squarely for the first time since he'd entered. "Your poetry, it somehow has a familiar ring, with a bit of strangeness."

"I composed it only a few minutes ago—how could it sound familiar?" He reached for the domed silver lid, ostensibly hiding the Beef Wellington underneath. "I warned you I was an attorney, not a poet—so that accounts for the strangeness. Poetry was not my best subject in school."

"Obviously." I was very interested in his expression. "Elizabeth Barrett Browning is sweet, but not your type."

"I did my best," he said with a wicked grin, meeting my eyes and challenging me before his gaze lowered to stare at the huge platter that held one hot dog and a small dab of cold canned beans. The disbelief in his eyes, his utter offended shock gave me so much satisfaction I almost liked him.

"You are now gazing upon Jory's favorite menu," I said, gloating. "It is exactly what he and I ate tonight for dinner, and since it was good enough for us, I thought it was good enough for you, so I saved some. Since I've already eaten, *all* of that is yours alone, and you may help yourself."

Scowling, he flashed me a burning, hard look, then savagely bit down into the hot dog which I'm sure had grown cold as the beans. But he gobbled down everything and drank his glass of milk, and for dessert I handed him a box of animal crackers. First he stared at the box in another expression of dumbfounded amazement, then ripped it open, seized up a lion and snapped off the head in one bite.

Only when he'd eaten every animal cracker and then picked up each crumb did he take the trouble to look at me with so much disapproval I should have shrunken to ant size. "I take it you are one of those despicable liberated women who refuses to do anything to please a man!"

"Wrong. I am liberated only with *some* men. Others I can worship, adore and wait on like a slave."

"You made me do what I did!" he objected strongly. "Do you think I planned it that way? I wanted us to find our relationship on an equal basis. Why did you wear that kind of dress?"

"It's the kind all chauvinist men prefer!"

"I am not a chauvinist—and I hate that kind of dress!"

"You like what I've got on better?" I sat up straighter to give him a better view of the old nappy sweater I had on. With it I wore faded blue jeans, with dirty sneakers on my feet, and my hair was skinned back and fastened in a granny's knot. Deliberately I'd pulled long strands free so they hung loose about my face, slovenly fringes to make me look more appealing. And no makeup prettied my face. He was dressed to kill.

"At least you look honest and ready to let me do the pursuing. If there is one thing I despise, it's women who come on strong, like you did last night. I expected better from you than that kind of sleazy dress that showed everything to take the thrill from discovering for myself." He knitted his brows and mumbled, "From a damned harlot's red dress to blue jeans. In the course of one day, she changes into a teenybopper."

"It was rose-colored, *not red!* And besides, Bart, strong men like you always adore weak and passive stupid women, because basically you're meek yourself and afraid of an aggressive woman!"

"I am not weak or meek or anything but a man who likes to feel a man, not to be used for your own purposes. And as for passive women I despise them as much as I do aggressive ones. I just don't like the feeling of being the victim of a huntress leading me into a trap. What the hell are you trying to do to me? Why dislike me so much? I sent you roses, diamonds, imitation poetry, and you can't even comb your hair and take the shine from your nose."

"You are looking at the natural me, and now that you've seen, you can leave." I got up and walked to the front door and swung it open. "We are wrong for each other. Go back to your wife. She can have you, for *I* don't want you."

He came quickly, as if to obey, then seized me in his arms and kicked the door closed. "I love you, God knows why I do, but it seems I've always loved you."

I stared up in his face, disbelieving him, even as he took the pins from my hair and let it spill down. Out of long habit I tossed it about so it fluffed out and arranged itself, and smiling a little he tilted my face to his. "May I kiss your *natural* lips? They are very beautiful lips." Without waiting for permission he brushed his lips gently over mine. Oh—the shivery sensation of such a feathery kiss! Why didn't all men know that was the right way to start? What woman wanted to be eaten alive, choked by a thrusting tongue? Not me, I wanted to be played like a violin, strummed pianissimo, in largo timing, fingered into legato, and let it grow into crescendo. Deliciously I wanted to head toward the ecstatic heights that could only happen for me when the right words were spoken and the right kind of kisses given before his hands came into play. If he'd done for me only a little last night, this night he used all the skills he had. This time he took me to the stars where we both exploded, still holding tight to each other, and doomed to do it again, and then again.

He was hairy all over. Julian had been hairless but for one thatch that grew in a thin line up to his navel. And Julian had never kissed my feet that smelled of roses from a long perfumed bath before I put on old work clothes. Toe by toe he mouthed before he started working upward. I felt the grandmother watching, blazing her hard, gray eyes to put us both in hell. I turned off my mind, shut her out, and gave in to my senses and to this man who was now treating me like a lover.

But he didn't love me, I knew that. Bart was using me as a substitute for his wife, and when she came back I'd never see him again. I knew it, knew it, but still I took and I gave until we fell asleep in each other's arms.

When I slept, I dreamed. Julian was in the silver music box my father had given me when I was six. Round and round he spun, his face ever turning toward me, accusing me with his jet eyes, and then he grew a mustache and was Paul, who only looked sad. I ran fast to set him free from death in a music box turned into a coffin—and then it was Chris inside, his eyes closed, his hands folded one over the other on his chest . . . dead, dead. Chris!

I awoke to find Bart gone and my pillow wet with tears. *Momma, why did you start this, why?*

Holding tight to my son's small hand I led him out into the cold morning air on my way to work. Faint and far away I heard someone calling my name, and with it came the scent of old-fashioned roses. Why don't you come, Paul, and save me from myself—why only call in your thoughts?

Part one was done. Part two would begin when my mother knew I had Bart's child—and then there was the grandmother who had to pay as well. And when I looked I saw that the mountains curved upward into a satisfied smirk. At last I had responded to their call. Their vengeful, tormenting wail.

The Grandmother, Revisited

Foxworth Hall was at the end of a cul-de-sac, the largest and most impressive of many fine, large homes and the only one that sat high, high on the hillside, looking down on all the others like a castle. For days I went to stare at it, making my plans.

Bart and I didn't have to sneak around furtively to meet. The houses where he lived were far apart and no one could see us when he came to me through the back door that opened out into a yard with a fence. In back of that was a country lane, shrubbed, and made private by many trees. Sometimes we met in a distant town and our lovemaking in a motel room was wild, sweet, tender, erotic and altogether satisfying, and yet I froze when he told me at lunch, "She called this morning, Cathy. She'll be home before Christmas."

"That's nice," I said and went right on eating my salad and anticipating the Beef Wellington that would show up soon. He frowned and his fork loaded with salad hesitated on the way to his mouth. "It means we won't be able to see as much of each other. Aren't you sorry?"

"We'll find ways."

"If you aren't the damndest woman!"

"Don't get so worked up over nothing. All women are monsters to men, and maybe to ourselves. We are our own worst enemies. You don't have to divorce her and give up your chance to inherit her fortune. Though she could outlive you and have the chance to buy another younger husband."

"Sometimes you are just as bitchy as she is! *She did not buy me!* I loved her! She loved me! I was crazy about her, as crazy for her as I am for you now. But she changed. When I met her she was sweet, charming, everything I wanted in a woman and wife, but she changed." He stabbed the salad fork toward his mouth and chewed viciously. "She's always been a mystery—like you."

"Bart, my love," I said, "very soon all mystery walls will crumble."

He went on, as if I hadn't interrupted, "That father of hers, he too was a mystery; you'd look at him and see a fine old gentleman, but underneath was a heart of steel. I thought I was his only attorney, but he had six others, each of us assigned to different tasks. Mine was to make out his wills. He changed them dozens of times, putting this family member in, and writing another out, and adding codicils like a mad man, though he was sane enough right up until the very end. The last codicil was the worst."

Of course, no children for him, ever. "Then you really were a practicing lawyer?" He smiled bitterly, then answered, "Of course I was. And now I am again. A man needs something meaningful to do. How many times can anyone tour Europe before boredom sets in? You see the same old faces, doing the same old things, laughing at the same jokes. The Beautiful People—what a laugh! Too much money buys everything but health, so they have no dreams left to purchase, and no aspirations, so in the end they are only bored."

"Why don't you divorce her and do something meaningful with your life?"

"She loves me." That's the way he said it. Short. Sweet. He stayed because she loved him, forcing me to say, "You told me when we first met that you loved her, and then you say you don't—which is it?" He thought about it for a long time.

"Honestly, ballerina, I'm ambivalent and resentful. I love her, I hate her. I thought she was what you seem to be now. So please, smother that bitchy side that reminds me of her and don't try and do to me what she did. You are putting a wall between us because you know something I don't. I don't fall in love easily, and I wish I *didn't* love you."

He seemed suddenly a small boy, wistful, as if his pet dog might betray him and life would never be good again. I was touched and dared to say, "Bart, I swear there will come a day when you know all my secrets and all of hers—but until that time comes say you love me, even if you don't mean it, for I can't enjoy being with you if I don't feel you love me just a little."

"A little? It seems I've loved you all my life. Even when I kissed you the first time it seemed I'd kissed you before—why is that?"

"Karma." I smiled at his baffled expression.

There was something I had to do before my mother came home. One day when I had no classes and Jory was in his special school I slipped over to Foxworth Hall, using all the hidden ways. At the back door I used the old wooden key that Chris had fashioned so long ago. It was Thursday. All the servants would be in town. Since Bart had told me in detail his routine, that also told me a lot of the grandmother's daily life. I knew at this time the nurse would be napping, as my grandmother had her rest time in the afternoon too. She'd be in the same little room beyond the library, the same room that had confined our grandfather during his last days, while upstairs we four children waited for him to pass on to his rewards, and death would set us free.

I strolled through all those rich, grand rooms and hungrily stared at all the fine furnishings and saw again the dual winding staircases in the front foyer large enough to be used as a ballroom. Where the curving staircases met was a balcony on the second floor, and from that rose another flight of stairs, straight up to the attic. I saw, the massive chest where Chris and I had hidden inside to watch a Christmas party going on below. So long ago, and yet my clock of time turned swiftly backward. I was twelve again and scared, afraid this mammoth house would swallow me down if I moved or spoke above a whisper. I was awed again by the three giant crystal chandeliers suspended from a ceiling some forty feet above the floor. And because it was a dance floor of mosaic tiles, I automatically had to dance just a little to see how it felt.

I ambled on, taking my time, admiring the paintings, the marble busts, the huge lamps, the fabulous wall hangings that only the super-rich, who could be so stingy in small ways, could buy. Imagine my grandmother buying bolts of gray taffeta just to save a few dollars, when they bought the best to furnish their rooms and they had millions!

The library was easy to find. Lessons learned at an early age and under miserable conditions could never be forgotten. Oh, such a library! Clairmont didn't have a library with so many fine books! Bart's photograph was on the ponderous desk that had been my grandfather's. Many things were there to indicate that Bart often used this room for his study, and to keep his mother-in-law company. His brown house-slippers were beneath a comfortable-looking chair near the immense stone fireplace with a mantel twenty feet long. French doors opened onto a terrace facing a formal garden with a fountain to spray water into a bird bath formed by a rock garden of steps, with the water trickling down into a pool. A nice, sunny place for an invalid to sit, protected from the wind.

At last I'd seen enough to satisfy my curiosity, harbored for years, and I sought out the heavy door at the far end of the library. Beyond that closed door was the witch-grandmother. Visions of her flashed through my mind. I saw her again as she'd been the first night we came, towering above us, her thick body strong, powerful, her cruel, hard eyes that swept over us all and showed no sympathy, no compassion for fatherless children who had lost so much, and she couldn't even smile to welcome us or touch the pretty round cheeks of the twins who had been so appealing at age five.

The second night flashed, when the grandmother ordered our mother to show us her naked back striped with red and bleeding welts. Even before we'd seen that horror she'd picked Carrie up by the hair and Cory had hurled himself against her, trying to inflict some pain with his small white shoe that kicked her leg and his small sharp teeth that bit—and with one powerful slap she'd sent him reeling. All because he had to defend his beloved twin who had screamed and screamed. Again I saw myself before the mirror in the bedroom without a stitch on, and her punishment had been so harsh, so heartless, trying to take from me what I admired the most, my hair. A whole day Chris had spent trying to take the tar from my hair and save it from the shears. Then no food or milk for two whole weeks! *Yes!* She deserved to see me again! Just as I'd vowed the day she whipped me that there would come a day in the future when she would be the helpless one and I would be the one to wield the whip and keep the food from her lips!

Ah, the sweet irony of it—that she would gloat to see her husband dead, and now she was in his bed and even more helpless—and alone! I took off my heavy winter coat, sat down to tug off my boots, and then I put on the white satin *pointes*. My leotards were white and sheer enough to let the pink of my skin show through. I unbound my hair so it fell in a luxuriant, golden cascade of rippling waves down my back. Now she would see and envy the hair the tar hadn't ruined after all.

Get ready, Grandmother! Here I come!

Very quietly I stole to her door. Then carefully I eased it open. She was on the high, high hospital bed, her eyes half-closed. The sun through the windows fell upon her pink and shining scalp, clearly revealing how nearly bald she was. And oh, how old she looked! So gaunt, so much smaller. Where was the giantess I used to know? Why wasn't she wearing a gray taffeta dress to whisper threats? Why did she have to look so pitiful?

I hardened my heart, closed out mercy, for she'd never had any for us. Apparently she was on the verge of sleep, but as the door opened slowly, slowly her eyes widened. Then her eyes bulged. She recognized me. Her thin, shriveled lips quivered. She was afraid! Glory hallelujah! My tune had come! Still, I paused in the open doorway, appalled. I had come for revenge and time had robbed me! Why wasn't she the monster I recalled? I wanted her that way, not what she was now, an old, sick woman with her hair so scant most of her scalp showed, and the hair left was pulled to the top of her head and fastened up there by a pink satin ribbon bow. The bow gave her a ghoulish-girlish look, and even bunched together as they were, the thin wisps were no wider than my small finger—just a tuft like a worn-out, bleached brush for watercolor painting.

Once she'd stood six feet tall and weighed over two hundred pounds and her huge breasts had been mountains of concrete. Now those breasts hung like old socks to reach her puffy abdomen. Her arms were withered old dry sticks, her hands corded, her fingers gnarled. Yet, as I stared and she stared in complete silence as a small clock ticked relentlessly on, her old despicable personality flared hot to let me know her outrage. She tried to speak to order me out. *Devil's issue, she'd scream* if she could, *get out of my house! Devil's spawn, out, out, out!* But she couldn't say it, any of it.

While I could greet her pleasantly, "Good afternoon, *dear* Grandmother. How very nice to see you again. Remember me?

I'm Cathy, one of the grandchildren you helped hide away, and each day you brought us food in a picnic basket—every day by six-thirty you were there, with your gallon thermos of milk, and your quart thermos of lukewarm soup—and canned soup at that. Why couldn't you have brought us hot soup at least once? Did you deliberately heat that soup to only warm? I stepped inside and closed the door behind me. And only then did she see the willow switch I'd hidden behind my back.

Casually I tapped the switch on my palm. "Grandmother," I said softly, "remember the day you whipped our mother? How you forced her to strip in front of her father, and then you whipped her, and she was an adult—a shameless, wicked, evil deed, don't you agree?"

Her terrified gray eyes fixed on the switch. A terrible struggle was going on in her brain—and I was *glad*, so *glad* Bart had told me she wasn't senile. Pale, watery, gray eyes, red-rimmed and crinkled all about with deep crow's feet, like cuts that never bled. Thin, crooked lips now shrunken to only a tiny buttonhole and puckered about by a radiating sunburst of deep lines, etching beneath her long hooked nose a spider-web design of crosshatch lines. And, believe it or not, to the high and severe neckline of that yellow cotton jacket was fastened *the* diamond brooch! Never had I seen her without the brooch pinned to the neckline of her gray taffeta dresses with the white crocheted collars.

"Grandmother," I chanted, "remember the twins? The dear little five-year-olds you enticed into this house, and not once while they were here did you ever speak their names— or any of our names. Cory's dead, and you know that—but did my mother tell you about Carrie? Carrie is dead too. She didn't grow very tall because she was robbed of sunlight and fresh air in the years when she needed it most. Robbed too of love and security and given trauma instead of happiness. Chris and I went onto the roof to sit and sun ourselves, but the twins were afraid of the high roof. Did you know we went

out there and we'd stay for hours and hours . . . no, you didn't
know, did you?"

She moved a bit, as if trying to shrink into the thin mattress. I gloated to see her fear, rejoiced that she could move
a little. Her eyes now were as mine used to be, windowpanes
to reveal all her terrified emotions—and she couldn't cry out
for help! At my mercy. "Remember the second night, dearest,
loving Grandmother? You lifted Carrie up by her hair, and you
must have known that hurt, yet you did it. Then you sent Cory
spinning with one blow, and that hurt too, and he was only trying to protect his sister. Poor Carrie, how she grieved for Cory.
She never got over his death, never stopped missing him. She
met a nice boy named Alex. They fell in love and were going to
be married when she found out he was going to be a minister.
That shook Carrie up. You see, you made us all deeply fearful
of religious people. The day Alex said he was going to be a minister Carrie went into a despairing depression. She had learned
the lesson you taught very well. You taught us that no one can
ever be perfect enough to please God. Something dormant
came to life the day Carrie was weakened by shock, depression
and the lack of the spirit to go on. Now listen to what she did—
because of you! Because you impressed on her young brain that
she was born evil and she'd be wicked no matter how much she
sought to be good! She believed you! Cory was dead. She knew
he had died from the arsenic put on sugared doughnuts. . . .
So when she felt she could no longer put up with life and all
the people who expected perfection, she bought rat poison! She
bought a package of twelve doughnuts and coated them with
that rat poison full of arsenic! She ate all but one—and that had
a bite mark. Now . . . shrink into your mattress and try and run
from the guilt that is yours! You and my mother killed her as
much as you killed Cory! I despise you, old woman!"

I didn't tell her I hated my mother more. The grandmother
had never loved us, so anything *she* did was to be expected. But
our mother who had borne us, who had cared for us, who had

loved us well when Daddy lived—that was another story—an unbearable horror story! And her time would come!

"Yes, Grandmother, Carrie is dead now too, because she wanted to die in the same way Cory had and be with him in heaven."

Her eyes squinched and a small shudder rippled the covers. I gloated.

I brought from behind my back the box containing a long length of Carrie's hair that had taken me hours to arrange and brush into one long, shimmering switch of molten gold. At one end it was tied with a red satin bow, and at the other, a bow of purple satin. "*Look old woman*, this is Carrie's hair, some of it. I have another box full of loose, tangled strands, for I can't bear to part with a piece of it. I saved it to keep not only for Chris and myself, but to show you and our mother . . . for the two of you killed Carrie as surely as you killed Cory!"

Oh, I was near mad with hate. Revenge blazed my eyes, my temper, and shook my hands. I could see Carrie as she lay near death, turning old, withered, bony until she was only a little skeleton covered by loose, pale skin, so translucent all her veins showed—and the remains had to be sealed quickly in a box of pretty metal to shut away the stench of decay.

I stepped nearer the bed and dangled the bright hair with its gay ribbons before her wide and frightened eyes. "Isn't this beautiful hair, old woman? Was yours ever so beautiful, so bountiful? *No! I know* it wasn't! Nothing about you could ever have been pretty, *nothing!* Not even when you were young! That's why you were so jealous of your husband's stepmother." I laughed to see her flinch. "Yes, dear Grandmother, I know a lot more about you now than I did. Your son-in-law has told me all the family secrets my mother told him. Your husband Malcolm was in love with his father's younger wife, ten times more beautiful and sweeter than you ever were! So when Alicia had a son, you suspected that child was your own husband's, and that's why you hated our father, and why you sent for him, deceiving him into believing he'd found a good home. And you educated him and gave him the best of everything so he'd have to taste of the good, rich live and to more hurt and disappointed later on, when you threw him out and left him nothing in your wills. But my father fooled you instead, didn't he? He stole your only daughter, whom you hated too, because her father loved her more than he loved you. And half-uncle married half-niece. Yet how wrong you were about Malcolm! She fought him off time and again—and the baby she had was not your husband's son! Though he would have been, if Malcolm had had his way!

Blankly she stared at me, as if the past was of no importance to her now. Only the present mattered, and the switch in my hand. "I'm going to tell you something now, old woman, that you need to know. There was never a better man born than my father or more honorable woman than his mother. But don't lie there and think I've inherited any of Alicia's or my fathers godly traits—for I am like *you!* Heartless! I never forget, never forgive! *I hate you for killing Cory and Carrie. I hate you for making of me what I am!"* I screamed this, out of control, forgetful of the nurse napping down the hall. I wanted to feed her arsenic by the handfuls and sit and watch her die and rot before my eyes, like Carrie had. I pirouetted round the room to release my frustrations, lashing my legs, showing off my fine young body, and then I drew up short and snapped in her face, "All those years you locked us up, and you never said our names, never looked at Chris because he was our father all over again—and your husband too, when he was young, and before you made him evil too. You blame everything wrong with human beings on their evil souls, and ignore the truth. *Money* is the god who rules in this house! It's *money* that's always made the worst things happen! You were married for your money and you knew it! And greed brought us here, and greed locked us up and stole three years and four months from our lives, and put us at your mercy and you didn't have any, not even for your grandchildren, the only grandchildren you'd ever have, and we never touched you, did we? Though we tried in the beginning, remember?" I jumped up on the bed and lashed at her with the length of Carrie's golden hair. A soft whip that didn't hurt, though she cringed from the touch. Then I tossed Carrie's precious hair to her bedside table and snapped the switch before her eyes. I danced and whirled on her bed, over her frozen body, displaying my fine agility as my long hair flared in a golden circle.

"Remember how you punished our mother before we grew to hate her too? I owe you for that," I said, legs apart and straddling her covered body. "From your neck down to your heels, I owe you that, plus the whip lashes you gave Chris and me, I owe you that too. And all the other things, each one of them is etched in my memory. Didn't I tell you there would come a day when I held the switch in my hand, and there would be food in the kitchen you'd never eat? *Well . . . that day is here, Grandmother.*"

The sunken gray eyes in her gaunt face sparkled hate, malicious and strong. Daring me to strike her—daring me!

"What shall I do first," I said as if to myself, "shall it be the switch, or the hot tar in your hair? Where did you get the tar, old woman? I always wondered where you got it. Did you plan it way in advance and wait for an excuse to use it? I'm going to confess something now you don't know. Chris never cut off all my hair, only the front part to fool you into thinking I was bald-headed. Beneath that towel I wrapped on my head was all the long hair he saved. Yes, old woman, love saved my hair from being cut off. He loved me enough to work for hours and hours to save what hair he could—more love than *you've* ever known, and from a brother."

Deep in her throat she made a strangling sound, and how I wished she could speak!

"Grandmother darling," I taunted, hands on my hips as I leaned to look down on her, "why don't you tell me where to get the tar? I haven't been able to find any. No road construction going on anywhere near—so I guess I'll have to use hot wax. *You* could have used melted wax, for it would have done the job just as well. Didn't you think of melting a few of your candles?" I smiled, menacingly, I hoped. "Oh, dear Grandmother, what *fun* you and I are going to have! And nobody will know, for *you can't talk* and *you can't write,* all you can do is lie there and suffer."

I didn't like myself or what I was saying or what I was feeling. My conscience hovered near the ceiling, looking down with shame at this released fury that was me in white tights. Aghast, I was up there feeling pity for this old woman who'd suffered through two strokes—but on the bed was another kind of me. A vicious, mean, vindictive Foxworth, with blue eyes as cold as hers used to be as I stared her down, and then suddenly, cruelly I bent; I yanked down the sheet and blanket that covered her and she was exposed. Her garment was like a hospital jacket that was slit and tied down the back, for there was no front opening. Just a plain yellow cotton thing with that incongruous diamond brooch at the throat. No doubt they would attach that brooch to her funeral garments.

Naked. She had to be stripped, as Momma was, as Chris had been, as I had been too. She had to suffer through the humiliation of being without clothes while contemptuous eyes made her shrivel even smaller. Relentlessly I seized hold of the hem of her stingy, cheap cotton garment and without compunction I yanked it upward to her armpits. In rumpled, unironed folds it half-hid her face, and carefully I pulled back the cloth that could hide from me any expression she might manage to reveal. Then I stared down at her body, expressing scorn and revulsion as she had expressed it with her hard eyes and knife-slashed lips when I was a child of fourteen and she had caught me looking at myself in the mirror, admiring the beauty of a figure I'd never seen before nude.

The body in its youth is a beautiful thing . . . a joy to

behold, the sweet young curves, the smooth unblemished skin, firm and taut flesh, but oh, to grow old! Those twin hills of concrete were flabby loose udders that sagged to her waist, and the nipples were at the very bottom, large brown, mottled and bumpy. The blue veins of her breasts stood up like thin ropes covered by a translucent sheath. The pasty whiteness of her skin was dimpled, furrowed, creased by stretch marks from childbirth, and a long scar from navel to her almost hairless mound of Venus showed she'd either had a hysterectomy or a caesarean section. It was an old scar, pale and shinier than the doughy, white, wrinkled skin around it. Her thin, long legs were gnarled old branches of a tired tree. I sighed—would *I* someday look like this?

Without pity or an attempt to be gentle I rolled her over and yanked her back into the center of the bed. And all the while I was babbling on of how Chris and I had joked she either nailed on her clothes or glued them in and never, of course, did she take off her underclothes unless she was in a closet with the light out. Her back showed fewer ravages than her front, though her buttocks were flat, flabby and too white.

"I'm going to whip you now. Grandmother," I said tonelessly, my heart gone out of this now. "I promised a long time ago I was going to do this if ever I had the chance and so I will do it!" And closing my eyes and, asking God to forgive me for what I was about to do, I lifted my arm high and then brought down that willow switch as hard as I could, and flat on her bare buttocks!

She shuddered. Some noise came from her throat. Then she seemed to sink into unconsciousness. She relaxed so much she released her bladder. I began to cry. Terrible sobs from *me* as I ran to the adjoining bath to find a washcloth and soap, and back I hurried with toilet tissue to clean her. Then I washed her and put salve on the awful welt I'd made.

I turned her over on the bed, straightened out her gown so she was covered modestly, neatly, and only then did I check to see if she was alive or dead. Her gray eyes were open and staring at me without expression as tears streaked *my* face. Next, slowly, as I sobbed on, her eyes began to gleam in unspoken triumph!

Mutely she called me *coward! I knew you couldn't be anything but a soft weakling! No spine, no starch! Kill me. Go on, kill me! I dare you, do it, do it, go on!*

Down from the bed I jumped, and I ran fast into the library and on into the parlor I'd seen. In a frenzy of anger I grabbed up the first candelabra I saw and dashed back to her—but I didn't have matches! Back again to the library where I rummaged through the desk Bart used. He smoked; he'd have matches or a cigarette lighter. I found a book of matches from a local disco.

The candles were ivory colored, dignified, like this house. Terror was in her iron eyes now. She *wanted* that bit of tufted hair tied with a pink ribbon. I lit a candle and watched it flame, then I held it angled over her head so the melting wax dribbled down drop by drop onto her hair and her scalp. Maybe six or seven drops fell before I could stand no more. She was right. I was a coward, I couldn't do to her what she'd done to us. I was a Foxworth twice over, and yet God had changed the mold so I didn't fit.

I blew out the ivory candle, replaced it in the candelabra, then left.

No sooner was I in the ballroom than I remembered I'd forgotten the precious length of Carrie's hair. I raced back to get it. I found the grandmother lying as I'd left her, only her head was turned and two huge glistening tears were in her eyes that stared at the switch of Carrie's beautiful hair. Ahh! Now I had my pound of flesh!

Bart spent more time at my small home than at his huge one. He plied me with gifts, as he did my son. He ate his breakfast, lunch and dinner with us on the days he didn't spend in his office, which I privately believed was more a facade for appearing useful than a functioning law office. My dancing school suffered from his attention, but it didn't matter. I was now a kept woman.

Paid to be his mistress.

Jory was delighted with the little leather boots Bart gave him. "Are *you* my daddy?" asked my son who would be four in February. "No. but I sure wish I was and I could be."

As soon as Jory was out in the yard, tromping around and staring down at his feet that fascinated him now that they sported cowboy boots, Bart turned to me and flung himself wearily down in a chair. "You'd never guess what happened over at our place. Some sadistic idiot put wax in my mother-in-law's hair. And there's a long welt on her buttocks that won't heal. The nurse can't explain it. I've questioned Olivia, and asked if it was anyone she knew, one of the servants, and she blinked her eyes twice, meaning no. Once is for yes. I'm mad as hell about it! It must have been one of the servants, yet I can't understand why one would be so cruel as to torment a helpless old woman who can't move to defend herself. She refuses to identify anyone I name. I promised Corrine I'd take good care of her, and now her bottom is such a raw mess she has to lie on her stomach two to four hours each day, and she is turned during the night."

"Oh," I breathed, feeling a bit sick. "How awful— why won't it heal?"

"Her circulation is bad. It would have to be, wouldn't it, since she can't move about normally?" He smiled then, brilliantly, like the sun coming out after a storm. "Don't concern yourself, darling. It's my problem, not yours—and, of course, hers." He held out his arms and I went quickly into them to snuggle in his lap, and he kissed fervently before he carried me into my bedroom. He laid me down and began to undress. "I could wring the neck of the fiend who did that to her!"

* * *

We lay entwined after our lovemaking, listening to the wind blending with Jory's shrill laughter, racing after the toy poodle Bart had given him. A few snow flurries were beginning to fall. I knew I had to get up soon so Jory wouldn't run in and catch us, just to tell us it was snowing. He couldn't remember other snows, and barely would the ground be sugar-coated than he'd want to make a snowman. Sighing first, I kissed Bart, then reluctantly pulled from his embrace. I turned my back to pull on bikini panties as he propped up on an elbow and watched. "You've got a lovely behind," he said. I said thanks. "What about my front?" He said it wasn't bad. I threw a shoe at him.

"Cathy, why don't you say you love me?"

I whirled about, startled. "Have you ever said it to me and meant it?" I snapped on a tiny bra.

"How do you know I don't mean it?" he asked with anger.

"Let me tell you how I know. When you love, you want that person with you all of the time. When you avoid the subject of divorce, that alone is an indication of how much you care for me and just where I belong in your life."

"Cathy, you've been hurt, haven't you? I don't want to hurt you more. You play games with me. I've always known that. What does it matter if it is only sex and not love? And tell me how to know where one ends and the other begins?"

His teasing words were a knife in my heart, for somehow, without meaning to let it happen, I'd fallen madly, idiotically in love with him.

According to Bart's enthusiastic report, his long gone wife came home from her rejuvenation trip looking smashingly young and beautiful. "She's lost twenty pounds. I swear, that face lift has done wonders! She looks sensational, and damn it, so unbelievably like you!"

It was easy to see how impressed he was with his new, younger-looking wife, and if he was only trying to take the wind from my too confident sails, I didn't let it show. Then he was telling me I was just as necessary to him as before in a tone that said I was not. "Cathy, while she was in Texas she changed. She's like she used to be, the sweet, loving woman I married."

Men! How gullible they were! Of course my mother was sweeter and nicer to him now—now that she knew he had a mistress who was very accessible, and that the other woman was her own daughter. She'd have to know, for it was whispered all about now—everyone knew.

"So, why are you here with me when your wife is back and so like me? Why don't you put your clothes on and say goodbye and never come back? Say it was sweet while it lasted, but it's all over now, and I'll say thank you for a wonderful time before I kiss you farewell"

"Well-ll," he drawled, pulling me hard against his naked body. "I didn't say she, was *that* sensational looking. And then again, there is something special about you. I can't name it. I can't understand it. But I don't know if I can live without you now." He said it seriously, truth in his dark eyes.

I'd won, won!

Quite by accident my mother and I met in the post office one day. She saw me and shivered. Her lovely head lifted higher as she turned it slightly away, pretending she didn't know me. She would deny me as she'd denied Carrie, even though it was so obvious that we were mother and daughter and not strangers. I wasn't Carrie. So I treated her as she treated me, indifferently, as if she were nobody special and never would be again. Yet, as I waited impatiently for my roll of stamps, I saw my mother dart her eyes to follow the restless prowl of my young son who had to stare at everything and everyone. He was handsome, graceful, a charming boy who drew the eyes of everyone who had to stop and admire him and pat his head. Jory moved with innate style, unstudied and relaxed, at ease wherever he was, because he thought the whole world was his, and he was loved by everyone. He turned to catch my mother's long stare and he smiled. "Hello," he greeted. "You're pretty—like my mommy."

Oh, the things children say! What innocent knowledge they had, to see so readily what others instinctively refused to acknowledge. He stepped closer to reach out and tentatively touch her fur coat. "My mommy's got a fur coat. My mommy is a dancer. Do you dance?"

She sighed, I held my breath. *See, Momma, there is the grandson your arms will never hold. You'll never hear him say your name . . . never!*

"No," she whispered, "I'm not a dancer." Tears filmed her eyes.

"My mommy can teach you how."

"I'm too old to learn," she whispered, backing off.

"No, you're not," said Jory, reaching for her hand as if he'd show her the way, but she pulled back, glanced at me, reddened, then fumbled in her purse for a handkerchief. "Do you have a little boy I can play with?" questioned my son, concerned to see her tears, as if having a son would make up for not knowing how to dance.

"No," she said in a quivering weak whisper, "I don't have any children."

That's when I moved in to say in a cold, harsh voice, "Some women don't deserve to have children." I paid for my roll of stamps and dropped them in my purse. "Some women like you, Mrs. Winslow, would rather have money than the bother of children who might get in the way of good times. Time itself will sooner or later let you know if you made the right decision."

She turned her back and shivered again as if all her furs couldn't keep her warm enough. Then she strode from the post office and headed toward a chauffeur-driven, black limousine. Like a queen she rode off, head held high, leaving Jory to ask, "Mommy, why don't you like that pretty lady? I like her a lot. She's like you, only not so pretty." I didn't comment, though it was on the tip of my tongue to say something so ugly he would never forget it.

In the twilight of that evening I sat near the windows, staring toward Foxworth Hall and wondering what Bart and my mother were doing. My hands were on my abdomen which was still flat, but soon it would be swelling with the child that might be started. One missed period didn't prove anything— except I wanted Bart's baby, and little things made me feel sure there was a baby. I let depression come and take me. He wouldn't leave her and her money to marry me and I'd have another fatherless child. What a fool to start all of this—but I'd always been a fool.

And then I saw a man slipping through the woods, coming to me, and I laughed, made confident again. He loved me! He did . . . and as soon as I knew for certain, I would tell him he was to be a father.

Then the wind came in with Bart and blew the vase of roses from the table. I stood and stared down at the crystal pieces and the petals scattered about. Why was the wind always trying to tell me something? Something I didn't want to hear!

Stacking the Deck

"Cathy, you told me there was no need for precautions!"

"There was no need. I want your baby."

"You want my baby? What the hell do you think I can do, marry you?"

"No. I did my own assuming. I presumed you'd have your fun with me and when it was over you'd go back to your wife and find yourself another playmate. And I'd have just what I set out to get—your baby. Now I can leave. So kiss me off, Bart, as just another of your little extramarital dalliances."

He looked furious. We were in my living room, while a fierce blizzard raged outside. Snow heaped in mounds window-high, and I was before the fireplace, knitting a baby bunting before I began a bootie. I was getting ready to slip a stitch then knit two together when Bart seized my knitting from my hands and hurled it away. "It's unraveling!" I cried in dismay.

"What the hell are you trying to do to me, Cathy? You know I can't marry you! I never lied and said I would. You're playing a game with me." He choked and covered his face with his hands, then took them down and pleaded, "I love you. God help me but I do. I want you near me always, and I want my child too. What kind of game are you playing now?"

"Just a woman's game. The only game she can play and be sure of winning."

"Look," he said, trying to regain his control of the situation, "explain what you mean, don't double talk. Nothing has to change because my wife is back. You'll always have a place in my life—"

"In your life? Don't you mean more correctly, on the fringes of your life?"

For the first time I heard humility in his voice. "Cathy, be reasonable. I love you, and I love my wife too. Sometimes I can't separate you from her. She came back different, as I told you, and now she is like she was when we first met. Maybe a more youthful figure and face has given her back some confidence she lost, and because of it she can be sweeter. Whatever the cause. I'm grateful. Even when I disliked her, I loved her. When she was hateful, I'd try and strike back by going to other women, but still I loved *her*. The one big issue we fight over is her unwillingness to have a child, even an adopted one. Of course she's too old to have one now. Please, Cathy, *stay! Don't leave!* Don't take my child away so I will never know what happens to him, or to her . . . or to you."

I laid it out flat. "All right, I will stay on one condition. If you divorce her and marry me, only then will you have the child you always wanted. Otherwise, I'm taking myself, and that means your child too, far away. Maybe I'll write to let you know if you have a son or a daughter, and maybe I won't. Either way, once I leave, you are out of my life for good." I thought, *look at him, acting as if that codicil weren't in the will forbidding his wife to have children.* Protecting her! Just like Chris, when all along he had to know. He'd drawn up the will. He had to know.

Before the fireplace he stood with his arm up on the

mantel, then he rested his forehead on that and stared down at the fire. His free hand was behind his back and clenched into a fist. His confused thoughts were so deep they reached out and touched me with pity. He turned then to face me, staring deep into my eyes. "My God," he said, shocked by his discovery. "You planned this all along, didn't you? You came here to accomplish what you have, but why? Why should you choose me to hurt? What have I ever done to you, Cathy, but love you? True, it started with sex, and sex only was what I wanted it to stay. But it has grown into something much more than that. I like being with you, just sitting and talking, or walking in the woods. I feel comfortable with you. I like the way you wait on me, and touch my cheek when you pass, and rumple my hair and kiss my neck, and the sweet, shy way you wake up and smile when you see me beside you. I like the clever games you play, keeping me always guessing, and always amused. I feel I have ten women in one, so now I feel I can't live without you. But I can't abandon my wife and marry you. She *needs* me!"

"You should have been an actor, Bart. Your words move me to tears."

"Damn you for taking this so lightly!" he bellowed. "You've got me on a rack and you're twisting the screws! Don't make me hate you and ruin the best months of my life!"

With that he stormed out of my cottage, and I was left alone, ruefully regretting that always I talked too much, for I would stay as long as he needed me.

Emma, Jory and I thought it a wonderful idea to make an excursion to Richmond and do some Christmas shopping. Jory had never seen Santa Claus that he could remember, and most fearfully he approached the red-suited, white-bearded man who held out his arms to encourage him. Tentatively he perched on Santa's knee in Thalhimers Department Store, and stared disbelievingly into twinkling blue eyes while I snapped pictures from every angle, even crawling to get what I wanted.

Next we visited a dress shop I'd heard about where I handed to them a sketch I'd drawn from memory. I selected the exact shade of dark green velvet, and then the lighter green chiffon for the skirt. "And make the straps of the velvet bodice shoestrings of rhinestones—and remember, the floating panels must reach the hem."

While Jory and Emma watched a Wait Disney movie. I had my hair cut and styled differently. Not just trimmed, as was my habit, but really cut shorter than I'd ever worn it. It was a style that flattered me, as it should, for it had flattered my mother when she wore her hair this way, fifteen years ago.

"Oh, Mommy!" cried Jory, distress in his voice. "You've lost your hair!" He began to cry. "Put your long hair back on—you don't look like my mommy now!"

No. that was the purpose. I didn't want to look like me this Christmas—not this special Christmas when I had to duplicate exactly what my mother had been when first I saw her dancing with Bart. Now, at long last, my chance—in a gown the same as hers, with her hair style, her younger face. I would confront my mother in her own home, on *my* terms. Woman to woman—and let the best one win! She'd be forty-eight, with a recent face lift—still I knew she was very beautiful. But she couldn't compete with her daughter who was twenty-one years younger! I laughed when I looked in the mirror after slipping on the new green gown. Oh, yes, I'd made myself into what she was—the kind of woman men just couldn't resist. I had her power, her beauty—and ten times more brains—how could she win?

Three days before Christmas I called Chris and asked if he'd like to go with me to Richmond. I'd forgotten a few necessary items the little local shops didn't have. "Cathy," he said sternly, his voice cold and hostile, "when you give up Bart Winslow you will see me again, but until you do. I don't care to be near you!"

"All right!" I flared. *"Stay where you are!* You can miss out

on *your* revenge, but I am not going to miss out on mine! Good-bye, Christopher Doll, and I hope *all the bedbugs bite!"* I hung up!

I didn't teach ballet class as often as I used to, but at recital times I was always there. My little dancers delighted in dressing up, and showing off before their parents, grandparents and friends. They looked adorable in their costumes for *The Nutcracker.* Even Jory had two minor roles to play, a snowflake and a sugarplum.

In my opinion there was no more magical way to spend at least one Christmas Eve than as a family attending a performance of *The Nutcracker.* And it was a thousand times more wonderful when one of those gifted, small, graceful children was your own small son, fifty-two days short of being four years old. The sweet babyness of him dancing on stage with so much passion drew applause time and again from the audience who stood up to cheer his solo performance that I'd choreographed especially for him.

And best of all, I'd made Bart swear he'd force my mother to attend that recital—and they were there; I checked by peeking through the curtains, front row center, Mr. and Mrs. Bartholomew Winslow. He looked happy; she looked grim. So I did have some control over Bart. It showed up in a huge bouquet of roses for the dance instructor, and a huge box for the solo performing snowflake.

"What can it be?" asked Jory, his face flushed, his happiness rebounding from the sky. "Can I open it now?"

"Sure, soon as we're home, and tomorrow morning Santa will leave a hundred gifts for you."

"Why?"

"Because he loves you."

"Why?" asked Jory.

"Because he couldn't help but love you—that's why."

"Oh."

Before five in the morning Jory was up, playing with the

electric train Bart had sent him. All over the living room floor were the splendid wrappings from hundreds of gifts from Paul, Henny, Chris, Bart, and Santa Claus. Emma gave him a box of homemade cookies that he polished off between ripping open the packages. "Gee, Mommy," he cried, "I thought it would be lonely without my uncles, but I'm not lonely. I'm having fun."

He wasn't lonely, but I was. I wanted Bart with me, not over there with her. I waited for him to make up some excuse to drive to the drug store and slip over to see me and Jory. But all I saw of Bart on Christmas morning was the two-inch wide diamond bracelet he enclosed in a box with two dozen red roses. His card read, "I love you, Ballerina."

If ever there was a woman who dressed more carefully than I did that night it must have been Marie Antoinette. Emma complained it was taking me forever. I painted my face as if a camera was going to shoot me close up for a magazine cover. Emma styled my hair as my mother had worn hers long ago. "Wave it back softly from the face, Emma, then catch it high at the crown with a cluster of curls, and make sure a few hang long enough to brush my shoulders."

When she finished, I gasped to see I was almost an exact duplicate of what my mother had been when I was twelve! My high cheekbones were emphasized just as hers had been with this hair style. As in a dream I never truly expected to happen I stepped into the green gown with the velvet bodice and chiffon skirt. This was the type of gown that never went out of fashion. I spun around before the mirror, getting the feel of being my mother with her power to control men, while Emma stood back and flattered me with compliments.

Even my perfume was the same. Musky with an Oriental garden scent. My slippers were straps of silver with four-inch heels. My silver evening bag matched. All I needed now was the emerald and diamond jewelry she had worn. Soon I'd have that too. Surely fate wouldn't let her be wearing green tonight. At some point in my life fate had to be on my side. I figured it was due tonight.

Tonight I'd deliver the surprises and the slaps. She would feel the pain of losing! What a pity Chris wouldn't come and enjoy the ending of a long, long play, started the day our father was killed on the highway.

I threw myself one more admiring glance, picked up the fur stole Bart had given me, gathered up my faltering courage, took a last peek at Jory who was curled up on his side and looking angelic. I leaned over to tenderly kiss his round, rosy cheek. "I love you, Jory," I whispered.

He partially awakened from a hazy dream and stared up at me as if I were part of that dream. "Oh, Mommy, you look so pretty!" His dark blue eyes shone with childish wonder as he asked quite seriously, "Are you going to a party to get me a new daddy?"

I smiled and again kissed him and said yes, in a way I was. "Thank you, darling, for thinking I look pretty. Now go back to sleep and dream of happy things, and tomorrow we'll build a snowman."

"Bring a daddy to help."

On the table by the front door was a note from Paul.

"Henny is very ill. It's a pity you can't give up your plans to visit her before it is too late. I wish you good luck, Catherine." With a sigh I put that note aside and picked up the note Henny had enclosed with Paul's written on festive red paper, with the letters made rooked because of painful arthritic knuckles.

Dear Fairy-Child,

   Henny is old; Henny is tired; Henny is glad own son is by her side, but unhappy because other children far away.

I tell you now, before I go on to better place, the simple secret of living happy. All you need do is say good-bye to yesterday's loves, and hello to the new. Look around and see who needs you most and you won't go wrong. Forget who needed you yesterday.

You write and say you have new baby inside you made by husband of your mother. Rejoice in child, even if mother's husband will stay married to her. Forgive your mother, even if once she did evil. Nobody all bad, and a lot of the good in her children must have come from her. When you can forgive and forget the past, peace and love will come again to you, and this time it will stay.

And if you never in this world see Henny again, remember that Henny loved you well, as her own daughter, just as I loved your angel-sister whom I expect to meet again soon.

                                  Soon to be in heaven,

                                  Henny

I put the note down with a heavy feeling of sadness in my chest, then shrugged my shoulders. What had to be done would be done. A long time ago I'd set my feet on this path, and I'd follow it, come what may.

How strange the wind wasn't blowing when I stepped out the door and turned to wave to Emma who was spending the night with Jory. With boots covering my silver slippers, I headed for my car. How hushed it was, like nature was holding back in suspense as it focused on me.

Soft as eiderdown snow began to drift down. I glanced up at the gray, leaden sky, so much like the grandmother's eyes. Resolved again, I turned the key in the ignition and headed toward Foxworth Hall, though I wasn't an invited guest. I'd stormed at Bart for that. "Why didn't you insist and force her to invite me?"

"Really. Cathy, isn't that a bit too much to ask? Can I insult my wife by asking my mistress to her party? I may be a fool, Cathy. but I am not that cruel."

That first Christmas of imprisonment when I was twelve I'd lain with my head on Chris's boyish chest, wistfully wishing to be grown up, with curves as shapely as my mother's, with a face as beautiful as hers, wearing clothes as stunning as hers. And most of all I'd wished to be in control of my life.

Some Christmas wishes did come true.

Revelations

Just a little after ten o'clock I used the wooden key Chris had carved so many years ago to slip unseen through a back door into Foxworth Hall. Already many guests were there and more were still arriving. The orchestra was playing a Christmas carol and faintly it drifted up to me. Music so sweetly haunting I was taken back to my childhood. Only this time I was alone in alien territory with no one to back me up as I stole quietly up the back stairs, keeping to the shadows, ready to hide quickly if necessary. I wended my solitary way to the grand central rotunda to stand near the cabinet where Chris and I had hidden to look down on another Christmas party. I gazed downward to spy upon Bart Winslow standing beside his wife who was wearing bright red lamé. His strong voice was hearty as he greeted his arriving guests warmly, shaking hands, kissing cheeks, acting the genial host in true fashion. My mother seemed somehow secondary to him, hardly needed at all in this huge mansion that was soon to be hers.

Smiling bitterly to myself, I stole on to my mother's grand suite of rooms. It took me back in time! Oh, golly-golly!

I used my little-girl exclamation of delight, of surprise, of dismay or frustration, though I had better and more accurate words at my disposal now. Tonight I had no frustrations, only a lilting sense of justification. Whatever happened, she had brought it upon herself. Look, I thought, there was the splendid swan bed, still there, with the little swan bed across the foot. I glanced around, seeing it was all the same, but for the brocade fabric on the walls—that was different.

Now it was a soft plum color, and not strawberry pink. There was a brass valet to hold a man's suit ready, and unwrinkled, until he put it on. That was new. I hurried on into my mother's dressing room. On my knees, I pulled out a special bottom drawer to feel around for the tiny button that had to be pushed in a certain combination of numbers to trigger the complicated lock. And would you believe it—she still used her birthday numbers of month, day and year! My! She was a trusting soul.

In no time at all I had the huge velvet tray on the floor before me, so I could help myself to the emeralds and diamonds she had worn to that Christmas party when first Chris and I beheld Bartholomew Winslow. How we'd loved her then, and how we'd resented *him*. We had been still in the shadow of our grief for our father, and hadn't wanted Momma to marry again—not ever again.

As in a dream I donned the emerald and diamond jewelry that went so well with my green velvet and chiffon gown. I glanced in the mirror to see if I looked as she had way back then. I was a few years younger, but yes, I did look like her. Not exactly, but almost—and enough to convince—for were two leaves from the same tree ever duplicates? I replaced the jewelry tray, put back the drawer, leaving everything as it had been. Except now I wore several hundred thousand dollars worth of gems I didn't own. One more look at my watch. Ten-thirty. Too soon. At twelve I wanted to make my grand entrance, like Cinderella in reverse.

With utmost caution, I crept stealthily along the long halls to the northern wing, and found that end room with the door locked. The wooden key still fitted. But my heart didn't seem to fit my chest. It beat too fast, too fierce, too loud and my pulse raced too excitedly. I had to keep calm, self-possessed, do everything right and not be intimidated by this awesome house that had done its best to destroy us.

When I stepped into that room with the two double beds, I stepped back into childhood. The gold-colored, quilted satin spreads were still on the beds, precisely made without a wrinkle. The ten-inch TV was still in the corner. The doll house with its porcelain people and antique made-to-scale furniture waited for Carrie's hands to bring it to life again. The old rocker that Chris had brought down from the attic, still there. *Why, it was as if in here time stood still and we'd never left!*

Even hell was still on the walls, gruesomely represented by three reproductions of masterpieces. Oh, God I hadn't known this room would make me feel so—so shredded inside. I couldn't afford to cry. That would make my mascara run. Yet I wanted to cry. All about me flitted the ghosts of Cory and Carrie, just five years old, laughing, crying, wanting outside, the sunlight, and all they could do was push tiny trucks to make-believe San Francisco or Los Angeles. There used to be train tracks that ran all over the room and under the furniture. Oh, where did the train tracks go—the coal cars, the engines? I pulled a tissue from my tiny evening bag and held it to the corner of one eye and then the other. I leaned to peer into the doll house. The porcelain maids were still cooking in the kitchen; the builder still stood near the front door to welcome the guests arriving in a coach pulled by two horses— and lo, when I looked in the nursery, the cradle was there! The missing cradle! For weeks we'd hunted to find it, fearful all the time the grandmother would notice it missing and punish Carrie—and there it was, just where it should be! But the baby wasn't in it, nor were the parents in the front parlor. Mr.

and Mrs. Parkins and baby Clara were now mine and never would they reside in this doll house again.

Had the grandmother herself stolen the cradle, so she could then see it missing, and ask Carrie where it was, and when it couldn't be produced, she'd have good reason to punish Carrie? And Cory as well, for he would automatically, without fear for himself, run to protect his twin sister. It was like her to do something mean and cruel like that. But if she had, why had she stayed her hand, and not played out her role to the end? I laughed bitterly to myself. She *had* played out her role to the end—not just a whipping, but something better, something *worse*. Poison. Arsenic on four sugared doughnuts.

I jumped then. It seemed I heard a child laugh. My imagination, of course. And then, when I should have known better, I headed for the closet and the high and narrow door at the very back end and the steep and narrow dark stairs. A million times I'd ascended these stairs. A million times in the dark, without a candle, or a flashlight. Up into the dark, eerie, gigantic attic, and only when I was there did I feel around for the place where Chris and I had hidden our candles and matches.

Still there. Time *did* stand still in this place. We'd had several candle holders, all of pewter with small handles to grasp. Holders we'd found in an old trunk along with boxes and boxes of short, stubby, clumsily made candles. We'd always presumed them to be homemade candles, for they had smelled so rank and old when they burned.

My breath caught! Oh! It was the same! The paper flowers still dangled down, mobiles to sway in the drafts, and the giant flowers were still on the walls. Only all the colors had faded to indistinct gray—ghost flowers. The sparkling gem centers we'd glued on had loosened, and now only a few daisies had sequins, or gleaming stones, for centers. Carrie's purple worm was there only now he too was a nothing color.

Cory's epileptic snail didn't appear a bright, lopsided beach ball now, it was more a tepid, half-rotten squashy orange. The BEWARE signs Chris and I had painted in red were still on the walls, and the swings still dangled down from the attic rafters. Over near the record player was the barre Chris had fashioned, then nailed to the wall so I could practice my ballet positions. Even my outgrown costumes hung limply from nails, dozens of them with matching leotards and worn out *pointe* shoes, all faded and dusty, rotten smelling.

As in an unhappy dream I was committed to, I drifted aimlessly toward the distant schoolroom, with the candlelight flickering. Ghosts were unsettled, memories and specters followed me as things began to wake up, yawn and whisper. No, I told myself, it was only the floating panels of my long chiffon wings . . . that was all. The spotted rocking-horse loomed up, scary and threatening, and my hand rose to my throat as I held back a scream. The rusty red wagon seemed to move by unseen hands pushing it, so my eyes took flight to the blackboard where I'd printed my enigmatic farewell message to those who came in the future. How was I to know it would be me?

> We lived in the attic,
> Christopher, Cory, Carrie and me—
> Now there are only three.

Behind the small desk that had been Cory's I scrunched down, and tried to fit my legs under. I wanted to put myself into a deep reverie that would call up Cory's spirit that would tell me where he lay.

As I sat there waiting, the wind outside began to blow, picking up strength so it howled and hurled the snow slantwise. Another blizzard was on, full force. With the storm came the drafts to blow out my candle! The darkness shrieked, and I had to run to get out! Run *fast* . . . run, run, run before I became one of *them!*

*   *   *

The next hour had been choreographed to the smallest detail. As the big grandfather clock began to strike twelve, I positioned myself in the center of the second-floor balcony. I did nothing spectacular to pull all eyes my way, just stood there with my flesh warmed by the flashing jewels. In her crimson dress of lamé, so high in front it reached her throat that was encircled with a lavish choker of diamonds, my mother slightly turned. I saw the backless gown made up for the severity in front, so a hint of her buttock cleavage showed. Her blond hair was styled shorter than I'd ever seen it, and fluffed out around her face in a flattering way. From this distance she looked very young and lovely, and nowhere near her actual age. Ahh . . . the last stroke of twelve sounded . . .

Some sixth sense must have warned her, for she turned her head slowly to look my way. I began my descent. She froze in shock. Her eyes grew wide and dark as her hand that held a cocktail glass trembled so much a bit of the liquid sloshed out and fell to the floor. Because she stared, Bart followed the direction of her gaze. He gawked as if at an apparition. Now that both host and hostess were mesmerized, each guest had to look where no doubt they expected to see Santa Claus, and it was only me. Only me as once my mother had been years ago, wearing the same gown, and before many, I was sure, of those very same people who were here that other Christmas when I was twelve. I even recognized a few, older, but I knew them! Oh, the joy to have them here!

This was my moment of triumph! Moving as only a ballerina can, I meant to play my role to the utmost of my dramatic ability. As the guests stared upward, clearly caught in thrall by time moved backward, I gloated to see my mother blanch. Then I rejoiced to see Bart's eyes widen more as they jumped from me, to her, then back to me. Slowly, in a dead silence, for the music had stopped, I descended the left side of the dual winding staircases, thinking I was Caraboose, the wicked fairy who put upon Aurora the curse of death. Then I made myself the Lilac Fairy to steal away Aurora's prince while she slept her sleep of one hundred years. (It was clever of me not to think of myself as my mother's daughter, and how soon I would destroy her. Very clever to make of this a stage production, when I was dealing with reality, and not fantasy and the blood that could be spilled.)

Gracefully I trailed my sparkling fingers along the rosewood railing, feeling my green chiffon wings fluttering and floating as step by step, and second by second, I neared the place where my mother and Bart were standing very close together. She was trembling all over, but managing to hold onto her poise. I thought I glimpsed a flicker of panic in the blue of her Dresden eyes. I kindly bestowed on her my most gracious smile while standing on the second step from the bottom. In this way I gave myself the height I needed to be taller than anyone else. All had to look up to me wearing four-inch silver heels on platform soles like Carrie's, so as to be on an even height with my mother when we met eye to eye. The better to see her dismay. Her discomfort. Her utter collapse!

"Merry Christmas!" I called to one and all in a loud clear voice. It resounded like a heralding trumpet to attract others from different, rooms, and they came in by the dozens, as if drawn more by the total silence but for my voice. "Mr. Winslow," I called invitingly, "come dance with me, just as you danced with my mother fifteen years ago, when I was twelve and hiding above, and she wore a gown just like the one I have on now." Bart was visibly jolted. Stunned shock made his dark eyes blacken, but he refused to move from my mother's side!

He forced me to do what I did next. As everyone stood there and waited, held in breathless suspense, expecting more explosive revelations, I gave them what they wanted.

"I'd like to introduce myself." My voice was high-pitched so it would carry well. "I am Catherine Leigh Foxworth, the firstborn daughter of Mrs. Bartholomew Winslow, whom most of you must remember was first married to my father, Christopher Foxworth. Remember too that he was my mother's half-uncle, the younger brother of Malcolm Neal Foxworth who disinherited his only daughter, his sole remaining heir, because she had the unholy temerity to wed his half-brother! What is more, I also have an older brother, named Christopher too—he's a doctor now. Once I had a younger brother and sister, twins seven years younger than I—but Cory and Carrie are dead now—for they were—" I stopped short for some reason, then went on. "That Christmas party fifteen years ago, Chris and I were hiding in the chest on the balcony, while the twins slept in the end room of the northern wing. Our playground was the attic, and never, never did we go downstairs. We were attic mice, unwanted and unloved once money came into the picture." And I would have screamed it all out, every last detail, but Bart came striding over to me.

"Bravo, Cathy!" he cried. "You play your part to perfection! Congratulations." He put his arm about my shoulders, charmingly smiled at me, then turned to the guests who appeared not to know what to think, or whom to believe, much less how to react. "Ladies, gentlemen," he said, "let me introduce to you Catherine Dahl, whom many of you must have seen on stage when she danced with her husband, Julian Marquet. And as you have just witnessed, she is also an actress of merit. Cathy here is a distant relative of my wife, and if you can see any resemblance, that explains it. In fact, Mrs. Julian Marquet is one of our neighbors now, you may know that. Since her resemblance to my wife is so remarkable, we cooked up this little farce between us, and did what we could to enliven and make different this party with our little joke."

He ruthlessly pinched my upper arm, before he caught my hand, put his arm about my waist and asked me to dance. "Come now, Cathy, certainly you want to show off your dancing ability after that fine dramatic performance." As the

music began to play, he forcefully made me dance! I turned
my head to see my mother sagging against a friend, her face
so pale her makeup stood out like livid blotches. Even so, she
couldn't take her eyes from me in the arms of her husband.

"You brazen little bitch!" Bart hissed at me. "How dare
you come in here and pull such a stunt? I thought I loved
you. I despise catty women with long claws. I won't have you
ruining my wife! You little idiot, whatever made you tell so
many lies?"

"You are the idiot, Bart," I said calmly, though I was panicked inside—what if he refused to believe? "Look at me.
How would I know she wore a gown like this, if I hadn't seen
her with it on? How would I know you went with her to see
her bedroom with the swan bed, if my brother, Chris, hadn't
hidden and heard and seen everything the two of you did up
on the second-floor rotunda."

He met my eyes, and he looked so strange, so distant and
strange.

"Yes, Bart darling, I *am* your wife's daughter, and I know
if your law firm finds out your wife had four children born
from the union of her first marriage, then you and she lose
everything. All that money. All your investments. Everything
you have bought will be taken back. Oh, the pity of that makes
me want to cry."

We danced on his cheek inches from mine. A smile was
fixed to his lips. "That gown you're wearing, how the hell did
you find out she had one exactly like that the first time I came
to this house to a party?"

I laughed with fake merriment. "Dear Bart, you are so
stupid. How do you think I know? I saw her in this gown. She
came to our room and showed us how pretty she looked, and
I was so envious of all her curves and the way Chris looked at
her with so much admiration. She wore her hair as I am wearing mine now. These jewels were taken from her safe in the
dressing room table drawer."

"You're lying," he said, but doubt was in his voice now.

"I know the combination," I went on softly, "she used her birthday numbers. She told me that when I was twelve. She *is* my mother. She did keep us locked in that room, waiting for her father to die, so she could inherit. And you know why she had to keep us a big, dark secret. You wrote the will, didn't you? Think back to a certain night when you fell asleep in her grand suite of rooms, and you dreamed a young girl wearing a short blue nightie stole in and kissed you. You weren't dreaming, Bart. That kiss was from me. I was fifteen then, and had snuck into your room to steal money—remember how you used to miss cash? You and she thought the servants were stealing, but it was Chris, and one time it was me . . . who didn't find anything because you were there to scare me away."

"Nooo," he said with a sigh. "*No! *She wouldn't do that to her own children!"

"Wouldn't she? She did. That big chest up there near the balcony balustrade has a backing of wire mesh screening. Chris and I could see just fine. We saw the caterers fixing crepes and waiters in red and black and a fountain spraying champagne, and there were two huge silver punch bowls. Chris and I could smell everything so delicious and we drooled to have a taste of what was down there. Our meals were so boring, and always cold or lukewarm. The twins hardly ate anything. Were you there the Thanksgiving Day dinner when she got up and down so much? Do you want to know why? She was preparing a tray of food to take up to us whenever the butler John was out of his pantry."

He shook his head, his eyes dazed.

"Yes, Bart, the woman you married had four children she hid away for three years and almost five months. Our playground was in the attic. Have you ever played in an attic in the summertime? In the winter? Do you think it was pleasant? Can you imagine how we felt, waiting year after year for an old man to die so our lives could begin? Do you know the trauma we suffered knowing she cared more for the money than she did for us, her own children? And the twins, they didn't grow. They stayed so small, grew so large-eyed and haunted looking, and she'd come and never look at them! She pretended not to notice their ill health!"

"Cathy, please! If you are lying, stop! Don't make me hate her!"

"Why not hate her? She deserves it," I went on as my mother went to lean against a wall, and looked sick enough to throw up. "Once I lay on the swan bed, with the little swan bed across the foot. You had a book in your nightstand drawer about sex, disguised under a dustjacket that read *How to Create and Design Your Own Needlepoint* or something like that."

"*How to Create Your Own Needlepoint Designs*," he corrected, looking sick and as pale as my mother, though he kept on smiling, hatefully smiling.

"You are making all of this up," he said in an odd tone that showed no sincerity. "You hate her because you want me, and connive to deceive me and destroy her."

I smiled and lightly brushed his cheek with my lips. "Then let me convince you more. Our grandmother always wore gray taffeta with hand-crocheted collars, and never without a diamond brooch with seventeen stones pinned at her throat. Very early each morning, before six-thirty, she brought us food and milk in a picnic hamper. At first she fed us rather well, but gradually, as her resentment grew, our meals grew worse and worse until we were fed mostly sandwiches of peanut butter and jelly and occasionally fried chicken and potato salad. She gave us a long list of rules to live by, including one that forbade us from opening the draperies to let in light. Year after year we lived in a dim room without sunlight. If only you knew how dreary life is, shut away, without light, feeling neglected, unwanted, unloved. Then there was another rule very hard to abide by. We were not supposed to even *look* at each other—especially one of the opposite sex."

"Oh, God!" he exclaimed, then sighed heavily. "That sounds like her. You say it was more than three years you were locked up there?"

"Three years and *almost* five months, and if that seems a long time to you, how do you think it was for small children of five, and one of twelve, and the other of fourteen? Back then, five minutes passed like five hours, and days were like months, and months were like years."

Doubt fought clearly with his legal mind that saw all the ramifications, if my tale were true. "Cathy, be honest, totally honest. You had two brothers and one sister—and all that time, when I was here too, you were living locked up?"

"In the beginning, we believed in her, every word she said, for we loved her, trusted her, she was our only hope, and our salvation. And we wanted her to inherit all that money from her father. We agreed to stay up there until the grandfather died, although when our mother explained how we were to live in Foxworth Hall she failed to mention we were to be hidden away. At first we thought it would only be for a day or so, but it went on and on. We filled our time by playing games—and we prayed a lot, slept a lot. We grew thin, half-sick, malnourished, and suffered through two weeks of starvation while you and our mother traveled throughout Europe on your honeymoon. And then you went to Vermont to visit your sister, where our mother bought a two-pound box of maple-sugar candy. But by then we'd already been eating, doughnuts with arsenic laced in the powdered sugar."

He gave me a hard, fierce look of terrible anger. "Yes. she did buy a box of that kind of candy in Vermont. But Cathy! whatever else you may say, I can never believe my wife would deliberately set out to poison her own children!" His scornful eyes raked over me, then back to my face. "*Yes, you do look like her!* You could be her daughter. I admit that! But to say Corrine would kill her own children. I can't believe that!"

I shoved him away forcefully, and whirled about. "*Listen*

everyone!" I yelled out. *"I am* the daughter of Corrine Foxworth Winslow! She *did* lock her four children in the end room of the northern wing. Our grandmother was in on the scheme and gave us the attic for our playroom. We decorated it with paper flowers, to make it pretty for our little twins, all so our mother could inherit. Our mother told us we *had* to hide, for if we didn't our grandfather would never have her written into his will. All of you know how he despised her for marrying his half-brother. Our mother persuaded us to come and live upstairs, and be as quiet as attic mice; we went, trusting and believing she would keep her word and let us out the day her father died. *But she didn't!* She didn't! She let us suffer up there for *nine* months after he was dead and buried!"

I had more to spill out. But my mother shrilled out in a loud voice, *"Stop!"* She stumbled forward; her arms outstretched as if she were blind. *"You lie!"* she screamed. "I've never seen you before! Get out of my house! Get out this instant before I call the police and have you thrown out! *Now you get out, and you stay out!"*

Everyone was staring at her now, not me. She, the ultra-poised and arrogant had lost control, was trembling, her face livid, wanting to scratch the eyes from my face! I don't think a soul there believed her then, not when they could see I was her very image—and I knew too many truths.

Bart left my side and went to his wife to whisper something in her ear. He put his arms consolingly around her, and kissed her cheek. She clung to him helplessly, with pale, shaky hands of desperation, beseeching his help with great teary eyes of cerulean blue—like mine, like Chris's, like the twins' blue eyes.

"Thank you again, Cathy, for a fine performance. Come into the library with me and I'll pay you your fee." He scanned over the guests clustered around and quietly he said, "I'm sorry, but my wife has been ill, and this little joke was ill-timed on my part. I should have known better than to plan such a show. So, if you will please forgive us, do go on with the party; enjoy yourselves; eat, drink and be merry; and stay as long as you like, Miss Catherine Dahl may have some more surprises in store for you."

How I hated him then!

As the guests milled about and whispered and looked from me to him, he picked up my mother and carried her toward the library. She was heavier than she used to be, but in his arms she seemed a feather. Bart glanced over his shoulder at me, gestured with his head that I was to follow, which I did.

I wanted Chris here with me, as he should be. It shouldn't be left up to me to confront her with the truth. I was strangely alone, defensive, as if in the end Bart would believe *her* and not me, no matter what I said, no matter what proof I gave him. And I had plenty of proof. I could describe to him the flowers in the attic, the snail, the worm, the cryptic message I'd written on the blackboard, and, most of all, I could show him the wooden key.

Bart reached the library and carefully put my mother into one of the leather chairs. He snapped an order my way. "Cathy, will you please close the door behind you."

Only then did I see who else was in the library! My grandmother was seated in the same wheelchair her husband had used. Ordinarily you can't tell one wheelchair from another, but this one was custom-made and much finer. She wore a gray-blue robe over her hospital jacket, and a lap robe covered her legs. The chair was placed near the fireplace so she could benefit from the heat of a roaring log fire. Her bald head shone as she turned it my way. Her flintstone gray eyes glowed maliciously.

A nurse was in the room with her. I didn't take the time to look at her face.

"Mrs. Mallory," said Bart, "will you please leave the room and leave Mrs. Foxworth here." It wasn't a request, but an order.

"Yes, sir," said the nurse who quickly got up and scuttled

to leave as fast as possible. "You just ring for me when Mrs. Foxworth wants to be put to bed, sir," she said at the door and then disappeared.

Bart seemed on the verge of exploding as he stalked the room, and what wrath he felt now seemed directed not only at me, but also at his wife. "All right," he said as soon as the nurse was gone, "let's have done with it, all of it. Corrine, I've always suspected you had a secret, a big secret. It occurred to me many times you didn't truly love me, but it never once crossed my mind you might have four children you hid away in the attic. *Why?* Why couldn't you have come to me and told me the truth?" He roared this, all control gone. "How could you be so selfishly heartless, so brutally cruel as to lock away your four children and then try and kill them with arsenic?"

Sagging limply in a brown leather chair, my mother closed her eyes. She seemed bloodless as she asked in a dull voice. "So, you are going to believe *her* and not me. You know I could never poison anyone, no matter what I had to gain. And you know that I don't have any children!"

I was stunned to know Bart believed me and not her, and then I guessed he didn't truly believe me, but was using a lawyer's trick, attacking and hoping to take her off guard, and maybe get to the truth. But that would never work, not with her. She'd trained herself over too many years for anyone to take her by surprise.

I strode forward to glare down at her, and in the harshest of voices I spoke. "Why don't you tell Bart about Cory, Momma? Go on, tell him how you and your mother came in the night and wrapped him in a green blanket and told us you were taking him to a hospital. Tell him how you came back the next day and told us he died from pneumonia. Lies! All lies! Chris sneaked downstairs and overheard that butler, John Amos Jackson, telling a maid of how the grandmother carried arsenic up to the attic to kill the little mice. *We were the little mice who ate those sugared doughnuts, Mother!* And we proved those doughnuts were poisoned. Remember Cory's little pet mouse that you used to ignore? He was fed only a bit of sugared doughnut and he died! Now sit there and cry, and deny who I am, and who Chris is, and who Cory and Carrie used to be!"

"I have never seen you before in my life," she said strongly, bolting upright and staring me straight in the eyes, "except when I went to the ballet in New York."

Bart narrowed his eyes, weighing her, then me. Then he looked at his wife again and his eyes grew even more slotlike and cunning. "Cathy," he said, still looking at her, "you are making very serious allegations against my wife. You accuse her of murder, premeditated murder. If you are proven right, she will face a jury trial for murder—is that what you want?"

"I want justice, that is all. No, I don't want to see her in prison or put in an electric chair—if they still do that in this state."

"She is lying," whispered my mother, "lying, lying, lying."

I had come prepared for accusations like this and calmly I pulled from my tiny purse duplicates of four birth certificates. I handed them to Bart who took them over to a lamp and bent to study them. Cruelly and with great satisfaction I smiled at my mother. "Dear mother, you were very foolish to sew those birth certificates in the lining of our old suitcases. Without them I wouldn't have had any proof at all to show your husband and, no doubt, he would go on believing you— for I am an actress and accustomed to putting on a good show.

"It's a pity he doesn't know *you* are an even better actress. Cringe away, Momma, but I have the proof!" I laughed wildly, near tears as I saw them begin to glisten in her eyes, for once I had loved her so well, and under all the hatred and animosity I felt for her, a little light of innate love still waxed and waned, and it hurt, oh, it did hurt to make her cry. Yet she deserved it, she did, I kept telling myself she did!

"You know something else. Momma. Carrie told me how

she met you on the street and you denied her, and shortly afterwards she became so ill she died—so you helped kill her too! And without the birth certificates you could have escaped all retribution, for that courthouse in Gladstone, Pennsylvania, burned down ten years ago. See how kind fate would have been to you, Mother? But you never did anything well. Why didn't you burn them? Why did you save them . . . ? That was very thoughtless of you, dearest loving Mother, to save the evidence; but then you were always careless, always thoughtless, always extravagant about everything. You thought if you killed your four children you could have others—but your father tricked you, didn't he?"

"Cathy! Sit down and let me handle this!" ordered Bart. "My wife has just undergone surgery and I'll not have you threaten her health. *Now sit before I push you down!"*

I sat.

He glanced at my mother, then at *her* mother.

"Corrine, if you have ever cared for me, loved me even a little—is any of what this woman says true? *Is she your daughter?"*

Very weakly my mother answered, ". . . Yes."

I sighed. I thought I heard the whole house sigh, and Bart along with it. I lifted my eyes to see my grandmother staring at me in the oddest way.

"Yes," she continued flatly, her dull eyes fixed on Bart. "I couldn't tell you, Bart. I wanted to tell you, but I was afraid you wouldn't want me if I came with four children and no money, and I loved and wanted you so much. I racked my brains trying to figure out a solution so I could keep you, my children and the money too." She sat up and made a ramrod of her spine as her head lifted regally high. "And I *did* figure out a solution! I *did!* It took me weeks and weeks of scheming, but I did figure a way!"

"Corrine," said Bart with ice in his voice as he towered above her, "murder is never a solution to anything! All you had to do was tell me, and I would have thought of a way to save your children and your inheritance."

"But don't you see," she cried out excitedly, "I figured out a way all by myself! I wanted you; I wanted my children and the money too. I thought my father *owed* me that money!" She laughed hysterically, beginning to lose control again, as if hell was at her heels and she had to speak fast to escape its burn. "Everyone thought I was stupid, a blond with a pretty face and figure but no brains. Well, I fooled you, Mother," she threw out at that old woman in the chair. And at a portrait on the wall she screamed, "And I fooled you too, Malcolm Foxworth!" Then at me she flared her eyes, "And you too, Catherine. You thought you had it so tough up there, locked away, missing out on schooldays and friends, but you don't realize how *good* you had it compared to what my father did to me! *You,* you and your accusations, always at me, *when could I let you out?* When down below my father was ordering me to do this, do that, for if you don't you won't inherit one penny and I'll tell your lover about your four children too!"

I gasped. Then jumped to my feet. "He knew about us? The grandfather knew?"

Again she laughed, hard, diamond-brittle laughter. "Yes, he knew, but I didn't tell him! The day Chris and I ran away from this horrible house he hired detectives to follow and keep tabs on us. Then, when my husband was killed in that accident, I was persuaded by my lawyer to seek their help. How my father rejoiced! Don't you see, Cathy," she said so fast her words piled one on the other, "he *wanted* me and my children in his house and under his thumb! He had it planned along with my mother, to deceive me and let me think he didn't know you were hidden upstairs. But he knew all the time! It was his plan to keep you locked up *for the rest of your lives!*"

I gasped and stared at her. I doubted her too; how could I trust anything she said now after she'd done so much? "The grandmother, she went along with his plan?" I asked, feeling a numbing sensation creeping up from my toes.

"Her?" said Momma, tossing her mother a hard look of contempt. "She'd do anything he said, for she hated me; she's always hated me; he loved me too much when I was a girl, and cared nothing at all about his sons whom she favored more. And after we were here, snared in his trap, he gloated to have his half-brother's children captured as animals in a cage, to keep locked up until they were dead. So, while you were up there, playing your games and decorating the attic, he kept at me, day in, day out. 'They should never have been born, should they?' he'd slyly say, and cunningly suggest you would all be better off dead than kept prisoners until you grew old, or sickened and died. I didn't truly believe he meant this at first. I thought it was only another of his ways to torture me. Each day he'd say you were wicked, flawed, evil children who should be destroyed. I'd cry, plead, go down on my knees and beg, and he'd laugh. One evening he raged at me. 'You fool,' he said. 'Were you idiot enough to think I could ever forgive you for sleeping with your half-uncle—the ultimate sin against God? Bearing his children?' And on and on he'd rave, screaming sometimes. Then he'd lash out with his walking cane, striking whatever he could reach. My mother would sit nearby and smirk with pleasure. Yet, he didn't let me know he knew you were up there for several weeks . . . and by that time, I was trapped." She pleaded with me to believe, to have mercy. "Can't you see how it was? I didn't know which way to turn! I didn't have any money, and I kept thinking his terrible temper tantrums would kill him, so I provoked him so he *would* die—but he kept on living, and berating me and my children. And every time I went into your room, you'd be pleading to be let out. *Especially you, Cathy—especially you.*"

"And what else did he do to make you keep us prisoners?" I asked sarcastically, "except scream and rail and hit you with his cane? It couldn't have been very hard, for he was very frail, and we never saw any marks on you after the first whipping. You were free to come and go as you wanted. You could have worked out some plan to slip us outside unknown to him. You wanted his money, and you didn't care what you had to do to get it! You wanted that money more than you wanted your four children!"

Before my very eyes her delicate and lovely restored face took on the aged look of *her* mother. She seemed to shrivel and grow haggard with the countless years she had yet to live with her regrets. Her gaze took wild flight, seeking some safe refuge in which to forever hide, not only from me, but from the fury she saw in her husband's eyes.

"Cathy," pleaded my mother, "I know you hate me, but—"

"Yes, Mother. I do hate you."

"You wouldn't if you understood—"

I laughed, hard and bitterly. "Dearest Mother, there is not one thing you could tell me to make me understand."

"Corrine," said Bart, his tone sterile, as if his heart had been removed. "Your daughter is right. You can sit there and cry, and talk about your father forcing you to poison your children—but how can I believe when I can't remember him even giving you a hard glance? He looked at you with love and pride. You did come and go as you chose. Your father lavished money on you, so you could buy new clothes and everything else you wanted. Now you come up with some ridiculous tale of how you were tortured by him, and forced by him to kill your hidden children. God, you sicken me!"

Her eyes took on a glassy stare; her pale and elegant hands trembled as they unfolded and fluttered up from her lap to her throat, and there they fingered over and over again the diamond choker that must be keeping her gown from falling off. "Bart, please, I'm not lying. . . . I admit I've lied to you in the past, and deceived you about my children—but I'm not lying now. Why can't you believe me?"

Bart stood with his feet spread apart, as a sailor would to brace himself on a rocky sea. His hands were behind his back and clenched into fists. "What kind of man do you think I am—or was?" he asked bitterly. "You could have told me any-thing then, and I would have understood. I loved you, Corrine. I would have done anything legally possible to thwart your father and help you gain his fortune, and at the same time keep your children alive, free to live normal lives. I'm not a monster, Corrine, and I didn't marry you for your money. I would have married you if you were penniless!"

"You couldn't outwit my father!" she cried, jumping up and beginning to pace the floor.

In that shiny crimson dress my mother appeared a bright lick of flame, a color that made her eyes dark purple as they darted from one to the other of us. Then, finally, when I couldn't stand to watch her as she was, broken, wild, with all her queenly poise gone, her eyes came to rest on *her* mother—that old woman who slumped in the wheelchair, as if with-out bones. Her gnarled fingers worked weakly at the afghan, but her gray zealot's eyes burned with a strong, mean fire. I watched as the eyes of mother and daughter clashed. Those gray eyes that never changed, never softened with old age or fear of the hell that must be lying in wait for her.

And, to my surprise, from this confrontation my mother rose straight and tall, the winner in this battle of wills. She began to speak in a dispassionate way, as if discussing some-one else. It was like hearing a woman talk who knew she was killing herself with each razored word, and yet she didn't care, not anymore—for I was the winner, after all, and to me, her most severe judge, she turned to appeal. "All right, Cathy. I knew sooner or later I would have to face up to you. I knew it would be *you* who would force the truth from me. It has always been *your* way to look through me, and guess I wasn't always what I wanted you to believe I was. Christopher loved me, trusted me. But you never would. Yet in the beginning, at the time your father was killed, I was trying to do the best I could by you. I told you what I believed to be the truth, when I asked you to come and live here hidden away until I won back my father's favor. I didn't truly think it would take more than one day, or possibly two."

I sat as frozen, staring at her. Her eyes pleaded mutely, *have mercy, Cathy, believe me! I speak the truth.*

She turned from me, and in great distress she appealed to Bart and spoke of their first meeting in a friend's home. "I didn't want to love you, Bart, and involve you in the mess I was in. I wanted to tell you about my children and the threat my father posed to them, but just when I would he'd worsen and appear ready to die, so I'd put it off and keep quiet. I prayed that when eventually I did tell you, you'd understand. It was stupid of me, for a secret kept too long becomes impossible to explain. You wanted to marry me. My father kept saying no. My children pleaded every day to be let out. Even though I knew they had every right to complain, I began to resent them, the way they kept harassing me, making me feel guilty and ashamed when I was trying to do the best I could for them. And it was Cathy, always it was Cathy, no matter how many gifts I gave her, who kept at it the most." She threw me another of her long, tormented looks, as if I'd tortured her beyond endurance.

"Cathy," she whispered then, her watery, drowning look of anguish brightening a little, as once more she turned to me. "I did do the best I could! I told my parents all of you did have hidden afflictions, especially Cory. They wanted to think God had punished my children, so they believed easily. And Cory was always having one cold after another, and his allergy. Can't you see what I tried to do, make all of you just a little sick, so I could rush you one by one to the hospital, then report back to my mother you died. I used a minute bit of arsenic, but not enough to kill you! All I wanted to do was make you a little bit sick, just enough to get you out!"

I was appalled by her stupidity to scheme in such a dangerous way. Then I guessed it was all a lie, just an excuse to satisfy Bart who was staring at her in the oddest way. I smiled at her then, while inside I was hurting so badly I could cry. "Momma," I said softly, interrupting her pleas, "have you forgotten your father was dead before the sugared doughnuts started coming? You didn't have to trick him in his grave."

She darted her tormented eyes to the grandmother who had a stern, forbidding look fixed on her daughter.

"Yes!" cried Momma, "I knew that! But for that codicil I would never have needed the arsenic! But my father let our butler John in on our secret, and he was alive to see that I followed through and kept you upstairs until each one of you was dead! And if he didn't, then my mother was to see he didn't inherit the fifty thousand dollars promised to him. Then there was my mother, who wanted John to inherit everything!"

A terrible silence came while I tried to digest this. The grandfather knew all the time and had wanted to keep us prisoners for life? And as if that weren't enough punishment, he then tried to force her to kill us? Oh, he must have been even more evil than I thought! Not human at all! Then, as I watched her and took note of her anxiously waiting blue eyes, her hands busily trying to twist an invisible rope of pearls, I knew she was lying. I glanced at the grandmother and saw her frown as she tried to speak. Fierce indignation was in her eyes, as if she would deny all my mother had said. But she hated Momma. She would want me to believe the worst—oh, God, how was I to find out the truth?

I glanced at Bart who stood before the fire, his dark eyes gazing at his wife as if he'd never seen her before, and what he was seeing now appalled him.

"Momma," I began in a flat voice, "what did you really do with Cory's body? We have looked in all the cemeteries around here and checked their records, and not one little boy of eight years died in that last week of October, 1960."

She swallowed first, then wrung her hands, flashing all the diamonds and other jewels. "I didn't know what to do with him," she whispered. "He died before I could reach the hospital. Suddenly he stopped breathing, and when I looked in the back seat I knew he was dead." She sobbed with the memory. "I hated myself then. I knew I could be charged with murder, and I hadn't meant to kill him! Only make him a little sick! So I threw his body in a deep ravine and covered him over with dead leaves, sticks and stones. . . ." Her huge desperate eyes pleaded with me to believe.

I too had to swallow, thinking of Cory in a deep dark ravine, left to decay there. "No, Momma, you didn't do that." My soft voice seemed to cut through the frozen atmosphere of the huge library. "I visited the end room of the northern wing before I came down here." I paused for better effect and made my next words more dramatic. "Before I came down the stairs to confront you I first used stairs that lead directly to the attic, then the hidden little stairway in the closet of our prison. Chris and I always suspected there was another way into the attic, and correctly we reasoned there had to be a door hidden behind the giant heavy armoires we couldn't shove out of the way no matter how hard we pushed. Momma . . . I found a small room we'd never seen before. There was a very peculiar odor in that room, like something dead and rotten."

For a moment she couldn't move. Her expression went totally blank. She stared at me with vacant eyes and then her mouth and her hands began to work, but she couldn't speak. She tried, but she couldn't speak. Bart started to say something, but she put her hands up to her ears to shut out anything anyone would say.

Suddenly the library door opened. I whirled in a fury.

My mother turned as in a nightmare to see why I kept staring. Chris pulled up short and gazed at her. She jumped then, as if terribly startled, then put up both her hands in a gesture that seemed to ward him off.

Was she seeing a ghost of our father? "Chris . . . ?" she asked. "Chris, I didn't mean to do it, really I didn't! Don't look at me like that, Chris! I loved them! I didn't want to give them the arsenic—but my father made me! He told me they should never have been born! He tried to tell me they were so evil they deserved to die, and that was the only way I could make amends for the sin I'd committed when I married you!" Tears streamed down her cheeks as she went on, though Chris kept shaking his head. "I loved my children! *Our* children! But what could I do? I only meant to make them a little sick—just enough to save them, that's all, that's all. . . . Chris, don't look at me like that! You know I wouldn't ever kill our children!"

His eyes turned icy blue as he stared at her. "Then you did deliberately feed us arsenic?" he asked. "I never fully believed it once we were free of this house and had time to think about it. But you did do it!"

She screamed then. In all my life I'd never heard such a scream as that one that rose and fell hysterically. Screams that sounded like the howls of the insane! On her heel she whirled about, still screaming, as she raced for a door I hadn't even known was there, and through it she ran and disappeared.

"Cathy," said Chris, tearing his eyes from the door and scanning the library to take note of Bart and the grandmother, "I've come to fetch you. I've had bad news. We have to go back to Clairmont immediately!"

Before I could answer Bart spoke up, "Are you Cathy's older brother, Chris?"

"Yes, of course. I came for Cathy. She's needed someplace else." He stretched out his hand as I drifted toward him.

"Wait a minute," said Bart. "I need to ask you a few questions. I've got to know the full truth. Was that woman in the red dress your mother?"

First Chris looked at me. I nodded to tell him Bart knew, and only then did Chris meet Bart's eyes with some hostility. "Yes, she is my mother and Cathy's mother, and once the mother of twins named Cory and Carrie."

"And she kept all four of you locked up in one room for more than three years?" asked Bart, as if he still didn't want to believe.

"Yes, three years and four months and sixteen days. And when she took Cory away one night she came back later and told us he died of pneumonia. And if you want more details, you will have to wait, for there are others we have to think about now. Come, Cathy," he said, reaching for my hand again. "We've got to hurry!" He looked then at the grandmother and gave her a wry smile. "Merry Christmas, Grandmother. I had hoped never to see you again, but now that I have I see time has worked its own revenge." He turned again to me. "Hurry, Cathy, where is your coat? I have Jory and Mrs. Lindstrom out in my car."

"Why?" I asked. Sudden panic filled me. What was the matter?

"No!" objected Bart. "Cathy can't leave! She's expecting my child and I want her here with me!"

Bart came to take me in his arms and tenderly he gazed with love at my face. "You have lifted the blinders from my eyes, Cathy. You were right. Certainly I was meant for better things than this. Perhaps I can still redeem my existence by doing something useful for a change."

I threw the grandmother a look of triumph and avoided looking directly at Chris, and with Bart's arm about my shoulders we left the library and the grandmother and strode through all the other rooms until we reached the grand foyer.

Bedlam had broken loose! Everyone was screaming, running, searching to find a wife or a husband. Smoke! I smelled smoke.

"My God, the house is on fire!" Bart cried. He shoved me toward Chris. "Take her outside and keep her safe! I've got to find my wife!" He looked wildly about, calling, "Corrine, Corrine, where are you?"

The milling throng were all headed for the same exit.

From the stairs above black smoke billowed down. Women fell and people stepped over them. The merry guests of the party were hell-bent now on getting out, and woe to those who didn't have the strength to fight their way to the door. Frantically I tried to follow Bart with my eyes. I saw him pick up a telephone, no doubt to call the fire department, and then he was racing up the right side of the dual staircase and into the very heart of the fire! *"No!"* I screamed. "Bart—don't go up there! You'll be killed! Bart—don't! Come back!"

I think he must have heard me, for he hesitated midway up and smiled back at me as I was frantically waving. He mouthed the words *I love you*—and then pointed toward the east. I didn't understand what he meant. But Chris took it that he was telling us of another way out.

Coughing and choking, Chris and I sped through another parlor, and finally I had the chance to see the grand dining room—but it was full of smoke too! "Look," cried Chris, pulling me on, "there are French doors—the fools, there must be a dozen or more exits on the first floor, and everyone rushes for the front door!"

We made it outside and finally over to the car I recognized as Chris's, and there Emma held Jory in her arms as she stared at the great house that was burning. Chris reached inside and pulled out a car robe to throw over my shoulders, and then he held to me as I leaned against him and sobbed for Bart—where was he? Why didn't he come out?

I heard the wail of fire engines winding around the hills, screaming in the night that was already wild with the wind and the snow. The snow that fell above the house on fire was speckled red dots that sizzled as they met the flames. Jory put out his arms, wanting me, and I held him close as Chris put his arms about me and held us both. "Don't worry, Cathy," he tried to comfort, "Bart must know all the ways to get out."

Then I saw my mother in her red flame dress, being restrained by two men. She screamed on and on, crying out her husband's name—and then that of the grandmother. "My mother! She's in there! She can't move!"

Bart was on the front steps when he heard her voice. He whirled about and sped back into the house. Oh, my God! He was going back to save the grandmother who didn't deserve to live! Risking his life—doing what he had to prove, after all, he wasn't just a lap dog.

This was the fire of my childhood nightmares! This was what I'd always feared more than anything! This was the reason I'd insisted we make the rope ladder of torn-up sheets so we could escape and reach the ground—just in case.

It was more than horrible to watch that mammoth house burn when once I would have been glad to see it go. The wind blew relentlessly and whipped the flames higher, higher until they lit up the night and fired the heavens. How easily old wood burned along with the antique furnishings, the priceless heirlooms that could never be replaced. If anything survived, despite what those heroic firemen did who raced about like crazy, connecting up hoses that squirted forth foam, it would be a miracle! Someone screamed, "People are trapped inside! Get them out!" I think it was me. The firemen worked with superhuman speed and agility to get them out while I cried wild and frantic. "Bart! I didn't want to kill you! I only wanted you to love me, that's all. Bart, don't die, please don't die!" My mother heard and she came running to where Chris was holding me tight in his arms.

"*You!*" she screamed, her distraught expression that of the insane, "*You think Bart loved you? That he would marry you? You are a fool!* You betrayed me! As you've always betrayed me, and now Bart will die because of you!"

"No, Mother," said Chris who tightened his arms about me, and his tone was that of ice, "it wasn't Cathy who cried out to remind your husband your mother was still inside. *You* did that. You must have seen he couldn't go back in that house and live. Perhaps you would rather see your husband dead than married to your daughter."

She stared at him. Her hands worked nervously. Her cerulean blue eyes were darkly shadowed by the pools of black mascara. And as I watched and Chris watched something in her eyes broke—some minute thing that had lent clarity and intelligence to the eyes dissolved and she seemed to shrink. "Christopher my son, my love, I'm your mother. Don't you love me anymore, Christopher? Why? Don't I bring you everything you need and ask for? New encyclopedias, games and clothes? What is it you lack? Tell me, so I can go out and buy it for you, please tell me what you want. I'll do anything, bring you anything to make up for what you're losing. A thousandfold over you will be rewarded when my father dies, and he will die any day, any hour, any second, I know! I swear you won't have to be up here much longer! No, not much longer, not much longer, not much longer." And on and on until I could have screamed. Instead I put my hands over my ears and pressed my face against Chris's broad chest.

He made some signal to one of the ambulance drivers, and warily they approached our mother who saw them, shrieked and then tried to run. I saw her stumble and fall, her heel caught in the long hem of her flaming red, glittering gown, and on the snow she fell flat, kicking, screaming and pounding her fists.

They took her away in a straightjacket, still screaming of how I had betrayed her, while Chris and I clung to one another and watched with wide eyes. We felt like children again, helpless with the fresh grief and shame we bore. I followed him about while he did what he could for those who had been burned. I only got in his way, but I couldn't let him out of my sight.

The body of Bart Winslow was found on the floor of the library with the skeletal grandmother still clutched in his arms—both suffocated by the smoke and not the flames. I stumbled over to fold down the green blanket and stared into his face to convince myself death had come again into my life. Again and again it kept coming! I kissed him, cried on his unyielding chest, I raised my head and he was looking straight at me—and through me—gone on to where I could never reach him and confess that I had loved him from the start—fifteen years ago.

"Cathy, please," said Chris, tugging me away. I sobbed when Bart's hand slipped from my grasp. "We have to go! There's no reason for us to stay on now that it is all over."

All over, all over—it was all over.

My eyes followed the ambulance with Bart's body inside, and my grandmother too. I didn't grieve for her—for she had got out of life what she put in.

I turned to Chris and cried again in his arms, for who would live long enough to let me keep the love I had to have? Who?

Hours and hours passed while Chris pleaded with me to leave this place that had brought us nothing but unhappiness and sorrow. Why hadn't I remembered that? Sadly I leaned to pick bits and pieces of craft paper that once had been orange and purple, and other pieces of our attic decorations blew on the wind, torn petals, jagged leaves, ripped from their stems.

It was dawn before the fire was brought under control. By that time the mammoth greatness that had once been Foxworth Hall was only a smoldering ruin. The eight chimneys still stood on the sturdy brick foundation, and, oddly enough, the dual winding staircases that curved up into nowhere still remained.

Chris was eager to depart, but I had to sit and watch until the last wisp of smoke was blown away and became part of the wind called nevermore. It was my salute, the final one to Bartholomew Winslow whom I'd first seen at the age of twelve. On first sight I'd given my heart to him. So much so that I had to have Paul grow a mustache so he'd look more like Bart. And I'd married Julian because his eyes were dark, dark like Bart's. . . . Oh, God, how could I live with the knowledge I had killed the one man I'd loved best?

"Please, please Cathy, the grandmother is gone and I can't say I'm sorry, though I am about Bart. It must have been our mother who started the fire. From what the police say, it began in that attic room at the top of the stairs."

His voice came to me as from a far distance, for I was locked up in a shell of my own making. I shook my head and tried to clear it. Who was I? Who was that man next to me— who was the little boy in the back seat asleep in the arms of an older woman?

"What's the matter with you, Cathy?" Chris said impatiently. "Listen, Henny had a massive stroke tonight! In trying to help her Paul suffered a heart attack! He needs us! Are you going to sit here all day too and grieve for a man you should have left alone, and let the one man who has done the most for us die?"

The grandmother had said a few things so right. I was evil, born unholy. Everything was my fault! All my fault! If I'd never come, if I'd never come, on and on I kept saying this to myself as I cried bitter tears for the loss of Bart.

Reaping the Harvest

It was autumn again, that passionate month of October. The trees this year were ablaze from the touch of early frost. I was on the back veranda of Paul's big white house, shelling peas and watching Bart's small son chase after his older half-brother Jory. We'd named Bart's son after him, thinking it only right, but his last name was Sheffield, not Winslow. I was now Paul's wife.

In a few months Jory would be seven years old, and though at first he'd been a bit jealous he was now delighted to have a younger brother to share his life—someone he could boss, instruct and patronize. However young, Bart was not the kind to take orders. He was his own person, right from the beginning.

"Catherine," called Paul's weak voice. I put the bowl of green peas quickly aside and hurried to his bedroom on the first floor. He was able to sit up in a chair for a few hours a day now, though on our wedding day, he'd been in bed. On our wedding night he'd slept in my arms, and that was all.

Paul had lost a great deal of weight; he looked gaunt. All

his youth and vitality, held on to so valiantly, had disappeared almost overnight. Yet he'd never moved me more than when he smiled at me and held out his arms. "I just called to see if you'd come. I ordered you to get out of this house for a change."

"You're talking too much," I cautioned. "You know you aren't supposed to talk but a little." This was a sore point with him, to only listen and not join in, but he tried to accept it. His next words took me by complete surprise. I could only stare at him, mouth agape and eyes wide. "Paul, you don't mean that!"

Solemnly he nodded, his still beautiful iridescent eyes holding mine. "Catherine, my love, it's been almost three years that you have been a slave to me, doing your best to make my last days happy. But I'm never going to get well. I could live on like this for years and years, like your grandfather did, while you grow older and older, and miss out on the best years of your life."

"I'm not missing out on anything," I said with a sob in my throat.

He smiled at me gently and held out his arms, and gladly I went to cuddle on his lap, though his arms about me no longer felt strong. He kissed me, and I held my breath. Oh, to be loved again . . . but I wouldn't let him, I wouldn't!

"Think about it, my darling. Your children need a father, the kind of father I can't be now."

"It's my fault!" I cried. "If I had married you years ago, instead of Julian, I could have kept you well, and forced you not to work so hard and drive yourself night and day. Paul, if we three hadn't come into your life, you wouldn't have had to earn so much money, enough to send Chris through college and me to ballet classes. . . ."

He put his hand over my mouth, and told me but for us, he would have died years ago from overwork. "Three years, Catherine," he said again. "And when you think about it, you will realize you are very much a prisoner, just as when you were in Foxworth Hall, waiting for your grandfather to die. I don't want you and Chris to grow to hate me . . . so think about it, and talk to him about it—and then decide."

"Paul, Chris is a doctor! You know he wouldn't agree!"

"Time is running out, Catherine, not only for me, but for you and Chris too. Soon Jory will be seven years old. He will be remembering everything more clearly. He will know Chris is his uncle, but if you leave now and forget about me, he will consider Chris his stepfather, not his uncle."

I sobbed. "No! Chris would never agree."

"Catherine, listen to me. It wouldn't be evil! You are now unable to have more children. Though I was terribly sorry you had such a difficult time giving birth to your last son, maybe it was a blessing in disguise. I'm impotent; I'm not a real husband, and soon you will be a widow again. And Chris has waited for so long. Can't you think about him, and forget the sin?"

And so, like Momma, we'd written our scripts too, Chris and I. And maybe ours were no better than hers, though I'd never plotted to kill anyone, nor had I meant to drive her over the brink of insanity so the rest of her life she'd live in a "convalescent" home. And the irony of ironies, when all that she'd inherited from her father had been taken away, it had reverted to her mother. The grandmother's will had been read and her entire fortune, plus the remains of Foxworth Hall, now belonged to a woman who could only sit in a mental institution and stare at four wails. Oh, Momma, if only you could have looked into the future when first you considered taking your four children back to Foxworth Hall! Cursed with millions—and unable to spend a cent. Nor would one penny come to us. When our mother died, it would be distributed to different charities.

*　　*　　*

In the spring of the following year we sat near the river water where Julia had led Scotty, then held him under so he drowned in the shallow, greenish water where my own two small sons sailed small boats and waded in water that only reached their ankles.

"Chris," I began falteringly, embarrassed, and yet happy too, "Paul made love to me last night for the first time. We were both so happy, we cried. It was safe enough, wasn't it?"

He bowed his head to hide his expression, and the sun blazed his golden hair. "I'm happy for the both of you. Yes, sex is safe enough now, as long as you don't work him up to a great pitch of excitement."

"We took it easy." After four severe heart attacks, it had to be easy sex.

"Good."

Jory shrieked out then he'd caught a fish. Was it too small? Would he have to throw back another? "Yes," called Chris, "that's just a baby. We don't eat baby fish, only the big ones."

"Come," I called, "let's head for home and dinner." They came running and laughing, my two sons, both so much alike they appeared whole brothers, and not halfs. And as yet we hadn't told them any different. Jory hadn't asked, and Bart was too young to question. But when they did, we would tell them the truth, as difficult as it was.

"We've got two daddies," cried Jory, flinging himself into Chris's arms as I picked up Bart. "Nobody at school but me has two daddies and they don't understand when I tell them . . . but maybe I don't tell it right."

"I'm sure you don't tell it right," said Chris with a small smile.

In Chris's new blue car we drove home to the big white house that had given us so much. As we had the first time we came, we saw a man on the front veranda with his white shoes propped up on the balustrade. As Chris took my sons into the house I went over to Paul and smiled to see him dozing with a pleased smile upon his face. The newspaper he'd been reading had slipped from his slack hand to fan on the veranda floor. "I'll go in and bathe the boys," whispered Chris, "and you can pick up the newspapers before the wind blows them onto our neighbors' lawns."

As quietly as you can try to pick up papers and fold them neatly, somehow they will crackle and rustle, and soon Paul half-opened his eyes and smiled at me. "Hi," he said sleepily. "Did you have a good day? Catch anything?"

"Two small fish bit on Jory's line, but he had to throw them back. What were you dreaming before you woke?" I asked, leaning to kiss him. "You looked so happy—was it a sexy dream?"

Again he smiled, sort of wistfully. "I was dreaming of Julia," he said. "She had Scotty with her, and they were both smiling at me. You know, she very seldom smiled at me after we married."

"Poor Julia," I said, kissing him again. "She missed out on so much. I promise my smiles will make up for all she didn't give."

"They already have." He reached to touch my cheek and stroked my hair. "It was my lucky day when you climbed my veranda steps on that Sunday. . . ."

"That damned Sunday," I corrected. He smiled. "Give me ten minutes more before you call me in to dinner. I'd like to get hold of that bus driver and tell him no Sundays are damned when you are on the bus."

I went in to help Chris with the boys, and while he buttoned up Jory's pj's I helped Bart Scott Winslow Sheffield with his yellow pajamas. We ate early, so we could dine with our children.

Soon the ten minutes were up and again I went to waken Paul. Three times I said his name softly and stroked his cheek gently, then blew in his ear. Still he slept on. I started to say his name again, and louder, when he made some small sound that sounded like my name. I looked, already trembling and afraid. Just the strangeness of the way he said that filled me with a terrible dread.

"Chris," I called weakly, "come quick and look at Paul."

He must have been in the hall, sent by Emma to see what was taking us so long, for he stepped out of the door immediately, then ran to Paul's side. He seized up his hand and felt for his pulse, and then in another second he was pulling his head back and holding his nose and breathing into his mouth. When that didn't work he struck him several times very hard on his chest. I ran into the house and called an ambulance.

But, of course, none of it did any good. Our benefactor, our savior, my husband was dead. Chris put his arm about my shoulder and drew me to his chest. "He's gone, Cathy, the way I would like to go, in my sleep, feeling well and happy. It's a good way for a good man to die, with no pain and no suffering—so don't look like that, it's not your fault!"

Nothing was ever my fault. Behind me lay a trail of dead men. But I wasn't responsible for the death of even one, was I? No, of course not. It was a wonder Chris had the nerve to climb in the car and sit beside me, heading his car west. Behind us, we trailed a U-Haul with all our worldly goods inside. Going west like the pioneers to seek a new future and find different kinds of lives. Paul had left everything he owned to me, including his family home. Though his will had stated, if I decided to sell, he wanted Amanda to have the final bid.

So at last Paul's sister had their ancestral home she had always wanted and schemed to get—but I made sure it was at a steep price.

Chris and I rented a home in California until we could have a custom-designed ranch house built to our specifications, with four bedrooms and two and a half baths. Plus we had another bath and bedroom for our maid, Emma Lindstrom. My sons call my brother Daddy. They both know they have other fathers who went on to heaven before they were born.

So far, they don't realize Chris is only their uncle. A long time ago. Jory forgot that. Maybe children too forget when they want to, and ask no questions that would be embarrassing to answer.

At least once a year we travel east to visit friends, including Madame Marisha and Madame Zolta. Both make a great to-do about the dancing abilities of Jory, and both try with fervent zeal to make Bart a dancer too. But so far, he doesn't have the inclination to be anything but a doctor. We visit all the graves of our beloved ones, and put flowers there. Always red and purple ones for Carrie, and roses of any color for Paul and Henny. We have even sought out our father's grave in Gladstone, and paid our respects to him too with flowers. And Julian is never overlooked, or Georges.

Last of all, we visit Momma.

She lives in a huge place that tries unsuccessfully to look homey. Usually she screams when she sees me. Then she jumps up and tries to tear the hair from my head. When she is restrained, she turns the hatred upon herself, trying time after time to mutilate her face, and free herself forever of any resemblance to me. Just as if she no longer looked in the mirrors that would tell her we no longer look alike. Remorse has made of her something terrible to see. And once she'd been so very beautiful. Her doctors allow only Chris to visit with her an hour or so, while I wait outside with my two sons. He reports back that if she recovers, she won't be faced with a murder charge, for both Chris and I have disclaimed there ever was a fourth child named Cory. She doesn't fully trust Chris, sensing he is under my evil influence, and if she lets go her facade of being insane, she will end up with a death penalty. So year after year passes as she clings to her calculated fallacy as a way to escape also the future with no one who really cares for her. Or perhaps, more truly, she seeks to torment me through Chris and the pity he insists on feeling for her. She is the one issue that keeps our relationship from being perfect.

So, the dreams of perfection, of fame, of fortune, of undying, ever-abiding love without one single flaw, like the toys and games of yesteryears, and all other youthful fantasies I have outgrown, I have put away.

Often I look at Chris, and wonder just what it is he sees in me. What is it that binds him to me in such a permanent way? I wonder too why he isn't afraid for his future and the length of it, since I am better at keeping pets alive than husbands. But he comes home jauntily, wearing a happy grin, as he strides into my welcoming arms that respond quickly to his greeting, "Come greet me with kisses if you love me."

His medical practice is large, but not too large, so he has time to work in our four acres of gardens with the marble statues we brought along from Paul's gardens. As much as possible we have duplicated what he had, except for the Spanish moss that clings, and clings, and then kills.

Emma Lindstrom, our cook, our housekeeper, friend, lives with us as Henny lived with Paul. She never asks questions. She has no family but us, and to us she is faithful, and our business is our own.

Pragmatic, blithe, the eternal, cockeyed optimist, Chris sings when he works in the gardens. When he shaves in the mornings he hums some ballet tune, feeling no trepidations, no regrets, as if long, long ago he had been the man who danced in the shadows of the attic and had never, never let me see his face. Did he know all along that just as he had won over me in all other games it would be him in the end?

Why hadn't I known?

Who had shut my eyes?

It must have been Momma who told me once, "Marry a man with dark, dark eyes, Cathy. Dark eyes feel so terribly intense about everything." What a laugh! As if blue eyes lacked some profound steadfastness; she should have known better.

I should know better too. It worries me because I went yesterday into our attic. In a little alcove to the side, I found

two single-size beds, long enough for two small boys to grow
into men.

Oh, my God! I thought, who did this? I would never lock
away my two sons, even if Jory did remember one day that
Chris was not his stepfather but his uncle. I wouldn't even
if he did tell Bart, our youngest. I could face the shame, the
embarrassment, and the publicity that would ruin Chris professionally. Yet . . . yet, today I bought a picnic hamper, the
kind with the double lids that open up from the center; the
very same kind of hamper the grandmother had used to bring
us food.

So, I go uneasily to bed and lie there awake, fearing the
worst in myself, and struggling to keep firm hold of the best.
It seems, as I turn over, and snuggle closer to the man I love,
that I can hear the cold wind blowing from the blue-misted
mountains so far away.

It's the past that I can never forget, that shadows all my
days, and hides furtively in the comers when Chris is home.
I do make an effort to be like he is, always optimistic, when
I am not at all the kind who can forget the tarnish on the
reverse side of the brightest coin.

But . . . I am not like her! I may look like her, but inside
I am honorable! I am stronger, more determined. The
best in me will win out in the end. I know it will. It has to
sometimes . . . doesn't it?

The secrets and scandals continue. . . .

IF THERE BE THORNS
SEEDS OF YESTERDAY

Which will be *your* first?

FROM SIMON PULSE

PUBLISHED BY SIMON & SCHUSTER